THE OXFORD BOOK OF

American Short Stories

The Oxford Book of

AMERICAN SHORT STORIES

Edited by

JOYCE CAROL OATES

OXFORD UNIVERSITY PRESS
Oxford New York

Oxford University Press

Oxford New York Toronto
Delhi Bombay Calcutta Madras Karachi
Kuala Lumpur Singapore Hong Kong Tokyo
Nairobi Dar es Salaam Cape Town
Melbourne Auckland Madrid

and associated companies in
Berlin Ibadan

First published in 1992 by Oxford University Press, Inc.,
198 Madison Avenue, New York, New York 10016-4314

First issued as an Oxford University Press paperback, 1994

Library of Congress Cataloging-in-Publication Data
The Oxford book of American short stories /
edited by Joyce Carol Oates.
p. cm. Includes index.
ISBN 0-19-507065-8
ISBN-13 978-0-19-509262-2 (pbk.)
ISBN 0-19-509262-7 (pbk.)

1. Short Stories, American.
I. Oates, Joyce Carol, 1938–
PS648.S5094 1992 813'.0108—dc20 92-1353

Cloth: 10 9 8

Paperback: 20

Printed in the United States of America
on acid-free paper

ACKNOWLEDGMENTS

The editor and publisher gratefully acknowledge permission to reprint the following material.

Alice Adams: "Alaska" from *Return Trips* by Alice Adams. Copyright © 1984 by Alice Adams. Reprinted by permission of Alfred A. Knopf, Inc.

Sherwood Anderson: "The Strength of God" from *Winesburg, Ohio* by Sherwood Anderson. Copyright 1919 by B. W. Huebsch. Copyright 1947 by Eleanor Copenhaver Anderson. Used by permission of Viking Penguin, a division of Penguin Books USA Inc.

James Baldwin: "Sonny's Blues." Copyright © 1957 by James Baldwin. From *Going to Meet the Man* by James Baldwin. Used by permission of Doubleday, a division of Bantam Doubleday Dell Publishing Group, Inc., and the James Baldwin Estate.

Donald Barthelme: "The School." Copyright © 1982 by Donald Barthelme. Reprinted by permission of Wylie, Aitken & Stone, Inc.

Saul Bellow: "Something To Remember Me By." Copyright © 1990 by Saul Bellow. Reprinted by permission of Harriet Wasserman Literary Agency, Inc.

Pinckney Benedict: "Town Smokes" from *Town Smokes.* Copyright © 1987 by Pinckney Benedict. Published by The Ontario Review Press and reprinted by permission of The Ontario Review Press, Princeton, New Jersey.

Paul Bowles: "A Distant Episode" from *A Distant Episode: The Selected Stories.* Copyright © 1988 by Paul Bowles. Published by The Ecco Press and reprinted by permission of The Ecco Press, New York, and Peter Owen Publishers, London.

Ray Bradbury: "There Will Come Soft Rains." Reprinted by permission of Don Congdon Associates, Inc. Copyright © 1950, renewed 1977 by Ray Bradbury. Poem by Sara Teasdale reprinted with permission of Macmillan Publishing Company from *Collected Poems of Sara Teasdale*. Copyright 1920 by Macmillan Publishing Company, renewed 1948 by Mamie T. Wheless.

Raymond Carver: "Are These Actual Miles?" first appeared in *Esquire* as "What Is It?" and included in *Will You Please Be Quiet, Please?*, published by McGraw-Hill and to be reissued by Vintage. Copyright © 1972 by Raymond Carver. Reprinted by permission of Tess Gallagher.

John Cheever: "The Death of Justina" from *The Stories of John Cheever*. Copyright © 1960 by John Cheever. Reprinted by permission of Alfred A. Knopf, Inc., and Jonathan Cape, Ltd.

Kate Chopin: "The Storm." Reprinted by permission of Louisiana State University Press from *The Complete Works of Kate Chopin*, by Per Seyersted, copyright © 1969.

Sandra Cisneros: "The House on Mango Street," "What Sally Said," "Linoleum Roses," and "A House of My Own" from *The House on Mango Street*. Copyright © 1989 by Sandra Cisneros. Published in the United States by Vintage Books, a division of Random House. Originally published in somewhat different form by Arte Publico Press in 1984; revised 1988. Reprinted by permission of Susan Bergholz Literary Services, New York.

Ralph Ellison: "Battle Royal" from *Invisible Man* by Ralph Ellison. Copyright 1948 by Ralph Ellison. Reprinted by permission of Random House, Inc.

Louise Erdrich: "Fleur" as it appeared in *Esquire*. Copyright © 1988 by Louise Erdrich. Reprinted by arrangement with the author.

William Faulkner: "That Evening Sun" from *Collected Stories of William Faulkner* by William Faulkner. Copyright 1931 and renewed 1959 by William Faulkner. Reprinted by permission of Random House, Inc., New York, and Curtis Brown, Ltd., London.

F. Scott Fitzgerald: "An Alcoholic Case." Reprinted with permission of Charles Scribner's Sons, an imprint of Macmillan Publishing Company, from *The Short Stories of F. Scott Fitzgerald*, edited by Malcolm Cowley. Copyright 1937 by

Esquire, Inc.; copyright renewal © 1965 by Frances Scott Fitzgerald Lanahan.

Ernest Hemingway: "A Clean, Well-Lighted Place." Reprinted with permission of Charles Scribner's Sons, an imprint of Macmillan Publishing Company, and Jonathan Cape Ltd., from *Winner Take Nothing* by Ernest Hemingway. Copyright 1933 by Charles Scribner's Sons; renewal copyright © 1961 by Mary Hemingway.

Langston Hughes: "Red-Headed Baby" from *The Ways of White Folks* by Langston Hughes. Copyright 1934 and renewed 1962 by Langston Hughes. Reprinted by permission of Alfred A. Knopf, Inc., and Harold Ober Associates, Inc.

David Leavitt: "Gravity" from *A Place I've Never Been* by David Leavitt. Copyright © 1990 by David Leavitt. Used by permission of Viking Penguin, a division of Penguin Books USA, Inc.

Ursula K. Le Guin: "Texts." Copyright © 1990 by Ursula K. Le Guin; first appeared in *American Short Fiction* by permission of the PEN Syndicated Fiction Project; reprinted from *The Sound of Writing* by permission of Ursula K. Le Guin and the PEN Syndicated Fiction Project.

Bernard Malamud: "My Son the Murderer" from *Rembrandt's Hat* by Bernard Malamud. Copyright © 1968, 1973 by Bernard Malamud. Reprinted by permission of Farrar, Straus and Giroux, Inc., and Russell & Volkening, Inc., as agents for the author.

Bobbie Ann Mason: "Big Bertha Stories" from *Love Life* by Bobbie Ann Mason. Copyright © 1988 by Bobbie Ann Mason. Reprinted by permission of HarperCollins Publishers.

Bharati Mukherjee: "The Management of Grief" from *The Middleman and Other Stories* by Bharati Mukherjee. Copyright © 1988 by Bharati Mukherjee. Reprinted by permission of Grove Press, Inc., Penguin Books Canada, Ltd., and Bharati Mukherjee.

Tim O'Brien: "The Things They Carried." Copyright © 1990 by Tim O'Brien. Reprinted by permission of Houghton Mifflin Company/Seymour Lawrence. All rights reserved.

Flannery O'Connor: "A Late Encounter with the Enemy" from *A Good Man Is Hard To Find and Other Stories.* Copyright 1953 by Flannery O'Connor and renewed 1981 by Mrs. Regina O'Connor, reprinted by permission of Harcourt Brace Jovanovich, Inc., and Harold Matson Company, Inc.

Joyce Carol Oates: "Heat" from *Heat.* Copyright © 1991 by The Ontario Review, Inc. Published by NAL/Dutton and reprinted by permission of The Ontario Review, Inc.

Cynthia Ozick: "The Shawl" from *The Shawl* by Cynthia Ozick. Copyright © 1980, 1983 by Cynthia Ozick. Originally appeared in *The New Yorker.* Reprinted by permission of Alfred A. Knopf, Inc., and Jonathan Cape, Ltd.

Katherine Anne Porter: "He" from *Flowering Judas and Other Stories.* Copyright 1930 and renewed 1958 by Katherine Anne Porter, reprinted by permission of Harcourt Brace Jovanovich, Inc., and Jonathan Cape, Ltd.

Leslie Marmon Silko: "Yellow Woman" from *The Storyteller* by Leslie Marmon Silko. Copyright © 1981 by Leslie Marmon Silko. Published by Seaver Books, New York.

Isaac Bashevis Singer: "The Lecture" from *The Seance and Other Stories* by Isaac Bashevis Singer. Copyright © 1968 by Isaac Bashevis Singer. Reprinted by permission of Farrar, Straus and Giroux, Inc., and Jonathan Cape, Ltd.

Amy Tan: "Two Kinds" from *The Joy Luck Club* by Amy Tan. Copyright © 1989 by Amy Tan. Reprinted by permission of The Putnam Publishing Group.

Peter Taylor: "Rain in the Heart" from *The Old Forest and Other Stories* by Peter Taylor. Copyright 1941, 1945, 1947, 1949, 1951, 1958, 1959, 1979, 1981, 1985, © 1986 by Peter Taylor. Used by permission of Doubleday, a division of Bantam Doubleday Dell Publishing Group, Inc., and Russell & Volkening, Inc., as agents of the author.

Jean Toomer: "Blood-Burning Moon" reprinted from *Cane* by Jean Toomer, by permission of Liveright Publishing Corporation. Copyright 1923 by Boni & Liveright. Copyright renewed 1951 by Jean Toomer.

John Updike: "The Persistence of Desire" from *Pigeon Feathers and Other Stories* by John Updike. Copyright © 1959 by John Updike. Reprinted by permission of Alfred A. Knopf, Inc., and Andre Deutsch Ltd.

Eudora Welty: "Where Is the Voice Coming From?" reprinted by permission of Russell & Volkening, Inc. as agents for the author. Copyright © 1963 by Eudora Welty, renewed in 1991 by Eudora Welty.

John Edgar Wideman: "Fever" from *Fever: Twelve Stories* by John Edgar Wideman. Copyright © 1989 by John Edgar Wideman. Reprinted by permission of Henry Holt and Company, Inc., and Wylie, Aitken & Stone, Inc.

William Carlos Williams: "The Girl with a Pimply Face" from *The Farmers' Daughters*. Copyright © 1961 by William Carlos Williams. Reprinted by permission of New Directions Publishing Corporation.

Tobias Wolff: "Hunters in the Snow" from *In the Garden of the North American Martyrs,* copyright © 1976, 1978, 1980, 1981 by Tobias Wolff. First published by The Ecco Press in 1981. Reprinted by permission.

Richard Wright: "The Man Who Was Almost a Man" from *Eight Men* by Richard Wright. Copyright © 1987 by the Estate of Richard Wright. Used by permission of the publisher, Thunder's Mouth Press, and Ellen Wright for the Estate of Richard Wright.

CONTENTS

THE OXFORD BOOK OF
American Short Stories

Introduction

Familiar names, unfamiliar titles: this, in part, was my initial inspiration in assembling *The Oxford Book of American Short Stories*. The challenge was to discover, wherever possible, short stories by our finest writers that were less known than the stories by these writers usually found in anthologies, yet of equal merit and interest; stories that, while reflecting authors' characteristic styles, visions, and subjects, suggested other aspects of sensibility. We Americans are justly proud of our literature, and a good deal of that pride stems from our awareness of the crucial role of the short story—in its earliest manifestations, the short tale or romance—as a form ideally suited to the expression of the imagination.

In my reading of many months I was enormously pleased to discover virtually unknown yet fascinating work by certain of our classic American writers, whose famous titles recur from anthology to anthology with dismaying predictability. Certainly, Nathaniel Hawthorne's "Young Goodman Brown" and "The Birthmark" are brilliant moral parables—but what of the more psychologically realistic "The Wives of the Dead," of which no one seems to have heard? Melville's "Bartleby the Scrivener" has entered our literary consciousness, deservedly, but what of "The Paradise of Bachelors and the Tartarus of Maids," with its eerily contemporary theme of sexual/class exploitation? (I first read this unclassifiable prose piece—hardly a "tale" in any conventional sense, still less a "story"—when I was an undergraduate at Syracuse University, and I have been haunted by its images ever since. Herman Melville, our first native feminist?—can it be so?) Henry James's aesthetic is nowhere more perfectly realized than in "The Beast in the Jungle," anthologized virtually everywhere; yet what of "The Middle Years," so much more direct, more human, more personal in its statement of the isolate's (or the artist's) life? It is in this lesser-known story that The Master speaks with painful candor, giving voice to what all artists know, yet perhaps would not want to express in such raw, unmediated terms:

We work in the dark—we do what we can—we give what we have. Our doubt is our passion and our passion is our task. The rest is the madness of art.

As schoolchildren we read and admired Mark Twain's early, frankly derivative tall tale, "The Celebrated Jumping Frog of Calaveras County," but the darker, more sinister, yes and funnier Twain, as represented in the mordant "Cannibalism in the Cars," is virtually unknown. (And why, in most general anthologies, is there no representation at all of Twain's great contemporary Harriet Beecher Stowe, whose popularity as a writer was by no means confined to her most famous work, *Uncle Tom's Cabin?*) So too with such familiar classics as Stephen Crane's "The Open Boat," Jack London's "To Build a Fire," Edith Wharton's "Roman Fever," Hemingway's "The Snows of Kilimanjaro" and "The Short Happy Life of Francis Macomber," Willa Cather's "Paul's Case," William Carlos Williams' "The Use of Force." These are certainly great works of art; at the very least, they have helped to define the range and depth of the short story in America. But the reader begins to feel frustration when they are encountered repeatedly, alternated now and then with a very few other titles of almost equal familiarity. Though among them F. Scott Fitzgerald, Eudora Welty, Flannery O'Connor, Saul Bellow, John Cheever, Peter Taylor, and John Updike have written literally hundreds of short stories, the same two or three titles by each writer are recycled continuously. Why, given such plenitude, is this so? Do editors of anthologies consult only other anthologies, instead of reading original collections of stories? But isn't the implicit promise of an anthology that it will, or aspires to, present something different, unexpected?

How ironic, it seemed to me, yet, perhaps, how symbolic, that in our age of rapid mass-production and the easy proliferation of consumer products, the richness and diversity of the American literary imagination should be so misrepresented in most anthologies and textbooks!

Of course, I must confess that, despite months of reading and rereading, I could not avoid reprinting certain very familiar favorites. Washington Irving's "Rip Van Winkle," Edgar Allan Poe's "The Tell-Tale Heart," Charlotte Perkins Gilman's "The Yellow Wallpaper," Ernest Hemingway's "A Clean, Well-Lighted Place," William Faulkner's "That Evening Sun"—the consequence of an ideal conjunction of quality of prose and quantity of pages. (All anthologies are compromises when a finitude of space is an issue.) James Baldwin's and Ralph Ellison's much-reprinted "Sonny's Blues" and "Battle Royal" are works by major American writers who did not cultivate the short story form, and so offer very few titles. Other old favorites which the scanning eye will note as absent—Ring Lardner's "Haircut," James Thurber's "The Secret Life of Walter Mitty," Shirley Jackson's "The Lottery"—were reluctantly excluded because they are so readily available elsewhere, and because, with space restrictions, I thought it more important to present outstanding titles by writers representing a broad spectrum of cultural traditions: Mary E. Wilkins Freeman, Jean Toomer, Zora Neale Hurston, Langston Hughes, Paul Bowles, Leslie Marmon Silko, Bharati Mukherjee, Amy Tan, David Leavitt, Sandra Cisneros, to name but a few.

"No creative writer can swallow another contemporary," Virginia Woolf once noted, as a way, perhaps, of rationalizing her own highly subjective tastes, "—the reception of living work is too coarse and partial if you're doing the same thing yourself." Even if one is not doing the same thing oneself, or anything approaching it, there remains an obvious difficulty in attempting an overview of the very landscape one inhabits.

As we move through the post-War era and into contemporary times, the proliferation of published stories and the immense diversities of talent make selection enormously difficult. What riches here, and what sorrow for the editor in having to exclude so much! Here indeed is American plenitude—not solely of talent but of distinct aesthetic agendas; distinct ethnic and minority voices; distinct regional themes. It will be evident that, beginning with Harriet Beecher Stowe, I have sought to include more women writers than commonly appear in such volumes; yet, in the past two decades, so many outstanding women writers have emerged, and are emerging still, often as "ethnic" voices, that a proportional representation of their work, in such limited space, is all but impossible. Ethnic and minority fiction has revitalized our contemporary literature and constitutes, it might be argued, a new regionalism. (Or is American literature at its core a literature of *regions?* Note how, in this volume, works by contemporaries so seemingly diverse as John Edgar Wideman and Sandra Cisneros, Eudora Welty and Saul Bellow, Leslie Silko, Louise Erdrich, and Bobbie Ann Mason, as well as John Updike, Peter Taylor, and John Cheever, are related along lines that have less to do with traditional American themes than with stories set in highly specific, brilliantly realized American *places.* Indeed, in writers so clearly linked to an idiomatic oral tradition as Flannery O'Connor and the young West Virginian Pinckney Benedict, place *is* voice.)

Because my emphasis in this anthology is on storytelling, often with a social and/or political theme, and not on literary experimentation, I have included, of the celebrated "meta-fictionalists" of the 1960's and 1970's, only Donald Barthelme, whose principal mode of fiction was the short story. Had I more space, I would have wished to include such dazzlingly inventive talents as John Barth, William Gass, John Hawkes, Robert Coover, Paul West, and Steven Millhauser, among others. Of writers associated with gender, I have included only David Leavitt, whose most representative fiction, though generally concerned with young gay Caucasian men of an educated middle class, transcends any labels; of the controversial "minimalists" of recent years, I have included only Raymond Carver, Bobbie Ann Mason, and Tobias Wolff—with the immediate qualification, which I assert with some urgency, that I, personally, do not consider these writers "minimalists" any more than Sherwood Anderson, Ernest Hemingway, and William Carlos Williams are "minimalists." Even to classify them as "realists" is reductive and misleading.

Other editors have remarked in print of a problem arguably unique to our time and nation, of the proliferation of published stories by serious, committed, highly gifted writers who are carving out careers for themselves that will, in time, not only rest upon a few distinguished works but upon solid bodies of work, which will, in turn, help to define our increasingly diversified and heterogeneous American literature. Obviously, I could include only a sampling of this richness. To do justice to the remarkable fecundity of the American short story would require not a single volume of this size, but a second.

Not that the story need be long,
but it will take a long while
to make it short.
Henry David Thoreau

Formal definitions of the short story are commonplace, yet there is none quite democratic enough to accommodate an art that includes so much variety and an art that so readily lends itself to experimentation and idiosyncratic voices. Perhaps length alone should be the sole criterion? Whenever critics try to impose other, more subjective strictures on the genre (as on any genre) too much work is excluded.

Yet length itself is problematic. No more than 10,000 words? Why not then 10,500? 11,000? Where, in fact, does a short story end and a novella begin? (Tolstoy's "The Death of Ivan Ilych" can be classified as both.) And there is the reverse problem, for, as short stories condense, they are equally difficult to define. What is the short-short story, precisely? What is that most teasing of prose works, the prose-poem? We can be guided by critical intuition in distinguishing between a newspaper article or an anecdote and a fully realized story, but intuition is notoriously difficult to define (or depend upon). Since the cultivation of the aesthetically subtle, minimally resolved short story by such masters as Chekhov, Lawrence, Joyce, and Hemingway, the definition of the "fully realized" story has become problematic as well.

My personal definition of the form is that it represents a concentration of imagination, and not an expansion; it *is* no more than 10,000 words; and, no matter its mysteries or experimental properties, it achieves closure—meaning that, when it ends, the attentive reader understand why.

That is to say, the short story is a prose piece that is not a mere concatenation of events, as in a news account or an anecdote, but an intensification of meaning by way of events. Its "plot" may be wholly interior, seemingly static, a matter of the progression of a character's thought. Its resolution need not be a formally articulated statement, as in many of Hawthorne's more didactic tales, or, in this collection, William Austin's once-famous cautionary tale, "Peter Rugg, the Missing Man," but it signals a tangible change of some sort; a distinct shift in consciousness; a deepening of insight. In the most elliptical of stories, a characteristic of the modern and contemporary story, the actual resolution frequently occurs in the reader's, and not the fictional characters', consciousness. To read stories as disparate as Katherine Anne Porter's "He," Paul Bowles's "A Distant Episode," Ray Bradbury's "There Will Come Soft Rains," Raymond Carver's "Are These Actual Miles?" and Tobias Wolff's

"Hunters in the Snow," among others in this volume, is to read stories so structured as to provide the reader, and not the characters themselves, with insight. Because the meaning of a story does not lie on its surface, visible and self-defining, does not mean that meaning does not exist. Indeed, the ambiguity of meaning, its inner, private quality, may well be part of the writer's vision.

In addition to these qualities, most short stories (but hardly all) are restricted in time and place; concentrate upon a very small number of characters; and move toward a single ascending dramatic scene or revelation. And all are generated by conflict.

The artist *is* the focal point of conflict. Lovers of pristine harmony, those who dislike being upset, shocked, made to think and to feel, are not naturally suited to appreciate art, at least not serious art; which, unlike television dramas and situation comedies, for instance, does not evoke conflict merely to solve it within a brief space of time. Rather, conflict is the implicit subject, itself; as conflict, the establishment of disequilibrium, is the impetus for the evolution of life, so is conflict the genesis, the prime mover, the secret heart of all art.

Discord, then, and not harmony, is the subject our writers share in common. Though the quelling of discord and the re-establishment of harmony may well be the point of the art.

The "literary" short story, the meticulously constructed short story, descends to us by way of the phenomenon of magazine publication, beginning in the nineteenth century, but has as its ancestor the oral tale.

We must assume that storytelling is as old as mankind, at least as old as spoken language. Reality is not enough for us—we crave the imagination's embellishments upon it. *In the beginning. Once upon a time. A long time ago there lived a princess who.* How the pulse quickens, hearing such beginnings! such promises of something new, strange, unexpected! The epic poem, the ballad, the parable, the beast-fable, sacred narratives, visionary prophecies—the fabulous mythopoetic "histories" of ancient cultures—the "divinely inspired" books of the Old and New Testament: all are forms of storytelling, expressions of the human imagination.

Like a river fed by countless small streams, the modern short story derives from a multiplicity of sources. Historically, the earliest literary documents of which we have knowledge are Egyptian papyri dating from 4000–3000 B.C., containing a work called, most intriguingly, *Tales of the Magicians.* The Middle Ages revered such secular works as fabliaux, ballads, and verse romances; the Arabian *Thousand and One Nights* and the Latin tales and anecdotes of the *Gesta Romanorum,* collected before the end of the thirteenth century, as well as the one hundred tales of Boccaccio's *The Decameron,* and Chaucer's *Canterbury Tales,* were enormously popular for centuries. Storytelling as an oral art, like the folk ballad, was, or is, characteristic of non-literate cultures, for obvious reasons. Even the prolongation of light (by artificial means) had an effect upon the storytelling tradition of our ancestors. The rise in literacy marked the ebbing of interest in old fairy tales and ballads, as did the gradual stabilization of languages and the cessation of local dialects in which the tales and ballads had been told most effectively. (The Brothers Grimm noted this phenomenon: if, in High German, a fairy tale gained in superficial clarity, it "lost in flavor, and no longer had such a firm hold of the kernel of meaning.")

One of the signal accomplishments of American literature, most famously exemplified by the great commercial and critical success of Samuel Clemens, is the reclamation of that "lost" flavor—the use, as style, of dialect, regional, and strongly (often comically) vernacular language. Of course, before Samuel Clemens cultivated the ingenuous-ironic persona of "Mark Twain," there were dialect writers and tale-tellers in America (for instance, Joel Chandler Harris, creator of the popular "Uncle Remus" stories); but Mark Twain was a phenomenon of a kind previously unknown here—our first American writer to be avidly read, coast to coast, by all classes of Americans, from the most high-born to the least cultured and minimally literate. The development of mass-market newspapers and subscription book sales made this success possible, but it was the brilliant reclamation of the vernacular in Twain's work (the early "The Celebrated Jumping Frog of Calaveras County," for instance) that made him into so uniquely *American* a writer, our counterpart to Dickens.

Twain's rapid ascent was by way of popular newspapers, which syndicated features coast to coast, and his crowd-pleasing public performances, but the more typical outlet for a short story writer, particularly of self-consciously "literary" work, was the magazine. Virtually every writer in this volume, from Washington Irving and Nathaniel Hawthorne onward, began his or her career publishing short fiction in magazines before moving on to book publication; in the nineteenth century, such highly regarded, and, in some cases, high-paying magazines as *The North American Review, Harper's Monthly, Atlantic Monthly, Scribner's Monthly* (later *The Century*), *The Dial*, and *Graham's Magazine* (briefly edited by Edgar Allan Poe) advanced the careers of writers who would otherwise have had financial difficulties in establishing themselves. In post-World War II America, the majority of short story writers publish in small-circulation "literary" magazines throughout their careers. It is all but unknown for a writer to publish a book of short stories without having published most of them in magazines beforehand.

Edgar Allan Poe's famous review-essay of Hawthorne's *Twice-Told Tales* (*Graham's Magazine*, 1842) is justly celebrated as one of the crucial documents in the establishment of the short story as a distinct literary genre. Poe's aesthetic is a curious admixture of the romantic and the classic: the intention of the art-work is to move the reader's soul deeply, but the means to this intention is coolly, if not chillingly, cerebral. Poe in his philosophy as in his practice is both visionary and manipulator:

> A skillful literary artist has constructed his tale. If wise, he has not fashioned his thoughts to accommodate his incidents; but having conceived, with deliberate care, a certain unique or single *effect* to be wrought out, he then invents such incidents—he then combines such events as may best aid him in establishing this preconceived effect.

Magazine publication is the ideal outlet for Poe's hypothesized tale, where works "requiring from a half-hour to one or two hours in [their] perusal" appeared. Indeed, the emphasis in Poe's review-essay is on the reader's experience of the work, and not upon the work itself; as if—can this be genius speaking? in the very language of the hack?—it scarcely matters *what* has been written, only *that* it has been written to a certain pre-conceived effect. (It should be noted too, and not incidentally, that Poe was a man of vast literary ambitions, and not simply, or not exclusively, a tormented Romantic driven to the composition of uncanny poetry and prose: he wrote for magazines, and he edited magazines, and it was his professional obsession from 1836 to his death in 1849 to found and edit a magazine, to be called *Penn Magazine.*)

As the literary short story derives from the oral tale, so, in Poe's aesthetic, the meticulously constructed short story relates to the poem. While the highest genius, arguably, is best employed in poetry ("not to exceed in length what might be perused in an hour"), the "loftiest talent" may turn to the prose tale, as exemplified by Nathaniel Hawthorne. Poe elevates the prose tale above much of poetry, in fact, and above the novel, for poetry brings the reader to too high a pitch of excitement to be sustained, and the novel is objectionable because of its "undue" length. By contrast, the brief tale enables the writer "to carry out the fulness of his intention. . . . During the hour of perusal the soul of the reader is at the writer's control. There are no external or extrinsic influences—resulting from weariness or interruption."

In Poe's somewhat Aristotelian terms, the secret of the short story's composition is its unity. Yet, within this, as within a well-made play, a multiplicity of modes or inflections of thought and expression—"the ratiocinative, for example, the sarcastic, or the humorous"—are available to the writer, as they are not available, apparently, to the poet. This concept, dogmatic even for its time, relates only incidentally to the stories Poe himself wrote, but provides an aesthetic anticipating the work of such masters of the genre as Chekhov, Joyce, Henry James, and Hemingway, in which everything is excluded that does not contribute to the general effect, or design, of the story. (Like most critics who are also artists, Poe was formulating an aesthetic to accommodate his own practice and his own limitations. Temperamentally, Poe was probably incapable of the sustained effort of the novelist; this helps to explain his envious disparagement of Charles Dickens, who, for all his apparent flaws in Poe's judgment, enjoyed the enormous popular success denied to Poe during his own lifetime.)

The American short story, however, has had no more thoughtful, visionary, and influential an early critic than Poe; just as the history of the short story itself in America is bound up with the unique work Poe published in 1840, *Tales of the Grotesque and Arabesque.*

A predominant vein connecting the majority of the stories in this volume, from Washington Irving and William Austin through to our contemporaries, is the quest, in some cases a distinctly *American* quest, for one's place in the world; one's cultural and spiritual identity, in terms of self and others.

For ours is the nation, so rare in human history, of self-determination; a theoretical experiment in newness, exploration, discovery. In theory at least, who our ancestors have been, what languages they have spoken, in what religions they believed—these factors cannot really help to define *us*. And it has been often noted that, in the New World, history itself has moved with extraordinary rapidity. Each generation constitutes a beginning-again, a new discovery, sometimes of language itself.

Washington Irving, who begins most volumes of American short fiction, was, in much of his work, a chronicler of tumultuous political change. Though English-oriented in his education, and immensely influenced by eighteenth-century English writers of the didactic and satirical sort, Irving's genius was to appropriate, in his most famous tales, a theme out of folklore: the comedy of the dislocated citizen, who, visited by the supernatural, ends up not knowing who he is. In "Rip Van Winkle," the theme is brilliantly applied to the hapless Rip who falls asleep in colonial America and wakes in post-Revolutionary America: waking to an irrevocably altered world.

Irving was born in 1783, at the end of the American Revolution. But, like Hawthorne, he derived great imaginative inspiration from the history of the region in which he lived. Not Irving's contemporary America, that vital, seething young nation, but Colonial America, in the quaintly sequestered world of the Kaatskill Mountains, is the setting for the robustly tall tale "Rip Van Winkle," a parable of dislocation. Rip, a descendant of Dutch settlers of the early eighteenth century, falls into an enchanted sleep, and, when he wakes, finds himself in post-Revolutionary America, where, to his astonishment, a new political language is spoken. The likeness of old King George has been metamorphosed into a dapper military portrait of someone called General Washington; Rip is no longer a subject of British rule, but a "free citizen of the United States"—which means nothing to him. It is a concept simply beyond his comprehension, as, Irving suggests, it is a concept beyond the comprehension of many citizens who had lived through the Revolution but were incapable of "revolutionizing" themselves. So, too, perhaps with the majority of men and women, in periods of violent social upheaval?

Where Irving's tone is jocular, tongue-in-cheek, William Austin's is grimly serious in his parable of Peter Rugg, the Missing Man. Here, the enchantment is clearly a curse, and Peter Rugg is a Flying Dutchman of sorts, doomed to ceaseless motion. Austin may have intended his archetypal hero to represent a newer species of man—a "lost" man—an atheist—who utters an oath that offends God, thus sealing his doom. Like certain of Hawthorne's similarly accursed heroes Rugg is dislocated yet more radically than Rip Van Winkle. To Rugg, the "new generation" of Bostonians are his enemies, and his home, his family, his very identity have been stripped from him. (Compare the equally desperate fate of the elderly Major Molineux in Hawthorne's "My Kinsman, Major Molineux.")

Another aspect of identity, that of "gendered" fate, at least as linked with the vicissitudes of social class, is taken up, with characteristic irony, by Melville in his linked sexual allegories "The Paradise of Bachelors and the Tartarus of Maids." The vision of sexual determinism—for the working-class female, her doom—strikes us as disturbingly contemporary. (Melville, in his great, brooding, idiosyncratic prose works, is *always* our contemporary.) How like the nightmare fate of Charlotte Perkins Gilman's heroine, trapped in her femaleness as in the yellow wallpaper of her confinement, these young factory workers: blank-looking girls, with blank, white folders in blank hands, blankly folding blank paper. Biological destiny and the position of the individual in a burgeoning industrial society are memorably linked, in Melville's vision of hell where Cupid himself is an overseer, and where the production of blank white soulless pulp is an image of the blankness—and inevitability—of human reproduction. Melville's protagonist-observer becomes spellbound—"What made the thing I saw so specially terrible to me was the metallic necessity, the unbudging fatality which governed it." Only Herman Melville could have fashioned out of "real" events (his visits to a gentleman's club in London and to a paper-mill factory in Dalton, Massachusetts) such harrowing and dreamlike allegorical fiction.

By Poe's criteria, "The Paradise of Bachelors and the Tartarus of Maids" is perhaps not a successful tale, lacking unity. Yet it is as horrific an image of man's (and woman's) fate as Poe himself created.

Questions of sexual and racial identity are taken up in more realistic terms by writers of subsequent generations, like Charles W. Chesnutt (whose "The Sheriff's Children" anticipates the obsessive father-son theme of Langston Hughes' work), Mary E. Wilkins Freeman (whose "Old Woman Magoun" anticipates radical feminist texts of our time), and Charlotte Perkins Gilman (whose "The Yellow Wallpaper," a Poe-inspired narration of lyric madness, has become in fact a celebrated feminist text of our time). Edith Wharton's unusually frank "A Journey" is a naturalistic allegory dramatizing a young wife's experience of her husband's dying; her resentment and terror of the burden his very body represents to her in death—as if she, yearning to live, will be stigmatized by his death, forced to disembark prematurely from the train (of life?). A similar moment of crisis is experienced—and transcended—by the hysterically repressed Presbyterian minister of Sherwood Anderson's "The Strength of God" (from *Winesburg, Ohio*): "God has appeared to me," the minister announces, "—in the person of Kate Swift, the school teacher, kneeling naked on a bed."

Arguably, most African-American writing is about racial identity: black cohesiveness and dispersion in a rapidly industrialized country; black experience (suffering, resignation, rebellion, rage, accommodation, integration, self-determination) in the face of historical white oppression. In broad theoretical images, the "white father's black son"—the unacknowledged progeny of the "white master"—is an emblem of the misbegotten and the rejected who returns as a powerful threat. The "Jesus" of William Faulkner's "That Evening Sun" is a bitter sort of savior; the degraded black man, the probable son of slaves, who revenges himself against the only victim available to him in his powerlessness—the black woman who is his wife. Faulkner's depiction of this tragedy is the more wrenching in that it is told to us obliquely, through the chattering and arguing of a self-absorbed white Mississippian family.

Striking a distinctly ominous note is Richard Wright's "The Man Who Was Almost a Man" (the black youth who is "almost" a murderer, and on his way to being one)—a story disturbing to white readers as the author's controversial *Native Son*, one of the seminal novels of black American experience. The young black men of Jean Toomer's "Blood-Burning Moon" and Ralph Ellison's "Battle Royal" inhabit a society divided along indisputably racist lines; Eudora Welty's "Where Is the Voice Coming From?" presents a deranged white murderer, the very voice of a retrograde Southern society of the 1960's. Only James Baldwin's "Sonny's Blues" ends with an image of transcendence and hope, however painfully won: "Then they all gathered around Sonny, and Sonny played. . . . Sonny's fingers filled the air with life, his life. But that life contained so many others." In a contemporary story by John Edgar Wideman, "Fever," blackness itself is perceived by whites as a contagion—"evil incarnate"—yet acquires a purposeful strength, the strength of bitterness, cunning, ironic detachment.

Among those writers with whom we associate literary Modernism (Ernest Hemingway, for instance) and those writers who are our contemporaries, questions of identity have become all-absorbing. The quintessential Hemingway hero is a paradigm for the hero (or heroine) of much twentieth-century fiction, whose predicament is: once one has stripped oneself of superfluities of identity, what remains? The terror of night?—nothingness? "Our nada who art in nada, nada be thy name," is the prayer of "A Clean, Well-Lighted Place"—as if God were nothing, and nothingness *is* God. Scott Fitzgerald's cartoonist-hero of the painfully autobiographical "An Alcoholic Case" looks into a corner of the hotel bathroom and sees death awaiting him: and nothing more. Perhaps the most extreme (and unforgettable) image of twentieth-century existential dislocation is the brutalized, tongueless American professor (of linguistics) of Paul Bowles's nightmare parable, "A Distant Episode."

In our contemporaries, the burden of history and politics as *personal* fate, weighing, at times, almost physically upon the shoulders of survivors and descendants, is dramatized in stories encompassing a wide range of subject matter, style, and vision—from Flannery O'Connor's mordant "A Late Encounter with the Enemy" (an aged Civil War veteran's hallucinatory descent into death, and into his identity) to Bernard Malamud's "My Son the Murderer" (generational conflict in the radicalized, despairing Sixties), Louise Erdrich's "Fleur" (a Native American "witch" resists the fate that would make her a victim) and Bharati Mukherjee's "The Management of Grief" (the surviving member of a Hindu family killed in a terrorist bombing detaches herself, through pain, from the paralysis of grief). The elliptical, poetic tales of Sandra Cisneros and the seemingly forthright, conversational "Two Kinds" by

Amy Tan take for granted a dominant Caucasian world outside the family—here, such abstractions as history and politics are realized in the experience of sensitive, yet representative, adolescent girls.

Meticulous chroniclers of lives less dramatically touched by history, though yet distinctly, often disturbingly American, are such writers as John Cheever, John Updike, Alice Adams, Ursula Le Guin, Raymond Carver, among others, who have taken for their subjects the lives (and what radically differing lives, told in what radically differing voices) of what might be called mainstream Americans of the Caucasian middle class. What these writers share is their artistry; their commitment to the short story; their faith in the imaginative reconstruction of reality that constitutes literature.

As Tolstoy said, talent is the capacity to direct concentrated attention upon the subject: "the gift of seeing what others have not seen."

Though it is hardly necessary, I suggest that the reader read this volume as it is assembled, more or less chronologically. A tale will unfold, by way of numerous tales, that is uniquely and wonderfully American.

WASHINGTON IRVING
(1783–1859)

Born in New York City on April 3, 1783, the last of eleven children of a wealthy Scottish merchant and an Englishwoman, Washington Irving is our first American writer to achieve a distinguished international reputation; the first to become a "classic" during his own lifetime. Well educated, cosmopolitan, imbued with a deep admiration for English literature and an interest in adapting such seemingly primitive forms as the ballad and the folklore for serious literary purposes, Irving strikes us as a highly conscious, even rather scholarly craftsman—an "imitator," as Melville would characterize him, rather than a "creative genius." Yet, so vividly rendered are certain of his fictitious characters (notably Rip Van Winkle and Ichabod Crane, of "The Legend of Sleepy Hollow"), so deeply imprinted have they become in the popular imagination, they strike us as mythopoetic figures—timeless, archetypal, transcending the circumstances of their own creation.

Rip Van Winkle and Ichabod Crane spring from the pages of The Sketch Book *(1820), Irving's most famous title, published under the pseudonym "Geoffrey Crayon." In an earlier phase of his long career, Irving had achieved remarkable celebrity, aged twenty-five, as "Diedrich Knickerbocker," the comically pedantic author of* A History of New York *(1809). Irving was a writer of sketches rather than fully realized stories, and his characters, like the luckless Rip Van Winkle, have an emblematic quality, illuminated by the hearty glare of comedy. He was a superb stylist, not a psychologist, for whom, as he said, a story is "merely a frame on which to sketch my materials."*

But what rich materials, and how elegantly constructed a frame.

Rip Van Winkle

A Posthumous Writing of Diedrich Knickerbocker

By Woden, God of Saxons,
From whence comes Wensday, that is Wodensday,
Truth is a thing that ever I will keep
Unto thylke day in which I creep into
My sepulchre—"

CARTWRIGHT

Whoever has made a voyage up the Hudson must remember the Kaatskill mountains. They are a dismembered branch of the great Appalachian family, and are seen away to the west of the river, swelling up to a noble height, and lording it over the surrounding country. Every change of season, every change of weather, indeed, every hour of the day, produces some change in the magical hues and shapes of these mountains, and they are regarded by all the good wives, far and near, as perfect barometers. When the weather is fair and settled, they are clothed in blue and purple, and print their bold outlines on the clear evening sky; but, sometimes, when the rest of the landscape is cloudless, they will gather a hood of gray vapors about their summits, which, in the last rays of the setting sun, will glow and light up like a crown of glory.

At the foot of these fairy mountains, the voyager may have descried the light smoke curling up from a village, whose shingle-roofs gleam among the trees, just where the blue tints of the upland melt away into the fresh green of the nearer landscape. It is a little village of great antiquity, having been founded by some of the Dutch colonists, in the early times of the province, just about the beginning of the government of the good Peter Stuyvesant, (may he rest in peace!) and there were some of the houses of the original settlers standing within a few years, built of small yellow bricks brought from Holland, having latticed windows and gable fronts, surmounted with weather-cocks.

In that same village, and in one of these very houses (which, to tell the precise truth, was sadly time-worn and weather-beaten), there lived many years since, while the country was yet a province of Great Britain, a simple good-natured fellow of the name of Rip Van Winkle. He was a descendant of the Van Winkles who figured so gallantly in the chivalrous days of Peter Stuyvesant, and accompanied him to the siege of Fort Christina. He inherited, however, but little of the martial character of his ancestors. I have observed that he was a simple, good-natured man; he was, moreover, a kind neighbor, and an obedient, hen-pecked husband. Indeed, to the latter circumstance might be owing that meekness of spirit which gained him such universal popularity; for those men are most apt to be obsequious and conciliating abroad, who are under the discipline of shrews at home. Their tempers, doubtless, are rendered pliant and malleable in the fiery furnace of domestic tribulation; and a curtain lecture is worth all the sermons in the world for teaching the virtues of patience and long-suffering. A termagant wife may, therefore, in some respects, be considered a tolerable blessing; and if so, Rip Van Winkle was thrice blessed.

Certain it is, that he was a great favorite among all the good wives of the village, who, as usual, with the amiable sex, took his part in all family squabbles; and never failed, whenever they talked those matters over in their evening gossipings, to lay all the blame on Dame Van Winkle. The children of the village, too, would shout with joy whenever he approached. He assisted at their sports, made their playthings, taught them to fly kites and shoot marbles, and told them long stories of ghosts, witches, and Indians. Whenever he went dodging about the village, he was surrounded by a troop of them, hanging on his skirts, clambering on his back, and playing a thousand tricks on him with impunity; and not a dog would bark at him throughout the neighborhood.

The great error in Rip's composition was an insuperable aversion to all kinds of profitable labor. It could not be from the want of assiduity or perseverance; for he would sit on a wet rock, with a rod as long and heavy as a Tartar's lance, and fish all day without a murmur, even though he should not be encouraged by a single nibble. He would carry a fowling-piece on his shoulder for hours together, trudging through woods and swamps, and up hill and down dale, to shoot a few squirrels or wild pigeons. He would never refuse to assist a neighbor even in the roughest toil, and was a foremost man at all country frolics for husking Indian corn, or building stone fences; the women of the village, too, used to employ him to run their errands, and to do such little odd jobs as their less obliging husbands would not do for them. In a word Rip was ready to attend to anybody's business but his own; but as to doing family duty, and keeping his farm in order, he found it impossible.

In fact, he declared it was of no use to work on his farm; it was the most pestilent little piece of ground in the whole country; everything about it went wrong, and would go wrong, in spite of him. His fences were continually falling to pieces; his cow would either go astray, or get among the cabbages; weeds were sure to grow quicker in his fields than anywhere else; the rain always made a point of setting in just as he had some out-door work to do; so that though his patrimonial estate had dwindled away under his management, acre by acre, until there was little more left than a mere patch of Indian corn and potatoes, yet it was the worst conditioned farm in the neighborhood.

His children, too, were as ragged and wild as if they belonged to nobody. His son Rip, an urchin begotten in his own likeness, promised to inherit the habits, with the old clothes of his father. He was generally seen trooping like a colt at his mother's heels, equipped in a pair of his father's cast-off galligaskins, which he had much ado to hold up with one hand, as a fine lady does her train in bad weather.

Rip Van Winkle, however, was one of those happy mortals, of foolish, well-oiled dispositions, who take the world easy, eat white bread or brown, whichever can be got with least thought or trouble, and would rather starve on a penny than work for a pound. If left to himself, he would have whistled life away in perfect contentment; but his wife kept continually dinning in his ears about his idleness, his carelessness, and the ruin he was bringing on his family. Morning, noon, and night, her tongue was incessantly going, and everything he said or did was sure to produce a torrent of household eloquence. Rip had but one way of replying to all lectures of the kind, and that, by frequent use, had grown into a habit. He shrugged his shoulders, shook his head, cast up his eyes, but said nothing. This, however, always provoked a fresh volley from his wife; so that he was fain to draw off his forces, and take to the outside of the house—the only side which, in truth, belongs to a hen-pecked husband.

Rip's sole domestic adherent was his dog Wolf, who was as much hen-pecked as his master; for Dame Van Winkle regarded them as companions in idleness, and even looked upon Wolf with an evil eye, as the cause of his master's going so often astray. True it is, in all points of spirit befitting an honorable dog, he was as courageous an animal as ever scoured the woods—but what courage can withstand the ever-during and all-be-setting terrors of a woman's tongue? The moment Wolf entered the house his crest fell, his tail drooped to the ground, or curled between his legs, he sneaked about with a gallows air, casting many a sidelong glance at Dame Van Winkle, and at the least flourish of a broomstick or ladle, he would fly to the door with yelping precipitation.

Times grew worse and worse with Rip Van Winkle as years of matrimony rolled on; a tart temper never mellows with age, and a sharp tongue is the only edged tool that grows keener with constant use. For a long while he used to console himself, when driven from home, by frequenting a kind of perpetual club of the sages, philosophers, and other idle personages of the village; which held its sessions on a bench before a small inn, designated by a rubicund portrait of His Majesty George the Third. Here they used to sit in the shade through a long lazy summer's day, talking listlessly over village gossip, or telling endless sleepy stories about nothing. But it would have been worth any statesman's money to have heard the profound discussions that sometimes took place, when by chance an old newspaper fell into their hands from some passing traveller. How solemnly they would listen to the contents, as drawled out by Derrick Van Bummel, the schoolmaster, a dapper learned little man, who was not to be daunted by the most gigantic word in the dictionary; and how sagely they would deliberate upon the public events some months after they had taken place.

The opinions of this junto were completely controlled by Nicholas Vedder, a patriarch of the village, and landlord of the inn, at the door of which he took his seat from morning till night, just moving sufficiently to avoid the sun and keep in the shade of a large tree; so that the neighbors could tell the hour by his movements as accurately as by a sun-dial. It is true he was rarely heard to speak, but smoked his pipe incessantly. His adherents, however (for every great man has his adherents), perfectly understood him, and knew how to gather his opinions. When any thing that was read or related displeased him, he was observed to smoke his pipe vehemently, and to send forth short, frequent and angry puffs; but when pleased, he would inhale the smoke slowly and tranquilly, and emit it in light and placid clouds; and sometimes, taking the pipe from his mouth, and letting the fragrant vapor curl about his nose, would gravely nod his head in token of perfect approbation.

From even this stronghold the unlucky Rip was at length routed by his termagant wife, who would suddenly break in upon the tranquillity of the assemblage and call the members all to naught; nor was that august personage, Nicholas Vedder himself, sacred from the daring tongue of this terrible virago, who charged him outright with encouraging her husband in habits of idleness.

Poor Rip was at last reduced almost to despair; and his only alternative, to escape from the labor of the farm and clamor of his wife, was to take gun in hand and stroll away into the woods. Here he would sometimes seat himself at the foot of a tree, and share the contents of his wallet with Wolf, with whom he sympathized as a fellow-sufferer in persecution. "Poor Wolf," he would say, "thy mistress leads thee a dog's life of it; but never mind, my lad, whilst I live thou shalt never want a friend to stand by thee!" Wolf would wag his tail, look wistfully in his master's face, and if dogs can feel pity I verily believe he reciprocated the sentiment with all his heart.

In a long ramble of the kind on a fine autumnal day, Rip had unconsciously scrambled to one of the highest parts of the Kaatskill mountains. He was after his favorite sport of squirrel shooting, and the still solitudes had echoed and re-echoed with the reports of his gun. Panting and fatigued, he threw himself, late in the afternoon, on a green knoll, covered with mountain herbage, that crowned the brow of a precipice. From an opening between the trees he could overlook all the lower country for many a mile of rich woodland. He saw at a distance the lordly Hudson, far, far below him, moving on its silent but majestic course, with the reflection of a purple cloud, or the sail of a lagging bark, here and there sleeping on its glassy bosom, and at last losing itself in the blue highlands.

On the other side he looked down into a deep mountain glen, wild, lonely, and shagged, the bottom filled with fragments from the impending cliffs, and scarcely lighted by the reflected rays of the setting sun. For some time Rip lay musing on this scene; evening was gradually advancing; the mountains began to throw their long blue shadows over the valleys; he saw that it would be dark long before he could reach the village, and he heaved a heavy sigh when he thought of encountering the terrors of Dame Van Winkle.

As he was about to descend, he heard a voice from a distance, hallooing, "Rip Van Winkle! Rip Van Winkle!" He looked round, but could see nothing but a crow winging its solitary flight across the mountain. He thought his fancy must have deceived him, and turned again to descend, when he heard the same cry ring through the still evening air: "Rip Van Winkle! Rip Van Winkle!"—at the same time Wolf bristled up his back, and giving a low growl, skulked to his master's side, looking fearfully down into the glen. Rip now felt a vague apprehension stealing over him; he looked anxiously in the same direction, and perceived a strange figure slowly toiling up the rocks, and bending under the weight of something he carried on his back. He was surprised to see any human being in this lonely and unfrequented place, but supposing it to be some one of the neighborhood in need of his assistance, he hastened down to yield it.

On nearer approach he was still more surprised at the singularity of the stranger's appearance. He was a short square-built old fellow, with thick bushy hair, and a grizzled beard. His dress was of the antique Dutch fashion—a cloth jerkin strapped round the waist—several pair of breeches, the outer one of ample volume, decorated with rows of buttons down the sides, and bunches at the knees. He bore on his shoulder a stout keg, that seemed full of liquor, and made signs for Rip to approach and assist him with the load. Though rather shy and distrustful of this new acquaintance, Rip complied with his usual alacrity; and mutually relieving one another, they clambered up a narrow gully, apparently the dry bed of a mountain torrent. As they ascended, Rip every now and then heard long rolling peals, like distant thunder, that seemed to issue out of a deep ravine, or rather cleft, between lofty rocks, toward which their rugged path conducted. He paused for an instant, but supposing it to be the muttering of one of those transient thunder-showers which often take place in mountain heights, he proceeded. Passing through the ravine, they came to a hollow, like a small amphitheatre, surrounded by perpendicular precipices, over the brinks of which impending trees shot their branches, so that you only caught glimpses of the azure sky and the bright evening cloud. During the whole time Rip and his companion had labored on in silence; for though the former marvelled greatly what could be the object of carrying a keg of liquor up this wild mountain, yet there was something strange and incomprehensible about the unknown, that inspired awe and checked familiarity.

On entering the amphitheatre, new objects of wonder presented themselves. On a level spot in the centre was a company of odd-looking personages playing at ninepins. They were dressed in a quaint outlandish fashion; some wore short doublets, others jerkins, with long knives in their belts, and most of them had enormous breeches, of similar style with that of the guide's. Their visages, too, were peculiar: one had a large beard, broad face, and small piggish eyes; the face of another seemed to consist entirely of nose, and was surmounted by a white sugar-loaf hat set off with a little red cock's tail. They all had beards, of various shapes and colors. There was one who seemed to be the commander. He was a stout old gentleman, with a weather-beaten countenance; he wore a laced doublet, broad belt and hanger, high-crowned hat and feather, red stockings, and high-heeled shoes, with roses in them. The whole group reminded Rip of the figures in an old Flemish painting, in the parlor of Dominie Van Shaick, the village parson, and which had been brought over from Holland at the time of the settlement.

What seemed particularly odd to Rip was, that though these folks were evidently amusing themselves, yet they maintained the gravest faces, the most mysterious silence, and were, withal, the most melancholy party of pleasure he had ever witnessed. Nothing interrupted the stillness of the scene but the noise of the balls, which, whenever they were rolled, echoed along the mountains like rumbling peals of thunder.

As Rip and his companion approached them, they suddenly desisted from their play, and stared at him with such fixed statue-like gaze, and such strange, uncouth, lack-lustre countenances, that his heart turned within him, and his knees smote together. His companion now emptied the contents of the keg into large flagons, and made signs to him to wait upon the company. He obeyed with fear and trembling; they quaffed the liquor in profound silence, and then returned to their game.

By degrees Rip's awe and apprehension subsided. He even ventured, when no eye was fixed upon him, to taste the beverage, which he found had much of the flavor of excellent Hollands. He was naturally a thirsty soul, and was soon tempted to repeat the draught. One taste provoked another; and he reiterated his visits to the flagon so often that at length his senses were overpowered, his eyes swam in his head, his head gradually declined, and he fell into a deep sleep.

On waking, he found himself on the green knoll whence he had first seen the old man of the glen. He rubbed his eyes—it was a bright sunny morning. The birds were hopping and twittering among the bushes, and the eagle was wheeling aloft, and breasting the pure mountain breeze. "Surely," thought Rip, "I have not slept here all night." He recalled the occurrences before he fell asleep. The strange man with a keg of liquor—the mountain ravine—the wild retreat among the rocks—the woe-begone party at ninepins—the flagon—"Oh! that flagon! that wicked flagon!" thought Rip—"what excuse shall I make to Dame Van Winkle!"

He looked round for his gun, but in place of the clean well-oiled fowling-piece, he found an old firelock lying by him, the barrel incrusted with rust, the lock falling off, and the stock worm-eaten. He now suspected that the grave roysters of the mountain had put a trick upon him, and, having dosed him with liquor, had robbed him of his gun. Wolf, too, had disappeared, but he might have strayed away after a squirrel or partridge. He whistled after him and shouted his name, but all in vain; the echoes repeated his whistle and shout, but no dog was to be seen.

He determined to revisit the scene of the last evening's gambol, and if he met with any of the party, to demand his dog and gun. As he rose to walk, he found himself stiff in the joints, and wanting in his usual activity. "These mountain beds do not agree with me," thought Rip, "and if this frolic should lay me up with a fit of the rheumatism, I shall have a blessed time with Dame Van Winkle." With some difficulty he got down into the glen: he found the gully up which he and his companion had ascended the preceding evening; but to his astonishment a mountain stream was now foaming down it, leaping from rock to rock, and filling the glen with babbling murmurs. He, however, made shift to scramble up its sides, working his toilsome way through thickets of birch, sassafras, and witch-hazel, and sometimes tripped up or entangled by the wild grapevines that twisted their coils or tendrils from tree to tree, and spread a kind of network in his path.

At length he reached to where the ravine had opened through the cliffs to the amphitheatre; but no traces of such opening remained. The rocks presented a high impenetrable wall, over which the torrent came tumbling in a sheet of feathery foam, and fell into a broad deep basin, black from the shadows of the surrounding forest. Here, then, poor Rip was brought to a stand. He again called and whistled after his dog; he was only answered by the cawing of a flock of idle crows, sporting high in air about a dry tree that overhung a sunny precipice; and who, secure in their elevation, seemed to look down and scoff at the poor man's perplexities. What was to be done? The morning was passing away, and Rip felt famished for want of his breakfast. He grieved to give up his dog and gun; he dreaded to meet his wife; but it would not do to starve among the mountains. He shook his head, shouldered the rusty firelock, and, with a heart full of trouble and anxiety, turned his steps homeward.

As he approached the village he met a number of people, but none whom he knew, which somewhat surprised him, for he had thought himself acquainted with everyone in the country round. Their dress, too, was of a different fashion from that to which he was accustomed. They all stared at him with equal marks of surprise, and whenever they cast their eyes upon him, invariably stroked their chins. The constant recurrence of this gesture induced Rip, involuntarily, to do the same, when, to his astonishment, he found his beard had grown a foot long!

He had now entered the skirts of the village. A troop of strange children ran at his heels, hooting after him, and pointing at his gray beard. The dogs, too, not one of which he recognized for an old acquaintance, barked at him as he passed. The very village was altered; it was larger and more populous. There were rows of houses which he had never seen before, and those which had been his familiar haunts had disappeared. Strange names were over the doors—strange faces at the windows—everything was strange. His mind now misgave him; he began to doubt whether both he and the world around him were not bewitched. Surely this was his native village, which he had left but the day before. There stood the Kaatskill mountains—there ran the silver Hudson at a distance—there was every hill and dale precisely as it had always been. Rip was sorely perplexed—"That flagon last night," thought he, "has addled my poor head sadly!"

It was with some difficulty that he found the way to his own house, which he approached with silent awe, expecting every moment to hear the shrill voice of Dame Van Winkle. He found the house gone to decay—the roof fallen in, the windows shattered, and the doors off the hinges. A half-starved dog that looked like Wolf was skulking about it. Rip called him by name, but the cur snarled, showed his teeth, and passed on. This was an unkind cut indeed—"My very dog," sighed poor Rip, "has forgotten me!"

He entered the house, which, to tell the truth, Dame Van Winkle had always kept in neat order. It was empty, forlorn, and apparently abandoned. This desolateness overcame all his connubial fears—he called loudly for his wife and children—the lonely chambers rang for a moment with his voice, and then all again was silence.

He now hurried forth, and hastened to his old resort, the village inn—but it too was gone. A large rickety wooden building stood in its place, with great gaping windows, some of them broken and mended with old hats and petticoats, and over the door was painted, "the Union Hotel, by Jonathan Doolittle." Instead of the great tree that used to shelter the quiet little Dutch inn of yore, there now was reared a tall naked pole, with something on the top that looked like a red night-cap, and from it was fluttering a flag, on which was a singular assemblage of stars and stripes—all this was strange and incomprehensible. He recognized on the sign, however, the ruby face of King George, under which he had smoked so many a peaceful pipe; but even this was singularly metamorphosed. The red coat was changed for one of blue and buff, a sword was held in the hand instead of a sceptre, the head was decorated with a cocked hat, and underneath, was painted in large characters, GENERAL WASHINGTON.

There was, as usual, a crowd of folk about the door, but none that Rip recollected. The very character of the people seemed changed. There was a busy, bustling, disputatious tone about it, instead of the accustomed phlegm and drowsy tranquillity. He looked in vain for the sage Nicholas Vedder, with his broad face, double chin, and fair long pipe, uttering clouds of tobacco-smoke instead of idle speeches; or Van Bummel, the schoolmaster, doling forth the contents of an ancient newspaper. In place of these, a lean, bilious-looking fellow, with his pockets full of handbills, was haranguing vehemently about rights of citizens—elections—members of Congress—liberty—Bunker's Hill—heroes of seventy-six—and other words, which were a perfect Babylonish jargon to the bewildered Van Winkle.

The appearance of Rip, with his long grizzled beard, his rusty fowling-piece, his uncouth dress, and an army of women and children at his heels, soon attracted the attention of the tavern politicians. They crowded round him, eying him from head to foot with great curiosity. The orator bustled up to him, and, drawing him partly aside, inquired "On which side he voted?" Rip stared in vacant stupidity. Another short but busy little fellow pulled him by the arm, and, rising on tiptoe, inquired in his ear, "Whether he was Federal or Democrat?" Rip was equally at a loss to comprehend the question; when a knowing, self-important old gentleman, in a sharp cocked hat, made his way through the crowd, putting them to the right and left with his elbows as he passed, and planting himself before Van Winkle, with one arm akimbo, the other resting on his cane, his keen eyes and sharp hat penetrating, as it were, into his very soul, demanded in an austere tone, "What brought him to the election with a gun on his shoulder, and a mob at his heels, and whether he meant to breed a riot in the village?"—"Alas! gentlemen," cried Rip, somewhat dismayed, "I am a poor quiet man, a native of the place, and a loyal subject of the king, God bless him!"

Here a general shout burst from the bystanders—"A tory! a tory! a spy! a refugee! hustle him! away with him!" It was with great difficulty that the self-important man in the cocked hat restored order; and, having assumed a tenfold austerity of brow, demanded again of the unknown culprit, what he came there for, and whom he was seeking? The poor man humbly assured him that he meant no harm, but merely came there in search of some of his neighbors, who used to keep about the tavern.

"Well—who are they?—name them."

Rip bethought himself a moment, and inquired. "Where's Nicholas Vedder?"

There was a silence for a little while, when an old man replied in a thin piping voice, "Nicholas Vedder! why, he is dead and gone these eighteen years! There was a wooden tombstone in the churchyard that used to tell all about him, but that's rotten and gone too."

"Where's Brom Dutcher?"

"Oh, he went off to the army in the beginning of the war; some say he was killed at the storming of Stony Point—others say he was drowned in a squall at the foot of Antony's Nose. I don't know—he never came back again."

"Where's Van Bummel, the schoolmaster?"

"He went off to the wars too, was a great militia general, and is now in Congress."

Rip's heart died away at hearing of these sad changes in his home and friends, and finding himself thus alone in the world. Every answer puzzled him too, by treating of such enormous lapses of time, and of matters which he could not understand: war—congress—Stony Point;—he had no courage to ask after any more friends, but cried out in despair, "Does nobody here know Rip Van Winkle?"

"Oh, Rip Van Winkle!" exclaimed two or three, "Oh, to be sure! that's Rip Van Winkle yonder, leaning against the tree."

Rip looked, and beheld a precise counterpart of himself, as he went up the mountain: apparently as lazy, and certainly as ragged. The poor fellow was now completely confounded. He doubted his own identity, and whether he was himself or another man. In the midst of his bewilderment, the man in the cocked hat demanded who he was, and what was his name?

"God knows," exclaimed he, at his wit's end; "I'm not myself—I'm somebody else—that's me yonder—no—that's somebody else got into my shoes—I was myself last night, but I fell asleep on the mountain, and they've changed my gun, and every thing's changed, and I'm changed, and I can't tell my name, or who I am!"

The bystanders began now to look at each other, nod, wink significantly, and tap their fingers against their foreheads. There was a whisper, also, about securing the gun, and keeping the old fellow from doing mischief, at the very suggestion of which the self-important man in the cocked hat retired with some precipitation. At this critical moment a fresh, comely woman pressed through the throng to get a peep at the gray-bearded man. She had a chubby child in her arms, which, frightened at his looks, began to cry. "Hush, Rip," cried she, "hush, you little fool; the old man won't hurt you." The name of the child, the air of the mother, the tone of her voice, all awakened a train of recollections in his mind. "What is your name, my good woman?" asked he.

"Judith Gardenier."

"And your father's name?"

"Ah, poor man, Rip Van Winkle was his name, but it's twenty years since he went away from home with his gun, and never has been heard of since—his dog came home without him; but whether he shot himself, or was carried away by the Indians, nobody can tell. I was then but a little girl."

Rip had but one question more to ask; but he put it with a faltering voice:

"Where's your mother?"

"Oh, she too had died but a short time since; she broke a blood-vessel in a fit of passion at a New England peddler."

There was a drop of comfort, at least, in this intelligence. The honest man could contain himself no longer. He caught his daughter and her child in his arms. "I am your father!" cried he—"Young Rip Van Winkle once—old Rip Van Winkle now!—Does nobody know poor Rip Van Winkle?"

All stood amazed, until an old woman, tottering out from among the crowd, put her hand to her brow, and peering under it in his face for a moment, exclaimed, "Sure enough! it is Rip Van Winkle—it is himself! Welcome home again, old neighbor—Why, where have you been these twenty long years?"

Rip's story was soon told, for the whole twenty years had been to him but as one night. The neighbors stared when they heard it; some were seen to wink at each other, and put their tongues in their cheeks; and the self-important man in the cocked hat, who, when the alarm was over, had returned to the field, screwed down the corners of his mouth, and shook his head—upon which there was a general shaking of the head throughout the assemblage.

It was determined, however, to take the opinion of old Peter Vanderdonk, who was seen slowly advancing up the road. He was a descendant of the historian of that name, who wrote one of the earliest accounts of the province. Peter was the most ancient inhabitant of the village, and well versed in all the wonderful events and traditions of the neighborhood. He recollected Rip at once, and corroborated his story in the most satisfactory manner. He assured the company that it was a fact, handed down from his ancestor the historian, that the Kaatskill mountains had always been haunted by strange beings. That it was affirmed that the great Hendrick Hudson, the first discoverer of the river and country, kept a kind of vigil there every twenty years, with his crew of the

Half-Moon; being permitted in this way to revisit the scenes of his enterprise, and keep a guardian eye upon the river, and the great city called by his name. That his father had once seen them in their old Dutch dresses playing at ninepins in a hollow of the mountain; and that he himself had heard one summer afternoon, the sound of their balls, like distant peals of thunders.

To make a long story short, the company broke up, and returned to the more important concerns of the election. Rip's daughter took him home to live with her; she had a snug, well-furnished house, and a stout cheery farmer for a husband, whom Rip recollected for one of the urchins that used to climb upon his back. As to Rip's son and heir, who was the ditto of himself, seen leaning against the tree, he was employed to work on the farm; but evinced an hereditary disposition to attend to anything else but his business.

Rip now resumed his old walks and habits; he soon found many of his former cronies, though all rather the worse for the wear and tear of time, and preferred making friends among the rising generation, with whom he soon grew into great favor.

Having nothing to do at home, and being arrived at that happy age when a man can be idle with impunity, he took his place once more on the bench at the inn door, and was reverenced as one of the patriarchs of the village, and a chronicle of the old times "before the war." It was some time before he could get into the regular track of gossip, or could be made to comprehend the strange events that had taken place during his torpor. How that there had been a revolutionary war—that the country had thrown off the yoke of old England—and that, instead of being a subject of his Majesty George the Third, he was now a free citizen of the United States. Rip, in fact, was no politician; the changes of states and empires made but little impression on him; but there was one species of despotism under which he had long groaned, and that was—petticoat government. Happily that was at an end; he had got his neck out of the yoke of matrimony, and could go in and out whenever he pleased, without dreading the tyranny of Dame Van Winkle. Whenever her name was mentioned, however, he shook his head, shrugged his shoulders, and cast up his eyes; which might pass either for an expression of resignation to his fate, or joy at his deliverance.

He used to tell his story to every stranger that arrived at Mr. Doolittle's hotel. He was observed, at first, to vary on some points every time he told it, which was, doubtless, owing to his having so recently awaked. It at last settled down precisely to the tale I have related, and not a man, woman, or child in the neighborhood, but knew it by heart. Some always pretended to doubt the reality of it, and insisted that Rip had been out of his head, and that this was one point on which he always remained flighty. The old Dutch inhabitants, however, almost universally gave it full credit. Even to this day they never hear a thunderstorm of a summer afternoon about the Kaatskill, but they say Hendrick Hudson and his crew are at their game of ninepins; and it is a common wish of all hen-pecked husbands in the neighborhood, when life hangs heavy on their hands, that they might have a quieting draught out of Rip Van Winkle's flagon.

WILLIAM AUSTIN
(1778–1841)

Now forgotten, his most famous story virtually unread, William Austin was a prominent literary figure of his time, trained in the law, and an acute critic of law and politics of the early nineteenth century. He was born in Lunenburg, Massachusetts, graduated from Harvard University in 1798, and wrote "Strictures on Harvard University" soon after graduation. He was also the author of the critical Letters from London *(1804), viewing English law and politics from the perspective of a New Englander. Not a prolific writer, Austin's concerns were with the social and moral condition of the America of his time, a newly formed, incompletely defined nation "cut off from the last age," like Peter Rugg, the Missing Man.*

It is difficult to believe today that this long-forgotten story, a parable reminiscent of the most characteristic work of Nathaniel Hawthorne, was one of the most famous stories of its time; and Peter Rugg, its doomed, self-deluded hero, one of the best-known fictitious figures of his time. Contemporary readers will be struck by the eerie foreshadowing of themes to be taken up, with greater psychological intensity, by a number of subsequent writers—not only Hawthorne, Melville, and Poe, but Franz Kafka and Borges. Presented as a document by an impartial witness, the nightmare tale of Peter Rugg reads as folktale and allegory; Rugg's damnation springs from a seemingly simple source—his profanity, which defies Heaven and sets him apart from the human community. How like the ending of Kafka's "A Country Doctor," these damning words out of nowhere: "There is nothing strange here but yourself, Mr. Rugg. . . . You were cut off from the last age, and you can never be fitted to the present. Your home is gone, and you can never have another home in this world."

Peter Rugg, the Missing Man

From Jonathan Dunwell of New York to Mr. Herman Krauff

Sir,—Agreeably to my promise, I now relate to you all the particulars of the lost man and child which I have been able to collect. It is entirely owing to the humane interest you seemed to take in the report, that I have pursued the inquiry to the following result.

You may remember that business called me to Boston in the summer of 1820. I sailed in the packet to Providence, and when I arrived there I learned that every seat in the stage was engaged. I was thus obliged either to wait a few hours or accept a seat with the driver, who civilly offered me that accommodation. Accordingly, I took my seat by his side, and soon found him intelligent and communicative. When we had travelled about ten miles, the horses suddenly threw their ears on their neck, as flat as a hare's. Said the driver, "Have you a surtout with you?"

"No," said I; "why do you ask?"

"You will want one soon," said he. "Do you observe the ears of all the horses?"

"Yes; and was just about to ask the reason."

"They see the storm-breeder, and we shall see him soon."

At this moment there was not a cloud visible in the firmament. Soon after, a small speck appeared in the road.

"There," said my companion, "comes the storm-breeder. He always leaves a Scotch mist behind him. By many a wet jacket do I remember him. I suppose the poor fellow suffers much himself,—much more than is known to the world."

Presently a man with a child beside him, with a large black horse, and a weather-beaten chair, once built for a chaise-body, passed in great haste, apparently at the rate of twelve miles an hour. He seemed to grasp the reins of his horse with firmness, and appeared to anticipate his speed. He seemed dejected, and looked anxiously at the passengers, particularly at the stage-driver and myself. In a moment after he passed us, the horse's ears were up, and bent themselves forward so that they nearly met.

"Who is that man?" said I; "he seems in great trouble."

"Nobody knows who he is, but his person and the child are familiar to me. I have met him more than a hundred times, and have been so often asked the way to Boston by that man, even when he was travelling directly from that town, that of late I have refused any communication with him; and that is the reason he gave me such a fixed look."

"But does he never stop anywhere?"

"I have never known him to stop anywhere longer than to inquire the way to Boston; and let him be where he may, he will tell you he cannot stay a moment, for he must reach Boston that night."

We were now ascending a high hill in Walpole; and as we had a fair view of the heavens, I was rather disposed to jeer the driver for thinking of his surtout, as not a cloud as big as a marble could be discerned.

"Do you look," said he, "in the direction whence the man came; that is the place to look. The storm never meets him; it follows him."

We presently approached another hill; and when at the height, the driver pointed out in an eastern direction a little black speck about as big as a hat. "There," said he, "is the seed-storm. We may possibly reach Polley's before it reaches us, but the wanderer and his child will go to Providence through rain, thunder, and lightning."

And now the horses, as though taught by instinct, hastened with increased speed. The little black cloud came on rolling over the turnpike, and doubled and trebled itself in all directions. The appearance of this cloud attracted the notice of all the passengers, for after it had spread itself to a great bulk it suddenly became more limited in circumference, grew more compact, dark, and consolidated. And now the successive flashes of chain lightning caused the whole cloud to appear like a sort of irregular net-work, and displayed a thousand fantastic images. The driver bespoke my attention to a remarkable configuration in the cloud. He said every flash of lightning near its centre discovered to him, distinctly, the form of a man sitting in an open carriage drawn by a black horse. But in truth I saw no such thing; the man's fancy was doubtless at fault. It is a very common thing for the imagination to paint for the senses, both in the visible and invisible world.

In the mean time the distant thunder gave notice of a shower at hand; and just as we reached Polley's tavern the rain poured down in torrents. It was soon over, the cloud passing in the direction of the turnpike toward Providence. In a few moments after, a respectable-looking man in a chaise stopped at the door. The man and child in the chair having excited some little sympathy among the passengers, the gentleman was asked if he had observed them. He said he had met them; that the man seemed bewildered, and inquired the way to Boston; that he was driving at great speed, as though he expected to outstrip the tempest; that the moment he had passed him, a thunder-clap broke directly over the man's head, and seemed to envelop both man and child, horse and carriage. "I stopped," said the gentleman, "supposing the lightning had struck him, but the horse only seemed to loom up and increase his speed; and as well as I could judge, he travelled just as fast as the thunder-cloud."

While this man was speaking, a pedler with a cart of tin merchandise came up, all dripping; and on being questioned, he said he had met that man and carriage, within a fortnight, in four different States; that at each time he had inquired the way to Boston; and that a thunder-shower like the present had each time deluged his wagon and his wares, setting his tin pots, etc. afloat, so that he had determined to get a marine insurance for the future. But that which excited his surprise most was the strange conduct of his horse, for long before he could distinguish the man in the chair, his own horse stood still in the road, and flung back his ears. "In short," said the pedler, "I wish never to see that man and horse again; they do not look to me as though they belonged to this world."

This was all I could learn at that time; and the occurrence soon after would have become with me, "like one of those things which had never happened," had I not, as I stood recently on the door-step of Bennett's hotel in Hartford, heard a man say, "There goes Peter Rugg and his child! he looks wet and weary, and farther from Boston than ever." I was satisfied it was the same man I had seen more than three years before; for whoever has once seen Peter Rugg can never after be deceived as to his identity.

"Peter Rugg!" said I; "and who is Peter Rugg?"

"That," said the stranger, "is more than any one can tell exactly. He is a famous traveller, held in light esteem by all innholders, for he never stops to eat, drink, or sleep. I wonder why the government does not employ him to carry the mail."

"Ay," said a by-stander, "that is a thought bright only on one side; how long would it take in that case to send a letter to Boston, for Peter has already, to my knowledge, been more than twenty years travelling to that place."

"But," said I, "does the man never stop anywhere; does he never converse with any one? I saw the same man more than three years since, near Providence, and I heard a strange story about him. Pray, sir, give me some account of this man."

"Sir," said the stranger, "those who know the most respecting that man, say the least. I have heard it asserted that Heaven sometimes sets a mark on a man, either for judgment or a trial. Under which Peter Rugg now labors, I cannot say; therefore I am rather inclined to pity than to judge."

"You speak like a humane man," said I; "and if you have known him so long, I pray you will give me some account of him. Has his appearance much altered in that time?"

"Why, yes. He looks as though he never ate, drank, or slept; and his child looks older than himself, and he looks like time broken off from eternity, and anxious to gain a resting-place."

"And how does his horse look?" said I.

"As for his horse, he looks fatter and gayer, and shows more animation and courage than he did twenty years ago. The last time Rugg spoke to me he inquired how far it was to Boston. I told him just one hundred miles."

" 'Why,' said he, 'how can you deceive me so? It is cruel to mislead a traveller. I have lost my way; pray direct me the nearest way to Boston.'

"I repeated, it was one hundred miles.

" 'How can you say so?' said he; 'I was told last evening it was but fifty, and I have travelled all night.'

" 'But,' said I, 'you are now travelling from Boston. You must turn back.'

" 'Alas,' said he, 'it is all turn back! Boston shifts with the wind, and plays all around the compass. One man tells me it is to the east, another to the west; and the guide-posts too, they all point the wrong way.'

" 'But will you not stop and rest?' said I; 'you seem wet and weary.'

" 'Yes,' said he, 'it has been foul weather since I left home.'

" 'Stop, then, and refresh yourself.'

" 'I must not stop; I must reach home to-night, if possible: though I think you must be mistaken in the distance to Boston.'

"He then gave the reins to his horse, which he restrained with difficulty, and disappeared in a moment. A few days afterward I met the man a little this side of Claremont, winding around the hills in Unity, at the rate, I believe, of twelve miles an hour."

"Is Peter Rugg his real name, or has he accidentally gained that name?"

"I know not, but presume he will not deny his name; you can ask him,—for see, he has turned his horse, and is passing this way."

In a moment a dark-colored, high-spirited horse approached, and would have passed without stopping, but I had resolved to speak to Peter Rugg, or whoever the man might be. Accordingly I stepped into the street; and as the horse approached, I made a feint of stopping him. The man immediately reined his horse. "Sir," said I, "may I be so bold as to inquire if you are not Mr. Rugg? for I think I have seen you before."

"My name is Peter Rugg," said he. "I have unfortunately lost my way; I am wet and weary, and will take it kindly of you to direct me to Boston."

"You live in Boston, do you; and in what street?"

"In Middle Street."

"When did you leave Boston?"

"I cannot tell precisely; it seems a considerable time."

"But how did you and your child become so wet? It has not rained here to-day."

"It has just rained a heavy shower up the river. But I shall not reach Boston to-night if I tarry. Would you advise me to take the old road or the turnpike?"

"Why, the old road is one hundred and seventeen miles, and the turnpike is ninety-seven."

"How can you say so? You impose on me; it is wrong to trifle with a traveller; you know it is but forty miles from Newburyport to Boston."

"But this is not Newburyport; this is Hartford."

"Do not deceive me, sir. Is not this town Newburyport, and the river that I have been following the Merrimack?"

"No, sir; this is Hartford, and the river the Connecticut."

He wrung his hands and looked incredulous. "Have the rivers, too, changed their courses, as the cities have changed places? But see! the clouds are gathering in the south, and we shall have a rainy night. Ah, that fatal oath!"

He would tarry no longer; his impatient horse leaped off, his hind flanks rising like wings: he seemed to devour all before him, and to scorn all behind.

I had now, as I thought, discovered a clew to the history of Peter Rugg; and I determined, the next time my business called me to Boston, to make a further inquiry. Soon after, I was enabled to collect the following particulars from Mrs. Croft, an aged lady in Middle Street, who has resided in Boston during the last twenty years. Her narration is this:

Just at twilight last summer a person stopped at the door of the late Mrs. Rugg. Mrs. Croft on coming to the door perceived a stranger, with a child by his side, in an old weather-beaten carriage, with a black horse. The stranger asked for Mrs. Rugg, and was informed that Mrs. Rugg had died at a good old age, more than twenty years before that time.

The stranger replied, "How can you deceive me so? Do ask Mrs. Rugg to step to the door."

"Sir, I assure you Mrs. Rugg has not lived here these twenty years; no one lives here but myself, and my name is Betsy Croft."

The stranger paused, looked up and down the street, and said, "Though the paint is rather faded, this looks like my house."

"Yes," said the child, "that is the stone before the door that I used to sit on to eat my bread and milk."

"But," said the stranger, "it seems to be on the wrong side of the street. Indeed, everything here seems to be misplaced. The streets are all changed, the people are all changed, the town seems changed, and what is strangest of all, Catherine Rugg has deserted her husband and child. Pray," continued the stranger, "has John Foy come home from sea? He went a long voyage; he is my kinsman. If I could see him, he could give me some account of Mrs. Rugg."

"Sir," said Mrs. Croft, "I never heard of John Foy. Where did he live?"

"Just above here, in Orange-tree Lane."

"There is no such place in this neighborhood."

"What do you tell me! Are the streets gone? Orange-tree Lane is at the head of Hanover Street, near Pemberton's Hill."

"There is no such lane now."

"Madam, you cannot be serious! But you doubtless know my brother, William Rugg. He lives in Royal Exchange Lane, near King Street."

"I know of no such lane; and I am sure there is no such street as King Street in this town."

"No such street as King Street! Why, woman you mock me! You may as well tell me there is no King George. However, madam, you see I am wet and weary, I must find a resting-place. I will go to Hart's tavern, near the market."

"Which market, sir? for you seem perplexed; we have several markets."

"You know there is but one market near the town dock."

"Oh, the old market; but no such person has kept there these twenty years."

Here the stranger seemed disconcerted, and uttered to himself quite audibly: "Strange mistake; how much this looks like the town of Boston! It certainly has a great resemblance to it; but I perceive my mistake now. Some other Mrs. Rugg, some other Middle Street.—Then," said he, "madam, can you direct me to Boston?"

"Why, this is Boston, the city of Boston; I know of no other Boston."

"City of Boston it may be; but it is not the Boston where I live. I recollect now, I came over a bridge instead of a ferry. Pray, what bridge is that I just came over?"

"It is Charles River bridge."

"I perceive my mistake: there is a ferry between Boston and Charlestown; there is no bridge. Ah, I perceive my mistake. If I were in Boston my horse would carry me directly to my own door. But my horse shows by his impatience that he is in a strange place. Absurd, that I should have mistaken this place for the old town of Boston! It is a much finer city than the town of Boston. It has been built long since Boston. I fancy Boston must lie at a distance from this city, as the good woman seems ignorant of it."

At these words his horse began to chafe, and strike the pavement with his forefeet. The stranger seemed a little bewildered, and said, "No home to-night;" and giving the reins to his horse, passed up the street, and I saw no more of him.

It was evident that the generation to which Peter Rugg belonged has passed away.

This was all the account of Peter Rugg I could obtain from Mrs. Croft; but she directed me to an elderly man, Mr. James Felt, who lived near her, and who had kept a record of the principal occurrences for the last fifty years. At my request she sent for him; and after I had related to him the object of my inquiry, Mr. Felt told me he had known Rugg in his youth, and that his disappearance had caused some surprise; but as it sometimes happens that men run away,—sometimes to be rid of others, and sometimes to be rid of themselves,—and Rugg took his child with him, and his own horse and chair, and as it did not appear that any creditors made a stir, the occurrence soon mingled itself in the stream of oblivion; and Rugg and his child, horse, and chair were soon forgotten.

"It is true," said Mr. Felt, "sundry stories grew out of Rugg's affair, whether true or false I cannot tell; but stranger things have happened in my day, without even a newspaper notice."

"Sir," said I, "Peter Rugg is now living. I have lately seen Peter Rugg and his child, horse, and chair; therefore I pray you to relate to me all you know or ever heard of him."

"Why, my friend," said James Felt, "that Peter Rugg is now a living man, I will not deny; but that you have seen Peter Rugg and his child, is impossible, if you mean a small child; for Jenny Rugg, if living, must be at least—let me see—Boston massacre, 1770—Jenny Rugg was about ten years old. Why, sir, Jenny Rugg, if living, must be more than sixty years of age. That Peter Rugg is living, is highly probable, as he was only ten years older than myself, and I was only eighty last March; and I am as likely to live twenty years longer as any man."

Here I perceived that Mr. Felt was in his dotage, and I despaired of gaining any intelligence from him on which I could depend.

I took my leave of Mrs. Croft, and proceeded to my lodgings at the Marlborough Hotel.

"If Peter Rugg," thought I, "has been travelling since the Boston massacre, there is no reason why he should not travel to the end of time. If the present generation know little of him, the next will know less, and Peter and his child will have no hold on this world."

In the course of the evening, I related my adventure in Middle Street.

"Ha!" said one of the company, smiling, "do you really think you have seen Peter Rugg? I have heard my grandfather speak of him, as though he seriously believed his own story."

"Sir," said I, "pray let us compare your grandfather's story of Mr. Rugg with my own."

"Peter Rugg, sir,—if my grandfather was worthy of credit,—once lived in Middle Street, in this city. He was a man of comfortable circumstances, had a wife and one daughter, and was generally esteemed for his sober life and manners. But unhappily, his temper, at times, was altogether ungovernable, and then his language was terrible. In these fits of passion, if a door stood in his way, he would never do less than kick a panel through. He would sometimes throw his heels over his head, and come down on his feet, uttering oaths in a circle; and thus in a rage, he was the first who performed a somerset, and did what others have since learned to do for merriment and money. Once Rugg was seen to bite a tenpenny nail in halves. In those days everybody, both men and boys, wore wigs; and Peter, at these moments of violent passion, would become so profane that his wig would rise up from his head. Some said it was on account of his terrible language; others accounted for it in a more philosophical way, and said it was caused by the expansion of his scalp, as violent passion, we know, will swell the veins and expand the head. While these fits were on him, Rugg had no respect for heaven or earth. Except this infirmity, all agreed that Rugg was a good sort of man; for when his fits were over, nobody was so ready to commend a placid temper as Peter.

"One morning, late in autumn, Rugg, in his own chair, with a fine large bay horse, took his daughter and proceeded to Concord. On his return a violent storm overtook him. At dark he stopped in Menotomy, now West Cambridge, at the door of a Mr. Cutter, a friend of his, who urged him to tarry the night. On Rugg's declining to stop, Mr. Cutter urged him vehemently. 'Why, Mr. Rugg,' said Cutter, 'the storm is overwhelming you. The night is exceedingly dark. Your little daughter will perish. You are in an open chair, and the tempest is increasing.' '*Let the storm increase,*' said Rugg, with a fearful oath, '*I will see home to-night, in spite of the last tempest, or may I never see home!*' At these words he gave his whip to his high-spirited horse and disappeared in a moment. But

Peter Rugg did not reach home that night, nor the next; nor, when he became a missing man, could he ever be traced beyond Mr. Cutter's, in Menotomy.

"For a long time after, on every dark and stormy night the wife of Peter Rugg would fancy she heard the crack of a whip, and the fleet tread of a horse, and the rattling of a carriage passing her door. The neighbors, too, heard the same noises, and some said they knew it was Rugg's horse; the tread on the pavement was perfectly familiar to them. This occurred so repeatedly that at length the neighbors watched with lanterns, and saw the real Peter Rugg, with his own horse and chair and the child sitting beside him, pass directly before his own door, his head turned toward his house, and himself making every effort to stop his horse, but in vain.

"The next day the friends of Mrs. Rugg exerted themselves to find her husband and child. They inquired at every public house and stable in town; but it did not appear that Rugg made any stay in Boston. No one, after Rugg had passed his own door, could give any account of him, though it was asserted by some that the clatter of Rugg's horse and carriage over the pavements shook the houses on both sides of the streets. And this is credible, if indeed Rugg's horse and carriage did pass on that night; for at this day, in many of the streets, a loaded truck or team in passing will shake the houses like an earthquake. However, Rugg's neighbors never afterward watched. Some of them treated it all as a delusion, and thought no more of it. Others of a different opinion shook their heads and said nothing.

"Thus Rugg and his child, horse, and chair were soon forgotten; and probably many in the neighborhood never heard a word on the subject.

"There was indeed a rumor that Rugg was seen afterward in Connecticut, between Suffield and Hartford, passing through the country at headlong speed. This gave occasion to Rugg's friends to make further inquiry; but the more they inquired, the more they were baffled. If they heard of Rugg one day in Connecticut, the next they heard of him winding round the hills in New Hampshire; and soon after a man in a chair, with a small child, exactly answering the description of Peter Rugg, would be seen in Rhode Island inquiring the way to Boston.

"But that which chiefly gave a color of mystery to the story of Peter Rugg was the affair at Charlestown bridge. The toll-gatherer asserted that sometimes, on the darkest and most stormy nights, when no object could be discerned, about the time Rugg was missing, a horse and wheel-carriage, with a noise equal to a troop, would at midnight, in utter contempt of the rates of toll, pass over the bridge. This occurred so frequently that the toll-gatherer resolved to attempt a discovery. Soon after, at the usual time, apparently the same horse and carriage approached the bridge from Charlestown square. The toll-gatherer, prepared, took his stand as near the middle of the bridge as he dared, with a large three-legged stool in his hand; as the appearance passed, he threw the stool at the horse, but heard nothing except the noise of the stool skipping across the bridge. The toll-gatherer on the next day asserted that the stool went directly through the body of the horse, and he persisted in that belief ever after. Whether Rugg, or whoever the person was, ever passed the bridge again, the toll-gatherer would never tell; and when questioned, seemed anxious to waive the subject. And thus Peter Rugg and his child, horse, and carriage, remain a mystery to this day."

This, sir, is all that I could learn of Peter Rugg in Boston.

Further Account of Peter Rugg
By Jonathan Dunwell

In the autumn of 1825 I attended the races at Richmond in Virginia. As two new horses of great promise were run, the race-ground was never better attended, nor was expectation ever more deeply excited. The partisans of Dart and Lightning, the two race-horses, were equally anxious and equally dubious of the result. To an indifferent spectator, it was impossible to perceive any difference. They were equally beautiful to behold, alike in color and height, and as they stood side by side they measured from heel to forefeet within half an inch of each other. The eyes of each were full, prominent, and resolute; and when at time they regarded each other, they assumed a lofty demeanor, seemed to shorten their necks, project their eyes, and rest their bodies equally on their four hoofs. They certainly showed signs of intelligence, and displayed a courtesy to each other unusual even with statesmen.

It was now nearly twelve o'clock, the hour of expectation, doubt, and anxiety. The riders mounted their horses; and so trim, light, and airy they sat on the animals as to seem a part of them. The spectators, many deep in a solid column, had taken their places, and as many thousand breathing statues were there as spectators. All eyes were turned to Dart and Lightning and their two fairy riders. There was nothing to disturb this calm except a busy woodpecker on a neighboring tree. The signal was given, and Dart and Lightning answered it with ready intelligence. At first they proceed at a slow trot, then they quicken to a canter, and then a gallop; presently they sweep the plain. Both horses lay themselves flat on the ground, their riders bending forward and resting their chins between their horses' ears. Had not the ground been perfectly level, had there been any undulation, the least rise and fall, the spectator would now and then have lost sight of both horses and riders.

While these horses, side by side, thus appeared, flying without wings, flat as a hare, and neither gaining on the other, all eyes were diverted to a new spectacle. Directly in the rear of Dart and Lightning, a majestic black horse of unusual size, drawing an old weather-beaten chair, strode over the plain; and although he appeared to make no effort, for he maintained a steady trot, before Dart and Lightning approached the goal the black horse and chair had overtaken the racers, who, on perceiving this new competitor pass them, threw back their ears, and suddenly stopped in their course. Thus neither Dart nor Lightning carried away the purse.

The spectators now were exceedingly curious to learn whence came the black horse and chair. With many it was the opinion that nobody was in the vehicle. Indeed, this began to be the prevalent opinion; for those at a short distance, so fleet was the black horse, could not easily discern who, if anybody, was in the carriage. But both the riders, very near to whom the black horse passed, agreed in this particular,—that a sad-looking man and a little girl were in the chair. When they stated this I was satisfied that the man was Peter Rugg. But what caused no little surprise, John Spring, one of the riders (he who rode Lightning) asserted that no earthly horse without breaking his trot could, in a carriage, outstrip his racehorse; and he persisted, with some passion, that it was not a horse,—or, he was sure it was not a horse, but a large black ox. "What a great black ox can do," said John, "I cannot pretend to say; but no race-horse, not even flying Childers, could out-trot Lightning in a fair race."

This opinion of John Spring excited no little merriment, for it was obvious to every one that it was a powerful black horse that interrupted the race; but John Spring, jealous of Lightning's reputation as a horse, would rather have it thought that any other beast, even an ox, had been the victor. However, the "horse-laugh" at John Spring's expense was soon suppressed; for as soon as Dart and Lightning began to breathe more freely, it was observed that both of them walked deliberately to the track of the race-ground, and putting their heads to the earth, suddenly raised them again and began to snort. They repeated this till John Spring said,—"These horses have discovered something strange; they suspect foul play. Let me go and talk with Lightning."

He went up to Lightning and took hold of his mane; and Lightning put his nose toward the ground and smelt of the earth without touching it, then reared his head very high, and snorted so loudly that the sound echoed from the next hill. Dart did the same. John Spring stooped down to examine the spot where Lightning had smelled. In a moment he raised himself up, and the countenance of the man was changed. His strength failed him, and he sidled against Lightning.

At length John Spring recovered from his stupor and exclaimed, "It was an ox! I told you it was an ox. No real horse ever yet beat Lightning."

And now, on a close inspection of the black horse's tracks in the path, it was evident to every one that the forefeet of the black horse were cloven. Notwithstanding these appearances, to me it was evident that the strange horse was in reality a horse. Yet when the people left the race-ground, I presume one half of all those present would have testified that a large black ox had distanced two of the fleetest coursers that ever trod the Virginia turf. So uncertain are all things called historical facts.

While I was proceeding to my lodgings, pondering on the events of the day, a stranger rode up to me, and accosted me thus,—"I think your name is Dunwell, sir."

"Yes, sir," I replied.

"Did I not see you a year or two since in Boston, at the Marlborough Hotel?"

"Very likely, sir, for I was there."

"And you heard a story about one Peter Rugg."

"I recollect it all," said I.

"The account you heard in Boston must be true, for here he was to-day. The man has found his way to Virginia, and for aught that appears, has been to Cape Horn. I have seen him before to-day, but never saw him travel with such fearful velocity. Pray, sir, where does Peter Rugg spend his winters, for I have seen him only in summer, and always in foul weather, except this time?"

I replied, "No one knows where Peter Rugg spends his winters; where or when he eats, drinks, sleeps, or lodges. He seems to have an indistinct idea of day and night, time and space, storm and sunshine. His only object is Boston. It appears to me that Rugg's horse has some control of the chair; and that Rugg himself is, in some sort, under the control of his horse."

I then inquired of the stranger where he first saw the man and horse.

"Why, sir," said he, "in the summer of 1824, I travelled to the North for my health; and soon after I saw you at the Marlborough Hotel I returned homeward to Virginia, and, if my memory's correct, I saw this man and horse in every State between here and Massachusetts. Sometimes he would meet me, but oftener overtake me. He never spoke but once, and that once was in Delaware. On his approach he checked his horse with some difficulty. A more beautiful horse I never saw; his hide was as fair and rotund and glossy as the skin of a Congo beauty. When Rugg's horse approached mine he reined in his neck, bent his ears forward until they met, and looked my horse full in the face. My horse immediately withered into half a horse, his hide curling up like a piece of burnt leather; spell-bound, he was fixed to the earth as though a nail had been driven through each hoof.

" 'Sir,' said Rugg, 'perhaps you are travelling to Boston; and if so, I should be happy to accompany you, for I have lost my way, and I must reach home to-night. See how sleepy this little girl looks; poor thing, she is a picture of patience.'

" 'Sir,' said I, 'it is impossible for you to reach home to-night, for you are in Concord, in the county of Sussex, in the State of Delaware.'

" 'What do you mean,' said he, 'by State of Delaware? If I were in Concord, that is only twenty miles from Boston, and my horse

Lightfoot could carry me to Charlestown ferry in less than two hours. You mistake, sir; you are a stranger here; this town is nothing like Concord. I am well acquainted with Concord. I went to Concord when I left Boston.'

" 'But,' said I, 'you are in Concord, in the State of Delaware.'

" 'What do you mean by State?' said Rugg.

" 'Why, one of the United States.'

" 'States!' said he, in a low voice; 'the man is a wag, and would persuade me I am in Holland.' Then, raising his voice, he said, 'You seem, sir, to be a gentleman, and I entreat you to mislead me not: tell me, quickly, for pity's sake, the right road to Boston, for you see my horse will swallow his bits, he has eaten nothing since I left Concord.'

" 'Sir, said I, 'this town is Concord,—Concord in Delaware, not Concord in Massachusetts; and you are now five hundred miles from Boston.'

"Rugg looked at me for a moment, more in sorrow than resentment, and then repeated, 'Five hundred miles! Unhappy man, who would have thought him deranged; but nothing in this world is so deceitful as appearances. Five hundred miles! This beats Connecticut River.'

"What he meant by Connecticut River, I know not; his horse broke away, and Rugg disappeared in a moment."

I explained to the stranger the meaning of Rugg's expression, "Connecticut River," and the incident respecting him that occurred at Hartford, as I stood on the door-stone of Mr. Bennett's excellent hotel. We both agreed that the man we had seen that day was the true Peter Rugg.

Soon after, I saw Rugg again, at the toll-gate on the turnpike between Alexandria and Middleburgh. While I was paying the toll. I observed to the toll-gatherer that the drought was more severe in his vicinity than farther south.

"Yes," said he, "the drought is excessive; but if I had not heard yesterday, by a traveller, that the man with the black horse was seen in Kentucky a day or two since, I should be sure of a shower in a few minutes."

I looked all around the horizon, and could not discern a cloud that could hold a pint of water.

"Look, sir," said the toll-gatherer, "you perceive to the eastward, just above that hill, a small black cloud not bigger than a blackberry, and while I am speaking it is doubling and trebling itself, and rolling up the turnpike steadily, as if its sole design was to deluge some object."

"True," said I, "I do perceive it; but what connection is there between a thunder-cloud and a man and horse?"

"More than you imagine, or I can tell you; but stop a moment, sir, I may need your assistance. I know that cloud; I have seen it several times before, and can testify to its identity. You will soon see a man and black horse under it."

While he was speaking, true enough, we began to hear the distant thunder, and soon the chain-lightning performed all the figures of a country-dance. About a mile distant we saw the man and black horse under the cloud; but before he arrived at the toll-gate, the thunder-cloud had spent itself, and not even a sprinkle fell near us.

As the man, whom I instantly knew to be Rugg, attempted to pass, the toll-gatherer swung the gate across the road, seized Rugg's horse by the reins, and demanded two dollars.

Feeling some little regard for Rugg, I interfered, and began to question the toll-gatherer, and requested him not to be wroth with the man. The toll-gatherer replied that he had just cause, for the man had run his toll ten times, and moreover that the horse had discharged a cannon-ball at him, to the great danger of his life; that the man had always before approached so rapidly that he was too quick for the rusty hinges of the toll-gate; "but now I will have full satisfaction."

Rugg looked wistfully at me, and said, "I entreat you, sir, to delay me not; I have found at length the direct road to Boston, and shall not reach home before night if you detain me. You see I am dripping wet, and ought to change my clothes."

The toll-gatherer then demanded why he had run his toll so many times.

"Toll! Why," said Rugg, "do you demand toll? There is no toll to pay on the king's highway."

"King's highway! Do you not perceive this is a turnpike?"

"Turnpike! there are no turnpikes in Massachusetts."

"That may be, but we have several in Virginia."

"Virginia! Do you pretend I am in Virginia?"

Rugg, then, appealing to me, asked how far it was to Boston.

Said I, "Mr. Rugg, I perceive you are bewildered, and am sorry to see you so far from home; you are, indeed, in Virginia."

"You know me, then, sir, it seems; and you say I am in Virginia. Give me leave to tell you, sir, you are the most impudent man alive; for I was never forty miles from Boston, and I never saw a Virginian in my life. This beats Delaware!"

"Your toll, sir, your toll!"

"I will not pay you a penny," said Rugg; "you are both of you highway robbers. There are no turnpikes in this country. Take toll on the king's highway! Robbers take toll on the king's highway!" Then in a low tone, he said, "Here is evidently a conspiracy against me; alas, I shall never see Boston! The highways refuse me a passage, the rivers change their courses, and there is no faith in the compass."

But Rugg's horse had no idea of stopping more than one minute; for in the midst of this altercation, the horse, whose nose was resting on the upper bar of the turnpike-gate, seized it between his teeth, lifted it gently off its staples, and trotted off with it. The toll-gatherer, confounded, strained his eyes after his gate.

"Let him go," said I, "the horse will soon drop your gate, and you will get it again."

I then questioned the toll-gatherer respecting his knowledge of this man; and he related the following particulars:—

"The first time," said he, "that man ever passed this toll-gate was in the year 1806, at the moment of the great eclipse. I thought the horse was frightened at the sudden darkness, and concluded he had run away with the man. But within a few days after, the same man and horse repassed with equal speed, without the least respect to the toll-gate or to me, except by a vacant stare. Some few years afterward, during the late war, I saw the same man approaching again, and I resolved to check his career. Accordingly I stepped into the middle of the road, and stretched wide both my arms, and cried, 'Stop, sir, on your peril!' At this the man said, 'Now, Lightfoot, confound the robber!' at the same time he gave the whip liberally to the flank of his horse, which bounded off with such force that it appeared to me two such horses, give them a place to stand, would overcome any check man could devise. An ammunition wagon which had just passed on to Baltimore had dropped an eighteen-pounder in the road; this unlucky ball lay in the way of the horse's heels, and the beast, with the sagacity of a demon, clinched it with one of his heels and hurled it behind him. I feel dizzy in relating the fact, but so nearly did the ball pass my head, that the wind thereof blew off my hat; and the ball embedded itself in that gate-post, as you may see if you will cast your eye on the post. I have permitted it to remain there in memory of the occurrence,—as the people of Boston, I am told, preserve the eighteen-pounder which is now to be seen half imbedded in Brattle Street church."

I then took leave of the toll-gatherer, and promised him if I saw or heard of his gate I would send him notice.

A strong inclination had possessed me to arrest Rugg and search his pockets, thinking great discoveries might be made in the examination; but what I saw and heard that day convinced me that no human force could detain Peter Rugg against his consent. I therefore determined if I ever saw Rugg again to treat him in the gentlest manner.

In pursuing my way to New York, I entered on the turnpike in Trenton; and when I arrived at New Brunswick, I perceived the road was newly macadamized. The small stones had just been laid thereon. As I passed this piece of road, I observed that, at regular distances of about eight feet, the stones were entirely displaced from spots as large as the circumference of a half-bushel measure. This singular appearance induced me to inquire the cause of it at the turnpike-gate.

"Sir," said the toll-gatherer, "I wonder not at the question, but I am unable to give you a satisfactory answer. Indeed, sir, I believe I am bewitched, and that the turnpike is under a spell of enchantment; for what appeared to me last night cannot be a real transaction, otherwise a turnpike-gate is a useless thing."

"I do not believe in witchcraft or enchantment," said I; "and if you will relate circumstantially what happened last night, I will endeavour to account for it by natural means."

"You may recollect the night was uncommonly dark. Well, sir, just after I had closed the gate for the night, down the turnpike, as far as my eye could reach, I beheld what at first appeared to be two armies engaged. The report of the musketry, and the flashes of their firelocks, were incessant and continuous. As this strange spectacle approached me with the fury of a tornado, the noise increased; and the appearance rolled on in one compact body over the surface of the ground. The most splendid fireworks rose out of the earth and encircled this moving spectacle. The divers tints of the rainbow, the most brilliant dyes that the sun lays in the lap of spring, added to the whole family of gems, could not display a more beautiful, radiant, and dazzling spectacle than accompanied the black horse. You would have thought all the stars of heaven had met in merriment on the turnpike. In the midst of this luminous configuration sat a man, distinctly to be seen, in a miserable-looking chair, drawn by a black horse. The turnpike-gate ought, by the laws of Nature and the laws of the State, to have made a wreck of the whole, and dissolved the enchantment; but no, the horse without an effort passed over the gate, and drew the man and chair horizontally after him without touching the bar. This is what I call enchantment. What think you, sir?"

"My friend," said I, "you have grossly magnified a natural occurrence. The man was Peter Rugg, on his way to Boston. It is true, his horse travelled with unequalled speed, but as he reared high his forefeet, he could not help displacing the thousand small stones on which he trod, which flying in all directions struck one another, and resounded and scintillated. The top bar of your gate is not more than two feet from the ground, and Rugg's horse at every vault could easily lift the carriage over that gate."

This satisfied Mr. McDoubt, and I was pleased at that occurrence; for otherwise Mr. McDoubt, who is a worthy man, late from the Highlands, might have added to his calendar of superstitions. Having thus disenchanted the macadamized road and the turnpike-gate, and also Mr. McDoubt, I pursued my journey homeward to New York.

Little did I expect to see or hear anything further of Mr. Rugg, for he was now more than twelve hours in advance of me. I could hear nothing of him on my way to Elizabethtown, and therefore concluded that during the past night he had turned off from the turnpike and pursued a westerly direction; but just before I arrived at Powles's Hook, I observed a considerable collection of passengers in the ferry-boat, all standing motionless, and steadily looking at the same object. One of the ferry-men, Mr. Hardy, who knew me well, observing my approach delayed a minute, in order to afford me a passage, and coming up, said, "Mr. Dunwell, we have a curiosity on board that would puzzle Dr. Mitchell."

"Some strange fish, I suppose, has found its way into the Hudson."

"No," said he, "it is a man who looks as if he had lain hidden in the ark, and had just now ventured out. He has a little girl with him, the counterpart of himself, and the finest horse you ever saw, harnessed to the queerest-looking carriage that ever was made."

"Ah, Mr. Hardy," said I, "you have, indeed, hooked a prize; no one before you could ever detain Peter Rugg long enough to examine him."

"Do you know the man?" said Mr. Hardy.

"No, nobody knows him, but everybody has seen him. Detain him as long as possible; delay the boat under any pretence, cut the gear of the horse, do anything to detain him."

As I entered the ferry-boat, I was struck at the spectacle before me. There, indeed, sat Peter Rugg and Jenny Rugg in the chair, and there stood the black horse, all as quiet as lambs, surrounded by more than fifty men and women, who seemed to have lost all their senses but one. Not a motion, not a breath, not a nestle. They were all eye. Rugg appeared to them to be a man not of this world; and they appeared to Rugg a strange generation of men. Rugg spoke not, and they spoke not: nor was I disposed to disturb the calm, satisfied to reconnoitre Rugg in a state of rest. Presently, Rugg observed in a low voice, addressed to nobody, "A new contrivance, horses instead of oars; Boston folks are full of notions."

It was plain that Rugg was of Dutch extraction. He had on three pairs of small-clothes, called in former days of simplicity breeches, not much the worse for wear; but time had proved the fabric, and shrunk one more than another, so that they showed at the knees their different qualities and colours. His several waistcoats, the flaps of which rested on his knees, made him appear rather corpulent. His capacious drab coat would supply the stuff for half a dozen modern ones; the sleeves were like meal bags, in the cuffs of which you might nurse a child to sleep. His hat, probably once black, now of a tan colour, was neither round nor crooked, but in shape much like the one President Monroe wore on his late tour. This dress gave the rotund face of Rugg an antiquated dignity. The man, though deeply sunburned, did not appear to be more than thirty years of age. He had lost his sad and anxious look, was quite composed, and seemed happy. The chair in which Rugg sat was very capacious, evidently made for service, and calculated to last for ages; the timber would supply material for three modern carriages. This chair, like a Nantucket coach, would answer for everything that ever went on wheels. The horse, too, was an object of curiosity; his majestic height, his natural mane and tail, gave him a commanding appearance, and his large open nostrils indicated inexhaustible wind. It was apparent that the hoofs of his forefeet had been split, probably on some newly macadamized road, and were now growing together again; so that John Spring was not altogether in the wrong.

How long this dumb scene would otherwise have continued I cannot tell. Rugg discovered no sign of impatience. But Rugg's horse having been quiet more than five minutes, had no idea of standing idle; he began to whinny, and in a moment after, with his right forefoot he started a plank. Said Rugg, "My horse is impatient, he sees the North End. You must be quick, or he will be ungovernable."

At these words, the horse raised his left forefoot; and when he laid it down every inch of the ferry-boat trembled. Two men immediately seized Rugg's horse by the nostrils. The horse nodded, and both of them were in the Hudson. While we were fishing up the men, the horse was perfectly quiet.

"Fret not the horse," said Rugg, "and he will do no harm. He is only anxious, like myself, to arrive at yonder beautiful shore; he sees the North Church, and smells his own stable."

"Sir," said I to Rugg, practising a little deception, "pray tell me, for I am a stranger here, what river is this, and what city is that opposite, for you seem to be an inhabitant of it?"

"This river, sir, is called Mystic River, and this is Winnisimmet ferry,—we have retained the Indian names,—and that town is Boston. You must, indeed, be a stranger in these parts, not to know that yonder is Boston, the capital of the New England provinces."

"Pray, sir, how long have you been absent from Boston?"

"Why, that I cannot exactly tell. I lately went with this little girl of mine to Concord, to see my friends; and I am ashamed to tell you, in returning lost the way, and have been travelling ever since. No one would direct me right. It is cruel to mislead a traveller. My horse, Lightfoot, has boxed the compass; and it seems to me he has boxed it back again. But, sir, you perceive my horse is uneasy; Lightfoot, as yet, has only given a hint and a nod. I cannot be answerable for his heels."

At these words Lightfoot reared his long tail, and snapped it as you would a whiplash. The Hudson reverberated with the sound. Instantly the six horses began to move the boat. The Hudson was a sea of glass, smooth as oil, not a ripple. The horses, from a smart trot, soon pressed into a gallop; water now ran over the gunwale; the ferry-boat was soon buried in an ocean of foam, and the noise of the spray was like the roaring of many waters. When we arrived at New York, you might see the beautiful white wake of the ferry-boat across the Hudson.

Though Rugg refused to pay toll at turnpikes, when Mr. Hardy reached his hand for the ferriage, Rugg readily put his hand into one of his many pockets, took out a piece of silver, and handed it to Mr. Hardy.

"What is this?" said Mr. Hardy.

"It is thirty shillings," said Rugg.

"It might once have been thirty shillings, old tenor," said Mr. Hardy, "but it is not at present."

"The money is good English coin," said Rugg; "my grandfather brought a bag of them from England, and had them hot from the mint."

Hearing this, I approached near to Rugg, and asked permission to see the coin. It was a half-crown, coined by the English Parliament, dated in the year 1649. On one side, "The Commonwealth of England,"and St. George's cross encircled with a wreath of laurel. On the other, "God with us," and a harp and St. George's cross united. I winked at Mr. Hardy, and pronounced it good current money; and said loudly, "I will not permit the gentleman to be imposed on, for I will exchange the money myself."

On this, Rugg spoke,—"Please to give me your name, sir."

"My name is Dunwell, sir," I replied.

"Mr. Dunwell," said Rugg, "you are the only honest man I have seen since I left Boston. As you are a stranger here, my house is your home; Dame Rugg will be happy to see her husband's friend. Step into my chair, sir, there is room enough; move a little, Jenny, for the gentleman, and we will be in Middle Street in a minute."

Accordingly I took a seat by Peter Rugg.

"Were you never in Boston before?" said Rugg.

"No," said I.

"Well, you will now see the queen of New England, a town second only to Philadelphia, in all North America.

"You forget New York," said I.

"Poh, New York is nothing; though I never was there. I am told you might put all New York in our mill-pond. No, sir, New York, I assure you, is but a sorry affair; no more to be compared with Boston than a wigwam with a palace."

As Rugg's horse turned into Pearl Street, I looked Rugg as fully in the face as good manners would allow, and said, "Sir, if this is Boston, I acknowledge New York is not worthy to be one of its suburbs."

Before we had proceeded far in Pearl Street, Rugg's countenance changed: his nerves began to twitch; his eyes trembled in their sockets; he was evidently bewildered. "What is the matter, Mr. Rugg? you seem disturbed."

"This surpasses all human comprehension; if you know, sir, where we are, I beseech you to tell me."

"If this place," I replied, "is not Boston, it must be New York."

"No, sir, it is not Boston; nor can it be New York. How could I be in New York, which is nearly two hundred miles from Boston?"

By this time we had passed into Broadway, and then Rugg, in truth, discovered a chaotic mind. "There is no such place as this in North America. This is all the effect of enchantment; this is a grand delusion, nothing real. Here is seemingly a great city, magnificent houses, shops and goods, men and women innumerable, and as busy as in real life, all sprung up in one night from the wilderness; or what is more probable, some tremendous convulsion of Nature has thrown London or Amsterdam on the shores of New England. Or, possibly, I may be dreaming, though the night seems rather long; but before now I have sailed in one night to Amsterdam, bought goods of Vandogger, and returned to Boston before morning."

At this moment a hue-and-cry was heard, "Stop the madmen, they will endanger the lives of thousands!" In vain hundreds attempted to stop Rugg's horse. Lightfoot interfered with nothing; his course was straight as a shooting-star. But on my part, fearful that before night I should find myself behind the Alleghanies, I addressed Mr. Rugg in a tone of entreaty, and requested him to restrain the horse and permit me to alight.

"My friend," said he, "we shall be in Boston before dark, and Dame Rugg will be most exceedingly glad to see us."

"Mr. Rugg," said I, "you must excuse me. Pray look to the west; see that thunder-cloud swelling with rage, as if in pursuit of us."

"Ah," said Rugg, "it is in vain to attempt to escape. I know that cloud; it is collecting new wrath to spend on my head." Then checking his horse, he permitted me to descend, saying, "Farewell, Mr. Dunwell, I shall be happy to see you in Boston; I live in Middle Street."

It is uncertain in what direction Mr. Rugg pursued his course, after he disappeared in Broadway; but one thing is sufficiently known to everybody,—that in the course of two months after he was seen in New York, he found his way most opportunely to Boston.

It seems the estate of Peter Rugg had recently fallen to the Commonwealth of Massachusetts for want of heirs; and the Legislature had ordered the solicitor-general to advertise and sell it at public auction. Happening to be in Boston at the time, and observing his advertisement, which described a considerable extent of land, I felt a kindly curiosity to see the spot where Rugg once lived. Taking the advertisement in my hand, I wandered a little way down Middle Street, and without asking a question of any one, when I came to a certain spot I said to myself, "This is Rugg's estate; I will proceed no farther. This must be the spot; it is a counterpart of Peter Rugg." The premises, indeed, looked as if they had fulfilled a sad prophecy. Fronting on Middle Street, they extended in the rear to Ann Street, and embraced about half an acre of land. It was not uncommon in former times to have half an acre for a house-lot; for an acre of land then, in many parts of Boston, was not more valuable than a foot in some places at present. The old mansion-house had become a powder-post, and been blown away. One other building, uninhabited, stood ominous, courting dilapidation. The street had been so much raised that the bed-chamber had descended to the kitchen and was level with the street. The house seemed conscious of its fate; and as though tired of standing there, the front was fast retreating from the rear, and waiting the next south wind to project itself into the street. If the most wary animals had sought a place of refuge, here they would have rendezvoused. Here, under the ridge-pole, the crow would have perched in security; and in the recesses below, you might have caught the fox and the weasel asleep. "The hand of destiny," said I, "has pressed heavy on this spot; still heavier on the former owners. Strange that so large a lot of land as this should want an heir! Yet Peter Rugg, at this day, might pass by his own door-stone, and ask, 'Who once lived here?' "

The auctioneer, appointed by the solicitor to sell this estate, was a man of eloquence, as many of the auctioneers of Boston are. The occasion seemed to warrant, and his duty urged, him to make a display. He addressed his audience as follows,—

"The estate, gentlemen, which we offer you this day, was once the property of a family now extinct. For that reason it has escheated to the Commonwealth. Lest any one of you should be deterred from bidding on so large an estate as this for fear of a disputed title, I am authorized by the solicitor-general to proclaim that the purchaser shall have the best of all titles,—a warranty-deed from the Commonwealth. I state this, gentlemen, because I know there is an idle rumour in this vicinity, that one Peter Rugg, the original owner of this estate, is still living. This rumour, gentlemen, has no foundation, and can have no foundation in the nature of things. It originated about two years since, from the incredible story of one Jonathan Dunwell, of New York. Mrs. Croft, indeed, whose husband I see present, and whose mouth waters for this estate, has countenanced this fiction. But, gentlemen, was it ever known that any estate, especially an estate of this value, lay unclaimed for nearly half a century, if any heir, ever so remote, were existing? For, gentlemen, all agree that old Peter Rugg, if living, would be at least one hundred years of age. It is said that he and his daughter, with a horse and chaise, were missed more than half a century ago; and because they never returned home, forsooth, they must be now living, and will some day come and claim this great estate. Such logic, gentlemen, never led to a good investment. Let not this idle story cross the noble purpose of consigning these ruins to the genius of architecture. If such a contingency could check the spirit of enterprise, farewell to all mercantile excitement. Your surplus money, instead of refreshing your sleep with the golden dreams of new sources of speculation, would turn to the nightmare. A man's money, if not employed, serves only to disturb his rest. Look, then, to the prospect before you. Here is half an acre of land,—more than twenty thousand square feet,—a corner lot, with wonderful capabilities; none of your contracted lots of forty feet by fifty, where in dog-days, you can breathe only through your scuttles. On the contrary, an architect cannot contemplate this lot of land without rapture, for here is room enough for his genius to shame the temple of Solomon. Then the prospect—how commanding! To the east, so near to the Atlantic that Neptune, freighted with the select treasures of the whole earth, can knock at your door with his trident. From the west, the produce of the river of Paradise—the Connecticut—will soon, by the blessings of steam, railways, and canals pass under your windows; and thus, on this spot, Neptune shall marry Ceres, and Pomona from Roxbury, and Flora from Cambridge, shall dance at the wedding.

"Gentlemen of science, men of taste, ye of the literary emporium,—for I perceive many of you present—to you this holy ground. If the spot on which in times past a hero left only the print of a footstep is now sacred, of what price is the birthplace of one who all the world knows was born in Middle Street, directly opposite to this lot; and who, if his birthplace were not well known, would now be claimed by more than seven cities. To you, then, the value of these premises must be inestimable. For ere long there will arise in full view of the edifice to be erected here, a monument, the wonder and veneration of the world. A column shall spring to the clouds; and on that column will be engraven one word which will convey all that is wise in intellect, useful in science, good in morals, prudent in counsel, and benevolent in principle,—a name of one who, when living, was the patron of the poor, the delight of the cottage, and the admiration of kings; now dead, worth the whole seven wise men of Greece. Need I tell you his name? He fixed the thunder and guided the lightning.

"Men of the North End! Need I appeal to your patriotism, in order to enhance the value of this lot? The earth affords no such scenery as this; there, around that corner, lived James Otis; here, Samuel Adams; there, Joseph Warren; and around that other corner, Josiah Quincy. Here was the birthplace of Freedom; here Liberty was born, and nursed, and grew to manhood. Here man was newly created. Here is the nursery of American Independence—I am too modest—here began the emancipation of the world; a thousand generations hence millions of men will cross the Atlantic just to look at the north end of Boston. Your fathers—what do I say—yourselves,—yes, this moment, I behold several attending this auction who lent a hand to rock the cradle of Independence.

"Men of speculation,—ye who are deaf to everything except the sound of money,—you, I know, will give me both of your ears when I tell you the city of Boston must have a piece of this estate in order to widen Ann Street. Do you hear me,—do you all hear me? I say the city must have a large piece of this land in order to widen Ann Street. What a chance! The city scorns to take a man's land for nothing. If it seizes your property, it is generous beyond the dreams of avarice. The only oppression is, you are in danger of being smothered under a load of wealth. Witness the old lady who lately died of a broken heart when the mayor paid her for a piece of her kitchen-garden. All the faculty agreed that the sight of the treasure, which the mayor incautiously paid her in dazzling dollars, warm from the mint, sped joyfully all the blood of her body into her heart, and rent it with raptures. Therefore, let him who purchases this estate fear his good fortune, and not Peter Rugg. Bid, then, liberally, and do not let the name of Rugg damp your ardor. How much will you give per foot for this estate?

Thus spoke the auctioneer, and gracefully waved his ivory hammer. From fifty to seventy-five cents per foot were offered in a few moments. The bidding labored from seventy-five to ninety. At length one dollar was offered. The auctioneer seemed satisfied; and looking at his watch, said he would knock off the estate in five minutes, if no one offered more.

There was a deep silence during this short period. While the hammer was suspended, a strange rumbling noise was heard, which arrested the attention of every one. Presently, it was like the sound of many shipwrights driving home the bolts of a seventy-four. As the sound approached nearer, some exclaimed, "The buildings in the new market are falling in promiscuous ruins." Others said, "No, it is an earthquake; we perceive the earth tremble." Others said, "Not so; the sounds proceeds from Hanover Street, and approaches nearer;" and this proved true, for presently Peter Rugg was in the midst of us.

"Alas, Jenny," said Peter, "I am ruined; our house has been burned, and here are all our neighbors around the ruins. Heaven grant your mother, Dame Rugg, is safe."

"They don't look like our neighbors," said Jenny; "but sure enough our house is burned, and nothing left but the door-stone and an old cedar post. Do ask where mother is."

In the mean time more than a thousand men had surrounded

Rugg and his horse and chair. Yet neither Rugg personally, nor his horse and carriage, attracted more attention than the auctioneer. The confident look and searching eyes of Rugg carried more conviction to every one present that the estate was his, than could any parchment or paper with signature and seal. The impression which the auctioneer had just made on the company was effaced in a moment; and although the latter words of the auctioneer were, "Fear not Peter Rugg," the moment the auctioneer met the eye of Rugg his occupation was gone; his arm fell down to his hips, his late lively hammer hung heavy in his hand, and the auction was forgotten. The black horse, too, gave his evidence. He knew his journey was ended; for he stretched himself into a horse and a half, rested his head over the cedar post, and whinnied thrice, causing his harness to tremble from headstall to crupper.

Rugg then stood upright in his chair, and asked with some authority, "Who has demolished my house in my absence, for I see no signs of conflagration? I demand by what accident this has happened, and wherefore this collection of strange people has assembled before my doorstep. I thought I knew every man in Boston, but you appear to me a new generation of men. Yet I am familiar with many of the countenances here present, and I can call some of you by name; but in truth I do not recollect that before this moment I ever saw any of you. There, I am certain, is a Winslow, and here a Sargent; there stands a Sewall, and next to him a Dudley. Will none of you speak to me,—or is this all a delusion? I see, indeed, many forms of men, and no want of eyes, but of motion, speech, and hearing, you seem to be destitute. Strange! Will no one inform me who has demolished my house?"

Then spake a voice from the crowd, but whence it came I could not discern: "There is nothing strange here but yourself, Mr. Rugg. Time, which destroys and renews all things, has dilapidated your house, and placed us here. You have suffered many years under an illusion. The tempest which you profanely defied at Menotomy has at length subsided; but you will never see home, for your house and wife and neighbors have all disappeared. Your estate, indeed, remains, but no home. You were cut off from the last age, and you can never be fitted to the present. Your home is gone, and you can never have another home in this world."

NATHANIEL HAWTHORNE
(1804–1864)

Long recognized as our earliest master of the short story and the "romance" (as distinct from the "novel"), Nathaniel Hawthorne endured, in fact, a long, humbling apprenticeship, with numerous false starts, before the publication, in 1837, of Twice-Told Tales. *Prolific out of necessity ("when a man has taken upon himself to beget children, he has no longer any right to a life of his own"), Hawthorne wrote with astonishing swiftness, as the dates of his work suggest:* Mosses from an Old Manse *(1846);* The Scarlet Letter *(1850);* The House of the Seven Gables *(1851);* The Blithedale Romance *(1852);* Tanglewood Tales *(1853);* The Marble Faun *(1860);* Our Old Home *(1863). His work is uniquely his: Gothic in tone and structure, mordantly analytical in narration, infused with a sense of life's profound and ironic mystery, and the tenuous place within it of human conscience. "The Wives of the Dead," the reader will note, is an unusual story for Hawthorne: its dreams entirely plausible, its plot neither fanciful nor strained. The dream as wish-fulfillment! Has anyone ever dramatized this melancholy fact of life with greater poignancy?*

Born on July 4, 1804, in Salem, Massachusetts, Hawthorne was a descendant of Puritan immigrants and the great-grandson of a judge who condemned men and women to death in the notorious Salem witchcraft trials. Through his writing career, Hawthorne considered the weight of history as it presses upon the present; his genius is for the examination of the individual in isolation, in uncertain relationships with other people and with a Higher Power. A more relaxed Hawthornian voice, unprogrammatic, even, at times, colloquial, is revealed in the marvelous, posthumously published American Notebooks.

The Wives of the Dead

The following story, the simple and domestic incidents of which may be deemed scarcely worth relating, after such a lapse of time, awakened some degree of interest, a hundred years ago, in a principal seaport of the Bay Province. The rainy twilight of an autumn day,—a parlor on the second floor of a small house, plainly furnished, as beseemed the middling circumstances of its inhabitants, yet decorated with little curiosities from beyond the sea, and a few delicate specimens of Indian manufacture,—these are the only particulars to be premised in regard to scene and season. Two young and comely women sat together by the fireside, nursing their mutual and peculiar sorrows. They were the recent brides of two brothers, a sailor and a landsman, and two successive days had brought tidings of the death of each, by the chances of Canadian warfare, and the tempestuous Atlantic. The universal sympathy excited by this bereavement drew numerous condoling guests to the habitation of the widowed sisters. Several, among whom was the minister, had remained till the verge of evening; when, one by one, whispering many comfortable passages of Scripture, that were answered by more abundant tears, they took their leave, and departed to their own happier homes. The mourners, though not insensible to the kindness of their friends, had yearned to be left alone. United, as they had been, by the relationship of the living, and now more closely so by that of the dead, each felt as if whatever consolation her grief admitted were to be found in the bosom of the other. They joined their hearts, and wept together silently. But after an hour of such indulgence, one of the sisters, all of whose emotions were influenced by her mild, quiet, yet not feeble character, began to recollect the precepts of resignation and endurance which piety had taught her, when she did not think to need them. Her misfortune, besides, as earliest known, should earliest cease to interfere with her regular course of duties; accordingly, having placed the table before the fire, and arranged a frugal meal, she took the hand of her companion.

"Come, dearest sister; you have eaten not a morsel to-day," she said. "Arise, I pray you, and let us ask a blessing on that which is provided for us."

Her sister-in-law was of a lively and irritable temperament, and the first pangs of her sorrow had been expressed by shrieks and passionate lamentation. She now shrunk from Mary's words, like a wounded sufferer from a hand that revives the throb.

"There is no blessing left for me, neither will I ask it!" cried Margaret, with a fresh burst of tears. "Would it were His will that I might never taste food more!"

Yet she trembled at these rebellious expressions, almost as soon as they were uttered, and, by degrees, Mary succeeded in bringing her sister's mind nearer to the situation of her own. Time went on, and their usual hour of repose arrived. The brothers and their brides, entering the married state with no more than the slender means which then sanctioned such a step, had confederated themselves in one household, with equal rights to the parlor, and claiming exclusive privileges in two sleeping rooms contiguous to it. Thither the widowed ones retired, after heaping ashes upon the dying embers of their fire, and placing a lighted lamp upon the hearth. The doors of both chambers were left open, so that a part of the interior of each, and the beds with their unclosed curtains, were reciprocally visible. Sleep did not steal upon the sisters at one and the same time. Mary experienced the effect often consequent upon grief quietly borne, and soon sunk into temporary forgetfulness, while Margaret became more disturbed and feverish, in proportion as the night advanced with its deepest and stillest hours. She lay listening to the drops of rain, that came down in monotonous succession, unswayed by a breath of wind; and a nervous impulse continually caused her to lift her head from the pillow, and gaze into Mary's chamber and the intermediate apartment. The cold light of the lamp threw the shadows of the furniture up against the wall, stamping them immovably there, except when they were shaken by a sudden flicker of the flame. Two vacant arm-chairs were in their old positions on opposite sides of the hearth, where the brothers had been wont to sit in young and laughing dignity, as heads of families; two humbler seats were near them, the true thrones of that little empire, where Mary and herself had exercised in love a power that love had won. The cheerful radiance of the fire had shone upon the happy circle, and the dead glimmer of the lamp might have befitted their reünion now. While Margaret groaned in bitterness, she heard a knock at the street-door.

"How would my heart have leapt at that sound but yesterday!" thought she, remembering the anxiety with which she had long awaited tidings from her husband. "I care not for it now; let them begone, for I will not arise."

But even while a sort of childish fretfulness made her thus resolve, she was breathing hurriedly, and straining her ears to catch a repetition of the summons. It is difficult to be convinced of the death of one whom we have deemed another self. The knocking was now renewed in slow and regular strokes, apparently given with the soft end of a doubled fist, and was accompanied by words, faintly heard through several thicknesses of wall. Margaret looked to her sister's chamber, and beheld her still lying in the depths of sleep. She arose, placed her foot upon the floor, and slightly arrayed herself, trembling between fear and eagerness as she did so.

"Heaven help me!" sighed she. "I have nothing left to fear, and methinks I am ten times more a coward than ever."

Seizing the lamp from the hearth, she hastened to the window that overlooked the street-door. It was a lattice, turning upon hinges; and having thrown it back, she stretched her head a little way into the moist atmosphere. A lantern was reddening the front of the house, and melting its light in the neighboring puddles, while a deluge of darkness overwhelmed every other object. As the window grated on its hinges, a man in a broad-brimmed hat and blanket-coat stepped from under the shelter of the projecting story, and looked upward to discover whom his application had aroused. Margaret knew him as a friendly innkeeper of the town.

"What would you have, Goodman Parker?" cried the widow.

"Lack-a-day, is it you, Mistress Margaret?" replied the innkeeper. "I was afraid it might be your sister Mary; for I hate to see a young woman in trouble, when I have n't a word of comfort to whisper to her."

"For Heaven's sake, what news do you bring?" screamed Margaret.

"Why, there has been an express through the town within this half-hour," said Goodman Parker, "travelling from the eastern jurisdiction with letters from the governor and council. He tarried at my house to refresh himself with a drop and a morsel, and I asked him what tidings on the frontiers. He tells me we had the better in the skirmish you wot of, and that thirteen men reported slain are well and sound, and your husband among them. Besides, he is appointed of the escort to bring the captivated Frenchers and Indians home to the province jail. I judged you would n't mind being broke of your rest, and so I stepped over to tell you. Good-night."

So saying, the honest man departed; and his lantern gleamed along the street, bringing to view indistinct shapes of things, and the fragments of a world, like order glimmering through chaos, or memory roaming over the past. But Margaret staid not to watch these picturesque effects. Joy flashed into her heart, and lighted it up at once; and breathless, and with winged steps, she flew to the bedside of her sister. She paused, however, at the door of the chamber, while a thought of pain broke in upon her.

"Poor Mary!" said she to herself. "Shall I waken her, to feel her sorrow sharpened by my happiness? No; I will keep it within my own bosom till the morrow."

She approached the bed, to discover if Mary's sleep were peaceful. Her face was turned partly inward to the pillow, and had been hidden there to weep; but a look of motionless contentment was now visible upon it, as if her heart, like a deep lake, had grown calm because its dead had sunk down so far within. Happy is it, and strange, that the lighter sorrows are those from which dreams are chiefly fabricated. Margaret shrunk from disturbing her sister-in-law, and felt as if her own better fortune had rendered her involuntarily unfaithful, and as if altered and diminished affection must be the consequence of the disclosure she had to make. With a sudden step, she turned away. But joy could not long be repressed, even by circumstances that would have excited heavy grief at another moment. Her mind was thronged with delightful thoughts, till sleep stole on, and transformed them to visions, more delightful and more wild, like the breath of winter (but what a cold comparison!) working fantastic tracery upon a window.

When the night was far advanced, Mary awoke with a sudden start. A vivid dream had latterly involved her in its unreal life, of which, however, she could only remember that it had been broken in upon at the most interesting point. For a little time, slumber hung about her like a morning mist, hindering her from perceiving the distinct outline of her situation. She listened with imperfect consciousness to two or three volleys of a rapid and eager knocking; and first she deemed the noise a matter of course, like the breath she drew; next, it appeared a thing in which she had no concern; and lastly, she became aware that it was a summons necessary to be obeyed. At the same moment, the pang of recollection darted into her mind; the pall of sleep was thrown back from the face of grief; the dim light of the chamber, and the objects therein revealed, had retained all her suspended ideas, and restored them as soon as she unclosed her eyes. Again there was a quick peal upon the street-door. Fearing that her sister would also be disturbed, Mary wrapped herself in a cloak and hood, took the lamp from the hearth, and hastened to the window. By some accident, it had been left unhasped, and yielded easily to her hand.

"Who's there?" asked Mary, trembling as she looked forth.

The storm was over, and the moon was up; it shone upon broken clouds above, and below upon houses black with moisture, and upon little lakes of the fallen rain, curling into silver beneath the quick enchantment of a breeze. A young man in a sailor's dress, wet as if he had come out of the depths of the sea, stood alone under the window. Mary recognized him as one whose livelihood was gained by short voyages along the coast; nor did she forget that, previous to her marriage, he had been an unsuccessful wooer of her own.

"What do you seek here, Stephen?" said she.

"Cheer up, Mary, for I seek to comfort you," answered the rejected lover. "You must know I got home not ten minutes ago, and the first thing my good mother told me was the news about your husband. So, without saying a word to the old woman, I clapped on my hat, and ran out of the house. I could n't have slept a wink before speaking to you, Mary, for the sake of old times."

"Stephen, I thought better of you!" exclaimed the widow, with gushing tears, and preparing to close the lattice; for she was no whit inclined to imitate the first wife of Zadig.

"But stop, and hear my story out," cried the young sailor. "I tell you we spoke a brig yesterday afternoon, bound in from Old England. And who do you think I saw standing on deck, well and hearty, only a bit thinner than he was five months ago?"

Mary leaned from the window, but could not speak.

"Why, it was your husband himself," continued the generous seaman. "He and three others saved themselves on a spar, when the Blessing turned bottom upwards. The brig will beat into the bay by daylight, with this wind, and you'll see him here to-morrow. There's the comfort I bring you, Mary, and so good-night."

He hurried away, while Mary watched him with a doubt of waking reality, that seemed stronger or weaker as he alternately entered the shade of the houses, or emerged into the broad streaks of moonlight. Gradually, however, a blessed flood of conviction swelled into her heart, in strength enough to overwhelm her, had its increase been more abrupt. Her first impulse was to rouse her sister-in-law, and communicate the new-born gladness. She opened the chamber-door, which had been closed in the course of the night, though not latched, advanced to the bedside, and was about to lay her hand upon the slumberer's shoulder. But then she remembered that Margaret would awake to thoughts of death and woe, rendered not the less bitter by their contrast with her own felicity. She suffered the rays of the lamp to fall upon the unconscious form of the bereaved one. Margaret lay in unquiet sleep, and the drapery was displaced around her; her young cheek was rosy-tinted, and her lips half opened in a vivid smile; an expression of joy, debarred its passage by her sealed eyelids, struggled forth like incense from the whole countenance.

"My poor sister! you will waken too soon from that happy dream," thought Mary.

Before retiring, she set down the lamp, and endeavored to arrange the bed-clothes so that the chill air might not do harm to the feverish slumberer. But her hand trembled against Margaret's neck, a tear also fell upon her cheek, and she suddenly awoke.

HERMAN MELVILLE

(1819–1891)

Of American writers, Herman Melville led, arguably, the most varied life. Born in New York City of English and Dutch colonial ancestry, one of eight children of an impoverished family, he went away to sea as a young man, acquiring experience for his early novels Typee *(1846),* Omoo *(1847),* Mardi *(1849),* Redburn *(1849), and* White-Jacket *(1850). (Note the rapid succession of titles! With* Moby-Dick *to come, in 1851). Celebrated as the first two novels were, for their South Seas exoticism and the accessibility of their boyish, firsthand narration, they scarcely characterize Melville's later, far more complex and demanding work; and led readers to expect writing that, for Melville, quickly came to seem the literary equivalent of "sawing wood."*

Astonishing as it seems to contemporary readers, the work of Melville's maturity failed to find any audience. Reviewers almost universally damned Moby-Dick; *the reception of* Pierre *(1852) was yet more virulent.* The Piazza Tales *(1856) and* The Confidence-Man *(1857) are more accessible, yet sold very poorly.* Clarel: A Poem and Pilgrimage in the Holy Land *was privately published in 1876;* Billy Budd, *completed in 1891, was posthumously published. It might be argued that, apart from his masterpiece* Moby-Dick, *Melville's most powerfully realized works of fiction are his idiosyncratic short stories and prose pieces: "Bartleby the Scrivener," "Benito Cereno," "The Encantadas," and the ingeniously paired surreal excursions into "The Paradise of Bachelors and the Tartarus of Maids."*

The Paradise of Bachelors and the Tartarus of Maids

I. THE PARADISE OF BACHELORS

It lies not far from Temple-Bar.

Going to it, by the usual way, is like stealing from a heated plain into some cool, deep glen, shady among harboring hills.

Sick with the din and soiled with the mud of Fleet Street—where the Benedick tradesmen are hurrying by, with ledger-lines ruled along their brows, thinking upon rise of bread and fall of babies—you adroitly turn a mystic corner—not a street—glide down a dim, monastic way, flanked by dark, sedate, and solemn piles, and still wending on, give the whole care-worn world the slip, and, disentangled, stand beneath the quiet cloisters of the Paradise of Bachelors.

Sweet are the oases in Sahara; charming the isle-groves of August prairies; delectable pure faith amidst a thousand perfidies: but sweeter, still more charming, most delectable the dreamy Paradise of Bachelors, found in the stony heart of stunning London.

In mild meditation pace the cloisters; take your pleasure, sip your leisure, in the garden waterward; go linger in the ancient library; go worship in the sculptured chapel; but little have you seen, just nothing do you know, not the sweet kernel have you tasted, till you dine among the banded Bachelors, and see their convivial eyes and glasses sparkle. Not dine in bustling commons, during term-time, in the hall; but tranquilly, by private hint, at a private table; some fine Templar's hospitably invited guest.

Templar? That's a romantic name. Let me see. Brian de Bois Gilbert was a Templar, I believe. Do we understand you to insinuate that those famous Templars still survive in modern London? May the ring of their armed heels be heard, and the rattle of their shields, as in mailed prayer the monk-knights kneel before the consecrated Host? Surely a monk-knight were a curious sight picking his way along the Strand, his gleaming corselet and snowy surcoat spattered by an omnibus. Long-bearded, too, according to his order's rule; his face furry as pard's; how would the grim ghost look among the crop-haired, close-shaven citizens? We know indeed—sad history recounts it—that a moral blight tainted at last this sacred Brotherhood. Though no sworded foe might outskill them in the fence, yet the worm of luxury crawled beneath their guard, gnawing the core of knightly troth, nibbling the monastic vow, till at last the monk's austerity relaxed to wassailing, and the sworn knights-bachelors grew to be but hypocrites and rakes.

But for all this, quite unprepared were we to learn that Knights-Templars (if at all in being) were so entirely secularized as to be reduced from carving out immortal fame in glorious battling for the Holy Land, to the carving of roast-mutton at a dinner-board. Like Anacreon, do these degenerate Templars now think it sweeter far to fall in banquet than in war? Or, indeed, how can there be any survival of that famous order? Templars in modern London! Templars in their red-cross mantles smoking cigars at the Divan! Templars crowded in a railway train, till, stacked with steel helmet, spear, and shield, the whole train looks like one elongated locomotive!

No. The genuine Templar is long since departed. Go view the wondrous tombs in the Temple Church; see there the rigidly-haughty forms stretched out, with crossed arms upon their stilly hearts, in everlasting and undreaming rest. Like the years before the flood, the bold Knights-Templars are no more. Nevertheless, the name remains, and the nominal society, and the ancient grounds, and some of the ancient edifices. But the iron heel is changed to a boot of patent-leather; the long two-handed sword to a one-handed quill, the monk-giver of gratuitous ghostly counsel now counsels for a fee; the defender of the sarcophagus (if in good practice with his weapon) now has more than one case to defend; the vowed opener and clearer of all highways leading to the Holy Sepulchre, now has it in particular charge to check, to clog, to hinder, and embarrass all the courts and avenues of Law; the knight-combatant of the Saracen, breasting spear-points at Acre, now fights law-points in Westminster Hall. The helmet is a wig. Struck by Time's enchanter's wand, the Templar is to-day a Lawyer.

But, like many others tumbled from proud glory's height—like the apple, hard on the bough, but mellow on the ground—the Templar's fall has but made him all the finer fellow.

I dare say those old warrior-priests were but gruff and grouty at the best; cased in Birmingham hardware, how could their crimped arms give yours or mine a hearty shake? Their proud, ambitious, monkish souls clasped shut, like horn-book missals, their very faces clapped in bomb-shells; what sort of genial men were these? But best of comrades, most affable of hosts, capital diner is the modern Templar. His wit and wine are both of sparkling brands.

The church and cloisters, courts and vaults, lanes and passages, banquet-halls, refectories, libraries, terraces, gardens, broad walks, domicils, and dessert-rooms, covering a very large space of ground, and all grouped in central neighborhood, and quite sequestered from the old city's surrounding din; and every thing about the place being kept in most bachelor-like particularity, no part of London offers to a quiet wight so agreeable a refuge.

The Temple is, indeed, a city by itself. A city with all the best appurtenances, as the above enumeration shows. A city with a park to it, and flower-beds, and a river-side—the Thames flowing by as openly, in one part, as by Eden's primal garden flowed the mild Euphrates. In what is now the Temple Garden the old Crusaders used to exercise their steeds and lances; the modern Templars now lounge on the benches beneath the trees, and, switching their patent-leather boots, in gay discourse exercise at repartee.

Long lines of stately portraits in the banquet-halls, show what great men of mark—famous nobles, judges, and Lord Chancellors—have in their time been Templars. But all Templars are not known to universal fame; though, if the having warm hearts and warmer welcomes, full minds and fuller cellars, and giving good advice and glorious dinners, spiced with rare divertisements of fun and fancy, merit immortal mention, set down, ye muses, the names of R. F. C. and his imperial brother.

Though to be a Templar, in the one true sense, you must needs be a lawyer, or a student at the law, and be ceremoniously enrolled as member of the order, yet as many such, though Templars, do not reside within the Temple's precincts, though they may have their offices there, just so, on the other hand, there are many residents of the hoary old domicils who are not admitted Templars. If being, say, a lounging gentleman and bachelor, or a quiet, unmarried, literary man, charmed with the soft seclusion of the spot, you much desire to pitch your shady tent among the rest in this serene encampment, then you must make some special friend among the order, and procure him to rent, in his name but at your charge, whatever vacant chamber you may find to suit.

Thus, I suppose, did Dr. Johnson, that nominal Benedick and

widower but virtual bachelor, when for a space he resided here. So, too, did that undoubted bachelor and rare good soul, Charles Lamb. And hundreds more, of sterling spirits, Brethren of the Order of Celibacy, from time to time have dined, and slept, and tabernacled here. Indeed, the place is all a honeycomb of offices and domicils. Like any cheese, it is quite perforated through and through in all directions with the snug cells of bachelors. Dear, delightful spot! Ah! when I bethink me of the sweet hours there passed, enjoying such genial hospitalities beneath those time-honored roofs, my heart only finds due utterance through poetry; and, with a sigh, I softly sing, "Carry me back to old Virginny!"

Such then, at large, is the Paradise of Bachelors. And such I found it one pleasant afternoon in the smiling month of May, when, sallying from my hotel in Trafalgar Square, I went to keep my dinner-appointment with that fine Barrister, Bachelor, and Bencher, R. F. C. (he *is* the first and second, and *should be* the third; I hereby nominate him), whose card I kept fast pinched between my gloved forefinger and thumb, and every now and then snatched still another look at the pleasant address inscribed beneath the name, "No.—, Elm Court, Temple."

At the core he was a right bluff, care-free, right comfortable, and most companionable Englishman. If on a first acquaintance he seemed reserved, quite icy in his air—patience; this Champagne will thaw. And if it never do, better frozen Champagne than liquid vinegar.

There were nine gentlemen, all bachelors, at the dinner. One was from "No.—, King's Bench Walk, Temple;" a second, third, and fourth, and fifth, from various courts or passages christened with some similarly rich resounding syllables. It was indeed a sort of Senate of the Bachelors, sent to this dinner from widely-scattered districts, to represent the general celibacy of the Temple. Nay it was, by representation, a Grand Parliament of the best Bachelors in universal London; several of those present being from distant quarters of the town, noted immemorial seats of lawyers and un-married men—Lincoln's Inn, Furnival's Inn; and one gentleman, upon whom I looked with a sort of collateral awe, hailed from the spot where Lord Verulam once abode a bachelor—Gray's Inn.

The apartment was well up toward heaven. I know not how many strange old stairs I climbed to get to it. But a good dinner, with famous company, should be well earned. No doubt our host had his dining-room so high with a view to secure the prior exercise necessary to the due relishing and digesting of it.

The furniture was wonderfully unpretending, old, and snug. No new shining mahogany, sticky with undried varnish; no uncomfortably luxurious ottomans, and sofas too fine to use, vexed you in this sedate apartment. It is a thing which every sensible American should learn from every sensible Englishman, that glare and glitter, gimcracks and gewgaws, are not indispensable to domestic solacement. The American Benedick snatches, down-town, a tough chop in a gilded show-box; the English bachelor leisurely dines at home on that incomparable South Down of his, off a plain deal board.

The ceiling of the room was low. Who wants to dine under the dome of St. Peter's? High ceilings! If that is your demand, and the higher the better, and you be so very tall, then go dine out with the topping giraffe in the open air.

In good time the nine gentlemen sat down to nine covers, and soon were fairly under way.

If I remember right, ox-tail soup inaugurated the affair. Of a rich russet hue, its agreeable flavor dissipated my first confounding of its main ingredient with teamster's gads and the rawhides of ushers. (By way of interlude, we here drank a little claret.) Neptune's was the next tribute rendered—turbot coming second; snowwhite, flaky, and just gelatinous enough, not too turtleish in its unctuousness.

(At this point we refreshed ourselves with a glass of sherry.) After these light skirmishers had vanished, the heavy artillery of the feast marched in, led by that well-known English generalissimo, roast beef. For aids-de-camp we had a saddle of mutton, a fat turkey, a chicken-pie, and endless other savory things; while for avant-couriers came nine silver flagons of humming ale. This heavy ordnance having departed on the track of the light skirmishers, a picked brigade of game-fowl encamped upon the board, their camp-fires lit by the ruddiest of decanters.

Tarts and puddings followed, with innumerable niceties; then cheese and crackers. (By way of ceremony, simply, only to keep up good old fashions, we here each drank a glass of good old port.)

The cloth was now removed; and like Blucher's army coming in at the death on the field of Waterloo, in marched a fresh detachment of bottles, dusty with their hurried march.

All these manœuvrings of the forces were superintended by a surprising old field-marshal (I can not school myself to call him by the inglorious name of waiter), with snowy hair and napkin, and a head like Socrates. Amidst all the hilarity of the feast, intent on important business, he disdained to smile. Venerable man!

I have above endeavored to give some slight schedule of the general plan of operations. But any one knows that a good, genial dinner is a sort of pell-mell, indiscriminate affair, quite baffling to detail in all particulars. Thus, I spoke of taking a glass of claret, and a glass of sherry, and a glass of port, and a mug of ale—all at certain specific periods and times. But those were merely the state bumpers, so to speak. Innumerable impromptu glasses were drained between the periods of those grand imposing ones.

The nine bachelors seemed to have the most tender concern for each other's health. All the time, in flowing wine, they most earnestly expressed their sincerest wishes for the entire well-being and lasting hygiene of the gentlemen on the right and on the left. I noticed that when one of these kind bachelors desired a little more wine (just for his stomach's sake, like Timothy), he would not help himself to it unless some other bachelor would join him. It seemed held something indelicate, selfish, and unfraternal, to be seen taking a lonely, unparticipated glass. Meantime, as the wine ran apace, the spirits of the company grew more and more to perfect genialness and unconstraint. They related all sort of pleasant stories. Choice experiences in their private lives were now brought out, like choice brands of Moselle or Rhenish, only kept for particular company. One told us how mellowly he lived when a student at Oxford; with various spicy anecdotes of most frank-hearted noble lords, his liberal companions. Another bachelor, a gray-headed man, with a sunny face, who, by his own account, embraced every opportunity of leisure to cross over into the Low Countries, on sudden tours of inspection of the fine old Flemish architecture there—this learned, white-haired, sunny-faced old bachelor, excelled in his descriptions of the elaborate splendors of those old guild-halls, town-halls, and stadthold-houses, to be seen in the land of the ancient Flemings. A third was a great frequenter of the British Museum, and knew all about scores of wonderful antiquities, of Oriental manuscripts, and costly books without a duplicate. A fourth had lately returned from a trip to Old Granada, and, of course, was full of Saracenic scenery. A fifth had a funny case in law to tell. A sixth was erudite in wines. A seventh had a strange characteristic anecdote of the private life of the Iron Duke, never printed, and never before announced in any public or private company. An eighth had lately been amusing his evenings, now and then, with translating a comic poem of Pulci's. He quoted for us the more amusing passages.

And so the evening slipped along, the hours told, not by a water-clock, like King Alfred's, but a wine-chronometer. Meantime the table seemed a sort of Epsom Heath; a regular ring, where the decanters galloped round. For fear one decanter should not with sufficient speed reach his destination, another was sent express after him to hurry him; and then a third to hurry the second; and so on with a fourth and fifth. And throughout all this nothing loud, nothing unmannerly, nothing turbulent. I am quite sure, from the scrupulous gravity and austerity of his air, that had Socrates, the field-marshal, perceived aught of indecorum in the company he served, he would have forthwith departed without giving warning. I afterward learned that, during the repast, an invalid bachelor in an adjoining chamber enjoyed his first sound refreshing slumber in three long, weary weeks.

It was the very perfection of quiet absorption of good living, good drinking, good feeling, and good talk. We were a band of brothers. Comfort—fraternal, household comfort, was the grand trait of the affair. Also, you could plainly see that these easy-hearted men had no wives or children to give an anxious thought. Almost all of them were travelers, too; for bachelors alone can travel freely, and without any twinges of their consciences touching desertion of the fireside.

The thing called pain, the bugbear styled trouble—those two legends seemed preposterous to their bachelor imaginations. How could men of liberal sense, ripe scholarship in the world, and capacious philosophical and convivial understandings—how could they suffer themselves to be imposed upon by such monkish fables? Pain! Trouble! As well talk of Catholic miracles. No such thing.—Pass the sherry, Sir.—Pooh, pooh! Can't be!—The port, Sir, if you please. Nonsense; don't tell me so.—The decanter stops with you, Sir, I believe.

And so it went.

Not long after the cloth was drawn our host glanced significantly upon Socrates, who, solemnly stepping to a stand, returned with an immense convolved horn, a regular Jericho horn, mounted with polished silver, and otherwise chased and curiously enriched; not omitting two life-like goat's heads, with four more horns of solid silver, projecting from opposite sides of the mouth of the noble main horn.

Not having heard that our host was a performer on the bugle, I was surprised to see him lift this horn from the table, as if he were about to blow an inspiring blast. But I was relieved from this and set quite right as touching the purposes of the horn, by his now inserting his thumb and forefinger into its mouth; whereupon a slight aroma was stirred up, and my nostrils were greeted with the smell of some choice Rappee. It was a mull of snuff. It went the rounds. Capital idea this, thought I, of taking snuff about this juncture. This goodly fashion must be introduced among my countrymen at home, further ruminated I.

The remarkable decorum of the nine bachelors—a decorum not to be affected by any quantity of wine—a decorum unassailable by any degree of mirthfulness—this was again set in a forcible light to me, by now observing that, though they took snuff very freely, yet not a man so far violated the proprieties, or so far molested the invalid bachelor in the adjoining room as to indulge himself in a sneeze. The snuff was snuffed silently, as if it had been some fine innoxious powder brushed off the wings of butterflies.

But fine though they be, bachelors' dinners, like bachelors' lives, can not endure forever. The time came for breaking up. One by one the bachelors took their hats, and two by two, and arm-in-arm they descended, still conversing, to the flagging of the court; some going to their neighboring chambers to turn over the Decameron ere retiring for the night; some to smoke a cigar, promenading in the garden on the cool river-side; some to make for the street, call a hack, and be driven snugly to their distant lodgings.

I was the last lingerer.

"Well," said my smiling host, "what do you think of the Temple here, and the sort of life we bachelors make out to live in it?"

"Sir," said I, with a burst of admiring candor—"Sir, this is the very Paradise of Bachelors!"

II. THE TARTARUS OF MAIDS

It lies not far from Woedolor Mountain in New England. Turning to the east, right out from among bright farms and sunny meadows, nodding in early June with odorous grasses, you enter ascendingly among bleak hills. These gradually close in upon a dusky pass, which, from the violent Gulf Stream of air unceasingly diving between its cloven walls of haggard rock, as well as from the tradition of a crazy spinster's hut having long ago stood somewhere here-abouts, is called the Mad Maid's Bellows'-pipe.

Winding along at the bottom of the gorge is a dangerously narrow wheel-road, occupying the bed of a former torrent. Following this road to its highest point, you stand as within a Dantean gateway. From the steepness of the walls here, their strangely ebon hue, and the sudden contraction of the gorge, this particular point is called the Black Notch. The ravine now expandingly descends into a great, purple, hopper-shapped hollow, far sunk among many Plutonian, shaggy-wooded mountains. By the country people this hollow is called the Devil's Dungeon. Sounds of torrents fall on all sides upon the ear. These rapid waters unite at last in one turbid brick-colored stream, boiling through a flume among enormous boulders. They call this strange-colored torrent Blood River. Gaining a dark precipice it wheels suddenly to the west, and makes one maniac spring of sixty feet into the arms of a stunted wood of gray-haired pines, between which it thence eddies on its further way down to the invisible lowlands.

Conspicuously crowning a rocky bluff high to one side, at the cataract's verge, is the ruin of an old saw-mill, built in those primitive times when vast pines and hemlocks superabounded throughout the neighboring region. The black-mossed bulk of those immense, rough-hewn, and spike-knotted logs, here and there tumbled all together, in long abandonment and decay, or left in solitary, perilous projection over the cataract's gloomy brink, impart to this rude wooden ruin not only much of the aspect of one of rough-quarried stone, but also a sort of feudal, Rhineland, and Thurmberg look, derived from the pinnacled wildness of the neighboring scenery.

Not far from the bottom of the Dungeon stands a large white-washed building, relieved, like some great whited sepulchre, against the sullen background of mountain-side firs, and other hardy evergreens, inaccessibly rising in grim terraces for some two thousand feet.

The building is a paper-mill.

Having embarked on a large scale in the seedsman's business (so extensively and broadcast, indeed, that at length my seeds were distributed through all the Eastern and Northern States, and even fell into the far soil of Missouri and the Carolinas), the demand for paper at my place became so great, that the expenditure soon amounted to a most important item in the general account. It need hardly be hinted how paper comes into use with seedsmen, as envelopes. These are mostly made of yellowish paper, folded square; and when filled, are all but flat, and being stamped, and superscribed with the nature of the seeds contained, assume not a little the appearance of business-letters ready for the mail. Of these small envelopes I used an incredible quantity—several hundreds of thousands in a year. For a time I had purchased my paper from the whole-sale dealers in a neighboring town. For economy's sake, and partly for the adventure of the trip, I now resolved to cross the mountains, some sixty miles, and order my future paper at the Devil's Dungeon paper-mill.

The sleighing being uncommonly fine toward the end of January, and promising to hold so for no small period, in spite of the bitter cold I started one gray Friday noon in my pung, well fitted with buffalo and wolf robes; and, spending one night on the road, next noon came in sight of Woedolor Mountain.

The far summit fairly smoked with frost; white vapors curled up from its white-wooded top, as from a chimney. The intense congelation made the whole country look like one petrifaction. The steel shoes of my pung craunched and gritted over the vitreous, chippy snow, as if it had been broken glass. The forests here and there skirting the route, feeling the same all-stiffening influence, their inmost fibres penetrated with the cold, strangely groaned—not in the swaying branches merely, but likewise in the vertical trunk—as the fitful gusts remorselessly swept through them. Brittle with excessive frost, many colossal tough-grained maples, snapped in twain like pipe-stems, cumbered the unfeeling earth.

Flaked all over with frozen sweat, white as a milky ram, his nostrils at each breath sending forth two horn-shaped shoots of heated respiration, Black, my good horse, but six years old, started at a sudden turn, where, right across the track—not ten minutes fallen—an old distorted hemlock lay, darkly undulatory as an anaconda.

Gaining the Bellows'-pipe, the violent blast, dead from behind, all but shoved my high-backed pung up-hill. The gust shrieked through the shivered pass, as if laden with lost spirits bound to the unhappy world. Ere gaining the summit, Black, my horse, as if exasperated by the cutting wind, slung out with his strong hind legs, tore the light pung straight up-hill, and sweeping grazingly through the narrow notch, sped downward madly past the ruined saw-mill. Into the Devil's Dungeon horse and cataract rushed together.

With might and main, quitting my seat and robes, and standing backward, with one foot braced against the dash-board, I rasped and churned the bit, and stopped him just in time to avoid collision, at a turn, with the bleak nozzle of a rock, couchant like a lion in the way—a road-side rock.

At first I could not discover the paper-mill.

The whole hollow gleamed with the white, except, here and there, where a pinnacle of granite showed one wind-swept angle bare. The mountains stood pinned in shrouds—a pass of Alpine corpses. Where stands the mill? Suddenly a whirling, humming sound broke upon my ear. I looked, and there, like an arrested avalanche, lay the large whitewashed factory. It was subordinately surrounded by a cluster of other and smaller buildings, some of which, from their cheap, blank air, great length, gregarious windows, and comfortless expression, no doubt were boarding-houses of the operatives. A snow-white hamlet amidst the snows. Various rude, irregular squares and courts resulted from the somewhat picturesque clusterings of these buildings, owing to the broken, rocky nature of the ground, which forbade all method in their relative arrangement. Several narrow lanes and alleys, too, partly blocked with snow fallen from the roof, cut up the hamlet in all directions.

When, turning from the traveled highway, jingling with bells of numerous farmers—who, availing themselves of the fine sleighing, were dragging their wood to market—and frequently diversified with swift cutters dashing from inn to inn of the scattered villages—when, I say, turning from that bustling main-road, I by degrees wound into the Mad Maid's Bellows'-pipe, and saw the grim

Black Notch beyond, then something latent, as well as something obvious in the time and scene, strangely brought back to my mind my first sight of dark and grimy Temple-Bar. And when Black, my horse, went darting through the Notch, perilously grazing its rocky wall, I remembered being in a runaway London omnibus, which in much the same sort of style, though by no means at an equal rate, dashed through the ancient arch of Wren. Though the two objects did by no means completely correspond, yet this partial inadequacy but served to tinge the similitude not less with the vividness than the disorder of a dream. So that, when upon reining up at the protruding rock I at last caught sight of the quaint groupings of the factory-buildings, and with the traveled highway and the Notch behind, found myself all alone, silently and privily stealing through deep-cloven passages into this sequestered spot, and saw the long, high-gabled main factory edifice, with a rude tower—for hoisting heavy boxes—at one end, standing among its crowded outbuildings and boarding-houses, as the Temple Church amidst the surrounding offices and dormitories, and when the marvelous retirement of this mysterious mountain nook fastened its whole spell upon me, then, what memory lacked, all tributary imagination furnished, and I said to myself, "This is the very counterpart of the Paradise of Bachelors, but snowed upon, and frost-painted to a sepulchre."

Dismounting, and warily picking my way down the dangerous declivity—horse and man both sliding now and then upon the icy ledges—at length I drove, or the blast drove me, into the largest square, before one side of the main edifice. Piercingly and shrilly the shotted blast blew by the corner; and redly and demoniacally boiled Blood River at one side. A long woodpile, of many scores of cords, all glittering in mail of crusted ice, stood crosswise in the square. A row of horse-posts, their north sides plastered with adhesive snow, flanked the factory wall. The bleak frost packed and paved the square as with some ringing metal.

The inverted similitude recurred—"The sweet, tranquil Temple-garden, with the Thames bordering its green beds," strangely meditated I.

But where are the gay bachelors?

Then, as I and my horse stood shivering in the wind-spray, a girl ran from a neighboring dormitory door, and throwing her thin apron over her bare head, made for the opposite building.

"One moment, my girl; is there no shed here-abouts which I may drive into?"

Pausing, she turned upon me a face pale with work, and blue with cold; an eye supernatural with unrelated misery.

"Nay," faltered I, "I mistook you. Go on; I want nothing."

Leading my horse close to the door from which she had come, I knocked. Another pale, blue girl appeared, shivering in the doorway as, to prevent the blast, she jealously held the door ajar.

"Nay, I mistake again. In God's name shut the door. But hold, is there no man about?"

That moment a dark-complexioned well-wrapped personage passed, making for the factory door, and spying him coming, the girl rapidly closed the other one.

"Is there no horse-shed here, Sir?"

"Yonder, to the wood-shed," he replied, and disappeared inside the factory.

With much ado I managed to wedge in horse and pung between the scattered piles of wood all sawn and split. Then, blanketing my horse, and piling my buffalo on the blanket's top, tucking in its edges well around the breast-hand and breeching, so that the wind might not strip him bare, I tied him fast, and ran lamely for the factory door, stiff with frost, and cumbered with my driver's dreadnaught.

Immediately I found myself standing in a spacious place, intolerably lighted by long rows of windows, focusing inward the snowy scene without.

At rows of blank-looking counters sat rows of blank-looking girls, with blank, white folders in the blank hands, all blankly folding blank paper.

In one corner stood some huge frame of ponderous iron, with a vertical thing like a piston periodically rising and falling upon a heavy wooden block. Before it—its tame minister—stood a tall girl, feeding the iron animal with half-quires of rose-hued note paper, which, at every downward dab of the piston-like machine, received in the corner the impress of a wreath of roses. I looked from the rosy paper to the pallid cheek, but said nothing.

Seated before a long apparatus, strung with long, slender strings like any harp, another girl was feeding it with foolscap sheets, which, so soon as they curiously traveled from her on the cords, were withdrawn at the opposite end of the machine by a second girl.

They came to the first girl blank; they went to the second girl ruled.

I looked upon the first girl's brow, and saw it was young and fair; I looked upon the second girl's brow, and saw it was ruled and wrinkled. Then, as I still looked, the two—for some small variety to the monotony—changed places; and where had stood the young, fair brow, now stood the ruled and wrinkled one.

Perched high upon a narrow platform, and still higher upon a high stool crowning it, sat another figure serving some other iron animal; while below the platform sat her mate in some sort of reciprocal attendance.

Not a syllable was breathed. Nothing was heard but the low, steady, overruling hum of the iron animals. The human voice was banished from the spot. Machinery—that vaunted slave of humanity—here stood menially served by human beings, who served mutely and cringingly as the slave serves the Sultan. The girls did not so much seem accessory wheels to the general machinery as mere cogs to the wheels.

All this scene around me was instantaneously taken in at one sweeping glance—even before I had proceeded to unwind the heavy fur tippet from around my neck. But as soon as this fell from me the dark-complexioned man, standing close by, raised a sudden cry, and seizing my arm, dragged me out into the open air, and without pausing for a word instantly caught up some congealed snow and began rubbing both my cheeks.

"Two white spots like the whites of your eyes," he said; "man, your cheeks are frozen."

"That may well be," muttered I, " 'tis some wonder the frost of the Devil's Dungeon strikes in no deeper. Rub away."

Soon a horrible, tearing pain caught at my reviving cheeks. Two gaunt blood-hounds, one on each side, seemed mumbling them. I seemed Actæon.

Presently, when all was over, I re-entered the factory, made known my business, concluded it satisfactorily, and then begged to be conducted throughout the place to view it.

"Cupid is the boy for that," said the dark-complexioned man. "Cupid!" and by this odd fancy-name calling a dimpled, red-cheeked, spirited-looking, forward little fellow, who was rather impudently, I thought, gliding about among the passive-looking girls—like a gold fish through hueless waves—yet doing nothing in particular that I could see, the man bade him lead the stranger through the edifice.

"Come first and see the water-wheel," said this lively lad, with the air of boyishly-brisk importance.

Quitting the folding-room, we crossed some damp, cold boards, and stood beneath a great wet shed, incessantly showering with foam, like the green barnacled bow of some East India-man in a gale. Round and round here went the enormous revolutions of the dark colossal water-wheel, grim with its one immutable purpose.

"This sets our whole machinery a-going, Sir; in every part of all these buildings; where the girls work and all."

I looked, and saw that the turbid waters of Blood River had not changed their hue by coming under the use of man.

"You make only blank paper; no printing of any sort, I suppose? All blank paper, don't you?"

"Certainly; what else should a paper-factory make?"

The lad here looked at me as if suspicious of my common-sense.

"Oh, to be sure!" said I, confused and stammering; "it only struck me as so strange that red waters should turn out pale chee—paper, I mean."

He took me up a wet and rickety stair to a great light room, furnished with no visible thing but rude, manger-like receptacles running all round its sides; and up to these mangers, like so many mares haltered to the rack, stood rows of girls. Before each was vertically thrust up a long, glittering scythe, immovably fixed at bottom to the manger-edge. The curve of the scythe, and its having no snath to it, made it look exactly like a sword. To and fro, across the sharp edge, the girls forever dragged long strips of rags, washed white, picked from baskets at one side; thus ripping asunder every seam, and converting the tatters almost into lint. The air swam with the fine, poisonous particles, which from all sides darted, subtilely, as motes in sunbeams, into the lungs.

"This is the rag-room," coughed the boy.

"You find it rather stifling here," coughed I, in answer; "but the girls don't cough."

"Oh, they are used to it."

"Where do you get such hosts of rags?" picking up a handful from a basket.

"Some from the country round about; some from far over sea—Leghorn and London."

" 'Tis not unlikely, then," murmured I, "that among these heaps of rags there may be some old shirts, gathered from the dormitories of the Paradise of Bachelors. But the buttons are all dropped off. Pray, my lad, do you ever find any bachelor's buttons hereabouts?"

"None grow in this part of the country. The Devil's Dungeon is no place for flowers."

"Oh! you mean the *flowers* so called—the Bachelor's Buttons?"

"And was not that what you asked about? Or did you mean the gold bosom-buttons of our boss, Old Bach, as our whispering girls all call him?"

"The man, then, I saw below is a bachelor, is he?"

"Oh, yes, he's a Bach."

"The edges of those swords, they are turned outward from the girls, if I see right; but their rags and fingers fly so, I can not distinctly see."

"Turned outward."

Yes, murmured I to myself; I see it now; turned outward; and each erected sword is so borne, edge-outward, before each girl. If my reading fails me not, just so, of old, condemned state-prisoners went from the hall of judgment to their doom: an officer before, bearing a sword, its edge turned outward, in significance of their fatal sentence. So, through consumptive pallors of this blank, raggy life, go these white girls to death.

"Those scythes look very sharp," again turning toward the boy.

"Yes; they have to keep them so. Look!"

That moment two of the girls, dropping their rags, plied each a whet-stone up and down the sword-blade. My unaccustomed blood curdled at the sharp shriek of the tormented steel.

Their own executioners; themselves whetting the very swords that slay them; meditated I.

"What makes those girls so sheet-white, my lad?"

"Why"—with a roguish twinkle, pure ignorant drollery, not knowing heartlessness—"I suppose the handling of such white bits of sheets all the time makes them so sheety."

"Let us leave the rag-room now, my lad."

More tragical and more inscrutably mysterious than any mystic sight, human or machine, throughout the factory, was the strange innocence of cruel-heartedness in this usage-hardened boy.

"And now," said he, cheerily, "I suppose you want to see our great machine, which cost us twelve thousand dollars only last autumn. That's the machine that makes the paper, too. This way, Sir."

Following him, I crossed a large, bespattered place, with two great round vats in it, full of a white, wet, woolly-looking stuff, not unlike the albuminous part of an egg, soft-boiled.

"There," said Cupid, tapping the vats carelessly, "these are the first beginnings of the paper, this white pulp you see. Look how it swims bubbling round and round, moved by the paddle here. From hence it pours from both vats into that one common channel yonder; and so goes, mixed up and leisurely, to the great machine. And now for that."

He led me into a room, stifling with a strange, blood-like, abdominal heat, as if here, true enough, were being finally developed the germinous particles lately seen.

Before me, rolled out like some long Eastern manuscript, lay stretched one continuous length of iron frame-work—multitudinous and mystical, with all sorts of rollers, wheels, and cylinders, in slowly-measured and unceasing motion.

"Here first comes the pulp now," said Cupid, pointing to the nighest end of the machine. "See; first it pours out and spreads itself upon this wide, sloping board; and then—look—slides, thin and quivering, beneath the first roller there. Follow on now, and see it as it slides from under that to the next cylinder. There; see how it has become just a very little less pulpy now. One step more, and it grows still more to some slight consistence. Still another cylinder, and it is so knitted—though as yet mere dragon-fly wing—that it forms an air-bridge here, like a suspended cobweb, between two more separated rollers; and flowing over the last one, and under again, and doubling about there out of sight for a minute among all those mixed cylinders you indistinctly see, it reappears here, looking now at last a little less like pulp and more like paper, but still quite delicate and defective yet awhile. But—a little further onward, Sir, if you please—here now, at this further point, it puts on something of a real look, as if it might turn out to be something you might possibly handle in the end. But it's not yet done, Sir. Good way to travel yet, and plenty more of cylinders must roll it."

"Bless my soul!" said I, amazed at the elongation, interminable convolutions, and deliberate slowness of the machine; "it must take a long time for the pulp to pass from end to end, and come out paper."

"Oh! not so long," smiled the precocious lad, with a superior and patronizing air; "only nine minutes. But look; you may try it for yourself. Have you a bit of paper? Ah! here's a bit on the floor. Now mark that with any word you please, and let me dab it on here, and we'll see how long before it comes out at the other end."

"Well, let me see," said I, taking out my pencil; "come, I'll mark it with your name."

Bidding me take out my watch, Cupid adroitly dropped the inscribed slip on an exposed part of the incipient mass.

Instantly my eye marked the second-hand on my dial-plate.

Slowly I followed the slip, inch by inch; sometimes pausing for full half a minute as it disappeared beneath inscrutable groups of the lower cylinders, but only gradually to emerge again; and so, on, and on, and on—inch by inch; now in open sight, sliding along like a freckle on the quivering sheet; and then again wholly vanished; and so, on, and on, and on—inch by inch; all the time the main sheet growing more and more to final firmness—when, suddenly, I saw a sort of paper-fall, not wholly unlike a water-fall; a scissory sound smote my ear, as of some cord being snapped; and down dropped an unfolded sheet of perfect foolscap, with my "Cupid" half faded out of it, and still moist and warm.

My travels were at an end, for here was the end of the machine.

"Well, how long was it?" said Cupid.

"Nine minutes to a second," replied I, watch in hand.

"I told you so."

For a moment a curious emotion filled me, not wholly unlike that which one might experience at the fulfillment of some mysterious prophecy. But how absurd, thought I again; the thing is a mere machine, the essence of which is unvarying punctuality and precision.

Previously absorbed by the wheels and cylinders, my attention was now directed to a sad-looking woman standing by.

"That is rather an elderly person so silently tending the machine-end here. She would not seem wholly used to it either."

"Oh," knowingly whispered Cupid, through the din, "she only came last week. She was a nurse formerly. But the business is poor in these parts, and she's left it. But look at the paper she is piling there."

"Ay, foolscap," handling the piles of moist, warm sheets, which continually were being delivered into the woman's waiting hands. "Don't you turn out any thing but foolscap at this machine?"

"Oh, sometimes, but not often, we turn out finer work—cream-laid and royal sheets, we call them. But foolscap being in chief demand, we turn out foolscap most."

It was very curious. Looking at that blank paper continually dropping, dropping, dropping, my mind ran on in wonderings of those strange uses to which those thousand sheets eventually would be put. All sorts of writings would be writ on those now vacant things—sermons, lawyers' briefs, physicians' prescriptions, love-letters, marriage certificates, bills of divorce, registers of births, death-warrants, and so on, without end. Then, recurring back to them as they here lay all blank, I could not but bethink me of that celebrated comparison of John Locke, who, in demonstration of his theory that man had no innate ideas, compared the human mind at birth to a sheet of blank paper; something destined to be scribbled on, but what sort of characters no soul might tell.

Pacing slowly to and fro along the involved machine, still humming with its play, I was struck as well by the inevitability as the evolvement-power in all its motions.

"Does that thin cobweb there," said I, pointing to the sheet in its more imperfect stage, "does that never tear or break? It is marvelous fragile, and yet this machine it passes through is so mighty."

"It never is known to tear a hair's point."

"Does it never stop—get clogged?"

"No. It *must* go. The machinery makes it go just *so;* just that very way, and at that very pace you there plainly *see* it go. The pulp can't help going."

Something of awe now stole over me, as I gazed upon this inflexible iron animal. Always, more or less, machinery of this ponderous, elaborate sort strikes, in some moods, strange dread into the human heart, as some living, panting Behemoth might. But what made the thing I saw so specially terrible to me was the metallic necessity, the unbudging fatality which governed it. Though, here and there, I could not follow the thin, gauzy vail of pulp in the course of its more mysterious or entirely invisible advance, yet it was indubitable that, at those points where it eluded me, it still marched on in unvarying docility to the autocratic cunning of the machine. A fascination fastened on me. I stood spellbound and wandering in my soul. Before my eyes—there, passing in slow procession along the wheeling cylinders, I seemed to see, glued to the pallid incipience of the pulp, the yet more pallid faces of all the pallid girls I had eyed that heavy day. Slowly, mournfully, beseechingly, yet unresistingly, they gleamed along, their agony dimly outlined on the imperfect paper, like the print of the tormented face on the handkerchief of Saint Veronica.

"Halloa! the heat of the room is too much for you," cried Cupid, staring at me.

"No—I am rather chill, if any thing."

"Come out, Sir—out—out," and, with the protecting air of a careful father, the precocious lad hurried me outside.

In a few moments, feeling revived a little, I went into the folding-room—the first room I had entered, and where the desk for transacting business stood, surrounded by the blank counters and blank girls engaged at them.

"Cupid here has led me a strange tour," said I to the dark-complexioned man before mentioned, whom I had ere this discovered not only to be an old bachelor, but also the principal proprietor. "Yours is a most wonderful factory. Your great machine is a miracle of inscrutable intricacy."

"Yes, all our visitors think it so. But we don't have many. We are in a very out-of-the-way corner here. Few inhabitants, too. Most of our girls come from far-off villages."

"The girls," echoed I, glancing round at their silent forms. "Why is it, Sir, that in most factories, female operatives, of whatever age, are indiscriminately called girls, never women?"

"Oh! as to that—why, I suppose, the fact of their being generally unmarried—that's the reason, I should think. But it never struck me before. For our factory here, we will not have married women; they are apt to be off-and-on too much. We want none but steady workers: twelve hours to the day, day after day, through the three hundred and sixty-five days, excepting Sundays, Thanksgiving, and Fastdays. That's our rule. And so, having no married women, what females we have are rightly enough called girls."

"Then these are all maids," said I, while some pained homage to their pale virginity made me involuntarily bow.

"All maids."

Again the strange emotion filled me.

"Your cheeks look whitish yet, Sir," said the man, gazing at me narrowly. "You must be careful going home. Do they pain you at all now? It's a bad sign, if they do."

"No doubt, Sir," answered I, "when once I have got out of the Devil's Dungeon, I shall feel them mending."

"Ah, yes; the winter air in valleys, or gorges, or any sunken place, is far colder and more bitter than elsewhere. You would hardly believe it now, but it is colder here than at the top of Woedolor Mountain."

"I dare say it is, Sir. But time presses me; I must depart."

With that, remuffling myself in dread-naught and tippet, thrusting my hands into my huge seal-skin mittens, I sallied out into the nipping air, and found poor Black, my horse, all cringing and doubled up with the cold.

Soon, wrapped in furs and meditations, I ascended from the Devil's Dungeon.

At the Black Notch I paused, and once more bethought me of Temple-Bar. Then, shooting through the pass, all alone with inscrutable nature, I exclaimed—Oh! Paradise of Bachelors! and oh! Tartarus of Maids!

EDGAR ALLAN POE
(1809–1849)

Though "The Raven" (1845) brought Edgar Allan Poe international fame, and poems like "Ulalume" and "The Bells" assured that fame, Poe's experience as a professional writer in mid-nineteenth-century America was as bitter and demoralizing as Melville's; and, in personal terms, yet more nightmarish. Orphaned at three, abandoned by the well-to-do Richmond merchant who adopted him, prone to illness, mental instability, and alcoholism through his short life, and, after his death, vilified by his very biographer, Poe has come to typify, in lurid excess, the fate of the imaginative genius who is forced to sell himself in the marketplace and to wear himself out tragically in the effort. Though his work is never autobiographical in any overt way, just as it is never "realistic," Poe's images and melodramatic Gothic plots seem but the reasonable analogues of his experience.

Except for The Raven and Other Poems *(1845), Poe's published works—*Tamerlane and Other Poems *(1827),* The Narrative of A. Gordon Pym *(1838),* Tales of the Grotesque and Arabesque *(1840),* Eureka *(1848)—brought in little income. The "Edgar Allan Poe" celebrated by contemporary critics is in fact a Poe distilled and heightened by foreign men of letters as diverse as Charles Baudelaire and Stéphane Mallarmé on the one hand and August Strindberg and George Bernard Shaw on the other: Poe as genius, not as frenzied hack writer. The value of Poe's best work for other writers lies in his bold use of surreal dream-images, the drama of his various deranged voices, the fluidity of his plots. "The Tell-Tale Heart" is at the very core of Poe: unhampered by the writerly turgidity of certain of his other stories, utterly convincing in its pathology, and in its obvious zest in its pathology. So much, so swiftly: this* is *genius.*

The Tell-Tale Heart

True!—nervous—very, very dreadfully nervous I had been and am; but why *will* you say that I am mad? The disease had sharpened my senses—not destroyed—not dulled them. Above all was the sense of hearing acute. I heard all things in the heaven and in the earth. I heard many things in hell. How, then, am I mad? Hearken! and observe how healthily—how calmly I can tell you the whole story.

It is impossible to say how first the idea entered my brain; but once conceived, it haunted me day and night. Object there was none. Passion there was none. I loved the old man. He had never wronged me. He had never given me insult. For his gold I had no desire. I think it was his eye! yes, it was this! One of his eyes resembled that of a vulture—a pale blue eye, with a film over it. Whenever it fell upon me, my blood ran cold; and so by degrees—very gradually—I made up my mind to take the life of the old man, and thus rid myself of the eye forever.

Now this is the point. You fancy me mad. Madmen know nothing. But you should have seen *me*. You should have seen how wisely I proceeded—with what caution—with what foresight—with what dissimulation I went to work! I was never kinder to the old man than during the whole week before I killed him. And every night, about midnight, I turned the latch of his door and opened it—oh, so gently! And then, when I had made an opening sufficient for my head, I put in a dark lantern, all closed, closed, so that no light shone out, and then I thrust in my head. Oh, you would have laughed to see how cunningly I thrust it in! I moved it slowly—very, very slowly, so that I might not disturb the old man's sleep. It took me an hour to place my whole head within the opening so far that I could see him as he lay upon his bed. Ha!—would a madman have been so wise as this? And then, when my head was well in the room, I undid the lantern cautiously—oh, so cautiously—cautiously (for the hinges creaked)—I undid it just so much that a single thin ray fell upon the vulture eye. And this I did for seven long nights—every night just at midnight—but I found the eye always closed; and so it was impossible to do the work; for it was not the old man who vexed me, but his Evil Eye. And every morning, when the day broke, I went boldly into the chamber, and spoke courageously to him, calling him by name in a hearty tone, and inquiring how he had passed the night. So you see he would have been a very profound old man, indeed, to suspect that every night, just at twelve, I looked in upon him while he slept.

Upon the eighth night I was more than usually cautious in opening the door. A watch's minute hand moves more quickly than did mine. Never before that night had I *felt* the extent of my own powers—of my sagacity. I could scarcely contain my feelings of triumph. To think that there I was, opening the door, little by little, and he not even to dream of my secret deeds or thoughts. I fairly chuckled at the idea; and perhaps he heard me, for he moved on the bed suddenly, as if startled. Now you may think that I drew back—but no. His room was as black as pitch with the thick darkness (for the shutters were close fastened, through fear of robbers), and so I knew that he could not see the opening of the door, and I kept pushing it on steadily, steadily.

I had my head in, and was about to open the lantern, when my thumb slipped upon the tin fastening, and the old man sprang up in the bed, crying out—"Who's there?"

I kept quite still and said nothing. For a whole hour I did not move a muscle, and in the meantime I did not hear him lie down. He was still sitting up in the bed, listening;—just as I have done, night after night, hearkening to the death watches in the wall.

Presently I heard a slight groan, and I knew it was the groan of mortal terror. It was not a groan of pain or of grief—oh, no!—it was the low stifled sound that arises from the bottom of the soul when overcharged with awe. I knew the sound well. Many a night, just at midnight, when all the world slept, it has welled up from my own bosom, deepening, with its dreadful echo, the terrors that distracted me. I say I knew it well. I knew what the old man felt, and pitied him, although I chuckled at heart. I knew that he had been lying awake ever since the first slight noise, when he had turned in the bed. His fears had been ever since growing upon him. He had been trying to fancy them causeless, but could not. He had been saying to himself—"It is nothing but the wind in the chimney—it is only a mouse crossing the floor," or "it is merely a cricket which has made a single chirp." Yes, he had been trying to comfort himself with these suppositions; but he had found all in vain. *All in vain;* because Death, in approaching him, had stalked with his black shadow before him, and enveloped the victim. And it was the mournful influence of the unperceived shadow that caused him to feel—although he neither saw nor heard—to *feel* the presence of my head within the room.

When I had waited a long time, very patiently, without hearing him lie down, I resolved to open a little—a very, very little crevice in the lantern. So I opened it—you cannot imagine how stealthily, stealthily—until, at length, a single dim ray, like the thread of the spider, shot from out the crevice and fell upon the vulture eye.

It was open—wide, wide open—and I grew furious as I gazed upon it. I saw it with perfect distinctness—all a dull blue, with a hideous veil over it that chilled the very marrow in my bones; but I could see nothing else of the old man's face or person; for I had directed the ray as if by instinct, precisely upon the damned spot.

And now have I not told you that what you mistake for madness is but over-acuteness of the senses?—now, I say, there came to my ears a low, dull, quick sound, such as a watch makes when enveloped in cotton. I knew *that* sound well, too. It was the beating of the old man's heart. It increased my fury, as the beating of a drum stimulates the soldier into courage.

But even yet I refrained and kept still. I scarcely breathed, I held the lantern motionless. I tried how steadily I could maintain the ray upon the eye. Meantime the hellish tattoo of the heart increased. It grew quicker and quicker, and louder and louder every instant. The old man's terror *must* have been extreme! It grew louder, I say, louder every moment!—do you mark me well? I have told you that I am nervous; so I am. And now at the dead hour of the night, amid the dreadful silence of that old house, so strange a noise as this excited me to uncontrollable terror. Yet, for some minutes longer I refrained and stood still. But the beating grew louder, louder! I thought the heart must burst. And now a new anxiety seized me—the sound would be heard by a neighbor! The old man's hour had come! With a loud yell, I threw open the lantern and leaped into the room. He shrieked once—once only. In an instant I dragged him to the floor, and pulled the heavy bed over him. I then smiled gaily, to find the deed so far done. But, for many minutes, the heart beat on with a muffled sound. This, however, did not vex me; it would not be heard through the wall.

At length it ceased. The old man was dead. I removed the bed and examined the corpse. Yes, he was stone, stone dead. I placed my hand upon the heart and held it there many minutes. There was no pulsation. He was stone dead. His eye would trouble me no more.

If still you think me mad, you will think so no longer when I describe the wise precautions I took for the concealment of the body. The night waned, and I worked hastily, but in silence. First of all I dismembered the corpse. I cut off the head and the arms and the legs.

I then took up three planks from the flooring of the chamber, and deposited all between the scantlings. I then replaced the boards so cleverly, so cunningly, that no human eye—not even *his*—could have detected anything wrong. There was nothing to wash out—no stain of any kind—no blood-spot whatever. I had been too wary for that. A tub had caught all—ha! ha!

When I had made an end of these labors, it was four o'clock—still dark as midnight. As the bell sounded the hour, there came a knocking at the street door. I went down to open it with a light heart,—for what had I *now* to fear? There entered three men who introduced themselves, with perfect suavity, as officers of the police. A shriek had been heard by a neighbor during the night; suspicion of foul play had been aroused; information had been lodged at the police office, and they (the officers) had been deputed to search the premises.

I smiled—for *what* had I to fear? I bade the gentlemen welcome. The shriek, I said, was my own in a dream. The old man, I mentioned, was absent in the country. I took my visitors all over the house. I bade them search—search *well*. I led them, at length, to *his* chamber. I showed them his treasures, secure, undisturbed. In the enthusiasm of my confidence, I brought chairs into the room, and desired them *here* to rest from their fatigues, while I myself, in the wild audacity of my perfect triumph, placed my own seat upon the very spot beneath which reposed the corpse of the victim.

The officers were satisfied. My *manner* had convinced them. I was singularly at ease. They sat, and while I answered cheerily, they chatted of familiar things. But, ere long, I felt myself getting pale and wished them gone. My head ached, and I fancied a ringing in my ears: but still they sat and still chatted. The ringing became more distinct:—it continued and became more distinct:—I talked more freely to get rid of the feeling: but it continued and gained definitiveness—until, at length, I found that the noise was *not* within my ears.

No doubt I now grew *very* pale;—but I talked more fluently, and with a heightened voice. Yet the sound increased—and what could I do? It was *a low, dull, quick sound—much such a sound as a watch makes when enveloped in cotton.* I gasped for breath—and yet the officers heard it not. I talked more quickly—more vehemently: but the noise steadily increased. I arose and argued about trifles, in a high key and with violent gesticulations; but the noise steadily increased. Why *would* they not be gone? I paced the floor to and fro with heavy strides, as if excited to fury by the observations of the men—but the noise steadily increased. Oh God! what *could* I do? I foamed—I raved—I swore! I swung the chair upon which I had been sitting, and grated it upon the boards, but the noise arose over all and continually increased. It grew louder—louder—*louder!* And still the men chatted pleasantly, and smiled. Was it possible they heard not? Almighty God!—no, no! They heard!—they suspected!—they *knew!*—they were making a mockery of my horror!—this I thought, and this I think. But anything was better than this agony! Anything was more tolerable than this derision! I could bear those hypocritical smiles no longer! I felt that I must scream or die!—and now—again!—hark! louder! louder! louder! *louder!*—

"Villains!" I shrieked, "dissemble no more! I admit the deed!—tear up the planks!—here, here!—it is the beating of his hideous heart!"

HARRIET BEECHER STOWE

(1811–1896)

"Is this the little lady who started such a big war?" Abraham Lincoln was reputed to have said to Harriet Beecher Stowe when they met during the Civil War. The author of Uncle Tom's Cabin *(1852), based upon the slave life she witnessed firsthand, Mrs. Stowe was not only the first American woman writer of significance, but one of the most popular and celebrated American writers in our history. Indeed, to consider Melville and Poe as "nineteenth-century American writers" if one considers Harriet Beecher Stowe as a "nineteenth-century American writer" is to have imagined a category broad, deep, and vertiginous as the Grand Canyon. Except in the most self-evident of terms, Melville and Poe do not belong to the same universe as Mrs. Stowe.*

Though Mrs. Stowe had some initial difficulty publishing Uncle Tom's Cabin *as a book, it was an immediate success when published, and was but the first of the author's numerous popular successes through a career of thirty-five years. Stowe published regularly in* Atlantic Monthly *and other prestigious magazines; among her more important works are the novels* The Pearl of Orr's Island *(1862) and* Oldtown Folks *(1869). "The Ghost in the Mill" is taken from* Sam Lawson's Oldtown Fireside Stories *(1872), which went through fourteen printings. The stories are linked by the children, primarily boys, of Oldtown, Massachusetts, who sit at the knee of Sam Lawson, a storyteller of scary but moral tales. Quaint by contemporary standards, and hardly adult fare, "The Ghost in the Mill" is intriguing for its depiction of the unassimilated Indian woman Ketury with her "scornful ways" and "snaky eyes," who appears elsewhere in the volume, empowered as an outsider of possibly demonic origin.*

The Ghost in the Mill

"Come, Sam, tell us a story," said I, as Harry and I crept to his knees, in the glow of the bright evening firelight; while Aunt Lois was busily rattling the tea-things, and grandmamma, at the other end of the fireplace, was quietly setting the heel of a blue-mixed yarn stocking.

In those days we had no magazines and daily papers, each reeling off a serial story. Once a week, "The Columbian Sentinel" came from Boston with its slender stock of news and editorial; but all the multiform devices—pictorial, narrative, and poetical—which keep the mind of the present generation ablaze with excitement, had not then even an existence. There was no theatre, no opera; there were in Oldtown no parties or balls, except, perhaps, the annual election, or Thanksgiving festival; and when winter came, and the sun went down at half-past four o'clock, and left the long, dark hours of evening to be provided for, the necessity of amusement became urgent. Hence, in those days, chimney-corner story-telling became an art and an accomplishment. Society then was full of traditions and narratives which had all the uncertain glow and shifting mystery of the firelit hearth upon them. They were told to sympathetic audiences, by the rising and falling light of the solemn embers, with the hearth-crickets filling up every pause. Then the aged told their stories to the young,—tales of early life; tales of war and adventure, of forest-days, of Indian captivities and escapes, of bears and wild-cats and panthers, of rattlesnakes, of witches and wizards, and strange and wonderful dreams and appearances and providences.

In those days of early Massachusetts, faith and credence were in the very air. Two-thirds of New England was then dark, unbroken forests, through whose tangled paths the mysterious winter wind groaned and shrieked and howled with weird noises and unaccountable clamors. Along the iron-bound shore, the stormful Atlantic raved and thundered, and dashed its moaning waters, as if to deaden and deafen any voice that might tell of the settled life of the old civilized world, and shut us forever into the wilderness. A good story-teller, in those days, was always sure of a warm seat at the hearth-stone, and the delighted homage of children; and in all Oldtown there was no better story-teller than Sam Lawson.

"Do, do, tell us a story," said Harry, pressing upon him, and opening very wide blue eyes, in which undoubting faith shone as in a mirror; "and let it be something strange, and different from common."

"Wal, I know lots o' strange things," said Sam, looking mysteriously into the fire. "Why, I know things, that ef I should tell,—why, people might say they wa'n't so; but then they *is* so for all that."

"Oh, *do*, do, tell us!"

"Why, I should scare ye to death, mebbe," said Sam doubtingly.

"Oh, pooh! no, you wouldn't," we both burst out at once.

But Sam was possessed by a reticent spirit, and loved dearly to be wooed and importuned; and so he only took up the great kitchen-tongs, and smote on the hickory forestick, when it flew apart in the middle, and scattered a shower of clear bright coals all over the hearth.

"Mercy on us, Sam Lawson!" said Aunt Lois in an indignant voice, spinning round from her dish-washing.

"Don't you worry a grain, Miss Lois," said Sam composedly. "I see that are stick was e'en a'most in two, and I thought I'd jest settle it. I'll sweep up the coals now," he added, vigorously applying a turkey-wing to the purpose, as he knelt on the hearth, his spare, lean figure glowing in the blaze of the firelight, and getting quite flushed with exertion.

"There, now!" he said, when he had brushed over and under and between the fire-irons, and pursued the retreating ashes so far into the red, fiery citadel, that his finger-ends were burning and tingling, "that are's done now as well as Hepsy herself could 'a' done it. I allers sweeps up the haarth: I think it's part o' the man's bisness when he makes the fire. But Hepsy's so used to seein' me a-doin' on't, that she don't see no kind o' merit in't. It's just as Parson Lothrop said in his sermon,—folks allers overlook their common marcies"—

"But come, Sam, that story," said Harry and I coaxingly, pressing upon him, and pulling him down into his seat in the corner.

"Lordy massy, these 'ere young uns!" said Sam. "There's never no contentin' on 'em: ye tell 'em one story, and they jest swallows it as a dog does a gob o' meat; and they're all ready for another. What do ye want to hear now?"

Now, the fact was, that Sam's stories had been told us so often, that they were all arranged and ticketed in our minds. We knew every word in them, and could set him right if he varied a hair from the usual track; and still the interest in them was unabated. Still we shivered, and clung to his knee, at the mysterious parts, and felt gentle, cold chills run down our spines at appropriate places. We were always in the most receptive and sympathetic condition. To-night, in particular, was one of those thundering stormy ones, when the winds appeared to be holding a perfect mad carnival over my grandfather's house. They yelled and squealed round the corners; they collected in troops, and came tumbling and roaring down chimney; they shook and rattled the buttery-door and the sinkroom-door and the cellar-door and the chamber-door, with a constant undertone of squeak and clatter, as if at every door were a cold, discontented spirit, tired of the chill outside, and longing for the warmth and comfort within.

"Wal, boys," said Sam confidentially, "what'll ye have?"

"Tell us 'Come down, come down!' " we both shouted with one voice. This was, in our mind, an "A No. 1" among Sam's stories.

"Ye mus'n't be frightened now," said Sam paternally.

"Oh, no! we ar'n't frightened *ever*," said we both in one breath.

"Not when ye go down the cellar arter cider?" said Sam with severe scrutiny. "Ef ye should be down cellar, and the candle should go out, now?"

"I ain't," said I: "I ain't afraid of any thing. I never knew what it was to be afraid in my life."

"Wal, then," said Sam, "I'll tell ye. This 'ere's what Cap'n Eb Sawin told me when I was a boy about your bigness, I reckon.

"Cap'n Eb Sawin was a most respectable man. Your gran'ther knew him very well; and he was a deacon in the church in Dedham afore he died. He was at Lexington when the fust gun was fired agin the British. He was a dreffle smart man, Cap'n Eb was, and driv team a good many years atween here and Boston. He married Lois Peabody, that was cousin to your gran'ther then. Lois was a rael sensible woman; and I've heard her tell the story as he told her, and it was jest as he told it to me,—jest exactly; and I shall never forget it if I live to be nine hundred years old, like Mathuselah.

"Ye see, along back in them times, there used to be a fellow come round these 'ere parts, spring and fall, a-peddlin' goods, with his pack on his back; and his name was Jehiel Lommedieu. Nobody rightly knew where he come from. He wasn't much of a talker; but the women rather liked him, and kind o' liked to have him round. Women will like some fellows, when men can't see no sort o' reason why they should; and they liked this 'ere Lommedieu, though he was kind o' mournful and thin and shad-bellied, and hadn't nothin' to say for himself. But it got to be so, that the women would count and calculate so many weeks afore 'twas time for Lommedieu to be along; and they'd make up ginger-snaps and preserves and pies, and make him stay to tea at the houses, and feed him up on the best there was: and the story went round, that he was a-courtin' Phebe Ann Parker, or Phebe Ann was a-courtin' him,—folks didn't rightly know which. Wal, all of a sudden, Lommedieu stopped comin' round; and nobody knew why,—only jest he didn't come. It turned out that Phebe Ann Parker had got a letter from him, sayin' he'd be along afore Thanksgiving; but he didn't come, neither afore nor at Thanksgiving time, nor arter, nor next spring: and finally the women they gin up lookin' for him. Some said he was dead; some said he was gone to Canada; and some said he hed gone over to the Old Country.

"Wal, as to Phebe Ann, she acted like a gal o' sense, and married 'Bijah Moss, and thought no more 'bout it. She took the right view on't, and said she was sartin that all things was ordered out for the best; and it was jest as well folks couldn't always have their own way. And so, in time, Lommedieu was gone out o' folks's minds, much as a last year's apple-blossom.

"It's relly affectin' to think how little these 'ere folks is missed that's so much sot by. There ain't nobody, ef they's ever so important, but what the world gets to goin' on without 'em, pretty much as it did with 'em, though there's some little flurry at fust. Wal, the last thing that was in anybody's mind was, that they ever should hear from Lommedieu agin. But there ain't nothin' but what has its time o' turnin' up; and it seems his turn was to come.

"Wal, ye see, 'twas the 19th o' March, when Cap'n Eb Sawin started with a team for Boston. That day, there come on about the biggest snow-storm that there'd been in them parts sence the oldest man could remember. 'Twas this 'ere fine, siftin' snow, that drives in your face like needles, with a wind to cut your nose off:

it made teamin' pretty tedious work. Cap'n Eb was about the toughest man in them parts. He'd spent days in the woods a-loggin', and he'd been up to the deestrict o' Maine a-lumberin', and was about up to any sort o' thing a man gen'ally could be up to; but these 'ere March winds sometimes does set on a fellow so, that neither natur' nor grace can stan' 'em. The cap'n used to say he could stan' any wind that blew one way 't time for five minutes; but come to winds that blew all four p'ints at the same minit,—why, they flustered him.

"Wal, that was the sort o' weather it was all day: and by sundown Cap'n Eb he got clean bewildered, so that he lost his road; and, when night came on, he didn't know nothin' where he was. Ye see the country was all under drift, and the air so thick with snow, that he couldn't see a foot afore him; and the fact was, he got off the Boston road without knowin' it, and came out at a pair o' bars nigh upon Sherburn, where old Cack Sparrock's mill is.

"Your gran'ther used to know old Cack, boys. He was a drefful drinkin' old crittur, that lived there all alone in the woods by himself a-tendin' saw and grist mill. He wa'n't allers jest what he was then. Time was that Cack was a pretty consid'ably likely young man, and his wife was a very respectable woman,—Deacon Amos Petengall's dater from Sherburn.

"But ye see, the year arter his wife died, Cack he gin up goin' to meetin' Sundays, and, all the tithing-men and selectmen could do, they couldn't get him out to meetin'; and, when a man neglects means o' grace and sanctuary privileges, there ain't no sayin' *what* he'll do next. Why, boys, jist think on't!—an immortal crittur lyin' round loose all day Sunday, and not puttin' on so much as a clean shirt, when all 'spectable folks has on their best close, and is to meetin' worshippin' the Lord! What can you 'spect to come of it, when he lies idlin' round in his old week-day close, fishing, or some sich, but what the Devil should be arter him at last, as he was arter old Cack?"

Here Sam winked impressively to my grandfather in the opposite corner, to call his attention to the moral which he was interweaving with his narrative.

"Wal, ye see, Cap'n Eb he told me, that when he come to them bars and looked up, and saw the dark a-comin' down, and the storm a-thickenin' up, he felt that things was gettin' pretty consid'able serious. There was a dark piece o' woods on ahead of him inside the bars; and he knew, come to get in there, the light would give out clean. So he jest thought he'd take the hoss out o' the team, and go ahead a little, and see where he was. So he driv his oxen up ag'in the fence, and took out the hoss, and got on him, and pushed along through the woods, not rightly knowin' where he was goin'.

"Wal, afore long he see a light through the trees and, sure enough, he come out to Cack Sparrock's old mill.

"It was a pretty consid'able gloomy sort of a place, that are old mill was. There was a great fall of water that come rushin' down the rocks, and fell in a deep pool; and it sounded sort o' wild and lonesome; but Cap'n Eb he knocked on the door with his whip-handle, and got in.

"There, to be sure, sot old Cack beside a great blazin' fire, with his rum-jug at his elbow. He was a drefful fellow to drink, Cack was! For all that, there was some good in him, for he was pleasant-spoken and 'bliging; and he made the cap'n welcome.

" 'Ye see, Cack,' said Cap'n Eb, 'I'm off my road and got snowed up down by your bars,' says he.

" 'Want ter know!' says Cack. 'Calculate you'll jest have to camp down here till mornin',' says he.

"Wal, so old Cack he got out his tin lantern, and went with Cap'n Eb back to the bars to help him fetch along his critturs. He told him he could put 'em under the mill-shed. So they got the critturs up to the shed, and got the cart under; and by that time the storm was awful.

"But Cack he made a great roarin' fire, 'cause, ye see, Cack allers had slab-wood a plenty from his mill; and a roarin' fire is jest so much company. It sort o' keeps a fellow's spirits up, a good fire does. So Cack he sot on his old teakettle, and made a swingeing lot o' toddy; and he and Cap'n Eb were havin' a tol'able comfortable time there. Cack was a pretty good hand to tell stories; and Cap'n Eb warn't no way backward in that line, and kep' up his end pretty well: and pretty soon they was a-roarin' and haw-hawin' inside about as loud as the storm outside; when all of a sudden, 'bout midnight, there come a loud rap on the door.

" 'Lordy massy! what's that?' says Cack. Folks is rather startled allers to be checked up sudden when they are a-carryin' on and laughin'; and it was such an awful blowy night, it was a little scary to have a rap on the door.

"Wal, they waited a minit, and didn't hear nothin' but the wind a-screechin' round the chimbley; and old Cack was jest goin' on with his story, when the rap come ag'in, harder'n ever, as if it'd shook the door open.

" 'Wal,' says old Cack, 'if 'tis the Devil, we'd jest as good's open, and have it out with him to onst,' says he; and so he got up and opened the door, and, sure enough, there was old Ketury there. Expect you've heard your grandma tell about old Ketury. She used to come to meetin's sometimes, and her husband was one o' the prayin' Indians; but Ketury was one of the rael wild sort, and you couldn't no more convert *her* than you could convert a wild-cat or a painter [panther]. Lordy massy! Ketury used to come to meetin', and sit there on them Indian benches; and when the second bell was a-tollin', and when Parson Lothrop and his wife was comin' up the broad aisle, and everybody in the house ris' up and stood, Ketury would sit there, and look at 'em out o' the corner o' her eyes; and folks used to say she rattled them necklaces o' rattle-snakes' tails and wild-cat teeth, and sich like heathen trumpery, and looked for all the world as if the spirit of the old Sarpent him-self was in her. I've seen her sit and look at Lady Lothrop out o' the corner o' her eyes; and her old brown baggy neck would kind o' twist and work; and her eyes they looked so, that 'twas enough to scare a body. For all the world, she looked jest as if she was a-workin' up to spring at her. Lady Lothrop was jest as kind to Ketury as she always was to every poor crittur. She'd bow and smile as gracious to her when meetin was over, and she come down the aisle, passin' out o' meetin'; but Ketury never took no notice. Ye see, Ketury's father was one o' them great powwows down to Martha's Vineyard; and people used to say she was set apart, when she was a child, to the sarvice o' the Devil: any way, she never could be made nothin' of in a Christian way. She come down to Parson Lothrop's study once or twice to be catechised; but he couldn't get a word out o' her, and she kind o' seemed to sit scorn-ful while he was a-talkin'. Folks said, if it was in old times, Ketury wouldn't have been allowed to go on so; but Parson Lothrop's so sort o' mild, he let her take pretty much her own way. Everybody thought that Ketury was a witch: at least, she knew consid'able more'n she ought to know, and so they was kind o' 'fraid on her. Cap'n Eb says he never see a fellow seem scareder than Cack did when he see Ketury a-standin' there.

"Why, ye see, boys, she was as withered and wrinkled and brown as an old frosted punkin-vine; and her little snaky eyes sparkled and snapped, and it made yer head kind o' dizzy to look at 'em; and folks used to say that anybody that Ketury got mad at was sure to get the worst of it fust or last. And so, no matter what day or hour Ketury had a mind to rap at anybody's door, folks gen'lly thought it was best to let her in; but then, they never thought her coming was for any good, for she was just like the wind,—she came when the fit was on her, she staid jest so long as it pleased her, and went when she got ready, and not before. Ketury understood English, and could talk it well enough, but always seemed to scorn it, and was allers mowin' and mutterin' to herself in Indian, and winkin' and blinkin' as if she saw more folks round than you did, so that she wa'n't no way pleasant company: and yet everybody took good care to be polite to her.

So old Cack asked her to come in, and didn't make no question where she come from, or what she come on; but he knew it was twelve good miles from where she lived to his hut, and the snow was drifted above her middle: and Cap'n Eb declared that there wa'n't no track, nor sign o' a track, of anybody's coming through that snow next morning."

"How did she get there, then?" said I.

"Didn't ye never see brown leaves a-ridin' on the wind? 'Well,' Cap'n Eb he says, 'she came on the wind,' and I'm sure it was strong enough to fetch her. But Cack he got her down into the warm corner, and he poured her out a mug o' hot toddy, and give her: but ye see her bein' there sort o' stopped the conversation; for she sot there a-rockin' back'ards and for'ards, a-sippin her toddy, and a-mutterin', and lookin' up chimbley.

"Cap'n Eb says in all his born days he never hearn such screeches and yells as the wind give over that chimbley; and old Cack got so frightened, you could fairly hear his teeth chatter.

"But Cap'n Eb he was a putty brave man, and he wa'n't goin' to have conversation stopped by no woman, witch or no witch; and so, when he see her mutterin', and lookin' up chimbley, he spoke up, and says he, 'Well, Ketury, what do you see?' says he. 'Come, out with it; don't keep it to yourself.' Ye see Cap'n Eb was a hearty fellow, and then he was a leetle warmed up with the toddy.

"Then he said he see an evil kind o' smile on Ketury's face, and she rattled her necklace o' bones and snakes' tails; and her eyes seemed to snap; and she looked up the chimbley, and called out, 'Come down, come down! let's see who ye be.'

"Then there was a scratchin' and a rumblin' and a groan; and a pair of feet come down the chimbley, and stood right in the middle of the haarth, the toes pi'ntin' out'rds, with shoes and silver buckles a-shinin' in the firelight. Cap'n Eb says he never come so near bein' scared in his life; and, as to old Cack, he jest wilted right down in his chair.

"Then old Ketury got up, and reached her stick up chimbley, and called out louder, 'Come down, come down! let's see who ye be.' And, sure enough, down came a pair o' legs, and j'ined right on to the feet: good fair legs they was, with ribbed stockings and leather breeches.

" 'Wal, we're in for it now,' says Cap'n Eb. 'Go it, Ketury, and let's have the rest on him.'

"Ketury didn't seem to mind him: she stood there as stiff as a stake, and kep' callin' out, 'Come down, come down! let's see who ye be.' And then come down the body of a man with a brown coat and yellow vest, and j'ined right on to the legs; but there wa'n't no arms to it. Then Ketury shook her stick up chimbley, and called, '*Come down, come down!*' And there came down a pair o' arms, and went on each side o' the body; and there stood a man all finished, only there wa'n't no head on him.

" 'Wal, Ketury,' says Cap'n Eb, 'this 'ere's getting serious. I 'spec' you must finish him up, and let's see what he wants of us.'

"Then Ketury called out once more, louder'n ever, 'Come down, come down! let's see who ye be.' And, sure enough, down comes a man's head, and settled on the shoulders straight enough; and Cap'n Eb, the minit he sot eyes on him, knew he was Jehiel Lommedieu.

"Old Cack knew him too; and he fell flat on his face, and prayed the Lord to have mercy on his soul: but Cap'n Eb he was for gettin' to the bottom of matters, and not have his scare for nothin'; so he says to him, 'What do you want, now you hev come?'

"The man he didn't speak; he only sort o' moaned, and p'inted to the chimbley. He seemed to try to speak, but couldn't; for ye see it isn't often that his sort o' folks is permitted to speak: but just then there came a screechin' blast o' wind, and blowed the door open, and blowed the smoke and fire all out into the room, and there seemed to be a whirlwind and darkness and moans and screeches; and, when it all cleared up, Ketury and the man was both gone, and only old Cack lay on the ground, rolling and moaning as if he'd die.

"Wal, Cap'n Eb he picked him up, and built up the fire, and sort o' comforted him up, 'cause the crittur was in distress o' mind that was drefful. The awful Providence, ye see, had awakened him, and his sin had been set home to his soul; and he was under such conviction, that it all had to come out,—how old Cack's father had murdered poor Lommedieu for his money, and Cack had been privy to it, and helped his father build the body up in that very chimbley; and he said that he hadn't had neither peace nor rest since then, and that was what had driv' him away from ordinances; for ye know sinnin' will always make a man leave prayin'. Wal, Cack didn't live but a day or two. Cap'n Eb he got the minister o' Sherburn and one o' the selectmen down to see him; and they took his deposition. He seemed railly quite penitent; and Parson Carryl he prayed with him, and was faithful in settin' home the providence to his soul: and so, at the eleventh hour, poor old Cack might have got in; at least it looks a leetle like it. He was distressed to think he couldn't live to be hung. He sort o' seemed to think, that if he was fairly tried, and hung, it would make it all square. He made Parson Carryl promise to have the old mill pulled down, and bury the body; and, after he was dead, they did it.

"Cap'n Eb he was one of a party o' eight that pulled down the chimbley; and there, sure enough, was the skeleton of poor Lommedieu.

"So there you see, boys, there can't be no iniquity so hid but what it'll come out. The wild Indians of the forest, and the stormy winds and tempests, j'ined together to bring out this 'ere."

"For my part," said Aunt Lois sharply, "I never believed that story."

"Why, Lois," said my grandmother, "Cap'n Eb Sawin was a regular church-member, and a most respectable man."

"Law, mother! I don't doubt he thought so. I suppose he and Cack got drinking toddy together, till he got asleep, and dreamed it. I wouldn't believe such a thing if it did happen right before my face and eyes. I should only think I was crazy, that's all."

"Come, Lois, if I was you, I wouldn't talk so like a Sadducee," said my grandmother. "What would become of all the accounts in Dr. Cotton Mather's 'Magnilly' if folks were like you?"

"Wal," said Sam Lawson, drooping contemplatively over the coals, and gazing into the fire, "there's a putty consid'able sight o' things in this world that's true; and then ag'in there's a sight o' things that ain't true. Now, my old gran'ther used to say, 'Boys,' says he, 'if ye want to lead a pleasant and prosperous life, ye must contrive allers to keep jest the *happy medium* between truth and falsehood.' Now, that are's my doctrine."

Aunt Lois knit severely.

"Boys," said Sam, "don't you want ter go down with me and get a mug o' cider?"

Of course we did, and took down a basket to bring up some apples to roast.

"Boys," says Sam mysteriously, while he was drawing the cider, "you jest ask your Aunt Lois to tell you what she knows 'bout Ruth Sullivan."

"Why, what is it?"

"Oh! you must ask *her*. These 'ere folks that's so kind o' toppin' about sperits and sich, come sift 'em down, you gen'lly find they knows one story that kind o' puzzles 'em. Now you mind, and jist ask your Aunt Lois about Ruth Sullivan."

SAMUEL CLEMENS
(1835–1910)

Like Harriet Beecher Stowe, Samuel Clemens, who marketed himself through a career of four decades as "Mark Twain," enjoyed a degree of renown rare to any imaginative artist. Clemens is generally considered America's most beloved humorist, though much of his humor, even in his seemingly artless first-person musings, is laced with a savagely cynical view of mankind. Indeed, part of the satirist's intention seems to be a mockery of the very audience, credulous and eager to be entertained, that made him a distinctly American success: forever looking backward to a mythical "regional" America, a place of childhood and simple homespun virtues, even as the mass-marketing strategies of his time—the proliferation of newspapers, for instance—allowed for a shrewd manufacturing and distribution of such visions.

Samuel Langhorne Clemens was born in Florida, Missouri, grew up in Hannibal, and began his writing career as a newspaperman in various parts of the country, including the Nevada Territory and California. His inspired retelling of a popular tall tale, "The Celebrated Jumping Frog of Calaveras County," published in 1865, brought him instant acclaim and a wide, uncritical readership. Subsequent titles assured the success of "Mark Twain": The Innocents Abroad *(1869),* Old Times on the Mississippi *(1875),* The Adventures of Tom Sawyer *(1876),* The Adventures of Huckleberry Finn *(1884),* The Tragedy of Pudd'nhead Wilson *(1894). The heavyhanded satire of "The Man That Corrupted Hadleyburg" (1900) and "What Is Man?" (1906) did nothing to mitigate Clemens' reputation as a master of a peculiarly American, idiomatic English. "Cannibalism in the Cars," a virtually unknown work, is quintessential Clemens in its comic hyperbole and the angry despair that runs beneath its anecdotal surface.*

Cannibalism in the Cars

I visited St. Louis lately, and on my way West, after changing cars at Terre Haute, Indiana, a mild, benevolent-looking gentleman of about forty-five, or maybe fifty, came in at one of the way stations and sat down beside me. We talked together pleasantly on various subjects for an hour, perhaps, and I found him exceedingly intelligent and entertaining. When he learned that I was from Washington, he immediately began to ask questions about various public men, and about congressional affairs; and I saw very shortly that I was conversing with a man who was perfectly familiar with the ins and outs of political life at the capital, even to the ways and manners, and customs of procedure of senators and representatives in the chambers of the national legislature. Presently two men halted near us for a single moment, and one said to the other: "Harris, if you'll do that for me, I'll never forget you, my boy."

My new comrade's eye lighted pleasantly. The words had touched upon a happy memory, I thought. Then his faced settled into thoughtfulness—almost into gloom. He turned to me and said, "Let me tell you a story, let me give you a secret chapter of my life—a chapter that has never been referred to by me since its events transpired. Listen patiently, and promise that you will not interrupt me."

I said I would not, and he related the following strange adventure, speaking sometimes with animation, sometimes with melancholy, but always with feeling and earnestness.

On the nineteenth of December, 1853, I started from St. Louis on the evening train bound for Chicago. There were only twenty-four passengers, all told. There were no ladies and no children. We were in excellent spirits, and pleasant acquaintanceships were soon formed. The journey bade fair to be a happy one; and no individual in the party, I think, had even the vaguest presentiment of the horrors we were soon to undergo.

At 11:00 P.M. it began to snow hard. Shortly after leaving the small village of Welden, we entered upon that tremendous prairie solitude that stretches its leagues on leagues of houseless dreariness far away toward the Jubilee Settlements. The winds, unobstructed by trees or hills, or even vagrant rocks, whistled fiercely across the level desert, driving the falling snow before it like spray from the crested waves of a stormy sea. The snow was deepening fast; and we knew, by the diminished speed of the train, that the engine was plowing through it with steadily increasing difficulty. Indeed, it almost came to a dead halt sometimes, in the midst of great drifts that piled themselves like colossal graves across the track. Conversation began to flag. Cheerfulness gave place to grave concern. The possibility of being imprisoned in the snow, on the bleak prairie, fifty miles from any house, presented itself to every mind, and extended its depressing influence over every spirit.

At two o'clock in the morning I was aroused out of an uneasy slumber by the ceasing of all motion about me. The appalling truth flashed upon me instantly—we were captives in a snowdrift! "All hands to the rescue!" Every man sprang to obey. Out into the wild night, the pitchy darkness, the billowy snow, the driving storm, every soul leaped, with the consciousness that a moment lost now might bring destruction to us all. Shovels, hands, boards—anything, everything that could displace snow, was brought into instant requisition. It was a weird picture, that small company of frantic men fighting the banking snows, half in the blackest shadow and half in the angry light of the locomotive's reflector.

One short hour sufficed to prove the utter uselessness of our efforts. The storm barricaded the track with a dozen drifts while we dug one away. And worse than this, it was discovered that the last grand charge the engine had made upon the enemy had broken the fore-and-aft shaft of the driving wheel! With a free track before us we should still have been helpless. We entered the car wearied with labor, and very sorrowful. We gathered about the stoves, and gravely canvassed our situation. We had no provisions whatever—in this lay our chief distress. We could not freeze, for there was a good supply of wood in the tender. This was our only comfort. The discussion ended at last in accepting the disheartening decision of the conductor, *viz.*, that it would be death for any man to attempt to travel fifty miles on foot through snow like that. We could not send for help, and even if we could it would not come. We must submit, and await, as patiently as we might, succor or starvation! I think the stoutest heart there felt a momentary chill when those words were uttered.

Within the hour conversation subsided to a low murmur here and there about the car, caught fitfully between the rising and falling of the blast; the lamps grew dim; and the majority of the castaways settled themselves among the flickering shadows to think—to forget the present, if they could—to sleep, if they might.

The eternal night—it surely seemed eternal to us—wore its lagging hours away at last, and the cold gray dawn broke in the east. As the light grew stronger the passengers began to stir and give signs of life, one after another, and each in turn pushed his slouched hat up from his forehead, stretched his stiffened limbs and glanced out of the windows upon the cheerless prospect. It was cheerless, indeed!—not a living thing visible anywhere, not a human habitation; nothing but a vast white desert; uplifted sheets of snow drifting hither and thither before the wind—a world of eddying flakes shutting out the firmament above.

All day we moped about the cars, saying little, thinking much. Another lingering dreary night—and hunger.

Another dawning—another day of silence, sadness, wasting hunger, hopeless watching for succor that could not come. A night of restless slumber, filled with dreams of feasting—wakings distressed with the gnawings of hunger.

The fourth day came and went—and the fifth! Five days of dreadful imprisonment! A savage hunger looked out at every eye. There was in it a sign of awful import—the foreshadowing of a something that was vaguely shaping itself in every heart—a something which no tongue dared yet to frame into words.

The sixth day passed—the seventh dawned upon as gaunt and haggard and hopeless a company of men as ever stood in the shadow of death. It must out now! That thing which had been growing up in every heart was ready to leap from every lip at last! Nature had been taxed to the utmost—she must yield. Richard H. Gaston of Minnesota, tall, cadaverous, and pale, rose up. All knew what was coming. All prepared—every emotion, every semblance of excitement was smothered—only a calm, thoughtful seriousness appeared in the eyes that were lately so wild.

"Gentlemen: It cannot be delayed longer! The time is at hand! We must determine which of us shall die to furnish food for the rest!"

MR. JOHN J. WILLIAMS of Illinois rose and said: "Gentlemen—I nominate the Reverend James Sawyer of Tennessee."

Mr. Wm. R. Adams of Indiana said: "I nominate Mr. Daniel Slote of New York."

Mr. Charles J. Langdon: "I nominate Mr. Samuel A. Bowen of St. Louis."

Mr. Slote: "Gentlemen—I desire to decline in favor of Mr. John A. Van Nostrand, Jr., of New Jersey."

Mr. Gaston: "If there be no objection, the gentleman's desire will be acceded to."

Mr. Van Nostrand objecting, the resignation of Mr. Slote was rejected. The resignations of Messrs. Sawyer and Bowen were also offered, and refused upon the same grounds.

Mr. A. L. Bascom of Ohio: "I move that the nominations now close, and that the House proceed to an election by ballot."

Mr. Sawyer: "Gentlemen—I protest earnestly against these proceedings. They are, in every way, irregular and unbecoming. I must beg to move that they be dropped at once, and that we elect a chairman of the meeting and proper officers to assist him, and then we can go on with the business before us understandingly."

Mr. Bell of Iowa: "Gentlemen—I object. This is no time to stand upon forms and ceremonious observances. For more than seven days we have been without food. Every moment we lose in idle discussion increases our distress. I am satisfied with the nominations that have been made—every gentleman present is, I believe—and I, for one, do not see why we should not proceed at once to elect one or more of them. I wish to offer a resolution—"

Mr. Gaston: "It would be objected to, and have to lie over one day under the rules, thus bringing about the very delay you wish to avoid. The gentleman from New Jersey—"

Mr. Van Nostrand: "Gentlemen—I am a stranger among you; I have not sought the distinction that has been conferred upon me, and I feel a delicacy—"

Mr. Morgan of Alabama (interrupting): "I move the previous question."

The motion was carried, and further debate shut off, of course. The motion to elect officers was passed, and under it Mr. Gaston was chosen chairman, Mr. Blake, secretary, Messrs. Holcomb, Dyer and Baldwin a committee on nominations, and Mr. R. M. Howland, purveyor, to assist the committee in making selections.

A recess of half an hour was then taken, and some little caucusing followed. At the sound of the gavel the meeting reassembled, and the committee reported in favor of Messrs. George Ferguson of Kentucky, Lucien Herrman of Louisiana and W. Messick of Colorado as candidates. The report was accepted.

Mr. Rogers of Missouri: "Mr. President—The report being properly before the House now, I move to amend it by substituting for the name of Mr. Herrman that of Mr. Lucius Harris of St. Louis, who is well and honorably known to us all. I do not wish to be understood as casting the least reflection upon the high character and standing of the gentleman from Louisiana—far from it. I respect and esteem him as much as any gentleman here present possibly can; but none of us can be blind to the fact that he had lost more flesh during the week that we have lain here than any among us—none of us can be blind to the fact that the committee has been derelict in its duty, either through negligence or a graver fault, in thus offering for our suffrages a gentleman who, however pure his own motives may be, has really less nutriment in him—"

The Chair: "The gentleman from Missouri will take his seat. The Chair cannot allow the integrity of the committee to be questioned save by the regular course, under the rules. What action will the House take upon the gentleman's motion?"

Mr. Halliday of Virginia: "I move to further amend the report by substituting Mr. Harvey Davis of Oregon for Mr. Messick. It may be urged by gentlemen that the hardships and privations of a frontier life have rendered Mr. Davis tough; but, gentlemen, is this a time to cavil at toughness? Is this a time to be fastidious concerning trifles? Is this a time to dispute about matters of paltry significance? No, gentlemen, bulk is what we desire—substance, weight, bulk—these are the supreme requisites now—not talent, not genius, not education. I insist upon my motion."

Mr. Morgan (excitedly): "Mr. Chairman—I do most strenuously object to this amendment. The gentleman from Oregon is old, and furthermore is bulky only in bone—not in flesh. I ask the gentleman from Virginia if it is soup we want instead of solid sustenance? if he would delude us with shadows? if he would mock our suffering with an Oregonian specter? I ask him if he can look upon the anxious faces around him, if he can gaze into our sad eyes, if he can listen to the beating of our expectant hearts, and still thrust this famine-stricken fraud upon us? I ask him if he can think of our desolate state, of our past sorrows, of our dark future, and still unpityingly foist upon us this wreck, this ruin, this tottering swindle, this gnarled and blighted and sapless vagabond from Oregon's inhospitable shores? Never! [Applause.]"

The amendment was put to vote, after a fiery debate, and lost. Mr. Harris was substituted on the first amendment. The balloting then began. Five ballots were held without a choice. On the sixth, Mr. Harris was elected, all voting for him but himself. It was then moved that his election should be ratified by acclamation, which was lost, in consequence of his again voting against himself.

Mr. Radway moved that the House now take up the remaining candidates, and go into an election for breakfast. This was carried.

On the first ballot there was a tie, half the members favoring one candidate on account of his youth, and half favoring the other on account of his superior size. The president gave the casting vote for the latter, Mr. Messick. This decision created considerable dissatisfaction among the friends of Mr. Ferguson, the defeated candidate, and there was some talk of demanding a new ballot; but in the midst of it a motion to adjourn was carried, and the meeting broke up at once.

The preparations for supper diverted the attention of the Ferguson faction from the discussion of their grievance for a long time, and then, when they would have taken it up again, the happy announcement that Mr. Harris was ready drove all thought of it to the winds.

We improvised tables by propping up the backs of car seats, and sat down with hearts full of gratitude to the finest supper that had blessed our vision for seven torturing days. How changed we were from what we had been a few short hours before! Hopeless, sad-eyed misery, hunger, feverish anxiety, desperation, then; thankfulness, serenity, joy too deep for utterance now. That I know was the cheeriest hour of my eventful life. The winds howled, and blew the snow wildly about our prison house, but they were powerless to distress us anymore. I liked Harris. He might have been better done, perhaps, but I am free to say that no man ever agreed with me better than Harris, or afforded me so large a degree of satisfaction. Messick was very well, though rather high-flavored, but for genuine nutritiousness and delicacy of fiber, give me Harris. Messick had his good points—I will not attempt to deny it, nor do I wish to do it—but he was no more fitted for breakfast than a mummy would be, sir—not a bit. Lean?—why, bless me!—and tough? Ah, he was very tough! You could not imagine it—you could never imagine anything like it.

"Do you mean to tell me that—"

"Do not interrupt me, please. After breakfast we elected a man by the name of Walker, from Detroit, for supper. He was very good. I wrote his wife so afterward. He was worthy of all praise. I shall always remember Walker. He was a little rare, but very good. And then the next morning we had Morgan of Alabama for breakfast. He was one of the finest men I ever sat down to—handsome, educated, refined, spoke several languages fluently—a perfect gentleman—he was a perfect gentleman, and singularly juicy. For supper we had that Oregon patriarch, and he *was* a fraud, there is no question about it—old, scraggy, tough, nobody can picture the reality. I finally said, 'Gentlemen, you can do as you like, but *I* will wait for another election.' And Grimes of Illinois said, 'Gentlemen, *I* will wait also. When you elect a man that has *something* to recommend him, I shall be glad to join you again.' It soon became evident that there was general dissatisfaction with Davis of Oregon, and so, to preserve the good will that had prevailed so pleasantly since we had had Harris, an election was called, and the result of it was that Baker of Georgia was chosen. He was splendid! Well, well—after that we had Doolittle, and Hawkins, and McElroy (there was some complaint about McElroy, because he was uncommonly short and thin), and Penrod, and two Smiths, and Bailey (Bailey had a wooden leg, which was clear loss, but he was otherwise good), and an Indian boy, and an organ-grinder and a gentleman by the name of Buckminster—a poor stick of a vagabond that wasn't any good for company and no account for breakfast. We were glad we got him elected before relief came."

"And so the blessed relief *did* come at last?"

"Yes, it came one bright, sunny morning, just after election. John Murphy was the choice, and there never was a better, I am willing to testify; but John Murphy came home with us, in the train that came to succor us, and lived to marry the widow Harris—"

"Relict of—"

"Relict of our first choice. He married her, and is happy and respected and prosperous yet. Ah, it was like a novel, sir—it was like a romance. This is my stopping-place, sir; I must bid you goodbye. Any time that you can make it convenient to tarry a day or two with me, I shall be glad to have you. I like you, sir; I have conceived an affection for you. I could like you as well as I liked Harris himself, sir. Good day, sir, and a pleasant journey."

He was gone. I never felt so stunned, so distressed, so bewildered in my life. But in my soul I was glad he was gone. With all his gentleness of manner and his soft voice, I shuddered whenever he turned his hungry eye upon me; and when I heard that I had achieved his perilous affection, and that I stood almost with the late Harris in his esteem, my heart fairly stood still!

I was bewildered beyond description. I did not doubt his word; I could not question a single item in a statement so stamped with the earnestness of truth as his; but its dreadful details overpowered me, and threw my thoughts into hopeless confusion. I saw the conductor looking at me. I said, "Who is that man?"

"He was a member of congress once, and a good one. But he got caught in a snowdrift in the cars, and like to have been starved to death. He got so frostbitten and frozen up generally, and used up for want of something to eat, that he was sick and out of his head two or three months afterward. He is all right now, only he is a monomaniac, and when he gets on that old subject he never stops till he has eat up that whole carload of people he talks about. He would have finished the crowd by this time, only he had to get out here. He has got their names as past as *ABC*. When he gets them all eat up but himself, he always says: 'Then the hour for the unusual election for breakfast having arrived, and there being no opposition, I was duly elected, after which, there being no objections offered, I resigned. Thus I am here.' "

I felt inexpressibly relieved to know that I had only been listening to the harmless vagaries of a madman instead of the genuine experiences of a bloodthirsty cannibal.

SARAH ORNE JEWETT

(1849–1909)

Born in South Berwick, Maine, the granddaughter of a prosperous sea captain and the daughter of an obstetrician, Sarah Orne Jewett grew up in a stable, middle-class household nurturing to a girl with literary aspirations. Out of her visits with her father to his rural patients came her novel A Country Doctor *(1884), which features a strong female protagonist.*

Jewett was precocious and industrious, writing both prose and poetry while still in her teens. Her earliest efforts were published by William Dean Howells in Atlantic Monthly, *and were subsequently gathered in her first collection of stories,* Deephaven *(1877). Other acclaimed and popular collections by Jewett are* A White Heron *(1886),* The King of Folly Island *(1888),* A Native of Winby *(1893), and* The Life of Nancy *(1895). Jewett's most famous single work is* The Country of the Pointed Firs *(1896) in which the lives of a small group of men and women are delineated with a quiet, sympathetic lyricism that transcends the merely local and "regional."*

"A White Heron," suspenseful and poetic at once, and, in its dialectics of male and female consciousness, strikingly contemporary, is representative of this fine writer at her best. Even the unabashed sentiment seems, in terms of the child Sylvia's limited experience, an expression of character: "Were the birds better friends than their hunter might have been,—who can tell?"

A White Heron

I

The woods were already filled with shadows one June evening, just before eight o'clock, though a bright sunset still glimmered faintly among the trunks of the trees. A little girl was driving home her cow, a plodding, dilatory, provoking creature in her behavior, but a valued companion for all that. They were going away from whatever light there was, and striking deep into the woods, but their feet were familiar with the path, and it was no matter whether their eyes could see it or not.

There was hardly a night the summer through when the old cow could be found waiting at the pasture bars; on the contrary, it was her greatest pleasure to hide herself away among the huckleberry bushes, and though she wore a loud bell she had made the discovery that if one stood perfectly still it would not ring. So Sylvia had to hunt for her until she found her, and call Co'! Co'! with never an answering Moo, until her childish patience was quite spent. If the creature had not given good milk and plenty of it, the case would have seemed very different to her owners. Besides, Sylvia had all the time there was, and very little use to make of it. Sometimes in pleasant weather it was a consolation to look upon the cow's pranks as an intelligent attempt to play hide and seek, and as the child had no playmates she lent herself to this amusement with a good deal of zest. Though this chase had been so long that the wary animal herself had given an unusual signal of her whereabouts, Sylvia had only laughed when she came upon Mistress Moolly at the swamp-side, and urged her affectionately homeward with a twig of birch leaves. The old cow was not inclined to wander farther, she even turned in the right direction for once as they left the pasture, and stepped along the road at a good pace. She was quite ready to be milked now, and seldom stopped to browse. Sylvia wondered what her grandmother would say because they were so late. It was a great while since she had left home at half-past five o'clock, but everybody knew the difficulty of making this errand a short one. Mrs. Tilley had chased the hornéd torment too many summer evenings herself to blame any one else for lingering, and was only thankful as she waited that she had Sylvia, nowadays, to give such valuable assistance. The good woman suspected that Sylvia loitered occasionally on her own account; there never was such a child for straying about out-of-doors since the world was made! Everybody said that it was a good change for a little maid who had tried to grow for eight years in a crowded manufacturing town, but, as for Sylvia herself, it seemed as if she never had been alive at all before she came to live at the farm. She thought often with wistful compassion of a wretched geranium that belonged to a town neighbor.

" 'Afraid of folks,' " old Mrs. Tilley said to herself, with a smile, after she had made the unlikely choice of Sylvia from her daughter's houseful of children, and was returning to the farm, " 'Afraid of folks,' they said! I guess she won't be troubled no great with 'em up to the old place!" When they reached the door of the lonely house and stopped to unlock it, and the cat came to purr loudly, and rub against them, a deserted pussy, indeed, but fat with young robins, Sylvia whispered that this was a beautiful place to live in, and she never should wish to go home.

The companions followed the shady wood-road, the cow taking slow steps and the child very fast ones. The cow stopped long at the brook to drink, as if the pasture were not half a swamp, and Sylvia stood still and waited, letting her bare feet cool themselves in the shoal water, while the great twilight moths struck softly against her. She waded on through the brook as the cow moved away, and listened to the thrushes with a heart that beat fast with pleasure. There was a stirring in the great boughs overhead. They were full of little birds and beasts that seemed to be wide awake, and going about their world, or else saying good-night to each other in sleepy twitters. Sylvia herself felt sleepy as she walked along. However, it was not much farther to the house, and the air was soft and sweet. She was not often in the woods so late as this, and it made her feel as if she were a part of the gray shadows and the moving leaves. She was just thinking how long it seemed since she first came to the farm a year ago, and wondering if everything went on in the noisy town just the same as when she was there; the thought of the great red-faced boy who used to chase and frighten her made her hurry along the path to escape from the shadow of the trees.

Suddenly this little woods-girl is horror-stricken to hear a clear whistle not very far away. Not a bird's-whistle, which would have a sort of friendliness, but a boy's whistle, determined, and somewhat aggressive. Sylvia left the cow to whatever sad fate might await her, and stepped discreetly aside into the brushes, but she was just too late. The enemy had discovered her, and called out in a very cheerful and persuasive tone, "Halloa, little girl, how far is it to the road?" and trembling Sylvia answered almost inaudibly, "A good ways."

She did not dare to look boldly at the tall young man, who carried a gun over his shoulder, but she came out of her bush and again followed the cow, while he walked alongside.

"I have been hunting for some birds," the stranger said kindly, "and I have lost my way, and need a friend very much. Don't be afraid," he added gallantly. "Speak up and tell me what your name is, and whether you think I can spend the night at your house, and go out gunning early in the morning."

Sylvia was more alarmed than before. Would not her grandmother consider her much to blame? But who could have foreseen such an accident as this? It did not seem to be her fault, and she hung her head as if the stem of it were broken, but managed to answer "Sylvy," with much effort when her companion again asked her name.

Mrs. Tilley was standing in the doorway when the trio came into view. The cow gave a loud moo by way of explanation.

"Yes, you'd better speak up for yourself, you old trial! Where'd she tucked herself away this time, Sylvy?" But Sylvia kept an awed silence; she knew by instinct that her grandmother did not comprehend the gravity of the situation. She must be mistaking the stranger for one of the farmer-lads of the region.

The young man stood his gun beside the door, and dropped a lumpy game-bag beside it; then he bade Mrs. Tilley good-evening, and repeated his wayfarer's story, and asked if he could have a night's lodging.

"Put me anywhere you like," he said. "I must be off early in the morning, before day; but I am very hungry, indeed. You can give me some milk at any rate, that's plain."

"Dear sakes, yes," responded the hostess, whose long slumbering hospitality seemed to be easily awakened. "You might fare better if you went out to the main road a mile or so, but you're welcome to what we've got. I'll milk right off, and you make yourself at home. You can sleep on husks or feathers," she proffered graciously. "I raised them all myself. There's good pasturing for geese just below here towards the ma'sh. Now step round and set a plate for the gentleman, Sylvy!" And Sylvia promptly stepped. She was glad to have something to do, and she was hungry herself.

It was a surprise to find so clean and comfortable a little dwelling in this New England wilderness. The young man had known the horrors of its most primitive housekeeping, and the dreary squalor of that level of society which does not rebel at the companionship of hens. This was the best thrift of an old-fashioned farmstead, though on such a small scale that it seemed like a hermitage. He listened eagerly to the old woman's quaint talk, he watched Sylvia's pale face and shining gray eyes with ever growing enthusiasm, and insisted that this was the best supper he had eaten for a month, and afterward the new-made friends sat down in the doorway together while the moon came up.

Soon it would be berry-time, and Sylvia was a great help at picking. The cow was a good milker, though a plaguy thing to keep track of, the hostess gossiped frankly, adding presently that she had buried four children, so Sylvia's mother, and a son (who might be dead) in California were all the children she had left. "Dan, my boy, was a great hand to go gunning," she explained sadly. "I never wanted for pa'tridges or gray squer'ls while he was to home. He's been a great wand'rer, I expect, and he 's no hand to write letters. There. I don't blame him, I'd ha' seen the world myself if it had been so I could."

"Sylvy takes after him," the grandmother continued affectionately, after a minute's pause. "There ain't a foot o' ground she don't know her way over, and the wild creaturs counts her one o' themselves. Squer'ls she'll tame to come an' feed right out o' her hands, and all sorts o' birds. Last winter she got the jaybirds to bangeing here, and I believe she'd 'a' scanted herself of her own meals to have plenty to throw out amongst 'em, if I had n't kep' watch. Anything but crows, I tell her, I'm willin' to help support—though Dan he had a tamed one o' them that did seem to have reason same as folks. It was round here a good spell after he went away. Dan an' his father they did n't hitch,—but he never held up his head ag'in after Dan had dared him an' gone off."

The guest did not notice this hint of family sorrows in his eager interest in something else.

"So Sylvy knows all about birds, does she?" he exclaimed, as he looked round at the little girl who sat, very demure but increasingly sleepy, in the moonlight. "I am making a collection of birds myself. I have been at it ever since I was a boy." (Mrs. Tilley smiled.) "There are two or three very rare ones I have been hunting for these five years. I mean to get them on my own ground if they can be found."

"Do you cage 'em up?" asked Mrs. Tilley doubtfully, in response to this enthusiastic announcement.

"Oh no, they 're stuffed and preserved, dozens and dozens of them," said the ornithologist, "and I have shot or snared every one myself. I caught a glimpse of a white heron a few miles from here on Saturday, and I have followed it in this direction. They have never been found in this district at all. The little white heron, it is," and he turned again to look at Sylvia with the hope of discovering that the rare bird was one of her acquaintances.

But Sylvia was watching a hop-toad in the narrow footpath.

"You would know the heron if you saw it," the stranger continued eagerly. "A queer tall white bird with soft feathers and long thin legs. And it would have a nest perhaps in the top of a high tree, made of sticks, something like a hawk's nest."

Sylvia's heart gave a wild beat; she knew that strange white bird, and had once stolen softly near where it stood in some bright green swamp grass, away over at the other side of the woods. There was an open place where the sunshine always seemed strangely yellow and hot, where tall, nodding rushes grew, and her grandmother had warned her that she might sink in the soft black mud underneath and never be heard of more. Not far beyond were the salt marshes just this side the sea itself, which Sylvia wondered and dreamed much about, but never had seen, whose great voice could sometimes be heard above the noise of the woods on stormy nights.

"I can't think of anything I should like so much as to find that heron's nest," the handsome stranger was saying. "I would give ten dollars to anybody who could show it to me," he added desperately, "and I mean to spend my whole vacation hunting for it if need be. Perhaps it was only migrating, or had been chased out of its own region by some bird of prey."

Mrs. Tilley gave amazed attention to all this, but Sylvia still watched the toad, not divining, as she might have done at some calmer time, that the creature wished to get to its hole under the door-step, and was much hindered by the unusual spectators at that hour of the evening. No amount of thought, that night, could decide how many wished-for treasures the ten dollars, so lightly spoken of, would buy.

The next day the young sportsman hovered about the woods, and Sylvia kept him company, having lost her first fear of the friendly lad, who proved to be most kind and sympathetic. He told her many things about the birds and what they knew and where they lived and what they did with themselves. And he gave her a jackknife, which she thought as great a treasure as if she were a desert-islander. All day long he did not once make her troubled or afraid except when he brought down some unsuspecting singing creature from its bough. Sylvia would have liked him vastly better without his gun; she could not understand why he killed the very birds he seemed to like so much. But as the day waned, Sylvia still watched the young man with loving admiration. She had never seen anybody so charming and delightful; the woman's heart, asleep in the child, was vaguely thrilled by a dream of love. Some premonition of that great power stirred and swayed these young creatures who traversed the solemn woodlands with soft-footed silent care. They stopped to listen to a bird's song; they pressed forward again eagerly, parting the branches—speaking to each other rarely and in whispers; the young man going first and Sylvia following, fascinated, a few steps behind, with her gray eyes dark with excitement.

She grieved because the longed-for white heron was elusive, but she did not lead the guest, she only followed, and there was no such thing as speaking first. The sound of her own unquestioned voice would have terrified her—it was hard enough to answer yes or no when there was need of that. At last evening began to fall, and they drove the cow home together, and Sylvia smiled with pleasure when they came to the place where she heard the whistle and was afraid only the night before.

II

Half a mile from home, at the farther edge of the woods, where the land was highest, a great pine-tree stood, the last of its generation. Whether it was left for a boundary mark, or for what reason, no one could say; the wood-choppers who had felled its mates were dead and gone long ago, and a whole forest of sturdy trees, pines and oaks and maples, had grown again. But the stately head of this old pine toward above them all and made a landmark for sea and shore miles and miles away. Sylvia knew it well. She had always believed that whoever climbed to the top of it could see the ocean; and the little girl had often laid her hand on the great rough trunk and looked up wistfully at those dark boughs that the wind always stirred, no matter how hot and still the air might be below. Now she thought of the tree with a new excitement, for why, if one climbed it at break of day could not one see all the world, and easily discover from whence the white heron flew, and mark the place, and find the hidden nest?

What a spirit of adventure, what wild ambition! What fancied triumph and delight and glory for the later morning when she could make known the secret! It was almost too real and too great for the childish heart to bear.

All night the door of the little house stood open and the whippoorwills came and sang upon the very step. The young sportsman and his old hostess were sound asleep, but Sylvia's great design kept her broad awake and watching. She forgot to think of sleep. The short summer night seemed as long as the winter darkness, and at last when the whippoorwills ceased, and she was afraid the morning would after all come too soon, she stole out of the house and followed the pasture path through the woods, hastening toward the open ground beyond, listening with a sense of comfort and companionship to the drowsy twitter of a half-awakened bird, whose perch she had jarred in passing. Alas, if the great wave of human interest which flooded for the first time this dull little life should sweep away the satisfactions of an existence heart to heart with nature and the dumb life of the forest!

There was the huge tree asleep yet in the paling moonlight, and small and silly Sylvia began with utmost bravery to mount to the top of it, with tingling, eager blood coursing the channels of her whole frame, with her bare feet and fingers, that pinched and held like bird's claws to the monstrous ladder reaching up, up, almost to the sky itself. First she must mount the white oak tree that grew alongside, where she was almost lost among the dark branches and the green leaves heavy and wet with dew; a bird fluttered off its nest, and a red squirrel ran to and fro and scolded pettishly at the harmless housebreaker. Sylvia felt her way easily. She had often climbed there, and knew that higher still one of the oak's upper branches chafed against the pine trunk, just where its lower boughs were set close together. There, when she made the dangerous pass from one tree to the other, the great enterprise would really begin.

She crept out along the swaying oak limb at last, and took the daring step across into the old pine-tree. The way was harder than she thought; she must reach far and hold fast, the sharp dry twigs caught and held her and scratched her like angry talons, the pitch made her thin little fingers clumsy and stiff as she went round and round the tree's great stem, higher and higher upward. The sparrows and robins in the woods below were beginning to wake and twitter to the dawn, yet it seemed much lighter there aloft in the pine-tree, and the child knew she must hurry if her project were to be of any use.

The tree seemed to lengthen itself out as she went up, and to reach farther and farther upward. It was like a great main-mast to the voyaging earth; it must truly have been amazed that morning through all its ponderous frame as it felt this determined spark of human spirit wending its way from higher branch to branch. Who knows how steadily the least twigs held themselves to advantage this light, weak creature on her way! The old pine must have loved his new dependent. More than all the hawks, and bats, and moths, and even the sweet voiced thrushes, was the brave, beating heart of the solitary gray-eyed child. And the tree stood still and frowned away the winds that June morning while the dawn grew bright in the east.

Sylvia's face was like a pale star, if one had seen it from the ground, when the last thorny bough was past, and she stood trembling and tired but wholly triumphant, high in the treetop. Yes, there was the sea with the dawning sun making a golden dazzle over it, and toward that glorious east flew two hawks with slow-moving pinions. How low they looked in the air from that height when one had only seen them before far up, and dark against the blue sky. Their gray feathers were as soft as moths; they seemed only a little way from the tree, and Sylvia felt as if she too could go flying away among the clouds. Westward, the woodlands and farms reached miles and miles into the distance; here and there were church steeples, and white villages, truly it was a vast and awesome world!

The birds sang louder and louder. At last the sun came up bewilderingly bright. Sylvia could see the white sails of ships out at sea, and the clouds that were purple and rose-colored and yellow at first began to fade away. Where was the white heron's nest in the sea of green branches, and was this wonderful sight and pageant of the world the only reward for having climbed to such a giddy height? Now look down again, Sylvia, where the green marsh is set among the shining birches and dark hemlocks; there where you saw the white heron once you will see him again; look, look! a white spot of him like a single floating feather comes up from the dead hemlock and grows larger, and rises, and comes close at last, and goes by the landmark pine with steady sweep of wing and outstretched slender neck and crested head. And wait! wait! do not move a foot or a finger, little girl, do not send an arrow of light and consciousness from your two eager eyes, for the heron has perched on a pine bough not far beyond yours, and cries back to his mate on the nest and plumes his feathers for the new day!

The child gives a long sigh a minute later when a company of shouting cat-birds comes also to the tree, and vexed by their fluttering and lawlessness the solemn heron goes away. She knows his secret now, the wild, light, slender bird that floats and wavers, and goes back like an arrow presently to his home in the green world beneath. Then Sylvia, well satisfied, makes her perilous way down again, not daring to look far below the branch she stands on, ready to cry sometimes because her fingers ache and her lamed feet slip. Wondering over and over again what the stranger would say to her, and what he would think when she told him how to find his way straight to the heron's nest.

"Sylvy, Sylvy!" called the busy old grandmother again and again, but nobody answered, and the small husk bed was empty and Sylvia had disappeared.

The guest waked from a dream, and remembering his day's pleasure hurried to dress himself that might it sooner begin. He was sure from the way the shy little girl looked once or twice yesterday that she had at least seen the white heron, and now she must really be made to tell. Here she comes now, paler than ever, and her worn old frock is torn and tattered, and smeared with pine pitch. The grandmother and the sportsman stand in the door together and question her, and the splendid moment has come to speak of the dead hemlock-tree by the green marsh.

But Sylvia does not speak after all, though the old grandmother fretfully rebukes her, and the young man's kind, appealing eyes are looking straight in her own. He can make them rich with money; he has promised it, and they are poor now. He is so well worth making happy, and he waits to hear the story she can tell.

No, she must keep silence! What is it that suddenly forbids her and makes her dumb? Has she been nine years growing and now, when the great world for the first time puts out a hand to her,

KATE CHOPIN
(1851–1904)

Born to a wealthy Catholic St. Louis family, Kate Chopin (née O'Flaherty) was treated as harshly by critics and the reading public as any writer in this volume, including even Melville and Poe. After a moderately successful early career, Chopin published a second novel, The Awakening *(1899), which was so viciously and universally condemned for its "morbid, poisonous, and vulgar" subject matter that she virtually gave up writing in the few remaining years of her life. Not only did Chopin, a mature artist of forty-eight at this time, have to bear the indignity of such public disapprobation, but she suffered social ostracism by friends and literary acquaintances in St. Louis. And all for having written a slender, carefully composed work of fiction in a Flaubertian vein, about a sensitive and passionate woman's adulterous romance and eventual suicide—a work now recognized as a brilliant tour de force, an American classic.*

Despite her relatively short writing career, Kate Chopin completed an early novel, At Fault *(1890), over one hundred fifty stories and sketches, and a considerable quantity of poetry, reviews, and criticism. A collection of stories of Louisiana rural life,* Bayou Folk *(1894) was well received; a second collection,* A Night in Acadie *(1897), established Chopin's reputation as a local colorist. The story included here, "The Storm," written shortly after* The Awakening, *could certainly never have been published in any magazine of Chopin's time, and was, apparently, never submitted for publication. It did not see print until 1969, in Per Seyersted's edition of* The Complete Works of Kate Chopin.

The Storm

I

The leaves were so still that even Bibi thought it was going to rain. Bobinôt, who was accustomed to converse on terms of perfect equality with his little son, called the child's attention to certain sombre clouds that were rolling with sinister intention from the west, accompanied by a sullen, threatening roar. They were at Friedheimer's store and decided to remain there till the storm had passed. They sat within the door on two empty kegs. Bibi was four years old and looked very wise.

"Mama'll be 'fraid, yes," he suggested with blinking eyes.

"She'll shut the house. Maybe she got Sylvie helpin' her this evenin'," Bobinôt responded reassuringly.

"No; she ent got Sylvie. Sylvie was helpin' her yistiday," piped Bibi.

Bobinôt arose and going across to the counter purchased a can of shrimps, of which Calixta was very fond. Then he returned to his perch on the keg and sat stolidly holding the can of shrimps while the storm burst. It shook the wooden store and seemed to be ripping great furrows in the distant field. Bibi laid his little hand on his father's knee and was not afraid.

II

Calixta, at home, felt no uneasiness for their safety. She sat at a side window sewing furiously on a sewing machine. She was greatly occupied and did not notice the approaching storm. But she felt very warm and often stopped to mop her face on which the perspiration gathered in beads. She unfastened her white sacque at the throat. It began to grow dark, and suddenly realizing the situation she got up hurriedly and went about closing windows and doors.

Out on the small front gallery she had hung Bobinôt's Sunday clothes to air and she hastened out to gather them before the rain fell. As she stepped outside, Alcée Laballière rode in at the gate. She had not seen him very often since her marriage, and never alone. She stood there with Bobinôt's coat in her hands, and the big rain drops began to fall. Alcée rode his horse under the shelter of a side projection where the chickens had huddled and there were plows and a harrow piled up in the corner.

"May I come and wait on your gallery till the storm is over, Calixta?" he asked.

"Come 'long in, M'sieur Alcée."

His voice and her own startled her as if from a trance, and she seized Bobinôt's vest. Alcée, mounting to the porch, grabbed the trousers and snatched Bibi's braided jacket that was about to be carried away by a sudden gust of wind. He expressed an intention to remain outside, but it was soon apparent that he might as well have been out in the open: the water beat in upon the boards in driving sheets, and he went inside, closing the door after him. It was even necessary to put something beneath the door to keep the water out.

"My! what a rain! It's good two years sence it rain' like that," exclaimed Calixta as she rolled up a piece of bagging and Alcée helped her to thrust it beneath the crack.

She was a little fuller of figure than five years before when she married; but she had lost nothing of her vivacity. Her blue eyes still retained their melting quality; and her yellow hair, dishevelled by the wind and rain, kinked more stubbornly than ever about her ears and temples.

The rain beat upon the low, shingled roof with a force and clatter that threatened to break an entrance and deluge them there. They were in the dining room—the sitting room—the general utility room. Adjoining was her bed room, with Bibi's couch along side her own. The door stood open, and the room with its white, monumental bed, its closed shutters, looked dim and mysterious.

Alcée flung himself into a rocker and Calixta nervously began to gather up from the floor the lengths of a cotton sheet which she had been sewing.

"If this keeps up, *Dieu sait* if the levees goin' to stan' it!" she exclaimed.

"What have you got to do with the levees?"

"I got enough to do! An' there's Bobinôt with Bibi out in that storm—if he only didn't left Friedheimer's!"

"Let us hope, Calixta, that Bobinôt's got sense enough to come in out of a cyclone."

She went and stood at the window with a greatly disturbed look on her face. She wiped the frame that was clouded with moisture. It was stiflingly hot. Alcée got up and joined her at the window, looking over her shoulder. The rain was coming down in sheets obscuring the view of far-off cabins and enveloping the distant wood in a gray mist. The playing of the lightning was incessant. A bolt struck a tall chinaberry tree at the edge of the field. It filled all visible space with a blinding glare and the crash seemed to invade the very boards they stood upon.

Calixta put her hands to her eyes, and with a cry, staggered backward. Alcée's arm encircled her, and for an instant he drew her close and spasmodically to him.

"*Bonté!*" she cried, releasing herself from his encircling arm and retreating from the window, "the house'll go next! If I only knew w'ere Bibi was!" She would not compose herself; she would not be seated. Alcée clasped her shoulders and looked into her face. The contact of her warm, palpitating body when he had unthinkingly drawn her into his arms, had aroused all the old-time infatuation and desire for her flesh.

"Calixta," he said, "don't be frightened. Nothing can happen. The house is too low to be struck, with so many tall trees standing about. There! aren't you going to be quiet? say, aren't you?" He pushed her hair back from her face that was warm and steaming. Her lips were as red and moist as pomegranate seed. Her white neck and a glimpse of her full, firm bosom disturbed him powerfully. As she glanced up at him the fear in her liquid blue eyes had given place to a drowsy gleam that unconsciously betrayed a sensuous desire. He looked down into her eyes and there was nothing for him to do but to gather her lips in a kiss. It reminded him of Assumption.

"Do you remember—in Assumption, Calixta?" he asked in a low voice broken by passion. Oh! she remembered; for in Assumption he had kissed her and kissed and kissed her; until his senses would well nigh fail, and to save her he would resort to a desperate flight. If she was not an immaculate dove in those days, she was still inviolate; a passionate creature whose very defenselessness had made her defense, against which his honor forbade him to prevail. Now—

well, now—her lips seemed in a manner free to be tasted, as well as her round, white throat and her whiter breasts.

They did not heed the crashing torrents, and the roar of the elements made her laugh as she lay in his arms. She was a revelation in that dim, mysterious chamber; as white as the couch she lay upon. Her firm, elastic flesh that was knowing for the first time its birthright, was like a creamy lily that the sun invites to contribute its breath and perfume to the undying life of the world.

The generous abundance of her passion, without guile or trickery, was like a white flame which penetrated and found response in depths of his own sensuous nature that had never yet been reached.

When he touched her breasts they gave themselves up in quivering ecstasy, inviting his lips. Her mouth was a fountain of delight. And when he possessed her, they seemed to swoon together at the very borderland of life's mystery.

He stayed cushioned upon her, breathless, dazed, enervated, with his heart beating like a hammer upon her. With one hand she clasped his head, her lips lightly touching his forehead. The other hand stroked with a soothing rhythm his muscular shoulders.

The growl of the thunder was distant and passing away. The rain beat softly upon the shingles, inviting them to drowsiness and sleep. But they dared not yield.

The rain was over; and the sun was turning the glistening green world into a palace of gems. Calixta, on the gallery, watched Alcée ride away. He turned and smiled at her with a beaming face; and she lifted her pretty chin in the air and laughed aloud.

III

Bobinôt and Bibi, trudging home, stopped without at the cistern to make themselves presentable.

"My! Bibi, w'at will yo' mama say! You ought to be ashame'. You oughtn' put on those good pants. Look at 'em! An' that mud on yo' collar! How you got that mud on yo' collar, Bibi? I never saw such a boy!" Bibi was the picture of pathetic resignation. Bobinôt was the embodiment of serious solicitude as he strove to remove from his own person and his son's the signs of their tramp over heavy roads and through wet fields. He scraped the mud off Bibi's bare legs and feet with a stick and carefully removed all traces from his heavy brogans. Then, prepared for the worst—the meeting with an over-scrupulous housewife, they entered cautiously at the back door.

Calixta was preparing supper. She had set the table and was dripping coffee at the hearth. She sprang up as they came in.

"Oh, Bobinôt! You back! My! but I was uneasy. W'ere you been during the rain? An' Bibi? he ain't wet? he ain't hurt?" She had clasped Bibi and was kissing him effusively. Bobinôt's explanations and apologies which he had been composing all along the way, died on his lips as Calixta felt him to see if he were dry, and seemed to express nothing but satisfaction at their safe return.

"I brought you some shrimps, Calixta," offered Bobinôt, hauling the can from his ample side pocket and laying it on the table.

"Shrimps! Oh, Bobinôt! you too good fo' anything!" and she gave him a smacking kiss on the cheek that resounded. *"J'vous réponds,* we'll have a feas' tonight! umph-umph!"

Bobinôt and Bibi began to relax and enjoy themselves, and when the three seated themselves at table they laughed much and so loud that anyone might have heard them as far away as Laballière's.

IV

Alcée Laballière wrote to his wife, Clarisse, that night. It was a loving letter, full of tender solicitude. He told her not to hurry back, but if she and the babies liked it at Biloxi, to stay a month longer. He was getting on nicely; and though he missed them, he was willing to bear the separation a while longer—realizing that their health and pleasure were the first things to be considered.

V

As for Clarisse, she was charmed upon receiving her husband's letter. She and the babies were doing well. The society was agreeable; many of her old friends and acquaintances were at the bay.

And the first free breath since her marriage seemed to restore the pleasant liberty of her maiden days. Devoted as she was to her husband, their intimate conjugal life was something which she was more than willing to forego for a while.

So the storm passed and everyone was happy.

CHARLES CHESNUTT
(1858–1932)

Charles Chesnutt, best known for his dialect stories The Conjure Woman *(1899) and* The Wife of His Youth and Other Stories of the Color Line *(1899), is generally considered the first black writer to find a white readership in America. Born in Cleveland, Ohio, and raised in Fayetteville, North Carolina, Chesnutt was precocious, and ambitious: he published his first story at the age of fourteen, and, like Jack London, subjected himself to a demanding regimen of self-education. He made his living primarily as a lawyer and court stenographer in Cleveland, but published in McClure's syndicated newspapers and in* Atlantic Monthly, *with the encouragement of William Dean Howells, who compared his work favorably with that of James, Turgenev, and Maupassant.*

Though Chesnutt's literary career, by his own decision, was short-lived, he published a number of books in addition to the short story collections, among them the novels The House Behind the Cedars *(1900),* The Marrow of Tradition *(1901), and* The Colonel's Dream *(1905); his* Frederick Douglass *appeared in 1899. Chesnutt was an astute social critic whose great subject was race in America: "The object of my writings would not be so much the elevation of the colored people as the elevation of the whites—for I consider the unjust spirit of caste which is so insidious as to pervade a whole nation . . . as a barrier to the moral progress of the American people."*

In this exemplary story, from The Wife of His Youth, *Chesnutt probes subtleties of conscience in an atmosphere of racial antagonism and misunderstanding. The expected does not happen; the unexpected, does. Here is a tragic drama powerfully abbreviated and given a vividly rendered local habitation.*

The Sheriff's Children

Branson County, North Carolina, is in a sequestered district of one of the staidest and most conservative States of the Union. Society in Branson County is almost primitive in its simplicity. Most of the white people own the farms they till, and even before the war there were no very wealthy families to force their neighbors, by comparison, into the category of "poor whites."

To Branson County, as to most rural communities in the South, the war is the one historical event that overshadows all others. It is the era from which all local chronicles are dated,—births, deaths, marriages, storms, freshets. No description of the life of any Southern community would be perfect that failed to emphasize the all pervading influence of the great conflict.

Yet the fierce tide of war that had rushed through the cities and along the great highways of the country had comparatively speaking but slightly disturbed the sluggish current of life in this region, remote from railroads and navigable streams. To the north in Virginia, to the west in Tennessee, and all along the seaboard the war had raged; but the thunder of its cannon had not disturbed the echoes of Branson County, where the loudest sounds heard were the crack of some hunter's rifle, the baying of some deep-mouthed hound, or the yodel of some tuneful negro on his way through the pine forest. To the east, Sherman's army had passed on its march to the sea; but no straggling band of "bummers" had penetrated the confines of Branson County. The war, it is true, had robbed the county of the flower of its young manhood; but the burden of taxation, the doubt and uncertainty of the conflict, and the sting of ultimate defeat, had been borne by the people with an apathy that robbed misfortune of half its sharpness.

The nearest approach to town life afforded by Branson County is found in the little village of Troy, the county seat, a hamlet with a population of four or five hundred.

Ten years make little difference in the appearance of these remote Southern towns. If a railroad is built through one of them, it infuses some enterprise; the social corpse is galvanized by the fresh blood of civilization that pulses along the farthest ramifications of our great system of commercial highways. At the period of which I write, no railroad had come to Troy. If a traveler, accustomed to the bustling life of cities, could have ridden through Troy on a summer day, he might easily have fancied himself in a deserted village. Around him he would have seen weather-beaten houses, innocent of paint, the shingled roofs in many instances covered with a rich growth of moss. Here and there he would have met a razor-backed hog lazily rooting his way along the principal thoroughfare; and more than once he would probably have had to disturb the slumbers of some yellow dog, dozing away the hours in the ardent sunshine, and reluctantly yielding up his place in the middle of the dusty road.

On Saturdays the village presented a somewhat livelier appearance, and the shade trees around the court-house square and along Front Street served as hitching-posts for a goodly number of horses and mules and stunted oxen, belonging to the farmer-folk who had come in to trade at the two or three local stores.

A murder was a rare event in Branson County. Every well-informed citizen could tell the number of homicides committed in the county for fifty years back, and whether the slayer, in any given instance, had escaped, either by flight or acquittal, or had suffered the penalty of the law. So, when it became known in Troy early one Friday morning in summer, about ten years after the war, that old Captain Walker, who had served in Mexico under Scott, and had left an arm on the field of Gettysburg, had been foully murdered during the night, there was intense excitement in the village. Business was practically suspended, and the citizens gathered in little groups to discuss the murder, and speculate upon the identity of the murderer. It transpired from testimony at the coroner's inquest, held during the morning, that a strange mulatto had been seen going in the direction of Captain Walker's house the night before, and had been met going away from Troy early Friday morning, by a farmer on his way to town. Other circumstances seemed to connect the stranger with the crime. The sheriff organized a posse to search for him, and early in the evening, when most of the citizens of Troy were at supper, the suspected man was brought in and lodged in the county jail.

By the following morning the news of the capture had spread to the farthest limits of the county. A much larger number of people than usual came to town that Saturday,—bearded men in straw hats and blue homespun shirts, and butternut trousers of great amplitude of material and vagueness of outline: women in homespun frocks and slat-bonnets, with faces as expressionless as the dreary sandhills which gave them a meagre sustenance.

The murder was almost the sole topic of conversation. A steady stream of curious observers visited the house of mourning, and gazed upon the rugged face of the old veteran, now stiff and cold in death; and more than one eye dropped a tear at the remembrance of the cheery smile, and the joke—sometimes superannuated, generally feeble, but always good-natured—with which the captain had been wont to greet his acquaintances. There was a growing sentiment of anger among these stern men, toward the murderer who had thus cut down their friend, and a strong feeling that ordinary justice was too slight a punishment for such a crime.

Toward noon there was an informal gathering of citizens in Dan Tyson's store.

"I hear it 'lowed that Square Kyahtah's too sick ter hol' co'te this evenin'," said one, "an' that the purlim'nary hearin' 'll haf ter go over 'tel nex' week."

A look of disappointment went round the crowd.

"Hit 's the durndes', meanes' murder ever committed in this caounty," said another, with moody emphasis.

"I s'pose the nigger 'lowed the Cap'n had some greenbacks," observed a third speaker.

"The Cap'n," said another, with an air of superior information, "has left two bairls of Confedrit money, which he 'spected 'ud be good some day er nuther."

This statement gave rise to a discussion of the speculative value of Confederate money; but in a little while the conversation returned to the murder.

"Hangin' air too good fer the murderer," said one; "he oughter be burnt, stidier bein' hung."

There was an impressive pause at this point, during which a jug of moonlight whiskey went the round of the crowd.

"Well," said a round-shouldered farmer, who, in spite of his peaceable expression and faded gray eye, was known to have been one of the most daring followers of a rebel guerrilla chieftain, "what air yer gwine ter do about it? Ef you fellers air gwine ter set down an' let a wuthless nigger kill the bes' white man in Branson, an' not say nuthin' ner do nuthin', *I'll* move outen the caounty."

This speech gave tone and direction to the rest of the conversation. Whether the fear of losing the round-shouldered farmer operated to bring about the result or not is immaterial to this narrative; but, at all events, the crowd decided to lynch the negro. They agreed that this was the least that could be done to avenge the death of their murdered friend, and that it was a becoming way in which to honor his memory. They had some vague notions of the majesty of the law and the rights of the citizen, but in the passion of the moment these sunk into oblivion; a white man had been killed by a negro.

"The Cap'n was an ole sodger," said one of his friends solemnly. "He'll sleep better when he knows that a co'te-martial has be'n hilt an' jestice done."

By agreement the lynchers were to meet at Tyson's store at five o'clock in the afternoon, and proceed thence to the jail, which was situated down the Lumberton Dirt Road (as the old turnpike antedating the plank-road was called), about half a mile south of the court-house. When the preliminaries of the lynching had been arranged, and a committee appointed to manage the affair, the crowd dispersed, some to go to their dinners, and some to secure recruits for the lynching party.

It was twenty minutes to five o'clock, when an excited negro, panting and perspiring, rushed up to the back door of Sheriff Campbell's dwelling, which stood at a little distance from the jail and somewhat farther than the latter building from the court-house. A turbaned colored woman came to the door in response to the negro's knock.

"Hoddy, Sis' Nance."

"Hoddy, Brer Sam."

"Is de shurff in," inquired the negro.

"Yas, Brer Sam, he's eatin' his dinner," was the answer.

"Will yer ax 'im ter step ter de do' a minute, Sis' Nance?"

The woman went into the dining-room, and a moment later the sheriff came to the door. He was a tall, muscular man, of a ruddier complexion than is usual among Southerners. A pair of keen, deep-set gray eyes looked out from under bushy eyebrows, and about his mouth was a masterful expression, which a full beard, once sandy in color, but now profusely sprinkled with gray, could not entirely conceal. The day was hot; the sheriff had discarded his coat and vest, and had his white shirt open at the throat.

"What do you want, Sam?" he inquired of the negro, who stood hat in hand, wiping the moisture from his face with a ragged shirt-sleeve.

"Shurff, dey gwine ter hang de pris'ner w'at's lock' up in de jail. Dey're comin' dis a-way now. I wuz layin' down on a sack er corn down at de sto', behine a pile er flour-bairls, w'en I hearn Doc' Cain en Kunnel Wright talkin' erbout it. I slip' outen de back do', en run here as fas' as I could. I hearn you say down ter de sto' once't dat you would n't let nobody take a pris'ner 'way fum you widout walkin' over yo' dead body, en I thought I'd let you know 'fo' dey come, so yer could pertec' de pris'ner."

The sheriff listened calmly, but his face grew firmer, and a determined gleam lit up his gray eyes. His frame grew more erect, and he unconsciously assumed the attitude of a soldier who momentarily expects to meet the enemy face to face.

"Much obliged, Sam," he answered. "I'll protect the prisoner. Who's coming?"

"I dunno who-all *is* comin'," replied the negro. "Dere's Mistah McSwayne, en Doc' Cain, en Maje' McDonal', en Kunnel Wright, en a heap er yuthers. I wuz so skeered I done furgot mo' d'n half un em. I spec' dey mus' be mos' here by dis time, so I'll git outen de way, fer I don' want nobody fer ter think I wuz mix' up in dis business." The negro glanced nervously down the road toward the town, and made a movement as if to go away.

"Won't you have some dinner first?" asked the sheriff.

The negro looked longingly in at the open door, and sniffed the appetizing odor of boiled pork and collards.

"I ain't got no time fer ter tarry, Shurff," he said, "but Sis' Nance mought gin me sump'n I could kyar in my han' en eat on de way."

A moment later Nancy brought him a huge sandwich of split corn-pone, with a thick slice of fat bacon inserted between the halves, and a couple of baked yams. The negro hastily replaced his ragged hat on his head, dropped the yams in the pocket of his capacious trousers, and, taking the sandwich in his hand, hurried across the road and disappeared in the woods beyond.

The sheriff reëntered the house, and put on his coat and hat. He then took down a double-barreled shotgun and loaded it with buckshot. Filling the chambers of a revolver with fresh cartridges, he slipped it into the pocket of the sack-coat which he wore.

A comely young woman in a calico dress watched these proceedings with anxious surprise.

"Where are you going, father?" she asked. She had not heard the conversation with the negro.

"I am goin' over to the jail," responded the sheriff. "There's a mob comin' this way to lynch the nigger we've got locked up. But they won't do it," he added, with emphasis.

"Oh, father! don't go!" pleaded the girl, clinging to his arm; "they'll shoot you if you don't give him up."

"You never mind me, Polly," said her father reassuringly, as he gently unclasped her hands from his arm. "I'll take care of myself and the prisoner, too. There ain't a man in Branson County that would shoot me. Besides, I have faced fire too often to be scared away from my duty. You keep close in the house," he continued, "and if any one disturbs you just use the old horse-pistol in the top bureau drawer. It's a little old-fashioned, but it did good work a few years ago."

The young girl shuddered at this sanguinary allusion, but made no further objection to her father's departure.

The sheriff of Branson was a man far above the average of the community in wealth, education, and social position. His had been one of the few families in the county that before the war had owned large estates and numerous slaves. He had graduated at the State University at Chapel Hill, and had kept up some acquaintance with current literature and advanced thought. He had traveled some in his youth, and was looked up to in the county as an authority on all subjects connected with the outer world. At first an ardent supporter of the Union, he had opposed the secession movement in his native State as long as opposition availed to stem the tide of public opinion. Yielding at last to the force of circumstances, he had entered the Confederate service rather late in the war, and served with distinction through several campaigns, rising in time to the rank of colonel. After the war he had taken the oath of allegiance, and had been chosen by the people as the most available candidate for the office of sheriff, to which he had been elected without opposition. He had filled the office for several terms, and was universally popular with his constituents.

Colonel or Sheriff Campbell, as he was indifferently called, as the military or civil title happened to be most important in the opinion of the person addressing him, had a high sense of the responsibility attaching to his office. He had sworn to do his duty faithfully, and he knew what his duty was, as sheriff, perhaps more clearly than he had apprehended it in other passages of his life. It was, therefore, with no uncertainty in regard to his course that he prepared his weapons and went over to the jail. He had no fears for Polly's safety.

The sheriff had just locked the heavy front door of the jail behind him when a half dozen horsemen, followed by a crowd of men on foot, came round a bend in the road and drew near the jail. They halted in front of the picket fence that surrounded the building, while several of the committee of arrangements rode on a few rods farther to the sheriff's house. One of them dismounted and rapped on the door with his riding-whip.

"Is the sheriff at home?" he inquired.

"No, he has just gone out," replied Polly, who had come to the door.

"We want the jail keys," he continued.

"They are not here," said Polly. "The sheriff has them himself." Then she added, with assumed indifference. "He is at the jail now."

The man turned away, and Polly went into the front room, from which she peered anxiously between the slats of the green blinds of a window that looked toward the jail. Meanwhile the messenger returned to his companions and announced his discovery. It looked as though the sheriff had learned of their design and was preparing to resist it.

One of them stepped forward and rapped on the jail door.

"Well, what is it?" said the sheriff, from within.

"We want to talk to you, Sheriff," replied the spokesman.

There was a little wicket in the door: this the sheriff opened, and answered through it.

"All right, boys, talk away. You are all strangers to me, and I don't know what business you can have." The sheriff did not think it necessary to recognize anybody in particular on such an occasion; the question of identity sometimes comes up in the investigation of these extra-judicial executions.

"We're a committee of citizens and we want to get into the jail."

"What for? It ain't much trouble to get into jail. Most people want to keep out."

The mob was in no humor to appreciate a joke, and the sheriff's witticism fell dead upon an unresponsive audience.

"We want to have a talk with the nigger that killed Cap'n Walker."

"You can talk to that nigger in the courthouse, when he's brought out for trial. Court will be in session here next week. I know what you fellows want, but you can't get my prisoner to-day. Do you want to take the bread out of a poor man's mouth? I get seventy-five cents a day for keeping this prisoner, and he's the only one in jail. I can't have my family suffer just to please you fellows."

One or two young men in the crowd laughed at the idea of Sheriff Campbell's suffering for want of seventy-five cents a day; but they were frowned into silence by those who stood near them.

"Ef yer don't let us in," cried a voice, "we'll bu's' the do' open."

"Bust away," answered the sheriff, raising his voice so that all could hear. "But I give you fair warning. The first man that tries it will be filled with buckshot. I'm sheriff of this county; I know my duty, and I mean to do it."

"What's the use of kicking, Sheriff?" argued one of the leaders of the mob. "The nigger is sure to hang anyhow; he richly deserves it; and we've got to do something to teach the niggers their places, or white people won't be able to live in the county."

"There's no use talking, boys," responded the sheriff. "I'm a white man outside, but in this jail I'm sheriff; and if this nigger's to be hung in this county, I propose to do the hanging. So you fellows might as well right-about-face, and march back to Troy. You've had a pleasant trip, and the exercise will be good for you. You know *me.* I've got powder and ball, and I've faced fire before now, with nothing between me and the enemy, and I don't mean to surrender this jail while I'm able to shoot." Having thus announced his determination, the sheriff closed and fastened the wicket, and looked around for the best position from which to defend the building.

The crowd drew off a little, and the leaders conversed together in low tones.

The Branson County jail was a small, two-story brick building, strongly constructed, with no attempt at architectural ornamentation. Each story was divided into two large cells by a passage running from front to rear. A grated iron door gave entrance from the passage to each of the four cells. The jail seldom had many prisoners in it, and the lower windows had been boarded up. When the sheriff had closed the wicket, he ascended the steep wooden stairs to the upper floor. There was no window at the front of the upper passage, and the most available position from which to watch the movements of the crowd below was the front window of the cell occupied by the solitary prisoner.

The sheriff unlocked the door and entered the cell. The prisoner was crouched in a corner, his yellow face, blanched with terror, looking ghastly in the semi-darkness of the room. A cold perspiration had gathered on his forehead, and his teeth were chattering with affright.

"For God's sake, Sheriff," he murmured hoarsely, "don't let 'em lynch me; I did n't kill the old man."

The sheriff glanced at the cowering wretch with a look of mingled contempt and loathing.

"Get up," he said sharply. "You will probably be hung sooner or later, but it shall not be to-day, if I can help it. I'll unlock your fetters, and if I can't hold the jail, you'll have to make the best fight you can. If I'm shot, I'll consider my responsibility at an end."

There were iron fetters on the prisoner's ankles, and handcuffs on his wrists. These the sheriff unlocked, and they fell clanking to the floor.

"Keep back from the window," said the sheriff. "They might shoot if they saw you."

The sheriff drew toward the window a pine bench which formed a part of the scanty furniture of the cell, and laid his revolver upon it. Then he took his gun in hand, and took his stand at the side of the window where he could with least exposure of himself watch the movements of the crowd below.

The lynchers had not anticipated any determined resistance. Of course they had looked for a formal protest, and perhaps a sufficient show of opposition to excuse the sheriff in the eye of any stickler for legal formalities. They had not however come prepared to fight a battle, and no one of them seemed willing to lead an attack upon the jail. The leaders of the party conferred together with a good deal of animated gesticulation, which was visible to the sheriff from his outlook, though the distance was too great for him to hear what was said. At length one of them broke away from the group, and rode back to the main body of the lynchers, who were restlessly awaiting orders.

"Well, boys," said the messenger, "we'll have to let it go for the present. The sheriff says he'll shoot, and he's got the drop on us this time. There ain't any of us that want to follow Cap'n Walker jest yet. Besides, the sheriff is a good fellow, and we don't want to hurt 'im. But," he added, as if to reassure the crowd, which began to show signs of disappointment, "the nigger might as well say his prayers, for he ain't got long to live."

There was a murmur of dissent from the mob, and several voices insisted that an attack be made on the jail. But pacific counsels finally prevailed, and the mob sullenly withdrew.

The sheriff stood at the window until they had disappeared around the bend in the road. He did not relax his watchfulness when the last one was out of sight. Their withdrawal might be a mere feint, to be followed by a further attempt. So closely, indeed, was his attention drawn to the outside, that he neither saw nor heard the prisoner creep stealthily across the floor, reach out his hand and secure the revolver which lay on the bench behind the sheriff, and creep as noiselessly back to his place in the corner of the room.

A moment after the last of the lynching party had disappeared there was a shot fired from the woods across the road; a bullet whistled by the window and buried itself in the wooden casing a few inches from where the sheriff was standing. Quick as thought, with the instinct born of a semi-guerrilla army experience, he raised his gun and fired twice at the point from which a faint puff of smoke showed the hostile bullet to have been sent. He stood a moment watching, and then rested his gun against the window, and reached behind him mechanically for the other weapon. It was not on the bench. As the sheriff realized this fact, he turned his head and looked into the muzzle of the revolver.

"Stay where you are, Sheriff," said the prisoner, his eyes glistening, his face almost ruddy with excitement.

The sheriff mentally cursed his own carelessness for allowing him to be caught in such a predicament. He had not expected anything of the kind. He had relied on the negro's cowardice and subordination in the presence of an armed white man as a matter of course. The sheriff was a brave man, but realized that the prisoner had him at an immense disadvantage. The two men stood thus for a moment, fighting a harmless duel with their eyes.

"Well, what do you mean to do?" asked the sheriff with apparent calmness.

"To get away, of course," said the prisoner, in a tone which caused the sheriff to look at him more closely, and with an involuntary feeling of apprehension; if the man was not mad, he was in a state of mind akin to madness, and quite as dangerous. The sheriff felt that he must speak the prisoner fair, and watch for a chance to turn the tables on him. The keen-eyed, desperate man before him was a different being altogether from the groveling wretch who had begged so piteously for life a few minutes before.

At length the sheriff spoke:—

"Is this your gratitude to me for saving your life at the risk of my own? If I had not done so, you would now be swinging from the limb of some neighboring tree."

"True," said the prisoner, "you saved my life, but for how long? When you came in, you said Court would sit next week. When the crowd went away they said I had not long to live. It is merely a choice of two ropes."

"While there's life there's hope," replied the sheriff. He uttered this commonplace mechanically, while his brain was busy in trying to think out some way of escape. "If you are innocent you can prove it."

The mulatto kept his eye upon the sheriff. "I didn't kill the old man," he replied; "but I shall never be able to clear myself. I was at his house at nine o'clock. I stole from it the coat that was on my back when I was taken. I would be convicted, even with a fair trial, unless the real murderer were discovered beforehand."

The sheriff knew this only too well. While he was thinking what argument next to use, the prisoner continued:—

"Throw me the keys—no, unlock the door."

The sheriff stood a moment irresolute. The mulatto's eye glittered ominously. The sheriff crossed the room and unlocked the door leading into the passage.

"Now go down and unlock the outside door."

The heart of the sheriff leaped within him. Perhaps he might make a dash for liberty, and gain the outside. He descended the narrow stairs, the prisoner keeping close behind him.

The sheriff inserted the huge iron key into the lock. The rusty bolt yielded slowly. It still remained for him to pull the door open.

"Stop!" thundered the mulatto, who seemed to divine the sheriff's purpose. "Move a muscle, and I'll blow your brains out."

The sheriff obeyed; he realized that his chance had not yet come.

"Now keep on that side of the passage, and go back upstairs."

Keeping the sheriff under cover of the revolver, the mulatto followed him up the stairs. The sheriff expected the prisoner to lock him into the cell and make his own escape. He had about come to the conclusion that the best thing he could do under the circumstances was to submit quietly, and take his chances of recapturing the prisoner after the alarm had been given. The sheriff had faced death more than once upon the battlefield. A few minutes before, well armed, and with a brick wall between him and them he had dared a hundred men to fight; but he felt instinctively that the desperate man confronting him was not to be trifled with, and he was too prudent a man to risk his life against such heavy odds. He had Polly to look after, and there was a limit beyond which devotion to duty would be quixotic and even foolish.

"I want to get away," said the prisoner, "and I don't want to be captured; for if I am I know I will be hung on the spot. I am afraid," he added somewhat reflectively, "that in order to save myself I shall have to kill you."

"Good God!" exclaimed the sheriff in involuntary terror: "you would not kill the man to whom you owe your own life."

"You speak more truly than you know," replied the mulatto. "I indeed owe my life to you."

The sheriff started. He was capable of surprise, even in that moment of extreme peril. "Who are you?" he asked in amazement.

"Tom, Cicely's son," returned the other. He had closed the door and stood talking to the sheriff through the grated opening. "Don't you remember Cicely—Cicely whom you sold, with her child, to the speculator on his way to Alabama?"

The sheriff did remember. He had been sorry for it many a time since. It had been the old story of debts, mortgages, and bad crops. He had quarreled with the mother. The price offered for her and her child had been unusually large, and he had yielded to the combination of anger and pecuniary stress.

"Good God!" he gasped, "you would not murder your own father?"

"My father?" replied the mulatto. "It were well enough for me to claim the relationship, but it comes with poor grace from you to ask anything by reason of it. What father's duty have you ever performed for me? Did you give me your name, or even your protection? Other white men gave their colored sons freedom and money, and sent them to the free States. *You* sold *me* to the rice swamps."

"I at least gave you the life you cling to," murmured the sheriff.

"Life?" said the prisoner, with a sarcastic laugh. "What kind of a life? You gave me your own blood, your features,—no man need look at us together twice to see that,—and you gave me a black mother. Poor wretch! She died under the lash, because she had enough womanhood to call her soul her own. You gave me a white man's spirit, and you made me a slave, and crushed it out."

"But you are free now," said the sheriff. He had not doubted, could not doubt, the mulatto's word. He knew whose passions coursed beneath that swarthy skin and burned in the black eyes opposite his own. He saw in this mulatto what he himself might have become had not the safeguards of parental restraint and public opinion been thrown around him.

"Free to do what?" replied the mulatto. "Free in name, but despised and scorned and set aside by the people to whose race I belong far more than to my mother's."

"There are schools," said the sheriff. "You have been to school." He had noticed that the mulatto spoke more eloquently and used better language than most Branson County people.

"I have been to school, and dreamed when I went that it would work some marvelous change in my condition. But what did I learn? I learned to feel that no degree of learning or wisdom will change the color of my skin and that I shall always wear what in my own country is a badge of degradation. When I think about it seriously I do not care particularly for such a life. It is the animal in me, not the man, that flees the gallows. I owe you nothing," he went on, "and expect nothing of you; and it would be no more than justice if I should avenge upon you my mother's wrongs and my own. But still I hate to shoot you; I have never yet taken human life—for I did *not* kill the old captain. Will you promise to give no alarm and make no attempt to capture me until morning, if I do not shoot?"

So absorbed were the two men in their colloquy and their own tumultuous thoughts that neither of them had heard the door below move upon its hinges. Neither of them had heard a light step come stealthily up the stairs, nor seen a slender form creep along the darkening passage toward the mulatto.

The sheriff hesitated. The struggle between his love of life and his sense of duty was a terrific one. It may seem strange that a man who could sell his own child into slavery should hesitate at such a moment, when his life was trembling in the balance. But the baleful influence of human slavery poisoned the very fountains of life, and created new standards of right. The sheriff was conscientious: his conscience had merely been warped by his environment. Let no one ask what his answer would have been: he was spared the necessity of a decision.

"Stop," said the mulatto, "you need not promise. I could not trust you if you did. It is your life for mine: there is but one safe way for me; you must die."

He raised his arm to fire, when there was a flash—a report from the passage behind him. His arm fell heavily at his side, and the pistol dropped at his feet.

The sheriff recovered first from his surprise, and throwing open the door secured the fallen weapon. Then seizing the prisoner he thrust him into the cell and locked the door upon him: after which he turned to Polly, who leaned half-fainting against the wall, her hands clasped over her heart.

"Oh, father. I was just in time!" she cried hysterically, and, wildly sobbing, threw herself into her father's arms.

"I watched until they all went away," she said. "I heard the shot from the woods and I saw you shoot. Then when you did not come out I feared something had happened, that perhaps you had been wounded. I got out the other pistol and ran over here. When I found the door open, I knew something was wrong and when I heard voices I crept upstairs, and reached the top just in time to hear him say he would kill you. Oh, it was a narrow escape!"

When she had grown somewhat calmer, the sheriff left her standing there and went back into the cell. The prisoner's arm was bleeding from a flesh wound. His bravado had given place to a stony apathy. There was no sign in his face of fear or disappointment or feeling of any kind. The sheriff sent Polly to the house for cloth, and bound up the prisoner's wound with a rude skill acquired during his army life.

"I'll have a doctor come and dress the wound in the morning," he said to the prisoner. "It will do very well until then, if you will keep quiet. If the doctor asks you how the wound was caused, you can say that you were struck by the bullet fired from the woods. It would do you no good to have it known that you were shot while attempting to escape."

The prisoner uttered no word of thanks or apology, but sat in sullen silence. When the wounded arm had been bandaged, Polly and her father returned to the house.

The sheriff was in an unusually thoughtful mood that evening. He put salt in his coffee at supper, and poured vinegar over his pancakes. To many of Polly's questions he returned random answers. When he had gone to bed he lay awake for several hours.

In the silent watches of the night, when he was alone with God, there came into his mind a flood of unaccustomed thoughts. An hour or two before, standing face to face with death, he had experienced a sensation similar to that which drowning men are said to feel—a kind of clarifying of the moral faculty, in which the veil of the flesh, with its obscuring passions and prejudices, is pushed aside for a moment, and all the acts of one's life stand out, in the clear light of truth, in their correct proportions and relations,—a state of mind in which one sees himself as God may be supposed to see him. In the reaction following his rescue, this feeling had given place for a time to far different emotions. But now, in the silence of midnight, something of this clearness of spirit returned to the sheriff. He saw that he had owed some duty to this son of his,—that neither law nor custom could destroy a responsibility inherent in the nature of mankind. He could not thus, in the eyes of God at least, shake off the consequences of his sin. Had he never sinned, this wayward spirit would never have come back from the vanished past to haunt him. As these thoughts came, his anger against the mulatto died away, and in its place there sprang up a great pity. The hand of parental authority might have restrained the passions he had seen burning in the prisoner's eyes when the desperate man spoke the words which had seemed to doom his father to death. The sheriff felt that he might have saved this fiery spirit from the slough of slavery; that he might have sent him to the free North, and given him there, or in some other land, an opportunity to turn to usefulness and honorable pursuits the talents that had run to crime, perhaps to madness; he might, still less, have given this son of his the poor simulacrum of liberty which men of his caste could possess in a slave-holding community; or least of all, but still something, he might have kept the boy on the plantation, where the burdens of slavery would have fallen lightly upon him.

The sheriff recalled his own youth. He had inherited an honored name to keep untarnished; he had had a future to make; the picture of a fair young bride had beckoned him on to happiness. The poor wretch now stretched upon a pallet of straw between the brick walls of the jail had had none of these things,—no name, no father, no mother—in the true meaning of motherhood,—and until the past few years no possible future, and then one vague and shadowy in its outline, and dependent for form and substance upon the slow solution of a problem in which there were many unknown quantities.

From what he might have done to what he might yet do was an easy transition for the awakened conscience of the sheriff. It oc-

CHARLOTTE PERKINS GILMAN

(1860–1935)

There are worse fates than being known for, indeed, exclusively identified with, a single title: in the case of Charlotte Perkins Gilman, author of numerous works of fiction and nonfiction, and, in her time, renowned as a leading feminist-theorist, that title is of course "The Yellow Wallpaper." Had Gilman written nothing else, she would yet be, so far as a general readership is concerned, as famous as she is now. In Gilman's own time, her most popular book was Women and Economics *(1898), called the "Bible" of the women's movement.*

Charlotte Perkins Gilman was born in 1860 in Hartford, Connecticut, where she was raised fatherless. In 1884 she married a Providence artist whom she divorced after four years, convinced that her domestic situation was driving her mad. The "dark fog" of mental illness that precipitated this break is brilliantly suggested by "The Yellow Wallpaper." (For more details of Gilman's self-scrutinized life as it relates to her art, see her autobiography, The Living of Charlotte Perkins Gilman, *published in 1935.)*

It might be noted in passing that Gilman was another important and unconventional talent singled out by William Dean Howells, who included "The Yellow Wallpaper" in his Great Modern American Stories *(1920).*

Gilman was a prominent feminist and woman of letters who lectured widely. Her most important titles include Man-Made World *(1911),* Herland *(1915),* His Religion and Hers *(1923). Apart from "The Yellow Wallpaper," she wrote a number of engaging short stories, among them the rather more light-hearted, "When I Was a Witch." But "The Yellow Wallpaper," a Poe-like descent into the mind, not of a murderer, but of a victim, a female victim, remains her masterpiece.*

The Yellow Wallpaper

It is very seldom that mere ordinary people like John and myself secure ancestral halls for the summer.

A colonial mansion, a hereditary estate, I would say a haunted house, and reach the height of romantic felicity—but that would be asking too much of fate!

Still I will proudly declare that there is something queer about it.

Else, why should it be let so cheaply? And why have stood so long untenanted?

John laughs at me, of course, but one expects that in man. John is practical in the extreme. He has no patience with faith, an intense horror of superstition, and he scoffs openly at any talk of things not to be felt and seen and put down in figures.

John is a physician, and *perhaps*—(I would not say it to a living soul, of course, but this is dead paper and a great relief to my mind)—*perhaps* that is one reason I do not get well faster.

You see he does not believe I am sick! And what can one do?

If a physician of high standing, and one's own husband, assures friends and relatives that there is really nothing the matter with one but temporary nervous depression—a slight hysterical tendency—what is one to do?

My brother is also a physician, and also of high standing, and he says the same thing.

So I take phosphates or phosphites—whichever it is—and tonics, and journeys, and air, and exercise, and am absolutely forbidden to "work" until I am well again.

Personally, I disagree with their ideas.

Personally, I believe that congenial work, with excitement and change, would do me good.

But what is one to do?

I did write for a while in spite of them; but it *does* exhaust me a good deal—having to be so sly about it, or else meet with heavy opposition.

I sometimes fancy that in my condition if I had less opposition and more society and stimulus—but John says the very worst thing

I can do is to think about my condition, and I confess it always makes me feel bad.

So I will let it alone and talk about the house.

The most beautiful place! It is quite alone, standing well back from the road, quite three miles from the village. It makes me think of English places that you read about, for there are hedges and walls and gates that lock, and lots of separate little houses for the gardeners and people.

There is a *delicious* garden! I never saw such a garden—large and shady, full of box-bordered paths, and lined with long grape-covered arbors with seats under them.

There were greenhouses, too, but they are all broken now.

There was some legal trouble, I believe, something about the heirs and co-heirs; anyhow, the place has been empty for years.

That spoils my ghostliness, I am afraid, but I don't care—there is something strange about the house—I can feel it.

I even said so to John one moonlight evening, but he said what I felt was a draught, and shut the window.

I get unreasonably angry with John sometimes. I'm sure I never used to be so sensitive. I think it is due to this nervous condition.

But John says if I feel so I shall neglect proper self-control; so I take pains to control myself—before him, at least, and that makes me very tired.

I don't like our room a bit. I wanted one downstairs that opened on the piazza and had roses all over the window, and such pretty old-fashioned chintz hangings! But John would not hear of it.

He said there was only one window and not room for two beds, and no near room for him if he took another.

He is very careful and loving, and hardly lets me stir without special direction.

I have a schedule prescription for each hour in the day; he takes all care from me, and so I feel basely ungrateful not to value it more.

He said we came here solely on my account; that I was to have perfect rest and all the air I could get. "Your exercise depends on your strength, my dear," said he, "and your food somewhat on your appetite; but air you can absorb all the time." So we took the nursery at the top of the house.

It is a big, airy room, the whole floor nearly, with windows that look all ways, and air and sunshine galore. It was nursery first and then playroom and gymnasium, I should judge; for the windows are barred for little children, and there are rings and things in the walls.

The paint and paper look as if a boys' school had used it. It is stripped off—the paper—in great patches all around the head of my bed, about as far as I can reach, and in a great place on the other side of the room low down. I never saw a worse paper in my life.

One of those sprawling flamboyant patterns committing every artistic sin.

It is dull enough to confuse the eye in following, pronounced enough constantly to irritate and provoke study, and when you follow the lame uncertain curves for a little distance they suddenly commit suicide—plunge off at outrageous angles, destroy themselves in unheard of contradictions.

The color is repellant, almost revolting; a smouldering unclean yellow, strangely faded by the slow-turning sunlight.

It is a dull yet lurid orange in some places, a sickly sulphur tint in others.

No wonder the children hated it! I should hate it myself if I had to live in this room long.

There comes John, and I must put this away—he hates to have me write a word.

We have been here two weeks, and I haven't felt like writing before, since that first day.

I am sitting by the window now, up in this atrocious nursery, and there is nothing to hinder my writing as much as I please, save lack of strength.

John is away all day, and even some nights when his cases are serious.

I am glad my case is not serious!

But these nervous troubles are dreadfully depressing.

John does not know how much I really suffer. He knows there is no *reason* to suffer, and that satisfies him.

Of course it is only nervousness. It does weigh on me so not to do my duty in any way!

I meant to be such a help to John, such a real rest and comfort, and here I am a comparative burden already!

Nobody would believe what an effort it is to do what little I am able—to dress and entertain, and order things.

It is fortunate Mary is so good with the baby. Such a dear baby!

And yet I *cannot* be with him, it makes me so nervous.

I suppose John never was nervous in his life. He laughs at me so about this wallpaper!

At first he meant to repaper the room, but afterwards he said that I was letting it get the better of me, and that nothing was worse for a nervous patient than to give way to such fancies.

He said that after the wallpaper was changed it would be the heavy bedstead, and then the barred windows, and then that gate at the head of the stairs, and so on.

"You know the place is doing you good," he said, "and really, dear, I don't care to renovate the house just for a three months' rental."

"Then do let us go downstairs," I said, "there are such pretty rooms there."

Then he took me in his arms and called me a blessed little goose, and said he would go down cellar, if I wished, and have it white-washed into the bargain.

But he is right enough about the beds and windows and things.

It is an airy and comfortable room as any one need wish, and, of course, I would not be so silly as to make him uncomfortable just for a whim.

I'm really getting quite fond of the big room, all but that horrid paper.

Out of one window I can see the garden, those mysterious deep-shaded arbors, the riotous old-fashioned flowers, and bushes and gnarly trees.

Out of another I get a lovely view of the bay and a little private wharf belonging to the estate. There is a beautiful shaded lane that runs down there from the house. I always fancy I see people walking in these numerous paths and arbors, but John has cautioned me not to give way to fancy in the least. He says that with my imaginative power and habit of story-making, a nervous weakness like mine is sure to lead to all manner of excited fancies, and that I ought to use my will and good sense to check the tendency. So I try.

I think sometimes that if I were only well enough to write a little it would relieve the press of ideas and rest me.

But I find I get pretty tired when I try.

It is so discouraging not to have any advice and companionship about my work. When I get really well, John says we will ask

Cousin Henry and Julia down for a long visit; but he says he would as soon put fireworks in my pillowcase as to let me have those stimulating people about now.

I wish I could get well faster.

But I must not think about that. This paper looks to me as if it *knew* what a vicious influence it had!

There is a recurrent spot where the pattern lolls like a broken neck and two bulbous eyes stare at you upside down.

I get positively angry with the impertinence of it and the everlastingness. Up and down and sideways they crawl, and those absurd, unblinking eyes are everywhere. There is one place where two breadths didn't match, and the eyes go all up and down the line, one a little higher than the other.

I never saw so much expression in an inanimate thing before, and we all know how much expression they have! I used to lie awake as a child and get more entertainment and terror out of blank walls and plain furniture than most children could find in a toy-store.

I remember what a kindly wink the knobs of our big, old bureau used to have, and there was one chair that always seemed like a strong friend.

I used to feel that if any of the other things looked too fierce I could always hop into that chair and be safe.

The furniture in this room is no worse than inharmonious, however, for we had to bring it all from downstairs. I suppose when this was used as a playroom they had to take the nursery things out, and no wonder! I never saw such ravages as the children have made here.

The wallpaper, as I said before, is torn off in spots, and it sticketh closer than a brother—they must have had perseverance as well as hatred.

Then the floor is scratched and gouged and splintered, the plaster itself is dug out here and there, and this great heavy bed which is all we found in the room, looks as if it had been through the wars.

But I don't mind it a bit—only the paper.

There comes John's sister. Such a dear girl as she is, and so careful of me! I must not let her find me writing.

She is a perfect and enthusiastic housekeeper, and hopes for no better profession. I verily believe she thinks it is the writing which made me sick!

But I can write when she is out, and see her a long way off from these windows.

There is one that commands the road, a lovely shaded winding road, and one that just looks off over the country. A lovely country, too, full of great elms and velvet meadows.

This wallpaper has a kind of sub-pattern in a different shade, a particularly irritating one, for you can only see it in certain lights, and not clearly then.

But in the places where it isn't faded and where the sun is just so—I can see a strange, provoking, formless sort of figure, that seems to skulk about behind that silly and conspicuous front design.

There's sister on the stairs!

Well, the Fourth of July is over! The people are all gone and I am tired out. John thought it might do me good to see a little company, so we just had mother and Nellie and the children down for a week.

Of course I didn't do a thing. Jennie sees to everything now.

But it tired me all the same.

John says if I don't pick up faster he shall send me to Weir Mitchell in the fall.

But I don't want to go there at all. I had a friend who was in his hands once, and she says he is just like John and my brother, only more so!

Besides, it is such an undertaking to go so far.

I don't feel as if it was worth while to turn my hand over for anything, and I'm getting dreadfully fretful and querulous.

I cry at nothing, and cry most of the time.

Of course I don't when John is here, or anybody else, but when I am alone.

And I am alone a good deal just now. John is kept in town very often by serious cases, and Jennie is good and lets me alone when I want her to.

So I walk a little in the garden or down that lovely lane, sit on the porch under the roses, and lie down up here a good deal.

I'm getting really fond of the room in spite of the wallpaper. Perhaps *because* of the wallpaper.

It dwells in my mind so!

I lie here on this great immovable bed—it is nailed down, I believe—and follow that pattern about by the hour. It is as good as gymnastics, I assure you. I start, we'll say, at the bottom, down in the corner over there where it has not been touched, and I determine for the thousandth time that I *will* follow that pointless pattern to some sort of a conclusion.

I know a little of the principle of design, and I know this thing was not arranged on any laws of radiation, or alternation, or repetition, or symmetry, or anything else that I ever heard of.

It is repeated, of course, by the breadths, but not otherwise.

Looked at in one way each breadth stands alone, the bloated curves and flourishes—a kind of "debased Romanesque" with delirium tremens—go waddling up and down in isolated columns of fatuity.

But, on the other hand, they connect diagonally, and the sprawling outlines run off in great slanting waves of optic horror, like a lot of wallowing sea-weeds in full chase.

The whole thing goes horizontally, too, at least it seems so, and I exhaust myself trying to distinguish the order of its going in that direction.

They have used a horizontal breadth for a frieze, and that adds wonderfully to the confusion.

There is one end of the room where it is almost intact, and there, when the crosslights fade and the low sun shines directly upon it, I can almost fancy radiation after all,—the interminable grotesques seem to form around a common centre and rush off in headlong plunges of equal distraction.

It makes me tired to follow it. I will take a nap I guess.

I don't know why I should write this.

I don't want to.

I don't feel able.

And I know John would think it absurd. But I *must* say what I feel and think in some way—it is such a relief!

But the effort is getting to be greater than the relief.

Half the time now I am awfully lazy, and lie down ever so much.

John says I mustn't lose my strength, and has me take cod liver oil and lots of tonics and things, to say nothing of ale and wine and rare meat.

Dear John! He loves me very dearly, and hates to have me sick. I tried to have a real earnest reasonable talk with him the other day, and tell him how I wish he would let me go and make a visit to Cousin Henry and Julia.

But he said I wasn't able to go, nor able to stand it after I got there; and I did not make out a very good case for myself, for I was crying before I had finished.

It is getting to be a great effort for me to think straight. Just this nervous weakness I suppose.

And dear John gathered me up in his arms, and just carried me upstairs and laid me on the bed, and sat by me and read to me till it tired my head.

He said I was his darling and his comfort and all he had, and that I must take care of myself for his sake, and keep well.

He says no one but myself can help me out of it, that I must use my will and self-control and not let any silly fancies run away with me.

There's one comfort, the baby is well and happy, and does not have to occupy this nursery with the horrid wallpaper.

If we had not used it, that blessed child would have! What a fortunate escape! Why, I wouldn't have a child of mine, an impressionable little thing, live in such a room for worlds.

I never thought of it before, but it is lucky that John kept me here after all, I can stand it so much easier than a baby, you see.

Of course I never mention it to them any more—I am too wise—but I keep watch for it all the same.

There are things in that paper that nobody knows but me, or ever will.

Behind that outside pattern the dim shapes get clearer every day.

It is always the same shape, only very numerous.

And it is like a woman stooping down and creeping about behind that pattern. I don't like it a bit. I wonder—I begin to think—I wish John would take me away from here!

It is so hard to talk with John about my case, because he is so wise, and because he loves me so.

But I tried it last night.

It was moonlight. The moon shines in all around just as the sun does.

I hate to see it sometimes, it creeps so slowly, and always comes in by one window or another.

John was asleep and I hated to waken him, so I kept still and watched the moonlight on that undulating wallpaper till I felt creepy.

The faint figure behind seemed to shake the pattern, just as if she wanted to get out.

I got up softly and went to feel and see if the paper *did* move, and when I came back John was awake.

"What is it, little girl?" he said. "Don't go walking about like that—you'll get cold."

I thought it was a good time to talk so I told him that I really was not gaining here, and that I wished he would take me away.

"Why darling!" said he, "our lease will be up in three weeks, and I can't see how to leave before.

"The repairs are not done at home, and I cannot possibly leave town just now. Of course if you were in any danger, I could and would, but you really are better, dear, whether you can see it or not. I am a doctor, dear, and I know. You are gaining flesh and color, your appetite is better, I feel really much easier about you."

"I don't weigh a bit more," said I, "nor as much; and my appetite may be better in the evening when you are here, but it is worse in the morning when you are away!"

"Bless her little heart!" said he with a big hug, "she shall be as sick as she pleases! But now let's improve the shining hours by going to sleep, and talk about it in the morning!"

"And you won't go away?" I asked gloomily.

"Why, how can I, dear? It is only three weeks more and then we will take a nice little trip of a few days while Jennie is getting the house ready. Really, dear, you are better!"

"Better in body perhaps—" I began, and stopped short, for he sat up straight and looked at me with such a stern, reproachful look that I could not say another word.

"My darling," said he, "I beg of you, for my sake and for our child's sake, as well as for your own, that you will never for one instant let that idea enter your mind! There is nothing so dangerous, so fascinating, to a temperament like yours. It is a false and foolish fancy. Can you not trust me as a physician when I tell you so?"

So of course I said no more on that score, and we went to sleep before long. He thought I was asleep first, but I wasn't, and lay there for hours trying to decide whether that front pattern and the back pattern really did move together or separately.

On a pattern like this, by daylight, there is a lack of sequence, a defiance of law, that is a constant irritant to a normal mind.

The color is hideous enough, and unreliable enough, and infuriating enough, but the pattern is torturing.

You think you have mastered it, but just as you get well underway in following, it turns a back-somersault and there you are. It slaps you in the face, knocks you down, and tramples upon you. It is like a bad dream.

The outside pattern is a florid arabesque, reminding one of a fungus. If you can imagine a toadstool in joints, an interminable string of toadstools, budding and sprouting in endless convolutions—why, that is something like it.

That is, sometimes!

There is one marked peculiarity about this paper, a thing nobody seems to notice but myself, and that is that it changes as the light changes.

When the sun shoots in through the east window—I always watch for that first, long, straight ray—it changes so quickly that I never can quite believe it.

That is why I watch it always.

By moonlight—the moon shines in all night when there is a moon—I wouldn't know it was the same paper.

At night in any kind of light, in twilight, candlelight, lamplight, and worst of all by moonlight, it becomes bars! The outside pattern I mean, and the woman behind it is as plain as can be.

I didn't realize for a long time what the thing was that showed behind, that dim sub-pattern, but now I am quite sure it is a woman.

By daylight she is subdued, quiet. I fancy it is the pattern that keeps her so still. It is so puzzling. It keeps me quiet by the hour.

I lie down ever so much now. John says it is good for me, and to sleep all I can.

Indeed he started the habit by making me lie down for an hour after each meal.

It is a very bad habit I am convinced, for you see I don't sleep.

And that cultivates deceit, for I don't tell them I'm awake—O, no!

The fact is I am getting a little afraid of John.

He seems very queer sometimes, and even Jennie has an inexplicable look.

It strikes me occasionally, just as a scientific hypothesis, that perhaps it is the paper!

I have watched John when he did not know I was looking, and come into the room suddenly on the most innocent excuses, and I've caught him several times *looking at the paper!* And Jennie too. I caught Jennie with her hand on it once.

She didn't know I was in the room, and when I asked her in a quiet, a very quiet voice, with the most restrained manner possible, what she was doing with the paper—she turned around as if she had been caught stealing, and looked quite angry—asked me why I should frighten her so!

Then she said that the paper stained everything it touched, that she had found yellow smooches on all my clothes and John's, and she wished we would be more careful!

Did not that sound innocent? But I know she was studying that pattern, and I am determined that nobody shall find it out but myself!

Life is very much more exciting now than it used to be. You see I have something more to expect, to look forward to, to watch. I really do eat better, and am more quiet than I was.

John is so pleased to see me improve! He laughed a little the other day, and said I seemed to be flourishing in spite of my wallpaper.

I turned it off with a laugh. I had no intention of telling him it was *because* of the wallpaper—he would make fun of me. He might even want to take me away.

I don't want to leave now until I have found it out. There is a week more, and I think that will be enough.

I'm feeling ever so much better! I don't sleep much at night, for it is so interesting to watch developments; but I sleep a good deal in the daytime.

In the daytime it is tiresome and perplexing.

There are always new shoots on the fungus, and new shades of yellow all over it. I cannot keep count of them, though I have tried conscientiously.

It is the strangest yellow, that wallpaper! It makes me think of all the yellow things I ever saw—not beautiful ones like buttercups, but old foul, bad yellow things.

But there is something else about that paper—the smell! I noticed it the moment we came into the room, but with so much air and sun it was not bad. Now we have had a week of fog and rain, and whether the windows are open or not, the smell is here.

It creeps all over the house.

I find it hovering in the dining-room, skulking in the parlor, hiding in the hall, lying in wait for me on the stairs.

It gets into my hair.

Even when I go to ride, if I turn my head suddenly and surprise it—there is that smell!

Such a peculiar odor, too! I have spent hours in trying to analyze it, to find what it smelled like.

It is not bad—at first, and very gentle, but quite the subtlest, most enduring odor I ever met.

In this damp weather it is awful, I wake up in the night and find it hanging over me.

It used to disturb me at first. I thought seriously of burning the house—to reach the smell.

But now I am used to it. The only thing I can think of that it is like is the *color* of the paper! A yellow smell.

There is a very funny mark on this wall, low down, near the mopboard. A streak that runs round the room. It goes behind every piece of furniture, except the bed, a long, straight, even *smooch*, as if it had been rubbed over and over.

I wonder how it was done and who did it, and what they did it for. Round and round and round—round and round and round—it makes me dizzy!

I really have discovered something at last.

Through watching so much at night, when it changes so, I have finally found out.

The front pattern *does* move—and no wonder! The woman behind shakes it!

Sometimes I think there are a great many women behind, and sometimes only one, and she crawls around fast, and her crawling shakes it all over.

Then in the very bright spots she keeps still, and in the very shady spots she just takes hold of the bars and shakes them hard.

And she is all the time trying to climb through. But nobody could climb through that pattern—it strangles so; I think that is why it has so many heads.

They get through, and then the pattern strangles them off and turns them upside down, and makes their eyes white!

If those heads were covered or taken off it would not be half so bad.

I think that woman gets out in the daytime!

And I'll tell you why—privately—I've seen her!

I can see her out of every one of my windows!

It is the same woman, I know, for she is always creeping, and most women do not creep by daylight.

I see her in that long shaded lane, creeping up and down. I see her in those dark grape arbors, creeping all around the garden.

I see her on that long road under the trees, creeping along, and when a carriage comes she hides under the blackberry vines.

I don't blame her a bit. It must be very humiliating to be caught creeping by daylight!

I always lock the door when I creep by daylight. I can't do it at night, for I know John would suspect something at once.

And John is so queer now, that I don't want to irritate him. I wish he would take another room! Besides, I don't want anybody to get that woman out at night but myself.

I often wonder if I could see her out of all the windows at once.

But, turn as fast as I can, I can only see out of one at one time.

And though I always see her, she *may* be able to creep faster than I can turn!

I have watched her sometimes away off in the open country, creeping as fast as a cloud shadow in a high wind.

If only that top pattern could be gotten off from the under one! I mean to try it, little by little.

I have found out another funny thing, but I shan't tell it this time! It does not do to trust people too much.

There are only two more days to get this paper off, and I believe John is beginning to notice. I don't like the look in his eyes.

And I heard him ask Jennie a lot of professional questions about me. She had a very good report to give.

She said I slept a good deal in the daytime.

John knows I don't sleep very well at night, for all I'm so quiet!

He asked me all sorts of questions, too, and pretended to be very loving and kind.

As if I couldn't see through him!

Still, I don't wonder he acts so, sleeping under this paper for three months.

It only interests me, but I feel sure John and Jennie are secretly affected by it.

Hurrah! This is the last day, but it is enough. John is to stay in town over night, and won't be out until this evening.

Jennie wanted to sleep with me—the sly thing! but I told her I should undoubtedly rest better for a night all alone.

That was clever, for really I wasn't alone a bit! As soon as it was moonlight and that poor thing began to crawl and shake the pattern, I got up and ran to help her.

I pulled and she shook, I shook and she pulled, and before morning we had peeled off yards of that paper.

A strip about as high as my head and half around the room.

And then when the sun came and that awful pattern began to laugh at me, I declared I would finish it to-day!

We go away to-morrow, and they are moving all my furniture down again to leave things as they were before.

Jennie looked at the wall in amazement, but I told her merrily that I did it out of pure spite at the vicious thing.

She laughed and said she wouldn't mind doing it herself, but I must not get tired.

How she betrayed herself that time!

But I am here, and no person touches this paper but Me—not *alive!*

She tried to get me out of the room—it was too patent! But I said it was so quiet and empty and clean now that I believed I would lie down again and sleep all I could; and not to wake me even for dinner—I would call when I woke.

So now she is gone, and the servants are gone, and the things are gone, and there is nothing left but that great bedstead nailed down, with the canvas mattress we found on it.

We shall sleep downstairs to-night, and take the boat home tomorrow.

I quite enjoy the room, now it is bare again.

How those children did tear about here!

This bedstead is fairly gnawed!

But I must get to work.

I have locked the door and thrown the key down into the front path.

I don't want to go out, and I don't want to have anybody come in, till John comes.

I want to astonish him.

I've got a rope up here that even Jennie did not find. If that woman does get out, and tries to get away, I can tie her!

But I forgot I could not reach far without anything to stand on!

This bed will *not* move!

I tried to lift and push it until I was lame, and then I got so angry I bit off a little piece at one corner—but it hurt my teeth.

Then I peeled off all the paper I could reach standing on the floor. It sticks horribly and the pattern just enjoys it! All those strangled heads and bulbous eyes and waddling fungus growths just shriek with derision!

I am getting angry enough to do something desperate. To jump out of the window would be admirable exercise, but the bars are too strong even to try.

Besides I wouldn't do it. Of course not. I know well enough that a step like that is improper and might be misconstrued.

I don't like to *look* out of the windows even—there are so many of those creeping women, and they creep so fast.

I wonder if they all come out of that wallpaper as I did?

But I am securely fastened now by my well-hidden rope—you don't get *me* out in the road there!

I suppose I shall have to get back behind the pattern when it comes night, and that is hard!

It is so pleasant to be out in this great room and creep around as I please!

I don't want to go outside. I won't, even if Jennie asks me to.

For outside you have to creep on the ground, and everything is green instead of yellow.

But here I can creep smoothly on the floor, and my shoulder just fits in that long smooch around the wall, so I cannot lose my way.

Why there's John at the door!

It is no use, young man, you can't open it!

How he does call and pound!

Now he's crying for an axe.

It would be a shame to break down that beautiful door!

"John dear!" said I in the gentlest voice, "the key is down by the front steps, under a plantain leaf!"

That silenced him for a few moments.

Then he said, very quietly indeed, "Open the door, my darling!"

"I can't," said I. "The key is down by the front door under a plantain leaf!"

And then I said it again, several times, very gently and slowly, and said it so often that he had to go and see, and he got it of course, and came in. He stopped short by the door.

"What is the matter?" he cried. "For God's sake, what are you doing!"

I kept on creeping just the same, but I looked at him over my shoulder.

"I've got out at last," said I, "in spite of you and Jane. And I've pulled off most of the paper, so you can't put me back!"

Now why should that man have fainted? But he did, and right across my path by the wall, so that I had to creep over him every time!

HENRY JAMES
(1843–1916)

With Henry James, we come to our first American theorist of fictional technique, whose extraordinary career encompassed any number of genres—the novel, the romance, the short story, the essay, the play, as well as countless prefaces, letters, notebooks, and reviews. Of American writers of the first rank, no one is more devoted to his craft than James; no one is more prolific, more fated for art—like the hapless Dencombe of "The Middle Years," perhaps, for whom the "infinite of life was gone" and all that remained was the "abyss of human illusion that was the real, the tideless deep." (Or is this mere playfulness on the part of James, who often sought, for diversity's sake, positions adversarial to his own?)

Henry James was born in New York City on April 15, 1843, to a well-to-do and distinguished family. His elder brother was William James, America's first psychologist and philosopher of significance. James set about consciously, and systematically, to make a career in international terms; he was to be no mere "American" writer, still less a writer bent upon popular success, but a self-determined literary master—one who would attempt to fashion, by way of such closely argued works as "The Art of Fiction," the very standards by which he would be judged. His early successes were The American *(1877),* Daisy Miller *(1878), and* The Portrait of a Lady *(1881); his middle, rather more ambitious works,* The Bostonians *(1886),* The Princess Casamassima *(1886), and* The Tragic Muse *(1890), were less popular. James' most ambitious novels are the later, writerly novels* The Wings of the Dove *(1902),* The Ambassadors *(1903), and* The Golden Bowl *(1904), though it might be argued that his most memorable works of fiction are short stories like "The Beast in the Jungle" and the novella* The Turn of the Screw, *in which vision, style, and a tightly imagined structure are brilliantly conjoined.*

The Middle Years

I

The April day was soft and bright, and poor Dencombe, happy in the conceit of reasserted strength, stood in the garden of the hotel, comparing, with a deliberation in which however there was still something of languor, the attractions of easy strolls. He liked the feeling of the south so far as you could have it in the north, he liked the sandy cliffs and the clustered pines, he liked even the colourless sea. "Bournemouth as a health-resort" had sounded like a mere advertisement, but he was thankful now for the commonest conveniences. The sociable country postman, passing through the garden, had just given him a small parcel which he took out with him, leaving the hotel to the right and creeping to a bench he had already haunted, a safe recess in the cliff. It looked to the south, to the tinted walls of the Island, and was protected behind by the sloping shoulder of the down. He was tired enough when he reached it, and for a moment was disappointed; he was better of course, but better, after all, than what? He should never again, as at one or two great moments of the past, be better than himself. The infinite of life was gone, and what remained of the dose a small glass scored like a thermometer by the apothecary. He sat and stared at the sea, which appeared all surface and twinkle, far shallower than the spirit of man. It was the abyss of human illusion that was the real, the tideless deep. He held his packet, which had come by book-post, unopened on his knee, liking, in the lapse of so many joys—his illness had made him feel his age—to know it was there, but taking for granted there could be no complete renewal of the pleasure, dear to young experience, of seeing one's self "just out." Dencombe, who had a reputation, had come out too often and knew too well in advance how he should look.

His postponement associated itself vaguely, after a little, with a group of three persons, two ladies and a young man, whom, beneath him, straggling and seemingly silent, he could see move slowly together along the sands. The gentleman had his head bent over a book and was occasionally brought to a stop by the charm of this volume, which, as Dencombe could perceive even at a distance, had a cover alluringly red. Then his companions, going a little further, waited for him to come up, poking their parasols into the beach, looking around them at the sea and sky and clearly sensible of the beauty of the day. To these things the young man with the book was still more clearly indifferent; lingering, credulous, absorbed, he was an object of envy to an observer from whose connexion with literature all such artlessness had faded. One of the ladies was large and mature; the other had the spareness of comparative youth and of a social situation possibly inferior. The large lady carried back Dencombe's imagination to the age of crinoline; she wore a hat of the shape of a mushroom, decorated with a blue veil, and had the air, in her aggressive amplitude, of clinging to a vanished fashion or even a lost cause. Presently her companion produced from under the folds of a mantle a limp portable chair which she stiffened out and of which the large lady took possession. This act, and something in the movement of either party, at once characterised the performers—they performed for Dencombe's recreation—as opulent matron and humble dependent. Where moreover was the virtue of an approved novelist if one couldn't establish a relation between such figures? the clever theory for instance that the young man was the son of the opulent matron and that the humble dependent, the daughter of a clergyman or an officer, nourished a secret passion for him. Was that not visible from the way she stole behind her protectress to look back at him?—back to where he had let himself come to a full stop when his mother sat down to rest. His book was a novel, it had the catchpenny binding; so that while the romance of life stood neglected at his side he lost himself in that of the circulating library. He moved mechanically to where the sand was softer and ended by plumping down in it to finish his chapter at his ease. The humble dependent, discouraged by his remoteness, wandered with a martyred droop of the head in another direction, and the exorbitant lady, watching the waves, offered a confused resemblance to a dying-machine that had broken down.

When his drama began to fail Dencombe remembered that he had after all another pastime. Though such promptitude on the part of the publisher was rare he was already able to draw from its wrapper his "latest," perhaps his last. The cover of "The Middle Years" was duly meretricious, the smell of the fresh pages the very odour of sanctity; but for the moment he went no further—he had become conscious of a strange alienation. He had forgotten what his book was about. Had the assault of his old ailment, which he had so fallaciously come to Bournemouth to ward off, interposed utter blankness as to what had preceded it? He had finished the revision of proof before quitting London, but his subsequent fortnight in bed had passed the sponge over colour. He couldn't have chanted to himself a single sentence, couldn't have turned with curiosity or confidence to any particular page. His subject had already gone from him, leaving scarce a superstition behind. He uttered a low moan as he breathed the chill of this dark void, so desperately it seemed to represent the completion of a sinister process. The tears filled his mild eyes; something precious had passed away. This was the pang that had been sharpest during the last few years—the sense of ebbing time, of shrinking opportunity; and now he felt not so much that his last chance was going as that it was gone indeed. He had done all he should ever do, and yet hadn't done what he wanted. This was the laceration—that practically his career was over: it was as violent as a grip at his throat. He rose from his seat nervously—a creature hunted by a dread; then he fell back in his weakness and nervously opened his book. It was a single volume; he preferred single volumes and aimed at a rare compression. He began to read and, little by little, in this occupation, was pacified and reassured. Everything came back to him, but came back with a wonder, came back above all with a high and magnificent beauty. He read his own prose, he turned his own leaves, and had as he sat there with the spring sunshine on the page an emotion peculiar and intense. His career was over, no doubt, but it was over, when all was said, with *that*.

He had forgotten during his illness the work of the previous year; but what he had chiefly forgotten was that it was extraordinarily good. He dived once more into his story and was drawn down, as by a siren's hand, to where, in the dim underworld of fiction, the great glazed tank of art, strange silent subjects float. He recognised his motive and surrendered to his talent. Never probably had that talent, such as it was, been so fine. His difficulties were still there, but what was also there, to his perception, though probably, alas! to nobody's else, was the art that in most cases had surmounted them. In his surprised enjoyment of this ability he had a glimpse of a possible reprieve. Surely its force wasn't spent—there was life and service in it yet. It hadn't come to him easily, it had been backward and roundabout. It was the child of time, the nursling of delay; he had struggled and suffered for it, making sacrifices not to be counted, and now that it was really mature was it to cease to yield, to confess itself brutally beaten? There was an infinite charm for Dencombe in feeling as he had never felt before that diligence *vincit omnia*. The result produced in his little book was somehow a result beyond his conscious intention: it was as if he had planted his genius, had trusted his method, and they had grown up and flowered with this sweetness. If the achievement had been real, however, the process had been painful enough. What he saw so intensely today, what he felt as a nail driven in, was that only now, at the very last, had he come into possession. His development had been abnormally slow, almost grotesquely gradual. He had been hindered and retarded by experience, he had for long periods only groped his way. It had taken too much of his life to produce too little of his art. The art had come, but it had come after everything else. At such a rate a first existence was too short—long enough only to collect material; so that to fructify, to use the material, one should have a second age, an extension. This extension was what poor Dencombe sighed for. As he turned the last leaves of his volume he murmured "Ah for another go, ah for a better chance!"

The three persons drawing his attention to the sands had vanished and then reappeared: they had now wandered up a path, an artificial and easy ascent, which led to the top of the cliff. Dencombe's bench was halfway down, on a sheltered ledge, and the large lady, a massive heterogeneous person with bold black eyes and kind red cheeks, now took a few moments to rest. She wore dirty gauntlets and immense diamond ear-rings: at first she looked vulgar, but she contradicted this announcement in an agreeable off-hand tone. While her companions stood waiting for her she spread her skirts on the end of Dencombe's seat. The young man had gold spectacles, through which, with his finger still in his red-covered book, he glanced at the volume, bound in the same shade of the same colour, lying on the lap of the original occupant of the bench. After an instant Dencombe felt him struck with a resemblance: he had recognised the gilt stamp on the crimson cloth, was reading "The Middle Years" and now noted that somebody else had kept pace with him. The stranger was startled, possibly even a little ruffled, to find himself not the only person favoured with an early copy. The eyes of the two proprietors met a moment, and Dencombe borrowed amusement from the expression of those of his competitor, those, it might even be inferred, of his admirer. They confessed to some resentment—they seemed to say: "Hang it, has he got it *already?* Of course he's a brute of a reviewer!" Dencombe shuffled his copy out of sight while the opulent matron, rising from her repose, broke out: "I feel already the good of this air!"

"I can't say I do," said the angular lady. "I find myself quite let down."

"I find myself horribly hungry. At what time did you order luncheon?" her protectress pursued.

The young person put the question by. "Doctor Hugh always orders it."

"I ordered nothing today—I'm going to make you diet," said their comrade.

"Then I shall go home and sleep. *Qui dort dine!*"

"Can I trust you to Miss Vernham?" asked Doctor Hugh of his elder companion.

"Don't I trust *you?*" she archly enquired.

"Not too much!" Miss Vernham, with her eyes on the ground, permitted herself to declare. "You must come with us at least to the house," she went on while the personage on whom they appeared to be in attendance began to mount higher. She had got a little out of ear-shot; nevertheless Miss Vernham became, so far as Dencombe was concerned, less distinctly audible to murmur to the young man: "I don't think you realise all you owe the Countess!"

Absently, a moment, Doctor Hugh caused his gold-rimmed spectacles to shine at her. "Is that the way I strike you? I see—I see!"

"She's awfully good to us," continued Miss Vernham, compelled by the lapse of the other's motion to stand there in spite of his discussion of private matters. Of what use would it have been that Dencombe should be sensitive to shades; hadn't he detected in that arrest a strange influence from the quiet old convalescent in the great tweed cape? Miss Vernham appeared suddenly to become aware of some such connexion, for she added in a moment: "If you want to sun yourself here you can come back after you've seen us home."

Doctor Hugh, at this, hesitated, and Dencombe, in spite of a desire to pass for unconscious, risked a covert glance at him. What his eyes met this time, as happened, was, on the part of the young lady, a queer stare, naturally vitreous, which made her remind him of some figure—he couldn't name it—in a play or a novel, some sinister governess or tragic old maid. She seemed to scan him, to challenge him, to say out of general spite: "What have you got to do with us?" At the same instant the rich humour of the Countess reached them from above: "Come, come, my little lambs; you should follow your old *bergère!*" Miss Vernham turned away for it, pursuing the ascent, and Doctor Hugh, after another mute appeal to Dencombe and a minute's evident demur, deposited his book on the bench as if to keep his place, or even as a gage of earnest return, and bounded without difficulty up the rougher part of the cliff.

Equally innocent and infinite are the pleasures of observation and the resources engendered by the trick of analysing life. It amused poor Dencombe, as he dawdled in his tepid air-bath, to believe himself awaiting a revelation of something at the back of a fine young mind. He looked hard at the book on the end of the bench, but wouldn't have touched it for the world. It served his purpose to have a theory that shouldn't be exposed to refutation. He already felt better of his melancholy; he had, according to his old formula, put his head at the window. A passing Countess could draw off the fancy when, like the elder of the ladies who had just retreated, she was as obvious as the giantess of a caravan. It was indeed general views that were terrible; short ones, contrary to an opinion sometimes expressed, were the refuge, were the remedy. Doctor Hugh couldn't possibly be anything but a reviewer who had understandings for early copies with publishers or with newspapers. He reappeared in a quarter of an hour with visible relief at finding Dencombe on the spot and the gleam of white teeth in an embarrassed but generous smile. He was perceptibly disappointed at the eclipse of the other copy of the book: it made a pretext the less for speaking to the quiet gentleman. But he spoke notwithstanding; he held up his own copy and broke out pleadingly: "*Do* say, if you have occasion to speak of it, that it's the best thing he has done yet!"

Dencombe responded with a laugh: "Done yet" was so amusing to him, made such a grand avenue of the future. Better still, the young man took *him* for a reviewer. He pulled out "The Middle Years" from under his cape, but instinctively concealed any telltale look of fatherhood. This was partly because a person was always a fool for insisting to others on his work. "Is that what you're going to say yourself?" he put to his visitor.

"I'm not quite sure I shall write anything. I don't, as a regular thing—I enjoy in peace. But it's awfully fine."

Dencombe just debated. If the young man had begun to abuse him he would have confessed on the spot to his identity, but there was no harm in drawing out any impulse to praise. He drew it out with such success that in a few moments his new acquaintance, seated by his side, was confessing candidly that the works of the author of the volumes before them were the only ones he could read a second time. He had come the day before from London, where a friend of his, a journalist, had lent him his copy of the last, the copy sent to the office of the journal and already the subject of a "notice" which, as was pretended there—but one had to allow for "swagger"—it had taken a full quarter of an hour to prepare. He intimated that he was ashamed for his friend, and in the case of a work demanding and repaying study, of such inferior manners; and, with his fresh appreciation and his so irregular wish to express it, he speedily became for poor Dencombe a remarkable, a delightful apparition. Chance had brought the weary man of letters face to face with the greatest admirer in the new generation of whom it was supposable he might boast. The admirer in truth was mystifying, so rare a case was it to find a bristling young doctor—he looked like a German physiologist—enamoured of literary form. It was an accident, but happier than most accidents, so that Dencombe, exhilarated as well as confounded, spent half an hour in making his visitor talk while he kept himself quiet. He explained his premature possession of "The Middle Years" by an allusion to the friendship of the publisher, who, knowing he was at Bournemouth for his health, had paid him this graceful attention. He allowed he had been ill, for Doctor Hugh would infallibly have guessed it; he even went so far as to wonder if he mightn't look for some hygienic "tip" from a personage combining so bright an enthusiasm with a presumable knowledge of the remedies now in vogue. It would shake his faith a little perhaps to have to take a doctor seriously who could take *him* so seriously, but he enjoyed this gushing modern youth and felt with an acute pang that there would still be work to do in a world in which such odd combinations were presented. It wasn't true, what he had tried for renunciation's sake to believe, that all the combinations were exhausted. They weren't by any means—they were infinite: the exhaustion was in the miserable artist.

Doctor Hugh, an ardent physiologist, was saturated with the spirit of the age—in other words he had just taken his degree: but he was independent and various, he talked like a man who would have preferred to love literature best. He would fain have made fine phrases, but nature had denied him the trick. Some of the finest in "The Middle Years" had struck him inordinately, and he took the liberty of reading them to Dencombe in support of his plea. He grew vivid, in the balmy air, to his companion, for whose deep refreshment he seemed to have been sent; and was particularly ingenuous in describing how recently he had become acquainted, and how instantly infatuated, with the only man who had put flesh between the ribs of an art that was starving on superstitions. He hadn't yet written to him—he was deterred by a strain of respect. Dencombe at this moment rejoiced more inwardly than ever that he had never answered the photographers. His visitor's attitude promised him a luxury of intercourse, though he was sure a due freedom for Doctor Hugh would depend not a little on the Countess. He learned without delay what type of Countess was involved, mastering as well the nature of the tie that united the curious trio. The large lady, an Englishwoman by birth and the daughter of a celebrated baritone, whose taste *minus* his talent she had inherited, was the widow of a French nobleman and mistress of all that remained of the handsome fortune, the fruit of her father's earnings, that had constituted her dower. Miss Vernham, an odd creature but an accomplished pianist, was attached to her person at a salary. The Countess was generous, independent, eccentric; she travelled with her minstrel and her medical man. Ignorant and passionate she had nevertheless moments in which she was almost irresistible. Dencombe saw her sit for her portrait in Doctor Hugh's free sketch, and felt the picture of his young friend's relation to her frame itself in his mind. This young friend, for a representative of the new psychology, was himself easily hypnotised, and if he became abnormally communicative it was only a sign of his real subjection. Dencombe did accordingly what he wanted with him, even without being known as Dencombe.

Taken ill on a journey in Switzerland the Countess had picked him up at an hotel, and the accident of his happening to please her had made her offer him, with her imperious liberality, terms that couldn't fail to dazzle a practitioner without patients and whose resources had been drained dry by his studies. It wasn't the way he would have proposed to spend his time, but it was time that would pass quickly, and meanwhile she was wonderfully kind. She exacted perpetual attention, but it was impossible not to like her. He gave details about his queer patient, a "type" if there ever was one, who had in connexion with her flushed obesity, and in addition to the morbid strain of a violent and aimless will, a grave organic disorder: but he came back to his loved novelist, whom he was so good as to pronounce more essentially a poet than many of those who went in for verse, with a zeal excited, as all his indiscretion had been excited, by the happy chance of Dencombe's sympathy and the coincidence of their occupation. Dencombe had confessed to a slight personal acquaintance with the author of "The Middle Years," but had not felt himself as ready as he could have wished when his companion, who had never yet encountered a being so privileged, began to be eager for particulars. He even divined in Doctor Hugh's eye at that moment a glimmer of suspicion. But the young man was too inflamed to be shrewd and repeatedly caught up the book to exclaim: "Did you notice this?" or "Weren't you immensely struck with that?" "There's a beautiful passage toward the end," he broke out; and again he laid his hand on the volume. As he turned the pages he came upon something else, while Dencombe saw him suddenly change colour. He had taken up as it lay on the bench Dencombe's copy instead of his own, and his neighbour at once guessed the reason of his start. Doctor Hugh looked grave an instant; then he said: "I see you've been altering the text!" Dencombe was a passionate corrector, a fingerer of style; the last thing he ever arrived at was a form final for himself. His ideal would have been to publish secretly, and then, on the published text, treat himself to the terrified revise, sacrificing always a first edition and beginning for posterity and even for the collectors, poor dears, with a second. This morning, in "The Middle Years," his pencil had pricked a dozen lights. He was amused at the effect of the young man's reproach; for an instant it made him change colour. He stammered at any rate ambiguously, then through a blur of ebbing consciousness saw Doctor Hugh's mystified eyes. He only had time to feel he was about to be ill again—that emotion, excitement, fatigue, the heat of the sun, the solicitation of the air, had combined to play him a trick, before, stretching out a hand to his visitor with a plaintive cry, he lost his senses altogether.

Later he knew he had fainted and that Doctor Hugh had got him home in a Bath-chair, the conductor of which, prowling within hail for custom, had happened to remember seeing him in the garden of the hotel. He had recovered his perception on the way, and had, in bed that afternoon, a vague recollection of Doctor Hugh's young face, as they went together, bent over him in a comforting laugh and expressive of something more than a suspicion of his identity. That identity was ineffaceable now, and all the more that he was rueful and sore. He had been rash, been stupid, had gone out too soon, stayed out too long. He oughtn't to have exposed himself to strangers, he ought to have taken his servant. He felt as if he had fallen into a hole too deep to descry any little patch of heaven. He was confused about the time that had passed—he pieced the fragments together. He had seen his doctor, the real one, the one who had treated him from the first and who had again been very kind. His servant was in and out on tiptoe, looking very wise after the fact. He said more than once something about the sharp young gentleman. The rest was vagueness in so far as it wasn't despair. The vagueness, however, justified itself by dreams, dozing anxieties from which he finally emerged to the consciousness of a dark room and a shaded candle.

"You'll be all right again—I know all about you now," said a voice near him that he felt to be young. Then his meeting with Doctor Hugh came back. He was too discouraged to joke about it yet, but made out after a little that the interest was intense for his visitor. "Of course I can't attend you professionally—you've got your own man, with whom I've talked and who's excellent," Doctor Hugh went on. "But you must let me come to see you as a good friend. I've just looked in before going to bed. You're doing beautifully, but it's a good job I was with you on the cliff. I shall come in early tomorrow. I want to do something for you. I want to do everything. You've done a tremendous lot for me." The young man held his hand, hanging over him, and poor Dencombe, weakly aware of this living pressure, simply lay there and accepted his devotion. He couldn't do anything less—he needed help too much.

The idea of the help he needed was very present to him that night, which he spent in a lucid stillness, an intensity of thought that constituted a reaction from his hours of stupor. He was lost, he was lost—he was lost if he couldn't be saved. He wasn't afraid of suffering, of death, wasn't even in love with life; but he had had a deep demonstration of desire. It came over him in the long quiet hours that only with "The Middle Years" had he taken his flight; only on that day, visited by soundless processions, had he recognised his kingdom. He had had a revelation of his range. What he dreaded was the idea that his reputation should stand on the unfinished. It wasn't with his past but with his future that it should properly be concerned. Illness and age rose before him like spectres with pitiless eyes: how was he to bribe such fates to give him the second chance? He had had the one chance that all men have—he had had the chance of life. He went to sleep again very late, and when he awoke Doctor Hugh was sitting at hand. There was already by this time something beautifully familiar in him.

"Don't think I've turned out your physician," he said; "I'm acting with his consent. He has been here and seen you. Somehow he seems to trust me. I told him how we happened to come together yesterday, and he recognises that I've a peculiar right."

Dencombe felt his own face pressing. "How have you squared the Countess?"

The young man blushed a little, but turned it off. "Oh never mind the Countess!"

"You told me she was very exacting."

Doctor Hugh had a wait. "So she is."

"And Miss Vernham's an *intrigante*."

"How do you know that?"

"I know everything. One *has* to, to write decently!"

"I think she's mad," said limpid Doctor Hugh.

"Well, don't quarrel with the Countess—she's a present help to you."

"I don't quarrel," Doctor Hugh returned. "But I don't get on with silly women." Presently he added: "You seem very much alone."

"That often happens at my age. I've outlived, I've lost by the way."

Doctor Hugh faltered; then surmounting a soft scruple: "Whom have you lost?"

"Every one."

"Ah no," the young man breathed, laying a hand on his arm.

"I once had a wife—I once had a son. My wife died when my child was born, and my boy, at school, was carried off by typhoid."

"I wish I'd been there!" cried Doctor Hugh.

"Well—if you're here!" Dencombe answered with a smile that, in spite of dimness, showed how he valued being sure of his companion's whereabouts.

"You talk strangely of your age. You're not old."

"Hypocrite—so early!"

"I speak physiologically."

"That's the way I've been speaking for the last five years, and it's exactly what I've been saying to myself. It isn't till we *are* old that we begin to tell ourselves we're not."

"Yet I know I myself am young," Doctor Hugh returned.

"Not so well as I!" laughed his patient, whose visitor indeed would have established the truth in question by the honesty with which he changed the point of view, remarking that it must be one of the charms of age—at any rate in the case of high distinction—to feel that one has laboured and achieved. Doctor Hugh employed the common phrase about earning one's rest, and it made poor Dencombe for an instant almost angry. He recovered himself, however, to explain, lucidly enough, that if, ungraciously, he knew nothing of such a balm, it was doubtless because he had wasted inestimable years. He had followed literature from the first, but he had taken a lifetime to get abreast of her. Only today at last had he begun to *see*, so that all he had hitherto shown was a movement without a direction. He had ripened too late and was so clumsily constituted that he had had to teach himself by mistakes.

"I prefer your flowers then to other people's fruit, and your mistakes to other people's successes," said gallant Doctor Hugh. "It's for your mistakes I admire you."

"You're happy—you don't know," Dencombe answered.

Looking at his watch the young man had got up; he named the hour of the afternoon at which he would return. Dencombe warned him against committing himself too deeply, and expressed again all his dread of making him neglect the Countess—perhaps incur her displeasure.

"I want to be like you—I want to learn by mistakes!" Doctor Hugh laughed.

"Take care you don't make too grave a one! But do come back," Dencombe added with the glimmer of a new idea.

"You should have had more vanity!" His friend spoke as if he knew the exact amount required to make a man of letters normal.

"No, no—I only should have had more time. I want another go."

"Another go?"

"I want an extension."

"An extension?" Again Doctor Hugh repeated Dencombe's words, with which he seemed to have been struck.

"Don't you know?—I want to what they call 'live.' "

The young man, for good-bye, had taken his hand, which closed with a certain force. They looked at each other hard. "You *will* live," said Doctor Hugh.

"Don't be superficial. It's too serious!"

"You *shall* live!" Dencombe's visitor declared, turning pale.

"Ah that's better!" And as he retired the invalid, with a troubled laugh, sank gratefully back.

All that day and all the following night he wondered if it mightn't be arranged. His doctor came again, his servant was attentive, but it was to his confident young friend that he felt himself mentally appeal. His collapse on the cliff was plausibly explained and his liberation, on a better basis, promised for the morrow; meanwhile, however, the intensity of his meditations kept him tranquil and made him indifferent. The idea that occupied him was none the less absorbing because it was a morbid fancy. Here was a clever son of the age, ingenious and ardent, who happened to have set him up for connoisseurs to worship. This servant of his altar had all the new learning in science and all the old reverence in faith; wouldn't he therefore put his knowledge at the disposal of his sympathy, his craft at the disposal of his love? Couldn't he be trusted to invent a remedy for a poor artist to whose art he had paid a tribute? If he couldn't the alternative was hard: Dencombe would have to surrender to silence unvindicated and undivined. The rest of the day and all the next he toyed in secret with this sweet futility. Who would work the miracle for him but the young man who could combine such lucidity with such passion? He thought of the fairy-tales of science and charmed himself into forgetting that he looked for a magic that was not of this world. Doctor Hugh was an apparition, and that placed him above the law. He came and went while his patient, who now sat up, followed him with supplicating eyes. The interest of knowing the great author had made the young man begin "The Middle Years" afresh and would help him to find a richer sense between its covers. Dencombe had told him what he "tried for"; with all his intelligence, on a first perusal, Doctor Hugh had failed to guess it. The baffled celebrity wondered then who in the world *would* guess it: he was amused once more at the diffused massive weight that could be thrown into the missing of an intention. Yet he wouldn't rail at the general mind to-day—consoling as that ever had been: the revelation of his own slowness had seemed to make all stupidity sacred.

Doctor Hugh, after a little, was visibly worried, confessing, on enquiry, to a source of embarrassment at home. "Stick to the Countess—don't mind me," Dencombe said repeatedly; for his companion was frank enough about the large lady's attitude. She was so jealous that she had fallen ill—she resented such a breach of allegiance. She paid so much for his fidelity that she must have it all: she refused him the right to other sympathies, charged him with scheming to make her die alone, for it was needless to point out how little Miss Vernham was a resource in trouble. When Doctor Hugh mentioned that the Countess would already have left Bournemouth if he hadn't kept her in bed, poor Dencombe held his arm tighter and said with decision: "Take her straight away." They had gone out together, walking back to the sheltered nook in which, the other day, they had met. The young man, who had given his companion a personal support, declared with emphasis that his conscience was clear—he could ride two horses at once. Didn't he dream for his future of a time when he should have to ride five hundred? Longing equally for virtue, Dencombe replied that in that golden age no patient would pretend to have contracted with him for his whole attention. On the part of the Countess wasn't such an avidity lawful? Doctor Hugh denied it, said there was no contract, but only a free understanding, and that a sordid servitude was impossible to a generous spirit: he liked moreover to talk about art, and that was the subject on which, this time, as they sat together on the sunny bench, he tried most to engage the author of "The Middle Years." Dencombe, soaring again a little on the weak wings of convalescence and still haunted by that happy notion of an organised rescue, found another strain of eloquence to plead the cause of a certain splendid "last manner," the very citadel, as it would prove, of his reputation, the stronghold into which his real treasure would be gathered. While his listener gave up the morning and the great still sea ostensibly waited he had a wondrous explanatory hour. Even for himself he was inspired as he told what his treasure would consist of; the precious metals he would dig from the mine, the jewels rare, strings of pearls, he would hang between the columns of his temple. He was wondrous for himself, so thick his convictions crowded, but still more wondrous for Doctor Hugh, who assured him none the less that the very pages he had just published were already encrusted with gems. This admirer, however, panted for the combinations to come and, before the face of the beautiful day, renewed to Dencombe his guarantee that his profession would hold itself responsible for such a life. Then he suddenly clapped his hand upon his watch-pocket and asked leave to absent himself for half an hour. Dencombe waited there for his return, but was at last recalled to the actual by the fall of a shadow across the ground. The shadow darkened into that of Miss Vernham, the young lady in attendance on the Countess; whom Dencombe, recognising her, perceived so clearly to have come to speak to him that he rose from his bench to acknowledge the civility. Miss Vernham indeed proved not particularly civil; she looked strangely agitated, and her type was now unmistakeable.

"Excuse me if I do ask," she said, "whether it's too much to hope that you may be induced to leave Doctor Hugh alone." Then before our poor friend, greatly disconcerted, could protest: "You ought to be informed that you stand in his light—that you may do him a terrible injury."

"Do you mean by causing the Countess to dispense with his services?"

"By causing her to disinherit him." Dencombe stared at this, and Miss Vernham pursued, in the gratification of seeing she could produce an impression: "It has depended on himself to come into something very handsome. He has had a grand prospect, but I think you've succeeded in spoiling it."

"Not intentionally, I assure you. Is there no hope the accident may be repaired?" Dencombe asked.

"She was ready to do anything for him. She takes great fancies, she lets herself go—it's her way. She has no relations, she's free to dispose of her money, and she's very ill," said Miss Vernham for a climax.

"I'm very sorry to hear it," Dencombe stammered.

"Wouldn't it be possible for you to leave Bournemouth? That's what I've come to see about."

He sank to his bench. "I'm very ill myself, but I'll try!"

Miss Vernham still stood there with her colourless eyes and the brutality of her good conscience. "Before it's too late, please!" she said; and with this she turned her back, in order, quickly, as if it had been a business to which she could spare but a precious moment, to pass out of his sight.

Oh yes, after this Dencombe was certainly very ill. Miss Vernham had upset him with her rough fierce news; it was the sharpest shock to him to discover what was at stake for a penniless young man of fine parts. He sat trembling on his bench, staring at the waste of waters, feeling sick with the directness of the blow. He was indeed too weak, too unsteady, too alarmed; but he would make the effort to get away, for he couldn't accept the guilt of interference and his honour was really involved. He would hobble home, at any rate, and then think what was to be done. He made his way back to the hotel and, as he went, had a characteristic vision of Miss Vernham's great motive. The Countess hated women of course—Dencombe was lucid about that; so the hungry pianist had no personal hopes and could only console herself with the bold conception of helping Doctor Hugh in order to marry him after he should get his money or else induce him to recognise her claim for compensation and buy her off. If she had befriended him at a fruitful crisis he would really, as a man of delicacy—and she knew what to think of that point—have to reckon with her.

At the hotel Dencombe's servant insisted on his going back to bed. The invalid had talked about catching a train and had begun with orders to pack; after which his racked nerves had yielded to a sense of sickness. He consented to see his physician, who immediately was sent for, but he wished it to be understood that his door was irrevocably closed to Doctor Hugh. He had his plan, which was so fine that he rejoiced in it after getting back to bed.

Doctor Hugh, suddenly finding himself snubbed without mercy, would, in natural disgust and to the joy of Miss Vernham, renew his allegiance to the Countess. When his physician arrived Dencombe learned that he was feverish and that this was very wrong: he was to cultivate calmness and try, if possible, not to think. For the rest of the day he wooed stupidity; but there was an ache that kept him sentient, the probable sacrifice of his "extension," the limit of his course. His medical adviser was anything but pleased: his successive relapses were ominous. He charged this personage to put out a strong hand and take Doctor Hugh off his mind—it would contribute so much to his being quiet. The agitating name, in his room, was not mentioned again, but his security was a smothered fear, and it was not confirmed by the receipt, at ten o'clock that evening, of a telegram which his servant opened and read him and to which, with an address in London, the signature of Miss Vernham was attached. "Beseech you to use all influence to make our friend join us here in the morning. Countess much the worse for dreadful journey, but everything may still be saved." The two ladies had gathered themselves up and had been capable in the afternoon of a spiteful revolution. They had started for the capital, and if the elder one, as Miss Vernham had announced, was very ill, she had wished to make it clear that she was proportionately reckless. Poor Dencombe, who was not reckless and who only desired that everything should indeed be "saved," sent this missive straight off to the young man's lodging and had on the morrow the pleasure of knowing that he had quitted Bournemouth by an early train.

Two days later he pressed in with a copy of a literary journal in his hand. He had returned because he was anxious and for the pleasure of flourishing the great review of "The Middle Years." Here at least was something adequate—it rose to the occasion; it was an acclamation, a reparation, a critical attempt to place the author in the niche he had fairly won. Dencombe accepted and submitted; he made neither objection nor enquiry, for old complications had returned and he had had two dismal days. He was convinced not only that he should never again leave his bed, so that his young friend might pardonably remain, but that the demand he should make on the patience of beholders would be of the most moderate. Doctor Hugh had been to town, and he tried to find in his eyes some confession that the Countess was pacified and his legacy clinched; but all he could see there was the light of his juvenile joy in two or three of the phrases of the newspaper. Dencombe couldn't read them, but when his visitor had insisted on repeating them more than once he was able to shake an unintoxicated head. "Ah no—but they would have been true of what I *could* have done!"

"What people 'could have done' is mainly what they've in fact done," Doctor Hugh contended.

"Mainly, yes; but I've been an idiot!" Dencombe said.

Doctor Hugh did remain; the end was coming fast. Two days later his patient observed to him, by way of the feeblest of jokes, that there would now be no question whatever of a second chance. At this the young man stared; then he exclaimed: "Why it has come to pass—it has come to pass! The second chance has been the public's—the chance to find the point of view, to pick up the pearl!"

"Oh the pearl!" poor Dencombe uneasily sighed. A smile as cold as a winter sunset flickered on his drawn lips as he added: "The pearl is the unwritten—the pearl is the unalloyed, the *rest,* the lost!"

From that hour he was less and less present, heedless to all appearance of what went on round him. His disease was definitely mortal, of an action as relentless, after the short arrest that had enabled him to fall in with Doctor Hugh, as a leak in a great ship. Sinking steadily, though this visitor, a man of rare resources, now cordially approved by his physician, showed endless art in guarding him from pain, poor Dencombe kept no reckoning of favour or neglect, betrayed no symptom of regret or speculation. Yet toward the last he gave a sign of having noticed how for two days Doctor Hugh hadn't been in his room, a sign that consisted of his suddenly opening his eyes to put a question. Had he spent those days with the Countess?

"The Countess is dead," said Doctor Hugh. "I knew that in a particular contingency she wouldn't resist. I went to her grave."

Dencombe's eyes opened wider. "She left you 'something handsome'?"

The young man gave a laugh almost too light for a chamber of woe. "Never a penny. She roundly cursed me."

"Cursed you?" Dencombe wailed.

"For giving her up. I gave her up for *you.* I had to choose," his companion explained.

"You chose to let a fortune go?"

"I chose to accept, whatever they might be, the consequences of my infatuation," smiled Doctor Hugh. Then as a larger pleasantry: "The fortune be hanged! It's your own fault if I can't get your things out of my head."

The immediate tribute to his humour was a long bewildered moan; after which, for many hours, many days, Dencombe lay motionless and absent. A response so absolute, such a glimpse of a definite result and such a sense of credit, worked together in his mind and, producing a strange commotion, slowly altered and transfigured his despair. The sense of cold submersion left him—he seemed to float without an effort. The incident was extraordinary as evidence, and it shed an intenser light. At the last he signed to Doctor Hugh to listen and, when he was down on his knees by the pillow, brought him very near. "You've made me think it all a delusion."

"Not your glory, my dear friend," stammered the young man.

"Not my glory—what there is of it! It *is* glory—to have been tested, to have had our little quality and cast our little spell. The thing is to have made somebody care. You happen to be crazy of course, but that doesn't affect the law."

"You're a great success!" said Doctor Hugh, putting into his young voice the ring of a marriage-bell.

Dencombe lay taking this in; then he gathered strength to speak once more. "A second chance—*that's* the delusion. There never was to be but one. We work in the dark—we do what we can—we give what we have. Our doubt is our passion and our passion is our task. The rest is the madness of art."

"If you've doubted, if you've despaired, you've always 'done' it," his visitor subtly argued.

"We've done something or other," Dencombe conceded.

"Something or other is everything. It's the feasible. It's *you!*"

"Comforter!" poor Dencombe ironically sighed.

"But it's true," insisted his friend.

"It's true. It's frustration that doesn't count."

"Frustration's only life," said Doctor Hugh.

"Yes, it's what passes." Poor Dencombe was barely audible, but he had marked with the words the virtual end of his first and only chance.

JACK LONDON
(1876–1916)

Hardly a refined literary theorist like Henry James, Jack London was as determined as James to make himself into a writer of significance, influence, and wealth. The prodigious regimen to which London subjected himself as a young man gave him an autodidact's stubborn faith in his own powers, which seems to have deserted him only at the very end of his foreshortened, feverishly productive career. Boasting that he wrote solely for money, London forced himself to produce a minimum of one thousand publishable words a day, six days a week; he died an alcoholic and a probable suicide, aged forty, by which time he was the highest paid American writer of the era and a world-renowned literary celebrity.

Born in San Francisco to an astrologer and a spiritualist-music teacher, Jack London supported himself, from earliest youth, in a variety of menial jobs. He traveled widely and restlessly, spending the winter of 1897–98 in the Klondike in a futile search for gold; he served time in jail for vagrancy; he became a disciple of Marx on the one hand and of Nietzsche and Darwin on the other. His obsession was the dramatization, in often brutally graphic terms, as in "In a Far Country" and the famous "To Build a Fire," of man's fate: to be a thinking creature of flesh in a supremely indifferent universe.

When London writes most vividly and powerfully, there is no one quite like him. Perhaps because his most characteristic works do not lend themselves to literary analysis, he tends to be undervalued in this country. Through the world, however, his most popular titles remain The Call of the Wild *(1903),* The Sea-Wolf *(1904),* White Fang *(1906), and the autobiographical* Martin Eden *(1909).*

In a Far Country

When a man journeys into a far country, he must be prepared to forget many of the things he has learned, and to acquire such customs as are inherent with existence in the new land; he must abandon the old ideals and the old gods, and oftentimes he must reverse the very codes by which his conduct has hitherto been shaped. To those who have the protean faculty of adaptability, the novelty of such change may even be a source of pleasure; but to those who happen to be hardened to the ruts in which they were created, the pressure of the altered environment is unbearable, and they chafe in body and in spirit under the new restrictions which they do not understand. This chafing is bound to act and react, producing divers evils and leading to various misfortunes. It were better for the man who cannot fit himself to the new groove to return to his own country; if he delay too long, he will surely die.

The man who turns his back upon the comforts of an elder civilization, to face the savage youth, the primordial simplicity of the North, may estimate success at an inverse ratio to the quantity and quality of his hopelessly fixed habits. He will soon discover, if he be a fit candidate, that the material habits are the less important. The exchange of such things as a dainty menu for rough fare, of the stiff leather shoe for the soft, shapeless moccasin, of the feather bed for a couch in the snow, is after all a very easy matter. But his pinch will come in learning properly to shape his mind's attitude toward all things, and especially toward his fellow man. For the courtesies of ordinary life, he must substitute unselfishness, forbearance, and tolerance. Thus, and thus only, can he gain that pearl of great price—true comradeship. He must not say "Thank you"; he must mean it without opening his mouth, and prove it by responding in kind. In short, he must substitute the deed for the word, the spirit for the letter.

When the world rang with the tale of Arctic gold, and the lure of the North gripped the heartstrings of men, Carter Weatherbee threw up his snug clerkship, turned the half of his savings over to his wife, and with the remainder bought an outfit. There was no romance in his nature—the bondage of commerce had crushed all that; he was simply tired of the ceaseless grind, and wished to risk great hazards in view of corresponding returns. Like many another fool, disdaining the old trails used by the Northland pioneers for a score of years, he hurried to Edmonton in the spring of the year; and there, unluckily for his soul's welfare, he allied himself with a party of men.

There was nothing unusual about this party, except its plans. Even its goal, like that of all the other parties, was the Klondike. But the route it had mapped out to attain that goal took away the breath of the hardiest native, born and bred to the vicissitudes of the Northwest. Even Jacques Baptiste, born of a Chippewa woman and a renegade *voyageur* (having raised his first whimpers in a deerskin lodge north of the sixty-fifth parallel, and had the same hushed by blissful sucks of raw tallow), was surprised. Though he sold his services to them and agreed to travel even to the never-opening ice, he shook his head ominously whenever his advice was asked.

Percy Cuthfert's evil star must have been in the ascendant, for he, too, joined this company of argonauts. He was an ordinary man, with a bank account as deep as his culture, which is saying a good deal. He had no reason to embark on such a venture—no reason in the world, save that he suffered from an abnormal development of sentimentality. He mistook this for the true spirit of romance and adventure. Many another man has done the like, and made as fatal a mistake.

The first break-up of spring found the party following the ice-run of Elk River. It was an imposing fleet, for the outfit was large, and they were accompanied by a disreputable contingent of half-breed *voyageurs* with their women and children. Day in and day out, they labored with the bateaux and canoes, fought mosquitoes and other kindred pests, or sweated and swore at the portages. Severe toil like this lays a man naked to the very roots of his soul, and ere Lake Athabasca was lost in the south, each member of the party had hoisted his true colors.

The two shirks and chronic grumblers were Carter Weatherbee and Percy Cuthfert. The whole party complained less of its aches and pains than did either of them. Not once did they volunteer for the thousand and one petty duties of the camp. A bucket of water to be brought, an extra armful of wood to be chopped, the dishes to be washed and wiped, a search to be made through the outfit for some suddenly indispensable article—and these two effete scions of civilization discovered sprains or blisters requiring instant attention. They were the first to turn in at night, with score of tasks yet undone; the last to turn out in the morning, when the start should be in readiness before the breakfast was begun. They were the first to fall to at meal-time, the last to have a hand in the cooking; the first to dive for a slim delicacy, the last to discover they had added to their own another man's share. If they toiled at the oars, they slyly cut the water at each stroke and allowed the boat's momentum to float up the blade. They thought nobody noticed; but their comrades swore under their breaths and grew to hate them, while Jacques Baptiste sneered openly and damned them from morning till night. But Jacques Baptiste was no gentleman.

At the Great Slave, Hudson Bay dogs were purchased, and the fleet sank to the guards with its added burden of dried fish and pemican. Then canoe and bateau answered to the swift current of the Mackenzie, and they plunged into the Great Barren Ground. Every likely-looking "feeder" was prospected, but the elusive "pay-dirt" danced ever to the north. At the Great Bear, overcome by the common dread of the Unknown Lands, their *voyageurs* began to desert, and Fort of Good Hope saw the last and bravest bending to the tow-lines as they bucked the current down which they had so treacherously glided. Jacques Baptiste alone remained. Had he not sworn to travel even to the never-opening ice?

The lying charts, compiled in main from hearsay, were now constantly consulted. And they felt the need of hurry, for the sun had already passed its northern solstice and was leading the winter south again. Skirting the shores of the bay, where the Mackenzie disembogues into the Arctic Ocean, they entered the mouth of the Little Peel River. Then began the arduous up-stream toil, and the two Incapables fared worse than ever. Tow-line and pole, paddle and tump-line, rapids and portages—such tortures served to give the one a deep disgust for great hazards, and printed for the other a fiery text on the true romance of adventure. One day they waxed mutinous, and being vilely cursed by Jacques Baptiste, turned, as worms sometimes will. But the half-breed thrashed the twain, and sent them, bruised and bleeding, about their work. It was the first time either had been man-handled.

Abandoning their river craft at the headwaters of the Little Peel, they consumed the rest of the summer in the great portage over the Mackenzie watershed to the West Rat. This little stream fed the Porcupine, which in turn joined the Yukon where that mighty highway of the North countermarches on the Arctic Circle. But they had lost in the race with winter, and one day they tied their rafts to the thick eddy-ice and hurried their goods ashore. That night the river jammed and broke several times; the following morning it had fallen asleep for good.

"We can't be more'n four hundred miles from the Yukon," concluded Sloper, multiplying his thumb nails by the scale of the map. The council, in which the two Incapables had whined to excellent disadvantage, was drawing to a close.

"Hudson Bay Post, long time ago. No use um now." Jacques Baptiste's father had made the trip for the Fur Company in the old days, incidentally marking the trail with a couple of frozen toes.

"Sufferin' cracky!" cried another of the party. "No whites?"

"Nary white," Sloper sententiously affirmed; "but it's only five hundred more up the Yukon to Dawson. Call it a rough thousand from here."

Weatherbee and Cuthfert groaned in chorus.

"How long'll that take, Baptiste?"

The half-breed figured for a moment. "Workum like hell, no man play out, ten—twenty—forty—fifty days. Um babies come" (designating the Incapables), "no can tell. Mebbe when hell freeze over; mebbe not then."

The manufacture of snowshoes and moccasins ceased. Somebody called the name of an absent member, who came out of an ancient cabin at the edge of the camp-fire and joined them. The cabin was one of the many mysteries which lurk in the vast recesses of the North. Built when and by whom, no man could tell. Two graves in the open, piled high with stones, perhaps contained the secret of those early wanderers. But whose hand had piled the stones?

The moment had come. Jacques Baptiste paused in the fitting of a harness and pinned the struggling dog in the snow. The cook made mute protest for delay, threw a handful of bacon into a noisy pot of beans, then came to attention. Sloper rose to his feet. His body was a ludicrous contrast to the healthy physiques of the Incapables. Yellow and weak, fleeing from a South American fever-hole, he had not broken his flight across the zones, and was still able to toil with men. His weight was probably ninety pounds, with the heavy hunting-knife thrown in, and his grizzled hair told of a prime which had ceased to be. The fresh young muscles of either Weatherbee or Cuthfert were equal to ten times the endeavor of his; yet he could walk them into the earth in a day's journey. And all this day he had whipped his stronger comrades into venturing a thousand miles of the stiffest hardship man can conceive. He was the incarnation of the unrest of his race, and the old Teutonic stubbornness, dashed with the quick grasp and action of the Yankee, held the flesh in the bondage of the spirit.

"All those in favor of going on with the dogs as soon as the ice sets, say ay."

"Ay!" rang out eight voices—voices destined to string a trail of oaths along many a hundred miles of pain.

"Contrary minded?"

"No!" For the first time the Incapables were united without some compromise of personal interests.

"And what are you going to do about it?" Weatherbee added belligerently.

"Majority rule! Majority rule!" clamored the rest of the party.

"I know the expedition is liable to fall through if you don't come," Sloper replied sweetly; "but I guess, if we try real hard, we can manage to do without you. What do you say, boys?"

The sentiment was cheered to the echo.

"But I say, you know," Cuthfert ventured apprehensively; "what's a chap like me to do?"

"Ain't you coming with us?"

"No-o."

"Then do as you damn well please. We won't have nothing to say."

"Kind o' calkilate yuh might settle it with that canoodlin' pardner of yourn," suggested a heavy-going Westerner from the Dakotas, at the same time pointing out Weatherbee. "He'll be shore to ask yuh what yur a-goin' to do when it comes to cookin' an' gatherin' the wood."

"Then we'll consider it all arranged," concluded Sloper. "We'll pull out to-morrow, if we camp within five miles—just to get everything in running order and remember if we've forgotten anything."

The sleds groaned by on their steel-shod runners, and the dogs strained low in the harnesses in which they were born to die. Jacques Baptiste paused by the side of Sloper to get a last glimpse of the cabin. The smoke curled up pathetically from the Yukon stovepipe. The two Incapables were watching them from the doorway.

Sloper laid his hand on the other's shoulder.

"Jacques Baptiste, did you ever hear of the Kilkenny cats?"

The half-breed shook his head.

"Well, my friend and good comrade, the Kilkenny cats fought till neither hide, nor hair, nor yowl, was left. You understand?—till nothing was left. Very good. Now, these two men don't like work. They'll be all alone in that cabin all winter—a mighty long, dark winter. Kilkenny cats—well?"

The Frenchman in Baptiste shrugged his shoulders, but the Indian in him was silent. Nevertheless, it was an eloquent shrug, pregnant with prophecy.

Things prospered in the little cabin at first. The rough badinage of their comrades had made Weatherbee and Cuthfert conscious of the mutual responsibility which had devolved upon them; besides, there was not so much work after all for two healthy men. And the removal of the cruel whiphand, or in other words the bulldozing half-breed, had brought with it a joyous reaction. At first, each strove to outdo the other, and they performed petty tasks with an unction which would have opened the eyes of their comrades who were now wearing out bodies and souls on the Long Trail.

All care was banished. The forest, which shouldered in upon them from three sides, was an inexhaustible woodyard. A few yards from their door slept the Porcupine, and a hole through its winter robe formed a bubbling spring of water, crystal clear and painfully cold. But they soon grew to find fault with even that. The hole would persist in freezing up, and thus gave them many a miserable hour of ice-chopping. The unknown builders of the cabin had extended the sidelogs so as to support a cache at the rear. In this was stored the bulk of the party's provisions. Food there was, without stint, for three times the men who were fated to live upon it. But the most of it was of the kind which built up brawn and sinew, but did not tickle the palate. True, there was sugar in plenty for two ordinary men; but these two were little else than children. They early discovered the virtues of hot water judiciously saturated with sugar, and they prodigally swam their flapjacks and soaked their crusts in the rich, white syrup. Then coffee and tea, and especially the dried fruits, made disastrous inroads upon it. The first words they had were over the sugar question. And it is a really serious thing when two men, wholly dependent upon each other for company, begin to quarrel.

Weatherbee loved to discourse blatantly on politics, while Cuthfert, who had been prone to clip his coupons and let the commonwealth jog on as best it might, either ignored the subject or delivered himself of startling epigrams. But the clerk was too obtuse to appreciate the clever shaping of thought, and this waste of ammunition irritated Cuthfert. He had been used to blinding people by his brilliancy, and it worked him quite a hardship, this loss of an audience. He felt personally aggrieved and unconsciously held his muttonhead companion responsible for it.

Save existence, they had nothing in common—came in touch on no single point. Weatherbee was a clerk who had known naught but clerking all his life; Cuthfert was a master of arts, a dabbler in oils, and had written not a little. The one was a lower-class man who considered himself a gentleman, and the other was a gentleman who knew himself to be such. From this it may be remarked that a man can be a gentleman without possessing the first instinct of true comradeship. The clerk was as sensuous as the other was aesthetic, and his love adventures, told at great length and chiefly coined from his imagination, affected the supersensitive master of arts in the same way as so many whiffs of sewer gas. He deemed the clerk a filthy, uncultured brute, whose place was in the muck with the swine, and told him so; and he was reciprocally informed that he was a milk-and-water sissy and a cad. Weatherbee could not have defined "cad" for his life; but it satisfied its purpose, which after all seems the main point in life.

Weatherbee flatted every third note and sang such songs as "The Boston Burglar" and "The Handsome Cabin Boy," for hours at a time, while Cuthfert wept with rage, till he could stand it no longer and fled into the outer cold. But there was no escape. The intense frost could not be endured for long at a time, and the little cabin crowded them—beds, stove, table, and all—into a space of ten by twelve. The very presence of either became a personal affront to the other, and they lapsed into sullen silences which increased in length and strength as the days went by. Occasionally, the flash of an eye or the curl of a lip got the better of them, though they strove to wholly ignore each other during these mute periods. And a great wonder sprang up in the breast of each, as to how God had ever come to create the other.

With little to do, time became an intolerable burden to them. This naturally made them still lazier. They sank into a physical lethargy which there was no escaping, and which made them rebel at the performance of the smallest chore. One morning when it was his turn to cook the common breakfast, Weatherbee rolled out of his blankets, and to the snoring of his companion, lighted first the slush-lamp and then the fire. The kettles were frozen hard, and there was no water in the cabin with which to wash. But he did not mind that. Waiting for it to thaw, he sliced the bacon and plunged into the hateful task of bread-making. Cuthfert had been slyly watching through his half-closed lids. Consequently there was a scene, in which they fervently blessed each other, and agreed, thenceforth, that each do his own cooking. A week later, Cuthfert neglected his morning ablutions, but none the less complacently ate the meal which he had cooked. Weatherbee grinned. After that the foolish custom of washing passed out of their lives.

As the sugar-pile and other little luxuries dwindled, they began to be afraid they were not getting their proper shares, and in order that they might not be robbed, they fell to gorging themselves. The luxuries suffered in this gluttonous contest, as did also the men. In the absence of fresh vegetables and exercise, their blood became impoverished, and a loathsome, purplish rash crept over their bodies. Yet they refused to heed the warning. Next, their muscles and joints began to swell, the flesh turning black, while their mouths, gums, and lips took on the color of rich cream. Instead of being drawn together by their misery, each gloated over the other's symptoms as the scurvy took its course.

They lost all regard for personal appearance, and for that matter, common decency. The cabin became a pigpen, and never once were the beds made or fresh pine boughs laid underneath. Yet they could not keep to their blankets, as they would have wished; for the frost was inexorable, and the fire box consumed much fuel. The hair of their heads and faces grew long and shaggy, while their garments would have disgusted a ragpicker. But they did not care. They were sick, and there was no one to see; besides, it was very painful to move about.

To all this was added a new trouble—the Fear of the North. This Fear was the joint child of the Great Cold and the Great Silence, and was born in the darkness of December, when the sun dipped below the horizon for good. It affected them according to their natures. Weatherbee fell prey to the grosser superstitions, and did his best to resurrect the spirits which slept in the forgotten graves. It was a fascinating thing, and in his dreams they came to him from out of the cold, and snuggled into his blankets, and told him of their toils and troubles ere they died. He shrank away from the clammy contact as they drew closer and twined their frozen limbs about him, and when they whispered in his ear of things to come, the cabin rang with his frightened shrieks. Cuthfert did not understand—for they no longer spoke—and when thus awakened he invariably grabbed for his revolver. Then he would sit up in bed, shivering nervously, with the weapon trained on the unconscious dreamer. Cuthfert deemed the man going mad, and so came to fear for his life.

His own malady assumed a less concrete form. The mysterious artisan who had laid the cabin, log by log, had pegged a wind-vane to the ridge-pole. Cuthfert noticed it always pointed south, and one day, irritated by its steadfastness of purpose, he turned it toward the east. He watched eagerly, but never a breath came by to disturb it. Then he turned the vane to the north, swearing never again to touch it till the wind did blow. But the air frightened him with its unearthly calm, and he often rose in the middle of the night to see if the vane had veered—ten degrees would have satisfied him. But no, it poised above him as unchangeable as fate. His imagination ran riot, till it became to him a fetich. Sometimes he followed the path it pointed across the dismal dominions, and allowed his soul to become saturated with the Fear. He dwelt upon the unseen and the unknown till the burden of eternity appeared to be crushing him. Everything in the Northland had that crushing effect—the absence of life and motion; the darkness; the infinite peace of the brooding land; the ghastly silence, which made the echo of each heart-beat a sacrilege; the solemn forest which seemed to guard an awful, inexpressible something, which neither word nor thought could compass.

The world he had so recently left, with its busy nations and great enterprises, seemed very far away. Recollections occasionally obtruded—recollections of marts and galleries and crowded thoroughfares, of evening dress and social functions, of good men and dear women he had known—but they were dim memories of a life he had lived long centuries agone, on some other planet. This phantasm was the Reality. Standing beneath the wind-vane, his eyes fixed on the polar skies, he could not bring himself to realize that the Southland really existed, that at that very moment it was a-roar with life and action. There was no Southland, no men being born of women, no giving and taking in marriage. Beyond his bleak sky-line there stretched vast solitudes, and beyond these still vaster solitudes. There were no lands of sunshine, heavy with the perfume of flowers. Such things were only old dreams of paradise. The sunlands of the West and the spicelands of the East, the smiling Arcadias and blissful Islands of the Blest—ha! ha! His laughter split the void and shocked him with its unwonted sound. There was no sun. This was the Universe, dead and cold and dark, and he its only citizen. Weatherbee? At such moments Weatherbee did not count. He was a Caliban, a monstrous phantom, fettered to him for untold ages, the penalty of some forgotten crime.

He lived with Death among the dead, emasculated by the sense of his own insignificance, crushed by the passive mastery of the slumbering ages. The magnitude of all things appalled him. Everything partook of the superlative save himself—the perfect cessation of wind and motion, the immensity of the snow-covered wildness, the height of the sky and the depth of the silence. That wind-vane—if it would only move. If a thunderbolt would fall, or the forest flare up in flame. The rolling up of the heavens as a scroll, the crash of Doom—anything, anything! But no, nothing moved; the Silence crowded in, and the Fear of the North laid icy fingers on his heart.

Once, like another Crusoe, by the edge of the river he came upon a track—the faint tracery of a snowshoe rabbit on the delicate snow-crust. It was a revelation. There was life in the Northland. He would follow it, look upon it, gloat over it. He forgot his swollen muscles, plunging through the deep snow in an ecstasy of anticipation. The forest swallowed him up, and the brief midday twilight vanished; but he pursued his quest till exhausted nature asserted itself and laid him helpless in the snow. There he groaned and cursed his folly, and knew the track to be the fancy of his brain; and late that night he dragged himself into the cabin on hands and knees, his cheeks frozen and a strange numbness about his feet. Weatherbee grinned malevolently, but made no offer to help him. He thrust needles into his toes and thawed them out by the stove. A week later mortification set in.

But the clerk had his own troubles. The dead men came out of their graves more frequently now, and rarely left him, waking or sleeping. He grew to wait and dread their coming, never passing the twin cairns without a shudder. One night they came to him in his sleep and led him forth to an appointed task. Frightened into inarticulate horror, he awoke between the heaps of stones and fled wildly to the cabin. But he had lain there for some time, for his feet and cheeks were also frozen.

Sometimes he became frantic at their insistent presence, and danced about the cabin, cutting the empty air with an axe, and smashing everything within reach. During these ghostly encounters, Cuthfert huddled into his blankets and followed the madman about with a cocked revolver, ready to shoot him if he came too near. But, recovering from one of these spells, the clerk noticed the weapon trained upon him. His suspicions were aroused, and thenceforth he, too, lived in fear of his life. They watched each other closely after that, and faced about in startled fright whenever either passed behind the other's back. The apprehensiveness became a mania which controlled them even in their sleep. Through mutual fear they tacitly let the slush-lamp burn all night, and saw to a plentiful supply of bacon-grease before retiring. The slightest movement on the part of one was sufficient to arouse the other, and many a still watch their gazes countered as they shook beneath their blankets with fingers on the trigger-guards.

What with the Fear of the North, the mental strain, and the ravages of the disease, they lost all semblance of humanity, taking on the appearance of wild beasts, hunted and desperate. Their cheeks and noses, as an aftermath of the freezing, had turned black. Their frozen toes had begun to drop away at the first and second joints. Every movement brought pain, but the fire box was insatiable, wringing a ransom of torture from their miserable bodies. Day in, day out, it demanded its food—a veritable pound of flesh—and they dragged themselves into the forest to chop wood on their knees. Once, crawling thus in search of dry sticks, unknown to each other they entered a thicket from opposite sides. Suddenly, without warning, two peering death's-heads confronted each other. Suffering had so transformed them that recognition was impossible. They sprang to their feet, shrieking with terror, and dashed away on their mangled stumps; and falling at the cabin's door, they clawed and scratched like demons till they discovered their mistake.

Occasionally they lapsed normal, and during one of these sane intervals, the chief bone of contention, the sugar, had been divided equally between them. They guarded their separate sacks, stored up in the cache, with jealous eyes; for there were but a few cupfuls left, and they were totally devoid of faith in each other. But one day Cuthfert made a mistake. Hardly able to move, sick with pain, with his head swimming and eyes blinded, he crept into the cache, sugar canister in hand, and mistook Weatherbee's sack for his own.

January had been born but a few days when this occurred. The sun had some time since passed its lowest southern declination, and at meridian now threw flaunting streaks of yellow light upon the northern sky. On the day following his mistake with the sugar-bag, Cuthfert found himself feeling better, both in body and in spirit. As noontime drew near and the day brightened, he dragged himself outside to feast on the evanescent glow, which was to him an earnest of the sun's future intentions. Weatherbee was also feeling somewhat better, and crawled out beside him. They propped themselves in the snow beneath the moveless wind-vane, and waited.

The stillness of death was about them. In other climes, when nature falls into such moods, there is a subdued air of expectancy, a waiting for some small voice to take up the broken strain. Not so in the North. The two men had lived seeming eons in this ghostly peace. They could remember no song of the past; they could conjure no song of the future. This unearthly calm had always been—the tranquil silence of eternity.

Their eyes were fixed upon the north. Unseen, behind their backs, behind the towering mountains to the south, the sun swept toward the zenith of another sky than theirs. Sole spectators of the mighty canvas, they watched the false dawn slowly grow. A faint flame began to glow and smoulder. It deepened in intensity, ringing the changes of reddish-yellow, purple, and saffron. So bright did it become that Cuthfert thought the sun must surely be behind it—

a miracle, the sun rising in the north! Suddenly, without warning and without fading, the canvas was swept clean. There was no color in the sky. The light had gone out of the day. They caught their breaths in half-sobs. But lo! the air was a-glint with particles of scintillating frost, and there, to the north, the wind-vane lay in vague outline of the snow. A shadow! A shadow! It was exactly midday. They jerked their heads hurriedly to the south. A golden rim peeped over the mountain's snowy shoulder, smiled upon them an instant, then dipped from sight again.

There were tears in their eyes as they sought each other. A strange softening came over them. They felt irresistibly drawn toward each other. The sun was coming back again. It would be with them to-morrow, and the next day, and the next. And it would stay longer every visit, and a time would come when it would ride their heaven day and night, never once dropping below the sky-line. There would be no night. The ice-locked winter would be broken; the winds would blow and the forests answer; the land would bathe in the blessed sunshine, and life renew. Hand in hand, they would quit this horrid dream and journey back to the Southland. They lurched blindly forward, and their hands met—their poor maimed hands, swollen and distorted beneath their mittens.

But the promise was destined to remain unfulfilled. The Northland is the Northland, and men work out their souls by strange rules, which other men, who have not journeyed into far countries, cannot come to understand.

An hour later, Cuthfert put a pan of bread into the oven, and fell to speculating on what the surgeons could do with his feet when he got back. Home did not seem so very far away now. Weatherbee was rummaging in the cache. Of a sudden, he raised a whirlwind of blasphemy, which in turn ceased with startling abruptness. The other man had robbed his sugar-sack. Still, things might have happened differently, had not the two dead men come out from under the stones and hushed the hot words in his throat. They led him quite gently from the cache, which he forgot to close. That consummation was reached; that something they had whispered to him in his dreams was about to happen. They guided him gently, very gently, to the woodpile, where they put the axe in his hands. Then they helped him shove open the cabin door, and he felt sure they shut it after him—at least he heard it slam and the latch fall sharply into place. And he knew they were waiting just without, waiting for him to do his task.

"Carter! I say, Carter!"

Percy Cuthfert was frightened at the look on the clerk's face, and he made haste to put the table between them.

Carter Weatherbee followed, without haste and without enthusiasm. There was neither pity nor passion in his face, but rather the patient, stolid look of one who has certain work to do and goes about it methodically.

"I say, what's the matter?"

The clerk dodged back, cutting off his retreat to the door, but never opening his mouth.

"I say, Carter, I say; let's talk. There's a good chap."

The master of arts was thinking rapidly, now, shaping a skillful flank movement on the bed where his Smith & Wesson lay. Keeping his eyes on the madman, he rolled backward on the bunk, at the same time clutching the pistol.

"Carter!"

The powder flashed full in Weatherbee's face, but he swung his weapon and leaped forward. The axe bit deeply at the base of the spine, and Percy Cuthfert felt all consciousness of his lower limbs leave him. Then the clerk fell heavily upon him, clutching him by the throat with feeble fingers. The sharp bite of the axe had caused Cuthfert to drop the pistol, and as his lungs panted for release, he fumbled aimlessly for it among the blankets. Then he remembered. He slid a hand up the clerk's belt to the sheath-knife; and they drew very close to each other in that last clinch.

Percy Cuthfert felt his strength leave him. The lower portion of his body was useless. The inert weight of Weatherbee crushed him—crushed him and pinned him there like a bear under a trap. The cabin became filled with a familiar odor, and he knew the bread to be burning. Yet what did it matter? He would never need it. And there were all of six cupfuls of sugar in the cache—if he had foreseen this he would not have been so saving the last several days. Would the wind-vane ever move? Why not? Had he not seen the sun to-day? He would go and see. No; it was impossible to move. He had not thought the clerk so heavy a man.

How quickly the cabin cooled! The fire must be out. The cold was forcing in. It must be below zero already, and the ice creeping up the inside of the door. He could not see it, but his past experience enabled him to gauge its progress by the cabin's temperature. The lower hinge must be white ere now. Would the tale of this ever reach the world? How would his friends take it? They would read it over their coffee, most likely, and talk it over at the clubs. He could see them very clearly. "Poor Old Cuthfert," they murmured; "not such a bad sort of a chap, after all." He smiled at their eulogies, and passed on in search of a Turkish bath. It was the same old crowd upon the streets. Strange, they did not notice his moosehide moccasins and tattered German socks! He would take a cab. And after the bath a shave would not be bad. No; he would eat first. Steak, and potatoes, and green things how fresh it all was! And what was that? Squares of honey, streaming liquid amber! But why did they bring so much? Ha! ha! he could never eat it all. Shine! Why certainly. He put his foot on the box. The bootblack looked curiously up at him, and he remembered his moosehide moccasins and went away hastily.

Hark! The wind-vane must be surely spinning. No; a mere singing in his ears. That was all—a mere singing. The ice must have passed the latch by now. More likely the upper hinge was covered. Between the moss-chinked roof-poles, little points of frost began to appear. How slowly they grew! No; not so slowly. There was a new one, and there another. Two—three—four; they were coming too fast to count. There were two growing together. And there, a third had joined them. Why, there were no more spots. They had run together and formed a sheet.

Well, he would have company. If Gabriel ever broke the silence of the North, they would stand together, hand in hand, before the great White Throne. And God would judge them, God would judge them!

Then Percy Cuthfert closed his eyes and dropped off to sleep.

MARY E. WILKINS FREEMAN

(1852–1930)

My first reading of "Old Woman Magoun" gave me one story; my second reading, another. Which is to suggest that there are subtleties of theme beneath the surface of this artfully told "woman's" story that may in fact suggest a critique, from within, of "woman's" sensibility.

Such subtleties, as well as the respectful attentiveness to place, voice, and characters, are typical of the work of this New England writer who, in her time, was a popular success and, along with Edith Wharton, in 1926, elected to membership in the previously all-male National Institute of Arts and Letters. Freeman was also awarded the Howells Medal for Fiction in 1926.

Born in Randolph, Massachusetts, the town in which she would spend most of her life, Mary E. Wilkins Freeman supported herself by writing when her family became destitute. She suffered from nightmares; may have become addicted to sedatives later in her life; had a difficult, late marriage to a doctor who became an alcoholic—yet, when she died at the age of seventy-eight, she had published twenty volumes of adult fiction, both novels and stories, as well as six volumes of children's stories. Her best-known titles are A Humble Romance and Other Stories *(1887) and* A New England Nun and Other Stories *(1891), from which "Old Woman Magoun" is taken. Freeman's story "The Revolt of 'Mother' " is her most frequently anthologized story, but the theme of female revolt, of various degrees of assertion, fuels such diverse stories as "A New England Nun" and "Old Woman Magoun"—the latter delineating a darker, more secret, and deadly, aspect of revolt.*

Old Woman Magoun

The hamlet of Barry's Ford is situated in a sort of high valley among the mountains. Below it the hills lie in moveless curves like a petrified ocean; above it they rise in green-cresting waves which never break. It is *Barry's* Ford because at one time the Barry family was the most important in the place; and *Ford* because just at the beginning of the hamlet the little turbulent Barry River is fordable. There is, however, now a rude bridge across the river.

Old Woman Magoun was largely instrumental in bringing the bridge to pass. She haunted the miserable little grocery, wherein whiskey and hands of tobacco were the most salient features of the stock in trade, and she talked much. She would elbow herself into the midst of a knot of idlers and talk.

"That bridge ought to be built this very summer," said Old Woman Magoun. She spread her strong arms like wings, and sent the loafers, half laughing, half angry, flying in every direction. "If I were a *man*," she said, "I'd go out this very minute and lay the fust log. If I were a passel of lazy men layin' round, I'd start up for once in my life, I would." The men cowered visibly—all except Nelson Barry; he swore under his breath and strode over to the counter.

Old Woman Magoun looked after him majestically. "You can cuss all you want to, Nelson Barry," said she; "I ain't afraid of you. I don't expect you to lay ary log of the bridge, but I'm goin' to have it built this very summer." She did. The weakness of the masculine element in Barry's Ford was laid low before such strenuous feminine assertion.

Old Woman Magoun and some other women planned a treat—two sucking pigs, and pies, and sweet cake—for a reward after the bridge should be finished. They even viewed leniently the increased consumption of ardent spirits.

"It seems queer to me," Old Woman Magoun said to Sally Jinks, "that men can't do nothin' without havin' to drink and chew to keep their sperits up. Lord! I've worked all my life and never done nuther."

"Men is different," said Sally Jinks.

"Yes, they be," assented Old Woman Magoun, with open contempt.

The two women sat on a bench in front of Old Woman Magoun's house, and little Lily Barry, her granddaughter, sat holding her doll on a small mossy stone near by. From where they sat they could see the men at work on the new bridge. It was the last day of the work.

Lily clasped her doll—a poor old rag thing—close to her childish bosom, like a little mother, and her face, round which curled her long yellow hair, was fixed upon the men at work. Little Lily had never been allowed to run with the other children of Barry's Ford. Her grandmother had taught her everything she knew—which was not much, but tending at least to a certain measure of spiritual growth—for she, as it were, poured the goodness of her own soul into this little receptive vase of another. Lily was firmly grounded in her knowledge that it was wrong to lie or steal or disobey her grandmother. She had also learned that one should be very industrious. It was seldom that Lily sat idly holding her doll-baby, but this was a holiday because of the bridge. She looked only a child, although she was nearly fourteen; her mother had been married at sixteen. That is, Old Woman Magoun said that her daughter, Lily's mother, had married at sixteen; there had been rumors, but no one had dared openly gainsay the old woman. She said that her daughter had married Nelson Barry, and he had deserted her. She had lived in her mother's house, and Lily had been born there, and she had died when the baby was only a week old. Lily's father, Nelson Barry, was the fairly dangerous degenerate of a good old family. Nelson's father before him had been bad. He was now the last of the family, with the exception of a sister of feeble intellect, with whom he lived in the old Barry house. He was a middle-aged man, still handsome. The shiftless population of Barry's Ford looked up to him as to an evil deity. They wondered how Old Woman Magoun dared brave him as she did. But Old Woman Magoun had within her a mighty sense of reliance upon herself as being on the right track in the midst of a maze of evil, which gave her courage. Nelson Barry had manifested no interest whatever in his daughter. Lily seldom saw her father. She did not often go to the store which was his favorite haunt. Her grandmother took care that she should not do so.

However, that afternoon she departed from her usual custom and sent Lily to the store.

She came in from the kitchen, whither she had been to baste the roasting pig. "There's no use talkin'," said she, "I've got to have some more salt. I've jest used the very last I had to dredge over that pig. I've got to go to the store."

Sally Jinks looked at Lily. "Why don't you send her?" she asked.

Old Woman Magoun gazed irresolutely at the girl. She was herself very tired. It did not seem to her that she could drag herself up the dusty hill to the store. She glanced with covert resentment at Sally Jinks. She thought that she might offer to go. But Sally Jinks said again, "Why don't you let her go?" and looked with a languid eye at Lily holding her doll on the stone.

Lily was watching the men at work on the bridge, with her childish delight in a spectacle of any kind, when her grandmother addressed her.

"Guess I'll let you go down to the store an' git some salt, Lily," said she.

The girl turned uncomprehending eyes upon her grandmother at the sound of her voice. She had been filled with one of the innocent reveries of childhood. Lily had in her the making of an artist or a poet. Her prolonged childhood went to prove it, and also her retrospective eyes, as clear and blue as blue light itself, which seemed to see past all that she looked upon. She had not come of the old Barry family for nothing. The best of the strain was in her, along with the splendid stanchness in humble lines which she had acquired from her grandmother.

"Put on your hat," said Old Woman Magoun; "the sun is hot, and you might git a headache." She called the girl to her, and put back the shower of fair curls under the rubber band which confined the hat. She gave Lily some money, and watched her knot it into a corner of her little cotton handkerchief. "Be careful you don't lose it," said she, "and don't stop to talk to anybody, for I am in a hurry for that salt. Of course, if anybody speaks to you answer them polite, and then come right along."

Lily started, her pocket-handkerchief weighted with the small silver dangling from one hand, and her rag doll carried over her shoulder like a baby. The absurd travesty of a face peeped forth from Lily's yellow curls. Sally Jinks looked after her with a sniff.

"She ain't goin' to carry that rag doll to the store?" said she.

"She likes to," replied Old Woman Magoun, in a half-shamed yet defiantly extenuating voice.

"Some girls at her age is thinkin' about beaux instead of rag dolls," said Sally Jinks.

The grandmother bristled. "Lily ain't big nor old for her age," said she. "I ain't in any hurry to have her git married. She ain't none too strong."

"She's got a good color," said Sally Jinks. She was crocheting white cotton lace, making her thick fingers fly. She really knew how to do scarcely anything except to crochet that coarse lace; somehow her heavy brain or her fingers had mastered that.

"I know she's got a beautiful color," replied Old Woman Magoun, with an odd mixture of pride and anxiety, "but it comes an' goes."

"I've heard that was a bad sign," remarked Sally Jinks, loosening some thread from her spool.

"Yes, it is," said the grandmother. "She's nothin' but a baby, though she's quicker than most to learn."

Lily Barry went on her way to the store. She was clad in a scanty short frock of blue cotton; her hat was tipped back, forming an oval frame for her innocent face. She was very small, and walked like a child, with the clap-clap of little feet of babyhood. She might have been considered, from her looks, under ten.

Presently she heard footsteps behind her; she turned around a little timidly to see who was coming. When she saw a handsome, well-dressed man, she felt reassured. The man came alongside and glanced down carelessly at first, then his look deepened. He smiled, and Lily saw he was very handsome indeed, and that his smile was not only reassuring but wonderfully sweet and compelling.

"Well, little one," said the man, "where are you bound, you and your dolly?"

"I am going to the store to buy some salt for grandma," replied Lily, in her sweet treble. She looked up in the man's face, and he fairly started at the revelation of its innocent beauty. He regulated his pace by hers, and the two went on together. The man did not speak again at once. Lily kept glancing timidly up at him, and every time that she did so the man smiled and her confidence increased. Presently when the man's hand grasped her little childish one hanging by her side, she felt a complete trust in him. Then she smiled up at him. She felt glad that this nice man had come along, for just here the road was lonely.

After a while the man spoke. "What is your name, little one?" he asked, caressingly.

"Lily Barry."

The man started. "What is your father's name?"

"Nelson Barry," replied Lily.

The man whistled. "Is your mother dead?"

"Yes, sir."

"How old are you, my dear?"

"Fourteen," replied Lily.

The man looked at her with surprise. "As old as that?"

Lily suddenly shrank from the man. She could not have told why. She pulled her little hand from his, and he let it go with no remonstrance. She clasped both her arms around her rag doll, in order that her hand should not be free for him to grasp again.

She walked a little farther away from the man, and he looked amused.

"You still play with your doll?" he said, in a soft voice.

"Yes, sir," replied Lily. She quickened her pace and reached the store.

When Lily entered the store, Hiram Gates, the owner, was behind the counter. The only man besides in the store was Nelson Barry. He sat tipping his chair back against the wall; he was half asleep, and his handsome face was bristling with a beard of several days' growth and darkly flushed. He opened his eyes when Lily entered, the strange man following. He brought his chair down on all fours, and he looked at the man—not noticing Lily at all—with a look compounded of defiance and uneasiness.

"Hullo, Jim!" he said.

"Hullo, old man!" returned the stranger.

Lily went over to the counter and asked for the salt, in her pretty little voice. When she had paid for it and was crossing the store, Nelson Barry was on his feet.

"Well, how are you, Lily? It is Lily, isn't it?" he said.

"Yes, sir," replied Lily, faintly.

Her father bent down and, for the first time in her life, kissed her, and the whiskey odor of his breath came into her face.

Lily involuntarily started, and shrank away from him. Then she rubbed her mouth violently with her little cotton handkerchief, which she held gathered up with the rag doll.

"Damn it all! I believe she is afraid of me," said Nelson Barry, in a thick voice.

"Looks a little like it," said the other man, laughing.

"It's that damned old woman," said Nelson Barry. Then he smiled again at Lily. "I didn't know what a pretty little daughter I was blessed with," said he, and he softly stroked Lily's pink cheek under her hat.

Now Lily did not shrink from him. Hereditary instincts and nature itself were asserting themselves in the child's innocent, receptive breast.

Nelson Barry looked curiously at Lily. "How old are you, anyway, child?" he asked.

"I'll be fourteen in September," replied Lily.

"But you still play with your doll?" said Barry, laughing kindly down at her.

Lily hugged her doll more tightly, in spite of her father's kind voice. "Yes, sir," she replied.

Nelson glanced across at some glass jars filled with sticks of candy. "See here, little Lily, do you like candy?" said he.

"Yes, sir."

"Wait a minute."

Lily waited while her father went over to the counter. Soon he returned with a package of the candy.

"I don't see how you are going to carry so much," he said, smiling. "Suppose you throw away your doll?"

Lily gazed at her father and hugged the doll tightly, and there was all at once in the child's expression something mature. It became the reproach of a woman. Nelson's face sobered.

"Oh, it's all right, Lily," he said; "keep your doll. Here, I guess you can carry this candy under your arm."

Lily could not resist the candy. She obeyed Nelson's instructions for carrying it, and left the store laden. The two men also left, and walked in the opposite direction, talking busily.

When Lily reached home, her grandmother, who was watching for her, spied at once the package of candy.

"What's that?" she asked, sharply.

"My father gave it to me," answered Lily, in a faltering voice. Sally regarded her with something like alertness.

"Your father?"

"Yes, ma'am."

"Where did you see him?"

"In the store."

"He gave you this candy?"

"Yes, ma'am."

"What did he say?"

"He asked me how old I was, and—"

"And what?"

"I don't know," replied Lily; and it really seemed to her that she did not know, she was so frightened and bewildered by it all, and, more than anything else, by her grandmother's face as she questioned her.

Old Woman Magoun's face was that of one upon whom a long-anticipated blow had fallen. Sally Jinks gazed at her with a sort of stupid alarm.

Old Woman Magoun continued to gaze at her grandchild with that look of terrible solicitude, as if she saw the girl in the clutch of a tiger. "You can't remember what else he said?" she asked, fiercely, and the child began to whimper softly.

"No, ma'am," she sobbed. "I—don't know, and—"

"And what? Answer me."

"There was another man there. A real handsome man."

"Did he speak to you?" asked Old Woman Magoun.

"Yes, ma'am; he walked along with me a piece," confessed Lily, with a sob of terror and bewilderment.

"What did *he* say to you?" asked Old Woman Magoun, with a sort of despair.

Lily told, in her little, faltering, frightened voice, all of the conversation which she could recall. It sounded harmless enough, but the look of the realization of a long-expected blow never left her grandmother's face.

The sun was getting low, and the bridge was nearing completion. Soon the workmen would be crowding into the cabin for their promised supper. There became visible in the distance, far up the road, the heavily plodding figure of another woman who had agreed to come and help. Old Woman Magoun turned again to Lily.

"You go right up-stairs to your own chamber now," said she.

"Good land! ain't you goin' to let that poor child stay up and see the fun?" said Sally Jinks.

"You jest mind your own business," said Old Woman Magoun, forcibly, and Sally Jinks shrank. "You go right up there now, Lily," said the grandmother, in a softer tone, "and grandma will bring you up a nice plate of supper."

"When be you goin' to let that girl grow up?" asked Sally Jinks, when Lily had disappeared.

"She'll grow up in the Lord's good time," replied Old Woman Magoun, and there was in her voice something both sad and threatening. Sally Jinks again shrank a little.

Soon the workmen came flocking noisily into the house. Old Woman Magoun and her two helpers served the bountiful supper. Most of the men had drunk as much as, and more than, was good for them, and Old Woman Magoun had stipulated that there was to be no drinking of anything except coffee during supper.

"I'll git you as good a meal as I know how," she said, "but if I see ary one of you drinkin' a drop, I'll run you all out. If you want anything to drink, you can go up to the store afterward. That's the place for you to go to, if you've got to make hogs of yourselves. I ain't goin' to have no hogs in my house."

Old Woman Magoun was implicitly obeyed. She had a curious authority over most people when she chose to exercise it. When the supper was in full swing, she quietly stole up-stairs and carried some food to Lily. She found the girl, with the rag doll in her arms, crouching by the window in her little rocking-chair—a relic of her infancy, which she still used.

"What a noise they are makin', grandma!" she said, in a terrified whisper, as her grandmother placed the plate before her on a chair.

"They've 'most all of 'em been drinkin'. They air a passel of hogs," replied the old woman.

"Is the man that was with—with my father down there?" asked Lily, in a timid fashion. Then she fairly cowered before the look in her grandmother's eyes.

"No, he ain't; and what's more, he never will be down there if I can help it," said Old Woman Magoun, in a fierce whisper. "I know who he is. They can't cheat me. He's one of them Willises—that family the Barrys married into. They're worse than the Barrys, ef they *have* got money. Eat your supper, and put him out of your mind, child."

It was after Lily was asleep, when Old Woman Magoun was

alone, clearing away her supper dishes, that Lily's father came. The door was closed, and he knocked, and the old woman knew at once who was there. The sound of that knock meant as much to her as the whir of a bomb to the defender of a fortress. She opened the door, and Nelson Barry stood there.

"Good-evening, Mrs. Magoun," he said.

Old Woman Magoun stood before him, filling up the doorway with her firm bulk.

"Good-evening, Mrs. Magoun," said Nelson Barry again.

"I ain't got no time to waste," replied the old woman, harshly. "I've got my supper dishes to clean up after them men."

She stood there and looked at him as she might have looked at a rebellious animal which she was trying to tame. The man laughed.

"It's no use," said he. "You know me of old. No human being can turn me from my way when I am once started in it. You may as well let me come in."

Old Woman Magoun entered the house, and Barry followed her.

Barry began without any preface. "Where is the child?" asked he.

"Up-stairs. She has gone to bed."

"She goes to bed early."

"Children ought to," returned the old woman, polishing a plate.

Barry laughed. "You are keeping her a child a long while," he remarked, in a soft voice which had a sting in it.

"She *is* a child," returned the old woman, defiantly.

"Her mother was only three years older when Lily was born."

The old woman made a sudden motion toward the man which seemed fairly menacing. Then she turned again to her dish-washing.

"I want her," said Barry.

"You can't have her," replied the old woman, in a still stern voice.

"I don't see how you can help yourself. You have always acknowledged that she was my child."

The old woman continued her task, but her strong back heaved. Barry regarded her with an entirely pitiless expression.

"I am going to have the girl, that is the long and short of it," he said, "and it is for her best good, too. You are a fool, or you would see it."

"Her best good?" muttered the old woman.

"Yes, her best good. What are you going to do with her, anyway? The girl is a beauty, and almost a woman grown, although you try to make out that she is a baby. You can't live forever."

"The Lord will take care of her," replied the old woman, and again she turned and faced him, and her expression was that of a prophetess.

"Very well, let Him," said Barry, easily. "All the same I'm going to have her, and I tell you it is for her best good. Jim Willis saw her this afternoon, and—"

Old Woman Magoun looked at him. "Jim Willis!" she fairly shrieked.

"Well, what of it?"

"One of them Willises!" repeated the old woman, and this time her voice was thick. It seemed almost as if she were stricken with paralysis. She did not enunciate clearly.

The man shrank a little. "Now what is the need of your making such a fuss?" he said. "I will take her, and Isabel will look out for her."

"Your half-witted sister?" said Old Woman Magoun.

"Yes, my half-witted sister. She knows more than you think."

"More wickedness."

"Perhaps. Well, a knowledge of evil is a useful thing. How are you going to avoid evil if you don't know what it is like? My sister and I will take care of my daughter."

The old woman continued to look at the man, but his eyes never fell. Suddenly her gaze grew inconceivably keen. It was as if she saw through all externals.

"I know what it is!" she cried. "You have been playing cards and you lost, and this is the way you will pay him."

Then the man's face reddened, and he swore under his breath.

"Oh, my God!" said the old woman; and she really spoke with her eyes aloft as if addressing something outside of them both. Then she turned again to her dish-washing.

The man cast a dogged look at her back. "Well, there is no use talking. I have made up my mind," said he, "and you know me and what that means. I am going to have the girl."

"When?" said the old woman, without turning around.

"Well, I am willing to give you a week. Put her clothes in good order before she comes."

The old woman made no reply. She continued washing dishes. She even handled them so carefully that they did not rattle.

"You understand," said Barry. "Have her ready a week from to-day."

"Yes," said Old Woman Magoun, "I understand."

Nelson Barry, going up the mountain road, reflected that Old Woman Magoun had a strong character, that she understood much better than her sex in general the futility of withstanding the inevitable.

"Well," he said to Jim Willis when he reached home, "the old woman did not make such a fuss as I expected."

"Are you going to have the girl?"

"Yes; a week from to-day. Look here, Jim; you've got to stick to your promise."

"All right," said Willis. "Go you one better."

The two were playing at cards in the old parlor, once magnificent, now squalid, of the Barry house. Isabel, the half-witted sister, entered, bringing some glasses on a tray. She had learned with her feeble intellect some tricks, like a dog. One of them was the mixing of sundry drinks. She set the tray on a little stand near the two men, and watched them with her silly simper.

"Clear out now and go to bed," her brother said to her, and she obeyed.

Early the next morning Old Woman Magoun went up to Lily's little sleeping-chamber, and watched her a second as she lay asleep, with her yellow locks spread over the pillow. Then she spoke. "Lily," said she—"Lily, wake up. I am going to Greenham across the new bridge, and you can go with me."

Lily immediately sat up in bed and smiled at her grandmother. Her eyes were still misty, but the light of awakening was in them.

"Get right up," said the old woman. "You can wear your new dress if you want to."

Lily gurgled with pleasure like a baby. "And my new hat?" asked she.

"I don't care."

Old Woman Magoun and Lily started for Greenham before Barry Ford, which kept late hours, was fairly awake. It was three miles to Greenham. The old woman said that, since the horse was a little lame, they would walk. It was a beautiful morning, with a diamond radiance of dew over everything. Her grandmother had curled Lily's hair more punctiliously than usual. The little face peeped like a rose out of two rows of golden spirals. Lily wore her new muslin dress with a pink sash, and her best hat of a fine white straw trimmed with a wreath of rosebuds; also the neatest black open-work stockings and pretty shoes. She even had white cotton gloves. When they set out, the old, heavily stepping woman, in her black gown and cape and bonnet, looked down at the little pink fluttering figure. Her face was full of the tenderest love and admiration, and yet there was something terrible about it. They crossed the new bridge—a primitive structure built of logs in a slovenly fashion. Old Woman Magoun pointed to a gap.

"Jest see that," said she. "That's the way men work."

"Men ain't very nice, be they?" said Lily, in her sweet little voice.

"No, they ain't, take them all together," replied her grandmother.

"That man that walked to the store with me was nicer than some, I guess," Lily said, in a wishful fashion. Her grandmother reached down and took the child's hand in its small cotton glove. "You hurt me, holding my hand so tight," Lily said presently, in a deprecatory little voice.

The old woman loosened her grasp. "Grandma didn't know how tight she was holding your hand," said she. "She wouldn't hurt you for nothin', except it was to save your life, or somethin' like that." She spoke with an undertone of tremendous meaning which the girl was too childish to grasp. They walked along the country road. Just before they reached Greenham they passed a stone wall overgrown with blackberry-vines, and, an unusual thing in that vicinity, a lusty spread of deadly nightshade full of berries.

"Those berries look good to eat, grandma," Lily said.

At that instant the old woman's face became something terrible to see. "You can't have any now," she said, and hurried Lily along.

"They look real nice," said Lily.

When they reached Greenham, Old Woman Magoun took her way straight to the most pretentious house there, the residence of the lawyer, whose name was Mason. Old Woman Magoun bade Lily wait in the yard for a few moments, and Lily ventured to seat herself on a bench beneath an oak-tree; then she watched with some wonder her grandmother enter the lawyer's office door at the right of the house. Presently the lawyer's wife came out and spoke to Lily under the tree. She had in her hand a little tray containing a plate of cake, a glass of milk, and an early apple. She spoke very kindly to Lily; she even kissed her, and offered her the tray of refreshments, which Lily accepted gratefully. She sat eating, with Mrs. Mason watching her, when Old Woman Magoun came out of the lawyer's office with a ghastly face.

"What are you eatin'?" she asked Lily, sharply. "Is that a sour apple?"

"I thought she might be hungry," said the lawyer's wife, with loving, melancholy eyes upon the girl.

Lily had almost finished the apple. "It's real sour, but I like it; it's real nice, grandma," she said.

"You ain't been drinkin' milk with a sour apple?"

"It was real nice milk, grandma."

"You ought never to have drunk milk and eat a sour apple," said her grandmother. "Your stomach was all out of order this mornin', an' sour apples and milk is always apt to hurt anybody."

"I don't know but they are," Mrs. Mason said, apologetically, as she stood on the green lawn with her lavender muslin sweeping around her. "I am real sorry, Mrs. Magoun. I ought to have thought. Let me get some soda for her."

"Soda never agrees with her," replied the old woman, in a harsh voice. "Come," she said to Lily, "it's time we were goin' home."

After Lily and her grandmother had disappeared down the road, Lawyer Mason came out of his office and joined his wife, who had seated herself on the bench beneath the tree. She was idle, and her face wore the expression of those who review joys forever past. She had lost a little girl, her only child, years ago, and her husband always knew when she was thinking about her. Lawyer Mason looked older than his wife; he had a dry, shrewd, slightly one-sided face.

"What do you think, Maria?" he said. "That old woman came to me with the most pressing entreaty to adopt that little girl."

"She is a beautiful little girl," said Mrs. Mason, in a slightly husky voice.

"Yes, she is a pretty child," assented the lawyer, looking pityingly at his wife; "but it is out of the question, my dear. Adopting a child is a serious measure, and in this case a child who comes from Barry's Ford."

"But the grandmother seems a very good woman," said Mrs. Mason.

"I rather think she is. I never heard a word against her. But the father! No, Maria, we cannot take a child with Barry blood in her veins. The stock has run out; it is vitiated physically and morally. It won't do, my dear."

"Her grandmother had her dressed up as pretty as a little girl could be," said Mrs. Mason, and this time the tears welled into her faithful, wistful eyes.

"Well, we can't help that," said the lawyer, as he went back to his office.

Old Woman Magoun and Lily returned, going slowly along the road to Barry's Ford. When they came to the stone wall where the blackberry-vines and the deadly nightshade grew, Lily said she was tired, and asked if she could not sit down for a few minutes. The strange look on her grandmother's face had deepened. Now and then Lily glanced at her and had a feeling as if she were looking at a stranger.

"Yes, you can set down if you want to," said Old Woman Magoun, deeply and harshly.

Lily started and looked at her, as if to make sure that it was her grandmother who spoke. Then she sat down on a stone which was comparatively free of the vines.

"Ain't you goin' to set down, grandma?" Lily asked, timidly.

"No; I don't want to get into that mess," replied her grandmother. "I ain't tired. I'll stand here."

Lily sat still; her delicate little face was flushed with heat. She extended her tiny feet in her best shoes and gazed at them. "My shoes are all over dust," said she.

"It will brush off," said her grandmother, still in that strange voice.

Lily looked around. An elm-tree in the field behind her cast a spray of branches over her head; a little cool puff of wind came on her face. She gazed at the low mountains on the horizon, in the midst of which she lived, and she sighed, for no reason that she knew. She began idly picking at the blackberry-vines; there were no berries on them; then she put her little fingers on the berries of the deadly nightshade. "These look like nice berries," she said.

Old Woman Magoun, standing stiff and straight in the road, said nothing.

"They look good to eat," said Lily.

Old Woman Magoun still said nothing, but she looked up into the ineffable blue of the sky, over which spread at intervals great white clouds shaped like wings.

Lily picked some of the deadly nightshade berries and ate them. "Why, they are real sweet," said she. "They are nice." She picked some more and ate them.

Presently her grandmother spoke. "Come," she said, "it is time we were going. I guess you have set long enough."

Lily was still eating the berries when she slipped down from the wall and followed her grandmother obediently up the road.

Before they reached home, Lily complained of being very thirsty. She stopped and made a little cup of a leaf and drank long at a mountain brook. "I am dreadful dry, but it hurts me to swallow," she said to her grandmother when she stopped drinking and joined the old woman waiting for her in the road. Her grandmother's face seemed strangely dim to her. She took hold of Lily's hand as they went on. "My stomach burns," said Lily, presently. "I want some more water."

"There is another brook a little farther on," said Old Woman Magoun, in a dull voice.

When they reached that brook, Lily stopped and drank again, but she whimpered a little over her difficulty in swallowing. "My stomach burns, too," she said, walking on, "and my throat is so dry, grandma." Old Woman Magoun held Lily's hand more tightly. "You hurt me holding my hand so tight, grandma," said Lily, looking up at her grandmother, whose face she seemed to see through a mist, and the old woman loosened her grasp.

When at last they reached home, Lily was very ill. Old Woman Magoun put her on her own bed in the little bedroom out of the kitchen. Lily lay there and moaned, and Sally Jinks came in.

"Why, what ails her?" she asked. "She looks feverish."

Lily unexpectedly answered for herself. "I ate some sour apples and drank some milk," she moaned.

"Sour apples and milk are dreadful apt to hurt anybody," said Sally Jinks. She told several people on her way home that Old Woman Magoun was dreadful careless to let Lily eat such things.

Meanwhile Lily grew worse. She suffered cruelly from the burning in her stomach, the vertigo, and the deadly nausea. "I am so sick, I am so sick, grandma," she kept moaning. She could no longer see her grandmother as she bent over her, but she could hear her talk.

Old Woman Magoun talked as Lily had never heard her talk before, as nobody had ever heard her talk before. She spoke from the depths of her soul; her voice was as tender as the coo of a dove, and it was grand and exalted. "You'll feel better very soon, little Lily," said she.

"I am so sick, grandma."

"You will feel better very soon, and then—"

"I am sick."

"You shall go to a beautiful place."

Lily moaned.

"You shall go to a beautiful place," the old woman went on.

"Where?" asked Lily, groping feebly with her cold little hands. Then she moaned again.

"A beautiful place, where the flowers grow tall."

"What color? Oh, grandma, I am so sick."

"A blue color," replied the old woman. Blue was Lily's favorite color. "A beautiful blue color, and as tall as your knees, and the flowers always stay there, and they never fade."

"Not if you pick them, grandma? Oh!"

"No, not if you pick them; they never fade, and they are so sweet you can smell them a mile off; and there are birds that sing, and all the roads have gold stones in them, and the stone walls are made of gold."

"Like the ring grandpa gave you? I am so sick, grandma."

"Yes, gold like that. And all the houses are built of silver and gold, and the people all have wings, so when they get tired walking they can fly, and—"

"I am so sick, grandma."

"And all the dolls are alive," said Old Woman Magoun. "Dolls like yours can run, and talk, and love you back again."

Lily had her poor old rag doll in bed with her, clasped close to her agonized little heart. She tried very hard with her eyes, whose pupils were so dilated that they looked black, to see her grandmother's face when she said that, but she could not. "It is dark," she moaned, feebly.

"There where you are going it is always light," said the grandmother, "and the commonest things shine like that breastpin Mrs. Lawyer Mason had on to-day."

Lily moaned pitifully, and said something incoherent. Delirium was commencing. Presently she sat straight up in bed and raved; but even then her grandmother's wonderful compelling voice had an influence over her.

"You will come to a gate with all the colors of the rainbow," said her grandmother; "and it will open, and you will go right in and walk up the gold street, and cross the field where the blue flowers come up to your knees, until you find your mother, and she will take you home where you are going to live. She has a little white room all ready for you, white curtains at the windows, and a little white looking-glass, and when you look in it you will see—"

"What will I see? I am so sick, grandma."

"You will see a face like yours, only it's an angel's; and there will be a little white bed, and you can lay down an' rest."

"Won't I be sick, grandma?" asked Lily. Then she moaned and babbled wildly, although she seemed to understand through it all what her grandmother said.

"No, you will never be sick any more. Talkin' about sickness won't mean anything to you."

It continued. Lily talked on wildly, and her grandmother's great voice of soothing never ceased, until the child fell into a deep sleep, or what resembled sleep; but she lay stiffly in that sleep, and a candle flashed before her eyes made no impression on them.

Then it was that Nelson Barry came. Jim Willis waited outside the door. When Nelson entered he found Old Woman Magoun on her knees beside the bed, weeping with dry eyes and a might of agony which fairly shook Nelson Barry, the degenerate of a fine old race.

"Is she sick?" he asked, in a hushed voice.

Old Woman Magoun gave another terrible sob, which sounded like the gasp of one dying.

"Sally Jinks said that Lily was sick from eating milk and sour apples," said Barry, in a tremulous voice. "I remember that her mother was very sick once from eating them."

Lily lay still, and her grandmother on her knees shook with her terrible sobs.

Suddenly Nelson Barry started. "I guess I had better go to Greenham for a doctor if she's as bad as that," he said. He went close to the bed and looked at the sick child. He gave a great start. Then he felt of her hands and reached down under the bedclothes for her little feet. "Her hands and feet are like ice," he cried out. "Good God! why didn't you send for some one—for me—before? Why, she's dying; she's almost gone!"

Barry rushed out and spoke to Jim Willis, who turned pale and came in and stood by the bedside.

"She's almost gone," he said, in a hushed whisper.

"There's no use going for the doctor; she'd be dead before he got here," said Nelson, and he stood regarding the passing child with a strange, sad face—unutterably sad, because of his incapability of the truest sadness.

"Poor little thing, she's past suffering, anyhow," said the other man, and his own face also was sad with a puzzled, mystified sadness.

Lily died that night. There was quite a commotion in Barry's Ford until after the funeral, it was all so sudden, and then everything went on as usual. Old Woman Magoun continued to live as she had done before. She supported herself by the produce of her tiny farm; she was very industrious, but people said that she was a trifle touched, since every time she went over the log bridge with her eggs or her garden vegetables to sell in Greenham, she carried with her, as one might have carried an infant, Lily's old rag doll.

STEPHEN CRANE
(1871–1900)

"Genius" and "prodigious" are the words that come most readily to mind in considering the elusive Stephen Crane, who died at an age (twenty-eight, of tuberculosis, poverty, and overwork) when most of the writers in this volume were just beginning their careers. Yet Crane left behind a remarkable body of work of fiction, nonfiction, and poetry, enough to fill a dozen volumes of a collected edition; his experimental, imagistic poems The Black Riders and Other Lines *(1895) alone would guarantee him a permanent place in the American literary canon. Like Jack London, whom he most resembles in terms of the unconventional and frequently dangerous life he led, Crane was clearly a phenomenon of youthful energy, drive, and audacity.*

Stephen Crane was born in Newark, New Jersey, the last of fourteen children; his father was a Methodist minister who died when Crane was nine years old. So precocious was Crane, and so determined to be a writer, he published his first novel, Maggie: A Girl of the Streets *(1893), at his own expense—at the age of twenty-two. His second novel, which was to make him famous,* The Red Badge of Courage *(1895), is generally considered the first American "realist" novel to find a reasonably wide audience. A tour de force by a young man who had never witnessed war, let alone participated in combat,* The Red Badge of Courage *was later described by Crane as a "pot-boiler."*

Crane's titles include two volumes of excellent short fiction, The Monster and Other Stories *(1899) and* Whilomville Stories *(1900). Though virtually unknown, "The Little Regiment" is as memorable an accomplishment as any of Crane's most frequently anthologized stories. Note the subtle employment of, even as the author detaches himself from, sentiment. Note the perfection of the story's final line.*

The Little Regiment

I

The fog made the clothes of the men of the column in the roadway seem of a luminous quality. It imparted to the heavy infantry overcoats a new colour, a kind of blue which was so pale that a regiment might have been merely a long, low shadow in the mist. However, a muttering, one part grumble, three parts joke, hovered in the air above the thick ranks, and blended in an undertoned roar, which was the voice of the column.

The town on the southern shore of the little river loomed spectrally, a faint etching upon the gray cloud-masses which were shifting with oily languor. A long row of guns upon the northern bank had been pitiless in their hatred, but a little battered belfry could be dimly seen still pointing with invincible resolution toward the heavens.

The enclouded air vibrated with noises made by hidden colossal things. The infantry tramplings, the heavy rumbling of the artillery, made the earth speak of gigantic preparation. Guns on distant heights thundered from time to time with sudden, nervous roar, as if unable to endure in silence a knowledge of hostile troops massing, other guns going to position. These sounds, near and remote, defined an immense battleground, described the tremendous width of the stage of the prospective drama. The voices of the guns, slightly casual, unexcited in their challenges and warnings, could not destroy the unutterable eloquence of the word in the air, a meaning of impending struggle which made the breath halt at the lips.

The column in the roadway was ankle-deep in mud. The men swore piously at the rain which drizzled upon them, compelling them to stand always very erect in fear of the drops that would sweep in under their coat-collars. The fog was as cold as wet cloths. The men stuffed their hands deep in their pockets, and huddled their muskets in their arms. The machinery of orders had rooted these soldiers deeply into the mud precisely as almighty nature roots mullein stalks.

They listened and speculated when a tumult of fighting came from the dim town across the river. When the noise lulled for a time they resumed their descriptions of the mud and graphically exaggerated the number of hours they had been kept waiting. The general commanding their division rode along the ranks, and they cheered admiringly, affectionately, crying out to him gleeful prophecies of the coming battle. Each man scanned him with a peculiarly keen personal interest, and afterward spoke of him with unquestioning devotion and confidence, narrating anecdotes which were mainly untrue.

When the jokers lifted the shrill voices which invariably belonged to them, flinging witticisms at their comrades, a loud laugh would sweep from rank to rank, and soldiers who had not heard would lean forward and demand repetition. When were borne past them some wounded men with gray and blood-smeared faces, and eyes that rolled in that helpless beseeching for assistance from the sky which comes with supreme pain, the soldiers in the mud watched intently, and from time to time asked of the bearers an account of the affair. Frequently they bragged of their corps, their division, their brigade, their regiment. Anon they referred to the mud and the cold drizzle. Upon this threshold of a wild scene of death they, in short, defied the proportion of events with that splendour of heedlessness which belongs only to veterans.

"Like a lot of wooden soldiers," swore Billie Dempster, moving his feet in the thick mass, and casting a vindictive glance indefinitely; "standing in the mud for a hundred years."

"Oh, shut up!" murmured his brother Dan. The manner of his words implied that this fraternal voice near him was an indescribable bore.

"Why should I shut up?" demanded Billie.

"Because you're a fool," cried Dan, taking no time to debate it; "the biggest fool in the regiment."

There was but one man between them, and he was habituated. These insults from brother to brother had swept across his chest, flown past his face, many times during two long campaigns. Upon this occasion he simply grinned first at one, then at the other.

The way of these brothers was not an unknown topic in regimental gossip. They had enlisted simultaneously, with each sneering loudly at the other for doing it. They left their little town, and went forward with the flag, exchanging protestations of undying suspicion. In the camp life they so openly despised each other that, when entertaining quarrels were lacking, their companions often contrived situations calculated to bring forth display of this fraternal dislike.

Both were large-limbed, strong young men, and often fought with friends in camp unless one was near to interfere with the other. This latter happened rather frequently, because Dan, preposterously willing for any manner of combat, had a very great horror of seeing Billie in a fight; and Billie, almost odiously ready himself, simply refused to see Dan stripped to his shirt and with his fists aloft. This sat queerly upon them, and made them the objects of plots.

When Dan jumped through a ring of eager soldiers and dragged forth his raving brother by the arm, a thing often predicted would almost come to pass. When Billie performed the same office for Dan, the prediction would again miss fulfilment by an inch. But indeed they never fought together, although they were perpetually upon the verge.

They expressed longing for such conflict. As a matter of truth, they had at one time made full arrangement for it, but even with the encouragement and interest of half of the regiment they somehow failed to achieve collision.

If Dan became a victim of police duty, no jeering was so destructive to the feelings as Billie's comment. If Billie got a call to appear at the headquarters, none would so genially prophesy his complete undoing as Dan. Small misfortunes to one were, in truth, invariably greeted with hilarity by the other, who seemed to see in them great re-enforcement of his opinion.

As soldiers, they expressed each for each a scorn intense and blasting. After a certain battle, Billie was promoted to corporal. When Dan was told of it, he seemed smitten dumb with astonishment and patriotic indignation. He stared in silence, while the dark blood rushed to Billie's forehead, and he shifted his weight from foot to foot. Dan at last found his tongue, and said: "Well, I'm durned!" If he had heard that an army mule had been appointed to the post of corps commander, his tone could not have had more derision in it. Afterward, he adopted a fervid insubordination, an almost religious reluctance to obey the new corporal's orders, which came near to developing the desired strife.

It is here finally to be recorded also that Dan, most ferociously profane in speech, very rarely swore in the presence of his brother; and that Billie, whose oaths came from his lips with the grace of falling pebbles, was seldom known to express himself in this manner when near his brother Dan.

At last the afternoon contained a suggestion of evening. Metallic cries rang suddenly from end to end of the column. They inspired at once a quick, business-like adjustment. The long thing stirred in the mud. The men had hushed, and were looking across the river. A moment later the shadowy mass of pale blue figures was moving steadily toward the stream. There could be heard from the town a clash of swift fighting and cheering. The noise of the shooting coming through the heavy air had its sharpness taken from it, and sounded in thuds.

There was a halt upon the bank above the pontoons. When the column went winding down the incline, and streamed out upon the bridge, the fog had faded to a great degree, and in the clearer dusk the guns on a distant ridge were enabled to perceive the crossing. The long whirling outcries of the shells came into the air above the men. An occasional solid shot struck the surface of the river, and dashed into view a sudden vertical jet. The distance was subtly illuminated by the lightning from the deep-booming guns. One by one the batteries on the northern shore aroused, the innumerable guns bellowing in angry oration at the distant ridge. The rolling thunder crashed and reverberated as a wild surf sounds on a still night, and to this music the column marched across the pontoons.

The waters of the grim river curled away in a smile from the ends of the great boats, and slid swiftly beneath the planking. The dark, riddled walls of the town upreared before the troops, and from a region hidden by these hammered and tumbled houses came incessantly the yells and firings of a prolonged and close skirmish.

When Dan had called his brother a fool, his voice had been so decisive, so brightly assured, that many men had laughed, considering it to be great humour under the circumstances. The incident happened to rankle deep in Billie. It was not any strange thing that his brother had called him a fool. In fact, he often called him a fool with exactly the same amount of cheerful and prompt conviction, and before large audiences, too. Billie wondered in his own mind why he took such profound offence in this case; but, at any rate, as he slid down the bank and on to the bridge with his regiment, he was searching his knowledge for something that would pierce Dan's blithesome spirit. But he could contrive nothing at this time, and his impotency made the glance which he was once able to give his brother still more malignant.

The guns far and near were roaring a fearful and grand introduction for this column which was marching upon the stage of death. Billie felt it, but only in a numb way. His heart was cased in that curious dissonant metal which covers a man's emotions at such times. The terrible voices from the hills told him that in this wide conflict his life was an insignificant fact, and that his death would be an insignificant fact. They portended the whirlwind to which he would be as necessary as a butterfly's waved wing. The solemnity, the sadness of it came near enough to make him wonder why he was neither solemn nor sad. When his mind vaguely adjusted events according to their importance to him, it appeared that the uppermost thing was the fact that upon the eve of battle, and before many comrades, his brother had called him a fool.

Dan was in a particularly happy mood. "Hurray! Look at 'em shoot," he said, when the long witches' croon of the shells came into the air. It enraged Billie when he felt the little thorn in him, and saw at the same time that his brother had completely forgotten it.

The column went from the bridge into more mud. At this southern end there was a chaos of hoarse directions and commands. Darkness was coming upon the earth, and regiments were being hurried up the slippery bank. As Billie floundered in the black mud, amid the swearing, sliding crowd, he suddenly resolved that, in the absence of other means of hurting Dan, he would avoid looking at him, refrain from speaking to him, pay absolutely no heed to his existence; and this done skilfully would, he imagined, soon reduce his brother to a poignant sensitiveness.

At the top of the bank the column again halted and rearranged itself, as a man after a climb rearranges his clothing. Presently the great steel-backed brigade, an infinitely graceful thing in the rhythm and ease of its veteran movement, swung up a little narrow, slanting street.

Evening had come so swiftly that the fighting on the remote borders of the town was indicated by thin flashes of flame. Some building was on fire, and its reflection upon the clouds was an oval of delicate pink.

II

All demeanour of rural serenity had been wrenched violently from the little town by the guns and by the waves of men which had surged through it. The hand of war laid upon this village had in an instant changed it to a thing of remnants. It resembled the place of a monstrous shaking of the earth itself. The windows, now mere unsightly holes, made the tumbled and blackened dwellings seem skeletons. Doors lay splintered to fragments. Chimneys had flung their bricks everywhere. The artillery fire had not neglected the rows of gentle shade-trees which had lined the streets. Branches and heavy trunks cluttered the mud in driftwood tangles, while a few shattered forms had contrived to remain dejectedly, mournfully upright. They expressed an innocence, a helplessness, which perforce created a pity for their happening into this cauldron of battle. Furthermore, there was under foot a vast collection of odd things reminiscent of the charge, the fight, the retreat. There were boxes and barrels filled with earth, behind which riflemen had lain snugly, and in these little trenches were the dead in blue with the dead in gray, the poses eloquent of the struggles for possession of the town until the history of the whole conflict was written plainly in the streets.

And yet the spirit of this little city, its quaint individuality, poised in the air above the ruins, defying the guns, the sweeping volleys; holding in contempt those avaricious blazes which had attacked many dwellings. The hard earthen sidewalks proclaimed the games that had been played there during long lazy days, in the careful shadows of the trees. "General Merchandise," in faint letters upon a long board, had to be read with a slanted glance, for the sign dangled by one end; but the porch of the old store was a palpable legend of wide-hatted men, smoking.

This subtle essence, this soul of the life that had been, brushed like invisible wings the thoughts of the men in the swift columns that came up from the river.

In the darkness a loud and endless humming arose from the great blue crowds bivouacked in the streets. From time to time a sharp spatter of firing from far picket lines entered this bass chorus. The smell from the smouldering ruins floated on the cold night breeze.

Dan, seated ruefully upon the doorstep of a shot-pierced house, was proclaiming the campaign badly managed. Orders had been issued forbidding camp-fires.

Suddenly he ceased his oration, and scanning the group of his comrades, said: "Where's Billie? Do you know?"

"Gone on picket."

"Get out! Has he?" said Dan. "No business to go on picket. Why don't some of them other corporals take their turn?"

A bearded private was smoking his pipe of confiscated tobacco, seated comfortably upon a horse-hair trunk which he had dragged from the house. He observed: "*Was* his turn."

"No such thing," cried Dan. He and the man on the horse-hair trunk held discussion in which Dan stoutly maintained that if his brother had been sent on picket it was an injustice. He ceased his argument when another soldier, upon whose arms could faintly be seen the two stripes of a corporal, entered the circle. "Humph," said Dan, "where you been?"

The corporal made no answer. Presently Dan said: "Billie, where you been?"

His brother did not seem to hear these inquiries. He glanced at the house which towered above them, and remarked casually to the man on the horse-hair trunk: "Funny, ain't it? After the pelting this town got, you'd think there wouldn't be one brick left on another."

"Oh," said Dan, glowering at his brother's back. "Getting mighty smart, ain't you?"

The absence of camp-fires allowed the evening to make apparent its quality of faint silver light in which the blue clothes of the throng became black, and the faces became white expanses, void of expression. There was considerable excitement a short distance from the group around the doorstep. A soldier had chanced upon a hoop-skirt, and arrayed in it he was performing a dance amid the applause of his companions. Billie and a greater part of the men immediately poured over there to witness the exhibition.

"What's the matter with Billie?" demanded Dan of the man upon the horse-hair trunk.

"How do I know?" rejoined the other in mild resentment. He arose and walked away. When he returned he said briefly, in a weather-wise tone, that it would rain during the night.

Dan took a seat upon one end of the horse-hair trunk. He was facing the crowd around the dancer, which in its hilarity swung this way and that way. At times he imagined that he could recognise his brother's face.

He and the man on the other end of the trunk thoughtfully talked of the army's position. To their minds, infantry and artillery were in a most precarious jumble in the streets of the town; but they did not grow nervous over it, for they were used to having the army appear in a precarious jumble to their minds. They had learned to accept such puzzling situations as a consequence of their position in the ranks, and were now usually in possession of a simple but perfectly immovable faith that somebody understood the jumble. Even if they had been convinced that the army was a headless monster, they would merely have nodded with the veteran's singular cynicism. It was none of their business as soldiers. Their duty was to grab sleep and food when occasion permitted, and cheerfully fight wherever their feet were planted until more orders came. This was a task sufficiently absorbing.

They spoke of other corps, and this talk being confidential, their voices dropped to tones of awe. "The Ninth"—"The First"—"The Fifth"—"The Sixth"—"The Third"—the simple numerals rang with eloquence, each having a meaning which was to float through many years as no intangible arithmetical mist, but as pregnant with individuality as the names of cities.

Of their own corps they spoke with a deep veneration, an idolatry, a supreme confidence which apparently would not blanch to see it match against everything.

It was as if their respect for other corps was due partly to a wonder that organizations not blessed with their own famous numeral could take such an interest in war. They could prove that their division was the best in the corps, and that their brigade was the best in the division. And their regiment—it was plain that no fortune of life was equal to the chance which caused a man to be born, so to speak, into this command, the keystone of the defending arch.

At times Dan covered with insults the character of a vague, unnamed general to whose petulance and busy-body spirit he ascribed the order which made hot coffee impossible.

Dan said that victory was certain in the coming battle. The other man seemed rather dubious. He remarked upon the fortified line of hills, which had impressed him even from the other side of the river. "Shucks," said Dan. "Why, we—" He pictured a splendid overflowing of these hills by the sea of men in blue. During the period of this conversation Dan's glance searched the merry throng about the dancer. Above the babble of voices in the street a far-away thunder could sometimes be heard—evidently from the very edge of the horizon—the boom-boom of restless guns.

III

Ultimately the night deepened to the tone of black velvet. The outlines of the fireless camp were like the faint drawings upon ancient tapestry. The glint of a rifle, the shine of a button, might have been of threads of silver and gold sewn upon the fabric of the night. There was little presented to the vision, but to a sense more subtle there was discernible in the atmosphere something like a pulse; a mystic beating which would have told a stranger of the presence of a giant thing—the slumbering mass of regiments and batteries.

With fires forbidden, the floor of a dry old kitchen was thought to be a good exchange for the cold earth of December, even if a shell had exploded in it and knocked it so out of shape that when a man lay curled in his blanket his last waking thought was likely to be of the wall that bellied out above him as if strongly anxious to topple upon the score of soldiers.

Billie looked at the bricks ever about to descend in a shower upon his face, listened to the industrious pickets plying their rifles on the border of the town, imagined some measure of the din of the coming battle, thought of Dan and Dan's chagrin, and rolling over in his blanket went to sleep with satisfaction.

At an unknown hour he was aroused by the creaking of boards. Lifting himself upon his elbow, he saw a sergeant prowling among the sleeping forms. The sergeant carried a candle in an old brass candle-stick. He would have resembled some old farmer on an unusual midnight tour if it were not for the significance of his gleaming buttons and striped sleeves.

Billie blinked stupidly at the light until his mind returned from the journeys of slumber. The sergeant stooped among the unconscious soldiers, holding the candle close, and peering into each face.

"Hello, Haines," said Billie. "Relief?"

"Hello, Billie," said the sergeant. "Special duty."

"Dan got to go?"

"Jameson, Hunter, McCormack, D. Dempster. Yes. Where is he?"

"Over there by the winder," said Billie, gesturing. "What is it for, Haines?"

"You don't think I know, do you?" demanded the sergeant. He began to pipe sharply but cheerily at men upon the floor. "Come, Mac, get up here. Here's a special for you. Wake up, Jameson. Come along, Dannie, me boy."

Each man at once took this call to duty as a personal affront. They pulled themselves out of their blankets, rubbed their eyes, and swore at whoever was responsible. "Them's orders," cried the sergeant. "Come! Get out of here." An undetailed head with dishevelled hair thrust out from a blanket, and a sleepy voice said: "Shut up, Haines, and go home."

When the detail clanked out of the kitchen, all but one of the remaining men seemed to be again asleep. Billie, leaning on his elbow, was gazing into darkness. When the footsteps died to silence, he curled himself into his blanket.

At the first cool lavender lights of daybreak he aroused again, and scanned his recumbent companions. Seeing a wakeful one he asked: "Is Dan back yet?"

The man said: "Hain't seem 'im."

Billie put both hands behind his head, and scowled into the air. "Can't see the use of these cussed details in the night-time," he muttered in his most unreasonable tones. "Darn nuisances. Why can't they—" He grumbled at length and graphically.

When Dan entered with the squad, however, Billie was convincingly asleep.

IV

The regiment trotted in double time along the street, and the colonel seemed to quarrel over the right of way with many artillery officers. Batteries were waiting in the mud, and the men of them, exasperated by the bustle of this ambitious infantry, shook their fists from saddle and caisson, exchanging all manner of taunts and jests. The slanted guns continued to look reflectively at the ground.

On the outskirts of the crumbled town a fringe of blue figures were firing into the fog. The regiment swung out into skirmish lines, and the fringe of blue figures departed, turning their backs and going joyfully around the flank.

The bullets began a low moan off toward a ridge which loomed faintly in the heavy mist. When the swift crescendo had reached its climax, the missiles zipped just overhead, as if piercing an invisible curtain. A battery on the hill was crashing with such tumult that it was as if the guns had quarrelled and had fallen pell-mell and snarling upon each other. The shells howled on their journey toward the town. From short range distance there came a spatter of musketry, sweeping along an invisible line and making faint sheets of orange light.

Some in the new skirmish lines were beginning to fire at various shadows discerned in the vapour, forms of men suddenly revealed by some humour of the laggard masses of clouds. The crackle of musketry began to dominate the purring of the hostile bullets. Dan, in the front rank, held his rifle poised, and looked into the fog keenly, coldly, with the air of a sportsman. His nerves were so steady that it was as if they had been drawn from his body, leaving him merely a muscular machine; but his numb heart was somehow beating to the pealing march of the fight.

The waving skirmish line went backward and forward, ran this way and that way. Men got lost in the fog, and men were found again. Once they got too close to the formidable ridge, and the thing burst out as if repulsing a general attack. Once another blue regiment was apprehended on the very edge of firing into them. Once a friendly battery began an elaborate and scientific process of extermination. Always as busy as brokers, the men slid here and there over the plain, fighting their foes, escaping from their friends, leaving a history of many movements in the wet yellow turf, cursing the atmosphere, blazing away every time they could identify the enemy.

In one mystic changing of the fog, as if the fingers of spirits were drawing aside these draperies, a small group of the gray skirmishers, silent, statuesque, were suddenly disclosed to Dan and those about him. So vivid and near were they that there was something uncanny in the revelation.

There might have been a second of mutual staring. Then each rifle in each group was at the shoulder. As Dan's glance flashed along the barrel of his weapon, the figure of a man suddenly loomed as if the musket had been a telescope. The short black beard, the slouch hat, the pose of the man as he sighted to shoot, made a quick picture in Dan's mind. The same moment, it would seem, he pulled his own trigger, and the man, smitten, lurched forward, while his exploding rifle made a slanting crimson streak in the air, and the slouch hat fell before the body. The billows of the fog, governed by singular impulses, rolled between.

"You got that feller such enough," said a comrade to Dan. Dan looked at him absent-mindedly.

V

When the next morning calmly displayed another fog, the men of the regiment exchanged eloquent comments; but they did not abuse it at length, because the streets of the town now contained enough galloping aides to make three troops of cavalry, and they knew that they had come to the verge of the great fight.

Dan conversed with the man who had once possessed a horse-hair trunk; but they did not mention the line of hills which had furnished them in more careless moments with an agreeable topic. They avoided it now as condemned men do the subject of death, and yet the thought of it stayed in their eyes as they looked at each other and talked gravely of other things.

The expectant regiment heaved a long sigh of relief when the sharp call: "Fall in," repeated indefinitely, arose in the streets. It was inevitable that a bloody battle was to be fought, and they wanted to get it off their minds. They were, however, doomed again to spend a long period planted firmly in the mud. They craned their necks, and wondered where some of the other regiments were going.

At last the mists rolled carelessly away. Nature made at this time all provisions to enable foes to see each other, and immediately the roar of guns resounded from every hill. The endless cracking of the skirmish had swelled to rolling crashes of musketry. Shells screamed with panther-like noises at the houses. Dan looked at the man of the horse-hair trunk, and the man said: "Well, here she comes!"

The tenor voices of younger officers and the deep and hoarse voices of the older ones rang in the streets. These cries pricked like spurs. The masses of men vibrated from the suddenness with which they were plunged into the situation of troops about to fight. That the orders were long-expected did not concern the emotion.

Simultaneous movement was imparted to all these thick bodies of men and horses that lay in the town. Regiment after regiment swung rapidly into the streets that faced the sinister ridge.

This exodus was theatrical. The little sober-hued village had been like the cloak which disguises the king of drama. It was now put aside, and an army, splendid thing of steel and blue, stood forth in the sunlight.

Even the soldiers in the heavy columns drew deep breaths at the sight, more majestic than they had dreamed. The heights of the enemy's position were crowded with men who resembled people come to witness some mighty pageant. But as the column moved steadily to their positions, the guns, matter-of-fact warriors, doubled their number, and shells burst with red thrilling tumult on the crowded plain. One came into the ranks of the regiment, and after the smoke and the wrath of it had faded, leaving motionless figures, everyone stormed according to the limits of his vocabulary, for veterans detest being killed when they are not busy.

The regiment sometimes looked sideways at its brigade companions composed of men who had never been in battle; but no frozen blood could withstand the heat of the splendour of this army before the eyes on the plain, these lines so long that the flanks were little streaks, this mass of men of one intention. The recruits carried themselves heedlessly. At the rear was an idle battery, and three artillery men in a foolish row on a caisson nudged each other and grinned at the recruits. "You'll catch it pretty soon," they called out. They were impersonally gleeful, as if they themselves were not also likely to catch it pretty soon. But with this picture of an army in their hearts, the new men perhaps felt the devotion which the drops may feel for the wave; they were of its power and glory; they smiled jauntily at the foolish row of gunners, and told them to go to blazes.

The column trotted across some little bridges, and spread quickly into lines of battle. Before them was a bit of plain, and back of the plain was the ridge. There was no time left for considerations. The men were staring at the plain, mightily wondering how it would feel to be out there, when a brigade in advance yelled and charged. The hill was all gray smoke and fire-points.

That fierce elation in the terrors of war, catching a man's heart and making it burn with such ardour that he becomes capable of dying, flashed in the faces of the men like coloured lights, and made them resemble leashed animals, eager, ferocious, daunting at nothing. The line was really in its first leap before the wild, hoarse crying of the orders.

The greed for close quarters which is the emotion of a bayonet charge, came then into the minds of the men and developed until it was a madness. The field, with its faded grass of a Southern winter, seemed to this fury miles in width.

High, slow-moving masses of smoke, with an odour of burning cotton, engulfed the line until the men might have been swimmers. Before them the ridge, the shore of this gray sea, was outlined, crossed, and recrossed by sheets of flame. The howl of the battle arose to the noise of innumerable wind demons.

The line, galloping, scrambling, plunging like a herd of wounded horses, went over a field that was sown with corpses, the records of other charges.

Directly in front of the black-faced, whooping Dan, carousing in this onward sweep like a new kind of fiend, a wounded man appeared, raising his shattered body, and staring at this rush of men down upon him. It seemed to occur to him that he was to be trampled; he made a desperate, piteous effort to escape; then finally huddled in a waiting heap. Dan and the soldier near him widened the interval between them without looking down, without appearing to heed the wounded man. This little clump of blue seemed to reel past them as boulders reel past a train.

Bursting through a smoke-wave, the scampering, unformed bunches came upon the wreck of the brigade that had preceded them, a floudering mass stopped afar from the hill by the swirling volleys.

It was as if a necromancer had suddenly shown them a picture of the fate which awaited them; but the line with muscular spasm hurled itself over this wreckage and onward, until men were stumbling amid the relics of other assaults, the point where the fire from the ridge consumed.

The men, panting, perspiring, with crazed faces, tried to push against it; but it was as if they had come to a wall. The wave halted, shuddered in an agony from the quick struggle of its two desires, then toppled, and broke into a fragmentary thing which has no name.

Veterans could now at last be distinguished from recruits. The new regiments were instantly gone, lost, scattered, as if they never had been. But the sweeping failure of the charge, the battle, could not make the veterans forget their business. With a last throe, the band of maniacs drew itself up and blazed a volley at the hill, insignificant to those iron intrenchments, but nevertheless expressing that singular final despair which enables men coolly to defy the walls of a city of death.

After this episode the men renamed their command. They called it the Little Regiment.

VI

"I seen Dan shoot a feller yesterday. Yes sir. I'm sure it was him that done it. And maybe he thinks about that feller now, and wonders if *he* tumbled down just about the same way. Them things come up in a man's mind."

Bivouac fires upon the sidewalks, in the streets, in the yards, threw high their wavering reflections, which examined, like slim, red fingers, the dingy, scarred walls and the piles of tumbled brick. The droning of voices again arose from great blue crowds.

The odour of frying bacon, the fragrance from countless little coffee-pails floated among the ruins. The rifles, stacked in the shadows, emitted flashes of steely light. Wherever a flag lay horizontally from one stack to another was the bed of an eagle which had led men into the mystic smoke.

The men about a particular fire were engaged in holding in check their jovial spirits. They moved whispering around the blaze, although they looked at it with a certain fine contentment, like labourers after a day's hard work.

There was one who sat apart. They did not address him save in tones suddenly changed. They did not regard him directly, but always in little sidelong glances.

At last a soldier from a distant fire came into this circle of light. He studied for a time the man who sat apart. Then he hesitatingly stepped closer, and said: "Got any news, Dan?"

"No," said Dan.

The new-comer shifted his feet. He looked at the fire, at the sky, at the other men, at Dan. His face expressed a curious despair; his tongue was plainly in rebellion. Finally, however, he contrived to say: "Well, there's some chance yet, Dan. Lots of the wounded are still lying out there, you know. There's some chance yet."

"Yes," said Dan.

The soldier shifted his feet again, and looked miserably into the air. After another struggle he said: "Well, there's some chance yet, Dan." He moved hastily away.

One of the men of the squad, perhaps encouraged by this example, now approached the still figure. "No news yet, hey?" he said, after coughing behind his hand.

"No," said Dan.

"Well," said the man, "I've been thinking of how he was fretting about you the night you went on special duty. You recollect? Well, sir, I was surprised. He couldn't say enough about it. I swan, I don't believe he slep' a wink after you left, but just lay awake cussing special duty and worrying. I was surprised. But there he lay cussing. He——"

Dan made a curious sound, as if a stone had wedged in his throat. He said: "Shut up, will you?"

Afterward the men would not allow this moody contemplation of the fire to be interrupted.

"Oh, let him alone, can't you?"

"Come away from there, Casey!"

"Say, can't you leave him be?"

They moved with reverence about the immovable figure, with its countenance of mask-like invulnerability.

VII

After the red round eye of the sun had stared long at the little plain and its burden, darkness, a sable mercy, came heavily upon it, and the wan hands of the dead were no longer seen in strange frozen gestures.

The heights in front of the plain shone with tiny camp-fires, and from the town in the rear, small shimmerings ascended from the blazes of the bivouac. The plain was a black expanse upon which, from time to time, dots of light, lanterns, floated slowly here and there. These fields were long steeped in grim mystery.

Suddenly, upon one dark spot, there was a resurrection. A strange thing had been groaning there, prostrate. Then it suddenly dragged itself to a sitting posture, and became a man.

The man stared stupidly for a moment at the lights on the hill, then turned and contemplated the faint colouring over the town. For some moments he remained thus, staring with dull eyes, his face unemotional, wooden.

Finally he looked around him at the corpses dimly to be seen. No change flashed into his face upon viewing these men. They seemed to suggest merely that his information concerning himself was not too complete. He ran his fingers over his arms and chest, bearing always the air of an idiot upon a bench at an almshouse door.

Finding no wound in his arms nor in his chest, he raised his hand to his head, and the fingers came away with some dark liquid upon them. Holding these fingers close to his eyes, he scanned them in the same stupid fashion, while his body gently swayed.

The soldier rolled his eyes again toward the town. When he arose, his clothing peeled from the frozen ground like wet paper. Hearing the sound of it, he seemed to see reason for deliberation. He paused and looked at the ground, then at his trousers, then at the ground.

Finally he went slowly off toward the faint reflection, holding his hands palm outward before him, and walking in the manner of a blind man.

VIII

The immovable Dan again sat unaddressed in the midst of comrades, who did not joke aloud. The dampness of the usual morning fog seemed to make the little camp-fires furious.

Suddenly a cry arose in the streets, a shout of amazement and delight. The men making breakfast at the fire looked up quickly. They broke forth in clamorous exclamation: "Well! Of all things! Dan! Dan! Look who's coming! Oh, Dan!"

Dan the silent raised his eyes and saw a man, with a bandage of the size of a helmet about his head, receiving a furious demonstration from the company. He was shaking hands, and explaining, and haranguing to a high degree.

Dan started. His face of bronze flushed to his temples. He seemed about to leap from the ground, but then suddenly he sank back, and resumed his impassive gazing.

The men were in a flurry. They looked from one to the other. "Dan! Look! See who's coming!" some cried again. "Dan! Look!"

He scowled at last, and moved his shoulders sullenly. "Well, don't I know it?"

But they could not be convinced that his eyes were in service. "Dan! Why can't you look? See who's coming!"

He made a gesture then of irritation and rage. "Curse it! Don't I know it?"

The man with a bandage of the size of a helmet moved forward, always shaking hands and explaining. At times his glance wandered to Dan, who saw with his eyes riveted.

After a series of shiftings, it occurred naturally that the man with the bandage was very near to the man who saw the flames. He paused, and there was a little silence. Finally he said: "Hello, Dan."

"Hello, Billie."

EDITH WHARTON
(1862–1937)

Born into a wealthy and socially prominent old New York City family, Edith Wharton (née Edith Newbold Jones) was to become an enormously successful and critically respected writer—a rarity for a woman of her time, as ours. Despite uncertain health she was tireless in her devotion to writing: she published fifty volumes of work, both fiction and nonfiction, and left a number of unpublished manuscripts at her death. A friend and confidante of Henry James, Wharton was one of the first women to be inducted into the National Institute of Arts and Letters and awarded the Pulitzer Prize.

Her early novel The House of Mirth *(1905) is the sharply observed tragi-comedy of an intelligent young woman doomed by a distorted image of herself. It became a bestseller and brought Wharton to immediate literary prominence. Subsequent titles—*Ethan Frome *(1911),* The Reef *(1912),* The Custom of the Country *(1913),* Summer *(1917),* The Age of Innocence *(1920), for which she was awarded the Pulitzer Prize—established her reputation as a major American writer. Less known as a short story writer, Wharton published a considerable number of excellent stories, including elegantly crafted tales of the supernatural.*

"A Journey," despite its obsessive, dream-like tone, is not a tale of the supernatural; neither is it one of Wharton's more typical works of short fiction, in which a female protagonist is viewed from without and within, in an ironically rendered social context. Here, the young wife, from a modest social background, is on the brink of acknowledging the fact that her life will diverge from her husband's—at the very hour, it seems, when her husband dies. This is a spare, mysterious story that ends, dramatically, at just the right moment.

A Journey

As she lay in her berth, staring at the shadows overhead, the rush of the wheels was in her brain, driving her deeper and deeper into circles of wakeful lucidity. The sleeping car had sunk into its night silence. Through the wet windowpane she watched the sudden lights, the long stretches of hurrying blackness. Now and then she turned her head and looked through the opening in the hangings at her husband's curtains across the aisle. . . .

She wondered restlessly if he wanted anything and if she could hear him if he called. His voice had grown very weak within the last months and it irritated him when she did not hear. This irritability, this increasing childish petulance seemed to give expression to their imperceptible estrangement. Like two faces looking at one another through a sheet of glass they were close together, almost touching, but they could not hear or feel each other: the conductivity between them was broken. She, at least, had this sense of separation, and she fancied sometimes that she saw it reflected in the look with which he supplemented his failing words. Doubtless the fault was hers. She was too impenetrably healthy to be touched by the irrelevancies of disease. Her self-reproachful tenderness was tinged with the sense of his irrationality: she had a vague feeling that there was a purpose in his helpless tyrannies. The suddenness of the change had found her so unprepared. A year ago their pulses had beat to one robust measure; both had the same prodigal confidence in an exhaustless future. Now their energies no longer kept step: hers still bounded ahead of life, pre-empting unclaimed regions of hope and activity, while his lagged behind, vainly struggling to overtake her.

When they married, she had such arrears of living to make up: her days had been as bare as the whitewashed schoolroom where she forced innutritious facts upon reluctant children. His coming had broken in on the slumber of circumstance, widening the present till it became the encloser of remotest chances. But imperceptibly the horizon narrowed. Life had a grudge against her: she was never to be allowed to spread her wings.

At first the doctors had said that six weeks of mild air would set him right; but when he came back this assurance was explained as having of course included a winter in a dry climate. They gave up their pretty house, storing the wedding presents and new furniture, and went to Colorado. She had hated it there from the first. Nobody knew her or cared about her; there was no one to wonder at the good match she had made, or to envy her the new dresses and the visiting cards which were still a surprise to her. And he kept growing worse. She felt herself beset with difficulties too evasive to be fought by so direct a temperament. She still loved him, of course; but he was gradually, undefinably ceasing to be himself. The man she had married had been strong, active, gently masterful: the male whose pleasure it is to clear a way through the material obstructions of life; but now it was she who was the protector, he who must be shielded from importunities and given his drops or his beef juice though the skies were falling. The routine of the sickroom bewildered her; this punctual administering of medicine seemed as idle as some uncomprehended religious mummery.

There were moments, indeed, when warm gushes of pity swept away her instinctive resentment of his condition, when she still found his old self in his eyes as they groped for each other through the dense medium of his weakness. But these moments had grown rare. Sometimes he frightened her: his sunken expressionless face seemed that of a stranger; his voice was weak and hoarse; his thin-lipped smile a mere muscular contraction. Her hand avoided his damp soft skin, which had lost the familiar roughness of health: she caught herself furtively watching him as she might have watched a strange animal. It frightened her to feel that this was the man she loved; there were hours when to tell him what she suffered seemed the one escape from her fears. But in general she judged herself more leniently, reflecting that she had perhaps been too long alone with him, and that she would feel differently when they were at home again, surrounded by her robust and buoyant family. How she had rejoiced when the doctors at last gave their consent to his going home! She knew, of course, what the decision meant; they both knew. It meant that he was to die; but they dressed the truth in hopeful euphemisms, and at times, in the joy of preparation, she really forgot the purpose of their journey, and slipped into an eager allusion to next year's plans.

At last the day of leaving came. She had a dreadful fear that they would never get away; that somehow at the last moment he would fail her; that the doctors held one of their accustomed treacheries in reserve; but nothing happened. They drove to the station, he was installed in a seat with a rug over his knees and a cushion at his back, and she hung out of the window waving unregretful farewells to the acquaintances she had really never liked till then.

The first twenty-four hours had passed off well. He revived a little and it amused him to look out of the window and to observe the humors of the car. The second day he began to grow weary and to chafe under the dispassionate stare of the freckled child with the lump of chewing gum. She had to explain to the child's mother that her husband was too ill to be disturbed: a statement received by that lady with a resentment visibly supported by the maternal sentiment of the whole car. . . .

That night he slept badly and the next morning his temperature frightened her: she was sure he was growing worse. The day passed slowly, punctuated by the small irritations of travel. Watching his tired face, she traced in its contractions every rattle and jolt of the train, till her own body vibrated with sympathetic fatigue. She felt the others observing him too, and hovered restlessly between him and the line of interrogative eyes. The freckled child hung about him like a fly; offers of candy and picture books failed to dislodge her: she twisted one leg around the other and watched him imperturbably. The porter, as he passed, lingered with vague proffers of help, probably inspired by philanthropic passengers swelling with the sense that "something ought to be done"; and one nervous man in a skull cap was audibly concerned as to the possible effect on his wife's health.

The hours dragged on in a dreary inoccupation. Towards dusk she sat down beside him and he laid his hand on hers. The touch startled her. He seemed to be calling her from far off. She looked at him helplessly and his smile went through her like a physical pang.

"Are you very tired?" she asked.

"No, not very."

"We'll be there soon now."

"Yes, very soon."

"This time tomorrow—"

He nodded and they sat silent. When she had put him to bed and crawled into her own berth she tried to cheer herself with the thought that in less than twenty-four hours they would be in New York. Her people would all be at the station to meet her—she pictured their round unanxious faces pressing through the crowd. She only hoped they would not tell him too loudly that he was looking splendidly and would be all right in no time: the subtler sympathies developed by long contact with suffering were making her aware of a certain coarseness of texture in the family sensibilities.

Suddenly she thought she heard him call. She parted the curtains and listened. No, it was only a man snoring at the other end of the car. His snores had a greasy sound, as though they passed through tallow. She lay down and tried to sleep. . . . Had she not heard him move? She started up trembling. . . . The silence frightened her more than any sound. He might not be able to make her hear—he might be calling her now. . . . What made her think of such things? It was merely the familiar tendency of an overtired mind to fasten itself on the most intolerable chance within the range of its forebodings. . . . Putting her head out, she listened: but she could not distinguish his breathing from that of the other pairs of lungs about her. She longed to get up and look at him, but she knew the impulse was a mere vent for her restlessness, and the fear of disturbing him restrained her. . . . The regular movement of his curtain reassured her, she knew not why; she remembered that he had wished her a cheerful good night; and the sheer inability to endure her fears a moment longer made her put them from her with an effort of her whole sound-tired body. She turned on her side and slept.

She sat up stiffly, staring out at the dawn. The train was rushing through a region of bare hillocks huddled against a lifeless sky. It looked like the first day of creation. The air of the car was close, and she pushed up her window to let in the keen wind. Then she looked at her watch: it was seven o'clock, and soon the people about her would be stirring. She slipped into her clothes, smoothed her disheveled hair and crept to the dressing room. When she had washed her face and adjusted her dress she felt more hopeful. It was always a struggle for her not to be cheerful in the morning. Her cheeks burned deliciously under the coarse towel and the wet hair about her temples broke into strong upward tendrils. Every inch of her was full of life and elasticity. And in ten hours they would be at home!

She stepped to her husband's berth: it was time for him to take his early glass of milk. The window shade was down, and in the dusk of the curtained enclosure she could just see that he lay sideways, with his face away from her. She leaned over him and drew up the shade. As she did so she touched one of his hands. It felt cold. . . .

She bent closer, laying her hand on his arm and calling him by name. He did not move. She spoke again more loudly; she grasped his shoulder and gently shook it. He lay motionless. She caught hold of his hand again: it slipped from her limply, like a dead thing. A dead thing?

Her breath caught. She must see his face. She leaned forward, and hurriedly, shrinkingly, with a sickening reluctance of the flesh, laid her hands on his shoulders and turned him over. His head fell back; his face looked small and smooth; he gazed at her with steady eyes.

She remained motionless for a long time, holding him thus; and they looked at each other. Suddenly she shrank back: the longing to scream, to call out, to fly from him, had almost overpowered her. But a strong hand arrested her. Good God! If it were known that he was dead they would be put off the train at the next station—

In a terrifying flash of remembrance there arose before her a scene she had once witnessed in traveling, when a husband and wife, whose child had died in the train, had been thrust out at some chance station. She saw them standing on the platform with the child's body between them; she had never forgotten the dazed look with which they followed the receding train. And this was what would happen to her. Within the next hour she might find herself on the platform of some strange station, alone with her husband's body. . . . Anything but that! It was too horrible—She quivered like a creature at bay.

As she cowered there, she felt the train moving more slowly. It was coming then—they were approaching a station! She saw again the husband and wife standing on the lonely platform; and with a violent gesture she drew down the shade to hide her husband's face.

Feeling dizzy, she sank down on the edge of the berth, keeping away from his outstretched body, and pulling the curtains close, so that he and she were shut into a kind of sepulchral twilight. She tried to think. At all costs she must conceal the fact that he was dead. But how? Her mind refused to act: she could not plan, combine. She could think of no way but to sit there, clutching the curtains, all day long. . . .

She heard the porter making up her bed; people were beginning to move about the car; the dressing-room door was being opened and shut. She tried to rouse herself. At length with a supreme effort she rose to her feet, stepping into the aisle of the car and drawing the curtains tight behind her. She noticed that they still parted slightly with the motion of the car, and finding a pin in her dress she fastened them together. Now she was safe. She looked round and saw the porter. She fancied he was watching her.

'Ain't he awake yet?' he inquired.

'No,' she faltered.

'I got his milk all ready when he wants it. You know you told me to have it for him by seven.'

She nodded silently and crept into her seat.

At half-past eight the train reached Buffalo. By this time the other passengers were dressed and the berths had been folded back for the day. The porter, moving to and fro under his burden of sheets and pillows, glanced at her as he passed. At length he said: 'Ain't he going to get up? You know we're ordered to make up the berths as early as we can.'

She turned cold with fear. They were just entering the station.

'Oh, not yet,' she stammered. 'Not till he's had his milk. Won't you get it, please?'

'All right. Soon as we start again.'

When the train moved on he reappeared with the milk. She took it from him and sat vaguely looking at it: her brain moved slowly from one idea to another, as though they were stepping-stones set far apart across a whirling flood. At length she became aware that the porter still hovered expectantly.

'Will I give it to him?' he suggested.

'Oh, no,' she cried, rising. 'He—he's asleep yet, I think—'

She waited till the porter had passed on; then she unpinned the curtains and slipped behind them. In the semiobscurity her husband's face stared up at her like a marble mask with agate eyes. The eyes were dreadful. She put out her hand and drew down the lids. Then she remembered the glass of milk in her other hand: what was she to do with it? She thought of raising the window and throwing it out; but to do so she would have to lean across his body and bring her face close to his. She decided to drink the milk.

She returned to her seat with the empty glass and after a while the porter came back to get it.

'When'll I fold up his bed?' he asked.

'Oh, not now—not yet; he's ill—he's very ill. Can't you let him stay as he is? The doctor wants him to lie down as much as possible.'

He scratched his head. 'Well, if he's *really* sick—'

He took the empty glass and walked away, explaining to the passengers that the party behind the curtains was too sick to get up just yet.

She found herself the center of sympathetic eyes. A motherly woman with an intimate smile sat down beside her.

'I'm really sorry to hear your husband's sick. I've had a remarkable amount of sickness in my family and maybe I could assist you. Can I take a look at him?'

'Oh, no—no please! He mustn't be disturbed.'

The lady accepted the rebuff indulgently.

'Well, it's just as you say, of course, but you don't look to me as if you'd had much experience in sickness and I'd have been glad to assist you. What do you generally do when your husband's taken this way?'

'I—I let him sleep.'

'Too much sleep ain't any too healthful either. Don't you give him any medicine?'

'Y—yes.'

'Don't you wake him to take it?'

'Yes.'

'When does he take the next dose?'

'Not for—two hours—'

The lady looked disappointed. 'Well, if I was you I'd try giving it oftener. That's what I do with my folks.'

After that many faces seemed to press upon her. The passengers were on their way to the dining car, and she was conscious that as they passed down the aisle they glanced curiously at the closed curtains. One lantern-jawed man with prominent eyes stood still and tried to shoot his projecting glance through the division between the folds. The freckled child, returning from breakfast, waylaid the passers with a buttery clutch, saying in a loud whisper, 'He's sick'; and once the conductor came by, asking for tickets. She shrank into her corner and looked out of the window at the flying trees and houses, meaningless hieroglyphs of an endlessly unrolled papyrus.

Now and then the train stopped, and the newcomers on entering the car stared in turn at the closed curtains. More and more people seemed to pass—their faces began to blend fantastically with the images surging in her brain. . . .

Later in the day a fat man detached himself from the mist of faces. He had a creased stomach and soft pale lips. As he pressed himself into the seat facing her she noticed that he was dressed in black broadcloth, with a soiled white tie.

'Husband's pretty bad this morning, is he?'

'Yes.'

'Dear, dear! Now that's terribly distressing, ain't it?' An apostolic smile revealed his gold-filled teeth. 'Of course you know there's no sech thing as sickness. Ain't that a lovely thought? Death itself is but a deloosion of our grosser senses. On'y lay yourself open to the influx of the sperrit, submit yourself passively to the action of the divine force, and disease and dissolution will cease to exist for you. If you could indooce your husband to read this little pamphlet—'

The faces about her again grew indistinct. She had a vague recollection of hearing the motherly lady and the parent of the freckled child ardently disputing the relative advantages of trying several medicines at once, or of taking each in turn; the motherly lady maintaining that the competitive system saved time; the other objecting that you couldn't tell which remedy had effected the cure; their voices went on and on, like bell buoys droning through a fog. . . . The porter came up now and then with questions that she did not understand, but somehow she must have answered since he went away again without repeating them; every two hours the motherly lady reminded her that her husband ought to have his drops; people left the car and others replaced them. . . .

Her head was spinning and she tried to steady herself by clutching at her thoughts as they swept by, but they slipped away from her like bushes on the side of a sheer precipice down which she seemed to be falling. Suddenly her mind grew clear again and she found herself vividly picturing what would happen when the train reached New York. She shuddered as it occurred to her that he would be quite cold and that someone might perceive he had been dead since morning.

She thought hurriedly: 'If they see I am not surprised they will suspect something. They will ask questions, and if I tell them the truth they won't believe me—no one would believe me! It will be terrible'—and she kept repeating to herself—'I must pretend I don't know. I must pretend I don't know. When they open the curtains I must go up to him quite naturally—and then I must scream!' She had an idea that the scream would be very hard to do.

Gradually new thoughts crowded upon her, vivid and urgent: she tried to separate and restrain them, but they beset her clamorously, like her school children at the end of a hot day, when she was too tired to silence them. Her head grew confused, and she felt a sick fear of forgetting her part, of betraying herself by some unguarded word or look.

'I must pretend I don't know,' she went on murmuring. The words had lost their significance, but she repeated them mechanically, as though they had been a magic formula, until suddenly she heard herself saying: 'I can't remember, I can't remember!'

Her voice sounded very loud, and she looked about her in terror; but no one seemed to notice that she had spoken.

As she glanced down the car her eye caught the curtains of her husband's berth, and she began to examine the monotonous arabesques woven through their heavy folds. The pattern was intricate and difficult to trace; she gazed fixedly at the curtains and as she did so the thick stuff grew transparent and through it she saw her husband's face—his dead face. She struggled to avert her look, but her eyes refused to move and her head seemed to be held in vice. At last, with an effort that left her weak and shaking, she turned away; but it was of no use; close in front of her, small and smooth, was her husband's face. It seemed to be suspended in the air between her and the false braids of the woman who sat in front of her. With an uncontrollable gesture she stretched out her hand to push the face away, and suddenly she felt the touch of his smooth skin. She repressed a cry and half started from her seat. The woman with the false braids looked around, and feeling that she must justify her movement in some way she rose and lifted her traveling bag from the opposite seat. She unlocked the bag and looked into it; but the first object her hand met was a small flask of her husband's, thrust there at the last moment, in the haste of departure. She locked the bag and closed her eyes . . . his face was there again, hanging between her eyeballs and lids like a waxen mask against a red curtain. . . .

She roused herself with a shiver. Had she fainted or slept? Hours seemed to have elapsed; but it was still broad day, and the people about her were sitting in the same attitudes as before.

A sudden sense of hunger made her aware that she had eaten nothing since morning. The thought of food filled her with disgust, but she dreaded a return of faintness, and remembering that she had some biscuits in her bag she took one out and ate it. The dry crumbs choked her, and she hastily swallowed a little brandy from her husband's flask. The burning sensation in her throat acted as a counterirritant, momentarily relieving the dull ache of her nerves. Then she felt a gently-stealing warmth, as though a soft air fanned her, and the swarming fears relaxed their clutch, receding through the stillness that enclosed her, a stillness soothing as the spacious quietude of a summer day. She slept.

Through her sleep she felt the impetuous rush of the train. It seemed to be life itself that was sweeping her on with headlong inexorable force—sweeping her into darkness and terror, and the awe of unknown days.—Now all at once everything was still—not a sound, not a pulsation. . . . She was dead in her turn, and lay beside him with smooth upstaring face. How quiet it was!—and yet she heard feet coming, the feet of the men who were to carry them away. . . . She could feel too—she felt a sudden prolonged vibration, a series of hard shocks, and then another plunge into darkness, the darkness of death this time—a black whirlwind on which they were both spinning like leaves, in wild uncoiling spirals, with millions and millions of the dead. . . .

She sprang up in terror. Her sleep must have lasted a long time, for the winter day had paled and the lights had been lit. The car was in confusion, and as she regained her self-possession she saw that the passengers were gathering up their wraps and bags. The woman with the false braids had brought from the dressing room a sickly ivy plant in a bottle, and the Christian Scientist was reversing his cuffs. The porter passed down the aisle with his impartial brush. An impersonal figure with a gold-banded cap asked for her husband's ticket. A voice shouted 'Baig-gage express!' and she heard the clicking of metal as the passengers handed over their checks.

Presently her window was blocked by an expanse of sooty wall, and the train passed into the Harlem tunnel. The journey was over; in a few minutes she would see her family pushing their joyous way through the throng at the station. Her heart dilated. The worst terror was past. . . .

'We'd better get him up now, hadn't we?' asked the porter, touching her arm.

He had her husband's hat in his hand and was meditatively revolving it under his brush.

She looked at the hat and tried to speak; but suddenly the car grew dark. She flung up her arms, struggling to catch at something, and fell face downward, striking her head against the dead man's berth.

SHERWOOD ANDERSON
(1876–1941)

Like Samuel Clemens, by whom, in fact, he was influenced, Sherwood Anderson has had an incalculable influence upon generations of American writers. The deceptively artless, unadorned, anecdotal Anderson voice has come to characterize, for many readers, the distinctive American voice—most recently reconstituted as Minimalism. Simple, often declarative sentences; "realistic" settings, characters, plots; a lack of interest in stylistic experimentation; an absence of philosophical exploration—this is the kind of fiction that many, or most, readers prefer, because it is so readily accessible. Except at its most brilliantly stylized, as in certain short fictions of Ernest Hemingway, the meanings and significance of the Anderson voice lie on the surface of narrative. Which is not to say that they are, or need be, superficial, as in Anderson's exemplary Winesburg, Ohio *(1919), from which "The Strength of God" is taken, and certain of his much-anthologized short stories like "The Egg," "I Want to Know Why," and "Death in the Woods."*

Anderson, born in southern Ohio of a nomadic family, became a writer in early middle age after a business career that seems to have pushed him into a nervous collapse. The author of a number of novels, including Windy McPherson's Son *(1916) and* Poor White *(1920), Anderson most realized his vision as a writer of short stories. These are collected in* The Triumph of the Egg *(1921),* Horses and Men *(1923), and* Death in the Woods and Other Stories *(1933). But his masterpiece remains* Winesburg, Ohio, *that "Book of the Grotesque"* sui generis.

The Strength of God

The Reverend Curtis Hartman was pastor of the Presbyterian Church of Winesburg, and had been in that position ten years. He was forty years old, and by his nature very silent and reticent. To preach, standing in the pulpit before the people, was always a hardship for him and from Wednesday morning until Saturday evening he thought of nothing but the two sermons that must be preached on Sunday. Early on Sunday morning he went into a little room called a study in the bell tower of the church and prayed. In his prayers there was one note that always predominated. "Give me strength and courage for Thy work, O Lord!" he plead, kneeling on the bare floor and bowing his head in the presence of the task that lay before him.

The Reverend Hartman was a tall man with a brown beard. His wife, a stout, nervous woman, was the daughter of a manufacturer of underwear at Cleveland, Ohio. The minister himself was rather a favorite in the town. The elders of the church liked him because he was quiet and unpretentious and Mrs. White, the banker's wife, thought him scholarly and refined.

The Presbyterian Church held itself somewhat aloof from the other churches of Winesburg. It was larger and more imposing and its minister was better paid. He even had a carriage of his own and on summer evenings sometimes drove about town with his wife. Through Main Street and up and down Buckeye Street he went, bowing gravely to the people, while his wife, afire with secret pride, looked at him out of the corners of her eyes and worried lest the horse become frightened and run away.

For a good many years after he came to Winesburg things went well with Curtis Hartman. He was not one to arouse keen enthusiasm among the worshippers in his church but on the other hand he made no enemies. In reality he was much in earnest and sometimes suffered prolonged periods of remorse because he could not go crying the word of God in the highways and byways of the town. He wondered if the flame of the spirit really burned in him and dreamed of a day when a strong sweet new current of power would come like a great wind into his voice and his soul and the people would tremble before the spirit of God made manifest in him. "I am a poor stick and that will never really happen to me," he mused dejectedly and then a patient smile lit up his features. "Oh well, I suppose I'm doing well enough," he added philosophically.

The room in the bell tower of the church, where on Sunday mornings the minister prayed for an increase in him of the power of God, had but one window. It was long and narrow and swung outward on a hinge like a door. On the window, made of little leaded panes, was a design showing the Christ laying his hand upon the head of a child. One Sunday morning in the summer as he sat by his desk in the room with a large Bible opened before him, and the sheets of his sermon scattered about, the minister was shocked to see, in the upper room of the house next door, a woman lying in her bed and smoking a cigarette while she read a book. Curtis Hartman went on tiptoe to the window and closed it softly. He was horror stricken at the thought of a woman smoking and trembled also to think that his eyes, just raised from the pages of the book of God, had looked upon the bare shoulders and white throat of a woman. With his brain in a whirl he went down into the pulpit and preached a long sermon without once thinking of his gestures or his voice. The sermon attracted unusual attention because of its power and clearness. "I wonder if she is listening, if my voice is carrying a message into her soul," he thought and began to hope that on future Sunday mornings he might be able to say words that would touch and awaken the woman apparently far gone in secret sin.

The house next door to the Presbyterian Church, through the windows of which the minister had seen the sight that had so upset him, was occupied by two women. Aunt Elizabeth Swift, a grey competent-looking widow with money in the Winesburg National Bank, lived there with her daughter Kate Swift, a school teacher. The school teacher was thirty years old and had a neat trim-looking figure. She had few friends and bore a reputation of having a sharp tongue. When he began to think about her, Curtis Hartman remembered that she had been to Europe and had lived for two years in New York City. "Perhaps after all her smoking means nothing," he thought. He began to remember that when he was a student in college and occasionally read novels, good, although somewhat worldly women, had smoked through the pages of a book that had once fallen into his hands. With a rush of new determination he worked on his sermons all through the week and forgot, in his zeal to reach the ears and the soul of this new listener, both his embarrassment in the pulpit and the necessity of prayer in the study on Sunday mornings.

Reverend Hartman's experience with women had been somewhat limited. He was the son of a wagon maker from Muncie, Indiana, and had worked his way through college. The daughter of the underwear manufacturer had boarded in a house where he lived during his school days and he had married her after a formal and prolonged courtship, carried on for the most part by the girl herself. On his marriage day the underwear manufacturer had given his daughter five thousand dollars and he promised to leave her at least twice that amount in his will. The minister had thought himself fortunate in marriage and had never permitted himself to think of other women. He did not want to think of other women. What he wanted was to do the work of God quietly and earnestly.

In the soul of the minister a struggle awoke. From wanting to reach the ears of Kate Swift, and through his sermons to delve into her soul, he began to want also to look again at the figure lying white and quiet in the bed. On a Sunday morning when he could not sleep because of his thoughts he arose and went to walk in the streets. When he had gone along Main Street almost to the old Richmond place he stopped and picking up a stone rushed off to the room in the bell tower. With the stone he broke out a corner of the window and then locked the door and sat down at the desk before the open Bible to wait. When the shade of the window to Kate Swift's room was raised he could see, through the hole, directly into her bed, but she was not there. She also had arisen and had gone for a walk and the hand that raised the shade was the hand of Aunt Elizabeth Swift.

The minister almost wept with joy at this deliverance from the carnal desire to "peep" and went back to his own house praising God. In an ill moment he forgot, however, to stop the hole in the window. The piece of glass broken out at the corner of the window just nipped off the bare heel of the boy standing motionless and looking with rapt eyes into the face of the Christ.

Curtis Hartman forgot his sermon on that Sunday morning. He talked to his congregation and in his talk said that it was a mistake for people to think of their minister as a man set aside and intended by nature to lead a blameless life. "Out of my own experience I know that we, who are the ministers of God's word, are beset by the same temptations that assail you," he declared. "I have been tempted and have surrendered to temptation. It is only the hand of God, placed beneath my head, that has raised me up. As he has raised me so also will he raise you. Do not despair. In your hour of sin raise your eyes to the skies and you will be again and again saved."

Resolutely the minister put the thoughts of the woman in the bed out of his mind and began to be something like a lover in the presence of his wife. One evening when they drove out together he turned the horse out of Buckeye Street and in the darkness on Gospel Hill, above Waterworks Pond, put his arm about Sarah Hartman's waist. When he had eaten breakfast in the morning and was ready to retire to his study at the back of his house he went around the table and kissed his wife on the cheek. When thoughts of Kate Swift came into his head, he smiled and raised his eyes to the skies. "Intercede for me, Master," he muttered, "keep me in the narrow path intent on Thy work."

And now began the real struggle in the soul of the brown-bearded minister. By chance he discovered that Kate Swift was in the habit of lying in her bed in the evenings and reading a book. A lamp stood on a table by the side of the bed and the light streamed down upon her white shoulders and bare throat. On the evening when he made the discovery the minister sat at the desk in the study from nine until after eleven and when her light was put out stumbled out of the church to spend two more hours walking and praying in the streets. He did not want to kiss the shoulders and the throat of Kate Swift and had not allowed his mind to dwell on such thoughts. He did not know what he wanted. "I am God's child and he must save me from myself," he cried, in the darkness under the trees as he wandered in the streets. By a tree he stood and looked at the sky that was covered with hurrying clouds. He began to talk to God intimately and closely. "Please, Father, do not forget me. Give me power to go to-morrow and repair the hole in the window. Lift my eyes again to the skies. Stay with me, Thy servant, in his hour of need."

Up and down through the silent streets walked the minister and for days and weeks his soul was troubled. He could not understand the temptation that had come to him nor could he fathom the reason for its coming. In a way he began to blame God, saying to himself that he had tried to keep his feet in the true path and had not run about seeking sin. "Through my days as a young man and all through my life here I have gone quietly about my work," he declared. "Why now should I be tempted? What have I done that this burden should be laid on me?"

Three times during the early fall and winter of that year Curtis Hartman crept out of his house to the room in the bell tower to sit in the darkness looking at the figure of Kate Swift lying in her bed and later went to walk and pray in the streets. He could not understand himself. For weeks he would go along scarcely thinking of the school teacher and telling himself that he had conquered the carnal desire to look at her body. And then something would happen. As he sat in the study of his own house, hard at work on a sermon, he would become nervous and begin to walk up and down the room. "I will go out into the streets," he told himself and even as he let himself in at the church door he persistently denied to himself the cause of his being there. "I will not repair the hole in the window and I will train myself to come here at night and sit in the presence of this woman without raising my eyes. I will not be defeated in this thing. The Lord has devised this temptation as a test of my soul and I will grope my way out of darkness into the light of righteousness."

One night in January when it was bitter cold and snow lay deep on the streets of Winesburg Curtis Hartman paid his last visit to the room in the bell tower of the church. It was past nine o'clock when he left his own house and he set out so hurriedly that he forgot to put on his overshoes. In Main Street no one was abroad but Hop Higgins the night watchman and in the whole town no one was awake but the watchman and young George Willard, who sat in the office of the *Winesburg Eagle* trying to write a story. Along the street to the church went the minister, plowing through the drifts and thinking that this time he would utterly give way to sin. "I want to look at the woman and to think of kissing her shoulders and I am going to let myself think what I choose," he declared bitterly and tears came into his eyes. He began to think that he would get out of the ministry and try some other way of life. "I shall go to some city and get into business," he declared. "If my nature is such that I cannot resist sin, I shall give myself over to sin. At least I shall not be a hypocrite, preaching the word of God with my mind thinking of the shoulders and neck of a woman who does not belong to me."

It was cold in the room of the bell tower of the church on that January night and almost as soon as he came into the room Curtis Hartman knew that if he stayed he would be ill. His feet were wet from tramping in the snow and there was no fire. In the room in the house next door Kate Swift had not yet appeared. With grim determination the man sat down to wait. Sitting in the chair and gripping the edge of the desk on which lay the Bible he stared into the darkness thinking the blackest thoughts of his life. He thought of his wife and for the moment almost hated her. "She has always been ashamed of passion and has cheated me," he thought. "Man has a right to expect living passion and beauty in a woman. He has no right to forget that he is an animal and in me there is something that is Greek. I will throw off the woman of my bosom and seek other women. I will besiege this school teacher. I will fly in the face of all men and if I am a creature of carnal lusts I will live then for my lusts."

The distracted man trembled from head to foot, partly from cold, partly from the struggle in which he was engaged. Hours passed and a fever assailed his body. His throat began to hurt and his teeth chattered. His feet on the study floor felt like two cakes of ice. Still he would not give up. "I will see this woman and will think the thoughts I have never dared to think," he told himself, gripping the edge of the desk and waiting.

Curtis Hartman came near dying from the effects of that night of waiting in the church, and also he found in the thing that happened what he took to be the way of life for him. On other evenings when he had waited he had not been able to see, through the little hole in the glass, any part of the school teacher's room except that occupied by her bed. In the darkness he had waited until the woman suddenly appeared sitting in the bed in her white night-robe. When the light was turned up she propped herself up among the pillows and read a book. Sometimes she smoked one of the cigarettes. Only her bare shoulders and throat were visible.

On the January night, after he had come near dying with cold and after his mind had two or three times actually slipped away into an odd land of fantasy so that he had by an exercise of will power to force himself back into consciousness, Kate Swift appeared. In the room next door a lamp was lighted and the waiting man stared into an empty bed. Then upon the bed before his eyes a naked woman threw herself. Lying face downward she wept and beat with her fists upon the pillow. With a final outburst of weeping she half arose, and in the presence of the man who had waited to look and to think thoughts the woman of sin began to pray. In the lamplight her figure, slim and strong, looked like the figure of the boy in the presence of the Christ on the leaded window.

Curtis Hartman never remembered how he got out of the church.

With a cry he arose, dragging the heavy desk along the floor. The Bible fell, making a great clatter in the silence. When the light in the house next door went out he stumbled down the stairway and into the street. Along the street he went and ran in at the door of the *Winesburg Eagle*. To George Willard, who was tramping up and down in the office undergoing a struggle of his own, he began to talk half incoherently. "The ways of God are beyond human understanding," he cried, running in quickly and closing the door. He began to advance upon the young man, his eyes glowing and his voice ringing with fervor. "I have found the light," he cried. "After ten years in this town, God has manifested himself to me in the body of a woman." His voice dropped and he began to whisper. "I did not understand," he said. "What I took to be a trial of my soul was only a preparation for a new and more beautiful fervor of the spirit. God has appeared to me in the person of Kate Swift, the school teacher, kneeling naked on a bed. Do you know Kate Swift? Although she may not be aware of it, she is an instrument of God, bearing the message of truth."

Reverend Curtis Hartman turned and ran out of the office. At the door he stopped, and after looking up and down the deserted street, turned again to George Willard. "I am delivered. Have no fear." He held up a bleeding fist for the young man to see. "I smashed the glass of the window," he cried. "Now it will have to be wholly replaced. The strength of God was in me and I broke it with my fist."

WILLA CATHER
(1873–1947)

Born in Virginia, Willa Cather moved with her family to Red Cloud, Nebraska, as a young child. Like Sarah Orne Jewett, whose New England stories first inspired her to write, Cather was a passionate chronicler of her time and place: "When I strike the open plains, something happens. I'm home. I breathe differently. That love of great spaces, of rolling open country like the sea,—it's the grand passion of my life."

Along with Edith Wharton, in many ways her antithesis, Willa Cather is the predominant American woman writer of her era. Her "grand passion" for the Midwest is matched by an equal fascination with the primordial American Southwest; and, as exemplified in this early story "A Death in the Desert," from her collection The Troll Garden *(1905), with the lives and fates of musical artists.*

Cather's literary output was considerable, and its high quality was recognized from the first. Among her outstanding titles are O Pioneers! *(1913),* The Song of the Lark *(1915),* My Ántonia *(1918),* A Lost Lady *(1923),* The Professor's House *(1925), and* Death Comes for the Archbishop *(1927). Her most frequently anthologized short stories are "Paul's Case" and "Neighbor Rosicky"; the story included here makes explicit the author's lifelong fascination with musical artists and with the seemingly impersonal destiny of one fated to serve, like the heroine of* The Song of the Lark, *"the madness of art"—an echo of the powerful concluding lines of Henry James's "The Middle Years."*

A Death in the Desert

Everett Hilgarde was conscious that the man in the seat across the aisle was looking at him intently. He was a large, florid man, wore a conspicuous diamond solitaire upon his third finger, and Everett judged him to be a travelling salesman of some sort. He had the air of an adaptable fellow who had been about the world and who could keep cool and clean under almost any circumstances.

The "High Line Flyer," as this train was derisively called among railroad men, was jerking along through the hot afternoon over the monotonous country between Holdrege and Cheyenne. Besides the blond man and himself the only occupants of the car were two dusty, bedraggled-looking girls who had been to the Exposition at Chicago, and who were earnestly discussing the cost of their first trip out of Colorado. The four uncomfortable passengers were covered with a sediment of fine, yellow dust which clung to their hair and eyebrows like gold powder. It blew up in clouds from the bleak, lifeless country through which they passed, until they were one colour with the sage-brush and sand-hills. The grey and yellow desert was varied only by occasional ruins of deserted towns, and the little red boxes of station-houses, where the spindling trees and sickly vines in the blue-grass yards made little green reserves fenced off in that confusing wilderness of sand.

As the slanting rays of the sun beat in stronger and stronger through the car-windows, the blond gentleman asked the ladies' permission to remove his coat, and sat in his lavender striped shirt-sleeves, with a black silk handkerchief tucked carefully about his collar. He had seemed interested in Everett since they had boarded the train at Holdrege, and kept glancing at him curiously and then looking reflectively out of the window, as though he were trying to recall something. But wherever Everett went someone was almost sure to look at him with that curious interest, and it had ceased to embarrass or annoy him. Presently the stranger, seeming satisfied with his observation, leaned back in his seat, half closed his eyes, and began softly to whistle the Spring Song from *Proserpine,* the cantata that a dozen years before had made its young composer famous in a night. Everett had heard that air on guitars in Old Mexico, on mandolins at college glees, on cottage organs in New England hamlets, and only two weeks ago he had heard it played on sleighbells at a variety theatre in Denver. There was literally no way of escaping his brother's precocity. Adriance could live on the other side of the Atlantic, where his youthful indiscretions were forgotten in his mature achievements, but his brother had never been able to outrun *Proserpine,* and here he found it again in the Colorado sand-hills. Not that Everett was exactly ashamed of *Proserpine;* only a man of genius could have written it, but it was the sort of thing that a man of genius outgrows as soon as he can.

Everett unbent a trifle and smiled at his neighbour across the aisle. Immediately the large man rose and coming over dropped into the seat facing Hilgarde, extending his card.

"Dusty ride, isn't it? I don't mind it myself; I'm used to it. Born and bred in de briar patch, like Br'er Rabbit. I've been trying to place you for a long time; I think I must have met you before."

"Thank you," said Everett, taking the card; "my name is Hilgarde. You've probably met my brother, Adriance; people often mistake me for him."

The travelling-man brought his hand down upon his knee with such vehemence that the solitaire blazed.

"So I was right after all, and if you're not Adriance Hilgarde you're his double. I thought I couldn't be mistaken. Seen him? Well, I guess! I never missed one of his recitals at the Auditorium, and he played the piano score of *Proserpine* through to us once at the Chicago Press Club. I used to be on the *Commercial* there before I began to travel for the publishing department of the concern. So you're Hilgarde's brother, and here I've run into you at the jumping-off place. Sounds like a newspaper yarn, doesn't it?"

The travelling-man laughed and offered Everett a cigar and plied him with questions on the only subject that people ever seemed to care to talk to Everett about. At length the salesman and the two girls alighted at a Colorado way station, and Everett went on to Cheyenne alone.

The train pulled into Cheyenne at nine o'clock, late by a matter of four hours or so; but no one seemed particularly concerned at its tardiness except the station agent, who grumbled about being kept in the office overtime on a summer night. When Everett alighted from the train he walked down the platform and stopped at the track crossing, uncertain as to what direction he should take to reach a hotel. A phaeton stood near the crossing and a woman held the reins. She was dressed in white, and her figure was clearly silhouetted against the cushions, though it was too dark to see her face. Everett had scarcely noticed her, when the switch-engine came puffing up from the opposite direction, and the headlight threw a strong glare of light on his face. Suddenly the woman in the phaeton uttered a low cry and dropped the reins. Everett started forward and caught the horse's head, but the animal only lifted its ears and whisked its tail in impatient surprise. The woman sat perfectly still, her head sunk between her shoulders and her handkerchief pressed to her face. Another woman came out of the depot and hurried toward the phaeton, crying, "Katharine, dear, what is the matter?"

Everett hesitated a moment in painful embarrassment, then lifted his hat and passed on. He was accustomed to sudden recognitions in the most impossible places, especially by women, but this cry out of the night had shaken him.

While Everett was breakfasting the next morning, the head waiter leaned over his chair to murmur that there was a gentleman waiting to see him in the parlour. Everett finished his coffee, and went in the direction indicated, where he found his visitor restlessly pacing the floor. His whole manner betrayed a high degree of agitation, though his physique was not that of a man whose nerves lie near the surface. He was something below medium height, square-shouldered and solidly built. His thick, closely cut hair was beginning to show grey about the ears, and his bronzed face was heavily lined. His square brown hands were locked behind him, and he held his shoulders like a man conscious of responsibilities, yet, as he turned to greet Everett, there was an incongruous diffidence in his address.

"Good-morning, Mr. Hilgarde," he said, extending his hand; "I found your name on the hotel register. My name is Gaylord. I'm afraid my sister startled you at the station last night, Mr. Hilgarde, and I've come around to apologize."

"Ah! the young lady in the phaeton? I'm sure I didn't know whether I had anything to do with her alarm or not. If I did, it is I who owe the apology."

The man coloured a little under the dark brown of his face.

"Oh, it's nothing you could help, sir, I fully understand that. You see, my sister used to be a pupil of your brother's, and it seems you favour him; and when the switch-engine threw a light on your face it startled her."

Everett wheeled about in his chair. "Oh! *Katharine* Gaylord! Is it possible! Now it's you who have given me a turn. Why, I used to know her when I was a boy. What on earth——"

"Is she doing here?" said Gaylord, grimly filling out the pause. "You've got at the heart of the matter. You knew my sister had been in bad health for a long time?"

"No, I had never heard a word of that. The last I knew of her she was singing in London. My brother and I correspond infrequently, and seldom get beyond family matters. I am deeply sorry to hear this. There are many reasons why I am [more] concerned than I can tell you."

The lines in Charley Gaylord's brow relaxed a little.

"What I'm trying to say, Mr. Hilgarde, is that she wants to see you. I hate to ask you, but she's so set on it. We live several miles out of town, but my rig's below, and I can take you out any time you can go."

"I can go now, and it will give me real pleasure to do so," said Everett, quickly. "I'll get my hat and be with you in a moment."

When he came downstairs Everett found a cart at the door, and Charley Gaylord drew a long sigh of relief as he gathered up the reins and settled back into his own element.

"You see, I think I'd better tell you something about my sister before you see her, and I don't know just where to begin. She travelled in Europe with your brother and his wife, and sang at a lot of his concerts, but I don't know just how much you know about her."

"Very little, except that my brother always thought her the most gifted of his pupils, and that when I knew her she was very young and very beautiful and turned my head sadly for a while."

Everett saw that Gaylord's mind was quite engrossed by his grief. He was wrought up to the point where his reserve and sense of proportion had quite left him, and his trouble was the one vital thing in the world. "That's the whole thing," he went on, flecking his horses with the whip.

"She was a great woman, as you say, and she didn't come of a great family. She had to fight her own way from the first. She got to Chicago and then to New York, and then to Europe, where she went up like lightning, and got a taste for it all; and now she's dying here like a rat in a hole, out of her own world, and she can't fall back into ours. We've grown apart, some way—miles and miles apart—and I'm afraid she's fearfully unhappy."

"It's a very tragic story that you are telling me, Gaylord," said Everett. They were well out into the country now, spinning along over the the dusty plains of red grass, with the ragged blue outline of the mountains before them.

"Tragic!" cried Gaylord, starting up in his seat, "my God, man, nobody will ever know how tragic. It's a tragedy I live with and eat with and sleep with, until I've lost my grip on everything. You see she had made a good bit of money, but she spent it all going to health resorts. It's her lungs, you know. I've got money enough to send her anywhere, but the doctors all say it's no use. She hasn't the ghost of a chance. It's just getting through the days now. I had no notion she was half so bad before she came to me. She just wrote that she was all run down. Now that she's here, I think she'd be happier anywhere under the sun, but she won't leave. She says it's easier to let go of life here, and that to go East would be dying twice. There was a time when I was a brakeman with a run out of Bird City, Iowa, and she was a little thing I could carry on my shoulder, when I could get her everything on earth she wanted, and she hadn't a wish my $80 a month didn't cover; and now, when I've got a little property together, I can't buy her a night's sleep!"

Everett saw that, whatever Charley Gaylord's present status in the world might be, he had brought the brakeman's heart up the ladder with him, and the brakeman's frank avowal of sentiment. Presently Gaylord went on:

"You can understand how she has outgrown her family. We're all a pretty common sort, railroaders from away back. My father was a conductor. He died when we were kids. Maggie, my other sister, who lives with me, was a telegraph operator here while I was getting my grip on things. We had no education to speak of. I have to hire a stenographer because I can't spell straight—the Almighty couldn't teach me to spell. The things that make up life to Kate are all Greek to me, and there's scarcely a point where we touch any more, except in our recollections of the old times when we were all young and happy together, and Kate sang in a church choir in Bird City. But I believe, Mr. Hilgarde, that if she can see just one person like you, who knows about the things and people she's interested in, it will give her about the only comfort she can have now."

The reins slackened in Charley Gaylord's hand as they drew up before a showily painted house with many gables and a round tower. "Here we are," he said, turning to Everett, "and I guess we understand each other."

They were met at the door by a thin, colourless woman, whom Gaylord introduced as "My sister, Maggie." She asked her brother to show Mr. Hilgarde into the music-room, where Katharine wished to see him alone.

When Everett entered the music-room he gave a little start of surprise, feeling that he had stepped from the glaring Wyoming sunlight into some New York studio that he had always known. He wondered which it was of those countless studios, high up under the roofs, over banks and shops and wholesale houses, that this room resembled, and he looked incredulously out of the window at the grey plain that ended in the great upheaval of the Rockies.

The haunting air of familiarity about the room perplexed him. Was it a copy of some particular studio he knew, or was it merely the studio atmosphere that seemed so individual and poignantly reminiscent here in Wyoming? He sat down in a reading-chair and looked keenly about him. Suddenly his eye fell upon a large photograph of his brother above the piano. Then it all became clear to him: this was veritably his brother's room. If it were not an exact copy of one of the many studios that Adriance had fitted up in various parts of the world, wearying of them and leaving almost before the renovator's varnish had dried, it was at least in the same tone. In every detail Adriance's taste was so manifest that the room seemed to exhale his personality.

Among the photographs on the wall there was one of Katharine Gaylord, taken in the days when Everett had known her, and when the flash of her eye or the flutter of her skirt was enough to set his boyish heart in a tumult. Even now, he stood before the portrait with a certain degree of embarrassment. It was the face of a woman already old in her first youth, thoroughly sophisticated and a trifle hard, and it told of what her brother had called her fight. The *camaraderie* of her frank, confident eyes was qualified by the deep lines about her mouth and the curve of the lips, which was both sad and cynical. Certainly she had more good-will than confidence toward the world, and the bravado of her smile could not conceal the shadow of an unrest that was almost discontent. The chief charm of the woman, as Everett had known her, lay in her superb figure and in her eyes, which possessed a warm, life-giving quality like the sunlight; eyes which glowed with a sort of perpetual *salutat* to the world. Her head, Everett remembered as peculiarly well shaped and proudly poised. There had been always a little of the imperatrix about her, and her pose in the photograph revived all his old impressions of her unattachedness, of how absolutely and valiantly she stood alone.

Everett was still standing before the picture, his hands behind him and his head inclined, when he heard the door open. A very tall woman advanced toward him, holding out her hand. As she started to speak she coughed slightly, then, laughing, said, in a low, rich voice, a trifle husky: "You see I make the traditional Camille entrance—with the cough. How good of you to come, Mr. Hilgarde."

Everett was acutely conscious that while addressing him she was not looking at him at all, and, as he assured her of his pleasure in coming, he was glad to have an opportunity to collect himself. He had not reckoned upon the ravages of a long illness. The long, loose folds of her white gown had been especially designed to conceal the sharp outlines of her emaciated body, but the stamp of her disease was there; simple and ugly and obtrusive, a pitiless fact that could not be disguised or evaded. The splendid shoulders were stooped, there was a swaying unevenness in her gait, her arms seemed disproportionately long, and her hands were transparently white, and cold to the touch. The changes in her face were less obvious; the proud carriage of the head, the warm, clear eyes, even the delicate flush of colour in her cheeks, all defiantly remained, though they were all in a lower key—older, sadder, softer.

She sat down upon the divan and began nervously to arrange the pillows. "I know I'm not an inspiring object to look upon, but you must be quite frank and sensible about that and get used to it at once, for we've no time to lose. And if I'm a trifle irritable you won't mind?—for I'm more than usually nervous."

"Don't bother with me this morning, if you are tired," urged Everett. "I can come quite as well to-morrow."

"Gracious, no!" she protested, with a flash of that quick, keen humour that he remembered as a part of her. "It's solitude that I'm tired to death of—solitude and the wrong kind of people. You see, the minister, not content with reading the prayers for the sick, called on me this morning. He happened to be riding by on his bicycle and felt it his duty to stop. Of course, he disapproves of my profession, and I think he takes it for granted that I have a dark past. The funniest feature of his conversation is that he is always excusing my own vocation to me—condoning it, you know—

and trying to patch up my peace with my conscience by suggesting possible noble uses for what he kindly calls my talent."

Everett laughed. "Oh! I'm afraid I'm not the person to call after such a serious gentleman—I can't sustain the situation. At my best I don't reach higher than low comedy. Have you decided to which one of the noble uses you will devote yourself?"

Katharine lifted her hands in a gesture of renunciation and exclaimed: "I'm not equal to any of them, not even the least noble. I didn't study that method."

She laughed and went on nervously: "The parson's not so bad. His English never offends me, and he has read Gibbon's 'Decline and Fall,' all five volumes, and that's something. Then, he has been to New York, and that's a great deal. But how we are losing time! Do tell me about New York; Charley says you're just on from there. How does it look and taste and smell just now? I think a whiff of the Jersey ferry would be as flagons of cod-liver oil to me. Who conspicuously walks the Rialto now, and what does he or she wear? Are the trees still green in Madison Square, or have they grown brown and dusty? Does the chaste Diana on the Garden Theatre still keep her vestal vows through all the exasperating changes of weather? Who has your brother's old studio now, and what misguided aspirants practise their scales in the rookeries about Carnegie Hall? What do people go to see at the theatres, and what do they eat and drink there in the world nowadays? You see, I'm homesick for it all, from the Battery to Riverside. Oh, let me die in Harlem!" she was interrupted by a violent attack of coughing, and Everett, embarrassed by her discomfort, plunged into gossip about the professional people he had met in town during the summer, and the musical outlook for the winter. He was diagraming with his pencil, on the back of an old envelope he found in his pocket, some new mechanical device to be used at the Metropolitan in the production of the *Rheingold*, when he became conscious that she was looking at him intently, and that he was talking to the four walls.

Katharine was lying back among the pillows, watching him through half-closed eyes, as a painter looks at a picture. He finished his explanation vaguely enough and put the envelope back in his pocket. As he did so, she said, quietly: "How wonderfully like Adriance you are!" and he felt as though a crisis of some sort had been met and tided over.

He laughed, looking up at her with a touch of pride in his eyes that made them seem quite boyish. "Yes, isn't it absurd? It's almost as awkward as looking like Napoleon—But, after all, there are some advantages. It has made some of his friends like me, and I hope it will make you."

Katharine smiled and gave him a quick, meaning glance from under her lashes. "Oh, it did that long ago. What a haughty, reserved youth you were then, and how you used to stare at people, and then blush and look cross if they paid you back in your own coin. Do you remember that night when you took me home from a rehearsal, and scarcely spoke a word to me?"

"It was the silence of admiration," protested Everett, "very crude and boyish, but very sincere and not a little painful. Perhaps you suspected something of the sort? I remember you saw fit to be very grown up and worldly."

"I believe I suspected a pose; the one that college boys usually affect with singers—'an earthen vessel in love with a star,' you know. But it rather surprised me in you, for you must have seen a good deal of your brother's pupils. Or had you an omnivorous capacity, and elasticity that always met the occasion?"

"Don't ask a man to confess the follies of his youth," said Everett, smiling a little sadly; "I am sensitive about some of them even now. But I was not so sophisticated as you imagined. I saw my brother's pupils come and go, but that was about all. Sometimes I was called on to play accompaniments, or to fill out a vacancy at a rehearsal, or to order a carriage for an infuriated soprano who had thrown up her part. But they never spent any time on me, unless it was to notice the resemblance you speak of."

"Yes," observed Katharine, thoughtfully, "I noticed it then, too; but it has grown as you have grown older. That is rather strange, when you have lived such different lives. It's not merely an ordinary family likeness of feature, you know, but a sort of interchangeable individuality; the suggestion of the other man's personality in your face—like an air transposed to another key. But I'm not attempting to define it; it's beyond me; something altogether unusual and a trifle—well, uncanny," she finished, laughing.

"I remember," Everett said, seriously, twirling the pencil between his fingers and looking, as he sat with his head thrown back, out under the red window-blind which was raised just a little, and as it swung back and forth in the wind revealed the glaring panorama of the desert—a blinding stretch of yellow, flat as the sea in dead calm, splotched here and there with deep purple shadows; and, beyond, the ragged blue outline of the mountains and the peaks of snow, white as the white clouds—"I remember, when I was a little fellow I used to be very sensitive about it. I don't think it exactly displeased me, or that I would have had it otherwise if I could, but it seemed to me like a birthmark, or something not to be lightly spoken of. People were naturally always fonder of Ad than of me, and I used to feel the chill of reflected light pretty often. It came into even my relations with my mother. Ad went abroad to study when he was absurdly young, you know, and mother was all broken up over it. She did her whole duty by each of us, but it was sort of generally understood among us that she'd have made burnt-offerings of us all for Ad any day. I was a little fellow then, and when she sat alone on the porch in the summer dusk, she used sometimes to call me to her and turn my face up in the light that streamed out through the shutters and kiss me, and then I always knew she was thinking of Adriance."

"Poor little chap," said Katharine, and her tone was a trifle huskier than usual. "How fond people have always been of Adriance! Now tell me the latest news of him. I haven't heard, except through the press, for a year or more. He was in Algiers then, in the valley of the Chelif, riding horseback night and day in an Arabian costume, and in his usual enthusiastic fashion he had quite made up his mind to adopt the Mahometan faith and become as nearly an Arab as possible. How many countries and faiths has he adopted, I wonder? Probably he was playing Arab to himself all the time. I remember he was a sixteenth-century duke in Florence once for weeks together."

"Oh, that's Adriance," chuckled Everett. "He is himself barely long enough to write checks and be measured for his clothes. I didn't hear from him while he was an Arab; I missed that."

"He was writing an Algerian *suite* for the piano then; it must be in the publisher's hands by this time. I have been too ill to answer his letter, and have lost touch with him."

Everett drew a letter from his pocket. "This came about a month ago. It's chiefly about his new opera, which is to be brought out in London next winter. Read it at your leisure."

"I think I shall keep it as a hostage, so that I may be sure you will come again. Now I want you to play for me. Whatever you like; but if there is anything new in the world, in mercy let me hear it. For nine months I have heard nothing but 'The Baggage Coach Ahead' and 'She is My Baby's Mother.' "

He sat down at the piano, and Katharine sat near him, absorbed in his remarkable physical likeness to his brother, and trying to discover in just what it consisted. She told herself that it was very much as though a sculptor's finished work had been rudely copied in wood. He was of a larger build than Adriance, and his shoulders were broad and heavy, while those of his brother were slender and rather girlish. His face was of the same oval mould, but it was grey, and darkened about the mouth by continual shaving. His eyes were of the same inconstant April colour, but they were reflective and rather dull; while Adriance's were always points of high light, and always meaning another thing than the thing they meant yesterday. But it was hard to see why this earnest young man should so continually suggest that lyric, youthful face that was as gay as his was grave. For Adriance, though he was ten years the elder, and though his hair was streaked with silver, had the face of a boy of twenty, so mobile that it told his thoughts before he could put them into words. A contralto, famous for the extravagance of her vocal methods and of her affections had once said of him that the shepherd-boys who sang in the Vale of Tempe must certainly have looked like young Hilgarde; and the comparison had been appropriated by a hundred shyer women who preferred to quote.

As Everett sat smoking on the veranda of the Inter-Ocean House that night, he was a victim to random recollections. His infatuation for Katharine Gaylord, visionary as it was, had been the most serious of his boyish love-affairs, and had long disturbed his bachelor dreams. He was painfully timid in everything relating to the emotions, and his hurt had withdrawn him from the society of women. The fact that it was all so done and dead and far behind him, and that the woman had lived her life out since then, gave him an oppressive sense of age and loss. He bethought himself of something he had read about "sitting by the hearth and remembering the faces of women without desire," and felt himself an octogenarian.

He remembered how bitter and morose he had grown during his stay at his brother's studio when Katharine Gaylord was working there, and how he had wounded Adriance on the night of his last concert in New York. He had sat there in the box while his brother and Katharine were called back again and again after the last number, watching the roses go up over the footlights until they were stacked half as high as the piano, brooding, in his sullen boy's heart, upon the pride those two felt in each other's work—spurring each other to their best and beautifully contending in song. The footlights had seemed a hard, glittering line drawn sharply between their life and his; a circle of flame set about those splendid children of genius. He walked back to his hotel alone, and sat in his window staring out on Madison Square until long after midnight, resolving to beat no more at doors that he could never enter, and realizing more keenly than ever before how far this glorious world of beautiful creations lay from the paths of men like himself. He told himself that he had in common with this woman only the baser uses of life.

Everett's week in Cheyenne stretched to three, and he saw no prospect of release except through the thing he dreaded. The bright, windy days of the Wyoming autumn passed swiftly. Letters and telegrams came urging him to hasten his trip to the coast, but he resolutely postponed his business engagements. The mornings he spent on one of Charley Gaylord's ponies, or fishing in the mountains, and in the evenings he sat in his room writing letters or reading. In the afternoon he was usually at his post of duty. Destiny, he reflected, seems to have very positive notions about the sort of parts we are fitted to play. The scene changes and the compensation varies, but in the end we usually find that we have played the same class of business from first to last. Everett had been a stop-gap all his life. He remembered going through a looking-glass labyrinth when he was a boy, and trying gallery after gallery, only at every turn to bump his nose against his own face—which, indeed, was not his own, but his brother's. No matter what his mission, east or west, by land or sea, he was sure to find himself employed in his brother's business, one of the tributary lives which helped to swell the shining current of Adriance Hilgarde's. It was not the first time that his duty had been to comfort, as best he could, one of the broken things his brother's imperious speed had cast aside and forgotten. He made no attempt to analyse the situation or to state it in exact terms; but he felt Katharine Gaylord's need for him, and he accepted it as a commission from his brother to help this woman to die. Day by day he felt her demands on him grow more imperious, her need for him grow more acute and positive; and day by day he felt that in his peculiar relation to her, his own individuality played a smaller and smaller part. His power to minister to her comfort, he saw, lay solely in his link with his brother's life. He understood all that his physical resemblance meant to her. He knew that she sat by him always watching for some common trick of gesture, some familiar play of expression, some illusion of light and shadow, in which he should seem wholly Adriance. He knew that she lived upon this and that her disease fed upon it; that it sent shudders of remembrance through her and that in the exhaustion which followed this turmoil of her dying senses, she slept deep and sweet, and dreamed of youth and art and days in a certain old Florentine garden, and not of bitterness and death.

The question which most perplexed him was, "How much shall I know? How much does she wish for me to know?" A few days after his first meeting with Katharine Gaylord, he had cabled his brother to write her. He had merely said that she was mortally ill; he could depend on Adriance to say the right thing—that was a part of his gift. Adriance always said not only the right thing, but the opportune, graceful, exquisite thing. His phrases took the colour of the moment and the then present condition, so that they never savoured of perfunctory compliment or frequent usage. He always caught the lyric essence of the moment, the poetic suggestion of every situation. Moreover, he usually did the right thing, the opportune, graceful, exquisite thing—except, when he did very cruel things—bent upon making people happy when their existence touched his, just as he insisted that his material environment should be beautiful; lavishing upon those near him all the warmth and radiance of his rich nature, all the homage of the poet and troubadour, and, when they were no longer near, forgetting—for that also was a part of Adriance's gift.

Three weeks after Everett had sent his cable, when he made his daily call at the gaily painted ranch-house, he found Katharine laughing like a school-girl. "Have you ever thought," she said, as he entered the music-room, "how much these séances of ours are like Heine's 'Florentine Nights,' except that I don't give you an opportunity to monopolize the conversation as Heine did?" She held his hand longer than usual as she greeted him, and looked searchingly up into his face. "You are the kindest man living, the kindest," she added, softly.

Everett's grey face coloured faintly as he drew his hand away, for he felt that this time she was looking at him and not at a whimsical caricature of his brother. "Why, what have I done now?" he asked, lamely. "I can't remember having sent you any stale candy or champagne since yesterday."

She drew a letter with a foreign postmark from between the leaves of a book and held it out, smiling. "You got him to write it. Don't say you didn't, for it came direct, you see, and the last address I gave him was a place in Florida. This deed shall be remembered of you when I am with the just in Paradise. But one thing you did not ask him to do, for you didn't know about it. He has sent me his latest work, the new sonata, the most ambitious thing he has ever done, and you are to play it for me directly, though it looks horribly intricate. But first for the letter; I think you would better read it aloud to me."

Everett sat down in a low chair facing the window-seat in which she reclined with a barricade of pillows behind her. He opened the letter, his lashes half-veiling his kind eyes, and saw to his satisfaction that it was a long one; wonderfully tactful and tender, even for Adriance, who was tender with his valet and his stable-boy, with his old gondolier and the beggar-women who prayed to the saints for him.

The letter was from Granada, written in the Alhambra, as he sat by the fountain of the Patio di Lindaraxa. The air was heavy with the warm fragrance of the South and full of the sound of splashing, running water, as it had been in a certain old garden in Florence, long ago. The sky was one great turquoise, heated until it glowed. The wonderful Moorish arches threw graceful blue shadows all about him. He had sketched an outline of them on the margin of his notepaper. The subtleties of Arabic decoration had cast an unholy spell over him, and the brutal exaggerations of Gothic art were a bad dream, easily forgotten. The Alhambra itself had, from the first, seemed perfectly familiar to him, and he knew that he must have trod that court, sleek and brown and obsequious, centuries before Ferdinand rode into Andalusia. The letter was full of confidences about his work, and delicate allusions to their old happy days of study and comradeship, and of her own work, still so warmly remembered and appreciatively discussed everywhere he went.

As Everett folded the letter he felt that Adriance had divined the thing needed and had risen to it in his own wonderful way. The letter was consistently egotistical, and seemed to him even a trifle patronizing, yet it was just what she had wanted. A strong realization of his brother's charm and intensity and power came over him; he felt the breath of that whirlwind of flame in which Adriance passed, consuming all in his path, and himself even more resolutely than he consumed others. Then he looked down at this white, burnt-out brand that lay before him. "Like him, isn't it?" she said, quietly.

"I think I can scarcely answer his letter, but when you see him next you can do that for me. I want you to tell him many things for me, yet they can all be summed up in this: I want him to grow wholly into his best and greatest self, even at the cost of the dear boyishness that is half his charm to you and me. Do you understand me?"

"I know perfectly well what you mean," answered Everett, thoughtfully. "I have often felt so about him myself. And yet it's difficult to prescribe for those fellows; so little makes, so little mars."

Katharine raised herself upon her elbow, and her face flushed with feverish earnestness. "Ah, but it is the waste of himself that I mean; his lashing himself out on stupid and uncomprehending people until they take him at their own estimate. He can kindle marble, strike fire from putty, but is it worth what it costs him?"

"Come, come," expostulated Everett, alarmed at her excitement. "Where is the new sonata? Let him speak for himself."

He sat down at the piano and began playing the first movement which was indeed the voice of Adriance, his proper speech. The sonata was the most ambitious work he had done up to that time, and marked the transition from his purely lyric vein to a deeper and nobler style. Everett played intelligently and with that sympathetic comprehension which seems peculiar to a certain lovable class of men who never accomplish anything in particular. When he had finished he turned to Katharine.

"How he has grown!" she cried. "What the three last years have done for him! He used to write only the tragedies of passion; but this is the tragedy of the soul, the shadow coexistent with the soul. This is the tragedy of effort and failure, the thing Keats called hell. This is my tragedy, as I lie here spent by the race-course, listening to the feet of the runners as they pass me—ah, God! the swift feet of the runners!"

She turned her face away and covered it with her straining hands.

Everett crossed over to her quickly and knelt beside her. In all the days he had known her she had never before, beyond an occasional ironical jest, given voice to the bitterness of her own defeat. Her courage had become a point of pride with him, and to see it going sickened him.

"Don't do it," he gasped. "I can't stand it, I really can't, I feel it too much. We mustn't speak of that; it's too tragic and too vast."

When she turned her face back to him there was a ghost of the old, brave, cynical smile on it, more bitter than the tears she could not shed. "No, I won't be ungenerous; I will save that for the watches of the night when I have no better company. Now you may mix me another drink of some sort. Formerly, when it was not *if* I should ever sing Brunhilda, but quite simply when I *should* sing Brunhilda, I was always starving myself, and thinking what I might drink and what I might not. But broken music-boxes may drink whatsoever they list, and no one cares whether they lose their figure. Run over that theme at the beginning again. That, at least, is not new. It was running in his head when we were in Venice years ago, and he used to drum it on his glass at the dinner-table. He had just begun to work it out when the late autumn came on, and the paleness of the Adriatic oppressed him, and he decided to go to Florence for the winter, and lost touch with the theme during his illness. Do you remember those frightful days? All the people who have loved him are not strong enough to save him from himself! When I got word from Florence that he had been ill, I was in Nice filling a concert engagement. His wife was hurrying to him from Paris, but I reached him first. I arrived at dusk, in a terrific storm. They had taken an old palace there for the winter, and I found him in the library—a long, dark room full of old Latin books and heavy furniture and bronzes. He was sitting by a wood fire at one end of the room, looking, oh, so worn and pale!—as he always does when he is ill, you know. Ah, it is so good that you *do* know! Even his red smoking-jacket lent no colour to his face. His first words were not to tell me how ill he had been, but that that morning he had been well enough to put the last strokes to the score of his '*Souvenirs d'Automne*,' and he was, as I most like to remember him; so calm and happy and tired; not gay, as he usually is, but just contented and tired with that heavenly tiredness that comes after a good work done at last. Outside, the rain poured down in torrents, and the wind moaned for the pain of all the world and sobbed in the branches of the shivering olives and about the walls of that desolated old palace. How that night comes back to me! There were no lights in the room, only the wood fire which glowed upon the hard features of the bronze Dante like the reflection of purgatorial flames, and threw long black shadows about us; beyond us it scarcely penetrated the gloom at all. Adriance sat staring at the fire with the weariness of all his life in his eyes, and of all the other lives that must aspire and suffer to make up one such life as his. Somehow the wind with all its world-pain had got into the room, and the cold rain was in our eyes, and the wave came up in both of us at once—that awful vague, universal pain, that cold fear of life and death and God and hope—and we were like two clinging together on a spar in mid-ocean after the ship-wreck of everything. Then we heard the front door open with a great gust of wind that shook even the walls, and the servants came running with lights, announcing that Madame had returned, '*and in the book we read no more that night.*' "

She gave the old line with a certain bitter humour, and with the hard, bright smile in which of old she had wrapped her weakness as in a glittering garment. That ironical smile, worn like a mask through so many years, had gradually changed even the lines of her face completely, and when she looked in the mirror she saw not herself, but the scathing critic, the amused observer and satirist of herself. Everett dropped his head upon his hand and sat looking at the rug. "How much you have cared!" he said.

"Ah, yes, I cared," she replied, closing her eyes with a long-drawn sigh of relief; and lying perfectly still, she went on: "You can't imagine what a comfort it is to have you know how I cared, what a relief it is to be able to tell it to some one. I used to want to shriek it out to the world in the long nights when I could not sleep. It seemed to me that I could not die with it. It demanded some sort of expression. And now that you know, you would scarcely believe how much less sharp the anguish of it is."

Everett continued to look helplessly at the floor. "I was not sure how much you wanted me to know," he said.

"Oh, I intended you should know from the first time I looked into your face, when you came that day with Charley. I flatter myself that I have been able to conceal it when I chose, though I suppose women always think that. The more observing ones may have seen, but discerning people are usually discreet and often kind, for we usually bleed a little before we begin to discern. But I wanted you to know; you are so like him that it is almost like telling him himself. At least, I feel now that he will know some day, and then I will be quite sacred from his compassion, for we none of us dare pity the dead. Since it was what my life has chiefly meant, I should like him to know. On the whole, I am not ashamed of it. I have fought a good fight."

"And has he never known at all?" asked Everett, in a thick voice.

"Oh! never at all in the way that you mean. Of course, he is accustomed to looking into the eyes of women and finding love there; when he doesn't find it there he thinks he must have been guilty of some discourtesy and is miserable about it. He has a genuine fondness for every one who is not stupid or gloomy, or old or preternaturally ugly. Granted youth and cheerfulness, and a moderate amount of wit and some tact, and Adriance will always be glad to see you coming around the corner. I shared with the rest; shared the smiles and the gallantries and the droll little sermons. It was quite like a Sunday-school picnic; we wore our best clothes and a smile and took our turns. It was his kindness that was hardest. I have pretty well used my life up at standing punishment."

"Don't; you'll make me hate him," groaned Everett.

Katharine laughed and began to play nervously with her fan. "It wasn't in the slightest degree his fault; that is the most grotesque part of it. Why, it had really begun before I ever met him. I fought my way to him, and I drank my doom greedily enough."

Everett rose and stood hesitating. "I think I must go. You ought to be quiet, and I don't think I can hear any more just now."

She put out her hand and took his playfully. "You've put in three weeks at this sort of thing, haven't you? Well, it may never be to your glory in this world, perhaps, but it's been the mercy of heaven to me, and it ought to square accounts for a much worse life than yours will ever be."

Everett knelt beside her, saying, brokenly: "I stayed because I wanted to be with you, that's all. I have never cared about other women since I met you in New York when I was a lad. You are a part of my destiny, and I could not leave you if I would."

She put her hands on his shoulders and shook her head. "No, no; don't tell me that. I have seen enough of tragedy, God knows: don't show me any more just as the curtain is going down. No, no, it was only a boy's fancy, and your divine pity and my utter pitiableness have recalled it for a moment. One does not love the dying, dear friend. If some fancy of that sort had been left over from boyhood, this would rid you of it, and that were well. Now go, and you will come again to-morrow, as long as there are to-morrows, will you not?" She took his hand with a smile that lifted the mask from her soul, that was both courage and despair, and full of infinite loyalty and tenderness, as she said softly,

> *"For ever and for ever, farewell, Cassius;*
> *If we do meet again, why, we shall smile;*
> *If not, why then, this parting was well made."*

The courage in her eyes was like the clear light of a star to him as he went out.

On the night of Adriance Hilgarde's opening concert in Paris, Everett sat by the bed in the ranch-house in Wyoming, watching over the last battle that we have with the flesh before we are done with it and free of it forever. At times it seemed that the serene soul of her must have left already and found some refuge from the storm, and only the tenacious animal life were left to do battle with death. She laboured under a delusion at once pitiful and merciful, thinking that she was in the Pullman on her way to New York, going back to her life and her work. When she aroused from her stupor, it was only to ask the porter to waken her half an hour out of Jersey City, or to remonstrate with him about the delays and the roughness of the road. At midnight Everett and the nurse were left alone with her. Poor Charley Gaylord had lain down on a couch outside the door. Everett sat looking at the sputtering night-lamp until it made his eyes ache. His head dropped forward on the foot of the bed, and he sank into a heavy, distressful slumber. He was dreaming of Adriance's concert in Paris, and of Adriance, the troubadour, smiling and debonair, with his boyish face and the touch of silver grey in his hair. He heard the applause and he saw the roses going up over the footlights until they were stacked half as high as the piano, and the petals fell and scattered, making crimson splotches on the floor. Down this crimson pathway came Adriance with his youthful step, leading his prima donna by the hand; a dark woman this time, with Spanish eyes.

The nurse touched him on the shoulder, he started and awoke. She screened the lamp with her hand. Everett saw that Katharine was awake and conscious, and struggling a little. He lifted her gently on his arm and began to fan her. She laid her hands lightly on his hair and looked into his face with eyes that seemed never to have wept or doubted. "Ah, dear Adriance, dear, dear," she whispered.

Everett went to call her brother, but when they came back the madness of art was over for Katharine.

Two days later Everett was pacing the station siding, waiting for the west-bound train. Charley Gaylord walked beside him, but the two men had nothing to say to each other. Everett's bags were piled on the truck, and his step was hurried and his eyes were full of impatience, as he gazed again and again up the track, watching for the train. Gaylord's impatience was not less than his own; these two, who had grown so close, had now become painful and impossible to each other, and longed for the wrench of farewell.

As the train pulled in, Everett wrung Gaylord's hand among the crowd of alighting passengers. The people of a German opera company, *en route* for the coast, rushed by them in frantic haste to snatch their breakfast during the stop. Everett heard an exclamation in a broad German dialect, and a massive woman whose figure persistently escaped from her stays in the most improbable places rushed up to him, her blond hair disordered by the wind, and glowing with joyful surprise she caught his coat-sleeve with her tightly gloved hands.

"*Herr Gott,* Adriance, *lieber Freund,*" she cried, emotionally.

Everett quickly withdrew his arm, and lifted his hat, blushing. "Pardon me, madame, but I see that you have mistaken me for Adriance Hilgarde. I am his brother," he said, quietly, and turning from the crestfallen singer he hurried into the car.

JEAN TOOMER
(1894–1967)

Of the writers represented in this gathering, Jean Toomer would seem to be among the most lyrically and imaginatively gifted. Yet, ironically, his fate was to write for decades in obscurity, leaving behind a voluminous quantity of unpublished work—short stories, novels, plays, an autobiography. His Cane *(1923) is a work of literary genius, but never again, perhaps by his own design, did he attempt a work of its type or quality.*

Jean Toomer was born in Washington, D.C., attended a number of colleges without earning a degree, and began writing in his middle twenties. From the first he aligned himself, not with the then-dominant literary mode of Naturalism, but with Modernist experimentation; he published poems in avant-garde magazines like Broom *and the* Little Review, *as well as in black publications. The dazzling* Cane, *though written within a few years of Anderson's* Winesburg, Ohio, *would seem to have sprung from entirely different sources, as from another planet.*

In this brilliant and unclassifiable composition, an isolated, yet deeply sensitive young black man tries to connect himself with his "folk" heritage, without success. Cane *is constructed as a collage, made up of poetry, prose-poetry, fiction, song, drama, and philosophical debate; Negro dialect is used like music, in aria-like interludes of great beauty and intensity. Throughout, and particularly in "Blood-Burning Moon," the selection included here, jazz rhythms underlie prose passages, and give a poetic resonance that, like both music and poetry, must be experienced to be understood. This is the lost, tragic, yet hauntingly beautiful world of the blues singer Robert Johnson, memorialized in prose.*

Blood-Burning Moon

1

Up from the skeleton stone walls, up from the rotting floor boards and the solid hand-hewn beams of oak of the pre-war cotton factory, dusk came. Up from the dusk the full moon came. Glowing like a fired pine-knot, it illumined the great door and soft showered the Negro shanties aligned along the single street of factory town. The full moon in the great door was an omen. Negro women improvised songs against its spell.

Louisa sang as she came over the crest of the hill from the white folks' kitchen. Her skin was the color of oak leaves on young trees in fall. Her breasts, firm and up-pointed like ripe acorns. And her singing had the low murmur of winds in fig trees. Bob Stone, younger son of the people she worked for, loved her. By the way the world reckons things, he had won her. By measure of that warm glow which came into her mind at thought of him, he had won her. Tom Burwell, whom the whole town called Big Boy, also loved her. But working in the fields all day, and far away from her, gave him no chance to show it. Though often enough of evenings he had tried to. Somehow, he never got along. Strong as he was with hands upon the ax or plow, he found it difficult to hold her. Or so he thought. But the fact was that he held her to factory town more firmly than he thought for. His black balanced, and pulled against, the white of Stone, when she thought of them. And her mind was vaguely upon them as she came over the crest of the hill, coming from the white folks' kitchen. As she sang softly at the evil face of the full moon.

A strange stir was in her. Indolently, she tried to fix upon Bob or Tom as the cause of it. To meet Bob in the canebrake, as she was going to do an hour or so later, was nothing new. And Tom's proposal which she felt on its way to her could be indefinitely put off. Separately, there was no unusual significance to either one. But for some reason, they jumbled when her eyes gazed vacantly at the rising moon. And from the jumble came the stir that was strangely within her. Her lips trembled. The slow rhythm of her song grew agitant and restless. Rusty black and tan spotted hounds, lying in the dark corners of porches or prowling around back yards, put their noses in the air and caught its tremor. They began plaintively to yelp and howl. Chickens woke up and cackled. Intermittently, all over the countryside dogs barked and roosters crowed as if heralding a weird dawn or some ungodly awakening. The women sang lustily. Their songs were cotton-wads to stop their ears. Louisa came down into factory town and sank wearily upon the step before her home. The moon was rising towards a thick cloud-bank which soon would hide it.

Red nigger moon. Sinner!
Blood-burning moon. Sinner!
Come out that fact'ry door.

2

Up from the deep dusk of a cleared spot on the edge of the forest a mellow glow arose and spread fan-wise into the low-hanging heavens. And all around the air was heavy with the scent of boiling cane. A large pile of cane-stalks lay like ribboned shadows upon the ground. A mule, harnessed to a pole, trudged lazily round and round the pivot of the grinder. Beneath a swaying oil lamp, a Negro alternately whipped out at the mule, and fed cane-stalks to the grinder. A fat boy waddled pails of fresh ground juice between the grinder and the boiling stove. Steam came from the copper boiling pan. The scent of cane came from the copper pan and drenched the forest and the hill that sloped to factory town, beneath its fragrance. It drenched the men in circle seated around the stove. Some of them chewed at the white pulp of stalks, but there was no need for them to, if all they wanted was to taste the cane. One tasted it in factory town. And from factory town one could see the soft haze thrown by the glowing stove upon the low-hanging heavens.

Old David Georgia stirred the thickening syrup with a long ladle, and ever so often drew it off. Old David Georgia tended his stove and told tales about the white folks, about moonshining and cotton picking, and about sweet nigger gals, to the men who sat there about his stove to listen to him. Tom Burwell chewed cane-stalk and laughed with the others till some one mentioned Louisa. Till some one said something about Louisa and Bob Stone, about the silk stockings she must have gotten from him. Blood ran up Tom's neck hotter than the glow that flooded from the stove. He sprang up. Glared at the men and said, "She's my gal." Will Manning laughed. Tom strode over to him. Yanked him up and knocked him to the ground. Several of Manning's friends got up to fight for him. Tom whipped out a long knife and would have cut them to shreds if they hadnt ducked into the woods. Tom had had enough. He nodded to Old David Georgia and swung down the path to factory town. Just then, the dogs started barking and the roosters began to crow. Tom felt funny. Away from the fight, away from the stove, chill got to him. He shivered. He shuddered when he saw the full moon rising towards the cloud-bank. He who didnt give a godam for the fears of old women. He forced his mind to fasten on Louisa. Bob Stone. Better not be. He turned into the street and saw Louisa sitting before her home. He went towards her, ambling, touched the brim of a marvelously shaped, spotted, felt hat, said he wanted to say something to her, and then found that he didnt know what he had to say, or if he did, that he couldnt say it. He shoved his big fists in his overalls, grinned, and started to move off.

"Youall want me, Tom?"

"Thats what us wants, sho, Louisa."

"Well, here I am—"

"An here I is, but that aint ahelpin none, all th same."

"You wanted to say something? . ."

"I did that, sho. But words is like th spots on dice: no matter how y fumbles em, there's times when they jes wont come. I dunno why. Seems like th love I feels fo yo done stole m tongue. I got it now. Whee! Louisa, honey, I oughtnt tell y, I feel I oughtnt cause yo is young an goes t church an I has had other gals, but Louisa I sho do love y. Lil gal, Ise watched y from them first days when youall sat right here befo yo door befo th well an sang some-times in a way that like t broke m heart. Ise carried y with me into th fields, day after day, an after that, an I sho can plow when yo is there, an I can pick cotton. Yassur! Come near beatin Barlo yesterday. I sho did. Yassur! An next year if ole Stone'll trust me, I'll have a farm. My own. My bales will buy yo what y gets from white flush of his cheeks turned purple. As if to balance this outer change, his mind became consciously a white man's. He passed the house with its huge open hearth which, in the days of slavery, was the plantation cookery. He saw Louisa bent over that hearth. He went in as a master should and took her. Direct, honest, bold. None of this sneaking that he had to go through now. The contrast was repulsive to him. His family had lost ground. Hell no, his family still owned the niggers, practically. Damned if they did, or he wouldnt have to duck around so. What would they think if they knew? His mother? His sister? He shouldnt mention them, shouldnt think of them in this connection. There in the dusk he blushed at doing so. Fellows about town were all right, but how about his friends up North? He could see them incredible, repulsed. They didnt know. The thought first made him laugh. Then, with their eyes still upon him, he began to feel embarrassed. He felt the need of explaining things to them. Explain hell. They wouldnt understand, and moreover, who ever heard of a Southerner getting on his knees to any Yankee, or anyone. No sir. He was going to see Louisa to-night, and love her. She was lovely—in her way. Nigger way. What way was that? Damned if he knew. Must know. He'd known her long enough to know. Was there something about niggers that you couldnt know? Listening to them at church didnt tell you anything. Looking at them didnt tell you anything. Talking to them didnt tell you anything—unless it was gossip, unless they wanted to talk. Of course, about farming, and licker, and craps—but those werent nigger. Nigger was something more. How much more? Something to be afraid of, more? Hell no. Who ever heard of being afraid of a nigger? Tom Burwell. Cartwell had told him that Tom went with Louisa after she reached home. No sir. No nigger had ever been with his girl. He'd like to see one try. Some position for him to be in. Him, Bob Stone, of the old Stone family, in a scrap with a nigger over a nigger girl. In the good old days . . . Ha! Those were the days. His family had lost ground. Not so much, though. Enough for him to have cut through old Lemon's canefield by way of the woods, that he might meet her. She was worth it. Beautiful nigger gal. Why nigger? Why not, just gal? No, it was because she was nigger that he went to her. Sweet . . . The scent of boiling cane came to him. Then he saw the rich glow of the stove. He heard the voices of the men circled around it. He was about to skirt the clearing when he heard his own name mentioned. He stopped. Quivering. Leaning against a tree, he listened.

"Bad nigger. Yassur, he sho is one bad nigger when he gets started."

"Tom Burwell's been on th gang three times fo cuttin men."

"What y think he's agwine t do t Bob Stone?"

"Dunno yet. He aint found out. When he does—Baby!"

"Aint no tellin."

"Young Stone aint no quitter an I ken tell y that. Blood of th old uns in his veins."

"Thats right. He'll scrap, sho."

"Be gettin too hot f niggers round this away."

"Shut up, nigger. Y dont know what y talkin bout."

Bob Stone's ears burned as though he had been holding them over the stove. Sizzling heat welled up within him. His feet felt as if they rested on red-hot coals. They stung him to quick movement. He circled the fringe of the glowing. Not a twig cracked beneath his feet. He reached the path that led to factory town. Plunged furiously down it. Halfway along, a blindness within him veered him aside. He crashed into the bordering canebrake. Cane leaves cut his face and lips. He tasted blood. He threw himself down and dug his fingers in the ground. The earth was cool. Caneroots took the fever from his hands. After a long while, or so it seemed to him, the thought came to him that it must be time to see Louisa. He got to his feet and walked calmly to their meeting place. No Louisa. Tom Burwell had her. Veins in his forehead bulged and distended. Saliva moistened the dried blood on his lips. He bit down on his lips. He tasted blood. Not his own blood; Tom Burwell's blood. Bob drove through the cane and out again upon the road. A hound swung down the path before him towards factory town. Bob couldnt see it. The dog loped aside to let him pass. Bob's blind rushing made him stumble over it. He fell with a thud that dazed him. The hound yelped. Answering yelps came from all over the countryside. Chickens cackled. Roosters crowed, heralding the bloodshot eyes of southern awakening. Singers in the town were silenced. They shut their windows down. Palpitant between the rooster crows, a chill hush settled upon the huddled forms of Tom and Louisa. A figure rushed from the shadow and stood before them. Tom popped to his feet.

"Whats y want?"

"I'm Bob Stone."

"Yassur—an I'm Tom Burwell. Whats y want?"

Bob lunged at him. Tom side-stepped, caught him by the shoulder, and flung him to the ground. Straddled him.

"Let me up."

"Yassur—but watch yo doins, Bob Stone."

A few dark figures, drawn by the sound of scuffle, stood about them. Bob sprang to his feet.

"Fight like a man, Tom Burwell, an I'll lick y."

Again he lunged. Tom side-stepped and flung him to the ground. Straddled him.

"Get off me, you godam nigger you."

"Yo sho has started somethin now. Get up."

Tom yanked him up and began hammering at him. Each blow sounded as if it smashed into a precious, irreplaceable soft something. Beneath them, Bob staggered back. He reached in his pocket and whipped out a knife.

"Thats my game, sho."

Blue flash, a steel blade slashed across Bob Stone's throat. He had a sweetish sick feeling. Blood began to flow. Then he felt a sharp twitch of pain. He let his knife drop. He slapped one hand against his neck. He pressed the other on top of his head as if to hold it down. He groaned. He turned, and staggered towards the crest of the hill in the direction of white town. Negroes who had seen the fight slunk into their homes and blew the lamps out. Louisa, dazed, hysterical, refused to go indoors. She slipped, crumbled, her body loosely propped against the woodwork of the well. Tom Burwell leaned against it. He seemed rooted there.

Bob reached Broad Street. White men rushed up to him. He collapsed in their arms.

"Tom Burwell. . . ."

White men like ants upon a forage rushed about. Except for the taut hum of their moving, all was silent. Shotguns, revolvers, rope, kerosene, torches. Two high-powered cars with glaring search-lights. They came together. The taut hum rose to a low roar. Then nothing could be heard but the flop of their feet in the thick dust of the road. The moving body of their silence preceded them over the crest of the hill into factory town. It flattened the Negroes beneath it. It rolled to the wall of the factory, where it stopped. Tom knew that they were coming. He couldnt move. And then he saw the search-lights of the two cars glaring down on him. A quick shock went through him. He stiffened. He started to run. A yell went up from the mob. Tom wheeled about and faced them. They poured down on him. They swarmed. A large man with dead-white face and flabby cheeks came to him and almost jabbed a gun-barrel through his guts.

"Hands behind y, nigger."

Tom's wrists were bound. The big man shoved him to the well. Burn him over it, and when the woodwork caved in, his body would drop to the bottom. Two deaths for a godam nigger. Louisa was driven back. The mob pushed in. Its pressure, its momentum was too great. Drag him to the factory. Wood and stakes already there. Tom moved in the direction indicated. But they had to drag him. They reached the great door. Too many to get in there. The mob divided and flowed around the walls to either side. The big man shoved him through the door. The mob pressed in from the sides. Taut humming. No words. A stake was sunk into the ground. Rotting floor boards piled around it. Kerosene poured on the rotting floor boards. Tom bound to the stake. His breast was bare. Nails' scratches let little lines of blood trickle down and mat into the hair. His face, his eyes were set and stony. Except for irregular breathing, one would have thought him already dead. Torches were flung onto the pile. A great flare muffled in black smoke shot upward. The mob yelled. The mob was silent. Now Tom could be seen within the flames. Only his head, erect, lean, like a blackened stone. Stench of burning flesh soaked the air. Tom's eyes popped. His head settled downward. The mob yelled. Its yell echoed against the skeleton stone walls and sounded like a hundred yells. Like a hundred mobs yelling. Its yell thudded against the thick front wall and fell back. Ghost of a yell slipped through the flames and out the great door of the factory. It fluttered like a dying thing down the single street of factory town. Louisa, upon the step before her home, did not hear it, but her eyes opened slowly. They saw the full moon glowing in the great door. The full moon, an evil thing, an omen, soft showering the homes of folks she knew. Where were they, these people? She'd sing, and perhaps they'd come out and

ERNEST HEMINGWAY
(1899–1961)

So profound has Ernest Hemingway's influence been upon American literature, and upon the short story in particular, any number of his stories might be singled out as "best" or "representative" work. "A Clean, Well-Lighted Place" is a model of compression and understated pathos; in its classical simplicity, as in other brief masterpieces by Hemingway, "A Very Short Story" and "Hills Like White Elephants," for instance, the author's stoical vision is memorably dramatized.

Ernest Hemingway was born in Oak Park, Illinois, but lived most of his adult life—in time, a disconcertingly public life—as an expatriate American. Indeed, Hemingway defined himself in bold opposition to the solidly church-going, middle-class Caucasian America that was his heritage. His first published story was "My Old Man," strongly influenced by Sherwood Anderson, and chosen for The Best American Short Stories 1923; *the author was twenty-four years old. His first book to appear in the United States,* In Our Time *(1925), is a gathering of linked short stories and prose sketches, published by way of Sherwood Anderson's intervention. Thereafter, each book by Ernest Hemingway would constitute a literary event, occasionally one of controversy:* The Sun Also Rises *(1926),* Men Without Women *(1927),* A Farewell to Arms *(1929),* Green Hills of Africa *(1938),* To Have and Have Not *(1937),* For Whom the Bell Tolls *(1940),* The Old Man and the Sea *(1952), among others. It is likely that, had Hemingway written only several of his greatest short stories—"The Snows of Kilimanjaro," "The Short Happy Life of Francis Macomber," "Soldier's Home," "Big Two-Hearted River," for instance—he would be as honored as a master of American prose as he is now.*

A Clean, Well-Lighted Place

It was late and every one had left the café except an old man who sat in the shadow the leaves of the tree made against the electric light. In the daytime the street was dusty, but at night the dew settled the dust and the old man liked to sit late because he was deaf and now at night it was quiet and he felt the difference. The two waiters inside the café knew that the old man was a little drunk, and while he was a good client they knew that if he became too drunk he would leave without paying, so they kept watch on him.

"Last week he tried to commit suicide," one waiter said.

"Why?"

"He was in despair."

"What about?"

"Nothing."

"How do you know it was nothing?"

"He has plenty of money."

They sat together at a table that was close against the wall near the door of the café and looked at the terrace where the tables were all empty except where the old man sat in the shadow of the leaves of the tree that moved slightly in the wind. A girl and a soldier went by in the street. The street light shone on the brass number on his collar. The girl wore no head covering and hurried beside him.

"The guard will pick him up," one waiter said.

"What does it matter if he gets what he's after?"

"He had better get off the street now. The guard will get him. They went by five minutes ago."

The old man sitting in the shadow rapped on his saucer with his glass. The younger waiter went over to him.

"What do you want?"

The old man looked at him. "Another brandy," he said.

"You'll be drunk," the waiter said. The old man looked at him. The waiter went away.

"He'll stay all night," he said to his colleague. "I'm sleepy now. I never get into bed before three o'clock. He should have killed himself last week."

The waiter took the brandy bottle and another saucer from the counter inside the café and marched out to the old man's table. He put down the saucer and poured the glass full of brandy.

"You should have killed yourself last week," he said to the deaf man. The old man motioned with his finger. "A little more," he said. The waiter poured on into the glass so that the brandy slopped over and ran down the stem into the top saucer of the pile. "Thank you," the old man said. The waiter took the bottle back inside the café. He sat down at the table with his colleague again.

"He's drunk now," he said.

"He's drunk every night."

"What did he want to kill himself for?"

"How should I know."

"How did he do it?"

"He hung himself with a rope."

"Who cut him down?"

"His niece."

"Why did they do it?"

"Fear for his soul."

"How much money has he got?"

"He's got plenty."

"He must be eighty years old."

"Anyway I should say he was eighty."

"I wish he would go home. I never get to bed before three o'clock. What kind of hour is that to go to bed?"

"He stays up because he likes it."

"He's lonely. I'm not lonely. I have a wife waiting in bed for me."

"He had a wife once too."

"A wife would be no good to him now."

"You can't tell. He might be better with a wife."

"His niece looks after him."

"I know. You said she cut him down."

"I wouldn't want to be that old. An old man is a nasty thing."

"Not always. This old man is clean. He drinks without spilling. Even now, drunk. Look at him."

"I don't want to look at him. I wish he would go home. He has no regard for those who must work."

The old man looked from his glass across the square, then over at the waiters.

"Another brandy," he said, pointing to his glass. The waiter who was in a hurry came over.

"Finished," he said, speaking with that omission of syntax stupid people employ when talking to drunken people or foreigners. "No more tonight. Close now."

"Another," said the old man.

"No. Finished." The waiter wiped the edge of the table with a towel and shook his head.

The old man stood up, slowly counted the saucers, took a leather coin purse from his pocket and paid for the drinks, leaving half a peseta tip.

The waiter watched him go down the street, a very old man walking unsteadily but with dignity.

"Why didn't you let him stay and drink?" the unhurried waiter asked. They were putting up the shutters. "It is not half-past two."

"I want to go home to bed."

"What is an hour?"

"More to me than to him."

"An hour is the same."

"You talk like an old man yourself. He can buy a bottle and drink at home."

"It's not the same."

"No, it is not," agreed the waiter with a wife. He did not wish to be unjust. He was only in a hurry.

"And you? You have no fear of going home before your usual hour?"

"Are you trying to insult me?"

"No, hombre, only to make a joke."

"No," the waiter who was in a hurry said, rising from pulling down the metal shutters. "I have confidence. I am all confidence."

"You have youth, confidence, and a job," the older waiter said. "You have everything."

"And what do you lack?"

"Everything but work."

"You have everything I have."

"No. I have never had confidence and I am not young."

"Come on. Stop talking nonsense and lock up."

"I am one of those who like to stay late at the café," the older waiter said. "With all those who do not want to go to bed. With all those who need a light for the night."

"I want to go home and into bed."

"We are of two different kinds," the older waiter said. He was now dressed to go home. "It is not only a question of youth and confidence although those things are very beautiful. Each night I am reluctant to close up because there may be some one who needs the café."

"Hombre, there are bodegas open all night long."

"You do not understand. This is a clean and pleasant café. It is well lighted. The light is very good and also, now, there are shadows of the leaves."

"Good night," said the younger waiter.

"Good night," the other said. Turning off the electric light he continued the conversation with himself. It is the light of course but it is necessary that the place be clean and pleasant. You do not want music. Certainly you do not want music. Nor can you stand before a bar with dignity although that is all that is provided for these hours. What did he fear? It was not fear or dread. It was a nothing that he knew too well. It was all a nothing and a man was nothing too. It was only that and light was all it needed and a certain cleanness and order. Some lived in it and never felt it but he knew it all was nada y pues nada y nada y pues nada. Our nada who art in nada, nada be thy name thy kingdom nada thy will be nada in nada as it is in nada. Give us this nada our daily nada and nada us our nada as we nada our nadas and nada us not into nada but deliver us from nada; pues nada. Hail nothing full of nothing, nothing is with thee. He smiled and stood before a bar with a shining steam pressure coffee machine.

"What's yours?" asked the barman.

"Nada."

"Otro loco mas," said the barman and turned away.

"A little cup," said the waiter.

The barman poured it for him.

"The light is very bright and pleasant but the bar is unpolished," the waiter said.

The barman looked at him but did not answer. It was too late at night for conversation.

"You want another copita?" the barman asked.

"No, thank you," said the waiter and went out. He disliked bars and bodegas. A clean, well-lighted café was a very different thing. Now, without thinking further, he would go home to his room. He would lie in the bed and finally, with daylight, he would go to sleep. After all, he said to himself, it is probably only insomnia. Many must have it.

F. SCOTT FITZGERALD
(1896–1940)

Born in St. Paul, Minnesota, of a middle-class family, F. Scott Fitzgerald enjoyed the most problematic of all good fortunes: early, immediate success and celebrity, for his first novel. This was This Side of Paradise *(1920), published when he was only twenty-four. Titles followed in rapid succession—the stories* Flappers and Philosophers *(1921) and* Tales of the Jazz Age *(1922) and a second novel,* The Beautiful and Damned *(1922)—and then, in effect, the fantasy was over. Fitzgerald was the supreme chronicler of the 1920's because he had shared uncritically in its excesses and delusions. After the Crash, and after Fitzgerald's own breakdown, he was the ideal chronicler of disillusion.*

In addition to a number of excellent, much-anthologized stories—"Babylon Revisited," "Winter Dreams," "The Diamond as Big as the Ritz"—Fitzgerald wrote two outstanding novels, The Great Gatsby *(1925) and* Tender is the Night *(1934);* The Last Tycoon *was uncompleted at the time of his premature death, aged forty-four.* The Last Tycoon *was posthumously published in 1941, and a miscellaneous collection of Fitzgerald's prose pieces, titled* The Crack-Up, *was published in 1945. The story included here, "An Alcoholic Case," was published in* Esquire *in early 1937, and, apart from its fluid, gripping narrative, it is fascinating as a document of rueful self-analysis. We see the doomed alcoholic from the point of view of a private nurse to whom he is an "alcoholic case"—the "well-known cartoonist, or artist, whatever . . . ." One of the most spare and least sentimental of Fitzgerald's 178 short stories, "An Alcoholic Case" is not readily forgotten.*

An Alcoholic Case

"Let—go—that—oh-h-h! Please, now, will you." *Don't* start drinking again! Come on—give me the bottle. I told you I'd stay awake givin it to you. Come on. If you do like that a-way—then what are you goin to be like when you go home. Come on—leave it with me—I'll leave half in the bottle. Pul-lease. You know what Dr. Carter says—I'll stay awake and give it to you, or else fix some of it in the bottle—come on—like I told you, I'm too tired to be fightin you all night. . . . All right, drink your fool self to death."

"Would you like some beer?" he asked.

"No, I don't want any beer. Oh, to think that I have to look at you drunk again. My God!"

"Then I'll drink the Coca-Cola."

The girl sat down panting on the bed.

"Don't you believe in anything?" she demanded.

"Nothing you believe in—please—it'll spill."

She had no business there, she thought, no business trying to help him. Again they struggled, but after this time he sat with his head in his hands awhile, before he turned around once more.

"Once more you try to get it I'll throw it down," she said quickly. "I will—on the tiles in the bathroom."

"Then I'll step on the broken glass—or you'll step on it."

"Then let go—oh you promised—"

Suddenly she dropped it like a torpedo, sliding underneath her hand and slithering with a flash of red and black and the words: SIR GALAHAD, DISTILLED LOUISVILLE GIN.

It was on the floor in pieces and everything was silent for awhile and she read *Gone With the Wind* about things so lovely that had happened long ago. She began to worry that he would have to go into the bathroom and might cut his feet, and looked up from time to time to see if he would go in. She was very sleepy—the last time she looked up he was crying and he looked like an old Jewish man she had nursed once in California; he had had to go to the bathroom many times. On this case she was unhappy all the time but she thought:

"I guess if I hadn't liked him I wouldn't have stayed on the case."

With a sudden resurgence of conscience she go up and put a chair in front of the bathroom door. She had wanted to sleep because he had got her up early that morning to get a paper with the Yale-Harvard game in it and she hadn't been home all day. That afternoon a relative of his had come in to see him and she had waited outside in the hall where there was a draft with no sweater to put over her uniform.

As well as she could she arranged him for sleeping, put a robe over his shoulders as he sat slumped over his chiffonier, and one on his knees. She sat down in the rocker but she was no longer sleepy; there was plenty to enter on the chart and treading lightly about she found a pencil and put it down:

Pulse 120

Respiration 25

Temp 98—98.4—98.2

Remarks—

—She could make so many:

Tried to get bottle of gin. Threw it away and broke it.

She corrected it to read:

In the struggle it dropped and was broken. Patient was generally difficult.

She started to add as part of her report: *I never want to go on an alcoholic case again,* but that wasn't in the picture. She knew she could wake herself at seven and clean up everything before his niece awakened. It was all part of the game. But when she sat down in the chair she looked at his face, white and exhausted, and counted his breathing again, wondering why it had all happened. He had been so nice today, drawn her a whole strip of his cartoon just for the fun and given it to her. She was going to have it framed and hang it in her room. She felt again his thin wrists wrestling against her wrist and remembered the awful things he had said, and she thought too of what the doctor had said to him yesterday:

"You're too good a man to do this to yourself."

She was tired and didn't want to clean up the glass on the bathroom floor, because as soon as he breathed evenly she wanted to get him over to the bed. But she decided finally to clean up the glass first; on her knees, searching a last piece of it, she thought:

—This isn't what I ought to be doing. And this isn't what *he* ought to be doing.

Resentfully she stood up and regarded him. Through the thin delicate profile of his nose came a light snore, sighing, remote, inconsolable. The doctor had shaken his head in a certain way, and she knew that really it was a case that was beyond her. Besides, on her card at the agency was written, on the advice of her elders, "No Alcoholics."

She had done her whole duty, but all she could think of was that when she was struggling about the room with him with that gin bottle there had been a pause when he asked her if she had hurt her elbow against a door and that she had answered: "You don't know how people talk about you, no matter how you think of yourself—" when she knew he had a long time ceased to care about such things.

The glass was all collected—as she got out a broom to make sure, she realized that the glass, in its fragments, was less than a window through which they had seen each other for a moment. He did not know about her sisters, and Bill Markoe whom she had almost married, and she did not know what had brought him to this pitch, when there was a picture on his bureau of his young wife and his two sons and him, all trim and handsome as he must have been five years ago. It was so utterly senseless—as she put a bandage on her finger where she had cut it while picking up the glass she made up her mind she would never take an alcoholic case again.

II

Some Halloween jokester had split the side windows of the bus and she shifted back to the Negro section in the rear for fear the glass might fall out. She had her patient's check but no way to cash it at this time of night; there was a quarter and a penny in her purse.

Two nurses she knew were waiting in the hall of Mrs. Hixson's Agency.

"What kind of case have you been on?"

"Alcoholic," she said.

"Oh yes—Gretta Hawks told me about it—you were on with that cartoonist who lives at the Forest Park Inn."

"Yes, I was."

"I hear he's pretty fresh."

"He's never done anything to bother me," she lied. "You can't treat them as if they were committed—"

"Oh, don't get bothered—I just heard that around town—oh, you know—they want you to play around with them—"

"Oh, be quiet," she said, surprised at her own rising resentment.

In a moment Mrs. Hixson came out and, asking the other two to wait, signaled her into the office.

"I don't like to put young girls on such cases," she began. "I got your call from the hotel."

"Oh, it wasn't bad, Mrs. Hixson. He didn't know what he was doing, and he didn't hurt me in any way. I was thinking much more of my reputation with you. He was really nice all day yesterday. He drew me—"

"I didn't want to send you on that case." Mrs. Hixson thumbed through the registration cards. "You take T.B. cases, don't you? Yes. I see you do. Now here's one—"

The phone rang in a continuous chime. The nurse listened as Mrs. Hixson's voice said precisely:

"I will do what I can—that is simply up to the doctor. . . . That is beyond my jurisdiction. . . . Oh, hello, Hattie, no, I can't now. Look, have you got any nurse that's good with alcoholics? There's somebody up at the Forest Park Inn who needs somebody. Call back, will you?"

She put down the receiver. "Suppose you wait outside. What sort of man is this, anyhow? Did he act indecently?"

"He held my hand away," she said, "so I couldn't give him an injection."

"Oh, an invalid he-man," Mrs. Hixson grumbled. "They belong in sanitaria. I've got a case coming along in two minutes that you can get a little rest on. It's an old woman—"

The phone rang again. "Oh, hello, Hattie. . . . Well, how about that big Svensen girl? She ought to be able to take care of any alcoholics. . . . How about Josephine Markham? Doesn't she live in your apartment house? . . . Get her to the phone." Then after a moment, "Jo, would you care to take the case of a well-known cartoonist, or artist, whatever they call themselves, at Forest Park Inn? . . . No. I don't know, but Doctor Carter is in charge and will be around about ten o'clock."

There was a long pause; from time to time Mrs. Hixson spoke:

"I see. . . . Of course, I understand your point of view. Yes, but this isn't supposed to be dangerous—just a little difficult. I never like to send girls to a hotel because I know what riff-raff you're liable to run into. . . . No, I'll find somebody. Even at this hour. Never mind and thanks. Tell Hattie I hope the hat matches the negligee. . . ."

Mrs. Hixson hung up the receiver and made notations on the pad before her. She was a very efficient woman. She had been a nurse and had gone through the worst of it, had been a proud, realistic, overworked probationer, suffered the abuse of smart interns and the insolence of her first patients who thought that she was something to be taken into camp immediately for premature commitment to the service of old age. She swung around suddenly from the desk.

"What kind of cases do you want? I told you I have a nice old woman—"

The nurse's brown eyes were alight with a mixture of thoughts—the movie she had just seen about Pasteur and the book they had all read about Florence Nightingale when they were student nurses. And their pride, swinging across the streets in the cold weather at Philadelphia General, as proud of their new capes as debutantes in their furs going in to balls at the hotels.

"I—I think I would like to try the case again," she said amid a cacophony of telephone bells. "I'd just as soon go back if you can't find anybody else."

"But one minute you say you'll never go on an alcoholic case again and the next minute you say you want to go back to one."

"I think I overestimated how difficult it was. Really, I think I could help him."

"That's up to you. But if he tried to grab your wrists."

"But he couldn't," the nurse said. "Look at my wrists: I played basket ball at Waynesboro High for two years. I'm quite able to take care of him."

Mrs. Hixson looked at her for a long minute. "Well, all right," she said. "But just remember that nothing they say when they're drunk is what they mean when they're sober—I've been all through that: arrange with one of the servants that you can call on him, because you never can tell—some alcoholics are pleasant and some of them are not, but all of them can be rotten."

"I'll remember," the nurse said.

It was an oddly clear night when she went out, with slanting particles of thin sleet making white of a blue-black sky. The bus was the same that had taken her into town but there seemed to be more windows broken now and the bus driver was irritated and talked about what terrible things he would do if he caught any kids. She knew he was just talking about the annoyance in general, just as she had been thinking about the annoyance of an alcoholic. When she came up to the suite and found him all helpless and distraught she would despise him and be sorry for him.

Getting off the bus she went down the long steps to the hotel, feeling a little exalted by the chill in the air. She was going to take care of him because nobody else would, and because the best people of her profession had been interested in taking care of the cases that nobody else wanted.

She knocked at his study door, knowing just what she was going to say.

He answered it himself. He was in dinner clothes even to a derby hat—but minus his studs and tie.

"Oh, hello," he said casually. "Glad you're back. I woke up a while ago and decided I'd go out. Did you get a night nurse?"

"I'm the night nurse too," she said. "I decided to stay on twenty-hour duty."

He broke into a genial, indifferent smile.

"I saw you were gone, but something told me you'd come back. Please find my studs. They ought to be either in a little tortoise shell box or—"

He shook himself a little more into his clothes, and hoisted the cuffs up inside his coat sleeves.

"I thought you had quit me," he said casually.

"I thought I had, too."

"If you look on that table," he said, "you'll find a whole strip of cartoons that I drew you."

"Who are you going to see?" she asked.

"It's the President's secretary," he said. "I had an awful time trying to get ready. I was about to give up when you came in. Will you order me some sherry?"

"One glass," she agreed wearily.

From the bathroom he called presently:

"Oh, nurse, nurse, Light of my Life, where is another stud?"

"I'll put it in."

In the bathroom she saw the pallor and the fever on his face and smelled the mixed peppermint and gin on his breath.

"You'll come up soon?" she asked. "Dr. Carter's coming at ten."

"What nonsense! You're coming down with me."

"Me?" she exclaimed. "In a sweater and skirt? Imagine!"

"Then I won't go."

"All right then, go to bed. That's where you belong anyhow. Can't you see these people tomorrow?"

"No, of course not."

"Of course not!"

She went behind him and reaching over his shoulder tied his tie—his shirt was already thumbed out of press where he had put in the studs, and she suggested:

"Won't you put on another one, if you've got to meet some people you like?"

"All right, but I want to do it myself."

"Why can't you let me help you?" she demanded in exasperation. "Why can't you let me help you with your clothes? What's a nurse for—what good am I doing?"

He sat down suddenly on the toilet seat.

"All right—go on."

"Now don't grab my wrist," she said, and then, "Excuse me."

"Don't worry. It didn't hurt. You'll see in a minute."

She had the coat, vest and stiff shirt off him but before she could pull his undershirt over his head he dragged at his cigarette, delaying her.

"Now watch this," he said. "One—two—three."

She pulled up the undershirt; simultaneously he thrust the crimson-grey point of the cigarette like a dagger against his heart. It crushed out against a copper plate on his left rib about the size of a silver dollar, and he said "ouch!" as a stray spark fluttered down against his stomach.

Now was the time to be hard-boiled, she thought. She knew there were three medals from the war in his jewel box, but she had risked many things herself: tuberculosis among them and one time something worse, though she had not known it and had never quite forgiven the doctor for not telling her.

"You've had a hard time with that, I guess," she said lightly as she sponged him. "Won't it ever heal?"

"Never. That's a copper plate."

"Well, it's no excuse for what you're doing to yourself."

He bent his great brown eyes on her, shrewd—aloof, confused. He signaled to her in one second, his Will to Die, and for all her training and experience she knew she could never do anything constructive with him. He stood up, steadying himself on the wash basin and fixing his eye on some place just ahead.

"Now, if I'm going to stay here you're not going to get at that liquor," she said.

Suddenly she knew he wasn't looking for that. He was looking at the corner where she had thrown the bottle this afternoon. She stared at his handsome face, weak and defiant—afraid to turn even half-way because she knew that death was in that corner where he was looking. She knew death—she had heard it, smelt its unmistakable odor, but she had never seen it before it entered into anyone, and she knew this man saw it in the corner of his bathroom: that it was standing there looking at him while he spit from a feeble cough and rubbed the result into the braid of his trousers. It shone there . . . crackling for a moment as evidence of the last gesture he ever made.

She tried to express it next day to Mrs. Hixson:

"It's not like anything you can beat—no matter how hard you try. This one could have twisted my wrists until he strained them and that wouldn't matter so much to me. It's just that you can't really help them and it's so discouraging—it's all for nothing."

WILLIAM CARLOS WILLIAMS
(1883–1963)

Born in Rutherford, New Jersey, and long associated with the nearby city of Paterson, William Carlos Williams is, along with Langston Hughes, the only writer in this volume to be better known as a poet than a prose fiction writer. He was trained as a physician and set himself in opposition to the more self-consciously literary experiments of Modernism; his attentiveness to the speech that is actually spoken *by Americans provided him, by his own account, with the forms and rhythms of his poetry. The spare, even laconic tone of Williams' short fictions, of which "The Girl with a Pimply Face" is exemplary, is in fact a poetic refinement of the Anderson-vernacular style, composed, like music, for the ear.*

During the 1930's, William Carlos Williams was active in the establishment of little magazines, as well as in political events. His leftist sympathies would one day cost him the post of consultant in poetry at the Library of Congress. The "politics" of his art, however, is intensely personal, grounded in a celebration of American individualism, as his work amply demonstrates. He was a tireless, prolific writer, and among his major titles are the short story collections The Knife of the Times *(1932) and* Life Along the Passaic River *(1938); the novels* White Mule *(1937) and* In the Money *(1940); the experimental volume of poetry and prose* Spring and All *(1923); and the late works* Paterson *(1946–1958) and* Pictures from Brueghel *(1962). Very possibly underestimated as a writer of prose, Williams has been enormously influential as a poet in America.*

The Girl with a Pimply Face

One of the local druggists sent in the call: 50 Summer St., second floor, the door to the left. It's a baby they've just brought from the hospital. Pretty bad condition I should imagine. Do you want to make it? I think they've had somebody else but don't like him, he added as an afterthought.

It was half past twelve. I was just sitting down to lunch. Can't they wait till after office hours?

Oh I guess so. But they're foreigners and you know how they are. Make it as soon as you can. I guess the baby's pretty bad.

It was two-thirty when I got to the place, over a shop in the business part of town. One of those street doors between plate glass show windows. A narrow entry with smashed mail boxes on one side and a dark stair leading straight up. I'd been to the address a number of times during the past years to see various people who had lived there.

Going up I found no bell so I rapped vigorously on the wavy-glass door-panel to the left. I knew it to be the door to the kitchen, which occupied the rear of that apartment.

Come in, said a loud childish voice.

I opened the door and saw a lank haired girl of about fifteen standing chewing gum and eyeing me curiously from beside the kitchen table. The hair was coal black and one of her eyelids drooped a little as she spoke. Well, what do you want? she said. Boy, she was tough and no kidding but I fell for her immediately. There was that hard, straight thing about her that in itself gives an impression of excellence.

I'm the doctor, I said.

Oh, you're the doctor. The baby's inside. She looked at me. Want to see her?

Sure, that's what I came for. Where's your mother?

She's out. I don't know when she's coming back. But you can take a look at the baby if you want to.

All right. Let's see her.

She led the way into the bedroom, toward the front of the flat, one of the unlit rooms, the only windows being those in the kitchen and along the facade of the building.

There she is.

I looked on the bed and saw a small face, emaciated but quiet, unnaturally quiet, sticking out of the upper end of a tightly rolled bundle made by the rest of the baby encircled in a blue cotton blanket. The whole wasn't much larger than a good sized loaf of rye bread. Hands and everything were rolled up. Just the yellowish face showed, tightly hatted and framed around by a corner of the blanket.

What's the matter with her, I asked.

I dunno, said the girl as fresh as paint and seeming about as indifferent as though it had been no relative of hers instead of her sister. I looked at my informer very much amused and she looked back at me, chewing her gum vigorously, standing there her feet well apart. She cocked her head to one side and gave it to me straight in the eye, as much as to say, Well? I looked back at her. She had one of those small, squeezed up faces, snub nose, overhanging eyebrows, low brow and a terrible complexion, pimply and coarse.

When's your mother coming back do you *think*, I asked again.

Maybe in an hour. But maybe you'd better come some time when my father's here. He talks English. He ought to come in around five I guess.

But can't you tell me something about the baby? I hear it's been sick. Does it have a fever?

I dunno.

But has it diarrhoea, are its movements green?

Sure, she said, I guess so. It's been in the hospital but it got worse so my father brought it home today.

What are they feeding it?

A bottle. You can see that yourself. There it is.

There was a cold bottle of half finished milk lying on the coverlet the nipple end of it fallen behind the baby's head.

How old is she? It's a girl, did you say?

Yeah, it's a girl.

Your sister?

Sure. Want to examine it?

No thanks, I said. For the moment at least I had lost all interest in the baby. This young kid in charge of the house did something to me that I liked. She was just a child but nobody was putting anything over on her if she knew it, yet the real thing about her was the complete lack of the rotten smell of a liar. She wasn't in the least presumptive. Just straight.

But after all she wasn't such a child. She had breasts you knew would be like small stones to the hand, good muscular arms and fine hard legs. Her bare feet were stuck into broken down leather sandals such as you see worn by children at the beach in summer.

She was heavily tanned too, wherever her skin showed. Just one of the kids you'll find loafing around the pools they have outside towns and cities everywhere these days. A tough little nut finding her own way in the world.

What's the matter with your legs? I asked. They were bare and covered with scabby sores.

Poison ivy, she answered, pulling up her skirts to show me.

Gee, but you ought to seen it two days ago. This ain't nothing. You're a doctor. What can I do for it?

Let's see, I said

She put her leg up on a chair. It had been badly bitten by mosquitoes, as I saw the thing, but she insisted on poison ivy. She had torn at the affected places with her finger nails and that's what made it look worse.

Oh that's not so bad, I said, if you'll only leave it alone and stop scratching it.

Yeah, I know that but I can't. Scratching's the only thing makes it feel better.

What's that on your foot.

Where? looking.

That big brown spot there on the back of your foot.

Dirt I guess. Her gum chewing never stopped and her fixed defensive non-expression never changed.

Why don't you wash it?

I do. Say, what could I do for my face?

I looked at it closely. You have what they call acne, I told her. All those blackheads and pimples you see there, well, let's see, the first thing you ought to do, I suppose is to get some good soap.

What kind of soap? Lifebuoy?

No. I'd suggest one of those cakes of Lux. Not the flakes but the cake.

Yeah, I know, she said. Three for seventeen.

Use it. Use it every morning. Bathe your face in very hot water. You know, until the skin is red from it. That's to bring the blood up to the skin. Then take a piece of ice. You have ice, haven't you?

Sure, we have ice.

Hold it in a face cloth—or whatever you have—and rub that all over your face. Do that right after you've washed it in the very hot water—before it has cooled. Rub the ice all over. And do it every day—for a month. Your skin will improve. If you like, you can take some cold cream once in a while, not much, just a little and rub that in last of all, if your face feels too dry.

Will that help me?

If you stick to it, it'll help you.

All right.

There's a lotion I could give you to use along with that. Remind me of it when I come back later. Why aren't you in school?

Agh, I'm not going any more. They can't make me. Can they?

They can try.

How can they? I know a girl thirteen that don't go and they can't make her either.

Don't you want to learn things?

I know enough already.

Going to get a job?

I got a job. Here. I been helping the Jews across the hall. They give me three fifty a week—all summer.

Good for you, I said. Think your father'll be here around five?

Guess so. He ought to be.

I'll come back then. Make it all the same call.

All right, she said, looking straight at me and chewing her gum as vigorously as ever.

Just then a little blond haired thing of about seven came in through the kitchen and walked to me looking curiously at my satchel and then at the baby.

What are you, a doctor?

See you later, I said to the older girl and went out.

At five-thirty I once more climbed the wooden stairs after passing two women at the street entrance who looked me up and down from where they were leaning on the brick wall of the building talking.

This time a woman's voice said, Come in, when I knocked on the kitchen door.

It was the mother. She was impressive, a bulky woman, growing toward fifty, in a black dress, with lank graying hair and a long seamed face. She stood by the enameled kitchen table. A younger, plumpish woman with blond hair, well cared for and in a neat house dress—as if she had dolled herself up for the occasion—was standing beside her.

The small blank child was there too and the older girl, behind the others, overshadowed by her mother, the two older women at least a head taller than she. No one spoke.

Hello, I said to the girl I had been talking to earlier. She didn't answer me.

Doctor, began the mother, save my baby. She very sick. The woman spoke with a thick, heavy voice and seemed overcome with grief and apprehension. Doctor! Doctor! she all but wept.

All right, I said to cut the woman short, let's take a look at her first.

So everybody headed toward the front of the house, the mother in the lead. As they went I lagged behind to speak to the second woman, the interpreter. What happened?

The baby was not doing so well. So they took it to the hospital to see if the doctors there could help it. But it got worse. So her husband took it out this morning. It looks bad to me.

Yes, said the mother who had overheard us. Me got seven children. One daughter married. This my baby, pointing to the child on the bed. And she wiped her face with the back of her hand. This baby no do good. Me almost crazy. Don't know who can help. What doctor, I don't know. Somebody tell me take to hospital. I think maybe do some good. Five days she there. Cost me two dollar every day. Ten dollar. I no got money. And when I see my baby, she worse. She look dead. I can't leave she there. No. No. I say to everybody, no. I take she home. Doctor, you save my baby. I pay you. I pay you everything—

Wait a minute, wait a minute, I said. Then I turned to the other woman. What happened?

The baby got like a diarrhoea in the hospital. And she was all dirty when they went to see her. They got all excited—

All sore behind, broke in the mother—

The younger woman said a few words to her in some language that sounded like Russian but it didn't stop her—

No. No. I send she to hospital. And when I see my baby like that I can't leave she there. My babies no that way. Never, she emphasized. Never! I take she home.

Take your time, I said. Take off her clothes. Everything off. This is a regular party. It's warm enough in here. Does she vomit?

She no eat. How she can vomit? said the mother.

But the other woman contradicted her. Yes, she was vomiting in the hospital, the nurse said.

It happens that this September we had been having a lot of such cases in my hospital also, an infectious diarrhoea which practically all the children got when they came in from any cause. I supposed that this was what happened to this child. No doubt it had been in a bad way before that, improper feeding, etc., etc. And then when they took it in there, for whatever had been the matter with it, the diarrhoea had developed. These things sometimes don't turn out so well. Lucky, no doubt, that they had brought it home when they did. I told them so, explaining at the same time: One nurse for ten or twenty babies, they do all they can but you can't run and change the whole ward every five minutes. But the infant looked too lifeless for that only to be the matter with it.

You want all clothes off, asked the mother again, hesitating and trying to keep the baby covered with the cotton blanket while undressing it.

Everything off, I said.

There it lay, just skin and bones with a round fleshless head at the top and the usual pot belly you find in such cases.

Look, said the mother, tilting the infant over on its right side with her big hands so that I might see the reddened buttocks. What kind of nurse that. My babies never that way.

Take your time, take your time, I told her. That's not bad. And it wasn't either. Any child with loose movements might have had the same half an hour after being cared for. Come on. Move away, I said and give me a chance. She kept hovering over the baby as if afraid I might expose it.

It had no temperature. There was no rash. The mouth was in reasonably good shape. Eyes, ears negative. The moment I put my stethoscope to the little boney chest, however, the whole thing became clear. The infant had a severe congenital heart defect, a roar when you listened over the heart that meant, to put it crudely, that she was no good, never would be.

The mother was watching me. I straightened up and looking at her told her plainly: She's got a bad heart.

That was the sign for tears. The big woman cried while she spoke. Doctor, she pleaded in blubbering anguish, save my baby.

I'll help her, I said, but she's got a bad heart. That will never be any better. But I knew perfectly well she wouldn't pay the least attention to what I was saying.

I give you anything, she went on. I pay you. I pay you twenty dollar. Doctor, you fix my baby. You good doctor. You fix.

All right, all right, I said. What are you feeding it?

They told me and it was a ridiculous formula, unboiled besides. I regulated it properly for them and told them how to proceed to make it up. Have you got enough bottles, I asked the young girl.

Sure, we got bottles, she told me.

O.K., then go ahead.

You think you cure she? The mother with her long, tearful face was at me again, so different from her tough female fifteen-year-old.

You do what I tell you for three days, I said, and I'll come back and see how you're getting on.

Tank you, doctor, so much. I pay you. I got today no money. I pay ten dollar to hospital. They cheat me. I got no more money. I pay you Friday when my husband get pay. You save my baby.

Boy! what a woman. I couldn't get away.

She my baby, doctor. I no want to lose. Me got seven children—

Yes, you told me.

But this my baby. You understand. She very sick. You good doctor—

Oh my God! To get away from her I turned again to the kid. You better get going after more bottles before the stores close. I'll come back Friday morning.

How about that stuff for my face you were gonna give me.

That's right. Wait a minute. And I sat down on the edge of the bed to write out a prescription for some lotio alba comp. such as we use in acne. The two older women looked at me in astonishment—wondering, I suppose, how I knew the girl. I finished writing the thing and handed it to her. Sop it on your face at bedtime, I said, and let it dry on. Don't get it into your eyes.

No, I won't.

I'll see you in a couple of days, I said to them all.

Doctor! the old woman was still after me. You come back. I pay you. But all a time short. Always tomorrow come milk man. Must pay rent, must pay coal. And no got money. Too much work. Too much wash. Too much cook. Nobody help. I don't know what's a matter. This door, doctor, this door. This house make sick. Make sick.

Do the best I can, I said as I was leaving.

The girl followed on the stairs. How much is this going to cost, she asked shrewdly holding the prescription.

Not much, I said, and then started to think. Tell them you only got half a dollar. Tell them I said that's all it's worth.

Is that right, she said.

Absolutely. Don't pay a cent more for it.

Say, you're all right, she looked at me appreciatively.

Have you got half a dollar.

Sure. Why not.

What's it all about, my wife asked me in the evening. She had heard about the case. Gee! I sure met a wonderful girl, I told her.

What! another?

Some tough baby. I'm crazy about her. Talk about straight stuff . . . And I recounted to her the sort of case it was and what I had done. The mother's an odd one too. I don't quite make her out.

Did they pay you?

No. I don't suppose they have any cash.

Going back?

Sure. Have to.

Well, I don't see why you have to do all this charity work. Now that's a case you should report to the Emergency Relief. You'll get at least two dollars a call from them.

But the father has a job, I understand. That counts me out.

What sort of a job?

I dunno. Forgot to ask.

What's the baby's name so I can put it in the book?

Damn it. I never thought to ask them that either. I think they must have told me but I can't remember it. Some kind of a Russian name—

You're the limit. Dumbbell, she laughed. Honestly—Who are they anyhow.

You know, I think it must be that family Kate was telling us about. Don't you remember. The time the little kid was playing there one afternoon after school, fell down the front steps and knocked herself senseless.

I don't recall.

Sure you do. That's the family. I get it now. Kate took the brat down there in a taxi and went up with her to see that everything was all right. Yop, that's it. The old woman took the older kid by the hair, because she hadn't watched her sister. And what a beating she gave her. Don't you remember Kate telling us afterward. She thought the old woman was going to murder the child she screamed and threw her around so. Some old gal. You can see they're all afraid of her. What a world. I suppose the damned brat drives her cuckoo. But boy, how she clings to that baby.

The last hope, I suppose, said my wife.

Yeah, and the worst bet in the lot. There's a break for you.

She'll love it just the same.

More, usually.

Three days later I called at the flat again. Come in. This time a resonant male voice. I entered, keenly interested.

By the same kitchen table stood a short, thickset man in baggy working pants and a heavy cotton undershirt. He seemed to have the stability of a cube placed on one of its facets, a smooth, highly colored Slavic face, long black moustaches and widely separated, perfectly candid blue eyes. His black hair, glossy and profuse stood out carelessly all over his large round head. By his look he reminded me at once of his blond haired daughter, absolutely unruffled. The shoulders of an ox. You the doctor, he said. Come in.

The girl and the small child were beside him, the mother was in the bedroom.

The baby no better. Won't eat, said the man in answer to my first question.

How are its bowels?

Not so bad.

Does it vomit?

No.

Then it is better, I objected. But by this time the mother had heard us talking and came in. She seemed worse than the last time. Absolutely inconsolable. Doctor! Doctor! she came up to me.

Somewhat irritated I put her aside and went in to the baby. Of course it was better, much better. So I told them. But the heart, naturally was the same.

How she heart? the mother pressed me eagerly. Today little better?

I started to explain things to the man who was standing back giving his wife precedence but as soon as she got the drift of what I was saying she was all over me again and the tears began to pour. There was no use my talking. Doctor, you good doctor. You do something fix my baby. And before I could move she took my left hand in both hers and kissed it through her tears. As she did so I realized finally that she had been drinking.

I turned toward the man, looking a good bit like the sun at noonday and as indifferent, then back to the woman and I felt deeply sorry for her.

Then, not knowing why I said it nor of whom, precisely I was speaking, I felt myself choking inwardly with the words: Hell! God damn it. The sons of bitches. Why do these things have to be?

The next morning as I came into the coat room at the hospital there were several of the visiting staff standing there with their cigarettes, talking. It was about a hunting dog belonging to one of the doctors. It had come down with distemper and seemed likely to die.

I called up half a dozen vets around here, one of them was saying. I even called up the one in your town, he added turning to me as I came in. And do you know how much they wanted to charge me for giving the serum to that animal?

Nobody answered.

They had the nerve to want to charge me five dollars a shot for it. Can you beat that? Five dollars a shot.

Did you give them the job, someone spoke up facetiously.

Did I? I should say I did not, the first answered. But can you beat that. Why we're nothing but a lot of slop-heels compared to those guys. We deserve to starve.

Get it out of them, someone rasped, kidding. That's the stuff.

Then the original speaker went on, buttonholing me as some of the others faded from the room. Did you ever see practice so rotten. By the way, I was called over to your town about a week ago to see a kid I delivered up here during the summer. Do you know anything about the case?

I probably got them on my list, I said. Russians?

Yeah, I thought as much. Has a job as a road worker or something. Said they couldn't pay me. Well, I took the trouble of going up to your court house and finding out what he was getting. Eighteen dollars a week. Just the type. And they had the nerve to tell me they couldn't pay me.

She told me ten.

She's a liar.

Natural maternal instinct, I guess.

Whisky appetite, if you should ask me.

Same thing.

O.K. buddy. Only I'm telling you. And did I tell *them*. They'll never call me down there again, believe me. I had that much satisfaction out of them anyway. You make 'em pay you. Don't you do anything for them unless they do. He's paid by the county. I tell you if I had taxes to pay down there I'd go and take it out of his salary.

You and how many others?

Say, they're bad actors, that crew. Do you know what they really do with their money? Whisky. Now I'm telling you. That old woman is the slickest customer you ever saw. She's drunk all the time. Didn't you notice it?

Not while I was there.

Don't you let them put any of that sympathy game over on you. Why they tell me she leaves that baby lying on the bed all day long screaming its lungs out until the neighbors complain to the police about it. I'm not lying to you.

Yeah, the old skate's got nerves, you can see that. I can imagine she's a bugger when she gets going.

But what about the young girl, I asked weakly. She seems like a pretty straight kid.

My confrere let out a wild howl. That thing! You mean that pimply faced little bitch. Say, if I had my way I'd run her out of the town tomorrow morning. There's about a dozen wise guys on her trail every night in the week. Ask the cops. Just ask them. They know. Only nobody wants to bring in a complaint. They say you'll stumble over her on the roof, behind the stairs anytime at all. Boy, they sure took you in.

Yes, I suppose they did, I said.

But the old woman's the ringleader. She's got the brains. Take my advice and make them pay.

The last time I went I heard the, Come in! from the front of the house. The fifteen-year-old was in there at the window in a rocking chair with the tightly wrapped baby in her arms. She got up. Her legs were bare to the hips. A powerful little animal.

What are you doing? Going swimming? I asked.

Naw, that's my gym suit. What the kids wear for Physical Training in school.

How's the baby?

She's all right.

Do you mean it?

Sure, she eats fine now.

Tell your mother to bring it to the office some day so I can weigh it. The food'll need increasing in another week or two anyway.

I'll tell her.

How's your face?

Gettin' better.

My God, it *is*, I said. And it was much better. Going back to school now?

Yeah, I had tuh.

KATHERINE ANNE PORTER

(1890–1980)

Katherine Anne Porter is a short story writer's short story writer—from the first, with the publication of her early stories "Maria Concepcion" and the much-anthologized "Flowering Judas," her reputation has been that of a supremely gifted stylist. Though her output of prose fiction is in fact small, its quality is uniformly high. Choosing a single story to represent Porter is a difficult task, for there are several Porter "voices"—including, most memorably, the muted, ironic voice of "He," a small masterpiece.

Born in Indian Creek, Texas, Katherine Anne Porter lived a long, varied, and at times tumultuous life. In the 1920's and 1930's she traveled a good deal, married and divorced twice, and published the first of her exquisitely crafted books, the story collection Flowering Judas *(1930), the novella* Noon Wine *(1937), and the collection* Pale Horse, Pale Rider *(1939). Her European experiences provided her with the rich background material of* The Leaning Tower and Other Stories *(1944). For decades, Porter worked intermittently on a long novel,* Ship of Fools, *which was finally published in 1962, as a major literary event. When Porter's* Collected Stories *appeared in 1965 it was awarded both the National Book Award and the Pulitzer Prize.*

The most powerful of Katherine Anne Porter's works of fiction are based upon memory—"the constant exercise of memory," as she spoke of it in her Journal. *The gritty details of "He," the slowly accumulating weight of resentment and bitterness, surely do derive from Porter's memory of rural Texas in the early years of this century; but the employment of these meager materials, and the subtlety of the narrating voice, are pure Porter—which is to say, inimitable.*

He

Life was very hard for the Whipples. It was hard to feed all the hungry mouths, it was hard to keep the children in flannels during the winter, short as it was: "God knows what would become of us if we lived north," they would say: keeping them decently clean was hard. "It looks like our luck won't never let up on us," said Mr. Whipple, but Mrs. Whipple was all for taking what was sent and calling it good, anyhow when the neighbors were in earshot. "Don't ever let a soul hear us complain," she kept saying to her husband. She couldn't stand to be pitied. "No, not if it comes to it that we have to live in a wagon and pick cotton around the country," she said, "nobody's going to get a chance to look down on us."

Mrs. Whipple loved her second son, the simple-minded one, better than she loved the other two children put together. She was forever saying so, and when she talked with certain of her neighbors, she would even throw in her husband and her mother for good measure.

"You needn't keep on saying it around," said Mr. Whipple, "you'll make people think nobody else has any feelings about Him but you."

"It's natural for a mother," Mrs. Whipple would remind him. "You know yourself it's more natural for a mother to be that way. People don't expect so much of fathers, some way."

This didn't keep the neighbors from talking plainly among themselves. "A Lord's pure mercy if He should die," they said. "It's the sins of the fathers," they agreed among themselves. "There's bad blood and bad doings somewhere, you can bet on that." This behind the Whipples' backs. To their faces everybody said, "He's not so bad off. He'll be all right yet. Look how He grows!"

Mrs. Whipple hated to talk about it, she tried to keep her mind off it, but every time anybody set foot in the house, the subject always came up, and she had to talk about Him first, before she could get on to anything else. It seemed to ease her mind. "I wouldn't have anything happen to Him for all the world, but it just looks like I can't keep Him out of mischief. He's so strong and active, He's always into everything; He was like that since He could walk. It's actually funny sometimes, the way He can do anything; it's laughable to see Him up to His tricks. Emly has more accidents; I'm forever tying up her bruises, and Adna can't fall a foot without cracking a bone. But He can do anything and not get a scratch. The preacher said such a nice thing once when he was here. He said, and I'll remember it to my dying day, 'The innocent walk with God—that's why He don't get hurt.' " Whenever Mrs. Whipple repeated these words, she always felt a warm pool spread in her breast, and the tears would fill her eyes, and then she could talk about something else.

He did grow and He never got hurt. A plank blew off the chicken house and struck Him on the head and He never seemed to know it. He had learned a few words, and after this He forgot them. He didn't whine for food as the other children did, but waited until it was given Him; He ate squatting in the corner, smacking and mumbling. Rolls of fat covered Him like an overcoat, and He could carry twice as much wood and water as Adna. Emly had a cold in the head most of the time—"she takes that after me," said Mrs. Whipple—so in bad weather they gave her the extra blanket off His cot. He never seemed to mind the cold.

Just the same, Mrs. Whipple's life was a torment for fear something might happen to Him. He climbed the peach trees much better than Adna and went skittering along the branches like a monkey, just a regular monkey. "Oh, Mrs. Whipple, you hadn't ought to let Him do that. He'll lose His balance sometime. He can't rightly know what He's doing."

Mrs. Whipple almost screamed out at the neighbor. "He *does* know what He's doing! He's as able as any other child! Come down out of there, you!" When He finally reached the ground she could hardly keep her hands off Him for acting like that before people, a grin all over His face and her worried sick about Him all the time.

"It's the neighbors," said Mrs. Whipple to her husband. "Oh, I do mortally wish they would keep out of our business. I can't afford to let Him do anything for fear they'll come nosing around about it. Look at the bees, now. Adna can't handle them, they sting him up so; I haven't got time to do everything, and now I don't dare let Him. But if He gets a sting He don't really mind."

"It's just because He ain't got sense enough to be scared of anything," said Mr. Whipple.

"You ought to be ashamed of yourself," said Mrs. Whipple,

"talking that way about your own child. Who's to take up for Him if we don't, I'd like to know? He sees a lot that goes on, He listens to things all the time. And anything I tell Him to do He does it. Don't never let anybody hear you say such things. They'd think you favored the other children over Him."

"Well, now I don't, and you know it, and what's the use of getting all worked up about it? You always think the worst of everything. Just let Him alone, He'll get along somehow. He gets plenty to eat and wear, don't He?" Mr. Whipple suddenly felt tired out. "Anyhow, it can't be helped now."

Mrs. Whipple felt tired too, she complained in a tired voice. "What's done can't never be undone, I know that as good as anybody; but He's my child, and I'm not going to have people say anything. I get sick of people coming around saying things all the time."

In the early fall Mrs. Whipple got a letter from her brother saying he and his wife and two children were coming over for a little visit next Sunday week. "Put the big pot in the little one," he wrote at the end. Mrs. Whipple read this part out loud twice, she was so pleased. Her brother was a great one for saying funny things. "We'll just show him that's no joke," she said, "we'll just butcher one of the sucking pigs."

"It's a waste and I don't hold with waste the way we are now," said Mr. Whipple. "That pig'll be worth money by Christmas."

"It's a shame and a pity we can't have a decent meal's vittles once in a while when my own family comes to see us," said Mrs. Whipple. "I'd hate for his wife to go back and say there wasn't a thing in the house to eat. My God, it's better than buying up a great chance of meat in town. There's where you'd spend the money!"

"All right, do it yourself then," said Mr. Whipple. "Christamighty, no wonder we can't get ahead!"

The question was how to get the little pig away from his ma, a great fighter, worse than a Jersey cow. Adna wouldn't try it: "That sow'd rip my insides out all over the pen." "All right, old fraidy," said Mrs. Whipple, "*He's* not scared. Watch *Him* do it." And she laughed as though it was all a good joke and gave Him a little push towards the pen. He sneaked up and snatched the pig right away from the teat and galloped back and was over the fence with the sow raging at His heels. The little black squirming thing was screeching like a baby in a tantrum, stiffening its back and stretching its mouth to the ears. Mrs. Whipple took the pig with her face stiff and sliced its throat with one stroke. When He saw the blood He gave a great jolting breath and ran away. "But He'll forget and eat plenty, just the same," thought Mrs. Whipple. Whenever she was thinking, her lips moved making words. "He'd eat it all if I didn't stop Him. He'd eat up every mouthful from the other two if I'd let Him."

She felt badly about it. He was ten years old now and a third again as large as Adna, who was going on fourteen. "It's a shame, a shame," she kept saying under her breath, "and Adna with so much brains!"

She kept on feeling badly about all sorts of things. In the first place it was the man's work to butcher; the sight of the pig scraped pink and naked made her sick. He was too fat and soft and pitiful-looking. It was simply a shame the way things had to happen. By the time she had finished it up, she almost wished her brother would stay at home.

Early Sunday morning Mrs. Whipple dropped everything to get Him all cleaned up. In an hour He was dirty again, with crawling under fences after a possum, and straddling along the rafters of the barn looking for eggs in the hayloft. "My Lord, look at you now after all my trying! And here's Adna and Emly staying so quiet. I get tired trying to keep you decent. Get off that shirt and put on another, people will say I don't half dress you!" And she boxed Him on the ears, hard. He blinked and blinked and rubbed His head, and His face hurt Mrs. Whipple's feelings. Her knees began to tremble, she had to sit down while she buttoned His shirt. "I'm just all gone before the day starts."

The brother came with his plump healthy wife and two great roaring hungry boys. They had a grand dinner, with the pig roasted to a crackling in the middle of the table, full of dressing, a pickled peach in his mouth and plenty of gravy for the sweet potatoes.

"This looks like prosperity all right," said the brother; "you're going to have to roll me home like I was a barrel when I'm done."

Everybody laughed out loud; it was fine to hear them laughing all at once around the table. Mrs. Whipple felt warm and good about it. "Oh, we've got six more of these; I say it's as little as we can do when you come to see us so seldom."

He wouldn't come into the dining room, and Mrs. Whipple passed it off very well. "He's timider than my other two," she said, "He'll just have to get used to you. There isn't everybody He'll make up with, you know how it is with some children, even cousins." Nobody said anything out of the way.

"Just like my Alty here," said the brother's wife. "I sometimes got to lick him to make him shake hands with his own grandmammy."

So that was over, and Mrs. Whipple loaded up a big plate for Him first, before everybody. "I always say He ain't to be slighted, no matter who else goes without," she said, and carried it to Him herself.

"He can chin Himself on the top of the door," said Emly, helping along.

"That's fine. He's getting along fine," said the brother.

They went away after supper. Mrs. Whipple rounded up the dishes, and sent the children to bed and sat down and unlaced her shoes. "You see?" she said to Mr. Whipple. "That's the way my whole family is. Nice and considerate about everything. No out-of-the-way remarks—they *have* got refinement. I get awfully sick of people's remarks. Wasn't that pig good?"

Mr. Whipple said, "Yes, we're out three hundred pounds of pork, that's all. It's easy to be polite when you come to eat. Who knows what they had in their minds all along?"

"Yes, that's like you," said Mrs. Whipple. "I don't expect anything else from you. You'll be telling me next that my own brother will be saying around that we made Him eat in the kitchen! Oh, my God!" She rocked her head in her hands, a hard pain started in the very middle of her forehead. "Now it's all spoiled, and everything was so nice and easy. All right, you don't like them and you never did—all right, they'll not come here again soon, never you mind! But they *can't* say He wasn't dressed every lick as good as Adna—oh, honest, sometimes I wish I was dead!"

"I wish you'd let up," said Mr. Whipple. "It's bad enough as it is."

It was a hard winter. It seemed to Mrs. Whipple that they hadn't ever known anything but hard times, and now to cap it all a winter like this. The crops were about half of what they had a right to expect; after the cotton was in it didn't do much more than cover the grocery bill. They swapped off one of the plow horses, and got cheated, for the new one died of the heaves. Mrs. Whipple kept thinking all the time it was terrible to have a man you couldn't depend on not to get cheated. They cut down on everything, but Mrs. Whipple kept saying there are things you can't cut down on, and they cost money. It took a lot of warm clothes for Adna and Emly, who walked four miles to school during the three-months session. "He sets around the fire a lot, He won't need so much," said Mr. Whipple. "That's so," said Mrs. Whipple, "and when He does the outdoor chores He can wear your tarpaullion coat. I can't do no better, that's all."

In February He was taken sick, and lay curled up under His blanket looking very blue in the face and acting as if He would choke. Mr. and Mrs. Whipple did everything they could for Him for two days, and then they were scared and sent for the doctor. The doctor told them they must keep Him warm and give Him plenty of milk and eggs. "He isn't as stout as He looks, I'm afraid," said the doctor. "You've got to watch them when they're like that. You must put more cover onto Him, too."

"I just took off His big blanket to wash," said Mrs. Whipple, ashamed. "I can't stand dirt."

"Well, you'd better put it back on the minute it's dry," said the doctor, "or He'll have pneumonia."

Mr. and Mrs. Whipple took a blanket off their own bed and put His cot in by the fire. "They can't say we didn't do everything for Him," she said, "even to sleeping cold ourselves on His account."

When the winter broke He seemed to be well again, but He walked as if His feet hurt Him. He was able to run a cotton planter during the season.

"I got it all fixed up with Jim Ferguson about breeding the cow next time," said Mr. Whipple. "I'll pasture the bull this summer and give Jim some fodder in the fall. That's better than paying out money when you haven't got it."

"I hope you didn't say such a thing before Jim Ferguson," said Mrs. Whipple. "You oughtn't to let him know we're so down as all that."

"Godamighty, that ain't saying we're down. A man is got to look ahead sometimes. He can lead the bull over today. I need Adna on the place."

At first Mrs. Whipple felt easy in her mind about sending Him for the bull. Adna was too jumpy and couldn't be trusted. You've got to be steady around animals. After He was gone she started thinking, and after a while she could hardly bear it any longer. She stood in the lane and watched for Him. It was nearly three miles to go and a hot day, but He oughtn't to be so long about it. She shaded her eyes and stared until colored bubbles floated in her eyeballs. It was just like everything else in life, she must always worry and never know a moment's peace about anything. After a long time she saw Him turn into the side lane, limping. He came on very slowly, leading the big hulk of an animal by a ring in the nose, twirling a little stick in His hand, never looking back or sideways, but coming on like a sleepwalker with His eyes half shut.

Mrs. Whipple was scared sick of bulls; she had heard awful stories about how they followed on quietly enough, and then suddenly pitched on with a bellow and pawed and gored a body to pieces. Any second now that black monster would come down on Him, my God, He'd never have sense enough to run.

She mustn't make a sound nor a move; she mustn't get the bull started. The bull heaved his head aside and horned the air at a fly. Her voice burst out of her in a shriek, and she screamed at Him to come on, for God's sake. He didn't seem to hear her clamor, but kept on twirling His switch and limping on, and the bull lumbered along behind him as gently as a calf. Mrs. Whipple stopped calling and ran towards the house, praying under her breath: "Lord, don't let anything happen to Him. Lord, you *know* people will say we oughtn't to have sent Him. You *know* they'll say we didn't take care of Him. Oh, get Him home, safe home, safe home, and I'll look out for Him better! Amen."

She watched from the window while He led the beast in, and tied him up in the barn. It was no use trying to keep up, Mrs. Whipple couldn't bear another thing. She sat down and rocked and cried with her apron over her head.

From year to year the Whipples were growing poorer and poorer. The place just seemed to run down of itself, no matter how hard they worked. "We're losing our hold," said Mrs. Whipple. "Why can't we do like other people and watch for our best chances? They'll be calling us poor white trash next."

"When I get to be sixteen I'm going to leave," said Adna. "I'm going to get a job in Powell's grocery store. There's money in that. No more farm for me."

"I'm going to be a schoolteacher," said Emly. "But I've got to finish the eighth grade, anyhow. Then I can live in town. I don't see any chances here."

"Emly takes after my family," said Mrs. Whipple. "Ambitious every last one of them, and they don't take second place for anybody."

When fall came Emly got a chance to wait on table in the railroad eating-house in the town near by, and it seemed such a shame not to take it when the wages were good and she could get her food too, that Mrs. Whipple decided to let her take it, and not bother with school until the next session. "You've got plenty of time," she said. "You're young and smart as a whip."

With Adna gone too, Mr. Whipple tried to run the farm with just Him to help. He seemed to get along fine, doing His work and part of Adna's without noticing it. They did well enough until Christmas time, when one morning He slipped on the ice coming up from the barn. Instead of getting up He thrashed round and round, and when Mr. Whipple got to Him, He was having some sort of fit.

They brought Him inside and tried to make Him sit up, but He blubbered and rolled, so they put Him to bed and Mr. Whipple rode to town for the doctor. All the way there and back he worried about where the money was to come from: it sure did look like he had about all the troubles he could carry.

From then on He stayed in bed. His legs swelled up double their size, and the fits kept coming back. After four months, the doctor said, "It's no use, I think you'd better put Him in the County Home for treatment right away. I'll see about it for you. He'll have good care there and be off your hands."

"We don't begrudge Him any care, and I won't let Him out of my sight," said Mrs. Whipple. "I won't have it said I sent my sick child off among strangers."

"I know how you feel," said the doctor. "You can't tell me anything about that, Mrs. Whipple. I've got a boy of my own. But you'd better listen to me. I can't do anything more for Him, that's the truth."

Mr. and Mrs. Whipple talked it over a long time that night after they went to bed. "It's just charity," said Mrs. Whipple, "that's what we've come to, charity! I certainly never looked for this."

"We pay taxes to help support the place just like everybody else," said Mr. Whipple, "and I don't call that taking charity. I think it would be fine to have Him where He'd get the best of everything . . . and besides, I can't keep up with these doctor bills any longer."

"Maybe that's why the doctor wants us to send Him—he's scared he won't get his money," said Mrs. Whipple.

"Don't talk like that," said Mr. Whipple, feeling pretty sick, "or we won't be able to send Him."

"Oh, but we won't keep Him there long," said Mrs. Whipple. "Soon's He's better, we'll bring Him right back home."

"The doctor has told you and told you time and again He can't ever get better, and you might as well stop talking," said Mr. Whipple.

"Doctors don't know everything," said Mrs. Whipple, feeling almost happy. "But anyhow, in the summer Emly can come home for a vacation, and Adna can get down for Sundays: we'll all work together and get on our feet again, and the children will feel they've got a place to come to."

All at once she saw it full summer again, with the garden going fine, and new white roller shades up all over the house, and Adna and Emly home, so full of life, all of them happy together. Oh, it could happen, things would ease up on them.

They didn't talk before Him much, but they never knew just how much He understood. Finally the doctor set the day and a neighbor who owned a double-seated carryall offered to drive them over. The hospital would have sent an ambulance, but Mrs. Whipple couldn't stand to see Him going away looking so sick as all that. They wrapped Him in blankets, and the neighbor and Mr. Whipple lifted Him into the back seat of the carryall beside Mrs. Whipple, who had on her black shirt waist. She couldn't stand to go looking like charity.

"You'll be all right, I guess I'll stay behind," said Mr. Whipple. "It don't look like everybody ought to leave the place at once."

"Besides, it ain't as if He was going to stay forever," said Mrs. Whipple to the neighbor. "This is only for a little while."

They started away, Mrs. Whipple holding to the edges of the blankets to keep Him from sagging sideways. He sat there blinking and blinking. He worked His hands out and began rubbing His nose with His knuckles, and then with the end of the blanket. Mrs. Whipple couldn't believe what she saw; He was scrubbing away big tears that rolled out of the corners of His eyes. He sniveled and made a gulping noise. Mrs. Whipple kept saying, "Oh, honey, you don't feel so bad, do you? You don't feel so bad, do you?" for He seemed to be accusing her of something. Maybe He remembered that time she boxed His ears, maybe He had been scared that day with the bull, maybe He had slept cold and couldn't tell her about it; maybe He knew they were sending Him away for good and all because they were too poor to keep Him. Whatever it was, Mrs. Whipple couldn't bear to think of it. She began to cry, frightfully, and wrapped her arms tight around Him. His head rolled on her shoulder: she had loved Him as much as she possibly could, there were Adna and Emly who had to be thought of too, there was nothing she could do to make up to Him for His life. Oh, what a mortal pity He was ever born.

They came in sight of the hospital, with the neighbor driving very fast, not daring to look behind him.

WILLIAM FAULKNER
(1897–1962)

Faulkner, sui generis. *One of the unquestionably great writers of the twentieth century. The extraordinary range and versatility of his work—the brilliance of his formal experimentation—the very ambition of his novels' structural designs: these are but the outward aspects of the man's genius. And that, born in Oxford, Mississippi, Faulkner should have spent virtually all of his writing life in that town, creating an immense body of work out of the soil of an undistinguished rural county in Mississippi, only deepens the wonder of his achievement.*

Faulkner's major titles are synonymous with some of the major titles of American literature. Among them are The Sound and the Fury *(1929),* As I Lay Dying *(1930),* Sanctuary *(1931),* Light in August *(1932),* Absalom, Absalom! *(1936),* The Hamlet *(1940). And there are the* Collected Stories *(1950), from which the story included here has been taken.*

Choosing a single story to represent Faulkner, too, is a difficult task. "That Evening Sun" is a masterpiece—but so are "A Rose for Emily," "Spotted Horses," "Barn Burning," among others. The particular appeal of "That Evening Sun" is that, for interested readers who have not yet read The Sound and the Fury, *Nancy's fate is divulged, in a chilling aside, in Quentin Compson's section of the novel. And the story seems to have been, for Faulkner, something of an experiment in dramatic form, rare in his work.*

That Evening Sun

I

Monday is no different from any other weekday in Jefferson now. The streets are paved now, and the telephone and electric companies are cutting down more and more of the shade trees—the water oaks, the maples and locusts and elms—to make room for iron poles bearing clusters of bloated and ghostly and bloodless grapes, and we have a city laundry which makes the rounds on Monday morning, gathering the bundles of clothes into bright-colored, specially-made motor cars: the soiled wearing of a whole week now flees apparitionlike behind alert and irritable electric horns, with a long diminishing noise of rubber and asphalt like tearing silk, and even the Negro women who still take in white people's washing after the old custom, fetch and deliver it in automobiles.

But fifteen years ago, on Monday morning the quiet, dusty, shady streets would be full of Negro women with, balanced on their steady, turbaned heads, bundles of clothes tied up in sheets, almost as large as cotton bales, carried so without touch of hand between the kitchen door of the white house and the blackened washpot beside a cabin door in Negro Hollow.

Nancy would set her bundle on the top of her head, then upon the bundle in turn she would set the black straw sailor hat which she wore winter and summer. She was tall, with a high, sad face sunken a little where her teeth were missing. Sometimes we would go a part of the way down the lane and across the pasture with her, to watch the balanced bundle and the hat that never bobbed nor wavered, even when she walked down into the ditch and up the other side and stooped through the fence. She would go down on her hands and knees and crawl through the gap, her head rigid, uptilted, the bundle steady as a rock or a balloon, and rise to her feet again and go on.

Sometimes the husbands of the washing women would fetch and deliver the clothes, but Jesus never did that for Nancy, even before father told him to stay away from our house, even when Dilsey was sick and Nancy would come to cook for us.

And then about half the time we'd have to go down the lane to Nancy's cabin and tell her to come on and cook breakfast. We would stop at the ditch, because father told us to not have anything to do with Jesus—he was a short black man, with a razor scar down his face—and we would throw rocks at Nancy's house until she came to the door, leaning her head around it without any clothes on.

"What yawl mean, chunking my house?" Nancy said. "What you little devils mean?"

"Father says for you to come on and get breakfast," Caddy said. "Father says it's over a half an hour now, and you've got to come this minute."

"I aint studying no breakfast," Nancy said. "I going to get my sleep out."

"I bet you're drunk," Jason said. "Father says you're drunk. Are you drunk, Nancy?"

"Who says I is?" Nancy said. "I got to get my sleep out. I aint studying no breakfast."

So after a while we quit chunking the cabin and went back home. When she finally came, it was too late for me to go to school. So we thought it was whisky until that day they arrested her again and they were taking her to jail and they passed Mr Stovall. He was the cashier in the bank and a deacon in the Baptist church, and Nancy began to say:

"When you going to pay me, white man? When you going to pay me, white man? It's been three times now since you paid me a cent—" Mr Stovall knocked her down, but she kept on saying, "When you going to pay me, white man? It's been three times now since—" until Mr Stovall kicked her in the mouth with his heel and the marshal caught Mr Stovall back, and Nancy lying in the street, laughing. She turned her head and spat out some blood and teeth and said, "It's been three times now since he paid me a cent."

That was how she lost her teeth, and all that day they told about Nancy and Mr Stovall, and all that night the ones that passed the jail could hear Nancy singing and yelling. They could see her hands holding to the window bars, and a lot of them stopped along the fence, listening to her and to the jailer trying to make her stop. She didn't shut up until almost daylight, when the jailer began to hear a bumping and scraping upstairs and he went up there and found Nancy hanging from the window bar. He said that it was cocaine and not whisky, because no nigger would try to commit suicide unless he was full of cocaine, because a nigger full of cocaine wasn't a nigger any longer.

The jailer cut her down and revived her; then he beat her, whipped her. She had hung herself with her dress. She had fixed it all right, but when they arrested her she didn't have on anything except a dress and so she didn't have anything to tie her hands with and she couldn't make her hands let go of the window ledge.

So the jailer heard the noise and ran up there and found Nancy hanging from the window, stark naked, her belly already swelling out a little, like a little balloon.

When Dilsey was sick in her cabin and Nancy was cooking for us, we could see her apron swelling out; that was before father told Jesus to stay away from the house. Jesus was in the kitchen, sitting behind the stove, with his razor scar on his black face like a piece of dirty string. He said it was a watermelon that Nancy had under her dress.

"It never come off of your vine, though," Nancy said.

"Off of what vine?" Caddy said.

"I can cut down the vine it did come off of," Jesus said.

"What makes you want to talk like that before these chillen?" Nancy said. "Whyn't you go on to work? You done et. You want Mr Jason to catch you hanging around his kitchen, talking that way before these chillen?"

"Talking what way?" Caddy said. "What vine?"

"I cant hang around white man's kitchen," Jesus said. "But white man can hang around mine. White man can come in my house, but I cant stop him. When white man want to come in my house, I aint got no house. I cant stop him, but he cant kick me outen it. He cant do that."

Dilsey was still sick in her cabin. Father told Jesus to stay off our place. Dilsey was still sick. It was a long time. We were in the library after supper.

"Isn't Nancy through in the kitchen yet?" mother said. "It seems to me that she has had plenty of time to have finished the dishes."

"Let Quentin go and see," father said. "Go and see if Nancy is through, Quentin. Tell her she can go on home."

I went to the kitchen. Nancy was through. The dishes were put away and the fire was out. Nancy was sitting in a chair, close to the cold stove. She looked at me.

"Mother wants to know if you are through," I said.

"Yes," Nancy said. She looked at me. "I done finished." She looked at me.

"What is it?" I said. "What is it?"

"I aint nothing but a nigger," Nancy said. "It aint none of my fault."

She looked at me, sitting in the chair before the cold stove, the sailor hat on her head. I went back to the library. It was the cold stove and all, when you think of a kitchen being warm and busy and cheerful. And with a cold stove and the dishes all put away, and nobody wanting to eat at that hour.

"Is she through?" mother said.

"Yessum," I said.

"What is she doing?" mother said.

"She's not doing anything. She's through."

"I'll go and see," father said.

"Maybe she's waiting for Jesus to come and take her home," Caddy said.

"Jesus is gone," I said. Nancy told us how one morning she woke up and Jesus was gone.

"He quit me," Nancy said. "Done gone to Memphis, I reckon. Dodging them city *po*lice for a while, I reckon."

"And a good riddance," father said. "I hope he stays there."

"Nancy's scaired of the dark," Jason said.

"So are you," Caddy said.

"I'm not," Jason said.

"Scairy cat," Caddy said.

"I'm not," Jason said.

"You, Candace!" mother said. Father came back.

"I am going to walk down the lane with Nancy," he said. "She says that Jesus is back."

"Has she seen him?" mother said.

"No. Some Negro sent her word that he was back in town. I wont be long."

"You'll leave me alone, to take Nancy home?" mother said. "Is her safety more precious to you than mine?"

"I wont be long," father said.

"You'll leave these children unprotected, with that Negro about?"

"I'm going too," Caddy said. "Let me go, Father."

"What would he do with them, if he were unfortunate enough to have them?" father said.

"I want to go, too," Jason said.

"Jason!" mother said. She was speaking to father. You could tell that by the way she said the name. Like she believed that all day father had been trying to think of doing the thing she wouldn't like the most, and that she knew all the time that after a while he would think of it. I stayed quiet, because father and I both knew that mother would want him to make me stay with her if she just thought of it in time. So father didn't look at me. I was the oldest. I was nine and Caddy was seven and Jason was five.

"Nonsense," father said. "We wont be long."

Nancy had her hat on. We came to the lane. "Jesus always been good to me," Nancy said. "Whenever he had two dollars, one of them was mine." We walked in the lane. "If I can just get through the lane," Nancy said, "I be all right then."

The lane was always dark. "This is where Jason got scared on Hallowe'en," Caddy said.

"I didn't," Jason said.

"Cant Aunt Rachel do anything with him?" father said. Aunt Rachel was old. She lived in a cabin beyond Nancy's, by herself. She had white hair and she smoked a pipe in the door, all day long; she didn't work any more. They said she was Jesus' mother. Sometimes she said she was and sometimes she said she wasn't any kin to Jesus.

"Yes, you did," Caddy said. "You were scairder than Frony. You were scairder than T.P. even. Scairder than niggers."

"Cant nobody do nothing with him," Nancy said. "He say I done woke up the devil in him and aint but one thing going to lay it down again."

"Well, he's gone now," father said. "There's nothing for you to be afraid of now. And if you'd just let white men alone."

"Let what white men alone?" Caddy said. "How let them alone?"

"He aint gone nowhere," Nancy said. "I can feel him. I can feel him now, in this lane. He hearing us talk, every word, hid somewhere, waiting. I aint seen him, and I aint going to see him again but once more, with that razor in his mouth. That razor on that string down his back, inside his shirt. And then I aint going to be even surprised."

"I wasn't scaired," Jason said.

"If you'd behave yourself, you'd have kept out of this," father said. "But it's all right now. He's probably in St. Louis now. Probably got another wife by now and forgot all about you."

"If he has, I better not find out about it," Nancy said. "I'd stand there right over them, and every time he wropped her, I'd cut that arm off. I'd cut his head off and I'd slit her belly and I'd shove—"

"Hush," father said.

"Slit whose belly, Nancy?" Caddy said.

"I wasn't scaired," Jason said. "I'd walk right down this lane by myself."

"Yah," Caddy said. "You wouldn't dare to put your foot down in it if we were not here too."

II

Dilsey was still sick, so we took Nancy home every night until mother said, "How much longer is this going on? I to be left alone in this big house while you take home a frightened Negro?"

We fixed a pallet in the kitchen for Nancy. One night we waked up, hearing the sound. It was not singing and it was not crying, coming up the dark stairs. There was a light in mother's room and we heard father going down the hall, down the back stairs, and Caddy and I went into the hall. The floor was cold. Our toes curled away from it while we listened to the sound. It was like singing and it wasn't like singing, like the sounds that Negroes make.

Then it stopped and we heard father going down the back stairs, and we went to the head of the stairs. Then the sound began again, in the stairway, not loud, and we could see Nancy's eyes halfway up the stairs, against the wall. They looked like cat's eyes do, like a big cat against the wall, watching us. When we came down the steps to where she was, she quit making the sound again, and we stood there until father came back up from the kitchen, with his pistol in his hand. He went back down with Nancy and they came back with Nancy's pallet.

We spread the pallet in our room. After the light in mother's room went off, we could see Nancy's eyes again. "Nancy," Caddy whispered, "are you asleep, Nancy?"

Nancy whispered something. It was oh or no, I dont know which. Like nobody had made it, like it came from nowhere and went nowhere, until it was like Nancy was not there at all; that I had looked so hard at her eyes on the stairs that they had got printed on my eyeballs, like the sun does when you have closed your eyes and there is no sun. "Jesus," Nancy whispered. "Jesus."

"Was it Jesus?" Caddy said. "Did he try to come into the kitchen?"

"Jesus," Nancy said. Like this: Jeeeeeeeeeeeeeeeesus, until the sound went out, like a match or a candle does.

"It's the other Jesus she means," I said.

"Can you see us, Nancy?" Caddy whispered. "Can you see our eyes too?"

"I aint nothing but a nigger," Nancy said. "God knows. God knows."

"What did you see down there in the kitchen?" Caddy whispered. "What tried to get in?"

"God knows," Nancy said. We could see her eyes. "God knows."

Dilsey got well. She cooked dinner. "You'd better stay in bed a day or two longer," father said.

"What for?" Dilsey said. "If I had been a day later, this place would be to rack and ruin. Get on out of here now, and let me get my kitchen straight again."

Dilsey cooked supper too. And that night, just before dark, Nancy came into the kitchen.

"How do you know he's back?" Dilsey said. "You aint seen him."

"Jesus is a nigger," Jason said.

"I can feel him," Nancy said. "I can feel him laying yonder in the ditch."

"Tonight?" Dilsey said. "Is he there tonight?"

"Dilsey's a nigger too," Jason said.

"You try to eat something," Dilsey said.

"I dont want nothing," Nancy said.

"I aint a nigger," Jason said.

"Drink some coffee," Dilsey said. She poured a cup of coffee for Nancy. "Do you know he's out there tonight? How come you know it's tonight?"

"I know," Nancy said. "He's there, waiting. I know. I done lived with him too long. I know what he is fixing to do fore he know it himself."

"Drink some coffee," Dilsey said. Nancy held the cup to her mouth and blew into the cup. Her mouth pursed out like a spreading adder's, like a rubber mouth, like she had blown all the color out of her lips with blowing the coffee.

"I aint a nigger," Jason said. "Are you a nigger, Nancy?"

"I hellborn, child," Nancy said. "I wont be nothing soon. I going back where I come from soon."

III

She began to drink the coffee. While she was drinking, holding the cup in both hands, she began to make the sound again. She made the sound into the cup and the coffee sploshed out onto her hands and her dress. Her eyes looked at us and she sat there, her elbows on her knees, holding the cup in both hands, looking at us across the wet cup, making the sound. "Look at Nancy," Jason said. "Nancy cant cook for us now. Dilsey's got well now."

"You hush up," Dilsey said. Nancy held the cup in both hands, looking at us, making the sound, like there were two of them: one looking at us and the other making the sound. "Whyn't you let Mr Jason telefoam the marshal?" Dilsey said. Nancy stopped then, holding the cup in her long brown hands. She tried to drink some coffee again, but it sploshed out of the cup, onto her hands and her dress, and she put the cup down. Jason watched her.

"I cant swallow it," Nancy said. "I swallows but it wont go down me."

"You go down to the cabin," Dilsey said. "Frony will fix you a pallet and I'll be there soon."

"Wont no nigger stop him," Nancy said.

"I aint a nigger," Jason said. "Am I, Dilsey?"

"I reckon not," Dilsey said. She looked at Nancy. "I dont reckon so. What you going to do, then?"

Nancy looked at us. Her eyes went fast, like she was afraid there wasn't time to look, without hardly moving at all. She looked at us, at all three of us at one time. "You member that night I stayed in yawls' room?" she said. She told about how we waked up early the next morning, and played. We had to play quiet, on her pallet, until father woke up and it was time to get breakfast. "Go and ask your maw to let me stay here tonight," Nancy said. "I wont need no pallet. We can play some more."

Caddy asked mother. Jason went too. "I cant have Negroes sleeping in the bedrooms," mother said. Jason cried. He cried until mother said he couldn't have any dessert for three days if he didn't stop. Then Jason said he could stop if Dilsey would make a chocolate cake. Father was there.

"Why dont you do something about it?" mother said. "What do we have officers for?"

"Why is Nancy afraid of Jesus?" Caddy said. "Are you afraid of father, mother?"

"What could the officers do?" father said. "If Nancy hasn't seen him, how could the officers find him?"

"Then why is she afraid?" mother said.

"She says he is there. She says she knows he is there tonight."

"Yet we pay taxes," mother said. "I must wait here alone in this big house while you take a Negro woman home."

"You know that I am not lying outside with a razor," father said.

"I'll stop if Dilsey will make a chocolate cake," Jason said. Mother told us to go out and father said he didn't know if Jason would get a chocolate cake or not, but he knew what Jason was going to get in about a minute. We went back to the kitchen and told Nancy.

"Father said for you to go home and lock the door, and you'll be all right," Caddy said. "All right from what, Nancy? Is Jesus mad at you?" Nancy was holding the coffee cup in her hands again, her elbows on her knees and her hands holding the cup between her knees. She was looking into the cup. "What have you done that made Jesus mad?" Caddy said. Nancy let the cup go. It didn't break on the floor, but the coffee spilled out, and Nancy sat there with her hands still making the shape of the cup. She began to make the sound again, not loud. Not singing and not unsinging. We watched her.

"Here," Dilsey said. "You quit that, now. You get aholt of yourself. You wait here. I going to get Versh to walk home with you." Dilsey went out.

We looked at Nancy. Her shoulders kept shaking, but she quit making the sound. We watched her. "What's Jesus going to do to you?" Caddy said. "He went away."

Nancy looked at us. "We had fun that night I stayed in yawls' room, didn't we?"

"I didn't," Jason said. "I didn't have any fun."

"You were asleep in mother's room," Caddy said. "You were not there."

"Let's go down to my house and have some more fun," Nancy said.

"Mother wont let us," I said "It's too late now."

"Dont bother her," Nancy said. "We can tell her in the morning. She wont mind."

"She wouldn't let us," I said.

"Don't ask her now," Nancy said. "Don't bother her now."

"She didn't say we couldn't go," Caddy said.

"We didn't ask," I said.

"If you go, I'll tell," Jason said.

"We'll have fun," Nancy said. "They wont mind, just to my house. I been working for yawl a long time. They wont mind."

"I'm not afraid to go," Caddy said. "Jason is the one that's afraid. He'll tell."

"I'm not," Jason said.

"Yes, you are," Caddy said. "You'll tell."

"I wont tell," Jason said. "I'm not afraid."

"Jason aint afraid to go with me," Nancy said. "Is you, Jason?"

"Jason is going to tell," Caddy said. The lane was dark. We passed the pasture gate. "I bet if something was to jump out from behind that gate, Jason would holler."

"I wouldn't," Jason said. We walked down the lane. Nancy was talking loud.

"What are you talking so loud for, Nancy?" Caddy said.

"Who; me?" Nancy said. "Listen at Quentin and Caddy and Jason saying I'm talking loud."

"You talk like there was five of us here," Caddy said. "You talk like father was here too."

"Who; me talking loud, Mr Jason?" Nancy said.

"Nancy called Jason 'Mister,' " Caddy said.

"Listen how Caddy and Quentin and Jason talk," Nancy said.

"We're not talking loud," Caddy said. "You're the one that's talking like father—"

"Hush," Nancy said; "hush, Mr Jason."

"Nancy called Jason 'Mister' aguh—"

"Hush," Nancy said. She was talking loud when we crossed the ditch and stooped through the fence where she used to stoop through with the clothes on her head. Then we came to her house. We were going fast then. She opened the door. The smell of the house was like the lamp and the smell of Nancy was like the wick, like they were waiting for one another to begin to smell. She lit the lamp and closed the door and put the bar up. Then she quit talking loud, looking at us.

"What're we going to do?" Caddy said.

"What do yawl want to do?" Nancy said.

"You said we would have some fun," Caddy said.

There was something about Nancy's house; something you could smell besides Nancy and the house. Jason smelled it, even. "I dont want to stay here," he said. "I want to go home."

"Go home, then," Caddy said.

"I dont want to go by myself," Jason said.

"We're going to have some fun," Nancy said.

"How?" Caddy said.

Nancy stood by the door. She was looking at us, only it was like she had emptied her eyes, like she had quit using them. "What do you want to do?" she said.

"Tell us a story," Caddy said. "Can you tell a story?"

"Yes," Nancy said.

"Tell it," Caddy said. We looked at Nancy. "You dont know any stories."

"Yes," Nancy said. "Yes, I do."

She came and sat in a chair before the hearth. There was a little fire there. Nancy built it up, when it was already hot inside. She built up a good blaze. She told a story. She talked like her eyes looked, like her eyes watching us and her voice talking to us did not belong to her. Like she was living somewhere else, waiting somewhere else. She was outside the cabin. Her voice was inside and the shape of her, the Nancy that could stoop under a barbed wire fence with a bundle of clothes balanced on her head as though without weight, like a balloon, was there. But that was all. "And so this here queen come walking up to the ditch, where that bad man was hiding. She was walking up to the ditch, and she say, 'If I can just get past this here ditch,' was what she say . . . "

"What ditch?" Caddy said. "A ditch like that one out there? Why did a queen want to go into a ditch?"

"To get to her house," Nancy said. She looked at us. "She had to cross the ditch to get into her house quick and bar the door."

"Why did she want to go home and bar the door?" Caddy said.

IV

Nancy looked at us. She quit talking. She looked at us. Jason's legs stuck straight out of his pants where he sat on Nancy's lap. "I dont think that's a good story," he said. "I want to go home."

"Maybe we had better," Caddy said. She got up from the floor. "I bet they are looking for us right now." She went toward the door.

"No," Nancy said. "Dont open it." She got up quick and passed Caddy. She didn't touch the door, the wooden bar.

"Why not?" Caddy said.

"Come back to the lamp," Nancy said. "We'll have fun. You dont have to go."

"We ought to go," Caddy said. "Unless we have a lot of fun." She and Nancy came back to the fire, the lamp.

"I want to go home," Jason said. "I'm going to tell."

"I know another story," Nancy said. She stood close to the lamp. She looked at Caddy, like when your eyes look up at a stick balanced on your nose. She had to look down to see Caddy, but her eyes looked like that, like when you are balancing a stick.

"I wont listen to it," Jason said. "I'll bang on the floor."

"It's a good one," Nancy said. "It's better than the other one."

"What's it about?" Caddy said. Nancy was standing by the lamp. Her hand was on the lamp, against the light, long and brown.

"Your hand is on that hot globe," Caddy said. "Dont it feel hot to your hand?"

Nancy looked at her hand on the lamp chimney. She took her hand away, slow. She stood there, looking at Caddy, wringing her long hand as though it were tied to her wrist with a string.

"Let's do something else," Caddy said.

"I want to go home," Jason said.

"I got some popcorn," Nancy said. She looked at Caddy and then at Jason and then at me and then at Caddy again. "I got some popcorn."

"I dont like popcorn," Jason said. "I'd rather have candy."

Nancy looked at Jason. "You can hold the popper." She was still wringing her hand; it was long and limp and brown.

"All right," Jason said. "I'll stay a while if I can do that. Caddy cant hold it. I'll want to go home again if Caddy holds the popper."

Nancy built up the fire. "Look at Nancy putting her hands in the fire," Caddy said. "What's the matter with you, Nancy?"

"I got popcorn," Nancy said. "I got some." She took the popper from under the bed. It was broken. Jason began to cry.

"Now we cant have any popcorn," he said.

"We ought to go home, anyway," Caddy said. "Come on, Quentin."

"Wait," Nancy said; "wait. I can fix it. Dont you want to help me fix it?"

"I dont think I want any," Caddy said. "It's too late now."

"You help me, Jason," Nancy said. "Dont you want to help me?"

"No," Jason said. "I want to go home."

"Hush," Nancy said; "hush. Watch. Watch me. I can fix it so Jason can hold it and pop the corn." She got a piece of wire and fixed the popper.

"It wont hold good," Caddy said.

"Yes, it will," Nancy said. "Yawl watch. Yawl help me shell some corn."

The popcorn was under the bed too. We shelled it into the popper and Nancy helped Jason hold the popper over the fire.

"It's not popping," Jason said. "I want to go home."

"You wait," Nancy said. "It'll begin to pop. We'll have fun then." She was sitting close to the fire. The lamp was turned up so high it was beginning to smoke.

"Why dont you turn it down some?" I said.

"It's all right," Nancy said. "I'll clean it. Yawl wait. The popcorn will start in a minute."

"I dont believe it's going to start," Caddy said. "We ought to start home, anyway. They'll be worried."

"No," Nancy said. "It's going to pop. Dilsey will tell um yawl with me. I been working for yawl long time. They won't mind if yawl at my house. You wait, now. It'll start popping any minute now."

Then Jason got some smoke in his eyes and he began to cry. He dropped the popper into the fire. Nancy got a wet rag and wiped Jason's face, but he didn't stop crying.

"Hush," she said. "Hush." But he didn't hush. Caddy took the popper out of the fire.

"It's burned up," she said. "You'll have to get some more popcorn, Nancy."

"Did you put all of it in?" Nancy said.

"Yes," Caddy said. Nancy looked at Caddy. Then she took the popper and opened it and poured the cinders into her apron and began to sort the grains, her hands long and brown, and we watching her.

"Haven't you got any more?" Caddy said.

"Yes," Nancy said; "yes. Look. This here ain't burnt. All we need to do is—"

"I want to go home," Jason said. "I'm going to tell."

"Hush," Caddy said. We all listened. Nancy's head was already turned toward the barred door, her eyes filled with red lamplight. "Somebody is coming," Caddy said.

Then Nancy began to make that sound again, not loud, sitting there above the fire, her long hands dangling between her knees; all of a sudden water began to come out on her face in big drops, running down her face, carrying in each one a little turning ball of firelight like a spark until it dropped off her chin. "She's not crying," I said.

"I aint crying," Nancy said. Her eyes were closed. "I aint crying. Who is it?"

"I dont know," Caddy said. She went to the door and looked out. "We've got to go now," she said. "Here comes father."

"I'm going to tell," Jason said. "Yawl made me come."

The water still ran down Nancy's face. She turned in her chair. "Listen. Tell him. Tell him we going to have fun. Tell him I take good care of yawl until in the morning. Tell him to let me come home with yawl and sleep on the floor. Tell him I won't need no pallet. We'll have fun. You member last time how we had so much fun?"

"I didn't have fun," Jason said. "You hurt me. You put smoke in my eyes. I'm going to tell."

V

Father came in. He looked at us. Nancy did not get up.

"Tell him," she said.

"Caddy made us come down here," Jason said. "I didn't want to."

Father came to the fire. Nancy looked up at him. "Cant you go to Aunt Rachel's and stay?" he said. Nancy looked up at father, her hands between her knees. "He's not here," father said. "I would have seen him. There's not a soul in sight."

"He in the ditch," Nancy said. "He waiting in the ditch yonder."

"Nonsense," father said. He looked at Nancy. "Do you know he's there?"

"I got the sign," Nancy said.

"What sign?"

"I got it. It was on the table when I come in. It was a hogbone, with blood meat still on it, laying by the lamp. He's out there. When yawl walk out that door, I gone."

"Gone where, Nancy?" Caddy said.

"I'm not a tattletale," Jason said.

"Nonsense," father said.

"He out there," Nancy said. "He looking through that window this minute, waiting for yawl to go. Then I gone."

"Nonsense," father said. "Lock up your house and we'll take you on to Aunt Rachel's."

"Twont do no good," Nancy said. She didn't look at father now, but he looked down at her, at her long, limp, moving hands. "Putting it off wont do no good."

"Then what do you want to do?" father said.

"I dont know," Nancy said. "I cant do nothing. Just put it off. And that dont do no good. I reckon it belong to me. I reckon what I going to get aint no more than mine."

"Get what?" Caddy said. "What's yours?"

"Nothing," father said. "You all must get to bed."

"Caddy made me come," Jason said.

"Go on to Aunt Rachel's," father said.

"It wont do no good," Nancy said. She sat before the fire, her elbows on her knees, her long hands between her knees. "When even your own kitchen wouldn't do no good. When even if I was sleeping on the floor in the room with your chillen, and the next morning there I am, and blood—"

"Hush," father said. "Lock the door and put out the lamp and go to bed."

"I scared of the dark," Nancy said. "I scared for it to happen in the dark."

"You mean you're going to sit right here with the lamp lighted?" father said. Then Nancy began to make the sound again, sitting before the fire, her long hands between her knees. "Ah, damnation," father said. "Come along, chillen. It's past bedtime."

"When yawl go home, I gone," Nancy said. She talked quieter now, and her face looked quiet, like her hands. "Anyway, I got my coffin money saved up with Mr Lovelady." Mr Lovelady was a short, dirty man who collected the Negro insurance, coming around to the cabins or the kitchens every Saturday morning, to collect fifteen cents. He and his wife lived at the hotel. One morning his wife committed suicide. They had a child, a little girl. He and the child went away. After a week or two he came back alone. We would see him going along the lanes and the back streets on Saturday mornings.

"Nonsense," father said. "You'll be the first thing I'll see in the kitchen tomorrow morning."

"You'll see what you'll see, I reckon," Nancy said. "But it will take the Lord to say what that will be."

VI

We left her sitting before the fire.

"Come and put the bar up," father said. But she didn't move. She didn't look at us again, sitting quietly there between the lamp and the fire. From some distance down the lane we could look back and see her through the open door.

"What, Father?" Caddy said. "What's going to happen?"

"Nothing," father said. Jason was on father's back, so Jason was the tallest of all of us. We went down into the ditch. I looked at it, quiet. I couldn't see much where the moonlight and the shadows tangled.

"If Jesus is hid here, he can see us, cant he?" Caddy said.

"He's not there," father said. "He went away a long time ago."

"You made me come," Jason said, high; against the sky it looked like father had two heads, a little one and a big one. "I didn't want to."

We went up out of the ditch. We could still see Nancy's house and the open door, but we couldn't see Nancy now, sitting before the fire with the door open, because she was tired. "I just done got tired," she said. "I just a nigger. It aint no fault of mine."

But we could hear her, because she began just after we came up out of the ditch, the sound that was not singing and not unsinging. "Who will do our washing now, Father?" I said.

"I'm not a nigger," Jason said, high and close above father's head.

"You're worse," Caddy said, "you are a tattletale. If something was to jump out, you'd be scairder than a nigger."

"I wouldn't," Jason said.

"You'd cry," Caddy said.
"Caddy," father said.
"I wouldn't!" Jason said.
"Scairy cat," Caddy said.
"Candace!" father said.

ZORA NEALE HURSTON
(1891–1960)

Zora Neale Hurston was born, significantly, in Eatonville, Florida, the first incorporated, self-governing, all-black town in the United States. Her father, a Baptist preacher, was three times elected mayor of Eatonville; her mother, who died when Hurston was a small child, nonetheless had a strong influence upon her, encouraging her independence.

Zora Neale Hurston published her most important work in the 1930's. During this time she was teaching, studying anthropology at Barnard, and working with the Federal Theatre Project in New York and with the Federal Writers' Project in Florida. She married twice and divorced twice. Her collection of folklore Mules and Men *(1935) and her novel* Their Eyes Were Watching God *(1937) established her as an important African-American writer, but, like much black writing of the era, the works were allowed to go out of print and have only recently been reissued.*

Hurston is rightly celebrated as a feminist as well as a superbly gifted black writer. Her independence—her "conservatism," as other black critics called it—brought her under attack during the 1940's and 1950's, after her publication of her autobiography Dust Tracks on a Road *(1942); when she published her last novel,* Seraph on the Suwanee *(1948), she had already become relatively isolated from the black literary community. This early story, "Sweat," originally published in 1926, is here taken from* I Love Myself When I Am Laughing . . . And Then Again When I Am Looking Mean and Impressive: A Zora Neale Hurston Reader *(1979). Its skillful employment of dialect and of an "outside" narrating language gives perspective to this ballad-like tale of revenge.*

Sweat

I

It was eleven o'clock of a Spring night in Florida. It was Sunday. Any other night, Delia Jones would have been in bed for two hours by this time. But she was a washwoman, and Monday morning meant a great deal to her. So she collected the soiled clothes on Saturday when she returned the clean things. Sunday night after church, she sorted and put the white things to soak. It saved her almost a half-day's start. A great hamper in the bedroom held the clothes that she brought home. It was so much neater than a number of bundles lying around.

She squatted on the kitchen floor beside the great pile of clothes, sorting them into small heaps according to color, and humming a song in a mournful key, but wondering through it all where Sykes, her husband, had gone with her horse and buckboard.

Just then something long, round, limp and black fell upon her shoulders and slithered to the floor beside her. A great terror took hold of her. It softened her knees and dried her mouth so that it was a full minute before she could cry out or move. Then she saw that it was the big bull whip her husband liked to carry when he drove.

She lifted her eyes to the door and saw him standing there bent over with laughter at her fright. She screamed at him.

"Sykes, what you throw dat whip on me like dat? You know it would skeer me—looks just like a snake, an' you knows how skeered Ah is of snakes."

"Course Ah knowed it! That's how come Ah done it." He slapped his leg with his hand and almost rolled on the ground in his mirth. "If you such a big fool dat you got to have a fit over a earth worm or a string, Ah don't keer how bad Ah skeer you."

"You ain't got no business doing it. Gawd knows it's a sin. Some day Ah'm gointuh drop dead from some of yo' foolishness. 'Nother thing, where you been wid mah rig? Ah feeds dat pony. He ain't fuh you to be drivin' wid no bull whip."

"You sho' is one aggravatin' nigger woman!" he declared and

stepped into the room. She resumed her work and did not answer him at once. "Ah done tole you time and again to keep them white folks' clothes outa dis house."

He picked up the whip and glared at her. Delia went on with her work. She went out into the yard and returned with a galvanized tub and set it on the washbench. She saw that Sykes had kicked all of the clothes together again, and now stood in her way truculently, his whole manner hoping, *praying*, for an argument. But she walked calmly around him and commenced to re-sort the things.

"Next time, Ah'm gointer kick'em outdoors," he threatened as he struck a match along the leg of his corduroy breeches.

Delia never looked up from her work, and her thin, stooped shoulders sagged further.

"Ah ain't for no fuss t'night Sykes. Ah just come from taking sacrament at the church house."

He snorted scornfully. "Yeah, you just come from de church house on a Sunday night, but heah you is gone to work on them clothes. You ain't nothing but a hypocrite. One of them amen-corner Christians—sing, whoop, and shout, then come home and wash white folks' clothes on the Sabbath."

He stepped roughly upon the whitest pile of things, kicking them helter-skelter as he crossed the room. His wife gave a little scream of dismay, and quickly gathered them together again.

"Sykes, you quit grindin' dirt into these clothes! How can Ah git through by Sat'day if Ah don't start on Sunday?"

"Ah don't keer if you never git through. Anyhow, Ah done promised Gawd and a couple of other men, Ah ain't gointer have it in mah house. Don't gimme no lip neither, else Ah'll throw 'em out and put mah fist up side yo' head to boot."

Delia's habitual meekness seemed to slip from her shoulders like a blown scarf. She was on her feet; her poor little body, her bare knuckly hands bravely defying the strapping hulk before her.

"Looka heah, Sykes, you done gone too fur. Ah been married to you fur fifteen years, and Ah been takin' in washin' fur fifteen years. Sweat, sweat, sweat! Work and sweat, cry and sweat, pray and sweat!"

"What's that got to do with me?" he asked brutally.

"What's it got to do with you, Sykes? Mah tub of suds is filled yo' belly with vittles more times than yo' hands is filled it. Mah sweat is done paid for this house and Ah reckon Ah kin keep on sweatin' in it."

She seized the iron skillet from the stove and struck a defensive pose, which act surprised him greatly, coming from her. It cowed him and he did not strike her as he usually did.

"Naw you won't," she panted, "that ole snaggle-toothed black woman you runnin' with ain't comin' heah to pile up on *mah* sweat and blood. You ain't paid for nothin' on this place, and Ah'm gointer stay right heah till Ah'm toted out foot foremost."

"Well, you better quit gittin' me riled up, else they'll be totin' you out sooner than you expect. Ah'm so tired of you Ah don't know whut to do. Gawd! How Ah hates skinny wimmen!"

A little awed by this new Delia, he sidled out of the door and slammed the back gate after him. He did not say where he had gone, but she knew too well. She knew very well that he would not return until nearly daybreak also. Her work over, she went on to bed but not to sleep at once. Things had come to a pretty pass!

She lay awake, gazing upon the debris that cluttered their matrimonial trail. Not an image left standing along the way. Anything like flowers had long ago been drowned in the salty stream that had been pressed from her heart. Her tears, her sweat, her blood. She had brought love to the union and he had brought a longing after the flesh. Two months after the wedding, he had given her the first brutal beating. She had the memory of his numerous trips to Orlando with all of his wages when he had returned to her penniless, even before the first year had passed. She was young and soft then, but now she thought of her knotty, muscled limbs, her harsh knuckly hands, and drew herself up into an unhappy little ball in the middle of the big feather bed. Too late now to hope for love, even if it were not Bertha it would be someone else. This case differed from the others only in that she was bolder than the others. Too late for everything except her little home. She had built it for her old days, and planted one by one the trees and flowers there. It was lovely to her, lovely.

Somehow, before sleep came, she found herself saying aloud: "Oh well, whatever goes over the Devil's back, is got to come under his belly. Sometime or ruther, Sykes, like everybody else, is gointer reap his sowing." After that she was able to build a spiritual earthworks against her husband. His shells could no longer reach her. AMEN. She went to sleep and slept until he announced his presence in bed by kicking her feet and rudely snatching the covers away.

"Gimme some kivah heah, an' get yo' damn foots over on yo' own side! Ah oughter mash you in yo' mouf fuh drawing dat skillet on me."

Delia went clear to the rail without answering him. A triumphant indifference to all that he was or did.

II

The week was as full of work for Delia as all other weeks, and Saturday found her behind her little pony, collecting and delivering clothes.

It was a hot, hot day near the end of July. The village men on Joe Clarke's porch even chewed cane listlessly. They did not hurl the cane-knots as usual. They let them dribble over the edge of the porch. Even conversation had collapsed under the heat.

"Heah come Delia Jones," Jim Merchant said, as the shaggy pony came 'round the bend of the road toward them. The rusty buckboard was heaped with baskets of crisp, clean laundry.

"Yep," Joe Lindsay agreed. "Hot or col', rain or shine, jes'ez reg'lar ez de weeks roll roun' Delia carries 'em an' fetches 'em on Sat'day."

"She better if she wanter eat," said Moss. "Syke Jones ain't wuth de shot an' powder hit would tek tuh kill 'em. Not to *huh* he ain't."

"He sho' ain't," Walter Thomas chimed in. "It's too bad, too, cause she wuz a right pretty li'l trick when he got huh. Ah'd uh mah'ied huh mahself if he hadnter beat me to it."

Delia nodded briefly at the men as she drove past.

"Too much knockin' will ruin *any* 'oman. He done beat huh 'nough tuh kill three women, let 'lone change they looks," said Elijah Moseley. "How Syke kin stommuck dat big black greasy Mogul he's layin' roun' wid, gits me. Ah swear dat eight-rock couldn't kiss a sardine can Ah done thowed out de back do' 'way las' yeah."

"Aw, she's fat, thass how come. He's allus been crazy 'bout fat women," put in Merchant. "He'd a' been tied up wid one long time ago if he could a' found one tuh have him. Did Ah tell yuh 'bout him come sidlin' roun' *mah* wife—bringin' her a basket uh peecans outa his yard fuh a present? Yessir, mah wife! She tol' him tuh take 'em right straight back home, 'cause Delia works so hard ovah dat washtub she reckon everything on de place taste lak sweat an' soapsuds. Ah jus' wisht Ah'd a' caught 'im 'roun' dere! Ah'd a' made his hips ketch on fiah down dat shell road."

"Ah know he done it, too. Ah sees 'im grinnin' at every 'oman dat passes," Walter Thomas said. "But even so, he useter eat some mighty big hunks uh humble pie tuh git dat li'l 'oman he got. She wuz ez pritty ez a speckled pup! Dat wuz fifteen years ago. He useter be so skeered uh losin' huh, she could make him do some parts of a husband's duty. Dey never wuz de same in de mind."

"There oughter be a law about him," said Lindsay. "He ain't fit tuh carry guts tuh a bear."

Clarke spoke for the first time. "Tain't no law on earth dat kin make a man be decent if it ain't in 'im. There's plenty men dat takes a wife lak dey do a joint uh sugar-cane. It's round, juicy an' sweet when dey gits it. But dey squeeze an' grind, squeeze an' grind an' wring tell dey wring every drop uh pleasure dat's in 'em out. When dey's satisfied dat dey is wrung dry, dey treats 'em jes' lak dey do a cane-chew. Dey thows 'em away. Dey knows whut dey is doin' while dey is at it, an' hates theirselves fuh it but they keeps on hangin' after huh tell she's empty. Den dey hates huh fuh bein' a cane-chew an' in de way."

"We oughter take Syke an' dat stray 'oman uh his'n down in Lake Howell swamp an' lay on de rawhide till they cain't say Lawd a' mussy. He allus wuz uh ovahbearin niggah, but since dat white 'oman from up north done teached 'im how to run a automobile, he done got too beggety to live—an' we oughter kill 'im," Old Man Anderson advised.

A grunt of approval went around the porch. But the heat was melting their civic virtue and Elijah Moseley began to bait Joe Clarke.

"Come on, Joe, git a melon outa dere an' slice it up for yo' customers. We'se all sufferin' wid de heat. De bear's done got *me!*"

"Thass right, Joe, a watermelon is jes' whut Ah needs tuh cure de eppizudicks," Walter Thomas joined forces with Moseley. "Come on dere, Joe. We all is steady customers an' you ain't set us up in a long time. Ah chooses dat long, bowlegged Floridy favorite."

"A god, an' be dough. You all gimme twenty cents and slice away," Clarke retorted. "Ah needs a col' slice m'self. Heah, everybody chip in. Ah'll lend y'all mah meat knife."

The money was all quickly subscribed and the huge melon brought forth. At that moment, Sykes and Bertha arrived. A determined silence fell on the porch and the melon was put away again.

Merchant snapped down the blade of his jackknife and moved toward the store door.

"Come on in, Joe, an' gimme a slab uh sow belly an' uh pound uh coffee—almost fuhgot 'twas Sat'day. Got to git on home." Most of the men left also.

Just then Delia drove past on her way home, as Sykes was ordering magnificently for Bertha. It pleased him for Delia to see.

"Git whutsoever yo' heart desires, Honey. Wait a minute, Joe. Give huh two bottles uh strawberry soda-water, uh quart parched ground-peas, an' a block uh chewin' gum."

With all this they left the store, with Sykes reminding Bertha that this was his town and she could have it if she wanted it.

The men returned soon after they left, and held their watermelon feast.

"Where did Syke Jones git da 'oman from nohow?" Lindsay asked.

"Ovah Apopka. Guess dey musta been cleanin' out de town when she lef'. She don't look lak a thing but a hunk uh liver wid hair on it."

"Well, she sho' kin squall," Dave Carter contributed. "When she gits ready tuh laff, she jes' opens huh mouf an' latches it back tuh de las' notch. No ole granpa alligator down in Lake Bell ain't got nothin' on huh."

III

Bertha had been in town three months now. Sykes was still paying her room-rent at Della Lewis'—the only house in town that would have taken her in. Sykes took her frequently to Winter Park to 'stomps'. He still assured her that he was the swellest man in the state.

"Sho' you kin have dat li'l ole house soon's Ah git dat 'oman outa dere. Everything b'longs tuh me an' you sho' kin have it. Ah sho' 'bominates uh skinny 'oman. Lawdy, you sho' is got one portly shape on you! You kin git *anything* you wants. Dis is *mah* town an' you sho' kin have it."

Delia's work-worn knees crawled over the earth in Gethsemane and up the rocks of Calvary many, many times during these months.

She avoided the villagers and meeting places in her efforts to be blind and deaf. But Bertha nullified this to a degree, by coming to Delia's house to call Sykes out to her at the gate.

Delia and Sykes fought all the time now with no peaceful interludes. They slept and ate in silence. Two or three times Delia had attempted a timid friendliness, but she was repulsed each time. It was plain that the breaches must remain agape.

The sun had burned July to August. The heat streamed down like a million hot arrows, smiting all things living upon the earth. Grass withered, leaves browned, snakes went blind in shedding and men and dogs went mad. Dog days!

Delia came home one day and found Sykes there before her. She wondered, but started to go on into the house without speaking, even though he was standing in the kitchen door and she must either stoop under his arm or ask him to move. He made no room for her. She noticed a soap box beside the steps, but paid no particular attention to it, knowing that he must have brought it there. As she was stooping to pass under his outstretched arm, he suddenly pushed her backward, laughingly.

"Look in de box dere Delia, Ah done brung yuh somethin'!"

She nearly fell upon the box in her stumbling, and when she saw what it held, she all but fainted outright.

"Syke! Syke, mah Gawd! You take dat rattlesnake 'way from heah! You *gottuh*. Oh, Jesus, have mussy!"

"Ah aint got tuh do nuthin' uh de kin'—fact is Ah ain't got tuh do nothin' but die. Tain't no use uh you puttin' on airs makin' out lak you skeered uh dat snake—he's gointer stay right heah tell he die. He wouldn't bite me cause Ah knows how tuh handle 'im. Nohow he wouldn't risk breakin' out his fangs 'gin *yo* skinny laigs."

"Naw, now Syke, don't keep dat thing 'round tryin' tuh skeer me tuh death. You knows Ah'm even feared uh earth worms. Thass de biggest snake Ah evah did see. Kill 'im Syke, please."

"Doan ast me tuh do nothin' fuh yuh. Goin' 'round tryin' tuh be so damn asterperious. Naw, Ah ain't gonna kill it. Ah think uh damn sight mo' uh him dan you! Dat's a nice snake an' anybody doan lak 'im kin jes' hit de grit."

The village soon heard that Sykes had the snake, and came to see and ask questions.

"How de hen-fire did you ketch dat six-foot rattler, Syke?" Thomas asked.

"He's full uh frogs so he cain't hardly move, thass how Ah eased up on 'm. But Ah'm a snake charmer an' knows how tuh handle 'em. Shux, dat ain't nothin'. Ah could ketch one eve'y day if Ah so wanted tuh."

"Whut he needs is a heavy hick'ry club leaned real heavy on his head. Dat's de bes' way tuh charm a rattlesnake."

"Naw, Walt, y'all jes' don't understand dese diamon' backs lak Ah do," said Sykes in a superior tone of voice.

The village agreed with Walter, but the snake stayed on. His box remained by the kitchen door with its screen wire covering. Two or three days later it had digested its meal of frogs and literally came to life. It rattled at every movement in the kitchen or the yard. One day as Delia came down the kitchen steps she saw his chalky-white fangs curved like scimitars hung in the wire meshes. This time she did not run away with averted eyes as usual. She stood for a long time in the doorway in a red fury that grew bloodier for every second that she regarded the creature that was her torment.

That night she broached the subject as soon as Sykes sat down to the table.

"Syke, Ah wants you tuh take dat snake 'way fum heah. You done starved me an' Ah put up widcher, you done beat me an Ah took dat, but you done kilt all mah insides bringin' dat varmint heah."

Sykes poured out a saucer full of coffee and drank it deliberately before he answered her.

"A whole lot Ah keer 'bout how you feels inside uh out. Dat snake ain't goin' no damn wheah till Ah gits ready fuh 'im tuh go. So fur as beatin' is concerned, yuh ain't took near all dat you gointer take ef yuh stay 'round *me*."

Delia pushed back her plate and got up from the table. "Ah hates you, Sykes," she said calmly. "Ah hates you tuh de same degree dat Ah useter love yuh. Ah done took an' took till mah belly is full up tuh mah neck. Dat's de reason Ah got mah letter fum de church an' moved mah membership tuh Woodbridge—so Ah don't haftuh take no sacrament wid yuh. Ah don't wantuh see yuh 'round me atall. Lay 'round wid dat 'oman all yuh wants tuh, but gwan 'way fum me an' mah house. Ah hates yuh lak uh suck-egg dog."

Sykes almost let the huge wad of corn bread and collard greens he was chewing fall out of his mouth in amazement. He had a hard time whipping himself up to the proper fury to try to answer Delia.

"Well, Ah'm glad you does hate me. Ah'm sho' tiahed uh you hangin' ontuh me. Ah don't want yuh. Look at yuh stringey ole neck! Yo' rawbony laigs an' arms is enough tuh cut uh man tuh death. You looks jes' lak de devvul's doll-baby tuh *me*. You cain't hate me no worse dan Ah hates you. Ah been hatin' *you* fuh years."

"Yo' ole black hide don't look lak nothin' tuh me, but uh passle uh wrinkled up rubber, wid yo' big ole yeahs flappin' on each side lak uh paih uh buzzard wings. Don't think Ah'm gointuh be run 'way fum mah house neither. Ah'm goin' tuh de white folks 'bout *you*, mah young man, de very nex' time you lay yo' han's on me. Mah cup is done run ovah." Delia said this with no signs of fear and Sykes departed from the house, threatening her, but made not the slightest move to carry out any of them.

That night he did not return at all, and the next day being Sunday, Delia was glad she did not have to quarrel before she hitched up her pony and drove the four miles to Woodbridge.

She stayed to the night service—'love feast'—which was very warm and full of spirit. In the emotional winds her domestic trials were borne far and wide so that she sang as she drove homeward,

Jurden water, black an' col
Chills de body, not de soul
An' Ah wantah cross Jurden in uh calm time.

She came from the barn to the kitchen door and stopped.

"Whut's de mattah, ol' Satan, you ain't kickin' up yo' racket?" She addressed the snake's box. Complete silence. She went on into the house with a new hope in its birth struggles. Perhaps her threat to go to the white folks had frightened Sykes! Perhaps he was sorry! Fifteen years of misery and suppression had brought Delia to the place where she would hope *anything* that looked towards a way over or through her wall of inhibitions.

She felt in the match-safe behind the stove at once for a match. There was only one there.

"Dat niggah wouldn't fetch nothin' heah tuh save his rotten neck, but he kin run thew whut Ah brings quick enough. Now he done toted off nigh on tuh haff uh box uh matches. He done had dat 'oman heah in mah house, too."

Nobody but a woman could tell how she knew this even before she struck the match. But she did and it put her into a new fury.

Presently she brought in the tubs to put the white things to soak. This time she decided she need not bring the hamper out of the bedroom; she would go in there and do the sorting. She picked up the pot-bellied lamp and went in. The room was small and the hamper stood hard by the foot of the white iron bed. She could sit and reach through the bedposts—resting as she worked.

"Ah wantah cross Jurden in uh calm time." She was singing again. The mood of the 'love feast' had returned. She threw back the lid of the basket almost gaily. Then, moved by both horror and terror, she sprang back toward the door. *There lay the snake in the basket!* He moved sluggishly at first, but even as she turned round and round, jumped up and down in an insanity of fear, he began to stir vigorously. She saw him pouring his awful beauty from the basket upon the bed, then she seized the lamp and ran as fast as she could to the kitchen. The wind from the open door blew out the light and the darkness added to her terror. She sped to the darkness of the yard, slamming the door after her before she thought to set down the lamp. She did not feel safe even on the ground, so she climbed up in the hay barn.

There for an hour or more she lay sprawled upon the hay a gibbering wreck.

Finally she grew quiet, and after that came coherent thought. With this stalked through her a cold, bloody rage. Hours of this. A period of introspection, a space of retrospection, then a mixture of both. Out of this an awful calm.

"Well, Ah done de bes' Ah could. If things ain't right, Gawd knows tain't mah fault."

She went to sleep—a twitch sleep—and woke up to a faint gray sky. There was a loud hollow sound below. She peered out. Sykes was at the wood-pile, demolishing a wire-covered box.

He hurried to the kitchen door, but hung outside there some minutes before he entered, and stood some minutes more inside before he closed it after him.

The gray in the sky was spreading. Delia descended without fear now, and crouched beneath the low bedroom window. The drawn shade shut out the dawn, shut in the night. But the thin walls held back no sound.

"Dat ol' scratch is woke up now!" She mused at the tremendous whirr inside, which every woodsman knows, is one of the sound illusions. The rattler is a ventriloquist. His whirr sounds to the right, to the left, straight ahead, behind, close under foot—everywhere but where it is. Woe to him who guesses wrong unless he is prepared to hold up his end of the argument! Sometimes he strikes without rattling at all.

Inside, Sykes heard nothing until he knocked a pot lid off the stove while trying to reach the match-safe in the dark. He had emptied his pockets at Bertha's.

The snake seemed to wake up under the stove and Sykes made a quick leap into the bedroom. In spite of the gin he had had, his head was clearing now.

"Mah Gawd!" he chattered, "ef Ah could on'y strack uh light!"

The rattling ceased for a moment as he stood paralyzed. He waited. It seemed that the snake waited also.

"Oh, fuh de light! Ah thought he'd be too sick"—Sykes was muttering to himself when the whirr began again, closer, right underfoot this time. Long before this, Sykes' ability to think had been flattened down to primitive instinct and he leaped—onto the bed.

Outside Delia heard a cry that might have come from a maddened chimpanzee, a stricken gorilla. All the terror, all the horror, all the rage that man possibly could express, without a recognizable human sound.

A tremendous stir inside there, another series of animal screams, the intermittent whirr of the reptile. The shade torn violently down from the window, letting in the red dawn, a huge brown hand seizing the window stick, great dull blows upon the wooden floor punctuating the gibberish of sound long after the rattle of the snake had abruptly subsided. All this Delia could see and hear from her place beneath the window, and it made her ill. She crept over to the four-o'clocks and stretched herself on the cool earth to recover.

She lay there. "Delia, Delia!" She could hear Sykes calling in a most despairing tone as one who expected no answer. The sun crept on up, and he called. Delia could not move—her legs had gone flabby. She never moved, he called, and the sun kept rising.

"Mah Gawd!" She heard him moan, "Mah Gawd fum Heben!"

She heard him stumbling about and got up from her flower-bed. The sun was growing warm. As she approached the door she heard him call out hopefully, "Delia, is dat you Ah heah?"

She saw him on his hands and knees as soon as she reached the door. He crept an inch or two toward her—all that he was able, and she saw his horribly swollen neck and his one open eye shining with hope. A surge of pity too strong to support bore her away from that eye that must, could not, fail to see the tubs. He would see the lamp. Orlando with its doctors was too far. She could scarcely reach the chinaberry tree, where she waited in the growing heat while inside she knew the cold river was creeping up and up to extinguish that eye which must know by now that she knew.

LANGSTON HUGHES

(1902–1967)

Brilliant in narration, powerful in impact, this story from The Ways of White Folks *(1934) cannot suggest the remarkable virtuosity of that volume of short fiction, which portrays, with sympathy, rage, horror, and satiric humor, the manifold relations between American blacks and whites. Any number of stories from the book might have been chosen to represent it, including its most ambitious concluding work, the near-novella "Father and Son."*

Langston Hughes is most celebrated as a poet, but his genius cut across a number of genres including short fiction, novels, and plays; during the 1930's, as the most popular writer connected with the Harlem Renaissance, he became something of a public figure, working as a journalist, lecturing, founding black theatres, and bringing out anthologies of black writing. Born in Joplin, Missouri, Hughes lived variously in Detroit, Cleveland, New York, and Chicago; his identification was "the bard of Harlem." Among African-American writers of our time, no one has been more honored than Hughes.

His output was considerable: more than thirty-five books. Of these, in addition to The Ways of White Folks, *the most significant are the poetry collections* The Weary Blues *(1926),* The Dream Keeper *(1932),* Montage of a Dream Deferred *(1951), and* The Panther and the Lash *(1967); the novel* Not Without Laughter *(1930); the humorous sketches* Simple Speaks His Mind *(1950); and the autobiographical* The Big Sea *(1940) and* I Wonder as I Wander *(1956).*

Red-Headed Baby

"Dead, dead as hell, these little burgs on the Florida coast. Lot of half-built skeleton houses left over from the boom. Never finished. Never will be finished. Mosquitoes, sand, niggers. Christ, I ought to break away from it. Stuck five years on same boat and still nothin' but a third mate puttin' in at dumps like this on a damned coast-wise tramp. Not even a good time to be had. Norfolk, Savannah, Jacksonville, ain't bad. Ain't bad. But what the hell kind of port's this? What the hell is there to do except get drunk and go out and sleep with niggers? Hell!"

Feet in the sand. Head under palms, magnolias, stars. Lights and the kid-cries of a sleepy town. Mosquitoes to slap at with hairy freckled hands and a dead hot breeze, when there is any breeze.

"What the hell am I walkin' way out here for? She wasn't nothin' to get excited over—last time I saw her. And that must a been a full three years ago. She acted like she was a virgin then. Name was Betsy. Sure ain't a virgin now, I know that. Not after we'd been anchored here damn near a month, the old man mixed up in some kind of law suit over some rich guy's yacht we rammed in a midnight squall off the bar. Damn good thing I wasn't on the bridge then. And this damn yellow gal, said she never had nothing to do with a seaman before. Lyin' I guess. Three years ago. She's probably on the crib-line now. Hell, how far was that house?"

Crossing the railroad track at the edge of town. Green lights. Sand in the road, seeping into oxfords and the cuffs of dungarees. Surf sounds, mosquito sounds, nigger-cries in the night. No street lights out here. There never is where niggers live. Rickety run-down huts, under palm trees. Flowers and vines all over. Always growing, always climbing. Never finished. Never will be finished climbing, growing. Hell of a lot of stars these Florida nights.

"Say, this ought to be the house. No light in it. Well, I remember this half-fallin'-down gate. Still fallin' down. Hell, why don't it go on and fall? Two or three years, and ain't fell yet. Guess *she's* fell a hell of a lot, though. It don't take them yellow janes long to get old and ugly. Said she was seventeen then. A wonder her old woman let me come in the house that night. They acted like it was the first time a white man had ever come in the house. They acted scared. But she was worth the money that time all right. She played like a kid. Said she liked my red hair. Said she'd never had a white man before. . . . Holy Jesus, the yellow wenches I've had, though. . . . Well, it's the same old gate. Be funny if she had another mule in my stall, now wouldn't it? . . . Say, anybody home there?"

"Yes, suh! Yes, suh! Come right in!"

"Hell, I know they can't recognize my voice. . . . It's the old woman, sure as a yard arm's long. . . . Hello! Where's Betsy?"

"Yes, suh, right here, suh. In de kitchen. Wait till I lights de light. Come in. Come in, young gentleman."

"Hell, I can't see to come in."

Little flare of oil light.

"Howdy! Howdy do, suh! Howdy, if 'tain't Mister Clarence, now, 'pon my word! Howdy, Mister Clarence, howdy! Howdy! After sich a long time."

"You must-a knowed my voice."

"No, suh, ain't recollected, suh. No, suh, but I knowed you was some white man comin' up de walk. Yes, indeedy! Set down, set down. Betsy be here directly. Set *right* down. Lemme call her. She's in de kitchen. . . . You Betsy!"

"Same old woman, wrinkled as hell, and still don't care where the money comes from. Still talkin' loud. . . . She knew it was some white man comin' up the walk, heh? There must be plenty of 'em, then, comin' here now. She knew it was some white man, heh! . . . What yuh sayin', Betsy, old gal? Damn if yuh ain't just as plump as ever. Them same damn moles on your cheek! Com'ere, lemme feel 'em."

Young yellow girl in a white house dress. Oiled hair. Skin like an autumn moon. Gold-ripe young yellow girl with a white house dress to her knees. Soft plump bare legs, color of the moon. Barefooted.

"Say, Betsy, here is Mister Clarence come back."

"Sure is! Claren—Mister Clarence! Ma, give him a drink."

"Keepin' licker in the house, now, heh? Yes? I thought you was church members last time I saw yuh? You always had to send out and get licker then."

"Well, we's expectin' company some of the times these days," smiling teeth like bright-white rays of moon, Betsy, nearly twenty, and still pretty.

"You usin' rouge, too, ain't yuh?"

"Sweet rouge."

"Yal?"

"Yeah, man, sweet and red like your hair."

"Yal?"

No such wise cracking three years ago. Too young and dumb for flirtation then: Betsy. Never like the old woman, talkative, "This here rum come right off de boats from Bermudy. Taste it, Mister Clarence. Strong enough to knock a mule down. Have a glass."

"Here's to you, Mister Clarence."

"Drinkin' licker, too, heh? Hell of a baby, ain't yuh? Yuh wouldn't even do that last time I saw yuh."

"Sure wouldn't, Mister Clarence, but three years a long time."

"Don't Mister Clarence *me* so much. Yuh know I christened yuh. . . . Auntie, yuh right about this bein' good licker."

"Yes, suh, I knowed you'd like it. It's strong."

"Sit on my lap, kid."

"Sure. . . ."

Soft heavy hips. Hot and browner than the moon—good licker. Drinking it down in little nigger house Florida coast palm fronds scratching roof hum mosquitoes night bugs flies ain't loud enough to keep a man named Clarence girl named Betsy old woman named Auntie from talking and drinking in a little nigger house on Florida coast dead warm night with the licker browner and more fiery than the moon. Yeah, man! A blanket of stars in the Florida sky—outside. In oil-lamp house you don't see no stars. Only a white man with red hair—third mate on a lousy tramp, a nigger girl, and Auntie wrinkled as an alligator bringing the fourth bottle of licker and everybody drinking—when the door . . . slowly . . . opens.

"Say, what the hell? Who's openin' that room door, peepin' in here? It can't be openin' itself?"

The white man stares intently, looking across the table, past the lamp, the licker bottles, the glasses and the old woman, way past the girl. Standing in the door from the kitchen—Look! a damn red-headed baby. Standing not saying a damn word, a damn runt of a red-headed baby.

"What the hell?"

"You Clar— . . . Mister Clarence, 'cuse me! . . . You hatian, you, get back to you' bed this minute—fo' I tan you in a inch o' yo' life!"

"Ma, let him stay."

Betsy's red-headed child stands in the door looking like one of those goggly-eyed dolls you hit with a ball at the County Fair. The child's face got no change in it. Never changes. Looks like never will change. Just staring—blue-eyed. Hell! God damn! A red-headed blue-eyed yellow-skinned baby!

"You Clarence! . . . 'Cuse me, Mister Clarence. I ain't talkin' to you suh. . . . You, Clarence, go to bed. . . . That chile near 'bout worries de soul-case out o' me. Betsy spiles him, that's why. De po' little thing can't hear, nohow. Just deaf as a post. And over two years old and can't even say, 'Da!' No, suh, can't say, 'Da!' "

"Anyhow, Ma, my child ain't blind."

"Might just as well be blind fo' all de good his eyesight do him. I show him a switch and he don't pay it no mind—'less'n I hit him."

"He's mighty damn white for a nigger child."

"Yes, suh, Mister Clarence. he really ain't got much colored blood in him, a-tall. Betsy's papa, Mister Clarence, now he were a white man, too. . . . Here, lemme pour you some licker. Drink, Mister Clarence, drink."

Damn little red-headed stupid-faced runt of a child, named Clarence. Bow-legged as hell, too. Three shots for a quarter like a loaded doll in a County Fair. Anybody take a chance. For Christ's sake, stop him from walking across the floor! Will yuh?

"Hey! Take your hands off my legs, you lousy little bastard!"

"He can't hear you, Mister Clarence."

"Tell him to stop crawlin' around then under the table before I knock his block off."

"You varmint. . . ."

"Hey! Take him up from there, will you?"

"Yes, suh, Mister Clarence."

"Hey!"

"You little . . ."

"Hurry! Go on! Get him out then! What's he doin' crawlin' round dumb as hell lookin' at me up at me. I said, *me*. Get him the hell out of here! Hey, Betsy, get him out!"

A red-headed baby. Moonlight-gone baby. No kind of yellow-white bow-legged goggled-eyed County Fair baseball baby. Get him the hell out of here pulling at my legs looking like me at me like me at myself like me red-headed as me.

"Christ!"

"Christ!"

Knocking over glasses by the oil lamp on the table where the night flies flutter Florida where skeleton houses left over from boom sand in the road and no lights in the nigger section across the railroad's knocking over glasses at edge of town where a moon-colored girl's got a red-headed baby deaf as a post like the dolls you wham at three shots for a quarter in the County Fair half full of licker and can't hit nothing.

"Lemme pay for those drinks, will yuh? How much is it?"

"Ain't you gonna stay, Mister Clarence?"

"Lemme pay for my licker, I said."

"Ain't you gonna stay all night?"

"Lemme pay for that licker."

"Why, Mister Clarence? You stayed before."

"How much is the licker?"

"Two dollars, Mister Clarence."

"Here."

"Thank you, Mister Clarence."

"Go'bye!"

"Go'bye."

RICHARD WRIGHT
(1908–1960)

"The Man Who Was Almost a Man" contrasts with, and in an oblique way amplifies, Langston Hughes's "Red-Headed Baby": for here we see a further development of certain thematic tensions, the logical, if unarticulated, next step. Its setting would seem to bear a close resemblance to the rural area near Natchez, Mississippi, where Wright was born to extreme poverty, familial disruption, and the violent bigotry of whites.

Like Zora Neale Hurston and Langston Hughes, Richard Wright left the South permanently. He too worked for the Writers' Project and did various freelance journalism; by 1935, he had started to write fiction, strongly influenced by the literary Naturalism of the era. The publication of the original and disturbing Native Son *in 1940 was a turning point in black American literary history, for the novel was unaccommodating in its portrayal of a vengeful black youth named Bigger Thomas, yet it became a bestseller, bought and read by a large audience of white readers. Bigger Thomas as character and symbol entered the American consciousness permanently, as a daemonic counterpart, it might be said, to Samuel Clemens' long-suffering Nigger Jim and Harriet Beecher Stowe's Christly Uncle Tom.*

Long associated with Marxist ideology, Richard Wright is nonetheless an artist of complexity and subtlety, as the story included here demonstrates. Apart from Native Son, *Wright's important titles are the stories* Uncle Tom's Children *(1938), the autobiographical* Black Boy *(1945), and the novel* The Outsider *(1953). An early novel,* Lawd Today, *was published posthumously; and a gathering of stories,* Eight Men, *from which "The Man Who Was Almost a Man" is taken, appeared in 1961.*

The Man Who Was Almost a Man

Dave struck out across the fields, looking homeward through paling light. Whut's the use talkin wid em niggers in the field? Anyhow, his mother was putting supper on the table. Them niggers can't understan nothing. One of these days he was going to get a gun and practice shooting, then they couldn't talk to him as though he were a little boy. He slowed, looking at the ground. Shucks, Ah ain scareda them even ef they are biggern me! Aw, Ah know whut Ahma do. Ahm going by ol Joe's sto n git that Sears Roebuck catlog n look at them guns. Mebbe Ma will lemme buy one when she gits mah pay from ol man Hawkins. Ahma beg her t gimme some money. Ahm ol ernough to hava gun. Ahm seventeen. Almost a man. He strode, feeling his long loose-jointed limbs. Shucks, a man oughta hava little gun aftah he done worked hard all day.

He came in sight of Joe's store. A yellow lantern glowed on the front porch. He mounted steps and went through the screen door, hearing it bang behind him. There was a strong smell of coal oil and mackerel fish. He felt very confident until he saw fat Joe walk in through the rear door, then his courage began to ooze.

"Howdy, Dave! Whutcha want?"

"How yuh, Mistah Joe? Aw, Ah don wanna buy nothing. Ah jus wanted t see ef yuhd lemme look at tha catlog erwhile."

"Sure! You wanna see it here?"

"Nawsuh. Ah wants t take it home wid me. Ah'll bring it back termorrow when Ah come in from the fiels."

"You plannin on buying something?"

"Yessuh."

"Your ma lettin you have your own money now?"

"Shucks. Mistah Joe, Ahm gittin t be a man like anybody else!"

Joe laughed and wiped his greasy white face with a red bandanna.

"What you plannin on buyin?"

Dave looked at the floor, scratched his head, scratched his thigh, and smiled. Then he looked up shyly.

"Ah'll tell yuh, Mistah Joe, ef yuh promise yuh won't tell."

"I promise."

"Waal, Ahma buy a gun."

"A gun? What you want with a gun?"

"Ah wanna keep it."

"You ain't nothing but a boy. You don't need a gun."

"Aw, lemme have the catlog, Mistah Joe. Ah'll bring it back."

Joe walked through the rear door. Dave was elated. He looked around at barrels of sugar and flour. He heard Joe coming back. He craned his neck to see if he were bringing the book. Yeah, he's got it. Gawddog, he's got it!

"Here, but be sure you bring it back. It's the only one I got."

"Sho, Mistah Joe."

"Say, if you wanna buy a gun, why don't you buy one from me? I gotta gun to sell."

"Will it shoot?"

"Sure it'll shoot."

"Whut kind is it?"

"Oh, it's kinda old . . . a left-hand Wheeler. A pistol. A big one."

"Is it got bullets in it?"

"It's loaded."

"Kin Ah see it?"

"Where's your money?"

"What yuh wan fer it?"

"I'll let you have it for two dollars."

"Just two dollahs? Shucks, Ah could buy tha when Ah git mah pay."

"I'll have it here when you want it."

"Awright, suh. Ah be in fer it."

He went through the door, hearing it slam again behind him. Ahma git some money from Ma n buy me a gun! Only two dollahs! He tucked the thick catalogue under his arm and hurried.

"Where yuh been, boy?" His mother held a steaming dish of black-eyed peas.

"Aw, Ma, Ah just stopped down the road t talk wid the boys."

"Yuh know bettah t keep suppah waiting."

He sat down, resting the catalogue on the edge of the table.

"Yuh git up from there and git to the well n wash yosef! Ah ain feedin no hogs in mah house!"

She grabbed his shoulder and pushed him. He stumbled out of the room, then came back to get the catalogue.

"Whut this?"

"Aw, Ma, it's jusa catlog."

"Who yuh git it from?"

"From Joe, down at the sto."

"Waal, thas good. We kin use it in the outhouse."

"Naw, Ma." He grabbed for it. "Gimme ma catlog, Ma."

She held onto it and glared at him.

"Quit hollerin at me! Whut's wrong wid yuh? Yuh crazy?"

"But Ma, please. It ain mine! It's Joe's! He tol me t bring it back t im termorrow."

She gave up the book. He stumbled down the back steps, hugging the thick book under his arm. When he had splashed water on his face and hands, he groped back to the kitchen and fumbled in a corner for the towel. He bumped into a chair; it clattered to the floor. The catalogue sprawled at his feet. When he had dried his eyes he snatched up the book and held it again under his arms. His mother stood watching him.

"Now, ef yuh gonna act a fool over that ol book, Ah'll take it n burn it up."

"Naw, Ma, please."

"Waal, set down n be still!"

He sat down and drew the oil lamp close. He thumbed page after page, unaware of the food his mother set on the table. His father came in. Then his small brother.

"Whutcha got there, Dave?" his father asked.

"Jusa catlog," he answered, not looking up.

"Yeah, here they is!" His eyes glowed at blue-and-black revolvers. He glanced up, feeling sudden guilt. His father was watching him. He eased the book under the table and rested it on his knees. After the blessing was asked, he ate. He scooped up peas and swallowed fat meat without chewing. Buttermilk helped to wash it down. He did not want to mention money before his father. He would do much better by cornering his mother when she was alone. He looked at his father uneasily out of the edge of his eye.

"Boy, how come yuh don quit foolin wid tha book n eat yo suppah?"

"Yessuh."

"How you n ol man Hawkins gitten erlong?"

"Suh?"

"Can't yuh hear? Why don yuh listen? Ah ast you how wuz yuh n ol man Hawkins gittin erlong?"

"Oh, swell, Pa. Ah plows mo lan than anybody over there."

"Waal, yuh oughta keep you mind on whut yuh doin."

"Yessuh."

He poured his plate full of molasses and sopped it up slowly with a chunk of cornbread. When his father and brother had left the kitchen, he still sat and looked again at the guns in the catalogue, longing to muster courage enough to present his case to his mother. Lawd, ef Ah only had tha pretty one! He could almost feel the slickness of the weapon with his fingers. If he had a gun like that he would polish it and keep it shining so it would never rust. N Ah'd keep it loaded, by Gawd!

"Ma?" His voice was hesitant.

"Hunh?"

"Ol man Hawkins give yuh mah money yit?"

"Yeah, but ain no usa yuh thinking about throwin nona it erway. Ahm keeping tha money sos yuh kin have cloes t go to school this winter."

He rose and went to her side with the open catalogue in his palms. She was washing dishes, her head bent low over a pan. Shyly he raised the book. When he spoke, his voice was husky, faint.

"Ma, Gawd knows Ah wans one of these."

"One of whut?" she asked, not raising her eyes.

"One of these," he said again, not daring even to point. She glanced up at the page, then at him with wide eyes.

"Nigger, is yuh gone plumb crazy?"

"Aw, Ma—"

"Git outta here! Don yuh talk t me bout no gun! Yuh a fool!"

"Ma, Ah kin buy one fer two dollahs."

"Not ef Ah knows it, yuh ain!"

"But yuh promised me one—"

"Ah don care what Ah promised! Yuh ain nothing but a boy yit!"

"Ma ef yuh lemme buy one Ah'll *never* ast yuh fer nothing no mo."

"Ah tol yuh t git outta here! Yuh ain gonna toucha penny of tha money fer no gun! Thas how come Ah has Mistah Hawkins t pay yu wages t me, cause Ah knows yuh ain got no sense."

"But, Ma, we needa gun. Pa ain got no gun. We needa gun in the house. Yuh kin never tell whut might happen."

"Now don yuh try to maka fool outta me, boy! Ef we did hava gun, yuh wouldn't have it!"

He laid the catalogue down and slipped his arm around her waist.

"Aw, Ma, Ah done worked hard alla summer n ain ast yuh fer nothing, is Ah, now?"

"Thas whut yuh spose t do!"

"But Ma, Ah wans a gun. Yuh kin lemme have two dollahs outta mah money. Please, Ma. I kin give it to Pa . . . Please, Ma! Ah loves yuh, Ma."

When she spoke her voice came soft and low.

"What yu wan wida gun, Dave? Yuh don need no gun. Yuh'll git in trouble. N ef yo pa jus thought Ah let yuh have money t buy a gun he'd hava fit."

"Ah'll hide it, Ma. It ain but two dollahs."

"Lawd, chil, whut's wrong wid yuh?"

"Ain nothin wrong, Ma. Ahm almos a man now. Ah wans a gun."

"Who gonna sell yuh a gun?"

"Ol Joe at the sto."

"N it don cos but two dollahs?"

"Thas all, Ma. Jus two dollahs. Please, Ma."

She was stacking the plates away; her hands moved slowly, reflectively. Dave kept an anxious silence. Finally, she turned to him.

"Ah'll let yuh git tha gun ef yuh promise me one thing."

"Whut's tha, Ma?"

"Yuh bring it straight back t me, yuh hear? It be fer Pa."

"Yessum! Lemme go now, Ma."

She stooped, turned slightly to one side, raised the hem of her dress, rolled down the top of her stocking, and came up with a slender wad of bills.

"Here," she said. "Lawd knows yuh don need no gun. But yer pa does. Yuh bring it right back t me, yuh hear? Ahma put it up. Now ef yuh don, Ahma have yuh pa lick yuh so hard yuh won fergit it."

"Yessum."

He took the money, ran down the steps, and across the yard.

"Dave! Yuuuuu Daaaaave!"

He heard, but he was not going to stop now. "Naw, Lawd!"

The first movement he made the following morning was to reach under his pillow for the gun. In the gray light of dawn he held it loosely, feeling a sense of power. Could kill a man with a gun like this. Kill anybody, black or white. And if he were holding his gun in his hand, nobody could run over him; they would have to respect him. It was a big gun, with a long barrel and a heavy handle. He raised and lowered it in his hand, marveling at its weight.

He had not come straight home with it as his mother had asked; instead he had stayed out in the fields, holding the weapon in his hand, aiming it now and then at some imaginary foe. But he had not fired it; he had been afraid that his father might hear. Also he was not sure he knew how to fire it.

To avoid surrendering the pistol he had not come into the house until he knew that they were all asleep. When his mother had tiptoed to his bedside late that night and demanded the gun, he had first played possum; then he had told her that the gun was hidden outdoors, that he would bring it to her in the morning. Now he lay turning it slowly in his hands. He broke it, took out the cartridges, felt them, and then put them back.

He slid out of bed, got a long strip of old flannel from a trunk, wrapped the gun in it, and tied it to his naked thigh while it was still loaded. He did not go in to breakfast. Even though it was not yet daylight, he started for Jim Hawkins' plantation. Just as the sun was rising he reached the barns where the mules and plows were kept.

"Hey! That you, Dave?"

He turned. Jim Hawkins stood eying him suspiciously.

"What're yuh doing here so early?"

"Ah didn't know Ah wuz gittin up so early, Mistah Hawkins. Ah was fixin t hitch up ol Jenny n take her t the fiels."

"Good. Since you're so early, how about plowing that stretch down by the woods?"

"Suits me, Mistah Hawkins."

"O.K. Go to it!"

He hitched Jenny to a plow and started across the fields. Hot dog! This was just what he wanted. If he could get down by the woods, he could shoot his gun and nobody would hear. He walked behind the plow, hearing the traces creaking, feeling the gun tied tight to his thigh.

When he reached the woods, he plowed two whole rows before he decided to take out the gun. Finally, he stopped, looked in all directions, then untied the gun and held it in his hand. He turned to the mule and smiled.

"Know whut this is, Jenny? Naw, yuh wouldn know! Yuhs jusa ol mule! Anyhow, this is a gun, n it kin shoot, by Gawd!"

He held the gun at arm's length. Whut t hell, Ahma shoot this thing! He looked at Jenny again.

"Lissen here, Jenny! When Ah pull this ol trigger, Ah don wan yuh to run n acka fool now?"

Jenny stood with head down, her short ears pricked straight. Dave walked off about twenty feet, held the gun far out from him at arm's length, and turned his head. Hell, he told himself, Ah ain afraid. The gun felt loose in his fingers; he waved it wildly for a moment. Then he shut his eyes and tightened his forefinger. Bloom! A report half deafened him and he thought his right hand was torn from his arm. He heard Jenny whinnying and galloping over the field, and he found himself on his knees, squeezing his fingers hard between his legs. His hand was numb; he jammed it into his mouth, trying to warm it, trying to stop the pain. The gun lay at his feet. He did not quite know what had happened. He stood up and stared at the gun as though it were a living thing. He gritted his teeth and kicked the gun. Yuh almos broke mah arm! He turned to look for Jenny; she was far over the fields, tossing her head and kicking wildly.

"Hol on there, ol mule!"

When he caught up with her she stood trembling, walling her big white eyes at him. The plow was far away; the traces had broken. Then Dave stopped short, looking, not believing. Jenny was bleeding. Her left side was red and wet with blood. He went closer. Lawd, have mercy! Wondah did Ah shoot this mule? He grabbed for Jenny's mane. She flinched, snorted, whirled, tossing her head.

"Hol on now! Hol on."

Then he saw the hole in Jenny's side, right between the ribs. It was round, wet, red. A crimson stream streaked down the front leg, flowing fast. Good Gawd! Ah wuzn't shootin at tha mule. He felt panic. He knew he had to stop that blood, or Jenny would bleed to death. He had never seen so much blood in all his life. He chased the mule for half a mile, trying to catch her. Finally she stopped, breathing hard, stumpy tail half arched. He caught her mane and led her back to where the plow and gun lay. Then he stooped and grabbed handfuls of damp black earth and tried to plug the bullet hole. Jenny shuddered, whinnied, and broke from him.

"Hol on! Hol on now!"

He tried to plug it again, but blood came anyhow. His fingers were hot and sticky. He rubbed dirt into his palms, trying to dry them. Then again he attempted to plug the bullet hole, but Jenny shied away, kicking her heels high. He stood helpless. He had to do something. He ran at Jenny; she dodged him. He watched a red stream of blood flow down Jenny's leg and form a bright pool at her feet.

"Jenny . . . Jenny," he called weakly.

His lips trembled. She's bleeding t death! He looked in the direction of home, wanting to go back, wanting to get help. But he saw the pistol lying in the damp black clay. He had a queer feeling that if he only did something, this would not be; Jenny would not be there bleeding to death.

When he went to her this time, she did not move. She stood with sleepy, dreamy eyes; and when he touched her she gave a low-pitched whinny and knelt to the ground, her front knees slopping in blood.

"Jenny . . . Jenny . . ." he whispered.

For a long time she held her neck erect; then her head sank, slowly. Her ribs swelled with a mighty heave and she went over.

Dave's stomach felt empty, very empty. He picked up the gun and held it gingerly between his thumb and forefinger. He buried it at the foot of a tree. He took a stick and tried to cover the pool of blood with dirt—but what was the use? There was Jenny lying with her mouth open and her eyes walled and glassy. He could not tell Jim Hawkins he had shot his mule. But he had to tell something. Yeah, Ah'll tell em Jenny started gittin ill n fell on the joint of the plow. . . . But that would hardly happen to a mule. He walked across the field slowly, head down.

It was sunset. Two of Jim Hawkins' men were over near the edge of the woods digging a hole in which to bury Jenny. Dave was surrounded by a knot of people, all of whom were looking down at the dead mule.

"I don't see how in the world it happened," said Jim Hawkins for the tenth time.

The crowd parted and Dave's mother, father, and small brother pushed into the center.

"Where Dave?" his mother called.

"There he is," said Jim Hawkins.

His mother grabbed him.

"Whut happened, Dave? Whut yuh done?"

"Nothin."

"C'mon, boy, talk," his father said.

Dave took a deep breath and told the story he knew nobody believed.

"Waal," he drawled. "Ah brung ol Jenny down here sos Ah could do mah plowin. Ah plowed bout two rows, just like yuh see." He stopped and pointed at the long rows of upturned earth. "Then somethin musta been wrong wid ol Jenny. She wouldn ack right a-tall. She started snortin n kickin her heels. Ah tried t hol her, but she pulled erway, rearin n goin in. Then when the point of the plow was stickin up in the air, she swung erroun n twisted herself back on it . . . She stuck herself n started t bleed. N fo Ah could do anything, she wuz dead."

"Did you ever hear of anything like that in all your life?" asked Jim Hawkins.

There were white and black standing in the crowd. They murmured. Dave's mother came close to him and looked hard into his face. "Tell the truth, Dave," she said.

"Looks like a bullet hole to me," said one man.

"Dave, whut yuh do wid tha gun?" his mother asked.

The crowd surged in, looking at him. He jammed his hands into his pockets, shook his head slowly from left to right, and backed away. His eyes were wide and painful.

"Did he hava gun?" asked Jim Hawkins.

"By Gawd, Ah tol yuh tha wuz a gun wound," said a man, slapping his thigh.

His father caught his shoulders and shook him till his teeth rattled.

"Tell whut happened, yuh rascal! Tell whut . . ."

Dave looked at Jenny's stiff legs and began to cry.

"Whut yuh do wid tha gun?" his mother asked.

"Whut wuz he doin wida gun?" his father asked.

"Come on and tell the truth," said Hawkins. "Ain't nobody going to hurt you . . ."

His mother crowded close to him.

"Did yuh shoot tha mule, Dave?"

Dave cried, seeing blurred white and black faces.

"Ahh ddinn gggo tt sshooot hher . . . Ah sswear tt Gawd Ahh ddin. . . . Ah wuz a-tryin t sssee ef the gggun would sshoot—"

"Where yuh git the gun from?" his father asked.

"Ah got it from Joe, at the sto."

"Where yuh git the money?"

"Ma give it t me."

"He kept worryin me, Bob. Ah had t. Ah tol im t bring the gun right back t me . . . It was fer yuh, the gun."

"But how yuh happen to shoot that mule?" asked Jim Hawkins.

"Ah wuzn shootin at the mule, Mistah Hawkins! The gun jumped when Ah pulled the trigger . . . N fo Ah knowed anythin Jenny was there a-bleedin."

Somebody in the crowd laughed. Jim Hawkins walked close to Dave and looked into his face.

"Well, looks like you have bought you a mule, Dave."

"Ah swear fo Gawd. Ah didn go t kill the mule, Mistah Hawkins!"

"But you killed her!"

All the crowd was laughing now. They stood on tiptoe and poked heads over one another's shoulders.

"Well, boy, looks like yuh done bought a dead mule! Hahaha!"

"Ain tha ershame."

"Hohohohoho."

Dave stood, head down, twisting his feet in the dirt.

"Well, you needn't worry about it, Bob," said Jim Hawkins to Dave's father. "Just let the boy keep on working and pay me two dollars a month."

"What yuh wan fer yo mule, Mistah Hawkins?"

Jim Hawkins screwed up his eyes.

"Fifty dollars."

"Whut yuh do wid tha gun?" Dave's father demanded.

Dave said nothing.

"Yuh wan me t take a tree n beat yuh till yuh talk!"

"Nawsuh!"

"Whut yuh do wid it?"

"Ah throwed it erway."

"Where?"

"Ah . . . Ah throwed it in the creek."

"Waal, c mon home. N firs thing in the mawnin git to tha creek n fin tha gun."

"Yessuh."

"Whut yuh pay fer it?"

"Two dollahs."

"Take tha gun n git yo money back n carry it t Mistah Hawkins, yuh hear? N don fergit Ahma lam you black bottom good fer this! Now march yoself on home, suh!"

Dave turned and walked slowly. He heard people laughing. Dave glared, his eyes welling with tears. Hot anger bubbled in him. Then he swallowed and stumbled on.

That night Dave did not sleep. He was glad that he had gotten out of killing the mule so easily, but he was hurt. Something hot seemed to turn over inside him each time he remembered how they had laughed. He tossed on his bed, feeling his hard pillow. N Pa says he's gonna beat me . . . He remembered other beatings, and his back quivered. Naw, naw, Ah sho don wan im t beat me tha way no mo. Dam em all! Nobody ever gave him anything. All he did was work. They treat me like a mule, n then they beat me. He gritted his teeth. N Ma had t tell on me.

Well, if he had to, he would take old man Hawkins that two dollars. But that meant selling the gun. And he wanted to keep that gun. Fifty dollars for a dead mule.

He turned over, thinking how he had fired the gun. He had an itch to fire it again. Ef other men kin shoota gun, by Gawd, Ah kin! He was still, listening. Mebbe they all sleepin now. The house was still. He heard the soft breathing of his brother. Yes, now! He would go down and get that gun and see if he could fire it! He eased out of bed and slipped into overalls.

The moon was bright. He ran almost all the way to the edge of the woods. He stumbled over the ground, looking for the spot where he had buried the gun. Yeah, here it is. Like a hungry dog scratching for a bone, he pawed it up. He puffed his black cheeks and blew dirt from the trigger and barrel. He broke it and found four cartridges unshot. He looked around; the fields were filled with silence and moonlight. He clutched the gun stiff and hard in his fingers. But, as soon as he wanted to pull the trigger, he shut his eyes and turned his head. Naw, Ah can't shoot wid mah eyes closed n mah head turned. With effort he held his eyes open; then he squeezed. *Blooooom!* He was stiff, not breathing. The gun was still in his hands. Dammit, he'd done it! He fired again. *Blooooom!* He smiled. *Blooooom! Blooooom! Click, click.* There! It was empty.

If anybody could shoot a gun, he could. He put the gun into his hip pocket and started across the fields.

When he reached the top of a ridge he stood straight and proud in the moonlight, looking at Jim Hawkins' big white house, feeling the gun sagging in his pocket. Lawd, ef Ah had just one mo bullet Ah'd taka shot at tha house. Ah'd like t scare ol man Hawkins jusa little . . . Jusa enough t let im know Dave Saunders is a man.

To his left the road curved, running to the tracks of the Illinois Central. He jerked his head, listening. From far off came a faint *hoooof-hoooof; hoooof-hoooof* . . . He stood rigid. Two dollahs a mont. Les see now . . . Tha means it'll take bout two years. Shucks! Ah'll be dam!

He started down the road, toward the tracks. Yeah, here she comes! He stood beside the track and held himself stiffly. Here she comes, erroun the ben . . . C mon, yuh slow poke! C mon! He had his hand on his gun; something quivered in his stomach. Then the train thundered past, the gray and brown box cars rumbling and clinking. He gripped the gun tightly; then he jerked his hand out of his pocket. Ah betcha Bill wouldn't do it! Ah betcha . . . The cars slid past, steel grinding upon steel. Ahm ridin yuh ternight, so hep me Gawd! He was hot all over. He hesitated just a moment; then he grabbed, pulled atop a car, and lay flat. He felt his pocket; the gun was still there. Ahead the long rails were glinting in the moonlight, stretching away, away to somewhere, somewhere where he could be a man . . .

PAUL BOWLES

(1910–   )

No one who reads this story ever forgets it, though one might well wish to forget it, like a bad dream that imposes itself, with ominous significance, upon the daylight, civilized world. Though "A Distant Episode" has become the most frequently anthologized of Paul Bowles's fiction, I could not resist including it here. It is both the highest achievement of this intransigent artist's work in fiction and representative of his imagination generally.

Born in New York City, Paul Bowles has had two distinct careers: as a composer, and as a writer and translator. During the 1930's and 1940's he was a music critic for the New York Herald Tribune, *and wrote musical scores for Broadway. Since 1945, he has lived in Tangier, and has concentrated upon literature. His first novel,* The Sheltering Sky, *was published in 1949 to considerable acclaim and notoriety; subsequent titles established his reputation as a chronicler of a world almost entirely devoid of the "manners" that constitute most works of fiction in our tradition. These are the story collections* The Delicate Prey *(1950),* The Time of Friendship *(1967), and* Collected Stories *(1979); the novels* Let It Come Down *(1952),* The Spider's House *(1955), and* Up Above the World *(1966). Bowles's nonfiction books include* Their Heads Are Green and Their Hands Are Blue: Scenes from the Non-Christian World *(1963) and* Things Gone and Things Still Here *(1977). His poetry has been collected in* Next to Nothing *(1981) and his autobiography, the enigmatic* Without Stopping, *was published in 1972.*

In 1991, in honor of his contribution to the short story as an art form, Paul Bowles was awarded the $25,000 Rea Award for the Short Story.

A Distant Episode

The September sunsets were at their reddest the week the Professor decided to visit Aïn Tadouirt, which is in the warm country. He came down out of the high, flat region in the evening by bus, with two small overnight bags full of maps, sun lotions and medicines. Ten years ago he had been in the village for three days; long enough, however, to establish a fairly firm friendship with the café-keeper, who had written him several times during the first year after his visit, if never since. "Hassan Ramani," the Professor said over and over, as the bus bumped downward through ever warmer layers of air. Now facing the flaming sky in the west, and now facing the sharp mountains, the car followed the dusty trail down the canyons into air which began to smell of other things besides the endless ozone of the heights: orange blossoms, pepper, sun-baked excrement, burning olive oil, rotten fruit. He closed his eyes happily and lived for an instant in a purely olfactory world. The distant past returned—what part of it, he could not decide.

The chauffeur, whose seat the Professor shared, spoke to him without taking his eyes from the road. "*Vous êtes géologue?*"

"A geologist? Ah, no! I'm a linguist."

"There are no languages here. Only dialects."

"Exactly. I'm making a survey of variations on Moghrebi."

The chauffeur was scornful. "Keep on going south," he said. "You'll find some languages you never heard of before."

As they drove through the town gate, the usual swarm of urchins rose up out of the dust and ran screaming beside the bus. The Professor folded his dark glasses, put them in his pocket; and as soon as the vehicle had come to a standstill he jumped out, pushing his way through the indignant boys who clutched at his luggage in vain, and walked quickly into the Grand Hotel Saharien. Out of its eight rooms there were two available—one facing the market and the other, a smaller and cheaper one, giving onto a tiny yard full of refuse and barrels, where two gazelles wandered about. He took the smaller room, and pouring the entire pitcher of water into the tin basin, began to wash the grit from his face and ears. The afterglow was nearly gone from the sky, and the pinkness in objects was disappearing, almost as he watched. He lit the carbide lamp and winced at its odor.

After dinner the Professor walked slowly through the streets to Hassan Ramani's café, whose back room hung hazardously out above the river. The entrance was very low, and he had to bend down slightly to get in. A man was tending the fire. There was one guest sipping tea. The *qaouaji* tried to make him take a seat at the other table in the front room, but the Professor walked airily ahead into the back room and sat down. The moon was shining through the reed latticework and there was not a sound outside but the occasional distant bark of a dog. He changed tables so he could see the river. It was dry, but there was a pool here and there that reflected the bright night sky. The *qaouaji* came in and wiped off the table.

"Does this café still belong to Hassan Ramani?" he asked him in the Moghrebi he had taken four years to learn.

The man replied in bad French: "He is deceased."

"Deceased?" repeated the Professor, without noticing the absurdity of the word. "Really? When?"

"I don't know," said the *qaouaji*. "One tea?"

"Yes. But I don't understand . . ."

The man was already out of the room, fanning the fire. The Professor sat still, feeling lonely, and arguing with himself that to do so was ridiculous. Soon the *qaouaji* returned with the tea. He paid him and gave him an enormous tip, for which he received a grave bow.

"Tell me," he said, as the other started away. "Can one still get those little boxes made from camel udders?"

The man looked angry. "Sometimes the Reguibat bring in those things. We do not buy them here." Then insolently, in Arabic: "And why a camel-udder box?"

"Because I like them," retorted the Professor. And then because he was feeling a little exalted, he added, "I like them so much I want to make a collection of them, and I will pay you ten francs for every one you can get me."

"*Khamstache*," said the *qaouaji*, opening his left hand rapidly three times in succession.

"Never. Ten."

"Not possible. But wait until later and come with me. You can give me what you like. And you will get camel-udder boxes if there are any."

He went out into the front room, leaving the Professor to drink his tea and listen to the growing chorus of dogs that barked and howled as the moon rose higher into the sky. A group of customers came into the front room and sat talking for an hour or so. When they had left, the *qaouaji* put out the fire and stood in the doorway putting on his burnous. "Come," he said.

Outside in the street there was very little movement. The booths were all closed and the only light came from the moon. An occasional pedestrian passed, and grunted a brief greeting to the *qaouaji*.

"Everyone knows you," said the Professor, to cut the silence between them.

"Yes."

"I wish everyone knew me," said the Professor, before he realized how infantile such a remark must sound.

"*No* one knows you," said his companion gruffly.

They had come to the other side of the town, on the promontory above the desert, and through a great rift in the wall the Professor saw the white endlessness, broken in the foreground by dark spots of oasis. They walked through the opening and followed a winding road between rocks, downward toward the nearest small forest of palms. The Professor thought: "He may cut my throat. But his café—he would surely be found out."

"Is it far?" he asked, casually.

"Are you tired?" countered the *qaouaji*.

"They are expecting me back at the Hotel Saharien," he lied.

"You can't be there and here," said the *qaouaji*.

The Professor laughed. He wondered if it sounded uneasy to the other.

"Have you owned Ramani's café long?"

"I work there for a friend." The reply made the Professor more unhappy than he had imagined it would.

"Oh. Will you work tomorrow?"

"That is impossible to say."

The Professor stumbled on a stone, and fell, scraping his hand. The *qaouaji* said: "Be careful."

The sweet black odor of rotten meat hung in the air suddenly.

"Agh!" said the Professor, choking. "What is it?"

The *qaouaji* had covered his face with his burnous and did not answer. Soon the stench had been left behind. They were on flat ground. Ahead the path was bordered on each side by a high mud wall. There was no breeze and the palms were quite still, but behind the walls was the sound of running water. Also, the odor of human excrement was almost constant as they walked between the walls.

The Professor waited until he thought it seemed logical for him to ask with a certain degree of annoyance: "But where are we going?"

"Soon," said the guide, pausing to gather some stones in the ditch.

"Pick up some stones," he advised. "Here are bad dogs."

"Where?" asked the Professor, but he stooped and got three large ones with pointed edges.

They continued very quietly. The walls came to an end and the bright desert lay ahead. Nearby was a ruined marabout, with its tiny dome only half standing, and the front wall entirely destroyed. Behind it were clumps of stunted, useless palms. A dog came running crazily toward them on three legs. Not until it got quite close did the Professor hear its steady low growl. The *qaouaji* let fly a large stone at it, striking it square in the muzzle. There was a strange snapping of jaws and the dog ran sideways in another direction, falling blindly against rocks and scrambling haphazardly about like an injured insect.

Turning off the road, they walked across the earth strewn with sharp stones, past the little ruin, through the trees, until they came to a place where the ground dropped abruptly away in front of them.

"It looks like a quarry," said the Professor, resorting to French for the word "quarry," whose Arabic equivalent he could not call to mind at the moment. The *qaouaji* did not answer. Instead he stood still and turned his head, as if listening. And indeed, from somewhere down below, but very far below, came the faint sound of a low flute. The *qaouaji* nodded his head slowly several times. Then he said: "The path begins here. You can see it well all the way. The rock is white and the moon is strong. So you can see well. I am going back now and sleep. It is late. You can give me what you like."

Standing there at the edge of the abyss which at each moment looked deeper, with the dark face of the *qaouaji* framed in its moonlit burnous close to his own face, the Professor asked himself exactly what he felt. Indignation, curiosity, fear, perhaps, but most of all relief and the hope that this was not a trick, the hope that the *qaouaji* would really leave him alone and turn back without him.

He stepped back a little from the edge, and fumbled in his pocket for a loose note, because he did not want to show his wallet. Fortunately there was a fifty-franc bill there, which he took out and handed to the man. He knew the *qaouaji* was pleased, and so he paid no attention when he heard him saying: "It is not enough. I have to walk a long way home and there are dogs. . . ."

"Thank you and good night," said the Professor, sitting down with his legs drawn up under him, and lighting a cigarette. He felt almost happy.

"Give me only one cigarette," pleaded the man.

"Of course," he said, a bit curtly, and he held up the pack.

The *qaouaji* squatted close beside him. His face was not pleasant to see. "What is it?" thought the Professor, terrified again, as he held out his lighted cigarette toward him.

The man's eyes were almost closed. It was the most obvious registering of concentrated scheming the Professor had ever seen. When the second cigarette was burning, he ventured to say to the still-squatting Arab: "What are you thinking about?"

The other drew on his cigarette deliberately, and seemed about to speak. Then his expression changed to one of satisfaction, but he did not speak. A cool wind had risen in the air, and the Professor shivered. The sound of the flute came up from the depths below at intervals, sometimes mingled with the scraping of nearby palm fronds one against the other. "These people are not primitives," the Professor found himself saying in his mind.

"Good," said the *qaouaji*, rising slowly. "Keep your money. Fifty francs is enough. It is an honor." Then he went back into French: "*Ti n'as qu'à discendre, to' droit.*" He spat, chuckled (or was the Professor hysterical?), and strode away quickly.

The Professor was in a state of nerves. He lit another cigarette, and found his lips moving automatically. They were saying: "Is this a situation or a predicament? This is ridiculous." He sat very still for several minutes, waiting for a sense of reality to come to him. He stretched out on the hard, cold ground and looked up at the moon. It was almost like looking straight at the sun. If he shifted his gaze a little at a time, he could make a string of weaker moons across the sky. "Incredible," he whispered. Then he sat up quickly and looked about. There was no guarantee that the *qaouaji* really had gone back to town. He got to his feet and looked over the edge of the precipice. In the moonlight the bottom seemed miles away. And there was nothing to give it scale; not a tree, not a house, not a person. . . . He listened for the flute, and heard only the wind going by his ears. A sudden violent desire to run back to the road seized him, and he turned and looked in the direction the *qaouaji* had taken. At the same time he felt softly of his wallet in his breast pocket. Then he spat over the edge of the cliff. Then he made water over it, and listened intently, like a child. This gave him the impetus to start down the path into the abyss. Curiously enough, he was not dizzy. But prudently he kept from peering to his right, over the edge. It was a steady and steep downward climb. The monotony of it put him into a frame of mind not unlike that which had been induced by the bus ride. He was murmuring "Hassan Ramani" again, repeatedly and in rhythm. He stopped, furious with himself for the sinister overtones the name now suggested to him. He decided he was exhausted from the trip. "And the walk," he added.

He was now well down the gigantic cliff, but the moon, being directly overhead, gave as much light as ever. Only the wind was left behind, above, to wander among the trees, to blow through the dusty streets of Aïn Tadouirt, into the hall of the Grand Hotel Saharien, and under the door of his little room.

It occurred to him that he ought to ask himself why he was doing this irrational thing, but he was intelligent enough to know that since he was doing it, it was not so important to probe for explanations at that moment.

Suddenly the earth was flat beneath his feet. He had reached the bottom sooner than he expected. He stepped ahead distrustfully still, as if he expected another treacherous drop. It was so hard to know in this uniform, dim brightness. Before he knew what had happened the dog was upon him, a heavy mass of fur trying to push him backwards, a sharp nail rubbing down his chest, a straining of muscles against him to get the teeth into his neck. The Professor thought: "I refuse to die this way." The dog fell back; it looked like an Eskimo dog. As it sprang again, he called out, very loud: "Ay!" It fell against him, there was a confusion of sensations and a pain somewhere. There was also the sound of voices very near to him, and he could not understand what they were saying. Something cold and metallic was pushed brutally against his spine as the dog still hung for a second by his teeth from a mass of clothing and perhaps flesh. The Professor knew it was a gun, and he raised his hands, shouting in Moghrebi: "Take away the dog!" But the gun merely pushed him forward, and since the dog, once it was back on the ground, did not leap again, he took a step ahead. The gun kept pushing; he kept taking steps. Again he heard voices, but the person directly behind him said nothing. People seemed to be running about; it sounded that way, at least. For his eyes, he discovered, were still shut tight against the dog's attack. He opened them. A group of men was advancing toward him. They were dressed in the black clothes of the Reguibat. "The Reguiba is a cloud across the face of the sun." "When the Reguiba appears the righteous man turns away." In how many shops and market-places he had heard these maxims uttered banteringly among friends. Never to a Reguiba, to be sure, for these men do not frequent towns. They send a representative in disguise, to arrange with shady elements there for the disposal of captured goods. "An opportunity," he thought quickly, "of testing the accuracy of such statements." He did not doubt for a moment that the adventure would prove to be a kind of warning against such foolishness on his part—a warning which in retrospect would be half sinister, half farcical.

Two snarling dogs came running from behind the oncoming men and threw themselves at his legs. He was scandalized to note that no one paid any attention to this breach of etiquette. The gun pushed him harder as he tried to sidestep the animals' noisy assault. Again he cried: "The dogs! Take them away!" The gun shoved him forward with great force and he fell, almost at the feet of the crowd of men facing him. The dogs were wrenching at his hands and arms. A boot kicked them aside, yelping, and then with increased vigor it kicked the Professor in the hip. Then came a chorus of kicks from different sides, and he was rolled violently about on the earth for a while. During this time he was conscious of hands reaching into his pockets and removing everything from them. He tried to say: "You have all my money; stop kicking me!" But his bruised facial muscles would not work; he felt himself pouting, and that was all. Someone dealt him a terrific blow on the head, and he thought: "Now at least I shall lose consciousness, thank Heaven." Still he went on being aware of the guttural voices he could not understand, and of being bound tightly about the ankles and chest. Then there was black silence that opened like a wound from time to time, to let in the soft, deep notes of the flute playing the same succession of notes again and again. Suddenly he felt excruciating pain everywhere—pain and cold. "So I have been unconscious, after all," he thought. In spite of that, the present seemed only like a direct continuation of what had gone before.

It was growing faintly light. There were camels near where he was lying; he could hear their gurgling and their heavy breathing. He could not bring himself to attempt opening his eyes, just in case it should turn out to be impossible. However, when he heard someone approaching, he found that he had no difficulty in seeing.

The man looked at him dispassionately in the gray morning light. With one hand he pinched together the Professor's nostrils. When the Professor opened his mouth to breathe, the man swiftly seized his tongue and pulled on it with all his might. The Professor was gagging and catching his breath; he did not see what was happening. He could not distinguish the pain of the brutal yanking from that of the sharp knife. Then there was an endless choking and spitting that went on automatically, as though he were scarcely a part of it. The word "operation" kept going through his mind; it calmed his terror somewhat as he sank back into darkness.

The caravan left sometime toward midmorning. The Professor, not unconscious, but in a state of utter stupor, still gagging and drooling blood, was dumped doubled-up into a sack and tied at one side of a camel. The lower end of the enormous amphitheater contained a natural gate in the rocks. The camels, swift *mehara,* were lightly laden on this trip. They passed through single file, and slowly mounted the gentle slope that led up into the beginning of the desert. That night, at a stop behind some low hills, the men took him out, still in a state which permitted no thought, and over the dusty rags that remained of his clothing they fastened a series of curious belts made of the bottoms of tin cans strung together. One after another of these bright girdles was wired about his torso, his arms and legs, even across his face, until he was entirely within a suit of armor that covered him with its circular metal scales. There was a good deal of merriment during this decking-out of the Professor. One man brought out a flute and a younger one did a not ungraceful caricature of an Ouled Naïl executing a cane dance. The Professor was no longer conscious; to be exact, he existed in the middle of the movements made by these other men. When they had finished dressing him the way they wished him to look, they stuffed some food under the tin bangles hanging over his face. Even though he chewed mechanically, most of it eventually fell out onto the ground. They put him back into the sack and left him there.

Two days later they arrived at one of their own encampments. There were women and children here in the tents, and the men had to drive away the snarling dogs they had left there to guard them. When they emptied the Professor out of his sack, there were screams of fright, and it took several hours to convince the last woman that he was harmless, although there had been no doubt from the start that he was a valuable possession. After a few days they began to move on again, taking everything with them, and traveling only at night as the terrain grew warmer.

Even when all his wounds had healed and he felt no more pain, the Professor did not begin to think again; he ate and defecated, and he danced when he was bidden, a senseless hopping up and down that delighted the children, principally because of the wonderful jangling racket it made. And he generally slept through the heat of the day, in among the camels.

Wending its way southeast, the caravan avoided all stationary civilization. In a few weeks they reached a new plateau, wholly wild and with a sparse vegetation. Here they pitched camp and remained, while the *mehara* were turned loose to graze. Everyone was happy here; the weather was cooler and there was a well only a few hours away on a seldom-frequented trail. It was here they conceived the idea of taking the Professor to Fogara and selling him to the Touareg.

It was a full year before they carried out this project. By this time the Professor was much better trained. He could do a handspring, make a series of fearful growling noises which had, nevertheless, a certain element of humor; and when the Reguibat removed the tin from his face they discovered he could grimace admirably while he danced. They also taught him a few basic obscene gestures which never failed to elicit delighted shrieks from the women. He was now brought forth only after especially abundant meals, when there was music and festivity. He easily fell in with their sense of ritual, and evolved an elementary sort of "program" to present when he was called for: dancing, rolling on the ground, imitating certain animals, and finally rushing toward the group in feigned anger, to see the resultant confusion and hilarity.

When three of the men set out for Fogara with him, they took four *mehara* with them, and he rode astride his quite naturally. No precautions were taken to guard him, save that he was kept among them, one man always staying at the rear of the party. They came within sight of the walls at dawn, and they waited among the rocks all day. At dusk the youngest started out, and in three hours he returned with a friend who carried a stout cane. They tried to put the Professor through his routine then and there, but the man from Fogara was in a hurry to get back to town, so they all set out on the *mehara*.

In the town they went directly to the villager's home, where they had coffee in the courtyard sitting among the camels. Here the Professor went into his act again, and this time there was prolonged merriment and much rubbing together of hands. An agreement was reached, a sum of money paid, and the Reguibat withdrew, leaving the Professor in the house of the man with the cane, who did not delay in locking him into a tiny enclosure off the courtyard.

The next day was an important one in the Professor's life, for it was then that pain began to stir again in his being. A group of men came to the house, among whom was a venerable gentleman, better clothed than those others who spent their time flattering him, setting fervent kisses upon his hands and the edges of his garments. This person made a point of going into classical Arabic from time to time, to impress the others, who had not learned a word of the Koran. Thus his conversation would run more or less as follows: "Perhaps at In Salah. The French there are stupid. Celestial vengeance is approaching. Let us not hasten it. Praise the highest and cast thine anathema against idols. With paint on his face. In case the police wish to look close." The others listened and agreed, nodding their heads slowly and solemnly. And the Professor in his stall beside them listened, too. That is, he was *conscious* of the sound of the old man's Arabic. The words penetrated for the first time in many months. Noises, then: "Celestial vengeance is approaching." Then: "It is an honor. Fifty francs is enough. Keep your money. Good." And the *qaouaji* squatting near him at the edge of the precipice. Then "anathema against idols" and more gibberish. He turned over panting on the sand and forgot about it.

But the pain had begun. It operated in a kind of delirium, because he had begun to enter into consciousness again. When the man opened the door and prodded him with his cane, he cried out in a rage, and everyone laughed.

They got him onto his feet, but he would not dance. He stood before them, staring at the ground, stubbornly refusing to move. The owner was furious, and so annoyed by the laughter of the others that he felt obliged to send them away, saying that he would await a more propitious time for exhibiting his property, because he dared not show his anger before the elder. However, when they had left he dealt the Professor a violent blow on the shoulder with his cane, called him various obscene things, and went out into the street, slamming the gate behind him. He walked straight to the street of the Ouled Naïl, because he was sure of finding the Reguibat there among the girls, spending the money. And there in a tent he found one of them still abed, while an Ouled Naïl washed the tea glasses. He walked in and almost decapitated the man before the latter had even attempted to sit up. Then he threw his razor on the bed and ran out.

The Ouled Naïl saw the blood, screamed, ran out of her tent into the next, and soon emerged from that with four girls who rushed together into the coffeehouse and told the *qaouaji* who had killed the Reguiba. It was only a matter of an hour before the French military police had caught him at a friend's house, and dragged him off to the barracks. That night the Professor had nothing to eat, and the next afternoon, in the slow sharpening of his consciousness caused by increasing hunger, he walked aimlessly about the courtyard and the rooms that gave onto it. There was no one. In one room a calendar hung on the wall. The Professor watched nervously, like a dog watching a fly in front of its nose. On the white paper were black objects that made sounds in his head. He heard them: "*Grande Epicerie du Sahel. Juin. Lundi, Mardi, Mercredi. . . .*"

The tiny ink marks of which a symphony consists may have been made long ago, but when they are fulfilled in sound they become imminent and mighty. So a kind of music of feeling began to play in the Professor's head, increasing in volume as he looked at the mud wall, and he had the feeling that he was performing what had been written for him long ago. He felt like weeping; he felt like roaring through the little house, upsetting and smashing the few breakable objects. His emotion got no further than this one overwhelming desire. So, bellowing as loud as he could, he attacked the house and its belongings. Then he attacked the door into the street, which resisted for a while and finally broke. He climbed through the opening made by the boards he had ripped apart, and still bellowing and shaking his arms in the air to make as loud a jangling as possible, he began to gallop along the quiet street toward the gateway of the town. A few people looked at him with great curiosity. As he passed the garage, the last building before the high mud archway that framed the desert beyond, a French soldier saw him. "*Tiens,*" he said to himself, "a holy maniac."

Again it was sunset time. The Professor ran beneath the arched gate, turned his face toward the red sky, and began to trot along the Piste d'In Salah, straight into the setting sun. Behind him, from the garage, the soldier took a potshot at him for good luck. The bullet whistled dangerously near the Professor's head, and his yelling rose into an indignant lament as he waved his arms more wildly, and hopped high into the air at every few steps, in an access of terror.

The soldier watched a while, smiling, as the cavorting figure grew smaller in the oncoming evening darkness, and the rattling of the tin became a part of the great silence out there beyond the gate. The wall of the garage as he leaned against it still gave forth heat, left there by the sun, but even then the lunar chill was growing in the air.

FLANNERY O'CONNOR
(1925–1964)

Flannery O'Connor is one of the most idiosyncratic and distinctive of American short story writers. Born in Savannah, she lived most of her life on a farm close by Milledgeville, Georgia; she died tragically young, of an inherited disease, lupus. An intensely religious writer, O'Connor took for her subject the provincial Southern world that surrounded her; a world permeated by the "grotesque" (O'Connor's term) that is the consequence of a secular and vulgarized society. Though O'Connor was a Roman Catholic, there is little in her fiction that suggests this faith. Indeed, it is the absence of faith that engages her adamantly unsentimental sympathies.

Flannery O'Connor published two short novels, Wise Blood *(1952) and* The Violent Bear It Away *(1960), but her genius was clearly for the short story. She published two collections of stories during her lifetime—*A Good Man Is Hard To Find *(1955), from which "A Late Encounter with the Enemy" is taken, and* Everything That Rises Must Converge *(1965); her* Collected Stories *(1979) contains these plus others previously uncollected. Her essays were collected in* Mystery and Manners *(1969) and her letters in* The Habit of Being *(1979).*

Flannery O'Connor's stories are widely anthologized, but it is always the same two or three stories that are represented. Her range was narrow, but, within that range, she is capable of subtle distinctions of strategy and tone. This wonderfully comic and unexpectedly moving story, though written early in the author's career, is vintage O'Connor; at the same time its ending, immersed in the hallucinatory consciousness of the dying old "general," gives it a human resonance of a kind missing in O'Connor's flatter and more satirical work.

A Late Encounter with the Enemy

General Sash was a hundred and four years old. He lived with his granddaughter, Sally Poker Sash, who was sixty-two years old and who prayed every night on her knees that he would live until her graduation from college. The General didn't give two slaps for her graduation but he never doubted he would live for it. Living had got to be such a habit with him that he couldn't conceive of any other condition. A graduation exercise was not exactly his idea of a good time, even if, as she said, he would be expected to sit on the stage in his uniform. She said there would be a long procession of teachers and students in their robes but that there wouldn't be anything to equal *him* in his uniform. He knew this well enough without her telling him, and as for the damm procession, it could march to hell and back and not cause him a quiver. He liked parades with floats full of Miss Americas and Miss Daytona Beaches and Miss Queen Cotton Products. He didn't have any use for processions and a procession full of schoolteachers was about as deadly as the River Styx to his way of thinking. However, he was willing to sit on the stage in his uniform so that they could see him.

Sally Poker was not as sure as he was that he would live until her graduation. There had not been any perceptible change in him for the last five years, but she had the sense that she might be cheated out of her triumph because she so often was. She had been going to summer school every year for the past twenty because when she started teaching, there were no such things as degrees. In those times, she said, everything was normal but nothing had been normal since she was sixteen, and for the past twenty summers, when she should have been resting, she had had to take a trunk in the burning heat to the state teacher's college; and though when she returned in the fall, she always taught in the exact way she had been taught not to teach, this was a mild revenge that didn't satisfy her sense of justice. She wanted the General at her graduation because she wanted to show what she stood for, or, as she said, "what all was behind her," and was not behind them. This *them* was not anybody in particular. It was just all the upstarts who had turned the world on its head and unsettled the ways of decent living.

She meant to stand on that platform in August with the General sitting in his wheel chair on the stage behind her and she meant to hold her head very high as if she were saying, "See him! See him! My kin, all you upstarts! Glorious upright old man standing for the old traditions! Dignity! Honor! Courage! See him!" One night in her sleep she screamed, "See him! See him!" and turned her head and found him sitting in his wheel chair behind her with a terrible expression on his face and with all his clothes off except the general's hat and she had waked up and had not dared to go back to sleep again that night.

For his part, the General would not have consented even to attend her graduation if she had not promised to see to it that he sit on the stage. He liked to sit on any stage. He considered that he was still a very handsome man. When he had been able to stand up, he had measured five feet four inches of pure game cock. He had white hair that reached to his shoulders behind and he would not wear teeth because he thought his profile was more striking without them. When he put on his full-dress general's uniform, he knew well enough that there was nothing to match him anywhere.

This was not the same uniform he had worn in the War between the States. He had not actually been a general in that war. He had probably been a foot soldier; he didn't remember what he had been; in fact, he didn't remember that war at all. It was like his feet, which hung down now shriveled at the very end of him, without feeling, covered with a blue-gray afghan that Sally Poker had crocheted when she was a little girl. He didn't remember the Spanish-American War in which he had lost a son; he didn't even remember the son. He didn't have any use for history because he never expected to meet it again. To his mind, history was connected with processions and life with parades and he liked parades. People were always asking him if he remembered this or that—a dreary black procession of questions about the past. There was only one event in the past that had any significance for him and that he cared to talk about; that was twelve years ago when he had received the general's uniform and had been in the premiere.

"I was in that preemy they had in Atlanta," he would tell visitors sitting on his front porch. "Surrounded by beautiful guls. It wasn't a thing local about it. It was nothing local about it. Listen here. It was a nashnul event and they had me in it—up onto the stage. There was no bob-tails at it. Every person at it had paid ten dollars to get in and had to wear his tuxseeder. I was in this uniform. A beautiful gul presented me with it that afternoon in a hotel room."

"It was in a suite in the hotel and I was in it too, Papa," Sally Poker would say, winking at the visitors. "You weren't alone with any young lady in a hotel room."

"Was, I'd a known what to do," the old General would say with a sharp look and the visitors would scream with laughter. "This was a Hollywood, California, gul," he'd continue. "She was from Hollywood, California, and didn't have any part in the pitcher. Out there they have so many beautiful guls that they don't need that they call them a extra and they don't use them for nothing but presenting people with things and having their pitchers taken. They took my pitcher with her. No, it was two of them. One on either side and me in the middle with my arms around each of them's waist and their waist ain't any bigger than a half a dollar."

Sally Poker would interrupt again. "It was Mr. Govisky that gave you the uniform, Papa, and he gave me the most exquisite corsage. Really, I wish you could have seen it. It was made with gladiola petals taken off and painted gold and put back together to look like a rose. It was exquisite. I wish you could have seen it, it was . . ."

"It was as big as her head," the General would snarl. "I was tellin it. They gimme this uniform and they gimme this soward and they say, 'Now General, we don't want you to start a war on us. All we want you to do is march right up on that stage when you're innerduced tonight and answer a few questions. Think you can do that?' 'Think I can do it!' I say. 'Listen here. I was doing things before you were born,' and they hollered."

"He was the hit of the show," Sally Poker would say, but she didn't much like to remember the premiere on account of what had happened to her feet at it. She had bought a new dress for the occasion—a long black crepe dinner dress with a rhinestone buckle and a bolero—and a pair of silver slippers to wear with it, because she was supposed to go up on the stage with him to keep him from falling. Everything was arranged for them. A real limousine came at ten minutes to eight and took them to the theater. It drew up under the marquee at exactly the right time, after the big stars and the director and the author and the governor and the mayor and some less important stars. The police kept traffic from jamming and there were ropes to keep the people off who wouldn't go. All the people who couldn't go watched them step out of the limousine into the lights. Then they walked down the red and gold foyer and an usherette in a Confederate cap and little short skirt conducted them to their special seats. The audience was already there and a group of UDC members began to clap when they saw the General in his uniform and that started everybody to clap. A few more celebrities came after them and then the doors closed and the lights went down.

A young man with blond wavy hair who said he represented the motion-picture industry came out and began to introduce everybody and each one who was introduced walked up on the stage and said how really happy he was to be here for this great event. The General and his granddaughter were introduced sixteenth on the program. He was introduced as General Tennessee Flintrock Sash of the Confederacy, though Sally Poker had told Mr. Govisky that his name was George Poker Sash and that he had only been a major. She helped him up from his seat but her heart was beating so fast she didn't know whether she'd make it herself.

The old man walked up the aisle slowly with his fierce white head high and his hat held over his heart. The orchestra began to play the Confederate Battle Hymn very softly and the UDC members rose as a group and did not sit down again until the General was on the stage. When he reached the center of the stage with Sally Poker just behind him guiding his elbow, the orchestra burst out in a loud rendition of the Battle Hymn and the old man, with real stage presence, gave a vigorous trembling salute and stood at attention until the last blast had died away. Two of the usherettes in Confederate caps and short skirts held a Confederate and a Union flag crossed behind them.

The General stood in the exact center of the spotlight and it caught a weird moon-shaped slice of Sally Poker—the corsage, the rhinestone buckle and one hand clenched around a white glove and handkerchief. The young man with the blond wavy hair inserted himself into the circle of light and said he was *really* happy to have here tonight for this great event, one, he said, who had fought and bled in the battles they would soon see daringly reacted on the screen, and "Tell me, General," he asked, "how old are you?"

"Niiiiiinnttty-two!" the General screamed.

The young man looked as if this were just about the most impressive thing that had been said all evening. "Ladies and gentlemen," he said, "let's give the General the biggest hand we've got!" and there was applause immediately and the young man indicated to Sally Poker with a motion of his thumb that she could take the old man back to his seat now so that the next person could be introduced; but the General had not finished. He stood immovable in the exact center of the spotlight, his neck thrust forward, his mouth slightly open, and his voracious gray eyes drinking in the glare and the applause. He elbowed his granddaughter roughly away. "How I keep so young," he screeched, "I kiss all the pretty guls!"

This was met with a great din of spontaneous applause and it was at just that instant that Sally Poker looked down at her feet and discovered that in the excitement of getting ready she had forgotten to change her shoes: two brown Girl Scout oxfords protruded from the bottom of her dress. She gave the General a yank and almost ran with him off the stage. He was very angry that he had not got to say how glad he was to be here for this event and on the way back to his seat, he kept saying as loud as he could, "I'm glad to be here at this preemy with all these beautiful guls!" but there was another celebrity going up the other aisle and nobody paid any attention to him. He slept through the picture, muttering fiercely every now and then in his sleep.

Since then, his life had not been very interesting. His feet were completely dead now, his knees worked like old hinges, his kidneys functioned when they would, but his heart persisted doggedly to beat. The past and the future were the same thing to him, one forgotten and the other not remembered; he had no more notion of dying than a cat. Every year on Confederate Memorial Day, he was bundled up and lent to the Capitol City Museum where he was displayed from one to four in a musty room full of old photographs, old uniforms, old artillery, and historic documents. All these were carefully preserved in glass cases so that children would not put their hands on them. He wore his general's uniform from the premiere and sat, with a fixed scowl, inside a small roped area. There was nothing about him to indicate that he was alive except an occasional movement in his milky gray eyes, but once when a bold child touched his sword, his arm shot forward and slapped the hand off in an instant. In the spring when the old homes were opened for pilgrimages, he was invited to wear his uniform and sit in some conspicuous spot and lend atmosphere to the scene. Some of these times he only snarled at the visitors but sometimes he told about the premiere and the beautiful girls.

If he had died before Sally Poker's graduation, she thought she would have died herself. At the beginning of the summer term, even before she knew if she would pass, she told the Dean that her grandfather, General Tennessee Flintrock Sash of the Confederacy, would attend her graduation and that he was a hundred and four years old and that his mind was still clear as a bell. Distinguished visitors were always welcome and could sit on the stage and be introduced. She made arrangements with her nephew, John Wesley Poker Sash, a Boy Scout, to come wheel the General's chair. She thought how sweet it would be to see the old man in his courageous gray and the young boy in his clean khaki—the old and the new, she thought appropriately—they would be behind her on the stage when she received her degree.

Everything went almost exactly as she had planned. In the summer while she was away at school, the General stayed with other relatives and they brought him and John Wesley, the Boy Scout, down to the graduation. A reporter came to the hotel where they stayed and took the General's picture with Sally Poker on one side of him and John Wesley on the other. The General, who had had his picture taken with beautiful girls, didn't think much of this. He had forgotten precisely what kind of event this was he was going to attend but he remembered that he was to wear his uniform and carry the sword.

On the morning of the graduation, Sally Poker had to line up in the academic procession with the B.S.'s in Elementary Education and she couldn't see to getting him on the stage herself—but John Wesley, a fat blond boy of ten with an executive expression, guaranteed to take care of everything. She came in her academic gown to the hotel and dressed the old man in his uniform. He was as frail as a dried spider. "Aren't you just thrilled, Papa?" she asked. "I'm just thrilled to death!"

"Put the soward acrost my lap, damm you," the old man said, "where it'll shine."

She put it there and then stood back looking at him. "You look just grand," she said.

"God damm it," the old man said in a slow monotonous certain tone as if he were saying it to the beating of his heart. "God damm every goddam thing to hell."

"Now, now," she said and left happily to join the procession.

The graduates were lined up behind the Science building and she found her place just as the line started to move. She had not slept much the night before and when she had, she had dreamed of the exercises, murmuring, "See him, see him?" in her sleep but waking up every time just before she turned her head to look at him behind her. The graduates had to walk three blocks in the hot sun in their black wool robes and as she plodded stolidly along she thought that if anyone considered this academic procession something impressive to behold, they need only wait until they saw that old General in his courageous gray and that clean young Boy Scout stoutly wheeling his chair across the stage with the sunlight catching the sword. She imagined that John Wesley had the old man ready now behind the stage.

The black procession wound its way up the two blocks and started on the main walk leading to the auditorium. The visitors stood on the grass, picking out their graduates. Men were pushing back their hats and wiping their foreheads and women were lifting their dresses slightly from the shoulders to keep them from sticking to their backs. The graduates in their heavy robes looked as if the last beads of ignorance were being sweated out of them. The sun blazed off the fenders of automobiles and beat from the columns of the buildings and pulled the eye from one spot of glare to another. It pulled Sally Poker's toward the big red Coca-Cola machine that had been set up by the side of the auditorium. Here she saw the General parked, scowling and hatless in his chair in the blazing sun while John Wesley, his blouse loose behind, his hip and cheek pressed to the red machine, was drinking a Coca-Cola. She broke from the line and galloped to them and snatched the bottle away. She shook the boy and thrust in his blouse and put the hat on the old man's head. "Now get him in there!" she said, pointing one rigid finger to the side door of the building.

For his part the General felt as if there were a little hole beginning to widen in the top of his head. The boy wheeled him rapidly down a walk and up a ramp and into a building and bumped him over the stage entrance and into position where he had been told and the General glared in front of him at heads that all seemed to flow together and eyes that moved from one face to another. Several figures in black robes came and picked up his hand and shook it. A black procession was flowing up each aisle and forming to stately music in a pool in front of him. The music seemed to be entering his head through the little hole and he thought for a second that the procession would try to enter it too.

He didn't know what procession this was but there was something familiar about it. It must be familiar to him since it had come to meet him, but he didn't like a black procession. Any procession that came to meet him, he thought irritably, ought to have floats with beautiful guls on them like the floats before the preemy. It must be something connected with history like they were always having. He had no use for any of it. What happened then wasn't anything to a man living now and he was living now.

When all the procession had flowed into the black pool, a black figure began orating in front of it. The figure was telling something about history and the General made up his mind he wouldn't listen, but the words kept seeping in through the little hole in his head. He heard his own name mentioned and his chair was shuttled forward roughly and the Boy Scout took a big bow. They called his name and the fat brat bowed. Goddam you, the old man tried to say, get out of my way, I can stand up!—but he was jerked back again before he could get up and take the bow. He supposed the noise they made was for him. If he was over, he didn't intend to listen to any more of it. If it hadn't been for the little hole in the top of his head, none of the words would have got to him. He thought of putting his finger up there into the hole to block them but the hole was a little wider than his finger and it felt as if it were getting deeper.

Another black robe had taken the place of the first one and was talking now and he heard his name mentioned again but they were not talking about him, they were still talking about history. "If we forget our past," the speaker was saying, "we won't remember our future and it will be as well for we won't have one." The General heard some of these words gradually. He had forgotten history and he didn't intend to remember it again. He had forgotten the name and face of his wife and the names and faces of his children or even if he had a wife and children, and he had forgotten the names of places and the places themselves and what had happened at them.

He was considerably irked by the hole in his head. He had not expected to have a hole in his head at this event. It was the slow black music that had put it there and though most of the music had stopped outside, there was still a little of it in the hole, going deeper and moving around in his thoughts, letting the words he heard into the dark places of his brain. He heard the words, Chickamauga, Shiloh, Johnston, Lee, and he knew he was inspiring all these words that meant nothing to him. He wondered if he had been a general at Chickamauga or at Lee. Then he tried to see himself and the horse mounted in the middle of a float full of beautiful girls, being driven slowly through downtown Atlanta. Instead, the old words began to stir in his head as if they were trying to wrench themselves out of place and come to life.

The speaker was through with that war and had gone on to the next one and now he was approaching another and all his words, like the black procession, were vaguely familiar and irritating. There was a long finger of music in the General's head, probing various spots that were words, letting in a little light on the words and helping them to live. The words began to come toward him and he said, Dammit! I ain't going to have it! and he started edging backwards to get out of the way. Then he saw the figure in the black robe sit down and there was a noise and the black pool in front of him began to rumble and to flow toward him from either side to the black slow music, and he said, Stop dammit! I can't do but one thing at a time! He couldn't protect himself from the words and attend to the procession too and the words were coming at him fast. He felt that he was running backwards and the words were coming at him like musket fire, just escaping him but getting nearer and nearer. He turned around and began to run as fast as he could but he found himself running toward the words. He was running into a regular volley of them and meeting them with quick curses. As the music swelled toward him, the entire past opened up on him out of nowhere and he felt his body riddled in a hundred places with sharp stabs of pain and he fell down, returning a curse for every hit. He saw his wife's narrow face looking at him critically through her round gold-rimmed glasses; he saw one of his squinting bald-headed sons; and his mother ran toward him with an anxious look; then a succession of places—Chickamauga, Shiloh, Marthasville—rushed at him as if the past were the only future now and he had to endure it. Then suddenly he saw that the black procession was almost on him. He recognized it, for it had been dogging all his days. He made such a desperate effort to see over it and find out what comes after the past that his hand clenched the sword until the blade touched bone.

The graduates were crossing the stage in a long file to receive their scrolls and shake the president's hand. As Sally Poker, who was near the end, crossed, she glanced at the General and saw him sitting fixed and fierce, his eyes wide open, and she turned her head forward again and held it a perceptible degree higher and received her scroll. Once it was all over and she was out of the auditorium in the sun again, she located her kin and they waited together on a bench in the shade for John Wesley to wheel the old man out. That crafty scout had bumped him out the back way and rolled him at high speed down a flagstone path and was waiting now, with the corpse, in the long line at the Coca-Cola machine.

JAMES BALDWIN
(1924–1987)

James Baldwin was not naturally a short story writer, though his much-anthologized "Sonny's Blues" is a short story classic. His gift was for longer, denser, more cohesive and combative forms: the novel, the essay, the speech, the memoir. Yet his most passionate nonfiction work, Notes of a Native Son *and* The Fire Next Time *for instance, have the force of fiction; just as the rich, meticulously detailed "Sonny's Blues" has the authenticity of memoir. In speaking of what it means to be black and American and—in such works as* Giovanni's Room*—homosexual, James Baldwin bore witness in a direct, unmediated way; he had no interest in formal or linguistic experimentation, like Ralph Ellison or the contemporary whom he most resembles, Norman Mailer.*

Born in Harlem, the first of nine children, Baldwin began his writing career early. His association with Richard Wright, whom he admired, led to his writing and publishing essays in the influential journal Partisan Review, *which were subsequently gathered into the collection* Notes of a Native Son *(1955). His first novel is the autobiographical* Go Tell It on the Mountain *(1953); his second, the more controversial* Giovanni's Room *(1956), which he had difficulty getting published.* Another Country *(1962) and* Tell Me How Long the Train's Been Gone *(1968) continue earlier themes of racial identity. The son of a Harlem preacher, and an intermittent preacher himself when a young man, Baldwin raised polemics to an art in his more celebrated works* Nobody Knows My Name *(1961),* The Fire Next Time *(1963), and* No Name in the Street *(1972). His collection of short stories is* Going to Meet the Man *(1965).*

Sonny's Blues

I read about it in the paper, in the subway, on my way to work. I read it, and I couldn't believe it, and I read it again. Then perhaps I just stared at it, at the newsprint spelling out his name, spelling out the story. I stared at it in the swinging lights of the subway car, and in the faces and bodies of the people, and in my own face, trapped in the darkness which roared outside.

It was not to be believed and I kept telling myself that as I walked from the subway station to the high school. And at the same time I couldn't doubt it. I was scared, scared for Sonny. He became real to me again. A great block of ice got settled in my belly and kept melting there slowly all day long, while I taught my classes algebra. It was a special kind of ice. It kept melting, sending trickles of ice water all up and down my veins, but it never got less. Sometimes it hardened and seemed to expand until I felt my guts were going to come spilling out or that I was going to choke or scream. This would always be at a moment when I was remembering some specific thing Sonny had once said or done.

When he was about as old as the boys in my classes his face had been bright and open, there was a lot of copper in it; and he'd had wonderfully direct brown eyes, and great gentleness and privacy. I wondered what he looked like now. He had been picked up, the evening before, in a raid on an apartment downtown, for peddling and using heroin.

I couldn't believe it: but what I mean by that is that I couldn't find any room for it anywhere inside me. I had kept it outside me for a long time. I hadn't wanted to know. I had had suspicions, but I didn't name them, I kept putting them away. I told myself that Sonny was wild, but he wasn't crazy. And he'd always been a good boy, he hadn't ever turned hard or evil or disrespectful, the way kids can, so quick, so quick, especially in Harlem. I didn't want to believe that I'd ever see my brother going down, coming to nothing, all that light in his face gone out, in the condition I'd already seen so many others. Yet it had happened and here I was, talking about algebra to a lot of boys who might, every one of them for all

I knew, be popping off needles every time they went to the head. Maybe it did more for them than algebra could.

I was sure that the first time Sonny had ever had horse, he couldn't have been much older than these boys were now. These boys, now, were living as we'd been living then, they were growing up with a rush and their heads bumped abruptly against the low ceiling of their actual possibilities. They were filled with rage. All they really knew were two darknesses, the darkness of their lives, which was now closing in on them, and the darkness of the movies, which had blinded them to that other darkness, and in which they now, vindictively, dreamed, at once more together than they were at any other time, and more alone.

When the last bell rang, the last class ended, I let out my breath. It seemed I'd been holding it for all that time. My clothes were wet—I may have looked as though I'd been sitting in a steam bath, all dressed up, all afternoon. I sat alone in the classroom a long time. I listened to the boys outside, downstairs, shouting and cursing and laughing. Their laughter struck me for perhaps the first time. It was not the joyous laughter which—God knows why—one associates with children. It was mocking and insular, its intent was to denigrate. It was disenchanted, and in this, also, lay the authority of their curses. Perhaps I was listening to them because I was thinking about my brother and in them I heard my brother. And myself.

One boy was whistling a tune, at once very complicated and very simple, it seemed to be pouring out of him as though he were a bird, and it sounded very cool and moving through all that harsh, bright air, only just holding its own through all those other sounds.

I stood up and walked over to the window and looked down into the courtyard. It was the beginning of the spring and the sap was rising in the boys. A teacher passed through them every now and again, quickly, as though he or she couldn't wait to get out of that courtyard, to get those boys out of their sight and off their minds. I started collecting my stuff. I thought I'd better get home and talk to Isabel.

The courtyard was almost deserted by the time I got downstairs. I saw this boy standing in the shadow of a doorway, looking just like Sonny. I almost called his name. Then I saw that it wasn't Sonny, but somebody we used to know, a boy from around our block. He'd been Sonny's friend. He'd never been mine, having been too young for me, and, anyway, I'd never liked him. And now, even though he was a grown-up man, he still hung around that block, still spent hours on the street corner, was always high and raggy. I used to run into him from time to time and he'd often work around to asking me for a quarter or fifty cents. He always had some real good excuse, too, and I always gave it to him, I don't know why.

But now, abruptly, I hated him. I couldn't stand the way he looked at me, partly like a dog, partly like a cunning child. I wanted to ask him what the hell he was doing in the school courtyard.

He sort of shuffled over to me, and he said, "I see you got the papers. So you already know about it."

"You mean about Sonny? Yes, I already know about it. How come they didn't get you?"

He grinned. It made him repulsive and it also brought to mind what he'd looked like as a kid. "I wasn't there. I stay away from them people."

"Good for you." I offered him a cigarette and I watched him through the smoke. "You come all the way down here just to tell me about Sonny?"

"That's right." He was sort of shaking his head and his eyes looked strange, as though they were about to cross. The bright sun deadened his damp dark brown skin and it made his eyes look yellow and showed up the dirt in his conked hair. He smelled funky. I moved a little away from him and I said, "Well, thanks. But I already know about it and I got to get home."

"I'll walk you a little ways," he said. We started walking. There were a couple of kids still loitering in the courtyard and one of them said good night to me and looked strangely at the boy beside me.

"What're you going to do?" he asked me. "I mean, about Sonny?"

"Look. I haven't seen Sonny for over a year, I'm not sure I'm going to do anything. Anyway, what the hell *can* I do?"

"That's right," he said quickly, "ain't nothing you can do. Can't much help old Sonny no more, I guess."

It was what I was thinking and so it seemed to me he had no right to say it.

"I'm surprised at Sonny, though," he went on—he had a funny

way of talking, he looked straight ahead as though he were talking to himself—"I thought Sonny was a smart boy, I thought he was too smart to get hung."

"I guess he thought so too," I said sharply, "and that's how he got hung. And how about you? You're pretty goddamn smart, I bet."

Then he looked directly at me, just for a minute. "I ain't smart," he said. "If I was smart, I'd have reached for a pistol a long time ago."

"Look. Don't tell *me* your sad story, if it was up to me, I'd give you one." Then I felt guilty—guilty, probably, for never having supposed that the poor bastard *had* a story of his own, much less a sad one, and I asked, quickly, "What's going to happen to him now?"

He didn't answer this. He was off by himself some place. "Funny thing," he said, and from his tone we might have been discussing the quickest way to get to Brooklyn, "when I saw the papers this morning, the first thing I asked myself was if I had anything to do with it. I felt sort of responsible."

I began to listen more carefully. The subway station was on the corner, just before us, and I stopped. He stopped, too. We were in front of a bar and he ducked slightly, peering in, but whoever he was looking for didn't seem to be there. The juke box was blasting away with something black and bouncy and I half watched the barmaid as she danced her way from the juke box to her place behind the bar. And I watched her face as she laughingly responded to something someone said to her, still keeping time to the music. When she smiled one saw the little girl, one sensed the doomed, still-struggling woman beneath the battered face of the semi-whore.

"I never *give* Sonny nothing," the boy said finally, "but a long time ago I come to school high and Sonny asked me how it felt." He paused, I couldn't bear to watch him, I watched the barmaid, and I listened to the music which seemed to be causing the pavement to shake. "I told him it felt great." The music stopped, the barmaid paused and watched the juke box until the music began again. "It did."

All this was carrying me some place I didn't want to go. I certainly didn't want to know how it felt. It filled everything, the people, the houses, the music, the dark, quicksilver barmaid, with menace; and this menace was their reality.

"What's going to happen to him now?" I asked again.

"They'll send him away some place and they'll try to cure him." He shook his head. "Maybe he'll even think he's kicked the habit. Then they'll let him loose"—he gestured, throwing his cigarette into the gutter. "That's all."

"What do you mean, that's *all?*"

But I knew what he meant.

"I *mean,* that's *all.*" He turned his head and looked at me, pulling down the corners of his mouth. "Don't you know what I mean?" he asked softly.

"How the hell *would* I know what you mean?" I almost whispered it, I don't know why.

"That's right," he said to the air, "how would *he* know what I mean?" He turned toward me again, patient and calm, and yet I somehow felt him shaking, shaking as though he were going to fall apart. I felt that ice in my guts again, the dread I'd felt all afternoon; and again I watched the barmaid, moving about the bar, washing glasses, and singing. "Listen. They'll let him out and then it'll just start all over again. That's what I mean."

"You mean—they'll let him out. And then he'll just start working his way back in again. You mean he'll never kick the habit. Is that what you mean?"

"That's right," he said, cheerfully. "*You* see what I mean."

"Tell me," I said at last, "why does he want to die? He must want to die, he's killing himself, why does he want to die?"

He looked at me in surprise. He licked his lips. "He don't want to die. He wants to live. Don't nobody want to die, ever."

Then I wanted to ask him—too many things. He could not have answered, or if he had, I could not have borne the answers. I started walking. "Well, I guess it's none of my business."

"It's going to be rough on old Sonny," he said. We reached the subway station. "This is your station?" he asked. I nodded. I took one step down. "Damn!" he said, suddenly. I looked up at him. He grinned again. "Damn if I didn't leave all my money home. You ain't got a dollar on you, have you? Just for a couple of days, is all."

All at once something inside gave and threatened to come pouring out of me. I didn't hate him any more. I felt that in another moment I'd start crying like a child.

"Sure," I said. "Don't sweat." I looked in my wallet and didn't have a dollar, I only had a five. "Here," I said. "That hold you?"

He didn't look at it—he didn't want to look at it. A terrible, closed look came over his face, as though he were keeping the number on the bill a secret from him and me. "Thanks," he said, and now he was dying to see me go. "Don't worry about Sonny. Maybe I'll write him or something."

"Sure," I said. "You do that. So long."

"Be seeing you," he said. I went on down the steps.

And I didn't write Sonny or send him anything for a long time. When I finally did, it was just after my little girl died, he wrote me back a letter which made me feel like a bastard.

Here's what he said:

Dear Brother,

You don't know how much I needed to hear from you. I wanted to write you many a time but I dug how much I must have hurt you and so I didn't write. But now I feel like a man who's been trying to climb up out of some deep, real deep and funky hole and just saw the sun up there, outside. I got to get outside.

I can't tell you much about how I got here. I mean I don't know how to tell you. I guess I was afraid of something or I was trying to escape from something and you know I have never been very strong in the head (smile). I'm glad Mama and Daddy are dead and can't see what's happened to their son and I swear if I'd known what I was doing I would never have hurt you so, you and a lot of other fine people who were nice to me and who believed in me.

I don't want you to think it had anything to do with me being a musician. It's more than that. Or maybe less than that. I can't get anything straight in my head down here and I try not to think about what's going to happen to me when I get outside again. Sometime I think I'm going to flip and *never* get outside and sometime I think I'll come straight back. I tell you one thing, though, I'd rather blow my brains out than go through this again. But that's what they all say, so they tell me. If I tell you when I'm coming to New York and if you could meet me, I sure would appreciate it. Give my love to Isabel and the kids and I was sorry to hear about little Gracie. I wish I could be like Mama and say the Lord's will be done, but I don't know it seems to me that trouble is the one thing that never does get stopped and I don't know what good it does to blame it on the Lord. But maybe it does some good if you believe it.

Your brother,
SONNY

Then I kept in constant touch with him and I sent him whatever I could and I went to meet him when he came back to New York. When I saw him many things I thought I had forgotten came flooding back to me. This was because I had begun, finally, to wonder about Sonny, about the life that Sonny lived inside. This life, whatever it was, had made him older and thinner and it had deepened the distant stillness in which he had always moved. He looked very unlike my baby brother. Yet, when he smiled, when we shook hands, the baby brother I'd never known looked out from the depths of his private life, like an animal waiting to be coaxed into the light.

"How you been keeping?" he asked me.

"All right. And you?"

"Just fine." He was smiling all over his face. "It's good to see you again."

"It's good to see you."

The seven years' difference in our ages lay between us like a chasm: I wondered if these years would ever operate between us as a bridge. I was remembering, and it made it hard to catch my breath. that I had been there when he was born; and I had heard the first words he had ever spoken. When he started to walk, he walked from our mother straight to me. I caught him just before he fell when he took the first steps he ever took in this world.

"How's Isabel?"

"Just fine. She's dying to see you."

"And the boys?"

"They're fine, too. They're anxious to see their uncle."

"Oh, come on. You know they don't remember me."

"Are you kidding? Of course they remember you."

He grinned again. We got into a taxi. We had a lot to say to each other, far too much to know how to begin.

As the taxi began to move, I asked, "You still want to go to India?"

He laughed. "You still remember that. Hell, no. This place is Indian enough for me."

"It used to belong to them," I said.

And he laughed again. "They damn sure knew what they were doing when they got rid of it."

Years ago, when he was around fourteen, he'd been all hipped on the idea of going to India. He read books about people sitting on rocks, naked, in all kinds of weather, but mostly bad, naturally, and walking barefoot through hot coals and arriving at wisdom. I used to say that it sounded to me as though they were getting away from wisdom as fast as they could. I think he sort of looked down on me for that.

"Do you mind," he asked, "if we have the driver drive alongside the park? On the west side—I haven't seen the city in so long."

"Of course not," I said. I was afraid that I might sound as though I were humoring him, but I hoped he wouldn't take it that way.

So we drove along, between the green of the park and the stony, lifeless elegance of hotels and apartment buildings, toward the vivid, killing streets of our childhood. These streets hadn't changed, though housing projects jutted up out of them now like rocks in the middle of a boiling sea. Most of the houses in which we had grown up had vanished, as had the stores from which we had stolen, the basements in which we had first tried sex, the rooftops from which we had hurled tin cans and bricks. But houses exactly like the houses of our past yet dominated the landscape, boys exactly like the boys we once had been found themselves smothering in these houses, came down into the streets for light and air and found themselves encircled by disaster. Some escaped the trap, most didn't. Those who got out always left something of themselves behind, as some animals amputate a leg and leave it in the trap. It might be said, perhaps, that I had escaped, after all, I was a school teacher; or that Sonny had, he hadn't lived in Harlem for years. Yet, as the cab moved uptown through streets which seemed, with a rush, to darken with dark people, and as I covertly studied Sonny's face, it came to me that what we both were seeking through our separate cab windows was that part of ourselves which had been left behind. It's always at the hour of trouble and confrontation that the missing member aches.

We hit 110th Street and started rolling up Lenox Avenue. And I'd known this avenue all my life, but it seemed to me again, as it had seemed on the day I'd first heard about Sonny's trouble, filled with a hidden menace which was its very breath of life.

"We almost there," said Sonny.

"Almost." We were both too nervous to say anything more.

We live in a housing project. It hasn't been up long. A few days after it was up it seemed uninhabitably new, now, of course, it's already run-down. It looks like a parody of the good, clean, faceless life—God knows the people who live in it do their best to make it a parody. The beat-looking grass lying around isn't enough to make their lives green, the hedges will never hold out the streets, and they know it. The big windows fool no one, they aren't big enough to make space out of no space. They don't bother with the windows, they watch the TV screen instead. The playground is most popular with the children who don't play at jacks, or skip rope, or roller skate, or swing, and they can be found in it after dark. We moved in partly because it's not too far from where I teach, and partly for the kids; but it's really just like the houses in which Sonny and I grew up. The same things happen, they'll have the same things to remember. The moment Sonny and I started into the house I had the feeling that I was simply bringing him back into the danger he had almost died trying to escape.

Sonny has never been talkative. So I don't know why I was sure he'd be dying to talk to me when supper was over the first night. Everything went fine, the oldest boy remembered him, and the youngest boy liked him, and Sonny had remembered to bring something for each of them; and Isabel, who is really much nicer than I am, more open and giving, had gone to a lot of trouble about dinner and was genuinely glad to see him. And she's always been able to tease Sonny in a way that I haven't. It was nice to see her face so vivid again and to hear her laugh and watch her make Sonny laugh. She wasn't, or, anyway, she didn't seem to be, at all uneasy or embarrassed. She chatted as though there were no subject which had to be avoided and she got Sonny past his first, faint stiffness. And thank God she was there, for I was filled with that icy dread again. Everything I did seemed awkward to me, and everything I said sounded freighted with hidden meaning. I was trying to remember everything I'd heard about dope addiction and I couldn't help watching Sonny for signs. I wasn't doing it out of malice. I was trying to find out something about my brother. I was dying to hear him tell me he was safe.

"Safe!" my father grunted, whenever Mama suggested trying to move to a neighborhood which might be safer for children. "Safe, hell! Ain't no place safe for kids, nor nobody."

He always went on like this, but he wasn't, ever, really as bad as he sounded, not even on weekends, when he got drunk. As a matter of fact, he was always on the lookout for "something a little better," but he died before he found it. He died suddenly, during a drunken weekend in the middle of the war, when Sonny was fifteen. He and Sonny hadn't ever got on too well. And this was partly because Sonny was the apple of his father's eye. It was because he loved Sonny so much and was frightened for him, that he was always fighting with him. It doesn't do any good to fight with Sonny. Sonny just moves back, inside himself, where he can't be reached. But the principal reason that they never hit it off is that they were so much alike. Daddy was big and rough and loud-talking, just the opposite of Sonny, but they both had—that same privacy.

Mama tried to tell me something about this, just after Daddy died. I was home on leave from the army.

This was the last time I ever saw my mother alive. Just the same, this picture gets all mixed up in my mind with pictures I had of her when she was younger. The way I always see her is the way she used to be on a Sunday afternoon, say, when the old folks were talking after the big Sunday dinner. I always see her wearing pale blue. She'd be sitting on the sofa. And my father would be sitting in the easy chair, not far from her. And the living room would be full of church folks and relatives. There they sit, in chairs all around the living room, and the night is creeping up outside, but nobody knows it yet. You can see the darkness growing against the window-panes and you hear the street noises every now and again, or maybe the jangling beat of a tambourine from one of the churches close by, but it's real quiet in the room. For a moment nobody's talking, but every face looks darkening, like the sky outside. And my mother rocks a little from the waist, and my father's eyes are closed. Everyone is looking at something a child can't see. For a minute they've forgotten the children. Maybe a kid is lying on the rug half asleep. Maybe somebody's got a kid on his lap and is absent-mindedly stroking the kid's head. Maybe there's a kid, quiet and big-eyed, curled up in a big chair in the corner. The silence, the darkness coming, and the darkness in the faces frightens the child obscurely. He hopes that the hand which strokes his forehead will never stop—will never die. He hopes that there will never come a time when the old folks won't be sitting around the living room, talking about where they've come from, and what they've seen, and what's happened to them and their kinfolk.

But something deep and watchful in the child knows that this is bound to end, is already ending. In a moment someone will get up and turn on the light. Then the old folks will remember the children and they won't talk any more that day. And when light fills the room, the child is filled with darkness. He knows that every time this happens he's moved just a little closer to that darkness outside. The darkness outside is what the old folks have been talking about. It's what they've come from. It's what they endure. The child knows that they won't talk any more because if he knows too much about what's happened to *them,* he'll know too much too soon, about what's going to happen to *him.*

The last time I talked to my mother, I remember I was restless. I wanted to get out and see Isabel. We weren't married then and we had a lot to straighten out between us.

There Mama sat, in black, by the window. She was humming an old church song, *Lord, you brought me from a long ways off.* Sonny was out somewhere. Mama kept watching the streets.

"I don't know," she said, "if I'll ever see you again, after you go off from here. But I hope you'll remember the things I tried to teach you."

"Don't talk like that," I said, and smiled. "You'll be here a long time yet."

She smiled, too, but she said nothing. She was quiet for a long time. And I said, "Mama, don't you worry about nothing. I'll be writing all the time, and you be getting the checks. . . ."

"I want to talk to you about your brother," she said, suddenly. "If anything happens to me he ain't going to have nobody to look out for him."

"Mama," I said, "ain't nothing going to happen to you *or* Sonny. Sonny's all right. He's a good boy and he's got good sense."

"It ain't a question of his being a good boy," Mama said, "nor of his having good sense. It ain't only the bad ones, nor yet the dumb ones that gets sucked under." She stopped, looking at me. "Your

Daddy once had a brother," she said, and she smiled in a way that made me feel she was in pain. "You didn't never know that, did you?"

"No," I said, "I never knew that," and I watched her face.

"Oh, yes," she said, "your Daddy had a brother." She looked out of the window again. "I know you never saw your Daddy cry. But *I* did—many a time, through all these years."

I asked her, "What happened to his brother? How come nobody's ever talked about him?"

This was the first time I ever saw my mother look old.

"His brother got killed," she said, "when he was just a little younger than you are now. I knew him. He was a fine boy. He was maybe a little full of the devil, but he didn't mean nobody no harm."

Then she stopped and the room was silent, exactly as it had sometimes been on those Sunday afternoons. Mama kept looking out into the streets.

"He used to have a job in the mill," she said, "and, like all young folks, he just liked to perform on Saturday nights. Saturday nights, him and your father would drift around to different places, go to dances and things like that, or just sit around with people they knew, and your father's brother would sing, he had a fine voice, and play along with himself on his guitar. Well, this particular Saturday night, him and your father was coming home from some place, and they were both a little drunk and there was a moon that night, it was bright like day. Your father's brother was feeling kind of good, and he was whistling to himself, and he had his guitar slung over his shoulder. They was coming down a hill and beneath them was a road that turned off from the highway. Well, your father's brother, being always kind of frisky, decided to run down this hill, and he did, with that guitar banging and clanging behind him, and he ran across the road, and he was making water behind a tree. And your father was sort of amused at him and he was still coming down the hill, kind of slow. Then he heard a car motor and that same minute his brother stepped from behind the tree, into the road, in the moonlight. And he started to cross the road. And your father started to run down the hill, he says he don't know why. This car was full of white men. They was all drunk, and when they seen your father's brother they let out a great whoop and holler and they aimed the car straight at him. They was having fun, they just wanted to scare him, the way they do sometimes, you know. But they was drunk. And I guess the boy, being drunk, too, and scared, kind of lost his head. By the time he jumped it was too late. Your father says he heard his brother scream when the car rolled over him, and he heard the wood of that guitar when it give, and he heard them strings go flying, and he heard them white men shouting, and the car kept on a-going and it ain't stopped till this day. And, time your father got down the hill, his brother weren't nothing but blood and pulp."

Tears were gleaming on my mother's face. There wasn't anything I could say.

"He never mentioned it," she said, "because I never let him mention it before you children. Your Daddy was like a crazy man that night and for many a night thereafter. He says he never in his life seen anything as dark as that road after the lights of that car had gone away. Weren't nothing, weren't nobody on that road, just your Daddy and his brother and that busted guitar. Oh, yes. Your Daddy never did really get right again. Till the day he died he weren't sure but that every white man he saw was the man that killed his brother."

She stopped and took out her handkerchief and dried her eyes and looked at me.

"I ain't telling you all this," she said, "to make you scared or bitter or to make you hate nobody. I'm telling you this because you got a brother. And the world ain't changed."

I guess I didn't want to believe this. I guess she saw this in my face. She turned away from me, toward the window again, searching those streets.

"But I praise my Redeemer," she said at last, "that He called your Daddy home before me. I ain't saying it to throw no flowers at myself, but, I declare, it keeps me from feeling too cast down to know I helped your father get safely through this world. Your father always acted like he was the roughest, strongest man on earth. And everybody took him to be like that. But if he hadn't had *me* there—to see his tears!"

She was crying again. Still, I couldn't move. I said, "Lord, Lord, Mama, I didn't know it was like that."

"Oh, honey," she said, "there's a lot that you don't know. But you are going to find it out." She stood up from the window and came over to me. "You got to hold on to your brother," she said, "and don't let him fall, no matter what it looks like is happening to him and no matter how evil you gets with him. You going to be evil with him many a time. But don't you forget what I told you, you hear?"

"I won't forget," I said. "Don't you worry, I won't forget. I won't let nothing happen to Sonny."

My mother smiled as though she were amused at something she saw in my face. Then, "You may not be able to stop nothing from happening. But you got to let him know you's *there*."

Two days later I was married, and then I was gone. And I had a lot of things on my mind and I pretty well forgot my promise to Mama until I got shipped home on a special furlough for her funeral.

And, after the funeral, with just Sonny and me alone in the empty kitchen, I tried to find out something about him.

"What do you want to do?" I asked him.

"I'm going to be a musician," he said.

For he had graduated, in the time I had been away, from dancing to the juke box to finding out who was playing what, and what they were doing with it, and he had bought himself a set of drums.

"You mean, you want to be a drummer?" I somehow had the feeling that being a drummer might be all right for other people but not for my brother Sonny.

"I don't think," he said, looking at me very gravely, "that I'll ever be a good drummer. But I think I can play a piano."

I frowned. I'd never played the role of the older brother quite so seriously before, had scarcely ever, in fact, *asked* Sonny a damn thing. I sensed myself in the presence of something I didn't really know how to handle, didn't understand. So I made my frown a little deeper as I asked: "What kind of musician do you want to be?"

He grinned. "How many kinds do you think there are?"

"Be *serious*," I said.

He laughed, throwing his head back, and then looked at me. "I *am* serious."

"Well, then, for Christ's sake, stop kidding around and answer a serious question. I mean, do you want to be a concert pianist, you want to play classical music and all that, or—or what?" Long before I finished he was laughing again. "For Christ's *sake*, Sonny!"

He sobered, but with difficulty. "I'm sorry. But you sound so—*scared!*" and he was off again.

"Well, you may think it's funny now, baby, but it's not going to be so funny when you have to make your living at it, let me tell you *that.*" I was furious because I knew he was laughing at me and I didn't know why.

"No," he said, very sober now, and afraid, perhaps, that he'd hurt me, "I don't want to be a classical pianist. That isn't what interests me. I mean"—he paused, looking hard at me, as though his eyes would help me to understand, and then gestured helplessly, as though perhaps his hand would help—"I mean, I'll have a lot of studying to do, and I'll have to study *everything*, but I mean, I want to play *with*—jazz musicians." He stopped. "I want to play jazz," he said.

Well, the word had never before sounded as heavy, as real, as it sounded that afternoon in Sonny's mouth. I just looked at him and I was probably frowning a real frown by this time. I simply couldn't see why on earth he'd want to spend his time hanging around night clubs, clowning around on bandstands, while people pushed each other around a dance floor. It seemed—beneath him, somehow. I had never thought about it before, had never been forced to, but I suppose I had always put jazz musicians in a class with what Daddy called "good-time people."

"Are you *serious?*"

"Hell, *yes*, I'm serious."

He looked more helpless than ever, and annoyed, and deeply hurt.

I suggested, helpfully: "You mean—like Louis Armstrong?"

His face closed as though I'd struck him. "No. I'm not talking about none of that old-time, down home crap."

"Well, look, Sonny, I'm sorry, don't get mad. I just don't altogether get it, that's all. Name somebody—you know, a jazz musician you admire."

"Bird."

"Who?"

"Bird! Charlie Parker! Don't they teach you nothing in the goddamn army?"

I lit a cigarette. I was surprised and then a little amused to discover that I was trembling. "I've been out of touch," I said. "You'll have to be patient with me. Now. Who's this Parker character?"

"He's just one of the greatest jazz musicians alive," said Sonny, sullenly, his hands in his pockets, his back to me. Maybe *the* greatest," he added, bitterly, "that's probably why *you* never heard of him."

"All right," I said. "I'm ignorant. I'm sorry. I'll go out and buy all the cat's records right away, all right?"

"It don't," said Sonny, with dignity, "make any difference to me. I don't care what you listen to. Don't do me no favors."

I was beginning to realize that I'd never seen him so upset before. With another part of my mind I was thinking that this would probably turn out to be one of those things kids go through and that I shouldn't make it seem important by pushing it too hard. Still, I didn't think it would do any harm to ask: "Doesn't all this take a lot of time? Can you make a living at it?"

He turned back to me and half leaned, half sat, on the kitchen table. "Everything takes time," he said, "and—well, yes, sure, I can make a living at it. But what I don't seem to be able to make you understand is that it's the only thing I want to do."

"Well Sonny," I said, gently, "you know people can't always do exactly what they *want* to do—"

"*No*, I don't know that," said Sonny, surprising me. "I think people *ought* to do what they want to do, what else are they alive for?"

"You getting to be a big boy," I said desperately, "it's time you started thinking about your future."

"I'm thinking about my future," said Sonny, grimly. "I think about it all the time."

I gave up. I decided, if he didn't change his mind, that we could always talk about it later. "In the meantime," I said, "you got to finish school." We had already decided that he'd have to move in with Isabel and her folks. I knew this wasn't the ideal arrangement because Isabel's folks are inclined to be dicty and they hadn't especially wanted Isabel to marry me. But I didn't know what else to do. "And we have to get you fixed up at Isabel's."

There was a long silence. He moved from the kitchen table to the window. "That's a terrible idea. You know it yourself."

"Do you have a *better* idea?"

He just walked up and down the kitchen for a minute. He was as tall as I was. He had started to shave. I suddenly had the feeling that I didn't know him at all.

He stopped at the kitchen table and picked up my cigarettes. Looking at me with a kind of mocking, amused defiance, he put one between his lips. "You mind?"

"You smoking already?"

He lit the cigarette and nodded, watching me through the smoke. "I just wanted to see if I'd have the courage to smoke in front of you." He grinned and blew a great cloud of smoke to the ceiling. "It was easy." He looked at my face. "Come on, now. I bet you was smoking at my age, tell the truth."

I didn't say anything but the truth was on my face, and he laughed. But now there was something very strained in his laugh. "Sure. And I bet that ain't all you was doing."

He was frightening me a little. "Cut the crap," I said. "We already decided that you was going to go and live at Isabel's. Now what's got into you all of a sudden?"

"*You* decided it," he pointed out. "*I* didn't decide nothing." He stopped in front of me, leaning against the stove, arms loosely folded. "Look, brother. I don't want to stay in Harlem no more, I really don't." He was very earnest. He looked at me, then over toward the kitchen window. There was something in his eyes I'd never seen before, some thoughtfulness, some worry all his own. He rubbed the muscle of one arm. "It's time I was getting out of here."

"Where do you want to *go*, Sonny?"

"I want to join the army. Or the navy, I don't care. If I say I'm old enough they'll believe me."

Then I got mad. It was because I was so scared. "You must be crazy. You goddamn fool, what the hell do you want to go and join the *army* for?"

"I just told you. To get out of Harlem."

"Sonny, you haven't even finished *school*. And if you really want to be a musician, how do you expect to study if you're in the *army?*"

He looked at me, trapped, and in anguish. "There's ways. I might be able to work out some kind of deal. Anyway, I'll have the G.I. Bill when I come out."

"*If* you come out." We stared at each other. "Sonny, please. Be reasonable. I know the setup is far from perfect. But we got to do the best we can."

"I ain't learning nothing in school," he said. "Even when I go." He turned away from me and opened the window and threw his cigarette out into the narrow alley. I watched his back. "At least,

I ain't learning nothing you'd want me to learn." He slammed the window so hard I thought the glass would fly out, and turned back to me. "And I'm sick of the stink of these garbage cans!"

"Sonny," I said, "I know how you feel. But if you don't finish school now, you're going to be sorry later that you didn't." I grabbed him by the shoulders. "And you only got another year. It ain't so bad. And I'll come back and I swear I'll help you do *whatever* you want to do. Just try to put up with it till I come back. Will you please do that? For me?"

He didn't answer and he wouldn't look at me.

"Sonny. You hear me?"

He pulled away. "I hear you. But you never hear anything *I* say."

I didn't know what to say to that. He looked out of the window and then back at me. "OK," he said, and sighed. "I'll try."

Then I said, trying to cheer him up a little, "They got a piano at Isabel's. You can practice on it."

And as a matter of fact, it did cheer him up for a minute. "That's right," he said to himself. "I forgot that." His face relaxed a little. But the worry, the thoughtfulness, played on it still, the way shadows play on a face which is staring into the fire.

But I thought I'd never hear the end of that piano. At first, Isabel would write me, saying how nice it was that Sonny was so serious about his music and how, as soon as he came in from school, or wherever he had been when he was supposed to be at school, he went straight to that piano and stayed there until suppertime. And, after supper, he went back to that piano and stayed there until everybody went to bed. He was at the piano all day Saturday and all day Sunday. Then he bought a record player and started playing records. He'd play one record over and over again, all day long sometimes, and he'd improvise along with it on the piano. Or he'd play one section of the record, one chord, one change, one progression, then he'd do it on the piano. Then back to the record. Then back to the piano.

Well, I really don't know how they stood it. Isabel finally confessed that it wasn't like living with a person at all, it was like living with sound. And the sound didn't make any sense to her, didn't make any sense to any of them—naturally. They began, in a way, to be afflicted by this presence that was living in their home.

It was as though Sonny were some sort of god, or monster. He moved in an atmosphere which wasn't like theirs at all. They fed him and he ate, he washed himself, he walked in and out of their door; he certainly wasn't nasty or unpleasant or rude, Sonny isn't any of those things; but it was as though he were all wrapped up in some cloud, some fire, some vision all his own; and there wasn't any way to reach him.

At the same time, he wasn't really a man yet, he was still a child, and they had to watch out for him in all kinds of ways. They certainly couldn't throw him out. Neither did they dare to make a great scene about that piano because even they dimly sensed, as I sensed, from so many thousands of miles away, that Sonny was at that piano playing for his life.

But he hadn't been going to school. One day a letter came from the school board and Isabel's mother got it—there had, apparently, been other letters but Sonny had torn them up. This day, when Sonny came in, Isabel's mother showed him the letter and asked where he'd been spending his time. And she finally got it out of him that he'd been down in Greenwich Village, with musicians and other characters, in a white girl's apartment. And this scared her and she started to scream at him and what came up, once she began—though she denies it to this day—was what sacrifices they were making to give Sonny a decent home and how little he appreciated it.

Sonny didn't play the piano that day. By evening, Isabel's mother had calmed down but then there was the old man to deal with, and Isabel herself. Isabel says she did her best to be calm but she broke down and started crying. She says she just watched Sonny's face. She could tell, by watching him, what was happening with him. And what was happening was that they penetrated his cloud, they had reached him. Even if their fingers had been a thousand times more gentle than human fingers ever are, he could hardly help feeling that they had stripped him naked and were spitting on that nakedness. For he also had to see that his presence, that music, which was life or death to him, had been torture for them and that they had endured it, not at all for his sake, but only for mine. And Sonny couldn't take that. He can take it a little better today than he could then but he's still not very good at it and, frankly, I don't know anybody who is.

The silence of the next few days must have been louder than the sound of all the music ever played since time began. One morning, before she went to work, Isabel was in his room for something and she suddenly realized that all of his records were gone. And she knew for certain that he was gone. And he was. He went as far as the navy would carry him. He finally sent me a postcard from some place in Greece and that was the first I knew that Sonny was still alive. I didn't see him any more until we were both back in New York and the war had long been over.

He was a man by then, of course, but I wasn't willing to see it. He came by the house from time to time, but we fought almost every time we met. I didn't like the way he carried himself, loose and dreamlike all the time, and I didn't like his friends, and his music seemed to be merely an excuse for the life he led. It sounded just that weird and disordered.

Then we had a fight, a pretty awful fight, and I didn't see him for months. By and by I looked him up, where he was living, in a furnished room in the Village, and I tried to make it up. But there were lots of other people in the room and Sonny just lay on his bed, and he wouldn't come downstairs with me, and he treated these other people as though they were his family and I weren't. So I got mad and then he got mad, and then I told him that he might just as well be dead as live the way he was living. Then he stood up and he told me not to worry about him any more in life, that he *was* dead as far as I was concerned. Then he pushed me to the door and the other people looked on as though nothing were happening, and he slammed the door behind me. I stood in the hallway, staring at the door. I heard somebody laugh in the room and then the tears came to my eyes. I started down the steps, whistling to keep from crying, I kept whistling to myself, *You going to need me, baby, one of these cold, rainy days.*

I read about Sonny's trouble in the spring. Little Grace died in the fall. She was a beautiful little girl. But she only lived a little over two years. She died of polio and she suffered. She had a slight fever for a couple of days, but it didn't seem like anything and we just kept her in bed. And we would certainly have called the doctor, but the fever dropped, she seemed to be all right. So we thought it had just been a cold. Then, one day, she was up, playing, Isabel was in the kitchen fixing lunch for the two boys when they'd come in from school, and she heard Grace fall down in the living room.

When you have a lot of children you don't always start running when one of them falls, unless they start screaming or something. And, this time, Grace was quiet. Yet, Isabel says that when she heard that *thump* and then that silence, something happened in her to make her afraid. And she ran to the living room and there was little Grace on the floor, all twisted up and the reason she hadn't screamed was that she couldn't get her breath. And when she did scream, it was the worst sound, Isabel says, that she'd ever heard in all her life, and she still hears it sometimes in her dreams. Isabel will sometimes wake me up with a low, moaning, strangled sound and I have to be quick to awaken her and hold her to me and where Isabel is weeping against me seems a mortal wound.

I think I may have written Sonny the very day that little Grace was buried. I was sitting in the living room in the dark, by myself, and I suddenly thought of Sonny. My trouble made his real.

One Saturday afternoon, when Sonny had been living with us, or, anyway, been in our house, for nearly two weeks, I found myself wandering aimlessly about the living room, drinking from a can of beer, and trying to work up the courage to search Sonny's room. He was out, he was usually out whenever I was home, and Isabel had taken the children to see their grandparents. Suddenly I was standing still in front of the living room window, watching Seventh Avenue. The idea of searching Sonny's room made me still. I scarcely dared to admit to myself what I'd be searching for. I didn't know what I'd do if I found it. Or if I didn't.

On the sidewalk across from me, near the entrance to a barbecue joint, some people were holding an old-fashioned revival meeting. The barbecue cook, wearing a dirty white apron, his conked hair reddish and metallic in the pale sun, and a cigarette between his lips, stood in the doorway, watching them. Kids and older people paused in their errands and stood there, along with some older men and a couple of very tough-looking women who watched everything that happened on the avenue, as though they owned it, or were maybe owned by it. Well, they were watching this, too. The revival was being carried on by three sisters in black, and a brother. All they had were their voices and their Bibles and a tambourine. The brother was testifying and while he testified two of the sisters stood together, seeming to say, Amen, and the third sister walked around with the tambourine outstretched and a couple of people dropped coins into it. Then the brother's testimony ended and the sister who had been taking up the collection dumped the coins into her palm and transferred them to the pocket of her long black robe. Then she raised both hands, striking the tambourine against the air, and then against one hand, and she started to sing. And the two other sisters and the brother joined in.

It was strange, suddenly, to watch, though I had been seeing these street meetings all my life. So, of course, had everybody else down there. Yet, they paused and watched and listened and I stood still at the window. *"Tis the old ship of Zion,"* they sang, and the sister with the tambourine kept a steady, jangling beat, *"It has rescued many a thousand!"* Not a soul under the sound of their voices was hearing this song for the first time, not one of them had been rescued. Nor had they seen much in the way of rescue work being done around them. Neither did they especially believe in the holiness of the three sisters and the brother, they knew too much about them, knew where they lived, and how. The woman with the tambourine, whose voice dominated the air, whose face was bright with joy, was divided by very little from the woman who stood watching her, a cigarette between her heavy, chapped lips, her hair a cuckoo's nest, her face scarred and swollen from many beatings, and her black eyes glittering like coal. Perhaps they both knew this, which was why, when, as rarely, they addressed each other, they addressed each other as Sister. As the singing filled the air the watching, listening faces underwent a change, the eyes focusing on something within; the music seemed to soothe a poison out of them; and time seemed, nearly, to fall away from the sullen, belligerent, battered faces, as though they were fleeing back to their first condition, while dreaming of their last. The barbecue cook half shook his head and smiled, and dropped his cigarette and disappeared into his joint. A man fumbled in his pockets for change and stood holding it in his hand impatiently, as though he had just remembered a pressing appointment further up the avenue. He looked furious. Then I saw Sonny, standing on the edge of the crowd. He was carrying a wide, flat notebook with a green cover, and it made him look, from where I was standing, almost like a schoolboy. The coppery sun brought out the copper in his skin, he was very faintly smiling, standing very still. Then the singing stopped, the tambourine turned into a collection plate again. The furious man dropped in his coins and vanished, so did a couple of the women, and Sonny dropped some change in the plate, looking directly at the woman with a little smile. He started across the avenue, toward the house. He has a slow, loping walk, something like the way Harlem hipsters walk, only he's imposed on this his own halfbeat. I had never really noticed it before.

I stayed at the window, both relieved and apprehensive. As Sonny disappeared from my sight, they began singing again. And they were still singing when his key turned in the lock.

"Hey," he said.

"Hey, yourself. You want some beer?"

"No. Well, maybe." But he came up to the window and stood beside me, looking out. "What a warm voice," he said.

They were singing *If I could only hear my mother pray again!*

"Yes," I said," and she can sure beat that tambourine."

"But what a terrible song," he said, and laughed. He dropped his notebook on the sofa and disappeared into the kitchen. "Where's Isabel and the kids?"

"I think they went to see their grandparents. You hungry?"

"No." He came back into the living room with his can of beer. "You want to come some place with me tonight?"

I sensed, I don't know how, that I couldn't possibly say No. "Sure. Where?"

He sat down on the sofa and picked up his notebook and started leafing through it. "I'm going to sit in with some fellows in a joint in the Village."

"You mean, you're going to play, tonight?"

"That's right." He took a swallow of his beer and moved back to the window. He gave me a sidelong look. "If you can stand it."

"I'll try," I said.

He smiled to himself and we both watched as the meeting across the way broke up. The three sisters and the brother, heads bowed, were singing *God be with you till we meet again.* The faces around them were very quiet. Then the song ended. The small crowd dispersed. We watched the three women and the lone man walk slowly up the avenue.

"When she was singing before," said Sonny, abruptly, "her voice reminded me for a minute of what heroin feels like sometimes—when it's in your veins. It makes you feel sort of warm and cool at the same time. And distant. And—and sure." He sipped his beer, very deliberately not looking at me. I watched his face. "It makes you feel—in control. Sometimes you've got to have that feeling."

"Do you?" I sat down slowly in the easy chair.

"Sometimes." He went to the sofa and picked up his notebook again. "Some people do."

"In order," I asked, "to play?" And my voice was very ugly, full of contempt and anger.

"Well"—he looked at me with great, troubled eyes, as though, in fact, he hoped his eyes would tell me things he could never otherwise say—"they *think* so. And *if* they think so—!"

"And what do *you* think?" I asked.

He sat on the sofa and put his can of beer on the floor. "I don't know," he said, and I couldn't be sure if he were answering my question or pursuing his thoughts. His face didn't tell me. "It's not so much to *play*. It's to *stand* it, to be able to make it at all. On any level." He frowned and smiled: "In order to keep from shaking to pieces."

"But these friends of yours," I said, "they seem to shake themselves to pieces pretty goddamn fast."

"Maybe." He played with the notebook. And something told me that I should curb my tongue, that Sonny was doing his best to talk, that I should listen. "But of course you only know the ones that've gone to pieces. Some don't—or at least they haven't *yet* and that's just about all *any* of us can say." He paused. "And then there are some who just live, really, in hell, and they know it and they see what's happening and they go right on. I don't know." He sighed, dropped the notebook, folded his arms. "Some guys, you can tell from the way they play, they on something *all* the time. And you can see that, well, it makes something real for them. But of course," he picked up his beer from the floor and sipped it and put the can down again, "they *want* to, too, you've got to see that. Even some of them that say they don't—*some*, not all."

"And what about you?" I asked—I couldn't help it. "What about you? Do *you* want to?"

He stood up and walked to the window and remained silent for a long time. Then he sighed. "Me," he said. Then: "While I was downstairs before, on my way here, listening to that woman sing, it struck me all of a sudden how much suffering she must have had to go through—to sing like that. It's *repulsive* to think you have to suffer that much."

I said: "But there's no way not to suffer—is there, Sonny?"

"I believe not," he said, and smiled, "but that's never stopped anyone from trying." He looked at me. "Has it?" I realized, with this mocking look, that there stood between us, forever, beyond the power of time or forgiveness, the fact that I had held silence—so long!—when he had needed human speech to help him. He turned back to the window. "No, there's no way not to suffer. But you try all kinds of ways to keep from drowning in it, to keep on top of it, and to make it seem—well, like *you*. Like you did something, all right, and now you're suffering for it. You know?" I said nothing. "Well you know," he said, impatiently, "why *do* people suffer? Maybe it's better to do something to give it a reason, *any* reason."

"But we just agreed," I said, "that there's no way not to suffer. Isn't it better, then, just to—take it?"

"But nobody just takes it," Sonny cried, "that's what I'm telling you! *Everybody* tries not to. You're just hung up on the *way* some people try—it's not *your* way!"

The hair on my face began to itch, my face felt wet. "That's not true," I said, "that's not true. I don't give a damn what other people do, I don't even care how they suffer. I just care how *you* suffer." And he looked at me. "Please believe me," I said, "I don't want to see you—die—trying not to suffer."

"I won't," he said, flatly, "die trying not to suffer. At least, not any faster than anybody else."

"But there's no need," I said, trying to laugh, "is there? in killing yourself."

I wanted to say more, but I couldn't. I wanted to talk about will power and how life could be—well, beautiful. I wanted to say that it was all within; but was it? or, rather, wasn't that exactly the trouble? And I wanted to promise that I would never fail him again. But it would all have sounded—empty words and lies.

So I made the promise to myself and prayed that I would keep it.

"It's terrible sometimes, inside," he said, "that's what's the trouble. You walk these streets, black and funky and cold, and there's not really a living ass to talk to, and there's nothing shaking, and there's no way of getting it out—that storm inside. You can't talk it and you can't make love with it, and when you finally try to get with it and play it, you realize *nobody's* listening. So *you've* got to listen. You got to find a way to listen."

And then he walked away from the window and sat on the sofa again, as though all the wind had suddenly been knocked out of him. "Sometimes you'll do *anything* to play, even cut your mother's throat." He laughed and looked at me. "Or your brother's." Then he sobered. "Or your own." Then: "Don't worry. I'm all right now and I think I'll *be* all right. But I can't forget—where I've been. I don't mean just the physical place I've been, I mean where I've *been*. And *what* I've been."

"What have you been, Sonny?" I asked.

He smiled—but sat sideways on the sofa, his elbow resting on the back, his fingers playing with his mouth and chin, not looking at me. "I've been something I didn't recognize, didn't know I could be. Didn't know anybody could be." He stopped, looking inward, looking helplessly young, looking old. "I'm not talking about it now because I feel *guilty* or anything like that—maybe it would be better if I did, I don't know. Anyway, I can't really talk about it. Not to you, not to anybody," and now he turned and faced me. "Sometimes, you know, and it was actually when I was most *out* of the world, I felt that I was in it, and that I was *with* it, really, and I could play or I didn't really have to *play*, it just came out of me, it was there. And I don't know how I played, thinking about it now, but I know I did awful things, those times, sometimes, to people. Or it wasn't that I *did* anything to them—it was that they weren't real." He picked up the beer can; it was empty; he rolled it between his palms: "And other times—well, I needed a fix, I needed to find a place to lean, I needed to clear a space to *listen*—and I couldn't find it, and I—went crazy, I did terrible things to *me*, I was terrible *for* me." He began pressing the beer can between his hands, I watched the metal begin to give. It glittered, as he played with it, like a knife, and I was afraid he would cut himself, but I said nothing. "Oh well. I can never tell you. I was all by myself at the bottom of something, stinking and sweating and crying and shaking, and I smelled it, you know? *my* stink, and I thought I'd die if I couldn't get away from it and yet, all the same, I knew that everything I was doing was just locking me in with it. And I didn't know," he paused, still flattening the beer can, "I didn't know, I still *don't* know, something kept telling me that maybe it was good to smell your own stink, but I didn't think that *that* was what I'd been trying to do—and—who can stand it?" and he abruptly dropped the ruined beer can, looking at me with a small, still smile, and then rose, walking to the window as though it were the lodestone rock. I watched his face, he watched the avenue. "I couldn't tell you when Mama died—but the reason I wanted to leave Harlem so bad was to get away from drugs. And then, when I ran away, that's what I was running from—really. When I came back, nothing had changed, *I* hadn't changed, I was just—older." And he stopped, drumming with his fingers on the windowpane. The sun had vanished, soon darkness would fall. I watched his face. "It can come again," he said, almost as though speaking to himself. Then he turned to me. "It can come again," he repeated. "I just want you to know that."

"All right," I said, at last. "So it can come again. All right."

He smiled, but the smile was sorrowful. "I had to try to tell you," he said.

"Yes," I said. "I understand that."

"You're my brother," he said, looking straight at me, and not smiling at all.

"Yes," I repeated, "yes. I understand that."

He turned back to the window, looking out. "All that hatred down there," he said, "all that hatred and misery and love. It's a wonder it doesn't blow the avenue apart."

We went to the only night club on a short, dark street, downtown. We squeezed through the narrow, chattering, jam-packed bar to the entrance of the big room, where the bandstand was. And we stood there for a moment, for the lights were very dim in this room and we couldn't see. Then, "Hello, boy," said a voice and an enormous black man, much older than Sonny or myself, erupted out of all that atmospheric lighting and put an arm around Sonny's shoulder. "I been sitting right here," he said, "waiting for you."

He had a big voice, too, and heads in the darkness turned toward us.

Sonny grinned and pulled a little away, and said, "Creole, this is my brother. I told you about him."

Creole shook my hand. "I'm glad to meet you, son," he said,

and it was clear that he was glad to meet me *there*, for Sonny's sake. And he smiled, "You got a real musician in *your* family," and he took his arm from Sonny's shoulder and slapped him, lightly, affectionately, with the back of his hand.

"Well. Now I've heard it all," said a voice behind us. This was another musician, and a friend of Sonny's, a coal-black, cheerful-looking man, built close to the ground. He immediately began confiding to me, at the top of his lungs, the most terrible things about Sonny, his teeth gleaming like a lighthouse and his laugh coming up out of him like the beginning of an earthquake. And it turned out that everyone at the bar knew Sonny, or almost everyone; some were musicians, working there, or nearby, or not working, some were simply hangers-on, and some were there to hear Sonny play. I was introduced to all of them and they were all very polite to me. Yet, it was clear that, for them, I was only Sonny's brother. Here, I was in Sonny's world. Or, rather: his kingdom. Here, it was not even a question that his veins bore royal blood.

They were going to play soon and Creole installed me, by myself, at a table in a dark corner. Then I watched them, Creole, and the little black man, and Sonny, and the others, while they horsed around, standing just below the bandstand. The light from the bandstand spilled just a little short of them and, watching them laughing and gesturing and moving about, I had the feeling that they, nevertheless, were being most careful not step into that circle of light too suddenly: that if they moved into the light too suddenly, without thinking, they would perish in flame. Then, while I watched, one of them, the small, black man, moved into the light and crossed the bandstand and started fooling around with his drums. Then—being funny and being, also, extremely ceremonious—Creole took Sonny by the arm and led him to the piano. A woman's voice called Sonny's name and a few hands started clapping. And Sonny, also being funny and being ceremonious, and so touched, I think, that he could have cried, but neither hiding it nor showing it, riding it like a man, grinned, and put both hands to his heart and bowed from the waist.

Creole then went to the bass fiddle and a lean, very bright-skinned brown man jumped up on the bandstand and picked up his horn. So there they were, and the atmosphere on the bandstand and in the room began to change and tighten. Someone stepped up to the microphone and announced them. Then there were all kinds of murmurs. Some people at the bar shushed others. The waitress ran around, frantically getting in the last orders, guys and chicks got closer to each other, and the lights on the bandstand, on the quartet, turned to a kind of indigo. Then they all looked different there. Creole looked about him for the last time, as though he were making certain that all his chickens were in the coop, and then he—jumped and struck the fiddle. And there they were.

All I know about music is that not many people ever really hear it. And even then, on the rare occasions when something opens within, and the music enters, what we mainly hear, or hear corroborated, are personal private, vanishing evocations. But the man who creates the music is hearing something else, is dealing with the roar rising from the void and imposing order on it as it hits the air. What is evoked in him, then, is of another order, more terrible because it has no words, and triumphant, too, for that same reason. And his triumph, when he triumphs, is ours. I just watched Sonny's face. His face was troubled, he was working hard, but he wasn't with it. And I had the feeling that, in a way, everyone on the bandstand was waiting for him, both waiting for him and pushing him along. But as I began to watch Creole, I realized that it was Creole who held them all back. He had them on a short rein. Up there, keeping the beat with his whole body, wailing on the fiddle, with his eyes half closed, he was listening to everything, but he was listening to Sonny. He was having a dialogue with Sonny. He wanted Sonny to leave the shore line and strike out for the deep water. He was Sonny's witness that deep water and drowning were not the same thing—he had been there, and he knew. And he wanted Sonny to know. He was waiting for Sonny to do the things on the keys which would let Creole know that Sonny was in the water.

And, while Creole listened, Sonny moved, deep within, exactly like someone in torment. I had never before thought of how awful the relationship must be between the musician and his instrument. He has to fill it, this instrument, with the breath of life, his own. He has to make it do what he wants it to do. And a piano is just a piano. It's made out of so much wood and wires and little hammers and big ones, and ivory. While there's only so much you can do with it, the only way to find this out is to try and make it do everything.

And Sonny hadn't been near a piano for over a year. And he wasn't on much better terms with his life, not the life that stretched before him now. He and the piano stammered, started one way, got scared, stopped; started another way, panicked, marked time, started again; then seemed to have found a direction, panicked again, got stuck. And the face I saw on Sonny I'd never seen before. Everything had been burned out of it, and, at the same time, things usually hidden were being burned in, by the fire and fury of the battle which was occurring in him up there.

Yet, watching Creole's face as they neared the end of the first set, I had the feeling that something had happened, something I hadn't heard. Then they finished, there was scattered applause, and then, without an instant's warning, Creole started into something else, it was almost sardonic, it was *Am I Blue*. And, as though he commanded, Sonny began to play. Something began to happen. And Creole let out the reins. The dry, low, black man said something awful on the drums, Creole answered, and the drums talked back. Then the horn insisted, sweet and high, slightly detached perhaps, and Creole listened, commenting now and then, dry, and driving, beautiful and calm and old. Then they all came together again, and Sonny was part of the family again. I could tell this from his face. He seemed to have found, right there beneath his fingers, a damn brand-new piano. It seemed that he couldn't get over it. Then, for awhile, just being happy with Sonny, they seemed to be agreeing with him that brand-new pianos certainly were a gas.

Then Creole stepped forward to remind them that what they were playing was the blues. He hit something in all of them, he hit something in me, myself, and the music tightened and deepened, apprehension began to beat the air. Creole began to tell us what the blues were all about. They were not about anything very new. He and his boys up there were keeping it new, at the risk of ruin, destruction, madness, and death, in order to find new ways to make us listen. For, while the tale of how we suffer, and how we are delighted, and how we may triumph is never new, it always must be heard. There isn't any other tale to tell, it's the only light we've got in all this darkness.

And this tale, according to that face, that body, those strong hands on those strings, has another aspect in every country, and a new depth in every generation. Listen, Creole seemed to be saying, listen. Now these are Sonny's blues. He made the little black man on the drums know it, and the bright, brown man on the horn. Creole wasn't trying any longer to get Sonny in the water. He was wishing him Godspeed. Then he stepped back, very slowly, filling the air with the immense suggestion that Sonny speak for himself.

Then they all gathered around Sonny and Sonny played. Every now and again one of them seemed to say, Amen. Sonny's fingers filled the air with life, his life. But that life contained so many others. And Sonny went all the way back, he really began with the spare, flat statement of the opening phrase of the song. Then he began to make it his. It was very beautiful because it wasn't hurried and it was no longer a lament. I seemed to hear with what burning he had made it his, with what burning we had yet to make it ours, how we could cease lamenting. Freedom lurked around us and I understood, at last, that he could help us to be free if we would listen, that he would never be free until we did. Yet, there was no battle in his face now. I heard what he had gone through, and would continue to go through until he came to rest in earth. He had made it his: that long line, of which we knew only Mama and Daddy. And he was giving it back, as everything must be given back, so that, passing through death, it can live forever. I saw my mother's face again, and felt, for the first time, how the stones of the road she had walked on must have bruised her feet. I saw the moonlit road where my father's brother died. And it brought something else back to me, and carried me past it, I saw my little girl again and felt Isabel's tears again, and I felt my own tears begin to rise. And I was yet aware that this was only a moment, that the world waited outside, as hungry as a tiger, and that trouble stretched above us, longer than the sky.

Then it was over. Creole and Sonny let out their breath, both soaking wet, and grinning. There was a lot of applause and some of it was real. In the dark, the girl came by and I asked her to take drinks to the bandstand. There was a long pause, while they talked up there in the indigo light and after awhile I saw the girl put a Scotch and milk on top of the piano for Sonny. He didn't seem to notice it, but just before they started playing again, he sipped from it and looked toward me, and nodded. Then he put it back on top of the piano. For me, then, as they began to play again, it glowed and shook above my brother's head like the very cup of trembling.

RALPH ELLISON

(1914–)

With the publication of his first novel, Invisible Man, *in 1952, Ralph Ellison entered the American literary canon. Deservedly, for* Invisible Man *is a memorable work; yet in a way ironically, for the novel's immediate success and the elevation of the author to the public role of "spokesman-for-his people" would seem to have precluded subsequent work of equal ambition and risk. Of the writers in this volume, only two or three have enjoyed the early success that Ellison has had. The rapid movement from "invisibility" to "visibility" is a phenomenon of our consumer culture yet to be fully investigated.*

Ralph Ellison was born in Oklahoma City, studied music at the Tuskegee Institute in Alabama, and moved to New York in 1936, where he began work with the Federal Writers' Project. He was an editor of Negro Quarterly *before serving in the Merchant Marine during World War II. Apart from* Invisible Man, *Ellison has published the prose collection* Shadow and Act *(1964) and several short stories, yet uncollected. Of these, "King of the Bingo Game" (1944) is frequently anthologized. "Battle Royal," which, slightly revised, became the opening chapter of* Invisible Man, *was in fact published as a short story in 1948. It is both a work of art complete in itself and a compelling introduction to* Invisible Man, *the chronicle of a black man's search in the United States of the mid-century—"It took me a long time and much painful boomeranging of my expectations to achieve a realization everyone else appears to have been born with: That I am nobody but myself. But first I had to discover that I am an invisible man!"*

Battle Royal

It goes a long way back, some twenty years. All my life I had been looking for something, and everywhere I turned someone tried to tell me what it was. I accepted their answers too, though they were often in contradiction and even self-contradictory. I was naïve. I was looking for myself and asking everyone except myself questions which I, and only I, could answer. It took me a long time and much painful boomeranging of my expectations to achieve a realization everyone else appears to have been born with: That I am nobody but myself. But first I had to discover that I am an invisible man!

And yet I am no freak of nature, nor of history. I was in the cards, other things having been equal (or unequal) eighty-five years ago. I am not ashamed of my grandparents for having been slaves. I am only ashamed of myself for having at one time been ashamed. About eighty-five years ago they were told they were free, united with others of our country in everything pertaining to the common good, and, in everything social, separate like the fingers of the hand. And they believed it. They exulted in it. They stayed in their place, worked hard, and brought up my father to do the same. But my grandfather is the one. He was an odd old guy, my grandfather, and I am told I take after him. It was he who caused the trouble. On his deathbed he called my father to him and said, "Son, after I'm gone I want you to keep up the good fight. I never told you, but our life is a war and I have been a traitor all my born days, a spy in the enemy's country ever since I give up my gun back in the Reconstruction. Live with your head in the lion's mouth. I want you to overcome 'em with yeses, undermine 'em with grins, agree 'em to death and destruction, let 'em swoller you till they vomit or bust wide open." They thought the old man had gone out of his mind. He had been the meekest of men. The younger children were rushed from the room, the shades drawn and the flame of the lamp turned so low that it sputtered on the wick like the old man's breathing. "Learn it to the younguns," he whispered fiercely; then he died.

But my folks were more alarmed over his last words than over his dying. It was as though he had not died at all, his words caused so much anxiety. I was warned emphatically to forget what he had said and, indeed, this is the first time it has been mentioned outside the family circle. It had a tremendous effect upon me, however. I could never be sure of what he meant. Grandfather had been a quiet old man who never made any trouble, yet on his deathbed he had called himself a traitor and a spy, and he had spoken of his meekness as a dangerous activity. It became a constant puzzle which lay unanswered in the back of my mind. And whenever things went well for me I remembered my grandfather and felt guilty and uncomfortable. It was as though I was carrying out his advice in spite of myself. And to make it worse, everyone loved me for it. I was praised by the most lily-white men in town. I was considered an example of desirable conduct—just as my grandfather had been. And what puzzled me was that the old man had defined it as *treachery*. When I was praised for my conduct I felt a guilt that in some way I was doing something that was really against the wishes of the white folks, that if they had understood they would have desired me to act just the opposite, that I should have been sulky and mean, and that that really would have been what they wanted, even though they were fooled and thought they wanted me to act as I did. It made me afraid that some day they would look upon me as a traitor and I would be lost. Still I was more afraid to act any other way because they didn't like that at all. The old man's words were like a curse. On my graduation day I delivered an oration in which I showed that humility was the secret, indeed, the very essence of progress. (Not that I believed this—how could I, remembering my grandfather?—I only believed that it worked.) It was a great success. Everyone praised me and I was invited to give the speech at a gathering of the town's leading white citizens. It was a triumph for the whole community.

It was in the main ballroom of the leading hotel. When I got there I discovered that it was on the occasion of a smoker, and I was told that since I was to be there anyway I might as well take part in the battle royal to be fought by some of my schoolmates as part of the entertainment. The battle royal came first.

All of the town's big shots were there in their tuxedoes, wolfing down the buffet foods, drinking beer and whiskey and smoking black cigars. It was a large room with a high ceiling. Chairs were arranged in neat rows around three sides of a portable boxing ring.

The fourth side was clear, revealing a gleaming space of polished floor. I had some misgivings over the battle royal, by the way. Not from a distaste for fighting but because I didn't care too much for the other fellows who were to take part. They were tough guys who seemed to have no grandfather's curse worrying their minds. No one could mistake their toughness. And besides, I suspected that fighting a battle royal might detract from the dignity of my speech. In those pre-invisible days I visualized myself as a potential Booker T. Washington. But the other fellows didn't care too much for me either, and there were nine of them. I felt superior to them in my way, and I didn't like the manner in which we were all crowded together in the servants' elevator. Nor did they like my being there. In fact, as the warmly lighted floors flashed past the elevator we had words over the fact that I, by taking part in the fight, had knocked one of their friends out of a night's work.

We were led out of the elevator through a rococo hall into an anteroom and told to get into our fighting togs. Each of us was issued a pair of boxing gloves and ushered out into the big mirrored hall, which we entered looking cautiously about us and whispering, lest we might accidentally be heard above the noise of the room. It was foggy with cigar smoke. And already the whiskey was taking effect. I was shocked to see some of the most important men of the town quite tipsy. They were all there—bankers, lawyers, judges, doctors, fire chiefs, teachers, merchants. Even one of the more fashionable pastors. Something we could not see was going on up front. A clarinet was vibrating sensuously and the men were standing up and moving eagerly forward. We were a small tight group, clustered together, our bare upper bodies touching and shining with anticipatory sweat: while up front the big shots were becoming increasingly excited over something we still could not see. Suddenly I heard the school superintendent, who had told me to come, yell, "Bring up the shines, gentlemen! Bring up the little shines!"

We were rushed up to the front of the ballroom, where it smelled even more strongly of tobacco and whiskey. Then we were pushed into place. I almost wet my pants. A sea of faces, some hostile, some amused, ringed around us, and in the center, facing us, stood a magnificent blonde—stark naked. There was dead silence. I felt a blast of cold air chill me. I tried to back away, but they were behind me and around me. Some of the boys stood with lowered heads, trembling. I felt a wave of irrational guilt and fear. My teeth chattered, my skin turned to goose flesh, my knees knocked. Yet I was strongly attracted and looked in spite of myself. Had the price of looking been blindness, I would have looked. The hair was yellow like that of a circus kewpie doll, the face heavily powdered and rouged, as though to form an abstract mask, the eyes hollow and smeared a cool blue, the color of a baboon's butt. I felt a desire to spit upon her as my eyes brushed slowly over her body. Her breasts were firm and round as the domes of East Indian temples, and I stood so close as to see the fine skin texture and beads of pearly perspiration glistening like dew around the pink and erected buds of her nipples. I wanted at one and the same time to run from the room, to sink through the floor, or go to her and cover her from my eyes and the eyes of the others with my body; to feel the soft thighs, to caress her and destroy her, to love her and to murder her, to hide from her, and yet to stroke where below the small American flag tattooed upon her belly her thighs formed a capital V. I had a notion that of all in the room she saw only me with her impersonal eyes.

And then she began to dance, a slow sensuous movement; the smoke of a hundred cigars clinging to her like the thinnest of veils. She seemed like a fair bird-girl girdled in veils calling to me from the angry surface of some gray and threatening sea. I was transported. Then I became aware of the clarinet playing and the big shots yelling at us. Some threatened us if we looked and others if we did not. On my right I saw one boy faint. And now a man grabbed a silver pitcher from a table and stepped close as he dashed ice water upon him and stood him up and forced two of us to support him as his head hung and moans issued from his thick bluish lips. Another boy began to plead to go home. He was the largest of the group, wearing dark red fighting trunks much too small to conceal the erection which projected from him as though in answer to the insinuating low-registered moaning of the clarinet. He tried to hide himself with his boxing gloves.

And all the while the blonde continued dancing, smiling faintly at the big shots who watched her with fascination, and faintly smiling at our fear. I noticed a certain merchant who followed her hungrily, his lips loose and drooling. He was a large man who wore diamond studs in a shirtfront which swelled with the ample paunch underneath, and each time the blonde swayed her undulating hips he ran his hand through the thin hair of his bald head and, with his arms upheld, his posture clumsy like that of an intoxicated panda, wound his belly in a slow and obscene grind. This creature was completely hypnotized. The music had quickened. As the dancer flung herself about with a detached expression on her face, the men began reaching out to touch her. I could see their beefy fingers sink into her soft flesh. Some of the others tried to stop them and she began to move around the floor in graceful circles, as they gave chase, slipping and sliding over the polished floor. It was mad. Chairs went crashing, drinks were spilt, as they ran laughing and howling after her. They caught her just as she reached a door, raised her from the floor, and tossed her as college boys are tossed at a hazing, and above her red, fixed-smiling lips I saw the terror and disgust in her eyes, almost like my own terror and that which I saw in some of the other boys. As I watched, they tossed her twice and her soft breasts seemed to flatten against the air and her legs flung wildly as she spun. Some of the more sober ones helped her to escape. And I started off the floor, heading for the anteroom with the rest of the boys.

Some were still crying and in hysteria. But as we tried to leave we were stopped and ordered to get into the ring. There was nothing to do but what we were told. All ten of us climbed under the ropes and allowed ourselves to be blindfolded with broad bands of white cloth. One of the men seemed to feel a bit sympathetic and tried to cheer us up as we stood with our backs against the ropes. Some of us tried to grin. "See that boy over there?" one of the men said. "I want you to run across at the bell and give it to him right in the belly. If you don't get him, I'm going to get you. I don't like his looks." Each of us was told the same. The blindfolds were put on. Yet even then I had been going over my speech. In my mind each word was as bright as a flame. I felt the cloth pressed into place, and frowned so that it would be loosened when I relaxed.

But now I felt a sudden fit of blind terror. I was unused to darkness, it was as though I had suddenly found myself in a dark room filled with poisonous cottonmouths. I could hear the bleary voices yelling insistently for the battle royal to begin.

"Get going in there!"

"Let me at that big nigger!"

I strained to pick up the school superintendent's voice, as though to squeeze some security out of that slightly more familiar sound.

"Let me at those black sonsabitches!" someone yelled.

"No, Jackson, no!" another voice yelled. "Here, somebody, help me hold Jack."

"I want to get at that ginger-colored nigger. Tear him limb from limb," the first voice yelled.

I stood against the ropes trembling. For in those days I was what they called ginger-colored, and he sounded as though he might crunch me between his teeth like a crisp ginger cookie.

Quite a struggle was going on. Chairs were being kicked about and I could hear voices grunting as with terrific effort. I wanted to see, to see more desperately than ever before. But the blindfold was as tight as a thick skin-puckering scab and when I raised my gloved hands to push the layers of white aside a voice yelled, "Oh, no you don't, black bastard! Leave that alone!"

"Ring the bell before Jackson kills him a coon!" someone boomed in the sudden silence. And I heard the bell clang and the sound of the feet scuffling forward.

A glove smacked against my head. I pivoted, striking out stiffly as someone went past, and felt the jar ripple along the length of my arm to my shoulder. Then it seemed as though all nine of the boys had turned upon me at once. Blows pounded me from all sides while I struck out as best I could. So many blows landed upon me that I wondered if I were not the only blindfolded fighter in the ring, or if the man called Jackson hadn't succeeded in getting me after all.

Blindfolded, I could no longer control my motions. I had no dignity. I stumbled about like a baby or a drunken man. The smoke had become thicker and with each new blow it seemed to sear and further restrict my lungs. My saliva became like hot bitter glue. A glove connected with my head, filling my mouth with warm blood. It was everywhere. I could not tell if the moisture I felt upon my body was sweat or blood. A blow landed hard against the nape of my neck. I felt myself going over, my head hitting the floor. Streaks of blue light filled the black world behind the blindfold. I lay prone, pretending that I was knocked out, but felt myself seized by hands and yanked to my feet. "Get going, black boy! Mix it up!" My arms were like lead, my head smarting from blows. I managed to feel my way to the ropes and held on, trying to catch my breath. A glove landed in my midsection and I went over again, feeling as though the smoke had become a knife jabbed into my guts. Pushed this way and that by the legs milling around me, I finally pulled erect and discovered that I could see the black, sweat-washed forms weaving in the smoky-blue atmosphere like drunken dancers weaving to the rapid drum-like thuds of blows.

Everyone fought hysterically. It was complete anarchy. Everybody fought everybody else. No group fought together for long. Two, three, four, fought one, then turned to fight each other, were themselves attacked. Blows landed below the belt and in the kidney, with the gloves open as well as closed, and with my eye partly opened now there was not so much terror. I moved carefully, avoiding blows, although not too many to attract attention, fighting group to group. The boys groped about like blind, cautious crabs crouching to protect their midsections, their heads pulled in short against their shoulders, their arms stretched nervously before them, with their fists testing the smoke-filled air like the knobbed feelers of hypersensitive snails. In one corner I glimpsed a boy violently punching the air and heard him scream in pain as he smashed his hand against a ring post. For a second I saw him bent over holding his hand, then going down as a blow caught his unprotected head. I played one group against the other, slipping in and throwing a punch then stepping out of range while pushing the others into the melee to take the blows blindly aimed at me. The smoke was agonizing and there were no rounds, no bells at three minute intervals to relieve our exhaustion. The room spun round me, a swirl of lights, smoke, sweating bodies surrounded by tense white faces. I bled from both nose and mouth, the blood spattering upon my chest.

The men kept yelling, "Slug him, black boy! Knock his guts out!"

"Uppercut him! Kill him! Kill that big boy!"

Taking a fake fall, I saw a boy going down heavily beside me as though we were felled by a single blow, saw a sneaker-clad foot shoot into his groin as the two who had knocked him down stumbled upon him. I rolled out of range, feeling a twinge of nausea.

The harder we fought the more threatening the men became. And yet, I had begun to worry about my speech again. How would it go? Would they recognize my ability? What would they give me?

I was fighting automatically when suddenly I noticed that one after another of the boys was leaving the ring. I was surprised, filled with panic, as though I had been left alone with an unknown danger. Then I understood. The boys had arranged it among themselves. It was the custom for the two men left in the ring to slug it out for the winner's prize. I discovered this too late. When the bell sounded two men in tuxedoes leaped into the ring and removed the blindfold. I found myself facing Tatlock, the biggest of the gang. I felt sick at my stomach. Hardly had the bell stopped ringing in my ears than it clanged again and I saw him moving swiftly toward me. Thinking of nothing else to do I hit him smash on the nose. He kept coming, bringing the rank sharp violence of stale sweat. His face was a black blank of a face, only his eyes alive—with hate of me and aglow with a feverish terror from what had happened to us all. I became anxious. I wanted to deliver my speech and he came at me as though he meant to beat it out of me. I smashed him again and again, taking his blows as they came. Then on a sudden impulse I struck him lightly and we clinched. I whispered, "Fake like I knocked you out, you can have the prize."

"I'll break your behind," he whispered hoarsely.

"For *them?*"

"For *me,* sonafabitch!"

They were yelling for us to break it up and Tatlock spun me half around with a blow, and as a joggled camera sweeps in a reeling scene, I saw the howling red faces crouching tense beneath the cloud of blue-gray smoke. For a moment the world wavered, unraveled, flowed, then my head cleared and Tatlock bounced before me. That fluttering shadow before my eyes was his jabbing left hand. Then falling forward, my head against his damp shoulder, I whispered.

"I'll make it five dollars more."

"Go to hell!"

But his muscles relaxed a trifle beneath my pressure and I breathed, "Seven?"

"Give it to your ma," he said, ripping me beneath the heart.

And while I still held him I butted him and moved away. I felt myself bombarded with punches. I fought back with hopeless desperation. I wanted to deliver my speech more than anything else in the world, because I felt that only these men could judge truly my ability, and now this stupid clown was ruining my chances. I began fighting carefully now, moving in to punch him and out again with my greater speed. A lucky blow to his chin and I had him going too—until I heard a loud voice yell, "I got my money on the big boy."

Hearing this, I almost dropped my guard. I was confused: Should I try to win against the voice out there? Would not this go against my speech, and was not this a moment for humility, for nonresistance? A blow to my head as I danced about sent my right eye popping like a jack-in-the-box and settled my dilemma. The room went red as I fell. It was a dream fall, my body languid and fastidious as to where to land, until the floor became impatient and smashed up to meet me. A moment later I came to. An hypnotic voice said FIVE emphatically. And I lay there, hazily watching a dark red spot of my own blood shaping itself into a butterfly, glistening and soaking into the soiled gray world of the canvas.

When the voice drawled TEN I was lifted up and dragged to a chair. I sat dazed. My eye pained and swelled with each throb of my pounding heart and I wondered if now I would be allowed to speak. I was wringing wet, my mouth still bleeding. We were grouped along the wall now. The other boys ignored me as they congratulated Tatlock and speculated as to how much they would be paid. One boy whimpered over his smashed hand. Looking up front, I saw attendants in white jackets rolling the portable ring away and placing a small square rug in the vacant space surrounded by chairs. Perhaps, I thought, I will stand on the rug to deliver my speech.

Then the M.C. called to us. "Come on up here boys and get your money."

We ran forward to where the men laughed and talked in their chairs, waiting. Everyone seemed friendly now.

"There it is on the rug," the man said. I saw the rug covered with coins of all dimensions and a few crumpled bills. But what excited me, scattered here and there, were the gold pieces.

"Boys, it's all yours," the man said. "You get all you grab."

"That's right, Sambo," a blond man said, winking at me confidentially.

I trembled with excitement, forgetting my pain. I would get the gold and the bills, I thought. I would use both hands. I would throw my body against the boys nearest me to block them from the gold.

"Get down around the rug now," the man commanded, "and don't anyone touch it until I give the signal."

"This ought to be good," I heard.

As told, we got around the square rug on our knees. Slowly the man raised his freckled hand as we followed it upward with our eyes.

I heard, "These niggers look like they're about to pray!"

Then, "Ready," the man said. "Go!"

I lunged for a yellow coin lying on the blue design of the carpet, touching it and sending a surprised shriek to join those around me. I tried frantically to remove my hand but could not let go. A hot, violent force tore through my body, shaking me like a wet rat. The rug was electrified. The hair bristled up on my head as I shook myself free. My muscles jumped, my nerves jangled, writhed. But I saw that this was not stopping the other boys. Laughing in fear and embarrassment, some were holding back and scooping up the coins knocked off by the painful contortions of others. The men roared above us as we struggled.

"Pick it up, goddamnit, pick it up!" someone called like a bass-voiced parrot. "Go on, get it!"

I crawled rapidly around the floor, picking up the coins, trying to avoid the coppers and to get greenbacks and the gold. Ignoring the shock by laughing, as I brushed the coins off quickly, I discovered that I could contain the electricity—a contradiction but it works. Then the men began to push us onto the rug. Laughing embarrassedly, we struggled out of their hands and kept after the coins. We were all wet and slippery and hard to hold. Suddenly I saw a boy lifted into the air, glistening with sweat like a circus seal, and dropped, his wet back landing flush upon the charged rug, heard him yell and saw him literally dance upon his back, his elbows beating a frenzied tattoo upon the floor, his muscles twitching like the flesh of a horse stung by many flies. When he finally rolled off, his face was gray and no one stopped him when he ran from the floor amid booming laughter.

"Get the money," the M.C. called. "That's good hard American cash!"

And we snatched and grabbed, snatched and grabbed. I was

careful not to come too close to the rug now, and when I felt the hot whiskey breath descend upon me like a cloud of foul air I reached out and grabbed the leg of a chair. It was occupied and I held on desperately.

"Leggo, nigger! Leggo!"

The huge face wavered down to mine as he tried to push me free. But my body was slippery and he was too drunk. It was Mr. Colcord, who owned a chain of movie houses and "entertainment palaces." Each time he grabbed me I slipped out of his hands. It became a real struggle. I feared the rug more than I did the drunk, so I held on, surprising myself for a moment by trying to topple *him* upon the rug. It was such an enormous idea that I found myself actually carrying it out. I tried not to be obvious, yet when I grabbed his leg, trying to tumble him out of the chair, he raised up roaring with laughter, and, looking at me with soberness dead in the eye, kicked me viciously in the chest. The chair leg flew out of my hand and I felt myself going and rolled. It was as though I had rolled through a bed of hot coals. It seemed a whole century would pass before I would roll free, a century in which I was seared through the deepest levels of my body to the fearful breath within me and the breath seared and heated to the point of explosion. It'll all be over in a flash, I thought as I rolled clear. It'll all be over in a flash.

But not yet, the men on the other side were waiting, red faces swollen as though from apoplexy as they bent forward in their chairs. Seeing their fingers coming toward me I rolled away as a fumbled football rolls off the receiver's fingertips, back into the coals. That time I luckily sent the rug sliding out of place and heard the coins ringing against the floor and the boys scuffling to pick them up and the M.C. calling, "All right, boys, that's all. Go get dressed and get your money."

I was limp as a dish rag. My back felt as though it had been beaten with wires.

When we had dressed the M.C. came in and gave us each five dollars, except Tatlock, who got ten for being the last in the ring. Then he told us to leave. I was not to get a chance to deliver my speech, I thought. I was going out into the dim alley in despair when I was stopped and told to go back. I returned to the ballroom, where the men were pushing back their chairs and gathering in small groups to talk.

The M.C. knocked on a table for quiet. "Gentlemen," he said, "we almost forgot an important part of the program. A most serious part, gentlemen. This boy was brought here to deliver a speech which he made at his graduation yesterday . . ."

"Bravo!"

"I'm told that he is the smartest boy we've got out there in Greenwood. I'm told that he knows more big words than a pocket-sized dictionary."

Much applause and laughter.

"So now, gentlemen, I want you to give him your attention."

There was still laughter as I faced them, my mouth dry, my eyes throbbing. I began slowly, but evidently my throat was tense, because they began shouting. "Louder! Louder!"

"We of the younger generation extol the wisdom of that great leader and educator," I shouted, "who first spoke these flaming words of wisdom: 'A ship lost at sea for many days suddenly sighted a friendly vessel. From the mast of the unfortunate vessel was seen a signal: "Water, water; we die of thirst!" The answer from the friendly vessel came back: "Cast down your bucket where you are." The captain of the distressed vessel, at last heeding the injunction, cast down his bucket, and it came up full of fresh sparkling water from the mouth of the Amazon River.' And like him I say, and in his words, 'To those of my race who depend upon bettering their condition in a foreign land, or who underestimate the importance of cultivating friendly relations with the Southern white man, who is his next-door neighbor, I would say: "Cast down your bucket where you are"—cast it down in making friends in every manly way of the people of all races by whom we are surrounded . . .' "

I spoke automatically and with such fervor that I did not realize that the men were still talking and laughing until my dry mouth, filling up with blood from the cut, almost strangled me. I coughed, wanting to stop and go to one of the tall brass, sand-filled spittoons to relieve myself, but a few of the men, especially the superintendent, were listening and I was afraid. So I gulped it down, blood, saliva and all, and continued. (What powers of endurance I had during those days! What enthusiasm! What a belief in the rightness of things!) I spoke even louder in spite of the pain. But still they talked and still they laughed, as though deaf with cotton in dirty ears. So I spoke with greater emotional emphasis. I closed my ears and swallowed blood until I was nauseated. The speech seemed a hundred times as long as before, but I could not leave out a single word. All had to be said, each memorized nuance considered, rendered. Nor was that all. Whenever I uttered a word of three or more syllables a group of voices would yell for me to repeat it. I used the phrase "social responsibility" and they yelled:

"What's the word you say, boy?"

"Social responsibility," I said.

"What?"

"Social . . ."

"Louder."

". . . responsibility."

"More!"

"Respon—"

"Repeat!"

"—sibility."

The room filled with the uproar of laughter until, no doubt, distracted by having to gulp down my blood, I made a mistake and yelled a phrase I had often seen denounced in newspaper editorials, heard debated in private.

"Social . . ."

"What?" they yelled.

". . . equality—"

The laughter hung smokelike in the sudden stillness. I opened my eyes, puzzled. Sounds of displeasure filled the room. The M.C. rushed forward. They shouted hostile phrases at me. But I did not understand.

A small dry mustached man in the front row blared out, "Say that slowly, son!"

"What, sir?"

"What you just said!"

"Social responsibility, sir," I said.

"You weren't being smart, were you boy?" he said, not unkindly.

"No, sir!"

"You sure that about 'equality' was a mistake?"

"Oh, yes, sir," I said. "I was swallowing blood."

"Well, you had better speak more slowly so we can understand. We mean to do right by you, but you've got to know your place at all times. All right, now, go on with your speech."

I was afraid. I wanted to leave but I wanted also to speak and I was afraid they'd snatch me down.

"Thank you, sir," I said, beginning where I had left off, and having them ignore me as before.

Yet when I finished there was a thunderous applause. I was surprised to see the superintendent come forth with a package wrapped in white tissue paper, and, gesturing for quiet, address the men.

"Gentlemen, you see that I did not overpraise the boy. He makes a good speech and some day he'll lead his people in the proper paths. And I don't have to tell you that this is important in these days and times. This is a good, smart boy, and so to encourage him in the right direction, in the name of the Board of Education I wish to present him a prize in the form of this . . ."

He paused, removing the tissue paper and revealing a gleaming calfskin briefcase.

". . . in the form of this first-class article from Shad Whitmore's shop."

"Boy," he said, addressing me, "take this prize and keep it well. Consider it a badge of office. Prize it. Keep developing as you are and some day it will be filled with important papers that will help shape the destiny of your people."

I was so moved that I could hardly express my thanks. A rope of bloody saliva forming a shape like an undiscovered continent drooled upon the leather and I wiped it quickly away. I felt an importance that I had never dreamed.

"Open it and see what's inside," I was told.

My fingers a-tremble, I complied, smelling fresh leather and finding an official-looking document inside. It was a scholarship to the state college for Negroes. My eyes filled with tears and I ran awkwardly off the floor.

I was overjoyed; I did not even mind when I discovered the gold pieces I had scrambled for were brass pocket tokens advertising a certain make of automobile.

When I reached home everyone was excited. Next day the neighbors came to congratulate me. I even felt safe from grandfather, whose deathbed curse usually spoiled my triumphs. I stood beneath his photograph with my briefcase in hand and smiled triumphantly into his stolid black peasant's face. It was a face that fascinated me. The eyes seemed to follow everywhere I went.

That night I dreamed I was at a circus with him and that he refused to laugh at the clowns no matter what they did. Then later he told me to open my briefcase and read what was inside and I did, finding an official envelope stamped with the state seal: and inside the envelope I found another and another, endlessly, and I thought I would fall of weariness. "Them's years," he said. "Now open that one." And I did and in it I found an engraved stamp containing a short message in letters of gold. "Read it," my grandfather said. "Out loud."

"To Whom It May Concern," I intoned. "Keep This Nigger-Boy Running."

I awoke with the old man's laughter ringing in my ears.

RAY BRADBURY

(1920–)

Like his fellow American writer of "science fiction," Isaac Asimov, Ray Bradbury is a phenomenon, not easily defined. Since he sold his first story (to a pulp magazine) at the age of twenty-one, he has published hundreds of short stories and has become one of our most widely read American writers here and abroad. Marginalized, at least in part, because of his association with what is perceived to be a nonliterary tradition, Bradbury is, in fact, in such stories as the finely crafted, elegiac work included here, in a vital and on-going tradition that includes Hawthorne and Poe; and, more generally, such visionaries as H. G. Wells, Karel Čapek, Aldous Huxley, and Stanislaw Lem. At his best, Bradbury is a poet of ominous prophecies—whose vision of a hellish future begins to seem, as the twentieth century reels to a close, ever more like realistic fiction and not fantasy.

Born in Waukegan, Illinois, Ray Bradbury has lived most of his adult life in California. His major titles are The Martian Chronicles *(1950), from which this selection has been taken,* The Illustrated Man *(1951),* Fahrenheit 451 *(1953),* Dandelion Wine *(1957),* Something Wicked This Way Comes *(1962) and* The Mummies of Guanajuato *(1978).* The Stories of Ray Bradbury *appeared in 1980.*

The title "There Will Come Soft Rains" is a line from a poem by Sara Teasdale, used to devastating irony here.

There Will Come Soft Rains

In the living room the voice-clock sang, *Tick-tock, seven o'clock, time to get up, time to get up, seven o'clock!* as if it were afraid that nobody would. The morning house lay empty. The clock ticked on, repeating and repeating its sounds into the emptiness. *Seven-nine, breakfast time, seven-nine!*

In the kitchen the breakfast stove gave a hissing sigh and ejected from its warm interior eight pieces of perfectly browned toast, eight eggs sunnyside up, sixteen slices of bacon, two coffees, and two cool glasses of milk.

"Today is August 4, 2026," said a second voice from the kitchen ceiling, "in the city of Allendale, California." It repeated the date three times for memory's sake. "Today is Mr. Featherstone's birthday. Today is the anniversary of Tilita's marriage. Insurance is payable, as are the water, gas, and light bills."

Somewhere in the walls, relays clicked, memory tapes glided under electric eyes.

Eight-one, tick-tock, eight-one o'clock, off to school, off to work, run, run, eight-one! But no doors slammed, no carpets took the soft tread of rubber heels. It was raining outside. The weather box on the front door sang quietly: "Rain, rain, go away; rubbers, raincoats for today . . ." And the rain tapped on the empty house, echoing.

Outside, the garage chimed and lifted its door to reveal the waiting car. After a long wait the door swung down again.

At eight-thirty the eggs were shriveled and the toast was like stone. An aluminum wedge scraped them into the sink, where hot water whirled them down a metal throat which digested and flushed them away to the distant sea. The dirty dishes were dropped into a hot washer and emerged twinkling dry.

Nine-fifteen, sang the clock, *time to clean.*

Out of warrens in the wall, tiny robot mice darted. The rooms were acrawl with the small cleaning animals, all rubber and metal. They thudded against chairs, whirling their mustached runners, kneading the rug nap, sucking gently at hidden dust. Then, like mysterious invaders, they popped into their burrows. Their pink electric eyes faded. The house was clean.

Ten o'clock. The sun came out from behind the rain. The house stood alone in a city of rubble and ashes. This was the one house left standing. At night the ruined city gave off a radioactive glow which could be seen for miles.

Ten-fifteen. The garden sprinklers whirled up in golden founts, filling the soft morning air with scatterings of brightness. The water pelted windowpanes running down the charred west side where the house had been burned evenly free of its white paint. The entire west face of the house was black, save for five places. Here the silhouette in paint of a man mowing a lawn. Here, as in a photograph, a woman bent to pick flowers. Still farther over, their images burned on wood in one titanic instant, a small boy, hands flung into the air; higher up, the image of a thrown ball, and opposite him a girl, hands raised to catch a ball which never came down.

The five spots of paint—the man, the woman, the children, the ball—remained. The rest was a thin charcoaled layer.

The gentle sprinkler rain filled the garden with falling light.

Until this day, how well the house had kept its peace. How carefully it had inquired, "Who goes there? What's the password?" and, getting no answer from lonely foxes and whining cats, it had shut up its windows and drawn shades in an old-maidenly preoccupation with self-protection which bordered on a mechanical paranoia.

It quivered at each sound, the house did. If a sparrow brushed a window, the shade snapped up. The bird, startled, flew off! No, not even a bird must touch the house!

The house was an altar with ten thousand attendants, big, small, servicing, attending, in choirs. But the gods had gone away, and the ritual of the religion continued senselessly, uselessly.

Twelve noon.

A dog whined, shivering, on the front porch.

The front door recognized the dog voice and opened. The dog, once huge and fleshy, but now gone to bone and covered with sores, moved in and through the house, tracking mud. Behind it whirred angry mice, angry at having to pick up mud, angry at inconvenience.

For not a leaf fragment blew under the door but what the wall panels flipped open and the copper scrap rats flashed swiftly out. The offending dust, hair, or paper, seized in miniature steel jaws, was raced back to the burrows. There, down tubes which fed into the cellar, it was dropped into the sighing vent of an incinerator which sat like evil Baal in a dark corner.

The dog ran upstairs, hysterically yelping to each door, at last realizing, as the house realized, that only silence was here.

If sniffed the air and scratched the kitchen door. Behind the door, the stove was making pancakes which filled the house with a rich baked odor and the scent of maple syrup.

The dog frothed at the mouth, lying at the door, sniffing, its eyes turned to fire. It ran wildly in circles, biting at its tail, spun in a frenzy, and died. It lay in the parlor for an hour.

Two o'clock, sang a voice.

Delicately sensing decay at last, the regiments of mice hummed out as softly as blown gray leaves in an electrical wind.

Two-fifteen.

The dog was gone.

In the cellar, the incinerator glowed suddenly and a whirl of sparks leaped up the chimney.

Two thirty-five.

Bridge tables sprouted from patio walls. Playing cards fluttered onto pads in a shower of pips. Martinis manifested on an oaken bench with egg-salad sandwiches. Music played.

But the tables were silent and the cards untouched.

At four o'clock the tables folded like great butterflies back through the paneled walls.

Four-thirty.

The nursery walls glowed.

Animals took shape: yellow giraffes, blue lions, pink antelopes, lilac panthers cavorting in crystal substance. The walls were glass. They looked out upon color and fantasy. Hidden films clocked through well-oiled sprockets, and the walls lived. The nursery floor was woven to resemble a crisp, cereal meadow. Over this ran aluminum roaches and iron crickets, and in the hot still air butterflies of delicate red tissue wavered among the sharp aroma of animal spoors! There was the sound like a great matted yellow hive of bees within a dark bellows, the lazy bumble of a purring lion. And there was the patter of okapi feet and the murmur of a fresh jungle rain, like other hoofs, falling upon the summer-starched grass. Now the walls dissolved into distances of parched weed, mile on mile, and warm endless sky. The animals drew away into thorn brakes and water holes.

It was the children's hour.

Five o'clock. The bath filled with clear hot water.

Six, seven, eight o'clock. The dinner dishes manipulated like magic tricks, and in the study a *click.* In the metal stand opposite the hearth where a fire now blazed up warmly, a cigar popped out, half an inch of soft gray ash on it, smoking, waiting.

Nine o'clock. The beds warmed their hidden circuits, for nights were cool here.

Nine-five. A voice spoke from the study ceiling:

"Mrs. McClellan, which poem would you like this evening?"

The house was silent.

The voice said at last, "Since you express no preference, I shall select a poem at random." Quiet music rose to back the voice. "Sara Teasdale. As I recall, your favorite. . . .

"There will come soft rains and the smell of the ground,
And swallows circling with their shimmering sound;

And frogs in the pools singing at night,
And wild plum-trees in tremulous white;

Robins will wear their feathery fire
Whistling their whims on a low fence-wire;

And not one will know of the war, not one
Will care at last when it is done.

Not one would mind, either bird nor tree
If mankind perished utterly;

And Spring herself, when she woke at dawn,
Would scarcely know that we were gone."

The fire burned on the stone hearth and the cigar fell away into a mound of quiet ash on its tray. The empty chairs faced each other between the silent walls, and the music played.

At ten o'clock the house began to die.

The wind blew. A falling tree bough crashed through the kitchen window. Cleaning solvent, bottled, shattered over the stove. The room was ablaze in an instant!

"Fire!" screamed a voice. The house lights flashed, water pumps shot water from the ceilings. But the solvent spread on the linoleum, licking, eating under the kitchen door, while the voices took it up in chorus: "Fire, fire, fire!"

The house tried to save itself. Doors sprang tightly shut, but the windows were broken by the heat and the wind blew and sucked upon the fire.

The house gave ground as the fire in ten billion angry sparks moved with flaming ease from room to room and then up the stairs. While scurrying water rats squeaked from the walls, pistoled their water, and ran for more. And the wall sprays let down showers of mechanical rain.

But too late. Somewhere, sighing, a pump shrugged to a stop. The quenching rain ceased. The reserve water supply which had filled baths and washed dishes for many quiet days was gone.

The fire crackled up the stairs. It fed upon Picassos and Matisses in the upper halls, like delicacies, baking off the oily flesh, tenderly crisping the canvases into black shavings.

Now the fire lay in beds, stood in windows, changed the colors of drapes!

And then, reinforcements.

From attic trapdoors, blind robot faces peered down with faucet mouths gushing green chemical.

The fire backed off, as even an elephant must at the sight of a dead snake. Now there were twenty snakes whipping over the floor, killing the fire with a clear cold venom of green froth.

But the fire was clever. It had sent flame outside the house, up through the attic to the pumps there. An explosion! The attic brain which directed the pumps was shattered into bronze shrapnel on the beams.

The fire rushed back into every closet and felt of the clothes hung there.

The house shuddered, oak bone on bone, its bared skeleton cringing from the heat, its wire, its nerves revealed as if a surgeon had torn the skin off to let the red veins and capillaries quiver in the scalded air. Help, help! Fire! Run, run! Heat snapped mirrors like the first brittle winter ice. And the voices wailed Fire, fire, run, run, like a tragic nursery rhyme, a dozen voices, high, low, like children dying in a forest, alone, alone. And the voices fading as the wires popped their sheathings like hot chestnuts. One, two, three, four, five voices died.

In the nursery the jungle burned. Blue lions roared, purple giraffes bounded off. The panthers ran in circles, changing color, and ten million animals, running before the fire, vanished off toward a distant steaming river. . . .

Ten more voices died. In the last instant under the fire avalanche, other choruses, oblivious, could be heard announcing the time, playing music, cutting the lawn by remote-control mower, or setting an umbrella frantically out and in the slamming and opening front door, a thousand things happening, like a clock shop when each clock strikes the hour insanely before or after the other, a scene of maniac confusion, yet unity; singing, screaming, a few last cleaning mice darting bravely out to carry the horrid ashes away! And one voice, with sublime disregard for the situation, read poetry aloud in the fiery study, until all the film spools burned, until all the wires withered and the circuits cracked.

The fire burst the house and let it slam flat down, puffing out skirts of spark and smoke.

In the kitchen, an instant before the rain of fire and timber, the stove could be seen making breakfasts at a psychopathic rate, ten dozen eggs, six loaves of toast, twenty dozen bacon strips, which, eaten by fire, started the stove working again, hysterically hissing!

The crash. The attic smashing into kitchen and parlor. The parlor into cellar, cellar into sub-cellar. Deep freeze, armchair, film tapes, circuits, beds, and all like skeletons thrown in a cluttered mound deep under.

Smoke and silence. A great quantity of smoke.

Dawn showed faintly in the east. Among the ruins, one wall stood alone. Within the wall, a last voice said, over and over again and again, even as the sun rose to shine upon the heaped rubble and steam:

"Today is August 5, 2026, today is August 5, 2026, today is . . ."

PETER TAYLOR

(1917–)

How difficult it is to write a credible love story; how much more difficult to write a love story that is both credible and, in the truest sense of the word, loving. Yet Peter Taylor, more generally known for his sophisticated serio-comic portraits of well-to-do Tennesseans embroiled in the complexities of their insular society, has achieved it with "Rain in the Heart." This is a story that is both different from most of Taylor's short fiction, yet, in its care and attentiveness to details of speech and behavior, supremely representative of the best of his work.

Born in Trenton, Tennessee, educated at Vanderbilt and Kenyon College, Peter Taylor has lived most of his life in the South. Though his short novel A Summons to Memphis *(1986) was published to much acclaim, and was awarded the Pulitzer Prize, Taylor has a reputation as one of the finest craftsmen writing in the short story form, and the bulk of his work has been in this genre. Among his titles are* A Long Fourth *(1948),* The Widows of Thornton *(1954),* A Woman of Means *(1950),* Miss Leonora When Last Seen *(1963), and* The Old Forest *(1985). His* Collected Stories *was published in 1986.*

Rain in the Heart

When the drilling was over they stopped at the edge of the field and the drill sergeant looked across the flat valley toward the woods on Peavine Ridge. Among the shifting lights on the treetops there in the late afternoon the drill sergeant visualized pointed roofs of houses that were on another, more thickly populated ridge seven miles to the west.

Lazily the sergeant rested the butt end of his rifle in the mud and turned to tell the squad of rookies to return to their own barracks. But they had already gone on without him and he stood a moment watching them drift back toward the rows of squat buildings, some with their rifles thrown over their shoulders, others toting them by the leader slings in suitcase fashion.

On the field behind the sergeant were the tracks which he and the twelve men had made during an hour's drilling. He turned and studied the tracks for a moment, wondering whether or not he could have told how many men had been tramping there if that had been necessary for telling the strength of an enemy. Then with a shrug of his shoulders he turned his face toward Peavine Ridge again, thinking once more of that other ridge in the suburban area where his bride had found furnished rooms. And seeing how the ridge before him stretched out endlessly north and south he was reminded of a long bus and streetcar ride that was before him on his journey to their rooms this night. Suddenly throwing the rifle over his shoulder, he began to make his way back toward his own barrack.

The immediate approach to the barrack of the noncommissioned officers was over a wide asphalt area where all formations were held. As the sergeant crossed the asphalt, it required a special effort for him to raise his foot each time. Since his furlough and wedding trip to the mountains, this was the first night the sergeant had been granted leave to go in to see his wife. When he reached the stoop before the entrance to the barrack he lingered by the bulletin board. He stood aimlessly examining the notices posted there. But finally drawing himself up straight he turned and walked erectly and swiftly inside. He knew that the barrack would be filled with men ready with stale, friendly, evil jokes.

As he hurried down the aisle of the barrack he removed his blue denim jacket, indicating his haste. It seemed at first that no one had noticed him. Yet he was still filled with a dread of the jokes which must inevitably be directed at him today. At last a copper-headed corporal who sat on the bunk next to his own, whittling his toenails with his knife, had begun to sing:

"Yes, she jumped in bed
And she covered up her head—"

Another voice across the aisle took up the song here:

> *"And she vowed he couldn't find her."*

Then other voices, some faking soprano, others simulating the deepest choir bass, from all points of the long room joined in:

> *"But she knew damned well*
> *That she lied like hell*
> *When he jumped right in beside her."*

The sergeant blushed a little, pretended to be very angry, and began to undress for his shower. Silently he reminded himself that when he started for town he must take with him the big volume of Civil War history, for it was past due at the city library. *She* could have it renewed for him tomorrow.

In the shower too the soldiers pretended at first to take no notice of him. They were talking of their own plans for the evening in town. One tall and bony sergeant with a head of wiry black hair was saying, "I've got a strong deal on tonight with a WAC from Vermont. But of course we'll have to be in by midnight."

Now the copper-headed corporal had come into the shower. He was smaller than most of the other soldiers, and beneath his straight copper-colored hair were a pair of a bright gray-green eyes. He had a hairy potbelly that looked like a football. "My deal's pretty strong tonight, too," he said, addressing the tall soldier beside him. "She lives down the road a way with her family, so I'll have to be in early too. But then you and me won't be all fagged out tomorrow, eh, Slim!"

"No," the tall and angular soldier said, "we'll be able to hold our backs up straight and sort of carry ourselves like soldiers, as some won't feel like doing."

The lukewarm shower poured down over the chest and back of the drill sergeant. This was the second year in the Army and now he found himself continually surprised at the small effect that the stream of words of the soldiers had upon him.

Standing in the narrow aisle between his own bunk and that of the copper-headed corporal, he pulled on his clean khaki clothes before an audience of naked soldiers who lounged on the two bunks.

"When I marry," the wiry-headed sergeant was saying, "I'll marry me a WAC who I can take right to the front with me."

"You shouldn't do that," the corporal said, "she might be wounded in action." He and the angular, wiry-headed sergeant laughed so bawdily and merrily that the drill sergeant joined in, hardly knowing what were the jokes they'd been making. But the other naked soldiers, of more regular shapes, found the jokes not plain enough, and they began to ask literally:

"Can a WAC and a soldier overseas get married?"

"If a married WAC gets pregnant, what happens?"

"When I get married, " said one soldier who was stretched out straight on his back with his eyes closed and a towel thrown across his loins, "it'll be to a nice girl like the sergeant here's married."

The sergeant looked at him silently.

"But wherever," asked Slim, "are *you* going to meet such a girl like that in such company as you keep?"

The soldier lying on his back opened one eye: "I wouldn't talk about my company if I was you. I've saw you and the corporal here with them biddy-dolls at Midway twicst."

The corporal's eyes shone. He laughed aloud and fairly shouted "And *he* got *me* the date both times, Buck."

"Well," said Buck, with his eyes still closed and his hands folded over his bare chest, "when I marry it won't be to one of them sort. Nor not to one of you WACs neither, Slim."

Slim said, "Blow it out your barracks bag."

One of those more regularly shaped soldiers seemed to rouse himself as from sleep to say, "That's why y'like 'em, ain't it, Slim? Y'like 'em because they know how?" His joke was sufficiently plain to bring laughter from all. They all looked toward Slim. Even the soldier who was lying down opened one eye and looked at him. And Slim, who was rubbing his wiry mop of black hair with a white towel, muttered, "At least I don't pollute little kids from the roller rink like some present."

The naked soldier named Buck who was stretched out on the cot opened his eyes and rolled them in the direction of Slim. Then he closed his eyes meditatively and suddenly opened them again. He sat up and swung his feet around to the floor. "Well, I did meet an odd number the other night," he said. "She was drinking beer alone in Conner's Café when I comes in and sits on her right, like this." He patted his hand on the olive-drab blanket, and all the while he talked he was not looking at the other soldiers. Rather his face was turned toward the window at the end of his cot, and with his lantern jaw raised and his small, round eyes squinting, he peered into the rays of sunlight. "She was an odd one and wouldn't give me any sort of talk as long as I sit there. Then I begun to push off and she says out of the clear, 'Soldier, what did the rat say to the cat?' I said that I don't know and she says, 'This pussy's killin' me.' " Now all the other soldiers began to laugh and hollo. But Buck didn't even smile. He continued to squint up into the light and to speak in the same monotone. "So I said, 'Come on,' and jerked her up by the arm. But, you know, she was odd. She never did say much but tell a nasty joke now and then. She didn't have a bunch of small talk, but she come along and did all right. But I do hate to hear a woman talk nasty."

The potbellied corporal winked at the drill sergeant and said, "Listen to him. He says he's going to marry a nice girl like yours, but I bet you didn't run up on yours in Conner's Café or the roller rink."

Buck whisked the towel from across his lap and drawing it back he quickly snapped it at the corporal's little, hairy potbelly. The drill sergeant laughed with the rest and watched for a moment the patch of white that the towel made on the belly which was otherwise still red from the hot shower.

Now the drill sergeant was dressed. He combed his sandy-colored hair before a square hand mirror which he had set on the windowsill. The sight of himself reminded him of her who would already be waiting for him on that other ridge. She with her soft, Southern voice, her small hands forever clasping a handkerchief. This was what his own face in the tiny mirror brought to mind. How unreal to him were these soldiers and their hairy bodies and all their talk and their rough ways. How temporary. How different from his own life, from his real life with her.

He opened his metal footlocker and took out the history book in which he had been reading of battles that once took place on this campsite and along the ridge where he would ride the bus tonight. He pulled his khaki overseas cap onto the right side of his head and slipped away, apparently unnoticed, from the soldiers gathered there. They were all listening now to Slim who was saying,

"Me and Pat McKenzie picked up a pretty little broad one night who was deaf and dumb. But when me and her finally got around to shacking up and she made the damnedest noises you ever heard."

With the book clasped under his arm the drill sergeant passed down the aisle between the rows of cots, observing here a half-dressed soldier picking up a pair of dirty socks, there another soldier shining a pair of prized garrison shoes or tying a khaki tie with meticulous care. The drill sergeant's thoughts were still on her whose brown curls fell over the white collar of her summer dress. And he could dismiss the soldiers as he passed them as good fellows each, saying, "So long, Smoky Joe," to one who seemed to be retiring even before sundown, and "So long, Happy Jack," to another who scowled at him. They were good rough-and-ready fellows all, Smoky Joe, Happy Jack, Slim, Buck, and the copper-headed one. But one of them called to him as he went out the door, "I wouldn't take no book along. What you think you want with a book this night?" And the laughter came through the open windows after he was outside on the asphalt.

The bus jostled him and rubbed him against the civilian workers from the camp and the mill workers who climbed aboard with their dinner pails at the first stop. He could feel the fat thighs of middle-aged women rubbing against the sensitive places of his body, and they—unaware of such personal feelings—leaned toward one another and swapped stories about their outrageous bosses. One of the women said that for a little she'd quit this very week. The men, also mostly middle-aged and dressed in overalls and shirt-sleeves, seemed sensible of nothing but that this suburban bus somewhere crossed Lake Road, Pidgeon Street, Jackson Boulevard, and that at some such intersection they must be ready to jerk the stop cord and alight. "The days are getting a little shorter," one of them said.

The sergeant himself alighted at John Ross Road and transferred to the McFarland Gap bus. The passengers on this bus were not as crowded as on the first. The men were dressed in linen and seersucker business suits, and the women carried purses and wore little tailored dresses and straw hats. Those who were crowded together did not make any conversation among themselves. Even those who seemed to know one another talked in whispers. The sergeant was standing in the aisle but he bent over now and again and looked out the windows at the neat bungalows and larger dwelling houses along the roadside. He would one day have a house such as one of those for his own. His own father's house was the like of these, with a screened porch on the side and a fine tile roof. He could hear his father saying, "A house is only as good as the roof over it." But weren't these the things that had once seemed prosaic and too binding for his notions? Before he went into the Army had there not been moments when the thought of limiting himself to a genteel suburban life seemed intolerable by its restrictions and confinement? Even by the confinement to the company of such people as those here on the bus with him? And yet now when he sometimes lay wakeful and lonesome at night in the long dark barrack among the carefree and garrulous soldiers or when he was kneed and elbowed by the worried and weary mill hands on a bus, he dreamed longingly of the warm companionship he would find with her and their sober neighbors in a house with a fine roof.

The rattling, bumping bus pulled along for several miles over the road atop the steep ridge which it had barely managed to climb in first gear. At the end of the bus line he stepped out to the roadside and waited for his streetcar. The handful of passengers that were still on the bus climbed out too and scattered to all parts of the neighborhood, disappearing into doorways of brick bungalows or clapboard two-storieds that were perched among evergreens and oak trees and maple and wild sumac on the crest and on the slopes of the ridge. *This* would be a good neighborhood to settle down in. The view was surely a prize—any way you chose to look.

But the sergeant had hardly more than taken his stand in the grass to wait for the streetcar, actually leaning a little against a low wall that bordered a sloping lawn, when he observed the figure of a woman standing in the shadow of a small chinaberry tree which grew beside the wall.

The woman came from behind the tree and stood by the wall. She was within three or four steps of the sergeant. He looked at her candidly, and her plainness from the very first made him want to turn his face away toward the skyline of the city in the valley. Her flat-chested and generally ill-shaped figure was clothed with a baglike gingham dress that hung at an uneven knee length. On her feet was a pair of flat-heeled brown oxfords. She wore white, ankle-length socks that emphasized the hairiness of her muscular legs. On her head a dark felt hat was drawn down almost to her eyebrows. Her hair was straight and of a dark color less rich than brown and yet more brown than black, and it was cut so that a straight not wholly greaseless strand hung over each cheek and turned upward just the slightest bit at the ends.

And in her hands before her the woman held a large bouquet of white and lavender sweet peas. She held them, however, as though they were a bunch of mustard greens. Or perhaps she held them more as a small boy holds flowers, half ashamed to be seen holding anything so delicate. Her eyes did not rest on them. Rather her eyes roved nervously up and down the car tracks. At last she turned her colorless, long face to the sergeant and asked with an artificial smile that showed her broad gums and small teeth, "Is this where the car stops?"

"I think so," he said. Then he did look away toward the city.

"I saw the yellow mark up there on the post, but I wasn't real sure," she pursued. He had to look back at her, and as he did so she said, "Don't that uniform get awful hot?"

"Oh yes," he said. He didn't want to say more. But finally a thought of his own good fortune and an innate kindness urged him to speak again. "I sometimes change it two or three times a day."

"I'd sure say it would get hot."

After a moment's silence the sergeant observed, "This is mighty hot weather."

"It's awful hot here in the summer," she said. "But it's always awful here in some way. Where are you from?"

He still wanted to say no more. "I'm from West Tennessee."

"What part?" she almost demanded.

"I'm from Memphis. It gets mighty hot there."

"I oncet know somebody from there."

"Memphis gets awfully hot in the summer too."

"Well," she said, drawing in a long breath, "you picked an awful hot place to come to. I don't mind heat so much. It's just an awful place to be. I've lived here all my life and I hate it here."

The sergeant walked away up the road and leaned forward looking for the streetcar. Then he walked back to the wall because he felt that she would think him a snob. Unable to invent another conversation, he looked at the flowers and said, "They're very pretty."

"Well, if you like 'em at all," she said, "you like 'em a great lot more than I do. I hate flowers. Only the other day I say to Mother that if I get sick and go the hospital don't bring any flowers around me. I don't want any. I don't like 'em."

"Why, those are pretty," he said. He felt for some reason that he must defend their worth. "I like all flowers. Those are especially hard to grow in West Tennessee."

"If you like 'em you like 'em more than I do. Only the other day I say to my Sunday School teacher that if I would die it'd save her a lot of money because I don't want anybody to send no flowers. I hate 'em. And it ain't just these. I hate all flowers."

"I think they're pretty," he insisted. "Did you pick 'em down there in the valley?"

"They was growing wild in a field and I picked them because I didn't have nothin' else to do. Here," she said, pushing the flowers into his hands, "you take 'em. I hate 'em."

"No, no, I wouldn't think of taking your flowers. Here, you must take them back."

"I don't want 'em. I'll just throw 'em away."

"Why, I can't take your flowers."

"You have 'em, and I ain't going to take 'em back. They'll just lay there and die if you put them on the wall."

"I feel bad accepting them. You must have gone to a lot of trouble to pick them."

"They was just growing wild at the edge of a field, and the lady said they was about to take her garden. I don't like flowers. I did her a favor, and you can do me one."

"There's nothing I like better," he said, feeling that he had been ungracious. "I guess I would like to raise flowers, and I used to work in the garden some." He leaned forward, listening for the sound of the streetcar.

For a minute or two neither of them spoke. She shifted from foot to foot and seemed to be talking to herself. From the corner of his eye he watched her lips moving. Finally she said aloud, "Some people act like they're doing you a favor to pay you a dollar a day."

"That's not much in these times," he observed.

"It's just like I was saying to a certain person the other day, 'If you are not willing to pay a dollar and a half a day you don't want nobody to work for you very bad.' But I work for a dollar just the same. This is half of it right here." She held up a half dollar between her thumb and forefinger. "But last week I pay for all my insurance for next year. I put my money away instead of buying things I really want. You can't say that for many girls."

"You certainly can't."

"Not many girls do that."

"I don't know many that do."

"No sirree," she said, snapping the fingers of her right hand, "the girls in this place was awful. I hate the way they act with soldiers downtown. They go to the honky-tonks and drink beer. I don't waste anybody's money drinking beer. I put my own money away instead of buying things I might really want."

The sergeant stepped out into the middle of the road and listened for the streetcar. As he returned to the wall, a Negro man and woman rode by in a large blue sedan. The woman standing by the wall watched the automobile go over the streetcar tracks and down the hill. "There's no Negro in this town that will do housework for less than two and a half a day, and they pay us whites only a dollar."

"Why will they pay Negroes more?" he asked.

"Because they can boss 'em," she said hastily. "Just because they can boss 'em around. I say to a certain person the other day, 'You can't boss me around like a nigger, no ma'am.' "

"I suppose that's it." He now began to walk up and down in front of her, listening and looking for the streetcar and occasionally raising the flowers to his nose to smell them. She continued to lean against the wall, motionless and with her humorless face turned upward the car wire where were hanging six or eight rolled newspapers tied in pairs by long dirty strings. "How y'reckon them papers come to be up there?" she asked.

"Some of the neighborhood kids or paperboys did it, I guess."

"Yea. That's it. Rich people's kids's just as bad as anybody's."

"Well, the paperboys probably did it whenever they had papers left over. I've done it myself when I was a kid."

"Yea," she said through her nose. "But kids just make me nervous. And I didn't much like bein' a kid neither."

The sergeant looked along one of the steel rails that still glimmered a little in the late sunlight and remembered good times he had had walking along the railroad tracks as a child. Suddenly he hoped his first child would be a boy.

"I'll tell you one thing, soldier," the woman beside him was saying, "I don't spend my money on lipstick and a lot of silly clothes.

I don't paint myself with a lot of lipstick and push my hair up on top of my head and walk around downtown so soldiers will look at me. You don't find many girls that don't do that in this awful place, do ya?"

"You certainly don't find many." The sergeant felt himself blushing.

"You better be careful, for you're going to drop some of them awful flowers. I don't know what you want with 'em."

"Why, they're pretty," he said as though he had not said it before.

Now the blue sedan came up the hill again and rolled quietly over the car tracks. Only the Negro man was in the sedan, and he was driving quite fast.

"How can a nigger like that own a car like that?"

"He probably only drives for some of the people who live along here."

"Yea. That's it. That's it. Niggers can get away with anything. I guess you've heard about 'em attacking that white girl down yonder."

"Yes . . . Yes."

"They ought to kill 'em all or send 'em all back to Africa."

"It's a real problem, I think."

"I don't care if no man black or white never looks at me if I have to put on a lot of lipstick and push my hair up and walk around without a hat."

The sergeant leaned forward, craning his neck.

"I'm just going to tell you what happened to me downtown the other day," she persisted. "I was standing looking in a store window on Broad when a soldier comes up behind me, and I'm just going to tell you what he said. He said he had a hotel room, and he asked me if I didn't want to go up to the room with him and later go somewhere to eat and that he'd give me some money too."

"I know," the sergeant said. "There's a mighty rough crowd in town now."

"But I just told him, 'No thanks. If I can't make money honest I don't want it,' is what I told him. I says, 'There's a girl on that corner yonder at Main that wants ya. Just go down there.' "

The sergeant stood looking down the track, shaking his head.

"He comes right up behind me, you understand, and tells me that he has a room in a hotel and that we can go there and do what we want to do and then go get something to eat and he will give me some money besides. And I just told him, 'No thanks. There's a girl on that corner yonder at Main that wants ya. Just go down there.' So I went off up the street a way and then I come back to where I was looking at a lot of silly clothes, and a man in a blue shirt who was standing there all the time says that the soldier had come back looking for me."

The sergeant stretched out his left arm so that his wristwatch appeared from under his sleeve. Then he crooked his elbow and looked at the watch.

"Oh, you have *some* wait yet," she said.

"How often do they run?"

"I don't know," she said without interest, "just every so often. I told him, y'see, if I can't make money honest I don't want it. You can't say that for many girls." Whenever his attention seemed to lag, her speech grew louder.

"No, you can't," he agreed.

"I save my money. Soldier, I've got two hundred and seven dollars in the bank, besides my insurance paid up for next year." She said nothing during what seemed to be several minutes. Then she asked, "Where do your mother and daddy live?"

"In West Tennessee."

"Where do you stay? Out at the camp?" She hardly gave him time to answer her questions now.

"Well, I stay out at camp some nights."

"*Some* nights? Where do you stay other nights?" She was grinning.

"I'm married and stay with my wife. I've just been married a little while but we have rooms up the way here."

"Oh, are you a married man? Where is she from? I hope she ain't from here."

"She's from Memphis. She's just finished school."

The woman frowned, blushed deeply, then she grinned again showing her wide gums. "I'd say you are goin' to take her the flowers. You won't have to buy her any."

"I do wish you'd take some of them back."

The woman didn't answer him for a long time. Finally, when he had almost forgotten what he had said last, she said without a sign of a grin, "I don't want 'em. The sight of 'em makes me sick."

And at last the streetcar came.

It was but a short ride now to the sergeant's stop. The car stopped just opposite the white two-story house. The sergeant alighted and had to stand on the other side of the track until the long yellow streetcar had rumbled away. It was as though an ugly, noisy curtain had at last been drawn back. He saw her face through an upstairs window of the white house with its precise cupola rising even higher than the tall brick chimneys and with fantastic lacy woodwork ornamenting the tiny porches and the cornices. He saw her through the only second-story window that was clearly visible between the foliage of trees that grew in the yard.

The house was older than most of the houses in the suburban neighborhood along this ridgetop, and an old-fashioned iron fence enclosed its yard. He had to stop a moment to unlatch the iron gate, and there he looked directly up into the smiling countenance at the open window. She spoke to him in a voice even softer than he remembered.

Now he had to pass through his landlady's front hall and climb a crooked flight of stairs before reaching his rooms, and an old-fashioned bell had tinkled when he opened the front door. At this tinkling sound an old lady's voice called from somewhere in the back of the house, "Yes?" But he made no answer. He hurried up the steps and was at last in the room with his wife.

They sat on the couch with their knees touching and her hand in his.

Just as her voice was softer, her appearance was fairer even than he had remembered. He told her that he had been rehearsing this moment during every second of the past two hours, and simultaneously he realized that what he was saying was true, that during all other conversations and actions his imagination had been going over and over the present scene.

She glanced at the sweet peas lying beside his cap on the table and said that when she had seen him in the gateway with the flowers she had felt that perhaps during the time they were separated she had not remembered him even as gentle and fine as he was. Yet she had been afraid until that moment by the window that in her heart she had exaggerated these virtues of his.

The sergeant did not tell her then how he had come into possession of the flowers. He knew that the incident of the cleaning woman would depress her good spirits as it had his own. And while he was thinking of the complete understanding and sympathy between them he heard her saying, "I know you are tired. You're probably not so tired from soldiering as from dealing with people of various sorts all day. I went to the grocery myself this morning and coming home on the bus I thought of how tiresome and boring the long ride home would be for you this evening when the buses are so crowded." He leaned toward her and kissed her, holding her until he realized that she was smiling. He released her, and she drew away with a laugh and said that she had supper to tend to and that she must put the sweet peas in water.

While she was stirring about the clean, closet-like kitchen, he surveyed in the late twilight the living room that was still a strange room to him, and without lighting the table or floor lamps he wandered into the bedroom, which was the largest room and from which an old-fashioned bay window overlooked the valley. He paused at the window and raised the shade. And he was startled by a magnificent view of the mountains that rose up on the other side of the city. And there he witnessed the last few seconds of a sunset—brilliant orange and brick red—beyond the blue mountains.

They ate at a little table that she drew out from the wall in the living room. "How have I merited such a good cook for a wife?" he said and smiled when the meal was finished. They stacked the dishes unwashed in the sink, for she had put her arms about his neck and whispered, "Why should I waste one moment of the time I have you here when the days are so lonesome and endless."

They sat in the living room and read aloud the letters that had come during the past few days.

For a little while she worked on the hem of a tablecloth, and they talked. They spoke of their friends at home. She showed him a few of their wedding presents that had arrived late. And they kept saying how fortunate they were to have found an apartment so comfortable as this. Here on the ridge it was cool almost every night.

Afterward he took out his pen and wrote a letter to his father. He read the letter aloud to her.

Still later it rained. The two of them hurried about putting down windows. Then they sat and heard it whipping and splashing against the window glass when the wind blew.

By the time they were both in their nightclothes the rain had stopped. He sat on a footstool by the bed reading in the heavy, dark history book. Once he read aloud a sentence which he thought impressive: "I have never seen the Federal dead lie so thickly on the ground save in front of the sunken wall at Fredericksburg." This was a Southern general writing of the battle fought along this ridgetop.

"What a very sad-sounding sentence," she said. She was brushing her hair in long, even strokes.

Finally he put down the book but remained sitting on the stool to polish his low-quartered military shoes. She at her dressing table looked at his reflection in the mirror before her, and said, "It's stopped raining."

"It stopped a good while ago," he said. And he looked up attentively, for there had seemed to be some regret in her voice.

"I'm sorry it stopped," she said, returning his gaze.

"You should be glad," he said. "I'd have to drill in all that mud tomorrow."

"Of course I'm glad," she said. "But hasn't the rain made us seem even more alone up here?"

The sergeant stood up. The room was very still and close. There was not even the sound of a clock. A light was burning on her dressing table, and through the open doorway he could see the table lamp that was still burning in the living room. The table there was a regular part of the furnishing of the apartment. But it was a piece of furniture they might have chosen themselves. He went to the door and stood a moment studying the effect she had achieved in her arrangement of objects on the table. On the dark octagonal top was the white lamp with the urn-shaped base. The light the lamp shed contrasted the shape of the urn with the global shape of a crystal vase from which sprigs of ivy mixed with periwinkle sprang in their individual wildness. And a square, crystal ashtray reflecting its exotic lights was placed at an angle to a small round silver dish.

He went to the living room to put out the light. Yet with his hand on the switch he hesitated because it was such a pleasing isolated arrangement of objects.

Once the light was out he turned immediately to go back into the bedroom. And now he halted in the doorway again, for as he entered the bedroom his eye fell on the vase of sweet peas she had arranged. It was placed on top of a high bureau and he had not previously noticed it. Up there the flowers looked somehow curiously artificial and not like the real sweet peas he had seen in the rough hands of the woman this afternoon. While he was gazing thus he felt his wife's eyes upon him. Yet without turning to her he went to the window, for he was utterly preoccupied with the impression he had just received and he had a strange desire to sustain the impression long enough to examine it. He kept thinking of that woman's hands.

Now he raised the shade and threw open the big window in the bay, and standing there barefoot on a small hooked rug he looked out at the dark mountains and at the lines and splotches of lights in the city below. He heard her switching off the two small lamps at her dressing table. He knew that it had disturbed her to see him so suddenly preoccupied, and it was as though he tried to cram all of a whole day's reflections into a few seconds. Had it really been the pale flowers that had impressed him so? Or had it been the setting of his alarm clock a few minutes before and the realization that after a few more hours here with her he must take up again that other life that the yellow streetcar had carried away with it this afternoon? He could hear the voices of the boys in the barrack, and he saw the figure of the woman by the stone wall under the chinaberry tree.

Now he could hear his wife moving to switch off the overhead light. There was a click. The room being dark, things outside seemed much brighter. On the slope of the ridge that dropped off steeply behind the house the dark treetops became visible. And again there were the voices of the boys in the barrack. Their crudeness, their hardness, even their baseness—qualities that seemed to be taking root in the very hearts of those men—kept passing like objects through his mind. And the bitterness of the woman waiting by the streetcar tracks pressed upon him.

His wife had come up beside him in the dark and slipped her arm about his waist. He folded his arms tightly about her. She spoke his name. Then she said, "These hours we have together are so isolated and few that they must sometimes not seem quite real to you when you are away." She too, he realized, felt a terrible unrelated diversity in things. In the warmth of her companionship, he felt a sudden contrast with the cold fighting he might take part in on a battlefield that was now distant and almost abstract.

The sergeant's eyes had now grown so accustomed to the darkness inside and outside that he could look down between the trees on the slope of the ridge. He imagined there the line after line of Union soldiers that had once been thrown into the battle to take this ridge at all cost. The Confederate general's headquarters were not more than two blocks away. If he and she had been living in those days he would have seen ever so clearly the Cause for that fighting. And *this* battlefield would not be abstract. He would have stood here holding back the enemy from the very land which was his own, from the house in which she awaited him.

But here the sergeant stopped and smiled at himself. He examined the sergeant he had just imagined in the Confederate ranks and it was not himself at all. He compared the Confederate sergeant to the sergeant on the field this afternoon who had stood a moment puzzling over the tracks that twelve rookies had made. *The sergeant is I,* he said to himself desperately, *but it is not that morning in December of '62 when the Federal dead were lying so thick on the ground.* He leaned down and kissed his wife's forehead, and taking her up in his arms he carried her to their bed. *It is only a vase of flowers,* he remarked silently, rhetorically to himself as his wife drew her arms tighter about his neck. *Three bunches from a stand of sweet peas that had taken the lady's garden.* As he let her down gently on the bed she asked, "Why did you look so strangely at the vase of flowers? What did they make you think about so long by the window?"

For a moment the sergeant was again overwhelmed by his wife's perception and understanding. He would tell her everything he had in his mind. What great fortune it was to have a wife who could understand and to have her here beside him to hear and to comprehend everything that was in his heart and mind. But as he lay in the dark trying to make out the line of her profile against the dim light of the window, there came through the rainwashed air outside the rumbling of a streetcar. And before he could even speak the thoughts which he had been thinking, all those things no longer seemed to matter. The noise of the streetcar, the irregular rumble and uncertain clanging, brought back to him once more all the incidents of the day. He and his wife were here beside each other, but suddenly he was hopelessly distracted by this new sensation. The streetcar had moved away now beyond his hearing, and he could visualize it casting its diffused light among the dark foliage and over the white gravel between the tracks. He was left with the sense that no moment in his life had any relation to an-

EUDORA WELTY
(1909–)

Born in Jackson, Mississippi, where she has lived most of her life, Eudora Welty, like Flannery O'Connor, is primarily a short story writer. She too takes for her immediate subject the Southern world of her experience, but her range is wider, her narrative voice more varied, and her compassion for her characters greater. Hers is the art of sympathy and of identification. In choosing this so atypical a Welty story, I wanted to suggest the virtuoso quality of that sympathy and identification. (The speaker is the imagined assassin of Medgar Evers.)

Eudora Welty came to immediate prominence with the publication of her first collection of stories, A Curtain of Green *(1941). Other story collections are* The Wide Net *(1943),* The Bride of the Innisfallen *(1955), and, most recently, her* Collected Stories *(1980). Her novels are* The Robber Bridegroom *(1942),* Delta Wedding *(1946),* The Ponder Heart *(1954),* Losing Battles *(1970), and* The Optimist's Daughter *(1972). Her most recent book is the much-acclaimed memoir* One Writer's Beginnings *(1983).*

Like "Why I Live at the P.O." and "Powerhouse," two of Eudora Welty's most frequently anthologized stories, "Where Is the Voice Coming From?" is a masterpiece of voice, rhythm, music. Except, in this case, the music is the music of death.

Where Is the Voice Coming From?

I says to my wife, "You can reach and turn it off. You don't have to set and look at a black nigger face no longer than you want to, or listen to what you don't want to hear. It's still a free country."

I reckon that's how I give myself the idea.

I says, I could find right exactly where in Thermopylae that nigger's living that's asking for equal time. And without a bit of trouble to me.

And I ain't saying it might not be because that's pretty close to where *I* live. The other hand, there could be reasons you might have yourself for knowing how to get there in the dark. It's where you all go for the thing you want when you want it the most. Ain't that right?

The Branch Bank sign tells you in lights, all night long even, what time it is and how hot. When it was quarter to four, and 92, that was me going by in my brother-in-law's truck. He don't deliver nothing at that hour of the morning.

So you leave Four Corners and head west on Nathan B. Forrest Road, past the Surplus & Salvage, not much beyond the Kum Back Drive-In and Trailer Camp, not as far as where the signs starts saying "Live Bait," "Used Parts," "Fireworks," "Peaches," and "Sister Peebles Reader and Adviser." Turn before you hit the city limits and duck back towards the I.C. tracks. And his street's been paved.

And there was his light on, waiting for me. In his garage, if you please. His car's gone. He's out planning still some other ways to do what we tell 'em they can't. I *thought* I'd beat him home. All I had to do was pick my tree and walk in close behind it.

I didn't come expecting not to wait. But it was so hot, all I did was hope and pray one or the other of us wouldn't melt before it was over.

Now, it wasn't no bargain I'd struck.

I've heard what you've heard about Goat Dykeman, in Mississippi. Sure, everybody knows about Goat Dykeman. Goat he got word to the Governor's Mansion he'd go up yonder and shoot that nigger Meredith clean out of school, if he's let out of the pen to do it. Old Ross turned *that* over in his mind before saying him nay, it stands to reason.

I ain't no Goat Dykeman, I ain't in no pen, and I ain't ask no Governor Barnett to give me one thing. Unless he wants to give me a pat on the back for the trouble I took this morning. But he don't have to if he don't want to. I done what I done for my own pure-D satisfaction.

As soon as I heard wheels, I knowed who was coming. That was him and bound to be him. It was the right nigger heading in a new white car up his driveway towards his garage with the light shining, but stopping before he got there, maybe not to wake 'em. That was him. I knowed it when he cut off the car lights and put his foot out and I knowed him standing dark against the light. I knowed him then like I know me now. I knowed him even by his still, listening back.

Never seen him before, never seen him since, never seen anything of his black face but his picture, never seen his face alive, any time at all, or anywheres, and didn't want to, need to, never hope to see that face and never will. As long as there was no question in my mind.

He had to be the one. He stood right still and waited against the light, his back was fixed, fixed on me like a preacher's eyeballs when he's yelling "Are you saved?" He's the one.

I'd already brought up my rifle, I'd already taken my sights. And I'd already got him, because it was too late then for him or me to turn by one hair.

Something darker than him, like the wings of a bird, spread on his back and pulled him down. He climbed up once, like a man under bad claws, and like just blood could weigh a ton he walked with it on his back to better light. Didn't get no further than his door. And fell to stay.

He was down. He was down, and a ton load of bricks on his back wouldn't have laid any heavier. There on his paved driveway, yes sir.

And it wasn't till the minute before, that the mockingbird had quit singing. He'd been singing up my sassafras tree. Either he was up early, or he hadn't never gone to bed, he was like me. And the mocker he'd stayed right with me, filling the air till come the crack, till I turned loose of my load. I was like him. I was on top of the world myself. For once.

I stepped to the edge of his light there, where he's laying flat. I says, "Roland? There was one way left, for me to be ahead of you and stay ahead of you, by Dad, and I just taken it. Now I'm alive and you ain't. We ain't never now, never going to be equals and you know why? One of us is dead. What about that, Roland?" I said. "Well, you seen to it, didn't you?"

I stood a minute—just to see would somebody inside come out long enough to pick him up. And there she comes, the woman. I doubt she'd been to sleep. Because it seemed to me she'd been in there keeping awake all along.

It was mighty green where I skint over the yard getting back. That nigger wife of his, she wanted nice grass! I bet my wife would hate to pay her water bill. And for burning her electricity. And there's my brother-in-law's truck, still waiting with the door open. "No Riders"—that didn't mean me.

There wasn't a thing I been able to think of since would have made it to go any nicer. Except a chair to my back while I was putting in my waiting. But going home, I seen what little time it takes after all to get a thing done like you really want it. It was 4:34, and while I was looking it moved to 35. And the temperature stuck where it was. All that night I guarantee you it had stood without dropping, a good 92.

My wife says, "What? Didn't the skeeters bite you?" She said, "Well, they been asking that—why somebody didn't trouble to load a rifle and get some of these agitators out of Thermopylae. Didn't the fella keep drumming it in, what a good idea? The one that writes a column ever' day?"

I says to my wife, "Find *some* way I don't get the credit."

"He says do it for Thermopylae," she says. "Don't you ever skim the paper?"

I says, "Thermopylae never done nothing for me. And I don't owe nothing to Thermopylae. Didn't do it for you. Hell, any more'n I'd do something or other for them Kennedys! I done it for my own pure-D satisfaction."

"It's going to get him right back on TV," says my wife. "You watch for the funeral."

I says, "You didn't even leave a light burning when you went to bed. So how was I supposed to even get me home or pull Buddy's truck up safe in our front yard?"

"Well, hear another good joke on you," my wife says next. "Didn't you hear the news? The N. double A.C.P. is fixing to send somebody to Thermopylae. Why couldn't you waited? You might could have got you somebody better. Listen and hear 'em say so."

I ain't but one. I reckon you have to tell *somebody*.

"Where's the gun, then?" my wife says. "What did you do with our protection?"

I says, "It was scorching! It was scorching!" I told her, "It's laying out on the ground in rank weeds, trying to cool off, that's what it's doing now."

"You dropped it," she says. "Back there."

And I told her, "Because I'm so tired of ever'thing in the world being just that hot to the touch! The keys to the truck, the doorknob, the bedsheet, ever'thing, it's all like a stove lid. There just ain't much going that's worth holding on to it no more," I says, "when it's a hundred and two in the shade by day and by night not too much difference. I wish *you'd* laid *your* finger to that gun."

"Trust you to come off and leave it," my wife says.

"Is that how no-'count I am?" she makes me ask. "*You* want to go back and get it?"

"You're the one they'll catch. I say it's so hot that even if you get to sleep you wake up feeling like you cried all night!" says my wife. "Cheer up, here's one more joke before time to get up. Heard what *Caroline* said? Caroline said, 'Daddy, I just can't wait to grow up big, so I can marry *James Meredith*.' I heard that where I work. One rich-bitch to another one, to make her cackle."

"At least I kept some dern teen-ager from North Thermopylae getting there and doing it first," I says. "Driving his own car."

On TV and in the paper, they don't know but half of it. They know who Roland Summers was without knowing who I am. His face was in front of the public before I got rid of him, and after I got rid of him there it is again—the same picture. And none of me. I ain't ever had one made. Not ever! The best that newspaper could do for me was offer a five-hundred-dollar reward for finding out who I am. For as long as they don't know who that is, whoever shot Roland is worth a good deal more right now than Roland is.

But by the time I was moving around uptown, it was hotter still. That pavement in the middle of Main Street was so hot to my feet I might've been walking the barrel of my gun. If the whole world could've just felt Main Street this morning through the soles of my shoes, maybe it would've helped some.

Then the first thing I heard 'em say was the N. double A. C. P. done it themselves, killed Roland Summers, and proved it by saying the shooting was done by a expert (I hope to tell you it was!) and at just the right hour and minute to get the whites in trouble.

You can't win.

"They'll never find him," the old man trying to sell roasted peanuts tells me to my face.

And it's so hot.

It looks like the town's on fire already, whichever ways you turn, ever' street you strike, because there's those trees hanging them pones of bloom like split watermelon. And a thousand cops crowding ever'where you go, half of 'em too young to start shaving, but all streaming sweat alike. I'm getting tired of 'em.

I was already tired of seeing a hundred cops getting us white people nowheres. Back at the beginning, I stood on the corner and I watched them new babyface cops loading nothing but nigger children into the paddy wagon and they come marching out of a little parade and into the paddy wagon singing. And they got in and sat down without providing a speck of trouble, and their hands held little new American flags, and all the cops could do was knock them flagsticks a-loose from their hands, and not let 'em pick 'em up, that was all, and give 'em a free ride. And children can just get 'em more flags.

Everybody: It don't get you nowhere to take nothing from nobody unless you make sure it's for keeps, for good and all, for ever and amen.

I won't be sorry to see them brickbats hail down on us for a change. Pop bottles too, they can come flying whenever they want to. Hundreds, all to smash, like Birmingham. I'm waiting on 'em to bring out them switchblade knives, like Harlem and Chicago. Watch TV long enough and you'll see it all to happen on Deacon Street in Thermopylae. What's holding it back, that's all?—Because it's *in* 'em.

I'm ready myself for that funeral.

Oh, they may find me. May catch me one day in spite of 'emselves. (But I grew up in the country.) May try to railroad me into the electric chair, and what that amounts to is something hotter than yesterday and today put together.

But I advise 'em to go careful. Ain't it about time us taxpayers starts to calling the moves? Starts to telling the teachers *and* the preachers *and* the judges of our so-called courts how far they can go?

Even the President so far, he can't walk in my house without being invited, like he's my daddy, just to say whoa. Not yet!

Once, I run away from my home. And there was a ad for me, come to be printed in our county weekly. My mother paid for it. It was from her. It says: "SON: You are not being hunted for anything but to find you." That time, I come on back home.

But people are dead now.

And it's so hot. Without it even being August yet.

Anyways, I seen him fall. I was evermore the one.

So I reach me down my old guitar off the nail in the wall. 'Cause I've got my guitar, what I've held on to from way back when, and I never dropped that, never lost or forgot it, never hocked it but to get it again, never give it away, and I set in my chair, with nobody home but me, and I start to play, and sing a-Down. And sing a-down, down, down, down. Sing a-down, down, down, down. Down.

ISAAC BASHEVIS SINGER
(1904–1991)

Born in Radzymin, Poland, on July 14, 1904, Isaac Bashevis Singer is distinguished from the other writers in this volume by the fact that, through his long and much-acclaimed career, he wrote his novels, short stories, memoirs, and children's books in Yiddish, which was then translated, with his supervision, into English. His logic is utterly appropriate to his work: "I like to write ghost stories and nothing fits a ghost story better than a dying language. The deader the language, the more alive the ghost."

In his early twenties, Isaac Bashevis Singer made the decision to leave rabbinical studies and to become a writer, partly under the influence of his older and successful brother, the novelist Israel Joshua Singer. In 1922 he began his literary career as an editor of a Yiddish literary journal in Poland, and in 1935 he emigrated to the United States, where his brother was already living. Most of his life—familial, social, literary—was spent in the neighborhood of Upper Broadway, New York City, in which many of his short stories are set; but his most memorable work, like the story included here, is illuminated by the willed or unwilled recollection of the Holocaust, that nightmare that continues to haunt those who managed to survive and begin life anew in North America.

Isaac Bashevis Singer's Collected Stories *appeared in 1982; his last novel,* Scum, *was published in 1991. In all, he wrote over forty books, including* Satan in Goray *(1955),* Gimpel the Fool *(1957),* Short Friday *(1964),* Enemies, A Love Story *(1972),* Passion *(1975),* Old Love *(1979),* The Penitent *(1983),* The Image and Other Stories *(1985), and* The Death of Methuselah *(1988).*

The Lecture

I was on my way to Montreal to deliver a lecture. It was midwinter and I had been warned that the temperature there was ten degrees lower than in New York. Newspapers reported that trains had been stalled by the snow and fishing villages cut off, so that food and medical supplies had to be dropped to them by plane.

I prepared for the journey as though it were an expedition to the North Pole. I put on a heavy coat over two sweaters and packed warm underwear and a bottle of cognac in case the train should be halted somewhere in the fields. In my breast pocket I had the manuscript that I intended to read—an optimistic report on the future of the Yiddish language.

In the beginning, everything went smoothly. As usual, I arrived at the station an hour before train departure and therefore could find no porter. The station teemed with travelers and I watched them, trying to guess who they were, where they were going, and why.

None of the men was dressed as heavily as I. Some even wore spring coats. The ladies looked bright and elegant in their minks and beavers, nylon stockings and stylish hats. They carried colorful bags and illustrated magazines, smoked cigarettes and chattered and laughed with a carefree air that has never ceased to amaze me. It was as though they knew nothing of the existence of world problems or eternal questions, as though they had never heard of death, sickness, war, poverty, betrayal, or even of such troubles as missing a train, losing a ticket, or being robbed. They flirted like young girls, exhibiting their blood-red nails. The station was chilly that morning, but no one except myself seemed to feel it. I wondered whether these people knew there had been a Hitler. Had they heard of Stalin's murder machine? They probably had, but what does one body care when another is tortured?

I was itchy from the woolen underwear. Now I began to feel hot. But from time to time a shiver ran through my body. The lecture, in which I predicted a brilliant future for Yiddish, troubled me. What had made me so optimistic all of a sudden? Wasn't Yiddish going under before my very eyes?

The prompt arrival of American trains and the ease in boarding them have always seemed like miracles to me. I remember journeys in Poland when Jewish passengers were not allowed into the cars and I had to hang on to the handrails. I remember railway strikes when trains were halted midway for many hours and it was impossible in the dense crowd to push through to the washroom.

But here I was, sitting on a soft seat, right by the window. The car was heated. There were no bundles, no high fur hats, no sheepskin coats, no boxes, and no gendarmes. Nobody was eating bread and lard. Nobody drank vodka from a bottle. Nobody was berating Jews for state treason. In fact, nobody discussed politics at all. As soon as the train started, a huge Negro in a white apron came in and announced lunch. The train was not rattling, it glided smoothly on its rails along the frozen Hudson. Outside, the landscape gleamed with snow and light. Birds that remained here for the winter flew busily over the icy river.

The farther we went, the wintrier the landscape. The weather seemed to change every few miles. Now we went through dense fog, and now the air cleared and the sun was shining again over silvery distances.

A heavy snowfall began. It suddenly turned dark. The day was flickering out. The express no longer ran but crept slowly and cautiously, as though feeling its way. The heating system in the train seemed to have broken down. It became chilly and I had to put on my coat. The other passengers pretended for a while that they did not notice anything, as though reluctant to admit too quickly that they were cold. But soon they began to tap their feet, grumble, grin sheepishly, and rummage in their valises for sweaters, scarves, boots, or whatever else they had brought along. Collars were turned up, hands stuffed into sleeves. The makeup on women's faces dried up and began to peel like plaster.

The American dream gradually dissolves and harsh Polish reality returns. Someone is drinking whiskey from a bottle. Someone is eating bread and sausage to warm his stomach. There is also a rush to the toilets. It is difficult to understand how it happened, but the floor of the car becomes wet and muddy. The windowpanes become crusted with ice and bloom with frost patterns.

Suddenly the train stops. I look out and see a sparse wood. The trees are thin and bent, and though they are covered with snow, they look bare and charred, as after a fire. The sun has already set, but purple stains still glow in the west. The snow on the ground is no longer white, but violet. Crows walk on it, flap their wings, and I can hear their cawing. The snow falls in gray, heavy lumps, as though the guardians of the Treasury of Snow up above had been too lazy to flake it more finely. Passengers walk from car to car, leaving the doors open. Conductors and other train employees run past; when they are asked questions, they do not stop, but mumble something rudely.

We are not far from the Canadian border, and Uncle Sam's domain is virtually at an end. Some passengers begin to take down their luggage; they may have to show it soon to the customs officials. A naturalized American citizen gets out his citizenship papers and studies his own photograph, as if trying to convince himself that the document is not a false one.

One or two passengers venture to step out of the train, but they sink up to their knees into the snow. It is not long before they clamber back into the car. The twilight lingers for a while, then night falls.

I see people using the weather as a pretext for striking up acquaintance. Women begin to talk among themselves and there is sudden intimacy. The men have also formed a group. Everyone picks up bits of information. People offer each other advice. But nobody pays any attention to me. I sit alone, a victim of my own isolation, shyness, and alienation from the world. I begin to read a book, and this provokes hostility, for reading a book at such a time seems like a challenge and an insult to the other passengers. I exclude myself from society, and all the faces say to me silently: You don't need us and we don't need you. Never mind, you will still have to turn to us, but we won't have to turn to you. . . .

I open my large, heavy valise, take out the bottle of cognac, and take a stealthy sip now and then. After that, I lean my face against the cold windowpane and try to look out. But all I see is the reflection of the interior of the car. The world outside seems to have disappeared. The solipsistic philosophy of Bishop Berkeley has won over all the other systems. Nothing remains but to wait patiently until God's idea of a train halted in its tracks by snowdrifts will give way to God's ideas of movement and arrival.

Alas for my lecture! If I arrive in the middle of the night, there will not even be anyone waiting for me. I shall have to look for a hotel. If only I had a return ticket. However, was Captain Scott, lost in the polar ice fields, in a better position after Amundsen had discovered the South Pole? How much would Captain Scott have given to be able to sit in a brightly lit railway car? No, one must not sin by complaining.

The cognac had made me warm. Drunken fumes rise from an empty stomach to the brain. I am awake and dozing at the same time. Whole minutes drift away, leaving only a blur. I hear talk, but I don't quite know what it means. I sink into blissful indifference. For my part, the train can stand here for three days and three nights. I have a box of crackers in my valise. I will not die of hunger. Various themes float through my mind. Something within me mutters dreamlike words and phrases.

The diesel engine must be straining forward. I am aware of dragging, knocking, growling sounds, as of a monstrous ox, a legendary steel bull. Most of the passengers have gone to the bar or the restaurant car, but I am too lazy to get up. I seem to have grown into the seat. A childish obstinacy takes possession of me: I'll show them all that I am not affected by any of this commotion; I am above the trivial happenings of the day.

Everyone who passes by—from the rear cars to the front, or the other way—glances at me; and it seems to me that each one forms some judgment of his own about the sort of person I am. But does anyone guess that I am a Yiddish writer late for his lecture? This, I am sure, occurs to no one. This is known only to the higher powers.

I take another sip, and another. I have never understood the passion for drinking, but now I see what power there is in alcohol. This liquid holds within itself the secrets of nirvana. I no longer look at my wristwatch. I no longer worry about a place to sleep. I mock in my mind the lecture I had prepared. What if it is not delivered? People will hear fewer lies! If I could open the window, I would throw the manuscript out into the woods. Let the paper and ink return to the cosmos, where there can be no errors and no lies. Atoms and molecules are guiltless; they are a part of the divine truth. . . .

2

The train arrived exactly at half past two. No one was waiting for me. I left the station and was caught in a blast of icy night wind that no coat or sweaters could keep out. All taxis were immediately taken. I returned to the station, prepared to spend the night sitting on a bench.

Suddenly I noticed a lame woman and a young girl looking at me and pointing with their fingers. I stopped and looked back. The lame woman leaned on two thick, short canes. She was wrinkled, disheveled, like an old woman in Poland, but her black eyes suggested that she was more sick and broken than old. Her clothes also reminded me of Poland. She wore a sort of sleeveless fur jacket. Her shoes had toes and heels I had not seen in years. On her shoulders she wore a fringed woolen shawl, like one of my mother's. The young woman, on the other hand, was stylishly dressed, but also rather slovenly.

After a moment's hesitation, I approached them.

The girl said: "Are you Mr. N.?"

I answered, "Yes, I am."

The lame woman made a sudden movement, as though to drop her canes and clap her hands. She immediately broke into a wailing cry so familiar to me.

"Dear Father in heaven!" she sang out. "I was telling my daughter it's he, and she said no. I recognized you! Where were you going with the valise? It's a wonder you came back. I'd never have forgiven myself! Well, Binele, what do you say now? Your mother still has some sense. I am only a woman, but I am a rabbi's daughter, and a scholar has an eye for people. I took one look and I thought to myself—it's he! But nowadays the eggs are cleverer than the chickens. She says to me: 'No, it can't be.' And in the meantime you disappear. I was already beginning to think, myself: Who knows, one's no more than human, anybody can make a mistake. But when I saw you come back, I knew it was you. My dear man, we've been waiting here since half past seven in the evening. We weren't alone; there was a whole group of teachers, educators, a few writers too. But then it grew later and later and people went home. They have wives, children. Some have to get up in the morning to go to work. But I said to my daughter, 'I won't go. I won't allow my favorite writer, whose every word I treasure as a pearl, to come here and find no one waiting for him. If you want, my child,' I said to her, 'you can go home and go to bed.' What's a night's sleep? When I was young, I used to think that if you missed a night's sleep the world would go under. But Hitler taught us a lesson. He taught us a lesson I won't forget until I lie with shards over my eyes. You look at me and you see an old, sick woman, a cripple, but I did hard labor in Hitler's camps. I dug ditches and loaded railway cars. Was there anything I didn't do? It was there that I caught my rheumatism. At night we slept on plank shelves not fit for dogs, and we were so hungry that—"

"You'll have enough time to talk later, Momma. It's the middle of the night," her daughter interrupted.

It was only then that I took a closer look at the daughter. Her figure and general appearance were those of a young girl, but she was obviously in her late twenties, or even early thirties. She was small, narrow, with yellowish hair combed back and tied into a bun. Her face was of a sickly pallor, covered with freckles. She had yellow eyes, a round forehead, a crooked nose, thin lips, and a long chin. Around her neck she wore a mannish scarf. She reminded me of a Hassidic boy.

The few words she spoke were marked by a provincial Polish accent I had forgotten during my years in America. She made me think of rye bread, caraway seeds, cottage cheese, and the water brought by water carriers from the well in pails slung on a wooden yoke over their shoulders.

"Thank you, but I have patience to listen," I said.

"When my mother begins to talk about those years, she can talk for a week and a day—"

"Hush, hush, your mother isn't as crazy as you think. It's true, our nerves were shattered out there. It is a wonder we are not running around stark mad in the streets. But what about her? As you see her, she too was in Auschwitz waiting for the ovens. I did not even know she was alive. I was sure she was lost, and you can imagine a mother's feelings! I thought she had gone the way of her three brothers; but after the liberation we found each other. What did they want from us, the beasts? My husband was a holy man, a scribe. My sons worked hard to earn a piece of bread, because inscribing mezuzahs doesn't bring much of an income. My husband, himself, fasted more often than he ate. The glory of God rested on his face. My sons were killed by the murderers—"

"Momma, will you please stop?"

"I'll stop, I'll stop. How much longer will I last, anyway? But she is right. First of all, my dear man, we must take care of you. The president gave me the name of a hotel—they made all the reservations for you—but my daughter didn't hear what he said, and I forgot it. This forgetting is my misfortune. I put something down and I don't know where. I keep looking for things, and that's how my whole days go by. So maybe, my dear writer, you'll spend the night with us? We don't have such a fine apartment. It's cold, it's shabby. Still, it's better than no place at all. I'd telephone the president, but I'm afraid to wake him up at night. He has such a temper, may he forgive me; he keeps shouting that we aren't civilized. So I say to him: 'The Germans are civilized, go to them. . . .' "

"Come with us, the night is three quarters gone, anyway," the daughter said to me. "He should have written it down instead of just saying it; and if he said it, he should have said it to me, not to my mother. She forgets everything. She puts on her glasses and cries, 'Where are my glasses?' Sometimes I have to laugh. Let me have your valise."

"What are you saying? I can carry it myself, it isn't heavy."

"You are not used to carrying things, but I have learned out there to carry heavy loads. If you would see the rocks I used to lift, you wouldn't believe your eyes. I don't even believe it myself anymore. Sometimes it seems to me it was all an evil dream. . . ."

"Heaven forbid, you will not carry my valise. That's all I need. . . ."

"He is a gentleman, he is a fine and gentle man. I knew it at once as soon as I read him for the first time," the mother said. "You wouldn't believe me, but we read your stories even in the camps. After the war, they began to send us books, and I came across one of your stories. I don't remember what it was called, but I read it and a darkness lifted off my heart. 'Binele,' I said—she was already with me then—'I've found a treasure.' Those were my words. . . ."

"Thank you, thank you very much."

"Don't thank me, don't thank me. It's we who have to thank you. All the troubles come from people being deaf and blind. They don't see the next man and so they torture him. We are wandering among blind evildoers. . . . Binele, don't let this dear man carry the valise. . . ."

"Yes, please give it to me!"

I had to plead with Binele to let me carry it. She almost tried to pull it out of my hands.

We went outside and a taxi drove up. It was not easy to get the mother into it. I still cannot understand how she had managed to come to the station. I had to lift her up and put her in. In the process, she dropped one of her canes, and Binele and I had to look for it in the snow. The driver had already begun to grumble and scold in his Canadian French. Afterward, the car began to pitch and roll over dimly lit streets covered with snow and overgrown with mountains of ice. The tires had chains on them, but the taxi skidded backward several times.

We finally drove into a street that was reminiscent of a small town in Poland: murky, narrow, with wooden houses. The sick woman hastily opened her purse, but I paid before she had time to take out her money. Both women chided me, and the driver demanded that we get out as quickly as possible. I virtually had to carry the crippled woman out of the taxi. Again, we had to look for her cane in the deep snow. Afterward, her daughter and I half led, half dragged her up a flight of steps. They opened the door and I was suddenly enveloped in odors I had long forgotten: moldy potatoes, rotting onions, chicory, and something else I could not even name. In some mysterious way the mother and daughter had managed to bring with them the whole atmosphere of wretched poverty from their old home in Poland.

They lit a kerosene lamp and I saw an apartment with tattered wallpaper, a rough wooden floor, and spider webs in every corner. The kerosene stove was out and the rooms were drafty. On a bench stood cracked pots, chipped plates, cups without handles. I even caught sight of a besom on a pile of sweepings. No stage director, I thought, could have done a better job of reproducing such a scene of old-country misery.

Binele began to apologize. "What a mess, no? We were in such a hurry to get to the station, we didn't even have time to wash the dishes. And what's the good of washing or cleaning here, anyway? It's an old, run-down shanty. The landlady knows only one thing: to come for the rent every month. If you're late one day, she's ready to cut your throat. Still, after everything we went through over there, this is a palace. . . ."

And Binele laughed, exposing a mouthful of widely spaced teeth with gold fillings that must have been made when she was still across the ocean.

3

They made my bed on a folding cot in a tiny room with barred windows. Binele covered me with two blankets and spread my coat on top of them. But it was still as cold as outside. I lay under all the coverings and could not warm up.

Suddenly I remembered my manuscript. Where was the manuscript of my lecture? I had had it in the breast pocket of my coat. Afraid to sit up, lest the cot should collapse, I tried to find it. But the manuscript was not there. I looked in my jacket, which hung on a chair nearby, but it was not there either. I was certain that I had not put it into the valise, for I had opened the valise only to get the cognac. I had intended to open it for the customs officers, but they had only waved me on, to indicate it was not necessary.

It was clear to me that I had lost the manuscript. But how? The mother and daughter had told me that the lecture was postponed to the next day, but what would I read? There was only one hope: perhaps it had dropped on the floor when Binele was covering me with the coat. I felt the floor, trying not to make a sound, but the cot creaked at the slightest movement. It even seemed to me that it began to creak in advance, when I only thought of moving. Inanimate things are not really inanimate. . . .

The mother and daughter were evidently not asleep. I heard a whispering, a mumbling from the next room. They were arguing about something quietly, but about what?

The loss of the manuscript, I thought, was a Freudian accident. I was not pleased with the essay from the very first. The tone I took in it was too grandiloquent. Still, what was I to talk about that evening? I might get confused from the very first sentences, like that speaker who had started his lecture with, "Peretz was a peculiar man," and could not utter another word.

If only I could sleep! I had not slept the previous night either. When I have to make a public appearance, I don't sleep for nights. The loss of the manuscript was a real catastrophe! I tried to close my eyes, but they kept opening by themselves. Something bit me; but as soon as I wanted to scratch, the cot shook and screamed like a sick man in pain.

I lay there, silent, stiff, wide-awake. A mouse scratched somewhere in a hole, and then I heard a sound, as of some beast with saw and fangs trying to saw through the floorboards. A mouse could not have raised such noise. It was some monster trying to cut down the foundations of the building. . . .

"Well, this adventure will be the end of me!" I said to myself. "I won't come out of here alive."

I lay benumbed, without stirring a limb. My nose was stuffed and I was breathing the icy air of the room through my mouth. My throat felt constricted. I had to cough, but I did not want to disturb the mother and daughter. A cough might also bring down the ramshackle cot. . . . Well, let me imagine that I had remained under Hitler in wartime. Let me get some taste of that, too. . . .

I imagined myself somewhere in Treblinka or Maidanek. I had done hard labor all day long. Now I was lying on a plank shelf. Tomorrow there would probably be a "selection," and since I was no longer well, I would be sent to the ovens. . . . I mentally began to say goodbye to the few people close to me. I must have dozed off, for I was awakened by loud cries. Binele was shouting: "Momma! Momma! Momma! . . ." The door flew open and Binele called me: "Help me! Mother is dead!"

I wanted to jump off the cot but it collapsed under me, and instead of jumping, I had to raise myself. I cried: "What happened?"

Binele screamed: "She is cold! Where are the matches? Call a doctor! Call a doctor! Put on the light! Oh, Momma! . . . Momma! Momma!"

I never carry matches with me, since I do not smoke. I went in my pajamas to the bedroom. In the dark I collided with Binele. I asked her: "How can I call a doctor?"

She did not answer, but opened the door into the hallway and shouted, "Help, people, help! My mother is dead!" She cried with all her strength, as women cry in the Jewish small towns in Poland, but nobody responded. I tried to look for matches, knowing in advance that I would not find them in this strange house. Binele returned and we collided again in the dark. She clung to me with unexpected force and wailed: "Help! Help! I have nobody else in the world! She was all I had!"

And she broke into a wild lament, leaving me stunned and speechless.

"Find a match! Light the lamp!" I finally cried out, although I knew that my words were wasted.

"Call a doctor! Call a doctor!" she screamed, undoubtedly realizing herself the senselessness of her demand.

She half led, half pulled me to the bed where her mother lay. I put out my hand and touched her body. I began to look for her hand, found it, and tried to feel her pulse, but there was no pulse. The hand hung heavy and limp. It was cold as only a dead thing is cold. Binele seemed to understand what I was doing and kept silent for a while.

"Well, well? She's dead? . . . She's dead! . . . She had a sick heart! . . . Help me! Help me!"

"What can I do? I can't see anything!" I said to her, and my words seemed to have double meaning.

"Help me! . . . Help me! . . . Momma!"

"Are there no neighbors in the house?" I asked.

"There is a drunkard over us. . . ."

"Perhaps we can get matches from him?"

Binele did not answer. I suddenly became aware of how cold I felt. I had to put something on or I would catch pneumonia. I shivered and my teeth chattered. I started out for the room where I had slept but found myself in the kitchen. I returned and nearly threw Binele over. She was, herself, half naked. Unwittingly I touched her breast.

"Put something on!" I told her. "You'll catch a cold!"

"I do not want to live! I do not want to live! . . . She had no right to go to the station! . . . I begged her, but she is so stubborn. . . . She had nothing to eat. She would not even take a glass of tea. . . . What shall I do now? Where shall I go? Oh, Momma, Momma!"

Then, suddenly, it was quiet. Binele must have gone upstairs to knock on the drunkard's door. I remained alone with a corpse in the dark. A long-forgotten terror possessed me. I had the eerie feeling that the dead woman was trying to approach me, to seize me with her cold hands, to clutch at me and drag me off to where she was now. After all, I was responsible for her death. The strain of coming out to meet me had killed her. I started toward the outside door, as though ready to run out into the street. I stumbled on a chair and struck my knee. Bony fingers stretched after me. Strange beings screamed at me silently. There was a ringing in my ears and saliva filled my mouth as though I were about to faint.

Strangely, instead of coming to the outside door, I found myself back in my room. My feet stumbled on the flattened cot. I bent down to pick up my overcoat and put it on. It was only then that I realized how cold I was and how cold it was in that house. The coat was like an ice bag against my body. I trembled as with ague. My teeth clicked, my legs shook. I was ready to fight off the dead woman, to wrestle with her in mortal combat. I felt my heart hammering frighteningly loud and fast. No heart could long endure such violent knocking. I thought that Binele would find two corpses when she returned, instead of one.

I heard talk and steps and saw a light. Binele had brought down the upstairs neighbor. She had a man's coat over her shoulders. The neighbor carried a burning candle. He was a huge man, dark, with thick black hair and a long nose. He was barefoot and wore a bathrobe over his pajamas. What struck me most in my panic was the enormous size of his feet. He went to the bed with his candle and shadows danced after him and wavered across the dim ceiling.

One glance at the woman told me that she was dead. Her face had altered completely. Her mouth had become strangely thin and sunken; it was no longer a mouth, but a hole. The face was yellow, rigid, and claylike. Only the gray hair looked alive. The neighbor muttered something in French. He bent over the woman and felt her forehead. He uttered a single word and Binele began to scream and wail again. He tried to speak to her, to tell her something else, but she evidently did not understand his language. He shrugged his shoulders, gave me the candle, and started back. My hand trembled so uncontrollably that the small flame tossed in all directions and almost went out. I let some tallow drip on the wardrobe and set the candle in it.

Binele began to tear her hair and let out such a wild lament that I cried angrily at her: "Stop screaming!"

She gave me a sidelong glance, full of hate and astonishment, and answered quietly and sensibly: "She was all I had in the world. . . ."

"I know, I understand. . . . But screaming won't help."

My words appeared to have restored her to her senses. She stood silently by the bed, looking down at her mother. I stood on the opposite side. I clearly remembered that the woman had had a short nose; now it had grown long and hooked, as though death had made manifest a hereditary trait that had been hidden during her lifetime. Her forehead and eyebrows had acquired a new and masculine quality. Binele's sorrow seemed for a while to have given way to stupor. She stared, wide-eyed, as if she did not recognize her own mother.

I glanced at the window. How long could a night last, even a winter night? Would the sun never rise? Could this be the moment of that cosmic catastrophe that David Hume had envisaged as a theoretical possibility? But the panes were just beginning to turn gray.

I went to the window and wiped the misty pane. The night outside was already intermingled with blurs of daylight. The contours of the street were becoming faintly visible; piles of snow, small houses, roofs. A street lamp glimmered in the distance, but it cast no light. I raised my eyes to the sky. One half was still full of stars; the other was already flushed with morning. For a few seconds I seemed to have forgotten all that had happened and gave myself up entirely to the birth of the new day. I saw the stars go out one by one. Streaks of red and rose and yellow stretched across the sky, as in a child's painting.

"What shall I do now? What shall I do now?" Binele began to cry again. "Whom shall I call? Where shall I go? Call a doctor! Call a doctor!" And she broke into sobs.

I turned to her. "What can a doctor do now?"

"But someone should be called."

"You have no relatives?"

"None. I've no one in the world."

"What about the members of your lecture club?"

"They don't live in this neighborhood. . . ."

I went to my room and began to dress. My clothes were icy. My suit, which had been pressed before my journey, was crumpled. My shoes looked like misshapen clodhoppers. I caught sight of my face in a mirror, and it shocked me. It was hollow, dirty, paper-gray, covered with stubble. Outside, the snow began to fall again.

"What can I do for you?" I asked Binele. "I'm a stranger here. I don't know where to go."

"Woe is me! What am I doing to you? You are the victim of our misfortune. I shall go out and telephone the police, but I cannot leave my mother alone."

"I'll stay here."

"You will? She loved you. She never stopped talking about you. . . . All day yesterday. . . ."

I sat down on a chair and kept my eyes away from the dead woman. Binele dressed herself. Ordinarily I would be afraid to remain alone with a corpse. But I was half frozen, half asleep. I was exhausted after the miserable night. A deep despair came over me. It was a long, long time since I had seen such wretchedness and so much tragedy. My years in America seemed to have been swept away by that one night and I was taken back, as though by magic, to my worst days in Poland, to the bitterest crisis of my life. I heard the outside door close. Binele was gone. I could no longer remain sitting in the room with the dead woman. I ran out to the kitchen. I opened the door leading to the stairs. I stood by the open door as though ready to escape as soon as the corpse began to do those tricks that I had dreaded since childhood. . . . I said to myself that it was foolish to be afraid of this gentle woman, this cripple who had loved me while alive and who surely did not hate me now, if the dead felt anything. But all the boyhood fears were back upon me. My ribs felt chilled, as if some icy fingers moved over them. My heart thumped and fluttered like the spring in a broken clock. . . . Everything within me was strained. The slightest rustle and I would have dashed down the stairs in terror. The door to the street downstairs had glass panes, but they were half frosted over, half misty. A pale glow filtered through them as at dusk. An icy cold came from below. Suddenly I heard steps. The corpse? I wanted to run, but I realized that the steps came from the upper floor. I saw someone coming down. It was the upstairs neighbor on his way to work, a huge man in rubber boots and a coat with a kind of cowl, a metal lunch box in his hands. He glanced at me curiously and began to speak to me in Canadian French. It was good to be with another human being for a moment. I nodded, gestured with my hands, and answered him in English. He tried again and again to say something in his unfamiliar language, as though he believed that if I listened more carefully I would finally understand him. In the end he mumbled something and threw up his arms. He went out and slammed the door. Now I was all alone in the whole house.

What if Binele should not return? I began to toy with the fantasy that she might run away. Perhaps I'd be suspected of murder?

Everything was possible in this world. I stood with my eyes fixed on the outside door. I wanted only one thing now—to return as quickly as possible to New York. My home, my job seemed totally remote and insubstantial, like memories of a previous incarnation. Who knows? Perhaps my whole life in New York had been no more than a hallucination? I began to search in my breast pocket. . . . Did I lose my citizenship papers, together with the text of my lecture? I felt a stiff paper. Thank God, the citizenship papers are here. I could have lost them, too. This document was now testimony that my years in America had not been an invention.

Here is my photograph. And my signature. Here is the government stamp. True, these were also inanimate, without life, but they symbolized order, a sense of belonging, law. I stood in the doorway and for the first time really read the paper that made me a citizen of the United States. I became so absorbed that I had almost forgotten the dead woman. Then the outside door opened and I saw Binele, covered with snow. She wore the same shawl that her mother had worn yesterday.

"I cannot find a telephone!"

She broke out crying. I went down to meet her, slipping the citizenship papers back into my pocket. Life had returned. The long nightmare was over. I put my arms around Binele and she did not try to break away. I became wet from the melting snow. We stood there midway up the stairs and rocked back and forth—a lost Yiddish writer, and a victim of Hitler and of my ill-starred lecture. I saw a number tattooed above her wrist and heard myself saying: "Binele, I won't abandon you. I swear by the soul of your mother. . . ."

Binele's body became limp in my arms. She raised her eyes and whispered: "Why did she do it? She just waited for your coming. . . ."

BERNARD MALAMUD

(1914–1986)

Bernard Malamud, like a number of the writers in this anthology, was gifted with an unusually sharp, sympathetic, mimetic ear for the cadences of speech; in Malamud's case, for the cadences of Jewish-American speech. (And this surprisingly—at least, for admirers who met with him in person. For, as it happened, Malamud spoke a rather formal, precise, uninflected American English.) Though his fiction is of a near-uniform quality, he was ambitious in its variety: now a chronicler of comic absurdities, now a poet of tragic, thwarted lives, now an Olympian gazing down, with a bemused eye, upon the follies of humankind. "My Son the Murderer" is a tour de force of pathos and betrayal; one of the most memorable, as it is surely one of the most succinct, testimonies to the generational dissonances of the 1960's in an America at war with Vietnam.

Born in Brooklyn, Bernard Malamud taught high school during the 1940's, until, with the publication of his early stories in such influential journals as Partisan Review *and* Commentary, *he began a long and distinguished career as a university teacher. Among his major titles are the novels* The Natural *(1952),* The Assistant *(1957),* The Fixer *(1966), and* Dubin's Lives *(1979), and the short story collections* The Magic Barrel *(1958), which received a National Book Award,* Idiots First *(1963),* Pictures of Fidelman *(1969), and* Rembrandt's Hat *(1973).* The Stories of Bernard Malamud *was published in 1983.*

My Son the Murderer

He wakes feeling his father is in the hallway, listening. He listens to him sleep and dream. Listening to him get up and fumble for his pants. He won't put on his shoes. To him not going to the kitchen to eat. Staring with shut eyes in the mirror. Sitting an hour on the toilet. Flipping the pages of a book he can't read. To his anguish, loneliness. The father stands in the hall. The son hears him listen.

My son the stranger, he won't tell me anything.

I open the door and see my father in the hall. Why are you standing there, why don't you go to work?

On account of I took my vacation in the winter instead of the summer like I usually do.

What the hell for if you spend it in this dark smelly hallway, watching my every move? Guessing what you can't see. Why are you always spying on me?

My father goes to the bedroom and after a while sneaks out in the hallway again, listening.

I hear him sometimes in his room but he don't talk to me and I don't know what's what. It's a terrible feeling for a father. Maybe someday he will write me a letter, My dear father . . .

My dear son Harry, open up your door. My son the prisoner.

My wife leaves in the morning to stay with my married daughter, who is expecting her fourth child. The mother cooks and cleans for her and takes care of the three children. My daughter is having a bad pregnancy, with high blood pressure, and lays in bed most of the time. This is what the doctor advised her. My wife is gone all day. She worries something is wrong with Harry. Since he graduated college last summer he is alone, nervous, in his own thoughts. If you talk to him, half the time he yells if he answers you. He reads the papers, smokes, he stays in his room. Or once in a while he goes for a walk in the street.

How was the walk, Harry?

A walk.

My wife advised him to go look for work, and a couple of times he went, but when he got some kind of an offer he didn't take the job.

It's not that I don't want to work. It's that I feel bad.

So why do you feel bad?

I feel what I feel. I feel what is.

Is it your health, sonny? Maybe you ought to go to a doctor?

I asked you not to call me by that name any more. It's not my health. Whatever it is I don't want to talk about it. The work wasn't the kind I want.

So take something temporary in the meantime, my wife said to him.

He starts to yell. Everything's temporary. Why should I add more to what's temporary? My gut feels temporary. The goddamn world is temporary. On top of that I don't want temporary work. I want the opposite of temporary, but where is it? Where do you find it?

My father listens in the kitchen.

My temporary son.

She says I'll feel better if I work. I say I won't. I'm twenty-two since December, a college graduate, and you know where you can stick that. At night I watch the news programs. I watch the war from day to day. It's a big burning war on a small screen. It rains bombs and the flames go higher. Sometimes I lean over and touch the war with the flat of my hand. I wait for my hand to die.

My son with the dead hand.

I expect to be drafted any day but it doesn't bother me the way it used to. I won't go. I'll go to Canada or somewhere I can go.

The way he is frightens my wife and she is glad to go to my daughter's house early in the morning to take care of the three children. I stay with him in the house but he don't talk to me.

You ought to call up Harry and talk to him, my wife says to my daughter.

I will sometime but don't forget there's nine years' difference between our ages. I think he thinks of me as another mother around and one is enough. I used to like him when he was a little boy but now it's hard to deal with a person who won't reciprocate to you.

She's got high blood pressure. I think she's afraid to call.

I took two weeks off from my work. I'm a clerk at the stamps window in the post office. I told the superintendent I wasn't feeling so good, which is no lie, and he said I should take sick leave. I said I wasn't that sick, I only needed a little vacation. But I told my friend Moe Berkman I was staying out because Harry has me worried.

I understand what you mean, Leo. I got my own worries and anxieties about my kids. If you got two girls growing up you got hostages to fortune. Still in all we got to live. Why don't you come to poker on this Friday night? We got a nice game going. Don't deprive yourself of a good form of relaxation.

I'll see how I feel by Friday, how everything is coming along. I can't promise you.

Try to come. These things, if you give them time, all pass away. If it looks better to you, come on over. Even if it don't look so good, come on over anyway because it might relieve your tension and worry that you're under. It's not so good for your heart at your age if you carry that much worry around.

It's the worst kind of worry. If I worry about myself I know what the worry is. What I mean, there's no mystery. I can say to myself, Leo you're a big fool, stop worrying about nothing—over what, a few bucks? Over my health that has always stood up pretty good although I have my ups and downs? Over that I'm now close to sixty and not getting any younger? Everybody that don't die by age fifty-nine gets to be sixty. You can't beat time when it runs along with you. But if the worry is about somebody else, that's the worst kind. That's the real worry because if he won't tell you, you can't get inside of the other person and find out why. You don't know where's the switch to turn off. All you do is worry more.

So I wait out in the hall.

Harry, don't worry so much about the war.

Please don't tell me what to worry about or what not to worry about.

Harry, your father loves you. When you were a little boy, every night when I came home you used to run to me. I picked you up and lifted you up to the ceiling. You liked to touch it with your small hand.

I don't want to hear about that any more. It's the very thing I don't want to hear. I don't want to hear about when I was a child.

Harry, we live like strangers. All I'm saying is I remember better days. I remember when we weren't afraid to show we loved each other.

He says nothing.

Let me cook you an egg.

An egg is the last thing in the world I want.

So what do you want?

He put his coat on. He pulled his hat off the clothes tree and went down into the street.

Harry walked along Ocean Parkway in his long overcoat and creased brown hat. His father was following him and it filled him with rage.

He walked at a fast pace up the broad avenue. In the old days there was a bridle path at the side of the walk where the concrete bicycle path was now. And there were fewer trees, their black branches cutting the sunless sky. At the corner of Avenue X, just about where you can smell Coney Island, he crossed the street and began to walk home. He pretended not to see his father cross over, though he was infuriated. The father crossed over and followed his son home. When he got to the house he figured Harry was upstairs already. He was in his room with the door shut. Whatever he did in his room he was already doing.

Leo took out his small key and opened the mailbox. There were three letters. He looked to see if one of them was, by any chance, from his son to him. My dear father, let me explain myself. The reason I act as I do . . . There was no such letter. One of the letters was from the Post Office Clerks Benevolent Society, which he slipped into his coat pocket. The other two letters were for Harry. One was from the draft board. He brought it up to his son's room, knocked on the door and waited.

He waited for a while.

To the boy's grunt he said, There is a draft-board letter here for you. He turned the knob and entered the room. His son was lying on his bed with his eyes shut.

Leave it on the table.

Do you want me to open it for you, Harry?

No, I don't want you to open it. Leave it on the table. I know what's in it.

Did you write them another letter?

That's my goddamn business.

The father left it on the table.

The other letter to his son he took into the kitchen, shut the door, and boiled up some water in a pot. He thought he would read it quickly and seal it carefully with a little paste, then go downstairs and put it back in the mailbox. His wife would take it out with her key when she returned from their daughter's house and bring it up to Harry.

The father read the letter. It was a short letter from a girl. The girl said Harry had borrowed two of her books more than six months ago and since she valued them highly she would like him to send them back to her. Could he do that as soon as possible so that she wouldn't have to write again?

As Leo was reading the girl's letter Harry came into the kitchen and when he saw the surprised and guilty look on his father's face, he tore the letter out of his hand.

I ought to murder you the way you spy on me.

Leo turned away, looking out of the small kitchen window into the dark apartment-house courtyard. His face burned, he felt sick.

Harry read the letter at a glance and tore it up. He then tore up the envelope marked personal.

If you do this again don't be surprised if I kill you. I'm sick of you spying on me.

Harry, you are talking to your father.

He left the house.

Leo went into his room and looked around. He looked in the dresser drawers and found nothing unusual. On the desk by the window was a paper Harry had written on. It said: Dear Edith, why don't you go fuck yourself? If you write me another letter I'll murder you.

The father got his hat and coat and left the house. He ran slowly for a while, running then walking, until he saw Harry on the other side of the street. He followed him, half a block behind.

He followed Harry to Coney Island Avenue and was in time to see him board a trolleybus going to the Island. Leo had to wait for the next one. He thought of taking a taxi and following the trolleybus, but no taxi came by. The next bus came by fifteen minutes later and he took it all the way to the Island. It was February and Coney Island was wet, cold, and deserted. There were few cars on Surf Avenue and few people on the streets. It felt like snow. Leo walked on the boardwalk amid snow flurries, looking for his son. The gray sunless beaches were empty. The hot-dog stands, shooting galleries, and bathhouses were shuttered up. The gunmetal ocean, moving like melted lead, looked freezing. A wind blew in off the water and worked its way into his clothes so that he shivered as he walked. The wind white-capped the leaden waves and the slow surf broke on the empty beaches with a quiet roar.

He walked in the blow almost to Sea Gate, searching for his son, and then he walked back again. On his way toward Brighton Beach he saw a man on the shore standing in the foaming surf. Leo hurried down the boardwalk stairs and onto the ribbed-sand beach. The man on the roaring shore was Harry, standing in water to the tops of his shoes.

Leo ran to his son. Harry, it was a mistake, excuse me, I'm sorry I opened your letter.

Harry did not move. He stood in the water, his eyes on the swelling leaden waves.

Harry, I'm frightened. Tell me what's the matter. My son, have mercy on me.

I'm frightened of the world, Harry thought. It fills me with fright.

He said nothing.

A blast of wind lifted his father's hat and carried it away over the beach. It looked as though it were going to be blown into the surf, but then the wind blew it toward the boardwalk, rolling like a wheel along the wet sand. Leo chased after his hat. He chased it one way, then another, then toward the water. The wind blew the hat against his legs and he caught it. By now he was crying. Breathless, he wiped his eyes with icy fingers and returned to his son at the edge of the water.

He is a lonely man. This is the type he is. He will always be lonely.

My son who made himself into a lonely man.

Harry, what can I say to you? All I can say to you is who says life is easy? Since when? It wasn't for me and it isn't for you. It's life, that's the way it is—what more can I say? But if a person don't want to live what can he do if he's dead? Nothing. Nothing is nothing, it's better to live.

Come home, Harry, he said. It's cold here. You'll catch a cold with your feet in the water.

Harry stood motionless in the water and after a while his father left. As he was leaving, the wind plucked his hat off his head and sent it rolling along the shore.

My father listens in the hallway. He follows me in the street. We meet at the edge of the water.

He runs after his hat.

My son stands with his feet in the ocean.

SAUL BELLOW
(1915–   )

Saul Bellow, born in Quebec, came of age in the Chicago of the 1920's and 1930's, "that gloomy city," which, by way of numerous works of fiction, he has virtually appropriated as his own. This recent story is both a valentine to that city and to the author's bemused recollection of his own idealistic youth.

One of the most publicly honored of American writers, Saul Bellow began his career with the sombre meditations of Dangling Man *(1944) and the tightly constructed* The Victim *(1947). Subsequent novels have been far freer, extravagant, colloquial, comic and didactic at once, establishing Bellow's reputation as a brilliant portraitist and stylist. Among his outstanding works are* The Adventures of Augie March *(1953), which can be read as a Jewish-American counterpart to Ralph Ellison's African-American* Invisible Man; Seize the Day *(1956),* Henderson the Rain King *(1959),* Herzog *(1964),* Mr. Sammler's Planet *(1970),* Humboldt's Gift *(1975), and* More Die of Heartbreak *(1987). Bellow has written comparatively few short stories, collected in* Mosby's Memoirs *(1968) and* Him with His Foot in His Mouth *(1984).*

"Something To Remember Me By," though distinctively Bellow, is cast in a sweetly rueful tone, as in a sepia print. It is one of the few stories addressed to a child—a story imagined as a gift, though not a gift of any conventional sort.

Something To Remember Me By

When there is too much going on, more than you can bear, you may choose to assume that nothing in particular is happening, that your life is going round and round like a turntable. Then one day you are aware that what you took to be a turntable, smooth, flat, and even, was in fact a whirlpool, a vortex. My first knowledge of the hidden work of uneventful days goes back to February 1933.

The exact date won't matter much to you. I like to think, however, that you, my only child, will want to hear about this hidden work as it relates to me. When you were a small boy you were keen on family history. You will quickly understand that I couldn't tell a child what I am about to tell you now. You don't talk about deaths and vortices to a kid, not nowadays. In my time my parents didn't hesitate to speak of death and dying. What they seldom mentioned was sex. We've got it the other way around. My mother died when I was an adolescent. I've often told you that. What I didn't tell you was that I knew she was dying and didn't allow myself to think about it—there's your turntable. The month was February, as I've said, adding that the exact date wouldn't matter to you. I should confess that I myself avoided fixing it. Chicago in winter, armored in gray ice, the sky low, the going heavy.

I was a high school senior, an indifferent student, generally unpopular, a background figure in the school. It was only as a high jumper that I performed in public. I had no form at all, a curious last-minute spring or convulsion put me over the bar. But this was what the school turned out to see.

Unwilling to study, I was bookish nevertheless. I was secretive about my family life. The truth is that I didn't want to talk about my mother. Besides, I had no language as yet for the oddity of my peculiar interests.

But let me get on with that significant day in the early part of February.

It began like any other winter school day in Chicago—grimly ordinary. The temperatures a few degrees above zero, botanical frost shapes on the windowpane, the snow swept up in heaps, the ice gritty and the streets, block after block, bound together by the iron of the sky. A breakfast of porridge, toast, and tea. Late as usual, I stopped for a moment to look into my mother's sickroom. I bent near and said, "It's Louie, going to school." She seemed to nod. Her eyelids were brown, her face was much lighter. I hurried off with my books on a strap over my shoulder.

When I came to the boulevard on the edge of the park, two small men rushed out of a doorway with rifles, wheeled around aiming upward, and fired at pigeons near the rooftop. Several birds fell straight down, and the men scooped up the soft bodies and ran indoors, dark little guys in fluttering white shirts. Depression hunters and their city game. Moments before, the police car had loafed by at ten miles an hour. The men had waited it out.

This had nothing to do with me. I mention it merely because it happened. I stepped around the blood spots and crossed into the park.

To the right of the path, behind the winter lilacs, the crust of the snow was broken. In the dead black night Stephanie and I had necked there, petted, my hands under her raccoon coat, under her sweater, under her skirt, adolescents kissing without restraint. Her coonskin cap had slipped to the back of her head. She opened the musky coat to me to have me closer.

I had to run to reach the school doors before the last bell. I was on notice from the family—no trouble with teachers, no summons from the principal at a time like this. And I did observe the rules, although I despised classwork. But I spent all the money I could lay hands on at Hammersmark's Bookstore. I read *Manhattan Transfer, The Enormous Room,* and *A Portrait of the Artist.* I belonged to the Cercle Français and the Senior Discussion Club. The club's topic for this afternoon was Von Hindenburg's choice of Hitler to form a new government. But I couldn't go to meetings now, I had an after-school job. My father had insisted that I find one.

After classes, on my way to work, I stopped at home to cut myself a slice of bread and a wedge of Wisconsin cheese, and to see whether my mother might be awake. During her last days she was heavily sedated and rarely said anything. The tall, square-shouldered bottle at her bedside was filled with clear red Nembutal. The color of this fluid was always the same, as if it could tolerate no shadow. Now that she could no longer sit up to have it washed, my mother's hair was cut short. This made her face more slender, and her lips were sober. Her breathing was dry and hard, obstructed. The window shade was halfway up. It was scalloped at the bottom and had white fringes. The street ice was dark gray. Snow was piled against the trees. Their trunks had a mineral-black look. Waiting out the winter in their alligator armor they gathered coal soot.

Even when she was awake, my mother couldn't find the breath to speak. She sometimes made signs. Except for the nurse, there was nobody in the house. My father was at business, my sister had a downtown job, my brothers hustled. The eldest, Albert, clerked for a lawyer in the Loop. My brother Len had put me onto a job on the Northwestern commuter trains, and for a while I was a candy butcher, selling chocolate bars and evening papers. When my mother put a stop to this because it kept me too late, I found other work. Just now I was delivering flowers for a shop on North Avenue and riding the streetcars carrying wreaths and bouquets to all parts of the city. Behrens the florist paid me fifty cents for an afternoon; with tips I could earn as much as a dollar. That gave me time to prepare my trigonometry lesson, and, very late at night, after I had seen Stephanie, to read my books. I sat in the kitchen when everyone was sleeping, in deep silence, snowdrifts under the windows and below, the janitor's shovel rasping on the cement and clanging on the furnace door. I read banned books circulated by my classmates, political pamphlets, read *Prufrock* and *Mauberley*. I also studied arcane books too far-out to discuss with anyone.

I read on the streetcars (called trolleys elsewhere). Reading shut out the sights. In fact there *were* no sights—more of the same and then more of the same. Shop fronts, garages, warehouses, narrow brick bungalows.

The city was laid out on a colossal grid, eight blocks to the mile, every fourth street a car line. The days shorts, the streetlights weak, the soiled snowbanks toward evening became a source of light. I carried my carfare in my mitten, where the coins mixed with lint worn away from the lining. Today I was delivering lilies to an uptown address. They were wrapped and pinned in heavy paper. Behrens, spelling out my errand for me, was pale, a narrow-faced man who wore nose glasses. Amid the flowers, he alone had no color—something like the price he paid for being human. He wasted no words: "This delivery will take an hour each way in this traffic, so it'll be your only one. I carry these people on the books, but make sure you get a signature on the bill."

I couldn't say why it was such a relief to get out of the shop, the damp, warm-earth smell, the dense mosses, the prickling cactuses, the glass iceboxes with orchids, gardenias, and sickbed roses. I preferred the brick boredom of the street, the paving stones and steel rails. I drew down the three peaks of my racing-skater's cap and hauled the clumsy package to Robey Street. When the car came panting up there was room for me on the long seat next to the door. Passengers didn't undo their buttons. They were chilled, guarded, muffled, miserable. I had reading matter with me—the remains of a book, the cover gone, the pages held together by binder's thread and flakes of glue. I carried these fifty or sixty pages in the pocket of my short sheepskin. With the one hand I had free I couldn't manage this mutilated book. And on the Broadway–Clark car, reading was out of the question. I had to protect my lilies from the balancing straphangers and people pushing toward the front.

I got down at Ainslie Street holding high the package, which had the shape of a padded kite. The apartment house I was looking for had a courtyard with iron palings. The usual lobby: a floor sinking in the middle, kernels of tile, gaps stuffed with dirt, and a panel of brass mailboxes with earpiece-mouthpieces. No voice came down when I pushed the button; instead, the lock buzzed, jarred, rattled, and I went from the cold of the outer lobby to the overheated mustiness of the inner one. On the second floor one of the two doors on the landing was open, and overshoes and galoshes and rubbers were heaped along the wall. At once I found myself in a crowd of drinkers. All the lights in the house were on, although it was a good hour before dark. Coats were piled on chairs and sofas. All whiskey in those days was bootleg, of course. Holding the flowers high, I parted the mourners. I was quasiofficial. The message went out, "Let the kid through. Go right on, buddy."

The long passageway was full, too, but the dining room was entirely empty. There, a dead girl lay in her coffin. Over her a cut-glass luster was hanging from a taped, deformed artery of wire pulled through the broken plaster. I hadn't expected to find myself looking down into a coffin.

You saw her as she was, without undertaker's makeup, a girl older than Stephanie, not so plump, thin, fair, her straight hair arranged on her dead shoulders. All buoyancy gone, a weight that counted totally on support, not so much lying as sunk in this gray rectangle. I saw what I took to be the pressure mark of fingers on her cheek. Whether she had been pretty or not was no consideration.

A stout woman (certainly the mother), wearing black, opened the swing door from the kitchen and saw me standing over the corpse. I thought she was displeased when she made a fist signal to come forward. As I passed her she drew both fists against her bosom. She said to put the flowers on the sink, and then she pulled the pins and crackled the paper. Big arms, thick calves, a bun of hair, her short nose thin and red. It was Behrens's practice to tie the stalks to slender green sticks. There was never any damage.

On the drainboard of the sink was a baked ham with sliced bread around the platter, a jar of French's mustard and wooden tongue depressors to spread it. I saw and I saw and I saw.

I was on my most discreet and polite behavior with the woman. I looked at the floor to spare her my commiserating face. But why should she care at all about my discreetness; how did I come into this except as a messenger and menial? If she wouldn't observe my behavior, whom was I behaving for? All she wanted was to settle the bill and send me on my way. She picked up her purse, holding it to her body as she had held her fists. "What do I owe Behrens?" she asked me.

"He said you could sign for this."

However, she wasn't going to deal in kindnesses. She said, "No." She said, "I don't want debts following me later on." She gave me a five-dollar bill, she added a tip of fifty cents, and it was I who signed the receipt, as well as I could on the enameled grooves of the sink. I folded the bill small and felt under the sheepskin coat for my watch pocket, ashamed to take money from her within sight of her dead daughter. I wasn't the object of the woman's severity, but her face somewhat frightened me. She leveled the same look at the walls, the door. I didn't figure here, however; this was no death of mine.

As if to take another reading of the girl's plain face, I looked again into the coffin on my way out. And then on the staircase I began to extract the pages from my sheepskin pocket, and in the lobby I hunted for the sentences I had read last night. Yes, here they were:

Nature cannot suffer the human form within her system of laws. When given to her charge, the human being before us is reduced to dust. Ours is the most perfect form to be found on earth. The visible world sustains us until life leaves, and then it must utterly destroy us. Where, then, is the world from which the human form comes?

If you swallowed some food and then died, that morsel of food that would have nourished you in life would hasten your disintegration in death.

This meant that nature didn't make life, it only housed it.

In those days I read many such books. But the one I had read the night before went deeper than the rest. You, my only child, are only too familiar with my lifelong absorption in or craze for further worlds. I used to bore you when I spoke of spirit, or pneuma, and of a continuum of spirit and nature. You were too well educated, respectably rational, to take stock in such terms. I might add, citing a famous scholar, that what is plausible can do without proof. I am not about to pursue this. However, there would be a gap in what I have to tell if I were to leave out my significant book, and this after all is a narrative, not an argument.

Anyway, I returned my pages to the pocket of my sheepskin, and then I didn't know quite what to do. At 4:00, with no more errands, I was somehow not ready to go home. So I walked through the snow to Argyle Street, where my brother-in-law practiced dentistry, thinking that we might travel home together. I prepared an explanation for turning up at his office. "I was on the North Side delivering flowers, saw a dead girl laid out, realized how close I was, and came here." Why did I need to account for my innocent behavior when it *was* innocent? Perhaps because I was always contemplating illicit things. Because I was always being accused. Because I ran a little truck farm of deceits—but self-examination, once so fascinating to me, has become tiresome.

My brother-in-law's office was a high, second-floor walk-up: PHILIP HADDIS D.D.S. Three bay windows at the rounded corner of the building gave you a full view of the street and of the lake, due east—the jagged flats of ice floating. The office door was open, and when I came through the tiny blind (windowless) waiting room and didn't see Philip at the big, back-tilted dentist's chair, I thought that he might have stepped into his lab. He was a good technician and did most of his own work, which was a big saving. Philip wasn't tall, but he was very big, a burly man. The sleeves of his white coat fitted tightly on his bare, thick forearms. The strength of his arms counted when it came to pulling teeth. Lots of patients were referred to him for extractions.

When he had nothing in particular to do he would sit in the chair himself, studying the *Racing Form* between the bent mantis leg of the drill, the gas flame, and the water spurting round and round in the green glass spit-sink. The cigar smell was always thick. Standing in the center of the dental cabinet was a clock under a glass bell. Four gilt weights rotated at its base. This was a gift from my mother. The view from the middle window was divided by a chain that couldn't have been much smaller than the one that stopped the British fleet on the Hudson. This held the weight of the druggist's sign—a mortar and pestle outlined in electric bulbs. There wasn't much daylight left. At noon it was poured out; by 4:00 it had drained away. From one side the banked snow was growing blue, from the other the shops were shining warmth on it.

The dentist's lab was in a cupboard. Easygoing Philip peed in the sink sometimes. It was a long trek to the toilet at the far end of the building, and the hallway was nothing but two walls—a plaster tunnel and a carpet runner edged with brass tape. Philip hated going to the end of the hall.

There was nobody in the lab, either. Philip might have been taking a cup of coffee at the soda fountain in the drugstore below. It was possible also that he was passing the time with Marchek, the doctor with whom he shared the suite of offices. The connecting door was never locked, and I had occasionally sat in Marchek's swivel chair with a gynecology book, studying the colored illustrations and storing up the Latin names.

Marchek's starred glass pane was dark, and I assumed his office to be empty, but when I went in I saw a naked woman lying on the examining table. She wasn't asleep, she seemed to be resting. Becoming aware that I was there, she stirred, and then without haste, disturbing herself as little as possible, she reached for her clothing heaped on Dr. Marchek's desk. Picking out her slip, she put it on her belly—she didn't spread it. Was she dazed, drugged? No, she simply took her sweet time about everything, she behaved with exciting lassitude. Wires connected her nice wrists to a piece of medical apparatus on a wheeled stand.

The right thing would have been to withdraw, but it was already too late for that. Besides, the woman gave no sign that she cared one way or another. She didn't draw the slip over her breasts, she didn't even bring her thighs together. The covering hairs were parted. There was salt, acid, dark, sweet odors. These were immediately effective; I was strongly excited. There was a gloss on her forehead, an exhausted look about the eyes. I believed that I had guessed what she had been doing, but then the room was half dark, and I preferred to avoid any definite thought. Doubt seemed much better, or equivocation.

I remembered that Philip, in his offhand, lazy way, had mentioned a "research project" going on next door. Dr. Marchek was measuring the reactions of partners in the sexual act. "He takes people from the street, he hooks them up and pretends he's collecting graphs. This is for kicks, the science part is horseshit."

The naked woman, then, was an experimental subject.

I had prepared myself to tell Philip about the dead girl on Ainslie Street, but the coffin, the kitchen, the ham, the flowers were as distant from me now as the ice floes on the lake and the killing cold of the water.

"Where did you come from?" the woman said to me.

"From next door—the dentist's office."

"The doctor was about to unstrap me, and I need to get loose. Maybe you can figure out these wires."

If Marchek should be in the inner room, he wouldn't come in now that he heard voices. As the woman raised both her arms so that I could undo the buckles, her breasts swayed, and when I bent over her the odor of her upper body made me think of the frilled brown papers in a box after the chocolates had been eaten—a sweet aftersmell and acrid cardboard mixed. Although I tried hard to stop it, my mother's chest mutilated by cancer surgery passed through my mind. Its gnarled scar tissue. I also called in Stephanie's closed eyes and kissing face—anything to spoil the attraction of this naked young woman. It occurred to me as I undid the clasps that instead of disconnecting her I was hooking myself. We were alone in the darkening office, and I wanted her to reach under the sheepskin and undo my belt for me.

But when her hands were free she wiped the jelly from her wrists and began to dress. She started with her bra, several times lowering her breasts into the cups, and when her arms went backward to fasten the snaps she bent far forward, as if she were passing under a low bough. The cells of my body were like bees, drunker and drunker on sexual honey (I expect that this will change the figure of Grandfather Louie, the old man remembered as this or that but never as a hive of erotic bees).

But I couldn't be blind to the woman's behavior even now. It was very broad, she laid it on. I saw her face in profile, and although it was turned downward there was no mistaking her smile. To use an expression from the Thirties, she was giving me the works. She knew I was about to fall on my face. She buttoned every small button with deliberate slowness, and her blouse had at least twenty such buttons, yet she was still bare from the waist down. Though we were so minor, she and I, a schoolboy and a floozy, we had such major instruments to play. And if we were to go further, whatever happened would never get beyond this room. It would be between the two of us and nobody would ever hear of it. Still, Marchek, that pseudoexperimenter, was probably biding his time in the next room. An old family doctor, he must have been embarrassed and angry. And at any moment, moreover, my brother-in-law Philip might come back.

When the woman slipped down from the leather table she gripped her leg and said she had pulled a muscle. She lifted one heel onto a chair and rubbed her calf, swearing under her breath and looking everywhere with swimming eyes. And then, after she had put on her skirt and fastened her stockings to the garter belt, she pushed her feet into her pumps and limped around the chair, holding it by the arm. She said, "Will you please reach me my coat? Just put it over my shoulders."

She, too, wore a raccoon. As I took it from the hook I wished it had been something else. But Stephanie's coat was newer than this one and twice as heavy. These pelts had dried out, and the fur was thin. The woman was already on her way out, and stooped as I laid the raccoon over her back. Marchek's office had its own exit to the corridor.

At the top of the staircase, the woman asked me to help her down. I said that I would, of course, but I wanted to look once more for my brother-in-law. As she tied the woolen scarf under her chin she smiled at me, with an Oriental wrinkling of her eyes.

Not to check in with Philip wouldn't have been right. My hope was that he would be returning, coming down the narrow corridor in his burly, sauntering, careless way. You won't remember your Uncle Philip. He had played college football, and he still had the look of a tackle, with his swelling, compact forearms. (At Soldier Field today he'd be physically insignificant; in his time, however, he was something of a strong man.)

But there was the long strip of carpet down the middle of the wall-valley, and no one was coming to rescue me. I turned back to his office. If only a patient were sitting in the chair and I could see Philip looking into his mouth, I'd be on track again, excused from taking the woman's challenge. One alternative was to say that I couldn't go with her, that Philip expected me to ride back with him to the Northwest Side. In the empty office I considered this lie, bending my head so that I wouldn't confront the clock with its soundless measured weights revolving. Then I wrote on Philip's memo pad: "Louie, passing by." I left it on the seat of the chair.

The woman had put her arms through the sleeves of the collegiate, rah-rah raccoon and was resting her fur-bundled rear on the bannister. She was passing her compact mirror back and forth, and when I came out she gave the compact a snap and dropped it into her purse.

"Still the charley horse?"

"My lower back, too."

We descended, very slow, both feet on each tread. I wondered what she would do if I were to kiss her. Laugh at me, probably. We were no longer between the four walls where anything might have happened. In the street, space was unlimited. I had no idea how far we were going, how far I would be able to go. Although she was the one claiming to be in pain, it was I who felt sick. She asked me to support her lower back with my hand, and there I discovered what an extraordinary action her hips could perform. At a party I had overheard an older woman saying to another lady, "I know how to make them burn." Hearing this was enough for me.

No special art was necessary with a boy of seventeen, not even so much as being invited to support her with my hand—to feel that intricate, erotic working of her back. I had already *seen* the woman on Marchek's examining table and had also felt the full weight of her when she leaned—when she laid her female substance on me. Moreover, she fully knew my mind. She was the thing I was thinking continually, and how often does thought find its object in circumstances like these—the object *knowing* that it has been found? The woman knew my expectations. She *was*, in the flesh, those expectations. I couldn't have sworn that she was a hooker, a tramp. She might have been an ordinary family girl with a taste for trampishness, acting loose, amusing herself with me, doing a comic sex turn as in those days people sometimes did.

"Where are we headed?"

"If you have to go, I can make it on my own," she said. "It's just Winona Street, the other side of Sheridan Road."

"No, no. I'll walk you there."

She asked whether I was still at school, pointing to the printed pages in my coat pocket.

I observed when we were passing a fruit shop (a boy of my own age emptying bushels of oranges into the lighted window) that, despite the woman's thick-cream color, her eyes were Far Eastern, black.

"You should be about seventeen," she said.

"Just."

She was wearing pumps in the snow and placed each step with care.

"What are you going to be, have you picked your profession?"

I had no use for professions. Utterly none. There were accountants and engineers in the soup lines. In the world slump, professions were useless. You were free, therefore, to make something extraordinary of yourself. I might have said, if I hadn't been excited to the point of sickness, that I didn't ride around the city on the cars to make a buck or to be useful to the family, but to take a reading of this boring, depressed, ugly, endless, rotting city. I couldn't have thought it then, but I now understand that my purpose was to interpret this place. Its power was tremendous. But so was mine, potentially. I refused absolutely to believe for a moment that people here were doing what they thought they were doing. Beneath the apparent life of these streets was their real life, beneath each face the real face, beneath each voice and its words the true tone and the real message. Of course, I wasn't about to say such things. It was beyond me at that time to say them. I was, however, a high-toned kid, "La-di-dah," my critical, satirical brother Albert called me. A high purpose in adolescence will expose you to that.

At the moment, a glamorous, sexual girl had me in tow. I couldn't guess where I was being led, nor how far, nor what she would surprise me with, nor the consequences.

"So the dentist is your brother?"

"In-law—my sister's husband. They live with us. You're asking what he's like? He's a good guy. He likes to lock his office on Friday and go to the races. He takes me to the fights. Also, at the back of the drugstore there's a poker game. . . ."

"*He* doesn't go around with books in his pocket."

"Well, no, he doesn't. He says, 'What's the use? There's too much to keep up or catch up with. You could never in a thousand years do it, so why knock yourself out?' My sister wants him to open a Loop office but that would be too much of a strain. I guess he's for inertia. He's not ready to do more than he's already doing."

"So what are you reading—what's it about?"

I didn't propose to discuss anything with her. I wasn't capable of it. What I had in mind just then was entirely different.

But suppose I had been able to explain. One does have a responsibility to answer genuine questions: "You see, miss, this is the visible world. We live in it, we breathe its air and eat its substance. When we die, however, matter goes to matter and then we're annihilated. Now, which world do we really belong to, this world of matter or another world from which matter takes its orders?"

Not many people were willing to talk about such notions. They made even Stephanie impatient. "When you die, that's it. Dead is dead," she would say. She loved a good time. And when I wouldn't take her downtown to the Oriental Theatre she didn't deny herself the company of other boys. She brought back off-color vaudeville jokes. I think the Oriental was part of a national entertainment circuit. Jimmy Savo, Lou Holtz, and Sophie Tucker played there. I was sometimes too solemn for Stephanie. When she gave imitations of Jimmy Savo singing "River, Stay Away from My Door," bringing her knees together and holding herself tight, she didn't break me up, and she was disappointed.

You would have thought that the book or book-fragment in my pocket was a talisman from a fairy tale to open castle gates or carry me to mountaintops. Yet when the woman asked me what it was, I was too scattered to tell her. Remember, I still kept my hand as instructed on her lower back, tormented by the sexual grind of her movements. I was discovering what the lady at the party had meant by saying, "I know how to make them burn." So of course I was in no condition to talk about the Ego and the Will, or about the secrets of the blood. Yes, I believed that higher knowledge was shared out among all human beings. What else was there to hold us together but this force hidden behind daily consciousness? But to be coherent about it now was absolutely out of the question.

"Can't you tell me?" she said.

"I bought this for a nickel from a bargain table."

"That's how you spend your money?"

I assumed her to mean that I didn't spend it on girls.

"And the dentist is a good-natured, lazy guy," she went on. "What has he got to tell you?"

I tried to review the mental record. What did Phil Haddis say? He said that a stiff prick has no conscience. At the moment it was all I could think of. It amused Philip to talk to me. He was a chum. Where Philip was indulgent, my brother Albert, your late uncle, was harsh. Albert might have taught me something if he had trusted me. He was then a night-school law student clerking for Rowland, the racketeer congressman. He was Rowland's bagman, and Rowland didn't hire him to read law but to make collections. Philip suspected that Albert was skimming, for he dressed sharply. He wore a derby (called, in those days, a Baltimore heater) and a camel's hair topcoat and pointed, mafioso shoes. Toward me, Albert was scornful. He said, "You don't understand fuck-all. You never will."

We were approaching Winona Street, and when we got to her building she'd have no further use for me and send me away. I'd see no more than the flash of the glass and then stare as she let herself in. She was already feeling in her purse for the keys. I was no longer supporting her back, preparing instead to mutter "bye-bye" when she surprised me with a sideward nod, inviting me to enter. I think I had hoped (with sex-polluted hope) that she would leave me in the street. I followed her through another tile lobby and through the inner door. The staircase was fiercely heated by coal-fueled radiators, the skylight three storeys up was wavering, the wallpaper had come unstuck and was curling and bulging. I swallowed my breath. I couldn't draw this heat into my lungs.

This had been a deluxe apartment house once, built for bankers, brokers, and well-to-do professionals. Now it was occupied by transients. In the big front room with its French windows there was a crap game. In the next room people were drinking or drowsing on the old chesterfields. The woman led me through what had once been a private bar—some of the fittings were still in place. Then I followed her through the kitchen—I would have gone anywhere, no questions asked. In the kitchen there were no signs of cooking, neither pots nor dishes. The linoleum was shredding, brown fibers standing like hairs. She led me into a narrower corridor, parallel to the main one. "I have what used to be a maid's room," she said. "It's got a nice view of the alley but there is a private bathroom."

And here we were—an almost empty space. So this was how whores operated—assuming that she was a whore: a bare floor, a narrow cot, a chair by the window, a lopsided clothespress against the wall. I stopped under the light fixture while she passed behind, as if to observe me. Then from the back she gave me a hug and a small kiss on the cheek, more promissory than actual. Her face powder, or perhaps it was her lipstick, had a sort of green-banana fragrance. My heart had never beaten as hard as this.

She said, "Why don't I go into the bathroom awhile and get ready while you undress and lie down in bed. You look like you were brought up neat, so lay your clothes on the chair. You don't want to drop them on the floor."

Shivering (this seemed the one cold room in the house), I began to pull off my things, beginning with the winter-wrinkled boots. The sheepskin I hung over the back of the chair. I pushed my socks into the boots and then my bare feet recoiled from the grit of the floor. I took off everything, as if to disassociate my shirt, my underthings from whatever it was that was about to happen, so that only my body could be guilty. The one thing that couldn't be excepted. When I pulled back the cover and got in I was thinking that the beds in the Bridewell prison would be like this. There was no pillowcase, my head lay on the ticking. What I saw of the outside was only the utility wires hung between the poles like lines on music paper, only sagging, and the glass insulators like clumps of notes. The woman had said nothing about money. Because she liked me. I couldn't believe my luck—luck with a hint of disaster. I blinded myself to the Bridewell metal cot, not meant for two. I felt also that I couldn't hold out if she kept me waiting long. And what feminine thing was she doing in there—undressing, washing, perfuming, changing?

Abruptly, she came out. She had been waiting, nothing else. She still wore the raccoon coat, even the gloves. Without looking at me she walked very quickly, almost running, and opened the window. As soon as the window shot up it let in a blast of cold air, and I stood up on the bed but it was too late to stop her. She took my clothes from the back of the chair and heaved them out. They fell into the alley. I shouted, "What are you doing!" She still refused to turn her head. As she ran away, tying the head scarf under her chin, she left the door open. I could hear her pumps beating double time in the hallway.

I couldn't run after her, could I, and show myself naked to the people in the flat? She had banked on this. When we came in, she must have given the high sign to the man she worked with, and he had been waiting in the alley. When I ran to look out, my things had already been gathered up. All I saw was the back of somebody with a bundle under his arm hurrying in the walkway between two garages. I might have picked up my boots—those she had left me—and jumped from the first-floor window, but I couldn't chase the man very far, and in a few minutes I would have wound up on Sheridan Road naked and freezing.

I had seen a drunk in his union suit, bleeding from the head after he had been rolled and beaten, staggering and yelling in the street. I didn't even have a shirt and drawers. I was as naked as the woman herself had been in the doctor's office, stripped of everything, including the five dollars I had collected for the flowers. And the sheepskin my mother had bought for me last year. Plus the book, the fragment of an untitled book, author unknown. This may have been the most serious loss of all.

Now I could think on my own about the world I really belonged to, whether it was this one or another.

I pulled down the window, and then I went to shut the door. The room didn't seem lived in, but suppose it had a tenant, and what if he were to storm in now and rough me up? Luckily there was a bolt to the door. I pushed it into its loop and then I ran around the room to see what I could find to wear. In the lopsided clothespress, nothing but wire hangers, and in the bathroom, only a cotton hand towel. I tore the blanket off the bed; if I were to slit it I might pull it over my head like a serape, but it was too thin to do me much good in freezing weather. When I pulled the chair over to the clothespress and stood on it, I found a woman's dress behind the molding, and a quilted bed jacket. In a brown paper bag there was a knitted brown tam. I had to put these things on, I had no choice.

It was now, I reckoned, about 5:00. Philip had no fixed schedule. He didn't hang around the office on the off chance that somebody might turn up with a toothache. After his last appointment he locked up and left. He didn't necessarily set out for home, he was not too keen to return to the house. If I wanted to catch him I'd have to run—boots, dress, tam, and jacket, I made my way out of the apartment. Nobody took the slightest interest in me. More people (Philip would have called them transients) had crowded in—it was even likely that the man who had snatched up my clothes in the alley had returned, was among them. The heat in the staircase now was stifling, and the wall paper smelled scorched, as if it were on the point of catching fire. In the street I was struck by a north wind straight from the Pole and the dress and sateen jacket counted for nothing. I was running, though, and had no time to feel it.

Philip would say, "Who was this floozy? Where did she pick you up?" Philip was unexcitable, always mild, amused by me. Anna would badger him with the example of her ambitious brothers—they hustled, they read books. You couldn't fault Philip for being pleased. I anticipate what he'd say—"Did you get in? Then at least you're not going to catch the clap." I depended on Philip now, for I had nothing, not even seven cents for carfare. I could be certain, however, that he wouldn't moralize at me, he'd set about dressing me, he'd scrounge a sweater among his neighborhood acquaintances or take me to the Salvation Army shop on Broadway if that should still be open. He'd go about this in his slow-moving, thick-necked, deliberate way. Not even dancing would speed him up, he spaced out the music to suit him when he did the fox-trot and pressed his cheek to Anna's. He wore a long, calm grin. My private term for this particular expression was Pussy-Veleerum. I saw Philip as fat but strong, strong but cozy, purring but inserting a joking comment. He gave a little suck at the corner of his mouth when he was about to take a swipe at you, and it was then that he was Pussy-Veleerum. A name it never occurred to me to speak aloud.

I sprinted past the windows of the fruit store, the delicatessen, the tailor's shop. I could count on help from Philip. My father, however, was an intolerant, hasty man. Slighter than his sons, handsome, with muscles of white marble (so they seemed to me), laying down the law. It would put him in a rage to see me like this. And it was true that I had failed to consider: my mother dying, the ground frozen, a funeral coming, the dug grave, the packet of sand from the Holy Land to be scattered on the shroud. If I were to turn up in this filthy dress, the old man, breaking under his burdens, would come down on me in a blind, Old Testament rage. I never thought of this as cruelty but as archaic right everlasting. Even Albert, who was already a Loop Lawyer, had to put up with the old man's blows—outraged, his eyes swollen and maddened, but he took it. It never seemed to any of us that my father was cruel. We had gone over the limit, and we were punished.

There were no lights in Philip's D.D.S office. When I jumped up the stairs the door with its blank starred glass was locked. Frosted panes were still rare. What we had was this star-marred product for toilets and other private windows. Marchek—whom nowadays we could call a voyeur—was also, angrily, gone. I had screwed up his experiment. I tried the doors, thinking that I could spend the night on the leather examining table where the beautiful nude had lain. From the office I could also make telephone calls. I did have a few friends, although there were none who might help me. I wouldn't have known how to explain my predicament to them. They'd think I was putting them on, that it was a practical joke—"This is Louie. A whore robbed me of my clothes and I'm stuck on the North Side without carfare. I'm wearing a dress. I lost my house keys. I can't get home."

I ran down to the drugstore to look for Philip there. He sometimes played five or six hands of poker in the druggist's back room, trying his luck before getting on the streetcar. I knew Kiyar, the druggist, by sight. He had no recollection of me—why should he have? He said, "What can I do for you, young lady?"

Did he really take me for a girl, or a tramp off the street, or a gypsy from one of the storefront fortune-teller camps? Those were now all over town. But not even a gypsy would wear this blue sateen quilted boudoir jacket instead of a coat.

"I wonder, is Phil Haddis the dentist in the back?"

"What do you want with Dr. Haddis, have you got a toothache, or what?"

"I need to see him."

The druggist was a compact little guy, and his full round bald head was painfully sensitive looking. In its sensitivity it could pick up any degree of disturbance, I thought. Yet there was a canny glitter coming through his specs, and Kiyar had the mark of a man whose mind never would change once he had made it up. Oddly enough, he had a small mouth, baby's lips. He had been on the street—how long? Forty years? In forty years you've seen it all and nobody can tell you a single thing.

"Did Dr. Haddis have an appointment with you? Are you a patient?"

He knew this was a private connection. I was no patient. "No. But if I was out here he'd want to know it. Can I talk to him one minute?"

"He isn't here."

Kiyar had walked behind the grille of the prescription counter. I mustn't lose him. If he went, what would I do next? I said, "This is important, Mr. Kiyar." He waited for me to declare myself. I wasn't about to embarrass Philip by setting off rumors. Kiyar said nothing. He may have been waiting for me to speak up. Declare myself. I assume he took pride in running a tight operation, giving nothing away. To cut through to the man I said, "I'm in a spot. I left Dr. Haddis a note, before, but when I came back I missed him."

At once I recognized my mistake. Druggists were always being appealed to. All these pills, remedy bottles, bright lights, medicine ads drew wandering screwballs and moochers. They all said they were in bad trouble.

"You can go to the Foster Avenue station."

"The police you mean."

I had thought of that too. I could always tell them my hard-luck story and they'd keep me until they checked it out and someone would come to fetch me. That would probably be Albert. Albert would love that. He'd say to me, "Well, aren't you the horny little bastard." He'd play up to the cops too, and amuse them.

"I'd freeze before I got to Foster Avenue," was my answer to Kiyar.

"There's always the squad car."

"Well, if Phil Haddis isn't in the back maybe he's still in the neighborhood. He doesn't always go straight home."

"Sometimes he goes over to the fights at Johnny Coulon's. It's a little early for that. You could try the speakeasy down the street, on Kenmore. It's an English basement, side entrance. You'll see a light by the fence. The guy at the slot is called Moose."

He didn't offer so much as a dime from his till. If I had said that I was in a scrape and that Phil was my sister's husband he'd probably have given me carfare. But I hadn't confessed, and there was a penalty for that.

Going out, I crossed my arms over the bed jacket and opened the door with my shoulder. I might as well have been wearing nothing at all. The wind cut at my legs, and I ran. Luckily I didn't have far to go. The iron pipe with the bulb at the end of it was halfway down the block. I saw it as soon as I crossed the street. These illegal drinking parlors were easy to find, they were meant to be. The steps were cement, four or five of them bringing me down to the door. The slot came open even before I knocked and instead of the doorkeeper's eyes, I saw his teeth.

"You Moose?"

"Yah. Who?"

"Kiyar sent me."

"Come on."

I felt as though I were falling into a big, warm, paved cellar. There was little to see, almost nothing. A sort of bar was set up, a few hanging fixtures, some tables from an ice cream parlor, wire-backed chairs. If you looked through the window of an English basement your eyes were at ground level. Here the glass was tarred over. There would have been nothing to see anyway: a yard, a wooden porch, a clothesline, wires, a back alley with ash heaps.

"Where did you come from, sister?" said Moose.

But Moose was a nobody here. The bartender, the one who counted, called me over and said, "What is it, sweetheart? You got a message for somebody?"

"Not exactly."

"Oh? You needed a drink so bad that you jumped out of bed and ran straight over—you couldn't stop to dress?"

"No, sir. I'm looking for somebody—Phil Haddis? The dentist?"

"There's only one customer. Is that him?"

It wasn't. My heart sank into river mud.

"It's not a drunk you're looking for?"

"No."

The drunk was on a high stool, thin legs hanging down, arms forward, and his head lay sidewise on the bar. Bottles, glasses, a beer barrel. Behind the barkeeper was a sideboard pried from the wall of an apartment. It had a long mirror—an oval laid on its side. Paper streamers curled down from the pipes.

"Do you know the dentist I'm talking about?"

"I might. Might not," said the barkeeper. He was a sloppy, long-faced giant—something of a kangaroo look about him. That was the long face in combination with the belly. He told me, "This is not a busy time. It's dinner, you know, and we're just a neighborhood speak."

It was no more than a cellar, just as the barman was no more than a Greek, huge and bored. Just as I myself, Louie, was no more than a naked male in a woman's dress. When you had named objects in this elementary way, hardly anything remained in them. The barman, on whom everything now depended, held his bare arms out at full reach and braced on his spread hands. The place smelled of yeast sprinkled with booze. He said, "You live around here?"

"No, about an hour on the streetcar."

"Say more."

"Humboldt Park is my neighborhood."

"Then you got to be a Uke, a Polack, a Scandihoof, or a Jew."

"Jew."

"I know my Chicago. And you didn't set out dressed like that. You'da frozen to death inside of ten minutes. It's for the boudoir, not winter wear. You don't have the shape of a woman, neither. The hips aren't there. Are you covering a pair of knockers? I bet not. So what's the story, are you a morphodite? Let me tell you, you got to give this Depression credit. Without it you'd never find out what kind of funny stuff is going on. But one thing I'll never believe is that you're a young girl and still got her cherry."

"You're right as far as that goes, but the rest of it is that I haven't got a cent, and I need carfare."

"Who took you, a woman?"

"Up in her room when I undressed, she grabbed my things and threw them out the window."

"Left you naked so you couldn't chase her . . . I would have grabbed her and threw her on the bed. I bet you didn't even get in."

Not even, I repeated to myself. Why didn't I push her down while she was still in her coat, as soon as we entered the room—pull up her clothes, as he would have done? Because he was born to that. While I was not. I wasn't intended for it.

"So that's what happened. You got taken by a team of pros. She set you up. You were the mark. Jewish fellows aren't supposed to keep company with those bad cunts. But when you get out of your house, into the world, you want action like anybody else. So. And where did you dig up this dress with the fancy big roses? I guess you were standing with your sticker sticking out and were lucky to find anything to put on. Was she a good looker?"

Her breasts, as she lay there, had kept their shape. They didn't slip sideward. The inward lines of her legs, thigh swelling toward thigh. The black crumpled hairs. Yes, a beauty, I would say.

Like the druggist, the barman saw the fun of the thing—an adolescent in a fix, a soiled dress, the rayon or sateen bed jacket. It was a lucky thing for me that business was at a standstill. If he had had customers, the barman wouldn't have given me the time of day. "In short, you got mixed up with a whore and she gave you the works."

For that matter, I had no sympathy for myself. I confessed that I had this coming, a high-minded Jewish school boy, too high-and-mighty to be orthodox and with his eye on a special destiny. At home, inside the house, an archaic rule; outside, the facts of life. The facts of life were having their turn. Their first effect was ridicule. To throw my duds into the alley was the woman's joke on me. The druggist with his pain-sensitive head was all irony. And now the barman was going to get his fun out of my trouble before he, maybe, gave me the seven cents for carfare. Then I could have a full hour of shame on the streetcar. My mother, with whom I might never speak again, used to say that I had a line of pride straight down the bridge of my nose, a foolish stripe that she could see.

I had no way of anticipating what her death would signify.

The barman, having me in place, was giving me the business. And Moose ("Moosey," the Greek called him) had come away from the door so as not to miss the entertainment. The Greek's kangaroo mouth turned up at the corners. Presently his hand went up to his head and he rubbed his scalp under the black, spiky hair. Some said they drank olive oil by the glass, these Greeks, to keep their hair so rich. "Now, give it to me again, about the dentist," said the barman.

"I came looking for him, but by now he's well on his way home."

He would by then be on the Broadway–Clark car, reading the Peach edition of the *Evening American,* a broad man with an innocent pout to his face, checking the race results. Anna had him dressed up as a professional man but he let the fittings—shirt, tie, buttons—go their own way. His instep was fat and swelled inside the narrow shoe she had picked for him. He wore the fedora correctly. Toward the rest he admitted no obligation.

Anna cooked dinner after work, and when Philip came in my father would begin to ask, "Where's Louie?" "Oh, he's out delivering flowers," they'd tell him. But the old man was nervous about his children after dark, and if they were late he waited up, walking—no, trotting—up and down the long apartment. When you tried to slip in he caught you and twisted you tight by the neckband. He was small, neat, slender, a gentleman, but abrupt, not unworldly—he wasn't ignorant of vices, he had lived in Odessa and even longer in St. Petersburg—but he had no patience. The least thing might craze him. Seeing me in this dress, he'd lose his head at once. *I* lost *mine* when that woman showed me her snatch with all the pink layers, when she raised up her arm and asked me to disconnect the wires, when I felt her skin and her fragrance came upward.

"What's your family, what does your dad do?" asked the barman.

"His business is wood fuel for bakers' ovens. It comes by freight car from northern Michigan. Also from Birnamwood, Wisconsin. He has a yard off Lake Street, east of Halsted."

I made an effort to give the particulars. I couldn't afford to be suspected of invention now.

"I know where that is. Now that's a neighborhood just full of hookers and cathouses. You think you can tell your old man what happened to you, that you got picked up by a cutie and she stole your clothes off you?"

The effect of this question was to make me tight in the face, dim in the ears. The whole cellar grew small and distant, toylike but not for play.

"How's your old man to deal with—tough?"

"Hard," I said.

"Slaps the kids around? This time you've got it coming. What's under the dress, a pair of bloomers?"

I shook my head.

"Your behind is bare? Now you know how it feels to go around like a woman."

The Greek's great muscles were dough-colored. You wouldn't

have wanted him to take a headlock on you. That's the kind of man the Organization hired. The Capone people were now in charge. The customers would be like celluloid Kewpie dolls to the Greek. He looked like one of those boxing kangaroos in the movies, and he could do a standing jump over the bar. Yet he enjoyed playing zany. He could curve his long mouth up at the corners like the happy face in a cartoon.

"What were you doing on the North Side?"

"Delivering flowers."

"Hustling after school but with ramming on your brain. You got a lot to learn, buddy boy. Well, enough of that. Now, Moosey, take this flashlight and see if you can scrounge up a sweater or something in the back basement for this down-on-his-luck kid. I'd be surprised if the old janitor hasn't picked the stuff over pretty good. If mice have nested in it, shake out the turds. It'll help on the trip home."

I followed Moose into the hotter half of the cellar. His flashlight picked out the laundry tubs with the hand-operated wringers mounted on them, the padlocked wooden storage bins. "Turn over some of these cardboard boxes. Mostly rags, is my guess. Dump 'em out, that's the easiest."

I emptied a couple of big cartons. Moose passed the light back and forth over the heaps. "Nothing much, like I said."

"Here's a flannel shirt," I said. I wanted to get out. The smell of heated burlap was hard to take. This was the only wearable article. I could have used a pullover or a pair of pants. We returned to the bar. As I was putting on the shirt, which revolted me (I come of finicky people whose fetish is cleanliness), the barman said, "I tell you what, you take this drunk home—this is about time for him, isn't it, Moosey?—he gets plastered here every night. See he gets home and it'll be worth half a buck to you."

"I'll do it," I said. "It all depends on how far away he lives. If it's far, I'll be frozen before I get there."

"It isn't far. Winona, west of Sheridan isn't far. I'll give you the directions. This guy is a city-hall payroller. He has no special job, he works direct for the ward committeeman. He's a lush with two little girls to bring up. If he's sober enough he cooks their dinner. Probably they take more care of him than he does of them."

"First I'll take charge of his money," said the barman. "I don't want my buddy here to be rolled. I don't say you would do it, but I owe this to a customer."

Bristle-faced Moose began to empty the man's pockets—his wallet, some keys, crushed cigarettes, a red bandanna that looked foul, matchbooks, greenbacks, and change. All these were laid out on the bar.

When I look back at past moments I carry with me an apperceptive mass that ripens and perhaps distorts, mixing what is memorable with what may not be worth mentioning. Thus I see the barman with one big hand gathering in the valuables as if they were his winnings, the pot in a poker game. And then I think that if the kangaroo giant had taken this drunk on his back he might have bounded home with him in less time than it would have taken me to support him as far as the corner. But what the barman actually said was, "I got a nice escort for you, Jim."

Moose led the man back and forth to make sure his feet were operating. His swollen eyes now opened and then closed again. "McKern," Moose said, briefing me. "Southwest corner of Winona and Sheridan, the second building on the south side of the street, and it's the second floor."

"You'll be paid when you get back," said the barman.

The freeze was now so hard that the snow underfoot sounded like metal foil. Though McKern may have sobered up in the street, he couldn't move very fast. Since I had to hold on to him I borrowed his gloves. He had a coat with pockets to put his hands in. I tried to keep behind him and get some shelter from the wind. That didn't work. He wasn't up to walking. I had to hold him. Instead of a desirable woman, I had a drunkard in my arms. This disgrace, you see, while my mother was surrendering to death. At about this hour, upstairs neighbors came down and relatives arrived and filled the kitchen and the dining room—a deathwatch. I should have been there, not on the far North Side. When I had earned the carfare, I'd still be an hour from home on a streetcar making four stops to the mile.

Toward the last, I was dragging McKern. I kept the street door open with my back while I pulled him into the dim lobby by the arms.

The little girls had been waiting and came down at once. They held the inner door for me while I brought their daddy upstairs with a fireman's-carry and laid him on his bed. The children had had plenty of practice at this. They undressed him down to the long johns and then stood silent on either side of the room. This, for them, was how things were. They took deep oddities calmly, as children generally will. I had spread his winter coat over him.

I had little sympathy for McKern, in the circumstances. I believe I can tell you why. He had surely passed out many times, and he would pass out again, dozens of times before he died. Drunkenness was common and familiar, and therefore accepted, and drunks could count on acceptance and support and relied on it. Whereas if your troubles were uncommon, unfamiliar, you could count on nothing. There was a convention about drunkenness established in part by drunkards. The founding proposition was that consciousness is terrible. Its lower, impoverished forms are perhaps the worst. Flesh and blood are poor and weak, susceptible to human shock. Here my descendant will hear the voice of Grandfather Louie giving one of his sermons on higher consciousness and interrupting the story he promised to tell. You will hold him to his word, as you have every right to do.

The older girl now spoke to me. She said, "The fellow phoned and said a man was bringing Daddy home, and you'd help with supper if Daddy couldn't cook it."

"Yes. Well? . . ."

"Only you're not a man, you've got a dress on."

"It looks like it, doesn't it. Don't you worry, I'll come to the kitchen with you."

"Are you a lady?"

"What do you mean—what does it look like? All right, I'm a lady."

"You can eat with us."

"Then show me where the kitchen is."

I followed them down a corridor, narrowed by clutter—boxes of canned groceries, soda biscuits, sardines, pop bottles. When I passed the bathroom, I slipped in for quick relief. The door had neither a hook nor a bolt, the string of the ceiling fixture had snapped off. A tiny night-light was plugged into the baseboard. I thanked God it was so dim. I put up the board while raising my skirt, and when I had begun I heard one of the children behind me. Over my shoulder I saw that it was the younger one, and as I turned my back (*everything* was happening today) I said, "Don't come in here."

But she squeezed past and sat on the edge of the tub. She grinned at me. She was expecting her second teeth. Today all females were making sexual fun of me, and even the infants were looking lewd. I stopped, letting the dress fall, and said to her, "What are you laughing about?"

"If you were a girl, you'd of sat down."

The kid wanted me to understand that she knew what she had seen. She pressed her fingers over her mouth, and I turned and went to the kitchen.

There the older girl was lifting the black cast-iron skillet with both hands. On dripping paper, the pork chops were laid out—nearby, a Mason jar of grease. I was competent enough at the gas range, which shone with old filth. Loath to touch the pork with my fingers, I forked the meat into the spitting fat. The chops turned my stomach. My thought was, "I'm into it now, up to the ears." The drunk in his bed, the dim secret toilet, the glaring tungsten twist over the gas range, the sputtering droplets stinging the hands. The older girl said, "There's plenty for you. Daddy won't be eating dinner."

"No, not me. I'm not hungry," I said.

All that my upbringing held in horror geysered up, my throat filling with it, my guts griping.

The children sat at the table, an enamel rectangle. Thick plates and glasses, a waxed package of sliced white bread, a milk bottle, a stick of butter, the burning fat clouding the room. The girls sat beneath the smoke, slicing their meat. I brought them salt and pepper from the range. They ate without conversation. My chore (my duty) done, there was nothing to keep me. I said, "I have to go."

I looked in at McKern, who had thrown down the coat and taken off his drawers. The parboiled face, the short nose pointed sharply, the life signs in the throat, the broken look of his neck, the black hair of his belly, the short cylinder between his legs ending in a spiral of loose skin, the white shine of the shins, the tragic expression of his feet. There was a stack of pennies on his bedside table. I helped myself to carfare but had no pocket for the coins. I opened the hall closet feeling quickly for a coat I might borrow, a pair of slacks. Whatever I took, Philip could return to the Greek barman tomorrow. I pulled a trench coat from a hanger, and a pair of trousers. For the third time I put on stranger's clothing—this is no time to mention stripes or checks or make exquisite notations. Escaping, desperate, I struggled into the pants on the landing, tucking in the dress, and pulled on the coat as I jumped down the stairs, knotting tight the belt and sticking the pennies, a fistful of them, into my pocket.

But still I went back to the alley under the woman's window to see if her light was on, and also to look for pages. The thief or pimp perhaps had chucked them away, or maybe they had dropped out when he snatched the sheepskin. Her window was dark. I found nothing on the ground. You may think this obsessive crankiness, a crazy dependency on words, on printed matter. But remember, there were no redeemers in the streets, no guides, no confessors, comforters, enlighteners, communicants to turn to. You had to take teaching wherever you could find it. Under the library dome downtown, in mosaic letters, there was a message from Milton, so moving but perhaps of no utility, perhaps aggravating difficulties: A GOOD BOOK, it said, IS THE PRECIOUS LIFE'S BLOOD OF A MASTER SPIRIT.

These are the plain facts, they have to be uttered. This, remember, is the New World, and here one of its mysterious cities. I should have hurried directly, to catch a car. Instead I was in a back alley hunting pages that would in any case have blown away.

I went back to Broadway—it *was* very broad—and waited on a safety island. Then the car came clanging, red, swaying on its tracks, a piece of Iron Age technology, double cane seats framed in brass. Rush hour was long past. I sat by a window, homebound, with flashes of thought like tracer bullets slanting into distant darkness. Like London in wartime. At home, what story would I tell? I wouldn't tell any. I never did. It was assumed anyway that I was lying. While I believed in honor, I did often lie. Is a life without lying conceivable? It was easier to lie than to explain myself. My father had one set of assumptions, I had another. Corresponding premises were not to be found.

I owed five dollars to Behrens. But I knew where my mother secretly hid her savings. Because I looked into all books, I had found the money in her Mahzor, the prayer book for the High Holidays, the days of awe. As yet I hadn't taken anything. She had hoped until this final illness to buy passage to Europe to see her mother and her sister. When she died I would turn the money over to my father, except for ten dollars, five for the florist and the rest for Von Hugel's *Eternal Life* and *The World as Will and Idea.*

The after-dinner guests and cousins would be gone when I reached home. My father would be on the lookout for me. It was the rear porch door that was locked after dark. The kitchen door was generally off the latch. I could climb over the wooden partition between the stairs and the porch. I often did that. Once you got your foot on the doorknob you could pull yourself over the partition and drop to the porch without noise. Then I could see into the kitchen and slip in as soon as my patrolling father had left it. The bedroom shared by all three brothers was just off the kitchen. I could borrow my brother Len's cast-off winter coat tomorrow. I knew which closet it hung in. If my father should catch me I could expect hard blows on my shoulders, on the top of my head, on my face. But if my mother had, tonight, just died, he wouldn't hit me.

This was when the measured, reassuring, sleep-inducing turntable of days became a whirlpool, a vortex darkening toward the bottom. I had had only the anonymous pages in the pocket of my lost sheepskin to interpret it to me. They told me that the truth of the universe was inscribed into our very bones. That the human skeleton was itself a hieroglyph. That everything we had ever known on earth was shown to us in the first days after death. That our experience of the world was desired by the cosmos, and needed by it for its own renewal.

I do not think that these pages, if I hadn't lost them, would have persuaded me forever or made the life I led a different one.

I am writing this account, or statement, in response to an eccentric urge swelling toward me from the earth itself.

Failed my mother! That may mean, will mean, little or nothing to you, my only child, reading this document.

I myself know the power of nonpathos, in these low, devious days.

On the streetcar, heading home, I braced myself, but all my preparations caved in like sand diggings. I got down at the North Avenue stop, avoiding my reflection in the shop-windows. After a death, mirrors were immediately covered. I can't say what this pious superstition means. Will the soul of your dead be reflected in a looking glass, or is this custom a check to the vanity of the living?

recall the old house where I was raised, where in midwinter Parma violets bloomed in a cold frame near the kitchen door and down the long corridor, past the seven views of Rome—up two steps and down three—one entered the library where all the books were in order, the lamps were bright, where there was a fire and a dozen bottles of good bourbon, locked in a cabinet with a veneer of tortoise shell whose silver key my father wore on his watch chain. Just let me give you one example and if you disbelieve me look honestly into your own past and see if you can't find a comparable experience. On Saturday the doctor told me to stop smoking and drinking and I did. I won't go into the commonplace symptoms of withdrawal, but I would like to point out that, standing at my window in the evening, watching the brilliant afterlight and the spread of darkness, I felt, through the lack of these humble stimulants, the force of some primitive memory in which the coming of night with its stars and its moon was apocalyptic. I thought suddenly of the neglected graves of my three brothers on the mountainside and that death is a loneliness much crueler than any loneliness hinted at in life. The soul (I thought) does not leave the body, but lingers with it through every degrading stage of decomposition and neglect, through heat, through cold, through the long winter nights when no one comes with a wreath or a plant and no one says a prayer. This unpleasant premonition was followed by anxiety. We were going out for dinner and I thought that the oil burner would explode in our absence and burn the house. The cook would get drunk and attack my daughter with a carving knife, or my wife and I would be killed in a collision on the main highway, leaving our children bewildered orphans with nothing in life to look forward to but sadness. I was able to observe, along with these foolish and terrifying anxieties, a definite impairment to my discretionary poles. I felt as if I were being lowered by ropes into the atmosphere of my childhood. I told my wife—when she passed through the living room—that I had stopped smoking and drinking but she didn't seem to care and who would reward me for my privations? Who cared about the bitter taste in my mouth and that my head seemed to be leaving my shoulders? It seemed to me that men had honored one another with medals, statuary and cups for much less and that abstinence is a social matter. When I abstain from sin it is more often a fear of scandal than a private resolve to improve on the purity of my heart, but here was a call for abstinence without the worldly enforcement of society, and death is not the threat that scandal is. When it was time for us to go out I was so light-headed that I had to ask my wife to drive the car. On Sunday I sneaked seven cigarettes in various hiding places and drank two Martinis in the downstairs coat closet. At breakfast on Monday my English muffin stared up at me from the plate. I mean I *saw* a face there in the rough, toasted surface. The moment of recognition was fleeting, but it was deep, and I wondered who it had been. Was it a friend, an aunt, a sailor, a ski instructor, a bartender or a conductor on a train? The smile faded off the muffin, but it had been there for a second—the sense of a person, a life, a pure force of gentleness and censure, and I am convinced that the muffin had contained the presence of some spirit. As you can see, I was nervous.

On Monday my wife's old cousin, Justina, came to visit her. Justina was a lively guest, although she must have been crowding eighty. On Tuesday my wife gave her a lunch party. The last guest left at three and a few minutes later, Cousin Justina, sitting on the living-room sofa with a glass of brandy, breathed her last. My wife called me at the office and I said that I would be right out. I was clearing my desk when my boss, MacPherson, came in.

"Spare me a minute," he asked. "I've been bird-dogging all over the place, trying to track you down. Pierson had to leave early and I want you to write the last Elixircol commercial."

"Oh, I can't, Mac," I said. "My wife just called. Cousin Justina is dead."

"You write that commercial," he said. His smile was satanic. "Pierson had to leave early because his grandmother fell off a stepladder."

Now I don't like fictional accounts of office life. It seems to me that if you're going to write fiction you should write about mountain-climbing and tempests at sea and I will go over my predicament with MacPherson briefly, aggravated as it was by his refusal to respect and honor the death of dear old Justina. It was like MacPherson. It was a good example of the way I've been treated. He is, I might say, a tall, splendidly groomed man of about sixty who changes his shirt three times a day, romances his secretary every afternoon between two and two-thirty and makes the habit of continuously chewing gum seem hygienic and elegant. I write his speeches for him and it has not been a happy arrangement for me. If the speeches are successful, MacPherson takes all the credit. I can see that his presence, his tailor and his fine voice are all a part of the performance, but it makes me angry never to be given credit for what was said. On the other hand, if the speeches are unsuccessful—if his presence and his voice can't carry the hour—his threatening and sarcastic manner is surgical and I am obliged to contain myself in the role of a man who can do no good in spite of the piles of congratulatory mail that my eloquence sometimes brings in. I must pretend, I must, like an actor, study and improve on my pretension, to have nothing to do with his triumphs and I must bow my head gracefully in shame when we have both failed. I am forced to appear grateful for injuries, to lie, to smile falsely and to play out a role as asinine and as unrelated to the facts as a minor prince in an operetta, but if I speak the truth it will be my wife and my children who will pay in hardships for my outspokenness. Now he refused to respect or even to admit the solemn fact of a death in our family and if I couldn't rebel it seemed as if I could at least hint at it.

The commercial he wanted me to write was for a tonic called Elixircol and was to be spoken on television by an actress who was neither young nor beautiful, but who had an appearance of ready abandon and who was anyhow the mistress of one of the sponsor's uncles. *Are you growing old?* I wrote. *Are you falling out of love with your image in the looking glass? Does your face in the morning seem racked and seamed with alcoholic and sexual excesses and does the rest of you appear to be a greyish-pink lump, covered all over with brindle hair? Walking in the autumn woods, do you feel that subtle distance has come between you and the smell of wood smoke? Have you drafted your obituary? Are you easily winded? Do you wear a girdle? Is your sense of smell fading, is your interest in gardening waning, is your fear of height increasing and are your sexual drives as ravening and intense as ever and does your wife look more and more to you like a stranger with sunken cheeks who has wandered into your bedroom by mistake? If this or any of this is true you need Elixircol, the true juice of youth. The small economy size* (business with the bottle) *costs seventy-five dollars and the giant family bottle comes at two hundred and fifty. It's a lot of scratch, God knows, but these are inflationary times and who can put a price on youth? If you don't have the cash, borrow it from your neighborhood loan shark or hold up the local bank.*

The odds are three to one that with a ten-cent water pistol and a slip of paper you can shake ten thousand out of any fainthearted teller. Everybody's doing it. (Music up and out.)

I sent this into MacPherson via Ralphie, the messenger boy, and took the 4:16 home, traveling through a landscape of utter desolation.

Now my journey is a digression and has no real connection to Justina's death, but what followed could only have happened in my country and in my time and since I was an American traveling across an American landscape, the trip may be part of the sum. There are some Americans who, although their fathers emigrated from the old world three centuries ago, never seem to have quite completed the voyage, and I am one of these. I stand, figuratively, with one wet foot on Plymouth Rock, looking with some delicacy, not into a formidable and challenging wilderness but onto a half-finished civilization embracing glass towers, oil derricks, suburban continents and abandoned movie houses and wondering why, in this most prosperous, equitable and accomplished world—where even the cleaning women practice the Chopin preludes in their spare time—everyone should seem to be so disappointed?

At Proxmire Manor I was the only passenger to get off the random, meandering and profitless local that carried its shabby lights off into the dusk like some game-legged watchman or beadle, making his appointed rounds. I went around to the front of the station to wait for my wife and to enjoy the traveler's fine sense of crises. Above me on the hill was my home and the homes of my friends, all lighted and smelling of fragrant wood smoke like the temples in a sacred grove, dedicated to monogamy, feckless childhood and domestic bliss, but so like a dream that I felt the lack of viscera with much more than poignance—the absence of that inner dynamism we respond to in some European landscapes. In short, I was disappointed. It was my country, my beloved country and there have been mornings when I could have kissed the earth that covers its many provinces and states. There was a hint of bliss—romantic and domestic bliss. I seemed to hear the jingle bells of the sleigh that would carry me to grandmother's house, although in fact grandmother spent the last years of her life working as a hostess on an ocean liner and was lost in the tragic sinking of the S.S. *Lorelei* and I was responding to a memory that I had not experienced. But the hill of light rose like an answer to some primitive dream of home-coming. On one of the highest lawns I saw the remains of a snow man who still smoked a pipe and wore a scarf and cap, but whose form was wasting away and whose anthracite eyes stared out at the view with terrifying bitterness. I sensed some disappointing greenness of spirit in the scene, although I knew in my bones, no less, how like yesterday it was that my father left the old world to found a new; and I thought of the forces that had brought stamina to the image: the cruel towns of Calabria with their cruel princes, the badlands northwest of Dublin, ghettos, despots, whorehouses, bread lines, the graves of children. Intolerable hunger, corruption, persecution and despair had generated these faint and mellow lights and wasn't it all a part of the great migration that is the life of man?

My wife's cheeks were wet with tears when I kissed her. She was distressed, of course, and really quite sad. She had been attached to Justina. She drove me home where Justina was still sitting on the sofa. I would like to spare you the unpleasant details, but I will say that both her mouth and her eyes were wide open. I went into the pantry to telephone Dr. Hunter. His line was busy. I poured myself a drink—the first since Sunday—and lighted a cigarette. When I called the doctor again he answered and I told him what had happened. "Well, I'm awfully sorry to hear about it, Moses," he said. "I can't get over until after six and there isn't much that I can do. This sort of thing has come up before and I'll tell you all I know. You see you live in a B zone—two-acre lots, no commercial enterprises, and so forth. A couple of years ago some stranger bought the old Plewett mansion and it turned out that he was planning to operate it as a funeral home. We didn't have any zoning provision at the time that would protect us and one was rushed through the village council at midnight and they overdid it. It seems that you not only can't have a funeral home in zone B—you can't bury anything there and you can't die there. Of course it's absurd, but we all make mistakes, don't we?

"Now there are two things you can do. I've had to deal with this before. You can take the old lady and put her into the car and drive her over to Chestnut Street where zone C begins. The boundary is just beyond the traffic light by the high school. As soon as you get her over to zone C, it's all right. You can just say she died in the car. You can do that or if this seems distasteful you can call the mayor and ask him to make an exception to the zoning laws. But I can't write you out a death certificate until you get her out of that neighborhood and of course no undertaker will touch her until you get a death certificate."

"I don't understand," I said, and I didn't, but then the possibility that there was some truth in what he had just told me broke against me or over me like a wave, exciting mostly indignation. "I've never heard such a lot of damned foolishness in my life," I said. "Do you mean to tell me that I can't die in one neighborhood and that I can't fall in love in another and that I can't eat. . . ."

"Listen. Calm down, Moses, I'm not telling you anything but the facts and I have a lot of patients waiting. I don't have the time to listen to you fulminate. If you want to move her, call me as soon as you get her over to the traffic light. Otherwise, I'd advise you to get in touch with the mayor or someone on the village council." He cut the connection. I was outraged, but this did not change the fact that Justina was still sitting on the sofa. I poured a fresh drink and lit another cigarette.

Justina seemed to be waiting for me and to be changing from an inert into a demanding figure. I tried to imagine carrying her out to the station wagon, but I couldn't complete the task in my imagination and I was sure that I couldn't complete it in fact. I then called the mayor, but this position in our village is mostly honorary and as I might have known he was in his New York law office and was not expected home until seven. I could cover her, I thought; that would be a decent thing to do, and I went up the back stairs to the linen closet and got a sheet. It was getting dark when I came back into the living room, but this was no merciful twilight. Dusk seemed to be playing directly into her hands and she had gained power and stature with the dark. I covered her with the sheet and turned on a lamp at the other end of the room, but the rectitude of the place with its old furniture, flowers, paintings, etc. was demolished by her monumental shape. The next thing to worry about was the children who would be home in a few minutes. Their knowledge of death, excepting their dreams and intuitions of which I know nothing, is zero and the bold figure in the parlor was bound to be traumatic. When I heard them coming up the walk I went out and told them what had happened and sent them up to their rooms. At seven I drove over to the mayor's.

He had not come home, but he was expected at any minute and I talked with his wife. She gave me a drink. By this time I was chain-smoking. When the mayor came in we went into a little office or library where he took up a position behind a desk, putting me in the low chair of a supplicant.

"Of course I sympathize with you, Moses," he said, settling back in his chair. "It's an awful thing to have happened, but the trouble is that we can't give you a zoning exception without a majority vote of the village council and all the members of the council happen to be out of town. Pete's in California and Jack's in Paris and Larry won't be back from Stowe until the end of the week."

I was sarcastic. "Then I suppose Cousin Justina will have to gracefully decompose in my parlor until Jack comes back from Paris."

"Oh, no," he said, "oh, *no.* Jack won't be back from Paris for another month, but I think you might wait until Larry comes from Stowe. Then we'd have a majority, assuming of course that they would agree to your appeal."

"For Christ's sake," I snarled.

"Yes, yes," he said, "it is difficult, but after all you must realize that this is the world you live in and the importance of zoning can't be overestimated. Why, if a single member of the council could give out zoning exceptions, I could give you permission right now to open a saloon in your garage, put up neon lights, hire an orchestra and destroy the neighborhood and all the human and commercial values we've worked so hard to protect."

"I don't want to open a saloon in my garage," I howled. "I don't want to hire an orchestra. I just want to bury Justina."

"I know, Moses, I know," he said. "I understand that. But it's just that it happened in the wrong zone and if I make an exception for you I'll have to make an exception for everyone, and this kind of morbidity, when it gets out of hand, can be very depressing. People don't like to live in a neighborhood where this sort of thing goes on all the time."

"Listen to me," I said. "You give me an exception and you give it to me now or I'm going home and dig a hole in my garden and bury Justina myself."

"But you can't do that, Moses. You can't bury anything in zone B. You can't even bury a cat."

"You're mistaken," I said. "I can and I will. I can't function as a doctor and I can't function as an undertaker, but I can dig a hole in the ground and if you don't give me my exception, that's what I'm going to do."

I got out of the low chair before I finished speaking and started for the door.

"Come back, Moses, come back," he said. "Please come back. Look. I'll give you an exception if you'll promise not to tell anyone. It's breaking the law, it's a forgery, but I'll do it if you promise to keep it a secret."

I promised to keep it a secret, he gave me the documents and I used his telephone to make the arrangements. Justina was removed a few minutes after I got home, but that night I had the strangest dream.

I dreamed that I was in a crowded supermarket. It must have been night because the windows were dark. The ceiling was paved with fluorescent light—brilliant, cheerful, but, considering our prehistoric memories, a harsh link in the chain of light that binds us to the past. Music was playing and there must have been at least a thousand shoppers pushing their wagons among the long corridors of comestibles and victuals. Now is there—or isn't there—something about the posture we assume when we push a wagon that unsexes us? Can it be done with gallantry? I bring this up because the multitude of shoppers seemed that evening, as they pushed their wagons, penitential and unsexed. There were all kinds, this being my beloved country. There were Italians. Finns, Jews, Negroes, Shropshiremen. Cubans—anyone who had heeded the voice of liberty—and they were dressed with that sumptuary abandon, that European caricaturists record with such bitter disgust. Yes, there were grandmothers in shorts, big-butted women in knitted pants, and men wearing such an assortment of clothing that it looked as if they had dressed hurriedly in a burning building. But this, as I say, is my own country and in my opinion the caricaturist who vilifies the old lady in shorts, vilifies himself. I am a native and I was wearing buckskin jump boots, chino pants cut so tight that my sexual organs were discernible and a rayon acetate pajama top printed with representations of the *Pinta*, the *Nina* and the *Santa Maria* in full sail. The scene was strange—the strangeness of a dream where we see familiar objects in an unfamiliar light, but as I looked more closely I saw that there were some irregularities. Nothing was labeled. Nothing was identified or known. The cans and boxes were all bare. The frozen-food bins were full of brown parcels, but they were such odd shapes that you couldn't tell if they contained a frozen turkey or a Chinese dinner. All the goods at the vegetable and the bakery counters were concealed in brown bags and even the books for sale had no titles. In spite of the fact that the contents of nothing was known, my companions of the dream—my thousands of bizarrely dressed compatriots—were deliberating gravely over these mysterious containers as if the choices they made were critical. Like any dreamer, I was omniscient—I was with them and I was withdrawn—and stepping above the scene for a minute I noticed the men at the check-out counters. They were brutes. Now sometimes in a crowd, in a bar or a street, you will see a face so full-blown in its obdurate resistance to the appeals of love, reason and decency—so lewd, so brutish and unregenerate—that you turn away. Men like these were stationed at the only way out and as the shoppers approached them they tore their packages open—I still couldn't see what they contained—but in every case the customer, at the sight of what he had chosen, showed all the symptoms of the deepest guilt; that force that brings us to our knees. Once their choice had been opened, to their shame they were pushed—in some cases kicked—toward the door and beyond the door I saw dark water and heard a terrible noise of moaning and crying in the air. They waited at the door in groups to be taken away in some conveyance that I couldn't see. As I watched, thousands and thousands pushed their wagons through the market, made their careful and mysterious choices and were reviled and taken away. What could be the meaning of this?

We buried Justina in the rain the next afternoon. The dead are not, God knows, a minority, but in Proxmire Manor their unexalted kingdom is on the outskirts, rather like a dump, where they are transported furtively as knaves and scoundrels and where they lie in an atmosphere of perfect neglect. Justina's life had been exemplary, but by ending it she seemed to have disgraced us all. The priest was a friend and a cheerful sight, but the undertaker and his helpers, hiding behind their limousines, were not, and aren't they at the root of most of our troubles with their claim that death is a violet-flavored kiss? How can a people who do not mean to understand death hope to understand love and who will sound the alarm?

I went from the cemetery back to my office.

The commercial was on my desk and MacPherson had written

across it in large letters in grease pencil: "Very funny, you broken-down bore. Do again."

I was tired but unrepentent and didn't seem able to force myself into a practical posture of usefulness and obedience. I did another commercial.

Don't lose your loved ones because of excessive radioactivity. Don't be a wallflower at the dance because of strontium 90 in your bones. Don't be a victim of fallout. When the tart on 36th Street gives you the big eye, does your body stride off in one direction and your imagination in another? Does your mind follow her up the stairs and taste her wares in revolting detail while your flesh goes off to Brooks Brothers or the foreign-exchange desk of the Chase Manhattan Bank? Haven't you noticed the size of the ferns, the lushness of the grass, the bitterness of the string beans and the brilliant markings on the new breeds of butterflies? You have been inhaling lethal atomic waste for the last twenty-five years and only Elixircol can save you.

I gave this copy to Ralphie and waited perhaps ten minutes, when it was returned, marked again with grease pencil. "Do," he wrote, "or you'll be dead."

I felt very tired. I returned to the typewriter, put another piece of paper into the machine and wrote: *The Lord is my Shepherd, therefore can I lack nothing. He shall feed me in a green pasture and lead me forth beside the waters of comfort. He shall convert my soul and bring me forth in the paths of righteousness for his Name's sake. Yea, though I walk through the valley of the shadow of death I will fear no evil for thou art with me; thy rod and thy staff comfort me. Thou shalt prepare a table for me in the presence of them that trouble me; thou hast anointed my head with oil and my cup shall be full. Surely thy loving kindness and thy mercy shall follow me all the days of my life and I will dwell in the house of the Lord forever.* I gave this to Ralphie and went home.

URSULA K. LE GUIN

(1929–   )

Like Ray Bradbury, Ursula K. Le Guin is celebrated as a writer of fantasy and science fiction; yet she writes what might be called mainstream literature as well—fiction, poetry, criticism. The author of fifteen novels, three books of poetry, seven books for children, two books of criticism, and five short story collections, Le Guin is a brilliant stylist for whom the imagination is transcendent. As the protagonist of "Texts," the elliptical story included here, believes, "texts"—messages to be decoded—confront us on all sides, if only we could read them: "Words were everywhere."

"Texts" is taken from Le Guin's most recent story collection, Searoad: Chronicles of Klatsand *(1991), a group of linked and interrelated stories set in a seaside town on the Oregon coast. The stories are "realistic"—though, as in all of Le Guin's work, they turn upon mystery and ambiguity.*

Born in Berkeley, California, daughter of writer Theodora Kroeber and anthropologist Alfred L. Kroeber, Ursula K. Le Guin studied at Radcliffe and Columbia, married the historian Charles A. Le Guin in 1953, and began publishing in the 1960's. She now lives in Oregon. Her work has been plentiful, and much acclaimed; the titles for which she is best known are the novels The Left Hand of Darkness *(1969),* The Dispossessed *(1974), and* Always Coming Home *(1985), but she is the author of outstanding collections of stories in the fantasy mode:* The Wind's Twelve Quarters *(1975),* Orsinian Tales *(1976),* The Compass Rose *(1982), and* Buffalo Gals *(1987).*

Such categories as "realism"—"fantasy"—"science fiction"—"mainstream" are revealed as hopelessly inadequate when we try to characterize writers of Ursula K. Le Guin's gifts.

Texts

Messages came, Johanna thought, usually years too late, or years before one could crack their code or had even learned the language they were in. Yet they came increasingly often and were so urgent, so compelling in their demand that she read them, that she do something, as to force her at last to take refuge from them. She rented, for the month of January, a little house with no telephone in a seaside town that had no mail delivery. She had stayed there several times in summer; winter, as she had hoped, was even quieter than summer. A whole day would go by without her hearing or speaking a word. She did not buy the paper or turn on the television, and the one morning she thought she ought to find some news on the radio she got a program in Finnish from Astoria. But the messages still came. Words were everywhere.

Literate clothing was no real problem. She remembered the first print dress she had ever seen, years ago, a genuine *print* dress with typography involved in the design—green on white, suitcases and hibiscus and the names *Riviera* and *Capri* and *Paris* occurring rather blobbily from shoulder-seam to hem, sometimes right side up, sometimes upside down. Then it had been, as the saleswoman said, very unusual. Now it was hard to find a T-shirt that did not urge political action, or quote lengthily from a dead physicist, or at least mention the town it was for sale in. All this she had coped with, she had even worn. But too many things were becoming legible.

She had noticed in earlier years that the lines of foam left by waves on the sand after stormy weather lay sometimes in curves that looked like handwriting, cursive lines broken by spaces, as if in words; but it was not until she had been alone for over a fortnight and had walked many times down to Wreck Point and back that she found she could read the writing. It was a mild day, nearly windless, so that she did not have to march briskly but could mosey along between the foam-lines and the water's edge where the sand reflected the sky. Every now and then a quiet winter breaker driving up and up the beach would drive her and a few gulls ahead of it onto the drier sand; then as the wave receded she and the gulls would follow it back. There was not another soul on the long beach. The sand lay as firm and even as a pad of pale brown paper, and on it a recent wave at its high mark had left a complicated series of curves and bits of foam. The ribbons and loops and lengths of white looked so much like handwriting in chalk that she stopped, the way she would stop, half willingly, to read what people scratched in the sand in summer. Usually it was "Jason + Karen" or paired initials in a heart; once, mysteriously and memorably, three initials and the dates 1973–1984, the only such inscription that spoke of a promise not made but broken. Whatever those eleven years had been, the length of a marriage? a child's life? they were gone, and the letters and numbers also were gone when she came back by where they had been, with the tide rising. She had wondered then if the person who wrote them had written them to be erased. But these foam words lying on the brown sand now had been written by the erasing sea itself. If she could read them they might tell her a wisdom a good deal deeper and bitterer than she could possibly swallow. Do I want to know what the sea writes? she thought, but at the same time she was already reading the foam, which though in vaguely cuneiform blobs rather than letters of any alphabet was perfectly legible as she walked along beside it. "Yes," it read, "esse hes hetu tokye to' ossusess ekyes. Seham hute' u." (When she wrote it down later she used the apostrophe to represent a kind of stop or click like the last sound in "Yep!") As she read it over, backing up some yards to do so, it continued to say the same thing, so she walked up and down it several times and memorised it. Presently, as bubbles burst and the blobs began to shrink, it changed here and there to read, "Yes, e hes etu kye to' ossusess kye. ham te u." She felt that this was not significant change but mere loss, and kept the original text in mind. The water of the foam sank into the sand and the bubbles dried away till the marks and lines lessened into a faint lacework of dots and scraps, half legible. It looked enough like delicate bits of fancywork that she wondered if one could also read lace or crochet.

When she got home she wrote down the foam words so that she would not have to keep repeating them to remember them, and then she looked at the machine-made Quaker lace tablecloth on the little round dining table. It was not hard to read but was, as one might expect, rather dull. She made out the first line inside the border as "pith wot pith wot pith wot" interminably, with a "dub" every thirty stitches where the border pattern interrupted.

But the lace collar she had picked up at a second-hand clothes store in Portland was a different matter entirely. It was handmade, hand written. The script was small and very even. Like the Spencerian hand she had been taught fifty years ago in the first grade, it was ornate but surprisingly easy to read. "My soul must go," was the border, repeated many times, "my soul must go, my soul must go," and the fragile webs leading inward read, "sister, sister, sister, light the light." And she did not know what she was to do, or how she was to do it.

DONALD BARTHELME

(1931–1989)

"Fragments are the only forms I trust," Donald Barthelme once said. Yet his brilliantly innovative short fictions have the unity of effect of completely imagined prose-poems; their curve is typically the logic of dream, selecting only the most significant of images and dropping out all else. Like the Surrealists Max Ernst, Marcel Duchamp, Man Ray, and René Magritte, who exercised a powerful influence upon his work, Barthelme's art is frequently the art of startling juxtapositions and collage. "The School" is atypical Barthelme, risking sentiment, sweetness, sincerity, unmediated yearning.

Donald Barthelme was born in Philadelphia and raised and educated in Houston, where his father worked as an architect. A graduate of the University of Houston, Barthelme worked as a newspaper reporter and museum director, helped edit a journal of art and literature called Location, *and began to publish short fiction in* The New Yorker *in the early 1960's. His major titles are* Come Back, Dr. Caligari *(1964),* Unspeakable Practices, Unnatural Acts *(1968),* City Life *(1970),* Guilty Pleasures *(1974), and* Sixty Stories *(1981)—short story collections; and* Snow White *(1967) and* The Dead Father *(1975)—novels. The posthumous novel* King Arthur *was published in 1991.*

The School

Well, we had all these children out planting trees, see, because we figured that . . . that was part of their education, to see how you know the root systems . . . and also the sense of responsibility, taking care of things, being individually responsible. You know what I mean. And the trees all died. They were orange trees. I don't know why they died, they just died. Something wrong with the soil possibly or maybe the stuff we got from the nursery wasn't the best. We complained about it. So we've got thirty kids there, each kid had his or her own little tree to plant, and we've got these thirty dead trees. All these kids looking at these little brown sticks. It was depressing.

It wouldn't have been so bad except that just a couple of weeks before the thing with the trees, the snakes all died. But I think that the snakes—well, the reason that the snakes kicked off was that . . . you remember, the boiler was shut off for four days because of the strike, and that was explicable. It was something you could explain to the kids because of the strike. I mean, none of their parents would let them cross the picket line and they knew there was a strike going on and what it meant. So when things got started up again and we found the snakes they weren't too disturbed.

With the herb gardens it was probably a case of overwatering, and at least now they know not to overwater. The children were very conscientious with the herb gardens and some of them probably . . . you know, slipped them a little extra water when we weren't looking. Or maybe . . . well, I don't like to think about sabotage, although it did occur to us. I mean, it was something that crossed our minds. We were thinking that way probably because before that the gerbils had died, and the white mice had died, and the salamander . . . well, now they know not to carry them around in plastic bags.

Of course we *expected* the tropical fish to die, that was no surprise. Those numbers, you look at them crooked and they're belly-up on the surface. But the lesson plan called for a tropical-fish input at that point, there was nothing we could do, it happens every year, you just have to hurry past it.

We weren't even supposed to have a puppy.

We weren't even supposed to have one, it was just a puppy the Murdoch girl found under a Gristede's truck one day and she was afraid the truck would run over it when the driver had finished making his delivery, so she stuck it in her knapsack and brought it to school with her. So we had this puppy. As soon as I saw the puppy I thought, Oh Christ, I bet it will live for about two weeks and then . . . And that's what it did. It wasn't supposed to be in the classroom at all, there's some kind of regulation about it, but you can't tell them they can't have a puppy when the puppy is already there, right in front of them, running around on the floor and yap yap yapping. They named it Edgar—that is, they named it after me. They had a lot of fun running after it and yelling "Here, Edgar! Nice Edgar!" Then they'd laugh like hell. They enjoyed the ambiguity. I enjoyed it myself. I don't mind being kidded. They made a little house for it in the supply closet and all that. I don't know what it died of. Distemper, I guess. It probably hadn't had any shots. I got it out of there before the kids got to school. I checked the supply closet each morning, routinely because I knew what was going to happen. I gave it to the custodian.

And then there was this Korean orphan that the class adopted through the Help the Children program, all the kids brought in a quarter a month, that was the idea. It was an unfortunate thing, the kid's name was Kim and maybe we adopted him too late or something. The cause of death was not stated in the letter we got, they suggested we adopt another child instead and sent us some interesting case histories, but we didn't have the heart. The class took it pretty hard, they began (I think, nobody ever said anything to me directly) to feel that maybe there was something wrong with the school. But I don't think there's anything wrong with the school, particularly, I've seen better and I've seen worse. It was just a run of bad luck. We had an extraordinary number of parents passing away, for instance. There were I think two heart attacks and two suicides, one drowning, and four killed together in a car accident. One stroke. And we had the usual heavy mortality rate among the grandparents, or maybe it was heavier this year, it seemed so. And finally the tragedy.

The tragedy occurred when Matthew Wein and Tony Mavrogordo were playing over where they're excavating for the new federal office building. There were all these big wooden beams stacked, you know, at the edge of the excavation. There's a court case coming out of that, the parents are claiming that the beams were poorly stacked. I don't know what's true and what's not. It's been a strange year.

I forgot to mention Billy Brandt's father, who was knifed fatally when he grappled with a masked intruder in his home.

One day, we had a discussion in class. They asked me, where did they go? The trees, the salamander, the tropical fish, Edgar, the poppas and mommas, Matthew and Tony, where did they go? And I said, I don't know, I don't know. And they said, who knows? and I said, nobody knows. And they said, is death that which gives meaning to life? And I said, no, life is that which gives meaning to life. Then they said, but isn't death, considered such a fundamental datum, the means by which the taken-for-granted mundanity of the everyday may be transcended in the direction of—

I said, yes, maybe.

They said, we don't like it.

I said, that's sound.

They said, it's a bloody shame!

I said, it is.

They said, will you make love now with Helen (our teaching assistant) so that we can see how it is done? We know you like Helen.

I do like Helen but I said that I would not.

We've heard so much about it, they said, but we've never seen it.

I said I would be fired and that it was never, or almost never, done as a demonstration. Helen looked out of the window.

They said, please, please make love with Helen, we require an assertion of value, we are frightened.

I said that they shouldn't be frightened (although I am often frightened) and that there was value everywhere. Helen came and embraced me. I kissed her a few times on the brow. We held each other. The children were excited. Then there was a knock on the door. I opened the door, and the new gerbil walked in. The children cheered wildly.

JOHN UPDIKE

(1932–   )

*Though celebrated as the creator of "Rabbit" Angstrom, the hero of the Rabbit quartet (*Rabbit, Run, *1961;* Rabbit Redux, *1971;* Rabbit Is Rich, *1981;* Rabbit at Rest, *1990), John Updike is equally admired as one of the finest practitioners of the short story in American literary history. His is an art of vigilance informed by compassion and humor; an art of both dissection and assimilation. This early story, with its oddly Magritte-like title, gives us a young hero already meditating upon mortality, even as he finds himself quickened to a renewal of an old, seemingly lost romance.*

One of our most prodigious and widely acclaimed writers, John Updike was born in Shillington, Pennsylvania, and, scarcely out of Harvard, began publishing stories in The New Yorker *in the mid-1950's. Among his titles are the story collections* The Same Door *(1959),* Pigeon Feathers *(1962),* The Music School *(1966),* Museums and Women *(1972),* Problems *(1979), and* Trust Me *(1987); the novels* The Centaur *(1963),* Couples *(1968),* The Coup *(1978), and* Roger's Version *(1986), in addition to the above named; the poetry collections* Midpoint *(1969) and* Facing Nature *(1985); the collections of essays and reviews* Hugging the Shore *(1983) and* Odd Jobs *(1991); and the memoir* Self-Consciousness *(1989).*

The perfectly realized "The Persistence of Desire" is quintessential Updike; a moment's epiphany firmly grounded in a life, a recognizable world. Here is the very poetry of realism. John Updike is that rarity in our time—the writer's writer who has also achieved popular success.

The Persistence of Desire

Pennypacker's office still smelled of linoleum, a clean, sad scent that seemed to lift from the checkerboard floor in squares of alternating intensity; this pattern had given Clyde as a boy a funny nervous feeling of intersection, and now he stood crisscrossed by a double sense of himself, his present identity extending down from Massachusetts to meet his disconsolate youth in Pennsylvania, projected upward from a distance of years. The enlarged, tinted photograph of a lake in the Canadian wilderness still covered one whole wall, and the walnut-stained chairs and benches continued their vague impersonation of the Shaker manner. The one new thing, set squarely on an orange end table, was a compact black clock constructed like a speedometer; it showed in Arabic numerals the present minute—1:28—and coiled invisibly in its works the two infinites of past and future. Clyde was early; the waiting room was empty. He sat down on a chair opposite the clock. Already it was 1:29, and while he watched, the digits slipped again; another drop into the brimming void. He glanced around for the comfort of a clock with a face and gracious, gradual hands. A stopped grandfather matched the other imitation antiques. He opened a magazine and immediately read, "Science reveals that the cells of the normal human body are replaced *in toto* every seven years."

The top half of a Dutch door at the other end of the room opened, and, framed in the square, Pennypacker's secretary turned the bright disc of her face toward him. "Mr. Behn?" she asked in a chiming voice. "Dr. Pennypacker will be back from lunch in a minute." She vanished backward into the maze of little rooms where Pennypacker, and eye, ear, nose, and throat man, had arranged his fabulous equipment. Through the bay window Clyde could see traffic, gayer in color than he remembered, hustle down Grand Avenue. On the sidewalk, haltered girls identical in all but name with girls he had known strolled past in twos and threes. Small town perennials, they moved rather mournfully under their burdens of bloom. In the opposite direction packs of the opposite sex carried baseball mitts.

Clyde became so lonely watching his old street that when, with a sucking exclamation, the door from the vestibule opened, he looked up gratefully, certain that the person, this being his home town, would be a friend. When he saw who it was, though every cell in his body had been replaced since he had last seen her, his hands jerked in his lap and blood bounded against his skin.

"Clyde Behn," she pronounced, with a matronly and patronizing yet frightened finality, as if he were a child and these words the moral of a story.

"Janet." He awkwardly rose from his chair and crouched, not so much in courtesy as to relieve the pressure on his heart.

"Whatever brings you back to these parts?" She was taking the pose that she was just anyone who once knew him.

He slumped back. "I'm always coming back. It's just you've never been here."

"Well, I've"—she seated herself on an orange bench and crossed her plump legs cockily—"been in Germany with my husband."

"He was in the Air Force."

"Yes." It startled her a little that he knew.

"And he's out now?" Clyde had never met him, but having now seen Janet again, he felt he knew him well—a slight, literal fellow, to judge from the shallowness of the marks he had left on her. He would wear eyebrow-style glasses, be a griper, have some not quite negotiable talent, like playing the clarinet or drawing political cartoons, and now be starting up a drab avenue of business. Selling insurance, most likely. Poor Janet, Clyde felt; except for the interval of himself—his splendid, perishable self—she would never see the light. Yet she had retained her beautiful calm, a sleepless tranquility marked by that pretty little blue puffiness below the eyes. And either she had grown slimmer or he had grown more tolerant of fat. Her thick ankles and the general *obstinacy* of her flesh used to goad him into being cruel.

"Yes." Her voice indicated that she had withdrawn; perhaps some ugliness of their last parting had recurred to her.

"I was 4-F." He was ashamed of this, and his confessing it, though she seemed unaware of the change, turned their talk inward. "A peacetime slacker," he went on, "what could be more ignoble?"

She was quiet a while, then asked, "How many children do you have?"

"Two. Age three and one. A girl and a boy; very symmetrical. Do you"—he blushed lightly, and brushed at his forehead to hide it—"have any?"

"No, we thought it wouldn't be fair, until we were more fixed."

Now the quiet moment was his to hold; she had matched him failing for failing. She recrossed her legs, and in a quaint strained way smiled.

"I'm trying to remember," he admitted, "the last time we saw each other. I can't remember how we broke up."

"I can't either," she said. "It happened so often."

Clyde wondered if with that sarcasm she intended to fetch his eyes to the brink of tears of grief. Probably not; premeditation had never been much of a weapon for her, though she had tried to learn it from him.

He moved across the linoleum to sit on the bench beside her. "I can't tell you," he said, "how much, of all the people in this town, you were the one I wanted to see." It was foolish, but he had prepared it to say, in case he ever saw her again.

"Why?" This was more like her: blunt, pucker-lipped curiosity. He had forgotten it.

"Well, hell. Any number of reasons. I wanted to say something."

"What?"

"Well, that if I hurt you, it was stupidity, because I was young. I've often wondered since if I did, because it seems now that you were the only person outside my family whoever, actually, *liked* me."

"Did I?"

"If you think by doing nothing but asking monosyllabic questions you're making an effect, you're wrong."

She averted her face, leaving, in a sense, only her body—the pale, columnar breadth of arm, the freckled crescent of shoulder muscle under the cotton strap of her summer dress—with him. "You're the one who's making effects." It was such a wan, senseless thing to say to defend herself; Clyde, virtually paralyzed by so heavy an injection of love, touched her arm icily.

With a quickness that suggested she had foreseen this, she got up and went to the table by the bay window, where rows of overlapping magazines were laid. She bowed her head to their titles, the nape of her neck in shadow beneath a half-collapsed bun. She had always had trouble keeping her hair pinned.

Clyde was blushing intensely. "Is your husband working around here?"

"He's looking for work." That she kept her back turned while saying this gave him hope.

"Mr. Behn?" The petite secretary-nurse, switching like a pendulum, led him back through the sanctums and motioned for him to sit in a high hinged chair padded with black leather. Pennypacker's equipment had always made him nervous; tons of it were marshalled through the rooms. A complex tree of tubes and lenses leaned over his left shoulder, and by his right elbow a porcelain basin was cupped expectantly. An eye chart crisply stated gibberish. In time Pennypacker himself appeared: a tall, stooped man with mottled cheekbones and an air of suppressed anger.

"Now what's the trouble, Clyde?"

"It's nothing: I mean it's very little," Clyde began, laughing inappropriately. During his adolescence he had developed a joking familiarity with his dentist and his regular doctor, but he had never become intimate with Pennypacker, who remained, what he had seemed at first, an aloof administrator of expensive humiliations. In the third grade he had made Clyde wear glasses. Later, he annually cleaned, with a shrill push of hot water, wax from Clyde's ears, and once had thrust two copper straws up Clyde's nostrils in a futile attempt to purge his sinuses. Clyde always felt unworthy of Pennypacker, felt himself a dirty conduit balking the smooth onward flow of the doctor's reputation and apparatus. He blushed to mention his latest trivial stoppage. "It's just that for over two months I've had this eyelid that twitters and it makes it difficult to think."

Pennypacker drew little circles with a pencil-sized flashlight in front of Clyde's right eye.

"It's the left lid," Clyde said, without daring to turn his head. "I went to a doctor up where I live, and he said it was like a rattle in the fender and there was nothing to do. He said it would go away, but it didn't and didn't, so I had my mother make an appointment for when I came down here to visit."

Pennypacker moved to the left eye and drew even closer. The distance between the doctor's eyes and the corners of his mouth was very long; the emotional impression of his face close up was like that of those first photographs taken from rockets, in which the earth's curvature was made apparent. "How do you like being in your home territory?" Pennypacker asked.

"Fine."

"Seem a little strange to you?"

The question itself seemed strange. "A little."

"Mm. That's interesting."

"About the eye, there were two things I thought. One was, I got some glasses made in Massachusetts by a man nobody else ever went to, and I thought his prescription might be faulty. His equipment seemed so ancient and kind of full of cobwebs; like a Dürer print." He never could decide how cultured Pennypacker was; the Canadian lake argued against it, but he was county-famous in his trade, in a county where doctors were as high as the intellectual scale went.

The flashlight, a tepid sun girdled by a grid of optical circles behind which Pennypacker's face loomed dim and colorless, came right to the skin of Clyde's eye, and the vague face lurched forward angrily, and Clyde, blind in a world of light, feared that Pennypacker was inspecting the floor of his soul. Paralyzed by panic, he breathed, "The other was that something might be in it. At night it feels as if there's a tiny speck deep in under the lid."

Pennypacker reared back and insolently raked the light back and forth across Clyde's face. "How long have you had this flaky stuff on your lids?"

The insult startled Clyde. "Is there any?"

"How long have you had it?"

"Some mornings I notice little grains like salt that I thought were what I used to call sleepy-dust—"

"This isn't sleepy-dust," the doctor said. He repeated, "This isn't sleepy-dust." Clyde started to smile at what he took to be kidding of his childish vocabulary, but Pennypacker cut him short with "Cases of this can lead to loss of the eyelashes."

"Really?" Clyde was vain of his lashes, which in his boyhood had been exceptionally long, giving his face the alert and tender look of a girl's. "Do you think it's the reason for the tic?" He imagined his face with the lids bald and the lashes lying scattered on his cheeks like insect legs. "What can I do?"

"Are you using your eyes a great deal?"

"Some. No more than I ever did."

Pennypacker's hands, blue after Clyde's dazzlement, lifted an intense brown bottle from a drawer. "It may be bacteria, it may be allergy; when you leave I'll give you something that should knock it out either way. Do you follow me? Now, Clyde"—his voice became murmurous and consolatory as he placed a cupped hand, rigid as an electrode, on the top of Clyde's head—"I'm going to put some drops in your eyes so we can check the prescription of the glasses you bought in Massachusetts."

Clyde didn't remember that the drops stung so; he gasped outright and wept while Pennypacker held the lids apart with his finger and worked them gently open and shut, as if he were playing with snapdragons. Pennypacker set preposterously small, circular dark brown glasses on Clyde's face and in exchange took away the stylish horn-rims Clyde had kept in his pocket. It was Pennypacker's method to fill his little rooms with waiting patients and wander from one to another like a dungeon-keeper.

Clyde heard, far off, the secretary's voice tinkle, and, amplified by the hollow hall, Pennypacker's rumble in welcome and Janet's respond. The one word "headaches," petulantly emphasized, stood up in her answer. Then a door was shut. Silence.

Clyde admired how matter-of-fact she had sounded. He had always admired this competence in her, her authority in the world peripheral to the world of love in which she was so servile. He remembered how she could outface waitresses and how she would bluff her mother when this vicious woman unexpectedly entered the screened porch where they were supposed to be playing cribbage. Potted elephant plants sat in the corners of the porch like faithful dwarfs; robins had built a nest in the lilac outside, inches from the screen. It had been taken as an omen, a blessing, when one evening their being on the glider no longer distressed the birds.

Unlike, say, the effects of Novocain, the dilation of pupils is impalpable. The wallpaper he saw through the open door seemed as distinct as ever. He held his fingernails close to his nose and was unable to distinguish the cuticles. He touched the sides of his nose, where tears had left trails. He looked at his fingers again, and they seemed fuzzier. He couldn't see his fingerprint whorls. The threads of his shirt had melted into an elusive liquid surface.

A door opened and closed, and another patient was ushered into a consulting room and imprisoned by Pennypacker. Janet's footsteps had not mingled with the others. Without ever quite sacrificing his reputation for good behavior, Clyde in high school had become fairly bold in heckling teachers he considered stupid or unjust. He got out of his chair, looked down the hall to where a white splinter of secretary showed, and quickly walked past a closed door to one ajar. His blood told him, This one.

Janet was sitting in a chair as upright as the one he had left, a two-pronged comb in her mouth, her back arched and her arms up, bundling her hair. As he slipped around the door, she plucked the comb from between her teeth and laughed at him. He saw in a little rimless mirror cocked above her head his own head, grimacing with stealth and grotesquely costumed in glasses like two chocolate coins, and appreciated her laughter, though it didn't fit with what he had prepared to say. He said it anyway: "Janet, are you happy?"

She rose with a practical face and walked past him and clicked the door shut. As she stood facing it, listening for a reaction from outside, he gathered her hair in his hand and lifted it from the nape of her neck, which he had expected to find in shadow but which was instead, to his distended eyes, bright as a candle. He clumsily put his lips to it.

"Don't you love your wife?" she asked.

"Incredibly much," he murmured into the fine neck-down.

She moved off, leaving him leaning awkwardly, and in front of the mirror smoothed her hair away from her ears. She sat down again, crossing her wrists in her lap.

"I just got told my eyelashes are going to fall out," Clyde said.

"Your pretty lashes," she said sombrely.

"Why do you hate me?"

"Shh. I don't hate you now."

"But you did once."

"No, I did *not* once. Clyde what *is* this bother? What are you after?"

"Son of a bitch, so I'm a bother. I knew it. You've just forgotten, all the time I've been remembering; you're so *damn* dense. I come in here a bundle of pain to tell you I'm sorry and I want you to be happy, and all I get is the back of your neck." Affected by what had happened to his eyes, his tongue had loosened, pouring out impressions; with culminating incoherence he dropped to his knees beside her chair, wondering if the thump would bring Pennypacker. "I must see you again," he blurted.

"Shh."

"I come back here and the only person who was ever pleasant to me I discover I maltreated so much she hates me."

"Clyde," she said, "you didn't maltreat me. You were a good boy to me."

Straightening up on his knees, he fumbled his fingers around the hem of the neck of her dress and pulled it out and looked down into the blurred cavity between her breasts. He had a remembrance of her freckles going down from her shoulders into her bathing suit. His glasses hit her cheek.

She stabbed the back of his hand with the points of her comb and he got to his feet, rearing high into a new, less sorrowful atmosphere. "When?" he asked, short of breath.

"No," she said.

"What's your married name?"

"Clyde, I thought you were successful. I thought you had beautiful children. Aren't you happy?"

"I am, I am; but"—the rest was so purely inspired its utterance only grazed his lips—"happiness isn't everything."

Footsteps ticked down the hall, toward their door, past it. Fear emptied his chest, yet with an excellent imitation of his old high-school flippancy he blew her a kiss, waited, opened the door, and whirled through it. His hand had left the knob when the secretary, emerging from the room where he should have been, confronted him in the linoleum-smelling hall. "Where could I get a drink of water?" he asked plaintively, assuming the hunch and whine of a blind beggar. In truth, he had, without knowing it, become thirsty.

"Once a year I pass through your territory," Pennypacker intoned as he slipped a growing weight of lenses into the tin frame on Clyde's nose. He had returned to Clyde more relaxed and chatty, now that all his little rooms were full. Clyde had tried to figure out from the pattern of noise, if Janet had been dismissed. He believed she had. The thought made his eyelid throb. He didn't even know her married name. "Down the Turnpike," Pennypacker droned on, while his face flickered in and out of focus, "up the New Jersey Pike, over the George Washington Bridge, up the Merritt, then up Route 7 all the way to Lake Champlain. To hunt the big bass. There's an experience for you."

"I notice you have a new clock in your waiting room."

"That's a Christmas present from the Alton Optical Company. Can you read that line?"

"H, L, F, Y, T, something that's either an S or an E—"

"K," Pennypacker said without looking. The poor devil, he had all those letters memorized, all that gibberish—abruptly, Clyde wanted to love him. The oculist altered one lens. "Is it better this way? . . . Or this way?"

At the end of the examination, Pennypacker said, "Though the man's equipment was dusty, he gave you a good prescription. In your right eye the axis of astigmatism has rotated several degrees, which is corrected in the lenses. If you have been experiencing a sense of strain, part of the reason, Clyde, is that those heavy frames are slipping down on your nose and giving you a prismatic effect. For a firm fit you should have metal frames, with adjustable nose pads."

"They leave such ugly dents on the sides of your nose."

"You should have them. Your bridge, you see"—he tapped his own—"is recessed. It takes a regular face to support unarticulated frames. Do you wear your glasses all the time?"

"For the movies and reading. When I got them in the third grade you told me that was all I needed them for."

"You should wear them all the time."

"Really? Even just for walking around?"

"All the time, yes. You have middle-aged eyes."

Pennypacker gave him a little plastic squeeze bottle of drops. "That is for the fungus on your lids."

"Fungus? There's a brutal thought. Well, will it cure the tic?"

Pennypacker impatiently snapped, "The tic is caused by muscular fatigue."

Thus Clyde was dismissed into a tainted world where things evaded his focus. He went down the hall in his sunglasses and was told by the secretary that he would receive a bill. The waiting room was full now, mostly with downcast old men and myopic children gnawing at their mothers. From out of this crowd a ripe young woman arose and came against his chest, and Clyde, included in the intimacy of the aroma her hair and skin gave off, felt weak and broad and grand, like a declining rose. Janet tucked a folded note into the pocket of his shirt and said conversationally, "He's waiting outside in the car."

The neutral, ominous "he" opened wide a conspiracy Clyde instantly entered. He stayed behind a minute, to give her time to get away. Ringed by the judging eyes of the young and old, he felt like an actor snug behind the blinding protection of the footlights; he squinted prolongedly at the speedometer-clock, which, like a letter delivered on the stage, in fact was blank. Then, smiling ironically toward both sides, he left the waiting room, coming into Pennypacker's entrance hall, a cubicle equipped with a stucco umbrella stand and a red rubber mat saying, in letters so large he could read them, WALK IN.

He had not expected to be unable to read her note. He held it at arm's length and slowly brought it toward his face, wiggling it in the light from outdoors. Though he did this several times, it didn't yield even the simplest word. Just wet blue specks. Under the specks, however, in their intensity and disposition, he believed he could make out the handwriting—slanted, open, unoriginal—familiar to him from other notes received long ago. This glimpse, through the skin of the paper, of her plain self quickened and sweetened his desire more than touching her had. He tucked the note back into his shirt pocket and its stiffness there made a shield for his heart. In this armor he stepped into the familiar street. The maples, macadam, shadows, houses, cement, were to his violated eyes as brilliant as a scene remembered; he became a child again in this town, where life was a distant adventure, a rumor, an always imminent joy.

ALICE ADAMS
(1926–)

Alice Adams, born in Fredericksburg, Virginia, and educated at Radcliffe, has lived for much of her adult life in San Francisco, the meticulously observed setting of a number of her short stories and novels. "Alaska" is typical of Alice Adams' exquisitely wrought fiction, in which dialogue is preeminent, recorded with a flawless ear; it is perhaps less typical in its protagonist, the cleaning lady of a wealthy woman.

Many times chosen to be represented in the annual O. Henry Prize Stories anthology, as well as in The Best American Short Stories, *Alice Adams is one of the most gifted of contemporary short story writers. Her short story collections are* Beautiful Girl *(1979),* To See You Again *(1982),* Return Trips *(1985), and* After You've Gone *(1989); her novels include* Careless Love *(1966),* Listening to Billie *(1978),* Rich Rewards *(1980),* Second Chances *(1988), and* Caroline's Daughters *(1991). Like Edith Wharton, John Cheever, and John Updike, Alice Adams is a superb social observer gifted with an unfailing eye for the revelatory detail. Social change as reflected in seemingly ordinary families of the middle and upper-middle classes, with an emphasis upon female experience, is a feature of her work, which typically shuns melodramatic extremes, as in the story included here.*

Alaska

Although Mrs. Lawson does not drink any more, not a drop since New Year's Day, 1961, in Juneau, Alaska, she sometimes feels a confusion in her mind about which husband she will meet, at the end of the day. She has been married five times, and she has lived, it seems to her, almost everywhere. Now she is a cleaning lady, in San Francisco, although some might say that she is too old for that kind of work. Her hair, for so many years dyed red, is now streaky gray, and her eyes are a paler blue than they once were. Her skin is a dark bronze color, but she thinks of herself as Negro—black, these days. From New Orleans, originally.

If someone came up and asked her, Who are you married to now, Lucille Lawson? of course she would answer, Charles, and we live in the Western Addition in San Francisco, two busses to get there from here.

But, not asked, she feels the presences of those other husbands—nameless, shadowy, lurking near the edges of her mind. And menacing, most of them, especially the one who tromped her in Juneau, that New Year's Day. He was the worst, by far, but none of them was worth a whole lot, come to think of it. And she was always working at one place or another, and always tired, at the end of her days, and then there were those husbands to come home to, and more work to do for them. Some husbands come honking for you in their cars, she remembers, but usually you have to travel a long way, busses and street cars, to get to where they are, to where you and them live.

These days Mrs. Lawson just cleans for Miss Goldstein, a rich white lady older than Mrs. Lawson is, who lives alone in a big house on Divisadero Street, near Union. She has lots of visitors, some coming to stay, all funny-looking folk. Many foreign, but not fancy. Miss Goldstein still travels a lot herself, to peculiar places like China and Cuba and Africa.

What Mrs. Lawson is best at is polishing silver, and that is what she mostly does, the tea service, coffee service, and all the flatware, although more than once Miss Goldstein has sighed and said that maybe it should all be put away, or melted down to help the poor people in some of the places she visits; all that silver around looks boastful, Miss Goldstein thinks. But it is something for Mrs. Lawson to do every day (Miss Goldstein does not come right out and say this; they both just know).

Along with the silver polishing she dusts, and sometimes she irons a little, some silk or linen shirts; Miss Goldstein does not get dressed up a lot, usually favoring sweaters and old pants. She gets the most dressed up when she is going off to march somewhere, which she does fairly often. Then she gets all gussied up in a black suit and her real pearls, and she has these posters to carry, NO NUKES IS GOOD NUKES, GRAY PANTHERS FOR PEACE. She would be a sight to behold, Mrs. Lawson thinks: she can hardly imagine Miss Goldstein with all the kinds of folks that are usually in those lines, the beards and raggedy blue jeans, the dirty old sweat shirts, big women wearing no bras. Thin, white-haired Miss Goldstein in her pearls.

To help with the heavy housework, the kitchen floor and the stove, bathtubs and all like that, Miss Goldstein has hired a young white girl, Gloria. At first Mrs. Lawson was mistrustful that a girl like that could clean anything, a blond-haired small little girl with these doll blue eyes in some kind of a white pants work outfit, but Gloria moves through that big house like a little bolt of white lightning, and she leaves everything behind her *clean*. Even with her eyesight not as good as it was Mrs. Lawson can see how clean the kitchen floor and the stove are, and the bathtubs. And she has *looked*.

Gloria comes at eight every morning, and she does all that in just two hours. Mrs. Lawson usually gets in sometime after nine, depending on how the busses run. And so there is some time when they are both working along, Mrs. Lawson at the sink with the silver, probably, or dusting off Miss Goldstein's bureau, dusting her books—and Gloria down on her knees on the bathroom floor (Gloria is right; the only way to clean a floor is on your knees, although not too many folks seem to know that, these days). Of course they don't talk much, both working, but Gloria has about twenty minutes before her next job, in that same neighborhood. Sometimes, then, Mrs. Lawson will take a break from her polishing, dusting, and heat up some coffee for the both of them, and they will talk a little. Gloria has a lot of worries, a lot on her mind, Mrs. Lawson can tell, although Gloria never actually says, beyond everyone's usual troubles, money and rent and groceries, and in Gloria's case car repairs, an old VW.

The two women are not friends, really, but all things considered they get along okay. Some days they don't either of them feel like talking, and they both just skim over sections of the newspaper, making comments on this and that, in the news. Other times they talk a little.

Gloria likes to hear about New Orleans, in the old days, when Mrs. Lawson's father had a drugstore and did a lot of doctoring there, and how later they all moved to Texas, and the Klan came after them, and they hid and moved again, to another town. And Gloria tells Mrs. Lawson how her sister is ashamed that she cleans houses for a living. The sister, Sharon, lives up in Alaska, but not in Juneau, where Mrs. Lawson lived. Gloria's sister lives in Fairbanks, where her husband is in forestry school.

However, despite her and Gloria getting along okay, in the late afternoons Mrs. Lawson begins to worry that Gloria will find something wrong there, when she comes first thing in the morning. Something that she, Mrs. Lawson, did wrong. She even imagines Gloria saying to Miss Goldstein, Honestly, how come you keep on that old Mrs. Lawson? She can't see to clean very good, she's too old to work.

She does not really think that Gloria would say a thing like that, and even if she did Miss Goldstein wouldn't listen, probably. Still, the idea is very worrying to her, and in an anxious way she sweeps up the kitchen floor, and dustmops the long front hall. And at the same time her mind is plagued with those images of husbands, dark ghosts, in Juneau and Oakland and Kansas City, husbands that she has to get home to, somehow. Long bus rides with cold winds at the places where you change, or else you have to wait a long time for the choked-up sound of them honking, until you get in their creaky old cars and drive, drive home, in the dark.

Mrs. Lawson is absolutely right about Gloria having serious troubles on her mind—more serious in fact than Mrs. Lawson could have thought of: Gloria's hideous, obsessive problem is a small lump on her leg, her right leg, mid-calf. A tiny knot. She keeps reaching to touch it, no matter what she is doing, and it is always there. She cannot make herself not touch it. She thinks constantly of that lump, its implications and probable consequences. Driving to work in her jumpy old VW, she reaches down to her leg, to check the lump. A couple of times she almost has accidents, as she concentrates on her fingers, reaching, what they feel as they touch her leg.

To make things even worse, the same week that she first noticed the lump Gloria met a really nice man, about her age: Dugald, neither married nor gay (a miracle, these days, in San Francisco). He is a bartender in a place where she sometimes goes with girlfriends, after a movie or something. In a way she has known Dugald for a long time, but in another way not—not known him until she happened to go into the place alone, thinking, Well, why not?

I'm tired (it was late one afternoon), a beer would be nice. And there was Dugald, and they talked, and he asked her out, on his next night off. And the next day she discovered the lump.

She went with Dugald anyway, of course, and she almost had a very good time—except that whenever she thought about what was probably wrong with her she went cold and quiet. She thinks that Dugald may not ever ask her out again, and even if he did, she can't get at all involved with anyone, not now.

Also, Gloria's sister, Sharon, in Fairbanks, Alaska, has invited her to come up and stay for a week, while Sharon's forestry-student husband is back in Kansas, visiting his folks; Sharon does not much like her husband's family. Gloria thinks she will go for ten days in June, while Miss Goldstein is in China, again. Gloria is on the whole pleased at the prospect of this visit; as she Ajaxes and Lysols Miss Goldstein's upstairs bathroom, she thinks, *Alaska*, and she imagines gigantic glaciers, huge wild animals, fantastic snow-capped mountains. (She will send a friendly postcard to Dugald, she thinks, and maybe one to old Lawson.) Smiling, for an instant she makes a small bet with herself, which is that at some point Sharon will ask her not to mention to anyone, *please*, what she, Gloria, does for a living. Well, Gloria doesn't care. Lord knows her work is not much to talk about; it is simply the most money she can get an hour, and not pay taxes (she is always afraid, when not preoccupied with her other, more terrible worries, that the IRS will somehow get to her). On the other hand, it is fun to embarrass Sharon.

At home though, lying awake at night, of course the lump is all that Gloria thinks about. And hospitals: when she was sixteen she had her tonsils out, and she decided then on no more operations, no matter what. If she ever has a baby she will do it at home. The hospital was so frightening, everyone was horrible to her, all the doctors and nurses (except for a couple of black aides who were sweet, really nice, she remembers). They all made her feel like something much less than a person. And a hospital would take all her money, and more, all her careful savings (someday she plans to buy a little cabin, up near Tahoe, and raise big dogs). She thinks about something being cut off. Her leg. Herself made so ugly, everyone trying not to look. No more men, no dates, not Dugald or anyone. No love or sex again, not ever.

In the daytime her terror is slightly more manageable, but it is still so powerful that the very idea of calling a doctor, showing him the lump, asking him what to do—chills her blood, almost stops her heart.

And she can feel the lump there, all the time. Probably growing.

Mrs. Lawson has told Gloria that she never goes to doctors; she can doctor herself, Mrs. Lawson says. She always has. Gloria has even thought of showing the lump to Mrs. Lawson.

But she tries to think in a positive way about Alaska. They have a cute little apartment right on the university campus, Sharon has written. Fairbanks is on a river; they will take an afternoon trip on a paddleboat. And they will spend one night at Mount McKinley, and go on a wild life tour.

"Fairbanks, now. I never did get up that way," says Mrs. Lawson, told of Sharon's invitation, Gloria's projected trip. "But I always heard it was real nice up there."

Actually she does not remember anything at all about Fairbanks, but for Gloria's sake she hopes that it is nice, and she reasons that any place would be better than Juneau, scrunched in between mountains so steep they look to fall down on you.

"I hope it's nice," says Gloria. "I just hope I don't get mauled by some bear, on that wild life tour."

Aside from not drinking and never going to doctors (she has read all her father's old doctor books, and remembers most of what she read) Mrs. Lawson believes that she gets her good health and her strength—considerable, for a person of her years—from her daily naps. Not a real sleep, just sitting down for a while in some place really comfortable, and closing her eyes.

She does that now, in a small room off Miss Goldstein's main library room (Miss Goldstein has already gone off to China, but even if she were home she wouldn't mind about a little nap). Mrs. Lawson settles back into a big old fat leather chair, and she slips her shoes off. And, very likely because of talking about Alaska that morning, Gloria's trip, her mind drifts off, in and out of Juneau. She remembers the bitter cold, cold rains of that winter up there, the winds, fogs thicker than cotton, and dark. Snow that sometimes kept them in the little hillside cabin for days, even weeks. Her and Charles: that husband had the same name as the one she now has, she just remembered—funny to forget a thing like that. They always used to drink a lot, her and the Charles in Alaska; you had to, to get through the winter. And pretty often they would fight, ugly drunk quarrels that she couldn't quite remember the words to, in the mornings. But that New Year's Eve they were having a real nice time; he was being real nice, laughing and all, and then all of a sudden it was like he turned into some other person, and he struck her. He grabbed up her hair, all of it red, at that time, and he called her a witch and he knocked her down to the floor, and he tromped her. Later of course he was sorry, and he said he had been feeling mean about not enough work, but still, he had tromped her.

Pulling herself out of that half dream, half terrible memory, Mrs. Lawson repeats, as though someone had asked her, that now she is married to Charles, in San Francisco. They live in the Western Addition; they don't drink, and this Charles is a nice man, most of the time.

She tries then to think about the other three husbands, one in Oakland, in Chicago, in Kansas City, but nothing much comes to mind, of them. No faces or words, just shadows, and no true pictures of any of those cities. The only thing she is perfectly clear about is that not one of those other men was named Charles.

On the airplane to Alaska, something terrible, horrible, entirely frightening happens to Gloria, which is: a girl comes and sits in the seat next to hers, and that girl has—the lower part of her right leg missing. Cut off. A pretty dark-haired girl, about the same size as Gloria, wearing a nice blazer, and a kind of long skirt. One boot. Metal crutches.

Gloria is so frightened—she knows that this is an omen, a sign meant for her—that she is dizzy, sick; she leans back and closes her eyes, as the plane bumps upward, zooming through clouds, and she stays that way for the rest of the trip. She tries not to think; she repeats numbers and meaningless words to herself.

At some point she feels someone touching her arm. Flinching, she opens her eyes to see the next-seat girl, who is asking, "Are you okay? Can I get you anything?"

"I'm all right. Just getting the flu, I think." Gloria smiles in a deliberately non-friendly way. The last thing in the world that she wants is a conversation with that girl: the girl at last getting around to her leg, telling Gloria, "It started with this lump I had, right here."

Doctors don't usually feel your legs, during physical examinations, Gloria thinks; she is standing beside Sharon on the deck of the big paddleboat that is slowly ploughing up the Natoma River. It would be possible to hide a lump for a long time, unless it grew a lot, she thinks, as the boat's captain announces over the bullhorn that they are passing what was once an Indian settlement.

Alaska is much flatter than Gloria had imagined its being, at least around Fairbanks—and although she had of course heard the words, midnight sun, she had not known they were a literal description; waking at three or four in the morning from bad dreams, her nighttime panics (her legs drawn up under her, one hand touching her calf, the lump) she sees brilliant sunshine, coming in through the tattered aluminum foil that Sharon has messily pasted to the window. It is all wrong—unsettling. Much worse than the thick dark fogs that come into San Francisco in the summer; she is used to them.

In fact sleeplessness and panic (what she felt at the sight of that girl with the missing leg has persisted; she knows it was a sign) have combined to produce in Gloria an almost trancelike state. She is so quiet, so passive that she can feel Sharon wondering about her, what is wrong. Gloria does not, for a change, say anything critical of Sharon's housekeeping, which is as sloppy as usual. She does not tell anyone that she, Gloria, is a cleaning person.

A hot wind comes up off the water, and Gloria remembers that tomorrow they go to Mount McKinley, and the wild life tour.

Somewhat to her disappointment, Mrs. Lawson does not get any postcards from Gloria in Alaska, although Gloria had mentioned that she would send one, with a picture.

What she does get is a strange phone call from Gloria on the day that she was supposed to come back. What is *strange* is that Gloria sounds like some entirely other person, someone younger even than Gloria actually is, younger and perfectly happy. It is Gloria's voice, all right, but lighter and quicker than it was, a voice without any shadows.

"I'm back!" Gloria bursts out, "but I just don't think I want to work today. I was out sort of late—" She laughs, in a bright new way, and then she asks, "She's not back yet, is she?"

Meaning Miss Goldstein. "No, not for another week," Mrs. Lawson tells her. "You had a good trip?"

"Fabulous! A miracle, really. I'll tell you all about it tomorrow."

Hanging up, Mrs. Lawson has an uneasy sense that some impersonator will come to work in Gloria's place.

But of course it is Gloria who is already down on her knees, cleaning the kitchen floor, when Mrs. Lawson gets there the following day.

And almost right away she begins to tell Mrs. Lawson about the wild life tour, from Mount McKinley, seemingly the focal point of her trip.

"It was really weird," says Gloria. "It looked like the moon, in that funny light." She has a lot to say, and she is annoyed that Mrs. Lawson seems to be paying more attention to her newspaper—is barely listening. Also, Lawson seems to have aged, while Gloria was away, or maybe Gloria just forgot how old she looks, since in a way she doesn't act very old; she moves around and works a lot harder than Sharon ever does, for one example. But it seems to Gloria today that Mrs. Lawson's skin is grayer than it was, ashy-looking, and her eyes, which are always strange, have got much paler.

Nevertheless, wanting more attention (her story has an important point to it) Gloria raises her voice, as she continues, "And every time someone spotted one of those animals he'd yell out, and the man would stop the bus. We saw caribou, and these funny white sheep, high up on the rocks, and a lot of moose, and some foxes. Not any bears. Anyway, every time we stopped I got real scared. We were on the side of a really steep mountain, part of Mount McKinley, I think, and the bus was so wide, like a school bus." She does not tell Mrs. Lawson that in a weird way she liked being so scared. What she thought was, if I'm killed on this bus I'll never even get to a doctor. Which was sort of funny, really, now that she can see the humor in it—now that the lump is mysteriously, magically gone!

However, she has reached the dramatic disclosure toward which this story of her outing has been heading. "Anyway, we got back all right," she says, "and two days after that, back in Fairbanks, do you know what the headlines were, in the local paper?" She has asked this (of course rhetorical) question in a slow, deepened voice, and now she pauses, her china-blue eyes gazing into Mrs. Lawson's paler, stranger blue.

"Well, I don't know," Lawson obliges.

"They said, BUS TOPPLES FROM MOUNTAIN, EIGHT KILLED 42 INJURED. Can you imagine? Our same bus, the very next day. What do you think that means?" This question too has been rhetorical; voicing it, Gloria smiles in a satisfied, knowing way.

A very polite woman, Mrs. Lawson smiles gently too. "It means you spared. You like to live fifty, sixty years more."

Eagerly Gloria bursts out, "Exactly! That's just the way I figured it, right away." She pauses, smiling widely, showing her little white teeth. "And then, that very same afternoon of the day we saw the paper," she goes on, "I was changing my clothes and I felt the calf of my leg where there'd been this lump that I was sort of worried about—and the lump was gone. I couldn't believe it. So I guess it was just a muscle, not anything bad."

"Them leg muscles can knot up that way, could of told you that myself," Mrs. Lawson mutters. "Heavy housework can do that to a person." But Gloria looks so happy, so bright-faced and shiny-eyed, that Mrs. Lawson does not want to bring her down, in any way, and so she adds, "But you sure are right about that bus accident. It's a sure sign you been spared."

"Oh, that's what I think too! And later we saw these really neat big dogs, in Fairbanks. I'm really thinking about getting a dog. This man I know really likes dogs too, last night we were talking." Her voice trails off in a happy reminiscence.

Later in the day, though, thinking about Gloria and her story, what she and Gloria said to each other, Mrs. Lawson is not really convinced about anything. The truth is, Gloria could perfectly well get killed by a bus in San Francisco, this very afternoon, or shot by some sniper; it's been saying in the paper about snipers, all over town, shooting folks. Or Gloria could find another lump, some place else, somewhere dangerous. Missing one bus accident is no sure sign that a person's life will always come up rosy, because nobody's does, not for long. Even Miss Goldstein, in China, could fall off of some Chinese mountain.

In a weary, discouraged way Mrs. Lawson moved through the rest of her day. It is true; she is too old and tired for the work she does. Through the big street-floor windows she watches the cold June fog rolling in from the bay, and she thinks how the weather in California has never seemed right to her. She thinks about Charles, and it comes to her that one Charles could change into the other, the same way that first Charles in such a sudden way turned violent, and wild.

That thought is enough to make her dread the end of her work, and the day, when although it is summer she will walk out into streets that are as dark and cold as streets are in Alaska.

RAYMOND CARVER

(1938–1988)

Of the writers in this anthology, Raymond Carver is one of the very few to have devoted himself to the art of the short story and the poem; to have devoted himself, in a sense, to the art of dramatically impacted brevity. In discussing Minimalism as a mode of fiction, Carver spoke of his practice as a form of realism in the Anderson-Hemingway tradition: "the gradual accretion of meaningful detail, the concrete word as opposed to the abstract or arbitrary or slippery word."

Raymond Carver was born in Clatskanie, Oregon, and educated at Humboldt State University and the University of Iowa. He had long been associated with Port Angeles, Washington, where he was living at the time of his death. Though he published relatively few volumes of short fiction, his influence upon younger writers has been considerable. His fiction titles are Will You Please Be Quiet, Please? *(1976),* What We Talk About When We Talk About Love *(1981),* Cathedral *(1983), and* Where I'm Calling From: New and Selected Stories *(1988). His poetry collections include* Winter Insomnia *(1970),* Ultramarine *(1986), and the posthumously published* A New Walk to the River *(1990).*

America is surely not the only culture in which a passion for material things has been elevated to romance, but it is surely one of the few cultures to have so thoroughly examined this romance. "Are These Actual Miles?" is vintage Carver, though written comparatively early in his career. In this wonderfully succinct tale, an entire marriage—an entire way of life—is given an emblematic shape in the lost car remembered "there in the drive, in the sun, gleaming."

Are These Actual Miles?

Fact is the car needs to be sold in a hurry, and Leo sends Toni out to do it. Toni is smart and has personality. She used to sell children's encyclopedias door to door. She signed him up, even though he didn't have kids. Afterward, Leo asked her for a date, and the date led to this. This deal has to be cash, and it has to be done tonight. Tomorrow somebody they owe might slap a lien on the car. Monday they'll be in court, home free—but word on them went out yesterday, when their lawyer mailed the letters of intention. The hearing on Monday is nothing to worry about, the lawyer has said. They'll be asked some questions, and they'll sign some papers, and that's it. But sell the convertible, he said—today, *tonight.* They can hold onto the little car, Leo's car, no problem. But they go into court with that big convertible, the court will take it, and that's that.

Toni dresses up. It's four o'clock in the afternoon. Leo worries the lots will close. But Toni takes her time dressing. She puts on a new white blouse, wide lacy cuffs, the new two-piece suit, new heels. She transfers the stuff from her straw purse into the new patent-leather handbag. She studies the lizard makeup pouch and puts that in too. Toni has been two hours on her hair and face. Leo stands in the bedroom doorway and taps his lips with his knuckles, watching.

"You're making me nervous," she says. "I wish you wouldn't just stand," she says. "So tell me how I look."

"You look fine," he says. "You look great. I'd buy a car from you anytime."

"But you don't have money," she says, peering into the mirror. She pats her hair, frowns. "And your credit's lousy. You're nothing," she says. "Teasing," she says and looks at him in the mirror. "Don't be serious," she says. "It has to be done, so I'll do it. You take it out, you'd be lucky to get three, four hundred and we both know it. Honey, you'd be lucky if you didn't have to pay *them.*" She gives her a hair a final pat, gums her lips, blots the lipstick with a tissue. She turns away from the mirror and picks up her purse. "I'll have to have dinner or something, I told you that already, that's the way they work, I know them. But don't worry, I'll get out of it," she says. "I can handle it."

"Jesus," Leo says, "did you have to say that?"

She looks at him steadily. "Wish me luck," she says.

"Luck," he says. "You have the pink slip?" he says.

She nods. He follows her through the house, a tall woman with a small high bust, broad hips and thighs. He scratches a pimple on his neck. "You're sure?" he says. "Make sure. You have to have the pink slip."

"I have the pink slip," she says.

"Make sure."

She starts to say something, instead looks at herself in the front window and then shakes her head.

"At least call," he says. "Let me know what's going on."

"I'll call," she says. "Kiss, kiss. Here," she says and points to the corner of her mouth. "Careful," she says.

He holds the door for her. "Where are you going to try first?" he says. She moves past him and onto the porch.

Ernest Williams looks from across the street. In his Bermuda shorts, stomach hanging, he looks at Leo and Toni as he directs a spray onto his begonias. Once, last winter, during the holidays, when Toni and the kids were visiting his mother's, Leo brought a woman home. Nine o'clock the next morning, a cold foggy Saturday, Leo walked the woman to the car, surprised Ernest Williams on the sidewalk with a newspaper in his hand. Fog drifted, Ernest Williams stared, then slapped the paper against his leg, hard.

Leo recalls that slap, hunches his shoulders, says, "You have someplace in mind first?"

"I'll just go down the line," she says. "The first lot, then I'll just go down the line."

"Open at nine hundred," he says. "Then come down. Nine hundred is low bluebook, even on a cash deal."

"I know where to start," she says.

Ernest Williams turns the hose in their direction. He stares at them through the spray of water. Leo has an urge to cry out a confession.

"Just making sure," he says.

"Okay, okay," she says. "I'm off."

It's her car, they call it her car, and that makes it all the worse. They bought it new that summer three years ago. She wanted something to do after the kids started school, so she went back selling. He was working six days a week in the fiber-glass plant. For a while they didn't know how to spend the money. Then they put a thousand on the convertible and doubled and tripled the payments until in a year they had it paid. Earlier, while she was dressing, he took the jack and spare from the trunk and emptied the glove compartment of pencils, matchbooks, Blue Chip stamps. Then he washed it and vacuumed inside. The red hood and fenders shine.

"Good luck," he says and touches her elbow.

She nods. He sees she is already gone, already negotiating.

"Things are going to be different!" he calls to her as she reaches the driveway. "We start over Monday. I mean it."

Ernest Williams looks at them and turns his head and spits. She gets into the car and lights a cigarette.

"This time next week!" Leo calls again. "Ancient history!"

He waves as she backs into the street. She changes gear and starts ahead. She accelerates and the tires give a little scream.

In the kitchen Leo pours Scotch and carries the drink to the backyard. The kids are at his mother's. There was a letter three days ago, his name penciled on the outside of the dirty envelope, the only letter all summer not demanding payment in full. We are having fun, the letter said. We like Grandma. We have a new dog called Mr. Six. He is nice. We love him. Good-bye.

He goes for another drink. He adds ice and sees that his hand trembles. He holds the hand over the sink. He looks at the hand for a while, sets down the glass, and holds out the other hand. Then he picks up the glass and goes back outside to sit on the steps. He recalls when he was a kid his dad pointing at a fine house, a tall white house surrounded by apple trees and a high white rail fence. "That's Finch," his dad said admiringly. "He's been in bankruptcy at least twice. Look at that house." But bankruptcy is a company collapsing utterly, executives cutting their wrists and throwing themselves from windows, thousands of men on the street.

Leo and Toni still had furniture. Leo and Toni had furniture and Toni and the kids had clothes. Those things were exempt. What else? Bicycles for the kids, but these he had sent to his mother's for safekeeping. The portable air-conditioner and the appliances, new washer and dryer, trucks came for those things weeks ago. What else did they have? This and that, nothing mainly, stuff that wore out or fell to pieces long ago. But there were some big parties back there, some fine travel. To Reno and Tahoe, at eighty with the top down and the radio playing. Food, that was one of the big items. They gorged on food. He figures thousands on luxury items alone. Toni would go to the grocery and put in everything she saw. "I had to do without when I was a kid," she says. "These kids are not going to do without," as if he'd been insisting they should. She joins all the book clubs. "We never had books around when I was a kid," she says as she tears open the heavy packages. They enroll in the record clubs for something to play on the new stereo. They sign up for it all. Even a pedigreed terrier named Ginger. He paid two hundred and found her run over in the street a week later. They buy what they want. If they can't pay, they charge. They sign up.

His undershirt is wet; he can feel the sweat rolling from his underarms. He sits on the step with the empty glass in his hand and watches the shadows fill up the yard. He stretches, wipes his face. He listens to the traffic on the highway and considers whether he should go to the basement, stand on the utility sink, and hang himself with his belt. He understands he is willing to be dead.

Inside he makes a large drink and he turns the TV on and he fixes something to eat. He sits at the table with chili and crackers and watches something about a blind detective. He clears the table. He washes the pan and the bowl, dries these things and puts them away, then allows himself a look at the clock.

It's after nine. She's been gone nearly five hours.

He pours Scotch, adds water, carries the drink to the living room. He sits on the couch but finds his shoulders so stiff they won't let him lean back. He stares at the screen and sips, and soon he goes for another drink. He sits again. A news program begins—it's ten o'clock—and he says, "God, what in God's name has gone wrong?" and goes to the kitchen to return with more Scotch. He sits, he closes his eyes, and opens them when he hears the telephone ringing.

"I wanted to call," she says.

"Where are you?" he says. He hears piano music, and his heart moves.

"I don't know," she says. "Someplace. We're having a drink,

then we're going someplace else for dinner. I'm with the sales manager. He's crude, but he's all right. He bought the car. I have to go now. I was on my way to the ladies and saw the phone."

"Did somebody buy the car?" Leo says. He looks out the kitchen window to the place in the drive where she always parks.

"I told you," she says. "I have to go now."

"Wait, wait a minute, for Christ's sake," he says. "Did somebody buy the car or not?"

"He had his checkbook out when I left," she says. "I have to go now. I have to go to the bathroom."

"Wait!" he yells. The line goes dead. He listens to the dial tone. "Jesus Christ," he says as he stands with the receiver in his hand.

He circles the kitchen and goes back to the living room. He sits. He gets up. In the bathroom he brushes his teeth very carefully. Then he uses dental floss. He washes his face and goes back to the kitchen. He looks at the clock and takes a clean glass from a set that has a hand of playing cards painted on each glass. He fills the glass with ice. He stares for a while at the glass he left in the sink.

He sits against one end of the couch and puts his legs up at the other end. He looks at the screen, realizes he can't make out what the people are saying. He turns the empty glass in his hand and considers biting off the rim. He shivers for a time and thinks of going to bed, though he knows he will dream of a large woman with gray hair. In the dream he is always leaning over tying his shoelaces. When he straightens up, she looks at him, and he bends to tie again. He looks at his hand. It makes a fist as he watches. The telephone is ringing.

"Where are you, honey?" he says slowly, gently.

"We're at this restaurant," she says, her voice strong, bright.

"Honey, which restaurant?" he says. He puts the heel of his hand against his eye and pushes.

"Downtown someplace," she says. "I think it's New Jimmy's. Excuse me," she says to someone off the line, "is this place New Jimmy's? This is New Jimmy's, Leo," she says to him. "Everything is all right, we're almost finished, then he's going to bring me home."

"Honey?" he says. He holds the receiver against his ear and rocks back and forth, eyes closed. "Honey?"

"I have to go," she says. "I wanted to call. Anyway, guess how much?"

"Honey," he says.

"Six and a quarter," she says. "I have it in my purse. He said there's no market for convertibles. I guess we're born lucky," she says and laughs. "I told him everything. I think I had to."

"Honey," Leo says.

"What?" she says.

"Please, honey," Leo says.

"He said he sympathizes," she says. "But he would have said anything." She laughs again. "He said personally he'd rather be classified a robber or a rapist than a bankrupt. He's nice enough, though," she says.

"Come home," Leo says. "Take a cab and come home."

"I can't," she says. "I told you, we're halfway through dinner."

"I'll come for you," he says.

"No," she says. "I said we're just finishing. I told you, it's part of the deal. They're out for all they can get. But don't worry, we're about to leave. I'll be home in a little while." She hangs up.

In a few minutes he calls New Jimmy's. A man answers. "New Jimmy's has closed for the evening," the man says.

"I'd like to talk to my wife," Leo says.

"Does she work here?" the man asks. "Who is she?"

"She's a customer," Leo says. "She's with someone. A business person."

"Would I know her?" the man says. "What is her name?"

"I don't think you know her," Leo says.

"That's all right," Leo says. "That's all right. I see her now."

"Thank you for calling New Jimmy's," the man says.

Leo hurries to the window. A car he doesn't recognize slows in front of the house, then picks up speed. He waits. Two, three hours later, the telephone rings again. There is no one at the other end when he picks up the receiver. There is only a dial tone.

"I'm right here!" Leo screams into the receiver.

Near dawn he hears footsteps on the porch. He gets up from the couch. The set hums, the screen glows. He opens the door. She bumps the wall coming in. She grins. Her face is puffy, as if she's been sleeping under sedation. She works her lips, ducks heavily and sways as he cocks his fist.

"Go ahead," she says thickly. She stands there swaying. Then she makes a noise and lunges, catches his shirt, tears it down the front. "Bankrupt!" she screams. She twists loose, grabs and tears his undershirt at the neck. "You son of a bitch," she says, clawing.

He squeezes her wrists, then lets go, steps back, looking for something heavy. She stumbles as she heads for the bedroom. "Bankrupt," she mutters. He hears her fall on the bed and groan.

He waits awhile, then splashes water on his face and goes to the bedroom. He turns the lights on, looks at her, and begins to take her clothes off. He pulls and pushes her from side to side undressing her. She says something in her sleep and moves her hand. He takes off her underpants, looks at them closely under the light, and throws them into a corner. He turns back the covers and rolls her in, naked. Then he opens her purse. He is reading the check when he hears the car come into the drive.

He looks through the front curtain and sees the convertible in the drive, its motor running smoothly, the headlamps burning, and he closes and opens his eyes. He sees a tall man come around in front of the car and up to the front porch. The man lays something on the porch and starts back to the car. He wears a white linen suit.

Leo turns on the porch light and opens the door cautiously. Her makeup pouch lies on the top step. The man looks at Leo across the front of the car, and then gets back inside and releases the handbrake.

"Wait!" Leo calls and starts down the steps. The man brakes the car as Leo walks in front of the lights. The car creaks against the brake. Leo tries to pull the two pieces of his shirt together, tries to bunch it all into his trousers.

"What is it you want?" the man says. "Look," the man says, "I have to go. No offense. I buy and sell cars, right? The lady left her makeup. She's a fine lady, very refined. What is it?"

Leo leans against the door and looks at the man. The man takes his hands off the wheel and puts them back. He drops the gear into reverse and the car moves backward a little.

"I want to tell you," Leo says and wets his lips.

The light in Ernest Williams' bedroom goes on. The shade rolls up.

Leo shakes his head, tucks in his shirt again. He steps back from the car. "Monday," he says.

"Monday," the man says and watches for sudden movement.

Leo nods slowly.

"Well, goodnight," the man says and coughs. "Take it easy, hear? Monday, that's right. Okay, then." He takes his foot off the brake, puts it on again after he has rolled back two or three feet. "Hey, one question. Between friends, are these actual miles?" The man waits, then clears his throat. "Okay, look, it doesn't matter either way," the man says. "I have to go. Take it easy." He backs into the street, pulls away quickly, and turns the corner without stopping.

Leo tucks at his shirt and goes back in the house. He locks the front door and checks it. Then he goes to the bedroom and locks that door and turns back the covers. He looks at her before he flicks the light. He takes off his clothes, folds them carefully on the floor, and gets in beside her. He lies on his back for a time and pulls the hair on his stomach, considering. He looks at the bedroom door, outlined now in the faint outside light. Presently he reaches out his hand and touches her hip. She does not move. He turns on his side and puts his hand on her hip. He runs his fingers over her hip and feels the stretch marks there. They are like roads, and he traces them in her flesh. He runs his fingers back and forth, first one, then another. They run everywhere in her flesh, dozens, perhaps hundreds of them. He remembers waking up the morning after they bought the car, seeing it, there in the drive, in the sun, gleaming.

LESLIE MARMON SILKO

(1948–)

Born in Albuquerque, New Mexico, of mixed ancestry—by her own description Laguna Pueblo, Mexican, and white—Leslie Marmon Silko grew up on the Laguna Pueblo Reservation, where members of her family had lived for generations, and where she learned traditional stories and legends from female relatives. Silko's first published book is the collection Laguna Woman: Poems *(1974) which draws richly upon her tribal ancestry.*

Silko has lived and taught in Arizona and Alaska as well as in New Mexico, where she currently resides. Her much-acclaimed novel Ceremony, *the story of a Native American of mixed ancestry who is a veteran of World War II, was published in 1977; her miscellany* Storyteller, *drawing upon Native American myths, and combining poetry, family history, fiction, and photographs, was published in 1981. Silko's correspondence with the poet James Wright was edited after Wright's death by his widow Anne Wright under the title* The Delicacy and Strength of Lace *(1986).*

"Yellow Woman" is a representative of Leslie Marmon Silko's seemingly effortless synthesis of realism and fantasy. Taken from Storyteller, *it has the air of a mystery; the reader, like the adventurous protagonist, comes to knowledge only by degrees, and then not fully. Is the romantic abductor merely a cattle-rustler, or is he a mountain spirit? Can he, perhaps, be both?*

Yellow Woman

My thigh clung to his with dampness, and I watched the sun rising up through the tamaracks and willows. The small brown water birds came to the river and hopped across the mud, leaving brown scratches in the alkali-white crust. They bathed in the river silently. I could hear the water, almost at our feet where the narrow fast channel bubbled and washed green ragged moss and fern leaves.

I looked at him beside me, rolled in the red blanket on the white river sand. I cleaned the sand out of the cracks between my toes, squinting because the sun was above the willow trees. I looked at him for the last time, sleeping on the white river sand.

I felt hungry and followed the river south the way we had come the afternoon before, following our footprints that were already blurred by lizard tracks and bug trails. The horses were still lying down, and the black one whinnied when he saw me but he did not get up—maybe it was because the corral was made out of thick cedar branches and the horses had not yet felt the sun like I had. I tried to look beyond the pale red mesas to the pueblo. I knew it was there, even if I could not see it, on the sandrock hill above the river, the same river that moved past me now and had reflected the moon last night.

The horse felt warm underneath me. He shook his head and pawed the sand. The bay whinnied and leaned against the gate trying to follow, and I remembered him asleep in the red blanket beside the river. I slid off the horse and tied him close to the other horse. I walked north with the river again, and the white sand broke loose in footprints over footprints.

"Wake up."

He moved in the blanket and turned his face to me with his eyes still closed. I knelt down to touch him.

"I'm leaving."

He smiled now, eyes still closed. "You are coming with me, remember?" He sat up now with his bare dark chest and belly in the sun.

"Where?"

"To my place."

"And will I come back?"

He pulled his pants on. I walked away from him, feeling him behind me and smelling the willows.

"Yellow Woman," he said.

I turned to face him. "Who are you?" I asked.

He laughed and knelt on the low, sandy bank, washing his face in the river. "Last night you guessed my name, and you knew why I had come."

I stared past him at the shallow moving water and tried to remember the night, but I could only see the moon in the water and remember his warmth around me.

"But I only said that you were him and that I was Yellow Woman—I'm not really her—I have my own name and I come from the pueblo on the other side of the mesa. Your name is Silva and you are a stranger I met by the river yesterday afternoon."

He laughed softly. "What happened yesterday has nothing to do with what you will do today, Yellow Woman."

"I know—that's what I'm saying—the old stories about the ka'tsina spirit and Yellow Woman can't mean us."

My old grandpa liked to tell those stories best. There is one about Badger and Coyote who went hunting and were gone all day, and when the sun was going down they found a house. There was a girl living there alone, and she had light hair and eyes and she told them that they could sleep with her. Coyote wanted to be with her all night so he sent Badger into a prairie-dog hole, telling him he thought he saw something in it. As soon as Badger crawled in, Coyote blocked up the entrance with rocks and hurried back to Yellow Woman.

"Come here," he said gently.

He touched my neck and I moved close to him to feel his breathing and to hear his heart. I was wondering if Yellow Woman had known who she was—if she knew that she would become part of the stories. Maybe she'd had another name that her husband and relatives called her so that only the ka'tsina from the north and the storytellers would know her as Yellow Woman. But I didn't go on; I felt him all around me, pushing me down into the white river sand.

Yellow Woman went away with the spirit from the north and lived with him and his relatives. She was gone for a long time, but then one day she came back and she brought twin boys.

"Do you know the story?"

"What story?" He smiled and pulled me close to him as he said this. I was afraid lying there on the red blanket. All I could know was the way he felt, warm, damp, his body beside me. This is the way it happens in the stories, I was thinking, with no thought beyond the moment she meets the ka'tsina spirit and they go.

"I don't have to go. What they tell in stories was real only then, back in time immemorial, like they say."

He stood up and pointed at my clothes tangled in the blanket. "Let's go," he said.

I walked beside him, breathing hard because he walked fast, his hand around my wrist. I had stopped trying to pull away from him, because his hand felt cool and the sun was high, drying the river bed into alkali. I will see someone, eventually I will see someone, and then I will be certain that he is only a man—some man from nearby—and I will be sure that I am not Yellow Woman. Because she is from out of time past and I live now and I've been to school and there are highways and pickup trucks that Yellow Woman never saw.

It was an easy ride north on horseback. I watched the change from the cottonwood trees along the river to the junipers that brushed past us in the foothills, and finally there were only piñons, and when I looked up at the rim of the mountain plateau I could see pine trees growing on the edge. Once I stopped to look down, but the pale sandstone had disappeared and the river was gone and the dark lava hills were all around. He touched my hand, not speaking, but always singing softly a mountain song and looking into my eyes.

I felt hungry and wondered what they were doing at home now—my mother, my grandmother, my husband, and the baby. Cooking breakfast, saying, "Where did she go?—maybe kidnaped," and Al going to the tribal police with the details: "She went walking along the river."

The house was made with black lava rock and red mud. It was high above the spreading miles of arroyos and long mesas. I smelled a mountain smell of pitch and buck brush. I stood there beside the black horse, looking down on the small, dim country we had passed, and I shivered.

"Yellow Woman, come inside where it's warm."

II

He lit a fire in the stove. It was an old stove with a round belly and an enamel coffeepot on top. There was only the stove, some faded Navajo blankets, and a bedroll and cardboard box. The floor was made of smooth adobe plaster, and there was one small window facing east. He pointed at the box.

"There's some potatoes and the frying pan." He sat on the floor with his arms around his knees pulling them close to his chest and he watched me fry the potatoes. I didn't mind him watching me because he was always watching me—he had been watching me since I came upon him sitting on the river bank trimming leaves from a willow twig with his knife. We ate from the pan and he wiped the grease from his fingers on his Levis.

"Have you brought women here before?" He smiled and kept chewing, so I said, "Do you always use the same tricks?"

"What tricks?" He looked at me like he didn't understand.

"The story about being a ka'tsina from the mountains. The story about Yellow Woman."

Silva was silent; his face was calm.

"I don't believe it. Those stories couldn't happen now," I said.

He shook his head and said softly, "But someday they will talk about us, and they will say, 'Those two lived long ago when things like that happened.' "

He stood up and went out. I ate the rest of the potatoes and thought about things—about the noise the stove was making and the sound of the mountain wind outside. I remembered yesterday and the day before, and then I went outside.

I walked past the corral to the edge where the narrow trail cut through the black rim rock. I was standing in the sky with nothing around me but the wind that came down from the blue mountain peak behind me. I could see faint mountain images in the distance miles across the vast spread of mesas and valleys and plains. I wondered who was over there to feel the mountain wind on those sheer blue edges—who walks on the pine needles in those blue mountains.

"Can you see the pueblo?" Silva was standing behind me.

I shook my head. "We're too far away."

"From here I can see the world." He stepped out on the edge. "The Navajo reservation begins over there." He pointed to the east. "The Pueblo boundaries are over here." He looked below us to the south, where the narrow trail seemed to come from. "The Texans have their ranches over there, starting with that valley, the Concho Valley. The Mexicans run some cattle over there too."

"Do you ever work for them?"

"I steal from them." Silva answered. The sun was dropping behind us and shadows were filling the land below. I turned away from the edge that dropped forever into the valleys below.

"I'm cold," I said; "I'm going inside." I started wondering about this man who could speak the Pueblo language so well but who lived on a mountain and rustled cattle. I decided that this man Silva must be Navajo, because Pueblo men didn't do things like that.

"You must be a Navajo."

Silva shook his head gently. "Little Yellow Woman," he said, "you never give up, do you? I have told you who I am. The Navajo people know me, too." He knelt down and unrolled the bedroll and spread the extra blankets out on a piece of canvas. The sun was down, and the only light in the house came from outside—the dim orange light from sundown.

I stood there and waited for him to crawl under the blankets.

"What are you waiting for?" he said, and I lay down beside him. He undressed me slowly like the night before beside the river—kissing my face gently and running his hands up and down my belly and legs. He took off my pants and then he laughed.

"Why are you laughing?"

"You are breathing so hard."

I pulled away from him and turned my back to him.

He pulled me around and pinned me down with his arms and chest. "You don't understand, do you, little Yellow Woman? You will do what I want."

And again he was all around me with his skin slippery against mine, and I was afraid because I understood that his strength could hurt me. I lay underneath him and I knew that he could destroy me. But later, while he slept beside me, I touched his face and I had a feeling—the kind of feeling for him that overcame me that morning along the river. I kissed him on the forehead and he reached out for me.

When I woke up in the morning he was gone. It gave me a strange feeling because for a long time I sat there on the blankets and looked around the little house for some object of his—some proof that he had been there or maybe that he was coming back. Only the blankets and the cardboard box remained. The .30-30 that had been leaning in the corner was gone, and so was the knife I had used the night before. He was gone, and I had my chance to go now. But first I had to eat, because I knew it would be a long walk home.

I found some dried apricots in the cardboard box, and I sat down on a rock at the edge of the plateau rim. There was no wind and the sun warmed me. I was surrounded by silence. I drowsed with apricots in my mouth, and I didn't believe that there were highways or railroads or cattle to steal.

When I woke up, I stared down at my feet in the black mountain dirt. Little black ants were swarming over the pine needles around my foot. They must have smelled the apricots. I thought about my family far below me. They would be wondering about me, because this had never happened to me before. The tribal police would file a report. But if old Grandpa weren't dead he would tell them what happened—he would laugh and say, "Stolen by a ka'tsina, a mountain spirit. She'll come home—they usually do." There are enough of them to handle things. My mother and grandmother will raise the baby like they raised me. Al will find someone else, and they will go on like before, except that there will be a story about the day I disappeared while I was walking along the river. Silva had come for me; he said he had. I did not decide to go. I just went. Moonflowers blossom in the sand hills before dawn, just as I followed him. That's what I was thinking as I wandered along the trail through the pine trees.

It was noon when I got back. When I saw the stone house I remembered that I had meant to go home. But that didn't seem important any more, maybe because there were little blue flowers growing in the meadow behind the stone house and the gray squirrels were playing in the pines next to the house. The horses were standing in the corral, and there was a beef carcass hanging on the shady side of a big pine in front of the house. Flies buzzed around the clotted blood that hung from the carcass. Silva was washing his hands in a bucket full of water. He must have heard me coming because he spoke to me without turning to face me.

"I've been waiting for you."

"I went walking in the big pine trees."

I looked into the bucket full of bloody water with brown-and-white animal hairs floating in it. Silva stood there letting his hands drip, examining me intently.

"Are you coming with me?"

"Where?" I asked him.

"To sell the meat in Marquez."

"If you're sure it's O.K."

"I wouldn't ask you if it wasn't," he answered.

He sloshed the water around in the bucket before he dumped it out and set the bucket upside down near the door. I followed him to the corral and watched him saddle the horses. Even beside the horses he looked tall, and I asked him again if he wasn't Navajo. He didn't say anything; he just shook his head and kept cinching up the saddle.

"But Navajos are tall."

"Get on the horse," he said, "and let's go."

The last thing he did before we started down the steep trail was to grab the .30-30 from the corner. He slid the rifle into the scabbard that hung from his saddle.

"Do they ever try to catch you?" I asked.

"They don't know who I am."

"Then why did you bring the rifle?"

"Because we are going to Marquez where the Mexicans live."

III

The trail leveled out on a narrow ridge that was steep on both sides like an animal spine. On one side I could see where the trail went around the rocky gray hills and disappeared into the southeast where the pale sandrock mesas stood in the distance near my home. On the other side was a trail that went west, and as I looked far into the distance I thought I saw the little town. But Silva said no, that I was looking in the wrong place, that I just thought I saw houses. After that I quit looking off into the distance; it was hot and the wildflowers were closing up their deep-yellow petals. Only the waxy cactus flowers bloomed in the bright sun, and I saw every color that a cactus blossom can be; the white ones and the red ones were still buds, but the purple and the yellow were blossoms, open full and the most beautiful of all.

Silva saw him before I did. The white man was riding a big gray horse, coming up the trail toward us. He was traveling fast and the gray horse's feet sent rocks rolling off the trail into the dry tumbleweeds. Silva motioned for me to stop and we watched the white man. He didn't see us right away, but finally his horse whinnied at our horses and he stopped. He looked at us briefly before he loped the gray horse across the three hundred yards that separated us. He stopped his horse in front of Silva, and his young fat face was shadowed by the brim of his hat. He didn't look mad, but his small, pale eyes moved from the blood-soaked gunny sacks hanging from my saddle to Silva's face and then back to my face.

"Where did you get the fresh meat?" the white man asked.

"I've been hunting," Silva said, and when he shifted his weight in the saddle the leather creaked.

"The hell you have, Indian. You've been rustling cattle. We've been looking for the thief for a long time."

The rancher was fat, and sweat began to soak through his white cowboy shirt and the wet cloth stuck to the thick rolls of belly fat. He almost seemed to be panting from the exertion of talking, and he smelled rancid, maybe because Silva scared him.

Silva turned to me and smiled. "Go back up the mountain, Yellow Woman."

The white man got angry when he heard Silva speak in a language he couldn't understand. "Don't try anything, Indian. Just keep riding to Marquez. We'll call the state police from there."

The rancher must have been unarmed because he was very frightened and if he had a gun he would have pulled it out then. I turned my horse around and the rancher yelled, "Stop!" I looked at Silva for an instant and there was something ancient and dark—something I could feel in my stomach—in his eyes, and when I glanced at his hand I saw his finger on the trigger of the .30-30 that was still in the saddle scabbard. I slapped my horse across the flank and the sacks of raw meat swung against my knees as the horse leaped up the trail. It was hard to keep my balance, and once I thought I felt the saddle slipping backward; it was because of this that I could not look back.

I didn't stop until I reached the ridge where the trail forked. The horse was breathing deep gasps and there was a dark film of sweat on its neck. I looked down in the direction I had come from, but I couldn't see the place. I waited. The wind came up and pushed warm air past me. I looked up at the sky, pale blue and full of thin clouds and fading vapor trails left by jets.

I think four shots were fired—I remember hearing four hollow explosions that reminded me of deer hunting. There could have been more shots after that, but I couldn't have heard them because my horse was running again and the loose rocks were making too much noise as they scattered around his feet.

Horses have a hard time running downhill, but I went that way instead of uphill to the mountain because I thought it was safer. I felt better with the horse running southeast past the round gray hills that were covered with cedar trees and black lava rock. When I got to the plain in the distance I could see the dark green patches of tamaracks that grew along the river; and beyond the river I could see the beginning of the pale sandrock mesas. I stopped the horse and looked back to see if anyone was coming; then I got off the horse and turned the horse around, wondering if it would go back to its corral under the pines on the mountain. It looked back at me for a moment and then plucked a mouthful of green tumbleweeds before it trotted back up the trail with its ears pointed forward, carrying its head daintily to one side to avoid stepping on the dragging reins. When the horse disappeared over the last hill, the gunny sacks full of meat were still swinging and bouncing.

I walked toward the river on a wood-hauler's road that I knew would eventually lead to the paved road. I was thinking about waiting beside the road for someone to drive by, but by the time I got to the pavement I had decided it wasn't very far to walk if I followed the river back the way Silva and I had come.

The river water tasted good, and I sat in the shade under a cluster of silvery willows. I thought about Silva, and I felt sad at leaving him; still, there was something strange about him, and I tried to figure it out all the way back home.

I came back to the place on the river bank where he had been sitting the first time I saw him. The green willow leaves that he had trimmed from the branch were still lying there, wilted in the sand. I saw the leaves and I wanted to go back to him—to kiss him and to touch him—but the mountains were too far away now. And I told myself, because I believe it, he will come back sometime and be waiting again by the river.

I followed the path up from the river into the village. The sun was getting low, and I could smell supper cooking when I got to the screen door of my house. I could hear their voices inside—my mother was telling my grandmother how to fix the Jell-O and my husband, Al, was playing with the baby. I decided to tell them that some Navajo had kidnaped me, but I was sorry that old Grandpa wasn't alive to hear my story because it was the Yellow Woman stories he liked to tell best.

CYNTHIA OZICK

(1928–)

Born, raised, and educated in New York City, Cynthia Ozick has been a longtime resident of New Rochelle, New York. Though most widely known for her short stories (among which "The Shawl" is the most celebrated), she is also the author of essays, poetry, criticism, translations, and novels. Her visionary conviction that the "Hebrew contribution to civilization" is the effort of bearing witness to the Holocaust, thereby making it a part of the human experience, lies at the center of her work in all its diversity.

Cynthia Ozick, by her own testimony, matured relatively late as a writer, after approximately twenty years of writing without significant publication. During these years, however, as the obsessive brilliance of her prose makes clear, she was acquiring an abundance of information and honing her literary skills. Hers is an art that, though cast in prose, employs the strategies of poetry.

Cynthia Ozick is the author of nine books, including her first novel Trust *(1966), the story collections* The Pagan Rabbi *(1971),* Bloodshed *(1976), and* Levitation *(1982). Her two collections of essays are* Art & Ardor *(1983) and* Metaphor and Myth *(1989); more recent novels are* The Cannibal Galaxy *(1983) and* The Messiah of Stockholm *(1987).* The Shawl *(1989) consists of the story included in this volume and a novella in which the heroine of the story, Rosa Lubin, is imagined as a Holocaust survivor living, many years later, in seclusion and near-squalor in Florida.*

The Shawl

Stella, cold, cold, the coldness of hell. How they walked on the roads together, Rosa with Magda curled up between sore breasts, Magda wound up in the shawl. Sometimes Stella carried Magda. But she was jealous of Magda. A thin girl of fourteen, too small, with thin breasts of her own, Stella wanted to be wrapped in a shawl, hidden away, asleep, rocked by the march, a baby, a round infant in arms. Magda took Rosa's nipple, and Rosa never stopped walking, a walking cradle. There was not enough milk; sometimes Magda sucked air; then she screamed. Stella was ravenous. Her knees were tumors on sticks, her elbows chicken bones.

Rosa did not feel hunger; she felt light, not like someone walking but like someone in a faint, in trance, arrested in a fit, someone who is already a floating angel, alert and seeing everything, but in the air, not there, not touching the road. As if teetering on the tips of her fingernails. She looked into Magda's face through a gap in the shawl: a squirrel in a nest, safe, no one could reach her inside the little house of the shawl's windings. The face, very round, a pocket mirror of a face; but it was not Rosa's bleak complexion, dark like cholera, it was another kind of face altogether, eyes blue as air, smooth feathers of hair nearly as yellow as the Star sewn into Rosa's coat. You could think she was one of *their* babies.

Rosa, floating, dreamed of giving Magda away in one of the villages. She could leave the line for a minute and push Magda into the hands of any woman on the side of the road. But if she moved out of line they might shoot. And even if she fled the line for half a second and pushed the shawl-bundle at a stranger, would the woman take it? She might be surprised, or afraid; she might drop the shawl, and Magda would fall out and strike her head and die. The little round head. Such a good child, she gave up screaming, and sucked now only for the taste of the drying nipple itself. The neat grip of the tiny gums. One mite of a tooth tip sticking up in the bottom gum, how shining, an elfin tombstone of white marble, gleaming there. Without complaining, Magda relinquished Rosa's teats, first the left, then the right; both were cracked, not a sniff of milk. The duct crevice extinct, a dead volcano, blind eye, chill hole, so Magda took the corner of the shawl and milked it instead. She sucked and sucked, flooding the threads with wetness. The shawl's good flavor, milk of linen.

It was a magic shawl, it could nourish an infant for three days and three nights. Magda lifted out of her mouth. She held her eyes open every moment, forgetting how to blink or nap, and Rosa and sometimes Stella studied their blueness. On the road they raised one burden of a leg after another and studied Magda's face. "Aryan," Stella said, in a voice grown as thin as a string; and Rosa thought how Stella gazed at Magda like a young cannibal. And the time that Stella said "Aryan," it sounded to Rosa as if Stella had really said "Let us devour her."

But Magda lived to walk. She lived that long, but she did not walk very well, partly because she was only fifteen months old, and partly because the spindles of her legs could not hold up her fat belly. It was fat with air, full and round. Rosa gave almost all her food to Magda. Stella gave nothing; Stella was ravenous, a growing child herself, but not growing much. Stella did not menstruate. Rosa did not menstruate. Rosa was ravenous, but also not; she learned from Magda how to drink the taste of a finger in one's mouth. They were in a place without pity, all pity was annihilated in Rosa, she looked at Stella's bones without pity. She was sure that Stella was waiting for Magda to die so she could put her teeth into the little thighs.

Rosa knew Magda was going to die very soon; she should have been dead already, but she had been buried away deep inside the magic shawl, mistaken there for the shivering mound of Rosa's breasts; Rosa clung to the shawl as if it covered only herself. No one took it away from her. Magda was mute. She never cried. Rosa hid her in the barracks, under the shawl, but she knew that one day someone would inform; or one day someone, not even Stella, would steal Magda to eat her. When Magda began to walk Rosa knew that Magda was going to die very soon, something would happen. She was afraid to fall asleep; she slept with the weight of her thigh on Magda's body; she was afraid she would smother Magda under her thigh. The weight of Rosa was becoming less and less; Rosa and Stella were slowly turning into air.

Magda was quiet, but her eyes were horribly alive, like blue tigers. She watched. Sometimes she laughed—it seemed a laugh, but how could it be? Magda had never seen anyone laugh. Still, Magda laughed at her shawl when the wind blew its corners, the bad wind with pieces of black in it, that made Stella's and Rosa's eyes tear. Magda's eyes were always clear and tearless. She watched like a tiger. She guarded her shawl. No one could touch it; only Rosa could touch it. Stella was not allowed. The shawl was Magda's own baby, her pet, her little sister. She tangled herself up in it and sucked on one of the corners when she wanted to be very still.

Then Stella took the shawl away and made Magda die.

Afterward Stella said: "I was cold."

And afterward she was always cold, always. The cold went into her heart: Rosa saw that Stella's heart was cold. Magda flopped onward with her little pencil legs scribbling this way and that, in search of the shawl; the pencils faltered at the barracks opening, where the light began. Rosa saw and pursued. But already Magda was in the square outside the barracks, in the jolly light. It was the roll-call arena. Every morning Rosa had to conceal Magda under the shawl against a wall of the barracks and go out and stand in the arena with Stella and hundreds of others, sometimes for hours, and Magda, deserted, was quiet under the shawl, sucking on her corner. Every day Magda was silent, and so she did not die. Rosa saw that today Magda was going to die, and at the same time a fearful joy ran in Rosa's two palms, her fingers were on fire, she was astonished, febrile: Magda, in the sunlight, swaying on her pencil legs, was howling. Ever since the drying up of Rosa's nipples, ever since Magda's last scream on the road, Magda had been devoid of any syllable; Magda was a mute. Rosa believed that something had gone wrong with her vocal cords, with her windpipe, with the cave of her larynx; Magda was defective, without a voice; perhaps she was deaf; there might be something amiss with her intelligence; Magda was dumb. Even the laugh that came when the ash-stippled wind made a clown out of Magda's shawl was only the air-blown showing of her teeth. Even when the lice, head lice and body lice, crazed her so that she became as wild as one of the big rats that plundered the barracks at daybreak looking for carrion, she rubbed and scratched and kicked and bit and rolled without a whimper. But now Magda's mouth was spilling a long viscous rope of clamor.

"Maaaa—"

It was the first noise Magda had ever sent out from her throat since the drying up of Rosa's nipples.

"Maaaa . . . aaa!"

Again! Magda was wavering in the perilous sunlight of the arena, scribbling on such pitiful little bent shins. Rosa saw. She saw that Magda was grieving for the loss of her shawl, she saw that Magda was going to die. A tide of commands hammered in Rosa's nipples: Fetch, get, bring! But she did not know which to go after first, Magda or the shawl. If she jumped out into the arena to snatch Magda up, the howling would not stop, because Magda would still not have the shawl; but if she ran back into the barracks to find the shawl, and if she found it, and if she came after Magda holding it and shaking it, then she would get Magda back, Magda would put the shawl in her mouth and turn dumb again.

Rosa entered the dark. It was easy to discover the shawl. Stella was heaped under it, asleep in her thin bones. Rosa tore the shawl free and flew—she could fly, she was only air—into the arena. The sunheat murmured of another life, of butterflies in summer. The light was placid, mellow. On the other side of the steel fence, far away, there were green meadows speckled with dandelions and deep-colored violets; beyond them, even farther, innocent tiger lilies, tall, lifting their orange bonnets. In the barracks they spoke of "flowers," of "rain": excrement, thick turd-braids, and the slow stinking maroon waterfall that slunk down from the upper bunks, the stink mixed with a bitter fatty floating smoke that greased Rosa's skin. She stood for an instant at the margin of the arena. Sometimes the electricity inside the fence would seem to hum; even Stella said it was only an imagining, but Rosa heard real sounds in the wire: grainy sad voices. The farther she was from the fence, the more clearly the voices crowded at her. The lamenting voices strummed so convincingly, so passionately, it was impossible to suspect them of being phantoms. The voices told her to hold up the shawl, high; the voices told her to shake it, to whip with it, to unfurl it like a flag. Rosa lifted, shook, whipped, unfurled. Far off, very far, Magda leaned across her air-fed belly, reaching out with the rods of her arms. She was high up, elevated, riding someone's shoulder. But the shoulder that carried Magda was not coming toward Rosa and the shawl, it was drifting away, the speck of Magda was moving more and more into the smoky distance. Above the shoulder a helmet glinted. The light tapped the helmet and sparkled it into a goblet. Below the helmet a black body like a domino and a pair of black boots hurled themselves in the direction of the electrified fence. The electric voices began to chatter wildly. "Maamaa, maaamaaa," they all hummed together. How far Magda was from Rosa now, across the whole square, past a dozen barracks, all the way on the other side! She was no bigger than a moth.

All at once Magda was swimming through the air. The whole of Magda traveled through loftiness. She looked like a butterfly touching a silver vine. And the moment Magda's feathered round head and her pencil legs and balloonish belly and zigzag arms splashed against the fence, the steel voices went mad in their growling, urging Rosa to run and run to the spot where Magda had fallen from her flight against the electrified fence; but of course Rosa did not obey them. She only stood, because if she ran they would shoot, and if she tried to pick up the sticks of Magda's body they would shoot, and if she let the wolf's screech ascending now through the ladder of her skeleton break out, they would shoot; so she took Magda's shawl and filled her own mouth with it, stuffed it in and stuffed it in, until she was swallowing up the wolf's screech and tasting the cinnamon and almond depth of Magda's saliva; and Rosa drank Magda's shawl until it dried.

JOYCE CAROL OATES

(1938–)

Born in Lockport, New York, and educated at Syracuse University and the University of Wisconsin, Joyce Carol Oates is the author of a number of volumes of short stories, including By the North Gate *(1963),* The Wheel of Love *(1970),* Marriages & Infidelities *(1972),* Night-Side *(1977),* A Sentimental Education *(1980),* Last Days *(1984),* Raven's Wing *(1986),* The Assignation *(1988),* Heat *(1991), and* Where *Is* Here? *(1992). Her novels include* Expensive People *(1968),* them *(1969),* Bellefleur *(1980),* A Bloodsmoor Romance *(1982),* You Must Remember This *(1987),* Because It Is Bitter, and Because It Is My Heart *(1990), and* Black Water *(1992). Since 1978 she has been on the faculty of Princeton University and is a co-editor of* The Ontario Review.

For the author, the formal challenge of "Heat" was to present a narrative in a seemingly acausal manner, analogous to the playing of a piano sans pedal; as if each paragraph, or chord, were separate from the rest. For how otherwise can we speak of the unspeakable, except through the prism of technique?

Heat

It was midsummer, the heat rippling above the macadam roads. Cicadas screaming out of the trees and the sky like pewter, glaring.

The days were the same day, like the shallow mud-brown river moving always in the same direction but so slow you couldn't see it. Except for Sunday: church in the morning, then the fat Sunday newspaper, the color comics and newsprint on your fingers.

Rhea and Rhoda Kunkel went flying on their rusted old bicycles, down the long hill toward the railroad yard, Whipple's Ice, the scrubby pastureland where dairy cows grazed. They'd stolen six dollars from their own grandmother who loved them. They were eleven years old, they were identical twins, they basked in their power.

Rhea and Rhoda Kunkel: it was always Rhea-and-Rhoda, never Rhoda-and-Rhea, I couldn't say why. You just wouldn't say the names that way. Not even the teachers at school would say them that way.

We went to see them in the funeral parlor where they were waked, we were made to. The twins in twin caskets, white, smooth, gleaming, perfect as plastic, with white satin lining puckered like the inside of a fancy candy box. And the waxy white lilies, and the smell of talcum powder and perfume. The room was crowded, there was only one way in and out.

Rhea and Rhoda were the same girl, they'd wanted it that way.

Only looking from one to the other could you see they were two.

The heat was gauzy, you had to push your way through like swimming. On their bicycles Rhea and Rhoda flew through it hardly noticing, from their grandmother's place on Main Street to the end of South Main where the paved road turned to gravel leaving town. That was the summer before seventh grade, when they died. Death was coming for them but they didn't know.

They thought the same thoughts sometimes at the same moment, had the same dream and went all day trying to remember it, bringing it back like something you'd be hauling out of the water on a tangled line. We watched them, we were jealous. None of us had a twin. Sometimes they were serious and sometimes, remembering, they shrieked and laughed like they were being killed. They stole things out of desks and lockers but if you caught them they'd hand them right back, it was like a game.

There were three floor fans in the funeral parlor that I could see, tall whirring fans with propellor blades turning fast to keep the warm air moving. Strange little gusts came from all directions making your eyes water. By this time Roger Whipple was arrested, taken into police custody. No one had hurt him. He would never stand trial, he was ruled mentally unfit, he would never be released from confinement.

He died there, in the state psychiatric hospital, years later, and was brought back home to be buried, the body of him I mean. His earthly remains.

Rhea and Rhoda Kunkel were buried in the same cemetery, the First Methodist. The cemetery is just a field behind the church.

In the caskets the dead girls did not look like anyone we knew really. They were placed on their backs with their eyes closed, and their mouths, the way you don't always in life when you're sleeping. Their faces were too small. Every eyelash showed, too perfect. Like angels everyone was saying and it was strange it was *so*. I stared and stared.

What had been done to them, the lower parts of them, didn't show in the caskets.

Roger Whipple worked for his father at Whipple's Ice. In the newspaper it stated he was nineteen, he'd gone to DeWitt Clinton until he was sixteen, my mother's friend Sadie taught there and remembered him from the special education class. A big slow sweet-faced boy with these big hands and feet, thighs like hams. A shy gentle boy with good manners and a hushed voice.

He wasn't simpleminded exactly, like the others in that class. He was watchful, he held back.

Roger Whipple in overalls squatting in the rear of his father's truck, one of his older brothers drove. There would come the sound of the truck in the driveway, the heavy block of ice smelling of cold, ice tongs over his shoulder. He was strong, round-shouldered like an older man. Never staggered or grunted. Never dropped anything. Pale washed-looking eyes lifting out of a big face, a soft mouth wanting to smile. We giggled and looked away. They said he'd never been the kind to hurt even an animal, all the Whipples swore.

Sucking ice, the cold goes straight into your jaws and deep into the bone.

People spoke of them as the Kunkel twins. Mostly nobody tried to tell them apart. Homely corkscrew-twisty girls you wouldn't know would turn up so quiet and solemn and almost beautiful, perfect little dolls' faces with the freckles powdered over, touches of rouge on the cheeks and mouths. I was tempted to whisper to them, kneeling by the coffins. Hey Rhea! Hey Rhoda! Wake *up!*

They had loud slip-sliding voices that were the same voice. They weren't shy. They were always first in line. One behind you and one in front of you and you'd better be wary of some trick. Flamey-orange hair and the bleached-out skin that goes with it, freckles like dirty raindrops splashed on their faces. Sharp green eyes they'd bug out until you begged them to stop.

Places meant to be serious, Rhea and Rhoda had a hard time

sitting still. In church, in school, a sideways glance between them could do it. Jamming their knuckles into their mouths, choking back giggles. Sometimes laughing escaped through their fingers like steam hissing. Sometimes it came out like snorting and then none of us could hold back. The worst time was in assembly, the principal up there telling us that Miss Flagler had died, we would all miss her. Tears shining in the woman's eyes behind her goggle-glasses and one of the twins gave a breathless little snort, you could feel it like flames running down the whole row of girls, none of us could hold back.

Sometimes the word "tickle" was enough to get us going, just that word.

I never dreamt about Rhea and Rhoda so strange in their caskets sleeping out in the middle of a room where people could stare at them, shed tears and pray over them. I never dream about actual things, only things I don't know. Places I've never been, people I've never seen. Sometimes the person I am in the dream isn't me. Who it is, I don't know.

Rhea and Rhoda bounced up the drive behind Whipple's Ice. They were laughing like crazy and didn't mind the potholes jarring their teeth, or the clouds of dust. If they'd had the same dream the night before, the hot sunlight erased it entirely.

When death comes for you you sometimes know and sometimes don't.

Roger Whipple was by himself in the barn, working. Kids went down there to beg him for ice to suck or throw around or they'd tease him, not out of meanness but for something to do. It was slow, the days not changing in the summer, heat sometimes all night long. He was happy with children that age, he was that age himself in his head, sixth grade learning abilities as the newspaper stated though he could add and subtract quickly. Other kinds of arithmetic gave him trouble.

People were saying afterward he'd always been strange. Watchful like he was, those thick soft lips. The Whipples did wrong, to let him run loose.

They said he'd always been a good gentle boy, went to Sunday school and sat still there and never gave anybody any trouble. He collected Bible cards, he hid them away under his mattress for safekeeping. Mr. Whipple started in early, disciplining him the way you might discipline a big dog or a horse. Not letting the creature know he has any power to be himself exactly. Not giving him the opportunity to test his will.

Neighbors said the Whipples worked him like a horse in fact. The older brothers were the most merciless. And why they all wore coveralls, heavy denim and long legs on days so hot, nobody knew. The thermometer above the First Midland Bank read 98° F. on noon of that day, my mother said.

Nights afterward my mother would hug me before I went to bed. Pressing my face hard against her breasts and whispering things I didn't hear, like praying to Jesus to love and protect *her* little girl and keep *her* from harm but I didn't hear, I shut my eyes tight and endured it. Sometimes we prayed together, all of us or just my mother and me kneeling by my bed. Even then I knew she was a good mother, there was this girl she loved as her daughter that was me and loved more than that girl deserved. There was nothing I could do about it.

Mrs. Kunkel would laugh and roll her eyes over the twins. In that house they were "double trouble"—you'd hear it all the time like a joke on the radio that keeps coming back. I wonder did she pray with them too. I wonder would they let her.

In the long night you forget about the day, it's like the other side of the world. Then the sun is there, and the heat. You forget.

We were running through the field behind school, a place where people dumped things sometimes and there was a dead dog there, a collie with beautiful fur but his eyes were gone from the sockets and the maggots had got him where somebody tried to lift him with her foot and when Rhea and Rhoda saw they screamed a single scream and hid their eyes.

They did nice things—gave their friends candy bars, nail polish, some novelty key chains they'd taken from somewhere, movie stars' pictures framed in plastic. In the movies they'd share a box of popcorn not noticing where one or the other of them left off and a girl who wasn't any sister of theirs sat.

Once they made me strip off my clothes where we'd crawled under the Kunkels' veranda. This was a large hollowed-out space where the earth dropped away at one end, you could sit without bumping your head, it was cool and smelled of dirt and stone. Rhea said all of a sudden, Strip! and Rhoda said at once, Strip!—come *on!* So it happened. They wouldn't let me out unless I took off my clothes, my shirt and shorts, yes and my panties too. Come *on* they said whispering and giggling, they were blocking the way out so I had no choice. I was scared but I was laughing too. This is to show our power over you, they said. But they stripped too just like me.

You have power over others you don't realize until you test it.

Under the Kunkels' veranda we stared at each other but we didn't touch each other. My teeth chattered because what if somebody saw us? Some boy, or Mrs. Kunkel herself? I was scared but I was happy too. Except for our faces, their face and mine, we could all be the same girl.

The Kunkel family lived in one side of a big old clapboard house by the river, you could hear the trucks rattling on the bridge, shifting their noisy gears on the hill. Mrs. Kunkel had eight children, Rhea and Rhoda were the youngest. Our mothers wondered why Mrs. Kunkel had let herself go—she had a moon-shaped pretty face but her hair was frizzed ratty, she must have weighed two hundred pounds, sweated and breathed so hard in the warm weather. They'd known her in school. Mr. Kunkel worked construction for the county. Summer evenings after work he'd be sitting on the veranda drinking beer, flicking cigarette butts out into the yard, you'd be fooled almost thinking they were fireflies. He went barechested in the heat, his upper body dark like stained wood. Flat little purplish nipples inside his chest hair the girls giggled to see. Mr. Kunkel teased us all, he'd mix Rhea and Rhoda up the way he'd mix the rest of us up like it was too much trouble to keep names straight.

Mr. Kunkel was in police custody, he didn't even come to the wake. Mrs. Kunkel was there in rolls of chin fat that glistened with sweat and tears, the makeup on her face was caked and discolored so you were embarrassed to look. It scared me, the way she grabbed me as soon as my parents and I came in. Hugging me against her big balloon breasts sobbing and all the strength went out of me, I couldn't push away.

The police had Mr. Kunkel, for his own good they said. He'd gone to the Whipples, though the murderer had been taken away, saying he would kill anybody he could get his hands on, the old man, the brothers. They were all responsible he said, his little girls were dead. Tear them apart with his bare hands he said but he had a tire iron.

Did it mean anything special, or was it just an accident, Rhea and Rhoda had taken six dollars from their grandmother an hour before? Because death was coming for them, it had to happen one way or another.

If you believe in God you believe that. And if you don't believe in God it's obvious.

Their grandmother lived upstairs over a shoe store downtown, an apartment looking out on Main Street. They'd bicycle down there for something to do and she'd give them grape juice or lemonade and try to keep them a while, a lonely old lady but she was nice, she was always nice to me, it was kind of nasty of Rhea and Rhoda to steal from her but they were like that. One was in the kitchen talking with her and without any plan or anything the other went to use the bathroom then slipped into her bedroom, got the money out of her purse like it was something she did every day of the week, that easy. On the stairs going down to the street Rhoda whispered to Rhea what did you *do?* knowing Rhea had done something she hadn't ought to have done but not knowing what it was or anyway how much money it was. They started in poking each other, trying to hold the giggles back until they were safe away.

On their bicycles they stood high on the pedals, coasting, going down the hill but not using their brakes. *What did you do! Oh what did you do!*

Rhea and Rhoda always said they could never be apart. If one didn't know exactly where the other was that one could die. Or the other could die. Or both.

Once they'd gotten some money from somewhere, they wouldn't say where, and paid for us all to go to the movies. And ice cream afterward too.

You could read the newspaper articles twice through and still not know what he did. Adults talked about it for a long time but not so we could hear. I thought probably he'd used an ice pick. Or maybe I heard somebody guess that who didn't know any more than me.

We liked it that Rhea and Rhoda had been killed, and all the stuff in the paper, and everybody talking about it, but we didn't like it that they were dead, we missed them.

Later, in tenth grade, the Kaufmann twins moved into our school district. Doris and Diane. But it wasn't the same thing.

Roger Whipple said he didn't remember any of it. Whatever he did, he didn't remember. At first everybody thought he was lying then they had to accept it as true, or true in some way, doctors from the state hospital examined him. He said over and over he hadn't done anything and he didn't remember the twins there that afternoon but he couldn't explain why their bicycles were where they were at the foot of his stairway and he couldn't explain why he'd taken a bath in the middle of the day. The Whipples admitted that wasn't a practice of Roger's or of any of them, ever, a bath in the middle of the day.

Roger Whipple was a clean boy, though. His hands always scrubbed so you actually noticed, swinging the block of ice off the truck and, inside the kitchen, helping to set it in the ice box. They said he'd go crazy if he got bits of straw under his nails from the ice house or inside his clothes. He'd been taught to shave and he shaved every morning without fail, they said the sight of the beard growing in, the scratchy feel of it, seemed to scare him.

A few years later his sister Linda told us how Roger was built like a horse. She was our age, a lot younger than him, she made a gesture toward her crotch so we'd know what she meant. She'd happened to see him a few times she said, by accident.

There he was squatting in the dust laughing, his head lowered watching Rhea and Rhoda circle him on their bicycles. It was a rough game where the twins saw how close they could come to hitting him, brushing him with the bike fenders and he'd lunge out not seeming to notice if his fingers hit the spokes, it was all happening so fast you maybe wouldn't feel pain. Out back of the ice house where the yard blended in with the yard of the old railroad depot next door that wasn't used any more. It was burning hot in the sun, dust rose in clouds behind the girls. Pretty soon they got bored with the game though Roger Whipple even in his heavy overalls wanted to keep going. He was red-faced with all the excitement, he was a boy who loved to laugh and didn't have much chance. Rhea said she was thirsty, she wanted some ice, so Roger Whipple scrambled right up and went to get a big bag of ice cubes!—he hadn't any more sense than that.

They sucked on the ice cubes and fooled around with them. He was panting and lolling his tongue pretending to be a dog and Rhea and Rhoda cried, Here doggie! Here doggie-doggie! tossing ice cubes at Roger Whipple he tried to catch in his mouth. That went on for a while. In the end the twins just dumped the rest of the ice onto the dirt then Roger Whipple was saying he had some secret things that belonged to his brother Eamon he could show them. Hidden under his bed mattress, would they like to see what the things were?

He wasn't one who could tell Rhea from Rhoda or Rhoda from Rhea. There was a way some of us knew, the freckles on Rhea's face were a little darker than Rhoda's. Rhea's eyes were just a little darker than Rhoda's. But you'd have to see the two side by side with no clowning around to know.

Rhea said okay, she'd like to see the secret things. She let her bike fall where she was straddling it.

Roger Whipple said he could only take one of them upstairs to his room at a time, he didn't say why.

Okay said Rhea. Of the Kunkel twins Rhea always had to be first.

She'd been born first, she said. Weighed a pound or two more.

Roger Whipple's room was in a strange place—on the second floor of the Whipple house above an unheated storage space that had been added after the main part of the house was built. There was a way of getting to the room from the outside, up a flight of rickety wood stairs. That way Roger could get in and out of his room without going through the rest of the house. People said the Whipples had him live there like some animal, they didn't want him tramping through the house but they denied it. The room had an inside door too.

Roger Whipple weighed about one-hundred ninety pounds that day. In the hospital he swelled up like a balloon, people said, bloated from the drugs, his skin was soft and white as bread dough and his hair fell out. He was an old man when he died aged thirty-one.

Exactly why he died, the Whipples never knew. The hospital just told them his heart had stopped in his sleep.

Rhoda shaded her eyes watching her sister running up the stairs with Roger Whipple behind her and felt the first pinch of fear, that something was wrong, or was going to be wrong. She called after them in a whining voice that she wanted to come along too, she didn't want to wait down there all alone, but Rhea just called back to her to be quiet and wait her turn, so Rhoda waited, kicking at the ice cubes melting in the dirt, and after a while she got restless and shouted up to them—the door was shut, the shade on the window was drawn—saying she was going home, damn them she was sick of waiting she said and she was going home. But nobody came to the door or looked out the window, it was like the place was empty. Wasps had built one of those nests that look like mud in layers under the eaves and the only sound was wasps.

Rhoda bicycled toward the road so anybody who was watching would think she was going home, she was thinking she hated Rhea! hated her damn twin sister! wished she was dead and gone, God damn her! She was going home and the first thing she'd tell their mother was that Rhea had stolen six dollars from Grandma: she had it in her pocket right that moment.

The Whipple house was an old farmhouse they'd tried to modernize by putting on red asphalt siding meant to look like brick. Downstairs the rooms were big and drafty, upstairs they were small, some of them unfinished and with bare floorboards, like Roger Whipple's room which people would afterward say based on what the police said was like an animal's pen, nothing in it but a bed shoved into a corner and some furniture and boxes and things Mrs. Whipple stored there.

Of the Whipples—there were seven in the family still living at home—only Mrs. Whipple and her daughter Iris were home that afternoon. They said they hadn't heard a sound except for kids playing in the back, they swore it.

Rhoda was bent on going home and leaving Rhea behind but at the end of the driveway something made her turn her bicycle wheel back . . . so if you were watching you'd think she was just cruising around for something to do, a red-haired girl with whitish skin and freckles, skinny little body, pedaling fast, then slow, then coasting, then fast again, turning and dipping and criss-crossing her path, talking to herself as if she was angry. She hated Rhea! She was furious at Rhea! But feeling sort of scared too and sickish in the pit of her belly knowing that she and Rhea shouldn't be in two places, something might happen to one of them or to both. Some things you know.

So she pedaled back to the house. Laid her bike down in the dirt next to Rhea's. The bikes were old hand-me-downs, the kickstands were broken. But their daddy had put on new Goodyear tires for them at the start of the summer and he'd oiled them too.

You never would see just one of the twins' bicycles anywhere, you always saw both of them laid down on the ground and facing in the same direction with the pedals in about the same position.

Rhoda peered up at the second floor of the house, the shade

drawn over the window, the door still closed. She called out Rhea? Hey Rhea? starting up the stairs making a lot of noise so they'd hear her, pulling on the railing as if to break it the way a boy would. Still she was scared. But making noise like that and feeling so disgusted and mad helped her get stronger, and there was Roger Whipple with the door open staring down at her flush-faced and sweaty as if he was scared too. He seemed to have forgotten her. He was wiping his hands on his overalls. He just stared, a lemony light coming up in his eyes.

Afterward he would say he didn't remember anything—didn't remember anything. Big as a grown man but round-shouldered so it was hard to judge how tall he was, or how old. His straw-colored hair falling in his eyes and his fingers twined together as if he was praying or trying with all his strength to keep his hands still. He didn't remember anything about the twins or anything in his room or in the ice house afterward but he cried a lot, he acted scared and guilty and sorry, they decided he shouldn't be put on trial, there was no point to it.

Mrs. Whipple kept to the house afterward, never went out not even to church or grocery shopping. She died of cancer just before Roger died, she'd loved him she said, she always said none of it had been his fault really, he wasn't the kind of boy even to hurt an animal, he'd loved kittens especially and was a good sweet obedient boy and religious too and whatever happened it must have been because those girls were teasing him, he'd had a lifetime of being teased and taunted by children, his heart broken by all the abuse, and something must have snapped that day, that was all.

The Whipples were the ones, though, who called the police. Mr. Whipple found the girls' bodies back in the ice house hidden under some straw and canvas.

He found them around nine that night, with a flashlight. He knew, he said. The way Roger was acting, and the fact the Kunkel girls were missing, word had gotten out. He knew but he didn't know what he knew or what he would find. Roger taking a bath like that in the middle of the day and washing his hair too and shaving for the second time and not answering when his mother spoke to him, just sitting there staring at the floor as if he was listening to something no one else could hear. He knew, Mr. Whipple said. The hardest minute of his life was in the ice house lifting that canvas to see what was under it.

He took it hard too, he never recovered. He hadn't any choice but to think what a lot of people thought—it had been his fault. He was an old-time Methodist, he took all that seriously, but none of it helped him. Believed Jesus Christ was his personal savior and He never stopped loving Roger or turned His face from him and if Roger did truly repent in his heart he would be saved and they would be reunited in Heaven, all the Whipples reunited. He believed, but none of it helped in his life.

The ice house is still there but boarded up and derelict, the Whipples' ice business ended long ago. Strangers live in the house and the yard is littered with rusting hulks of cars and pickup trucks. Some Whipples live scattered around the county but none in town. The old train depot is still there too.

After I'd been married some years I got involved with this man, I won't say his name, his name is not a name I say, but we would meet back there sometimes, back in that old lot that's all weeds and scrub trees. Wild as kids and on the edge of being drunk. I was crazy for this guy, I mean crazy like I could hardly think of anybody but him or anything but the two of us making love the way we did, with him deep inside me I wanted it never to stop just fuck and fuck and fuck I'd whisper to him and this went on for a long time, two or three years then ended the way these things do and looking back on it I'm not able to recognize that woman as if she was someone not even not-me but a crazy woman I would despise, making so much of such a thing, risking her marriage and her kids finding out and her life being ruined for such a thing, my God. The things people do.

It's like living out a story that has to go its own way.

Behind the ice house in his car I'd think of Rhea and Rhoda and what happened that day upstairs in Roger Whipple's room. And the funeral parlor with the twins like dolls laid out and their eyes like dolls' eyes too that shut when you tilt them back. One night when I wasn't asleep but wasn't awake either I saw my parents standing in the doorway of my bedroom watching me and I knew their thoughts, how they were thinking of Rhea and Rhoda and of me their daughter wondering how they could keep me from harm and there was no clear answer.

In his car in his arms I'd feel my mind drift. After we'd made love or at least after the first time. And I saw Rhoda Kunkel hesitating on the stairs a few steps down from Roger Whipple. I saw her white-faced and scared but deciding to keep going anyway, pushing by Roger Whipple to get inside the room, to find Rhea, she had to brush against him where he was standing as if he meant to block her but not having the nerve exactly to block her and he was smelling of his body and breathing hard but not in imitation of any dog now, not with his tongue flopping and lolling to make them laugh. Rhoda was asking where was Rhea?—she couldn't see well at first in the dark little cubbyhole of a room because the sunshine had been so bright outside.

Roger Whipple said Rhea had gone home. His voice sounded scratchy as if it hadn't been used in some time. She'd gone home he said and Rhoda said right away that Rhea wouldn't go home without her and Roger Whipple came toward her saying yes she did, yes she *did* as if he was getting angry she wouldn't believe him. Rhoda was calling, Rhea? Where are you? Stumbling against something on the floor tangled with the bedclothes.

Behind her was this big boy saying again and again yes she did, yes she *did*, his voice rising but it would never get loud enough so that anyone would hear and come save her.

I wasn't there, but some things you know.

TOBIAS WOLFF

(1945–   )

Born in Birmingham, Alabama, Tobias Wolff lived with his divorced mother in Connecticut, Florida, Utah, and Washington State, where he grew up. He attended the Hill School in Pennsylvania (see Wolff's brief, cryptic account in his memoir This Boy's Life*); joined the army before finishing high school; and spent four years in the paratroops, including a tour in Vietnam. Discharged from the army, Wolff continued his education at Oxford University, where he read English and received his B.A. in 1972. Returning to the United States, he worked variously as a reporter, a teacher, a night watchman, and a waiter before receiving a Stegner Fellowship at Stanford University in 1975. Since 1980, he has been writer-in-residence at Syracuse University where he lives with his wife Catherine and their three children.*

Tobias Wolff is the author of two collections of short stories, In the Garden of the North American Martyrs *(1981), from which "Hunters in the Snow" is taken, and* Back in the World *(1985). His short novel* The Barracks Thief *was published in 1984 and his much-celebrated memoir* This Boy's Life *in 1989. In these works, pathos, black humor, and an unsentimental intelligence are melded by way of an understated prose style elastic enough to accommodate the surreal while suggesting only the real, as in a trompe l'oeil painting.*

Of the wonderfully grotesque, yet entirely plausible, "Hunters in the Snow," Tobias Wolff has said: "I began this story as an act of recognition of the violence I grew up with, and that dominated my life for some years. By design it was to be a dark, sober piece, but it got away from me and made me laugh."

Hunters in the Snow

Tub had been waiting for an hour in the falling snow. He paced the sidewalk to keep warm and stuck his head out over the curb whenever he saw lights approaching. One driver stopped for him, but before Tub could wave the man on he saw the rifle on Tub's back and hit the gas. The tires spun on the ice.

The fall of snow thickened. Tub stood below the overhang of a building. Across the road the clouds whitened just above the rooftops, and the streetlights went out. He shifted the rifle strap to his other shoulder. The whiteness seeped up the sky.

A truck slid around the corner, horn blaring, rear end sashaying. Tub moved to the sidewalk and held up his hand. The truck jumped the curb and kept coming, half on the street and half on the sidewalk. It wasn't slowing down at all. Tub stood for a moment, still holding up his hand, then jumped back. His rifle slipped off his shoulder and clattered on the ice; a sandwich fell out of his pocket. He ran for the steps of the building. Another sandwich and a package of cookies tumbled onto the new snow. He made the steps and looked back.

The truck had stopped several feet beyond where Tub had been standing. He picked up his sandwiches and his cookies and slung the rifle and went to the driver's window. The driver was bent against the steering wheel, slapping his knees and drumming his feet on the floorboards. He looked like a cartoon of a person laughing, except that his eyes watched the man on the seat beside him.

"You ought to see yourself," said the driver. "He looks just like a beach ball with a hat on, doesn't he? Doesn't he, Frank?"

The man beside him smiled and looked off.

"You almost ran me down," said Tub. "You could've killed me."

"Come on, Tub," said the man beside the driver. "Be mellow, Kenny was just messing around." He opened the door and slid over to the middle of the seat.

Tub took the bolt out of his rifle and climbed in beside him. "I waited an hour," he said. "If you meant ten o'clock, why didn't you say ten o'clock?"

"Tub, you haven't done anything but complain since we got here," said the man in the middle. "If you want to piss and moan all day you might as well go home and bitch at your kids. Take your pick." When Tub didn't say anything, he turned to the driver. "O.K., Kenny, let's hit the road."

Some juvenile delinquents had heaved a brick through the windshield on the driver's side, so the cold and snow tunneled right into the cab. The heater didn't work. They covered themselves with a couple of blankets Kenny had brought along and pulled down the muffs on their caps. Tub tried to keep his hands warm by rubbing them under the blanket, but Frank made him stop.

They left Spokane and drove deep into the country, running along black lines of fences. The snow let up, but still there was no edge to the land where it met the sky. Nothing moved in the chalky fields. The cold bleached their faces and made the stubble stand out on their cheeks and along their upper lips. They had to stop and have coffee several times before they got to the woods where Kenny wanted to hunt.

Tub was for trying some place different; two years in a row they'd been up and down this land and hadn't seen a thing. Frank didn't care one way or the other; he just wanted to get out of the goddamned truck. "Feel that," Frank said. He spread his feet and closed his eyes and leaned his head way back and breathed deeply. "Tune in on that energy."

"Another thing," said Kenny. "This is open land. Most of the land around here is posted."

Frank breathed out. "Stop bitching, Tub. Get centered."

"I wasn't bitching."

"Centered," said Kenny. "Next thing you'll be wearing a nightgown, Frank. Selling flowers out at the airport."

"Kenny," said Frank. "You talk too much."

"O.K.," said Kenny. "I won't say a word. Like I won't say anything about a certain baby-sitter."

"What baby-sitter?" asked Tub.

"That's between us," said Frank, looking at Kenny. "That's confidential. You keep your mouth shut."

Kenny laughed.

"You're asking for it," said Frank.

"Asking for what?"

"You'll see."

"Hey," said Tub. "Are we hunting or what?"

Frank just smiled.

They started off across the field. Tub had trouble getting through the fences. Frank and Kenny could have helped him; they could have lifted up on the top wire and stepped on the bottom wire, but they didn't. They stood and watched him. There were a lot of fences and Tub was puffing when they reached the woods.

They hunted for over two hours and saw no deer, no tracks, no sign. Finally they stopped by the creek to eat. Kenny had several slices of pizza and a couple of candy bars; Frank had a sandwich, an apple, two carrots, and a square of chocolate; Tub put out one hard-boiled egg and a stick of celery.

"You ask me how I want to die today," said Kenny. "I'll tell you, burn me at the stake." He turned to Tub. "You still on that diet?" He winked at Frank.

"What do you think? You think I like hard-boiled eggs?"

"All I can say is, it's the first diet I ever heard of where you gained weight from it."

"Who said I gained weight?"

"Oh, pardon me. I take it back. You're just wasting away before my very eyes. Isn't he, Frank?"

Frank had his fingers fanned out, tips against the bark of the stump where he'd laid his food. His knuckles were hairy. He wore a heavy wedding band, and on his right pinky was another gold ring with a flat face and "F" printed out in what looked like diamonds. He turned it this way and that. "Tub," he said, "you haven't seen your own balls in ten years."

Kenny doubled over laughing. He took off his hat and slapped his leg with it.

"What am I supposed to do?" said Tub. "It's my glands."

They left the woods and hunted along the creek. Frank and Kenny worked one bank and Tub worked the other, moving upstream. The snow was light, but the drifts were deep and hard to move through. Wherever Tub looked, the surface was smooth, undisturbed, and after a time he lost interest. He stopped looking for tracks and just tried to keep up with Frank and Kenny on the other side. A moment came when he realized he hadn't seen them in a long time. The breeze was moving from him to them; when it stilled he could sometimes hear them arguing but that was all. He quickened his pace, breasting hard into the drifts, fighting the snow away with his knees and elbows. He heard his heart and felt the flush on his face, but he never once stopped.

Tub caught up with Frank and Kenny at a bend in the creek. They were standing on a log that stretched from their bank to his. Ice had backed up behind the log. Frozen reeds stuck out, barely nodding when the air moved.

"See anything?" asked Frank.

Tub shook his head.

There wasn't much daylight left, and they decided to head back toward the road. Frank and Kenny crossed the log and started downstream, using the trail Tub had broken. Before they had gone very far, Kenny stopped. "Look at that," he said, and pointed to some tracks going from the creek back into the woods. Tub's footprints crossed right over them. There on the bank, plain as day, were several mounds of deer sign.

"What do you think that is, Tub?" Kenny kicked at it. "Walnuts on vanilla icing?"

"I guess I didn't notice."

Kenny looked at Frank.

"I was lost."

"You were lost. Big deal."

They followed the tracks into the woods. The deer had gone over a fence half buried in drifting snow. A no-hunting sign was nailed to the top of one of the posts. Frank laughed and said the son of a bitch could read. Kenny wanted to go after him, but Frank said no way—the people out here didn't mess around. He thought maybe the farmer who owned the land would let them use it if they asked, though Kenny wasn't so sure. Anyway, he figured that by the time they walked to the truck and drove up the road and doubled back it would be almost dark.

"Relax," said Frank. "You can't hurry nature. If we're meant to get that deer, we'll get it. If we're not, we won't."

They started back toward the truck. This part of the woods was mainly pine. The snow was shaded and had a glaze on it. It held up Kenny and Frank, but Tub kept falling through. As he kicked forward, the edge of the crust bruised his shins. Kenny and Frank pulled ahead of him, to where he couldn't even hear their voices any more. He sat down on a stump and wiped his face. He ate both the sandwiches and half the cookies, taking his own sweet time. It was dead quiet.

When Tub crossed the last fence into the road, the truck started moving. Tub had to run for it and just managed to grab hold of the tailgate and hoist himself into the bed. He lay there panting. Kenny looked out the rear window and grinned. Tub crawled into the lee of the cab to get out of the freezing wind. He pulled his earflaps low and pushed his chin into the collar of his coat. Someone rapped on the window, but Tub would not turn around.

He and Frank waited outside while Kenny went into the farmhouse to ask permission. The house was old, and paint was curling off the sides. The smoke streamed westward off the top of the chimney, fanning away into a thin gray plume. Above the ridge of the hills another ridge of blue clouds was rising.

"You've got a short memory," said Tub.

"What?" said Frank. He had been staring off.

"I used to stick up for you."

"O.K., so you used to stick up for me. What's eating you?"

"You shouldn't have just left me back there like that."

"You're a grown-up, Tub. You can take care of yourself. Anyway, if you think you're the only person with problems, I can tell you that you're not."

"Is something bothering you, Frank?"

Frank kicked at a branch poking out of the snow. "Never mind," he said.

"What did Kenny mean about the baby-sitter?"

"Kenny talks too much," said Frank. "You just mind your own business."

Kenny came out of the farmhouse and gave the thumbs up, and they began walking back toward the woods. As they passed the barn, a large black hound with a grizzled snout ran out and barked at them. Every time he barked he slid backward a bit, like a cannon going off. Kenny got down on all fours and snarled and barked back at him, and the dog slunk away into the barn, looking over his shoulder and peeing a little as he went.

"That's an old-timer," said Frank. "A real graybeard. Fifteen years, if he's a day."

"Too old," said Kenny.

Past the barn they cut off through the fields. The land was unfenced, and the crust was freezing up thick, and they made good time. They kept to the edge of the field until they picked up the tracks again and followed them into the woods, farther and farther back toward the hills. The trees started to blur with the shadows, and the wind rose and needled their faces with the crystals it swept off the glaze. Finally they lost the tracks.

Kenny swore and threw down his hat. "This is the worst day of hunting I ever had, bar none." He picked up his hat and brushed off the snow. "This will be the first season since I was fifteen that I haven't got any deer."

"It isn't the deer," said Frank. "It's the hunting. There are all these forces out here and you just have to go with them."

"You go with them," said Kenny. "I came out here to get me a deer, not listen to a bunch of hippie bullshit. And if it hadn't been for Dimples here, I would have, too."

"That's enough," said Frank.

"And you . . . you're so busy thinking about that little jailbait of yours, you wouldn't know a deer if you saw one."

"I'm warning you," said Frank.

Kenny laughed. "I think maybe I'll have me a talk with a certain jailbait's father," he said. "Then you can warn him, too."

"Drop dead," said Frank and turned away.

Kenny and Tub followed him back across the fields. When they were coming up to the barn, Kenny stopped and pointed. "I hate that post," he said. He raised his rifle and fired. It sounded like a dry branch cracking. The post splintered along its right side, up toward the top.

"There," said Kenny. "It's dead."

"Knock it off," said Frank, walking ahead.

Kenny looked at Tub and smiled. "I hate that tree," he said, and fired again. Tub hurried to catch up with Frank. He started to speak, but just then the dog ran out of the barn and barked at them. "Easy, boy," said Frank.

"I hate that dog." Kenny was behind them.

"That's enough," said Frank. "You put that gun down."

Kenny fired. The bullet went in between the dog's eyes. He sank right down into the snow, his legs splayed out on each side, his yellow eyes open and staring. Except for the blood, he looked like a small bearskin rug. The blood ran down the dog's muzzle into the snow.

They all looked at the dog lying there.

"What did he ever do to you?" asked Tub. "He was just barking."

Kenny turned to Tub. "I hate you."

Tub shot from the waist. Kenny jerked backward against the fence and buckled to his knees. He folded his hands across his stomach. "Look," he said. His hands were covered with blood. In the dusk his blood was more blue than red. It seemed to belong to the shadows. It didn't seem out of place. Kenny eased himself onto his back. He sighed several times, deeply. "You shot me," he said.

"I had to," said Tub. He knelt beside Kenny. "Oh, God," he said. "Frank. Frank."

Frank hadn't moved since Kenny killed the dog.

"Frank!" Tub shouted.

"I was just kidding around," said Kenny. "It was a joke. Oh!" he said, and arched his back suddenly. "Oh!" he said again, and dug his heels into the snow and pushed himself along on his head for several feet. Then he stopped and lay there, rocking back and forth on his heels and head like a wrestler doing warm-up exercises.

Frank roused himself. "Kenny," he said. He bent down and put his gloved hand on Kenny's brow. "You shot him," he said to Tub.

"He made me," said Tub.

"No, no, no," said Kenny.

Tub was weeping from the eyes and nostrils. His whole face was wet. Frank closed his eyes, then looked down at Kenny again. "Where does it hurt?"

"Everywhere," said Kenny. "Just everywhere."

"Oh, God," said Tub.

"I mean where did it go in?" said Frank.

"Here." Kenny pointed at the wound in his stomach. It was welling slowly with blood.

"You're lucky," said Frank. "It's on the left side. It missed your appendix. If it had hit your appendix, you'd really be in the soup." He turned and threw up onto the snow, holding his sides as if to keep warm.

"Are you all right?" asked Tub.

"There's some aspirin in the truck," said Kenny.

"I'm all right," said Frank.

"We'd better call an ambulance," said Tub.

"Jesus," said Frank, "what are we going to say?"

"Exactly what happened," said Tub. "He was going to shoot me but I shot him first."

"No, sir!" said Kenny. "I wasn't either!"

Frank patted Kenny on the arm. "Easy does it, partner." He stood. "Let's go."

Tub picked up Kenny's rifle as they walked down toward the farmhouse. "No sense leaving this around," he said. "Kenny might get ideas."

"I can tell you one thing," said Frank. "You've really done it this time. This definitely takes the cake."

They had to knock on the door twice before it was opened by a thin man with lank hair. The room behind him was filled with smoke. He squinted at them. "You get anything?" he asked.

"No," said Frank.

"I knew you wouldn't. That's what I told the other fellow."

"We've had an accident."

The man looked past Frank and Tub into the gloom. "Shoot your friend, did you?"

Frank nodded.

"I did," said Tub.

"I suppose you want to use the phone."

"If it's O.K."

The man in the door looked behind him, then stepped back. Frank and Tub followed him into the house. There was a woman sitting by the stove in the middle of the room. The stove was smoking badly. She looked up and then down again at the child asleep in her lap. Her face was white and damp; strands of hair were pasted across her forehead. Tub warmed his hands over the stove while Frank went into the kitchen to call. The man who had let them in stood at the window, his hands in his pockets.

"My partner shot your dog," said Tub.

The man nodded without turning around. "I should have done it myself. I just couldn't."

"He loved that dog so much," the woman said. The child squirmed and she rocked it.

"You asked him to?" said Tub. "You asked him to shoot your dog?"

"He was old and sick. Couldn't chew his food any more. I would have done it myself but I don't have a gun."

"You couldn't have anyway," said the woman. "Never in a million years."

The man shrugged.

Frank came out of the kitchen. "We'll have to take him ourselves. The nearest hospital is fifty miles from here and all their ambulances are out anyway."

The woman knew a shortcut, but the directions were complicated and Tub had to write them down. The man told where they could find some boards to carry Kenny on. He didn't have a flashlight, but he said he would leave the porch light on.

It was dark outside. The clouds were low and heavy-looking and the wind blew in shrill gusts. There was a screen loose on the house, and it banged slowly and then quickly as the wind rose again. They could hear it all the way to the barn. Frank went for the boards while Tub looked for Kenny, who was not where they had left him. Tub found him farther up the drive, lying on his stomach. "You O.K.?" said Tub.

"It hurts."

"Frank says it missed your appendix."

"I already had my appendix out."

"All right," said Frank, coming up to them. "We'll have you in a nice warm bed before you can say Jack Robinson." He put the two boards on Kenny's right side.

"Just as long as I don't have one of those male nurses," said Kenny.

"Ha ha," said Frank. "That's the spirit. Get ready, set, over you go," and he rolled Kenny onto the boards. Kenny screamed and kicked his legs in the air. When he quieted down, Frank and Tub lifted the boards and carried him down the drive. Tub had the back end, and with the snow blowing into his face he had trouble with his footing. Also he was tired and the man inside had forgotten to turn the porch light on. Just past the house Tub slipped and threw out his hands to catch himself. The boards fell and Kenny tumbled out and rolled to the bottom of the drive, yelling all the way. He came to rest against the right front wheel of the truck.

"You fat moron," said Frank. "You aren't good for diddly."

Tub grabbed Frank by the collar and backed him hard up against the fence. Frank tried to pull his hands away, but Tub shook him and snapped his head back and forth and finally Frank gave up.

"What do you know about fat?" said Tub. "What do you know about glands?" As he spoke, he kept shaking Frank. "What do you know about me?"

"All right," said Frank.

"No more," said Tub.

"All right."

"No more talking to me like that. No more watching. No more laughing."

"O.K., Tub. I promise."

Tub let go of Frank and leaned his forehead against the fence. His arms hung straight at his sides.

"I'm sorry, Tub." Frank touched him on the shoulder. "I'll be down at the truck."

Tub stood by the fence for a while and then got the rifles off the porch. Frank had rolled Kenny back onto the boards and they lifted him into the bed of the truck. Frank spread the seat blankets over him. "Warm enough?" he asked.

Kenny nodded.

"O.K. Now how does reverse work on this thing?"

"All the way to the left and up." Kenny sat up as Frank started forward to the cab. "Frank!"

"What?"

"If it sticks, don't force it."

The truck started right away. "One thing," said Frank, "you've got to hand it to the Japanese. A very ancient, very spiritual culture and they can still make a hell of a truck." He glanced over at Tub. "Look, I'm sorry. I didn't know you felt that way, honest to God, I didn't. You should have said something."

"I did."

"When? Name one time."

"A couple of hours ago."

"I guess I wasn't paying attention."

"That's true, Frank," said Tub. "You don't pay attention very much."

"Tub," said Frank, "what happened back there—I should have been more sympathetic. I realize that. You were going through a lot. I just want you to know it wasn't your fault. He was asking for it."

"You think so?"

"Absolutely. I would have done the same thing in your shoes, no question."

The wind was blowing into their faces. The snow was a moving white wall in front of their lights; it swirled into the cab through the hole in the windshield and settled on them. Tub clapped his hands and shifted around to stay warm, but it didn't work.

"I'm going to have to stop," said Frank. "I can't feel my fingers."

Up ahead they saw some lights off the road. It was a tavern. Outside in the parking lot were several jeeps and trucks. A couple of them had deer strapped across their hoods. Frank parked and they went back to Kenny. "How you doing, partner?" said Frank.

"I'm cold."

"Well, don't feel like the Lone Ranger. It's worse inside, take my word for it. You should get that windshield fixed."

"Look," said Tub, "he threw the blankets off." They were lying in a heap against the tailgate.

"Now look, Kenny," said Frank, "it's no use whining about being cold if you're not going to try and keep warm. You've got to do your share." He spread the blankets over Kenny and tucked them in at the corners.

"They blew off."

"Hold on to them then."

"Why are we stopping, Frank?"

"Because if me and Tub don't get warmed up we're going to freeze solid and then where will you be?" He punched Kenny lightly in the arm. "So just hold your horses."

The bar was full of men in colored jackets, mostly orange. The waitress brought coffee. "Just what the doctor ordered," said Frank, cradling the steaming cup in his hand. His skin was bone white. "Tub, I've been thinking. What you said about me not paying attention, that's true."

"It's O.K."

"No. I really had that coming. I guess I've just been a little too interested in old number one. I've had a lot on my mind—not that that's any excuse."

"Forget it, Frank. I sort of lost my temper back there. I guess we're all a little on edge."

Frank shook his head. "It isn't just that."

"You want to talk about it?"

"Just between us, Tub?"

"Sure, Frank. Just between us."

"Tub, I think I'm going to be leaving Nancy."

"Oh, Frank. Oh, Frank." Tub sat back. "What's the problem? Has she been seeing someone?"

"No. I wish she was, Tub. I wish to God she was." He reached out and laid his hand on Tub's arm. "Tub, have you ever been really in love?"

"Well . . ."

"I mean *really* in love." He squeezed Tub's wrist. "With your whole being."

"I don't know. When you put it like that."

"You haven't, then. Nothing against you, but you'd know it if you had." Frank let go of Tub's arm. "Nancy hasn't been running around, Tub. I have."

"Oh, Frank."

"Running around's not the right word for it. It isn't like that. She's not just some bit of fluff."

"Who is she, Frank?"

Frank paused. He looked into his empty cup. "Roxanne Brewer."

"Cliff Brewer's kid? The baby-sitter?"

"You can't just put people into categories like that, Tub. That's why the whole system is wrong. And that's why this country is going to hell in a rowboat."

"But she can't be more than . . ." Tub shook his head.

"Fifteen. She'll be sixteen in May." Frank smiled. "May fourth, three twenty-seven P.M. Hell, Tub, a hundred years ago she'd have been an old maid by that age. Juliet was only thirteen."

"Juliet? Juliet Miller? Jesus, Frank, she doesn't even have breasts. She doesn't even wear a top to her bathing suit. She's still collecting frogs."

"Not Juliet Miller—the real Juliet. Tub, don't you see how you're dividing people up into categories? He's an executive, she's a secretary, he's a truck driver, she's fifteen years old. Tub, this so-called baby-sitter, this so-called fifteen-year-old has more in her little finger than most of us have in our entire bodies. I can tell you this little lady is something special."

Tub nodded. "I know the kids like her."

"She's opened up whole worlds to me that I never knew were there."

"What does Nancy think about all of this?"

"Nothing, Tub. She doesn't know."

"You haven't told her?"

"Not yet. It's not so easy. She's been damned good to me all these years. Then there's the kids to consider." The brightness in Frank's eyes trembled and he wiped quickly at them with the back of his hand. "I guess you think I'm a complete bastard."

"No, Frank. I don't think that."

"Well, you *ought* to."

"Frank, when you've got a friend it means you've always got someone on your side, no matter what. That's how I feel about it anyway."

"You mean that, Tub?"

"Sure I do."

Frank smiled. "You don't know how good it feels to hear you say that."

Kenny had tried to get out of the truck but he hadn't made it. He was jackknifed over the tailgate, his head hanging above the bumper. They lifted him back into the bed and covered him again. He was sweating and his teeth chattered. "It hurts, Frank."

"It wouldn't hurt so much if you just stayed put. Now we're going to the hospital. Got that? Say it: 'I'm going to the hospital.' "

"I'm going to the hospital."

"Again."

"I'm going to the hospital."

"Now just keep saying that to yourself and before you know it we'll be there."

After they had gone a few miles, Tub turned to Frank. "I just pulled a real boner," he said.

"What's that?"

"I left the directions on the table back there."

"That's O.K. I remember them pretty well."

The snowfall lightened and the clouds began to roll back off the fields, but it was no warmer and after a time both Frank and Tub were bitten through and shaking. Frank almost didn't make it around a curve, and they decided to stop at the next roadhouse.

There was an automatic hand dryer in the bathroom and they took turns standing in front of it, opening their jackets and shirts and letting the jet of hot air breathe across their faces and chests.

"You know," said Tub, "what you told me back there, I appreciate it. Trusting me."

Frank opened and closed his fingers in front of the nozzle. "The way I look at it, Tub, no man is an island. You've got to trust someone."

"Frank . . ."

Frank waited.

"When I said that about my glands, that wasn't true. The truth is I just shovel it in."

"Well, Tub . . ."

"Day and night, Frank. In the shower. On the freeway." He turned and let the air play over his back. "I've even got stuff in the paper towel machine at work."

"There's nothing wrong with your glands at all?" Frank had taken his boots and socks off. He held first his right, then his left foot up to the nozzle.

"No. There never was."

"Does Alice know?" The machine went off and Frank started lacing up his boots.

"Nobody knows. That's the worst of it, Frank, not the being fat—I never got any big kick out of being thin—but the lying. Having to lead a double life like a spy or a hit man. This sounds strange but I feel sorry for those guys, I really do. I know what they go through. Always having to think about what you say and do. Always feeling like people are watching you, trying to catch you at something. Never able to just be yourself. Like when I make a big deal about only having an orange for breakfast and then scarf all the way to work. Oreos, Mars bars, Twinkies, Sugar Babies, Snickers." Tub glanced at Frank and looked quickly away. "Pretty disgusting, isn't it?"

"Tub. Tub." Frank shook his head. "Come on." He took Tub's arm and led him into the restaurant half of the bar. "My friend is hungry," he told the waitress. "Bring four orders of pancakes, plenty of butter and syrup."

"Frank . . ."

"Sit down."

When the dishes came, Frank carved out slabs of butter and just laid them on the pancakes. Then he emptied the bottle of syrup, moving it back and forth over the plates. He leaned forward on his elbows and rested his chin on one hand. "Go on, Tub."

Tub ate several mouthfuls, then started to wipe his lips. Frank took the napkin away from him. "No wiping," he said. Tub kept at it. The syrup covered his chin; it dripped to a point like a goatee. "Weigh in, Tub," said Frank, pushing another fork across the table. "Get down to business." Tub took the fork in his left hand and lowered his head and started really chowing down. "Clean your plate," said Frank when the pancakes were gone, and Tub lifted each of the four plates and licked it clean. He sat back, trying to catch his breath.

"Beautiful," said Frank. "Are you full?"

"I'm full," said Tub. "I've never been so full."

Kenny's blankets were bunched up against the tailgate again.

"They must have blown off," said Tub.

"They're not doing him any good," said Frank. "We might as well get some use out of them."

Kenny mumbled. Tub bent over him. "What? Speak up."

"I'm going to the hospital," said Kenny.

"Attaboy," said Frank.

The blankets helped. The wind still got their faces and Frank's hands but it was much better. The fresh snow on the road and the trees sparkled under the beam of the headlight. Squares of light from farmhouse windows fell onto the blue snow in the fields.

"Frank," said Tub after a time, "you know that farmer? He told Kenny to kill the dog."

"You're kidding!" Frank leaned forward, considering. "That Kenny. What a card." He laughed and so did Tub. Tub smiled out the back window. Kenny lay with his arms folded over his stomach, moving his lips at the stars. Right overhead was the Big Dipper, and behind, hanging between Kenny's toes in the direction of the hospital, was the North Star, pole star, help to sailors. As the truck twisted through the gentle hills, the star went back and forth between Kenny's boots, staying always in his sight. "I'm going to the hospital," said Kenny, but he was wrong. They had taken a different turn a long way back.

TIM O'BRIEN

(1946–)

William Timothy O'Brien was born in Worthington, Minnesota, and educated at Macalester College in St. Paul. Shortly after graduation he was drafted to serve in the Vietnam War where he was a foot soldier from 1969 to 1970; he was wounded near My Lai. In 1970 he began graduate studies in government at Harvard and worked for the national affairs desk of The Washington Post. *The Vietnam War—its history, its politics, its effect upon individual men and women—has provided the dominant theme of Tim O'Brien's work, which, as suggested by his best-known story, "The Things They Carried," is characterized by a distinctive narrative voice and a highly poetic distillation of experience.*

Tim O'Brien is both a short story writer and a novelist—in three of his books, he is both at the same time. If I Die in a Combat Zone *(1973),* Going After Cacciato *(1978), and* The Things They Carried *(1990) are novels constructed out of skillfully linked short stories, in which the form (disjointed, with abrupt stops and starts, yet informed by a single unifying vision) most effectively expresses content.* Northern Lights *(1974) and* The Nuclear Age *(1985) are more conventionally structured novels set in the United States and focusing upon a smaller number of characters.*

The phenomenon of the Vietnam War—that most divisive of foreign wars in our American history—has resulted in an outpouring of imaginative work (prose fiction, memoirs, poetry, plays, films) of high quality. Among these hundreds, indeed thousands, of works, Tim O'Brien's Going After Cacciato *and* The Things They Carried *are generally considered outstanding.*

The Things They Carried

First Lieutenant Jimmy Cross carried letters from a girl named Martha, a junior at Mount Sebastian College in New Jersey. They were not love letters, but Lieutenant Cross was hoping, so he kept them folded in plastic at the bottom of his rucksack. In the late afternoon, after a day's march, he would dig his foxhole, wash his hands under a canteen, unwrap the letters, hold them with the tips of his fingers, and spend the last hour of light pretending. He would imagine romantic camping trips into the White Mountains in New Hampshire. He would sometimes taste the envelope flaps, knowing her tongue had been there. More than anything, he wanted Martha to love him as he loved her, but the letters were mostly chatty, elusive on the matter of love. She was a virgin, he was almost sure. She was an English major at Mount Sebastian, and she wrote beautifully about her professors and roommates and midterm exams, about her respect for Chaucer and her great affection for Virginia Woolf. She often quoted lines of poetry; she never mentioned the war, except to say, Jimmy, take care of yourself. The letters weighed 10 ounces. They were signed Love, Martha, but Lieutenant Cross understood that Love was only a way of signing and did not mean what he sometimes pretended it meant. At dusk, he would carefully return the letters to his rucksack. Slowly, a bit distracted, he would get up and move among his men, checking the perimeter, then at full dark he would return to his hole and watch the night and wonder if Martha was a virgin.

The things they carried were largely determined by necessity. Among the necessities or near-necessities were P-38 can openers, pocket knives, heat tabs, wristwatches, dog tags, mosquito repellent, chewing gum, candy, cigarettes, salt tablets, packets of Kool-Aid, lighters, matches, sewing kits, Military Payment Certificates, C rations, and two or three canteens of water. Together, these items weighed between 15 and 20 pounds, depending upon a man's habits or rate of metabolism. Henry Dobbins, who was a big man, carried extra rations; he was especially fond of canned peaches in heavy syrup over pound cake. Dave Jensen, who practiced field hygiene, carried a toothbrush, dental floss, and several hotel-sized bars of soap he'd stolen on R&R in Sydney, Australia. Ted Lavender, who was scared, carried tranquilizers until he was shot in the head outside the village of Than Khe in mid-April. By necessity, and because it was SOP, they all carried steel helmets that weighed 5 pounds including the liner and camouflage cover. They carried the standard fatigue jackets and trousers. Very few carried underwear. On their feet they carried jungle boots—2.1 pounds—and Dave Jensen carried three pairs of socks and a can of Dr. Scholl's foot powder as a precaution against trench foot. Until he was shot, Ted Lavender carried six or seven ounces of premium dope, which for him was a necessity. Mitchell Sanders, the RTO, carried condoms. Norman Bowker carried a diary. Rat Kiley carried comic books. Kiowa, a devout Baptist, carried an illustrated New Testament that had been presented to him by his father, who taught Sunday school in Oklahoma City, Oklahoma. As a hedge against bad times, however, Kiowa also carried his grandmother's distrust of the white man, his grandfather's old hunting hatchet. Necessity dictated. Because the land was mined and booby-trapped, it was SOP for each man to carry a steel-centered, nylon-covered flak jacket, which weighed 6.7 pounds, but which on hot days seemed much heavier. Because you could die so quickly, each man carried at least one large compress bandage, usually in the helmet band for easy access. Because the nights were cold, and because the monsoons were wet, each carried a green plastic poncho that could be used as a raincoat or groundsheet or makeshift tent. With its quilted liner, the poncho weighed almost two pounds, but it was worth every ounce. In April, for instance, when Ted Lavender was shot, they used his poncho to wrap him up, then to carry him across the paddy, then to lift him into the chopper that took him away.

They were called legs or grunts.

To carry something was to hump it, as when Lieutenant Jimmy Cross humped his love for Martha up the hills and through the swamps. In its intransitive form, to hump meant to walk, or to march, but it implied burdens far beyond the intransitive.

Almost everyone humped photographs. In his wallet, Lieutenant Cross carried two photographs of Martha. The first was a Kodacolor snapshot signed Love, though he knew better. She stood against a brick wall. Her eyes were gray and neutral, her lips slightly open as she stared straight-on at the camera. At night, sometimes, Lieutenant Cross wondered who had taken the picture, because he knew she had boyfriends, because he loved her so much, and because he could see the shadow of the picture-taker spreading out against the brick wall. The second photograph had been clipped from the 1968 Mount Sebastian yearbook. It was an action shot—women's volleyball—and Martha was bent horizontal to the floor, reaching, the palms of her hands in sharp focus, the tongue taut, the expression frank and competitive. There was no visible sweat. She wore white gym shorts. Her legs, he thought, were almost certainly the legs of a virgin, dry and without hair, the left knee cocked and carrying her entire weight, which was just over one hundred pounds. Lieutenant Cross remembered touching that left knee. A dark theater, he remembered, and the movie was *Bonnie and Clyde*, and Martha wore a tweed skirt, and during the final scene, when he touched her knee, she turned and looked at him in a sad, sober way that made him pull his hand back, but he would always remember the feel of the tweed skirt and the knee beneath it and the sound of the gunfire that killed Bonnie and Clyde, how embarrassing it was, how slow and oppressive. He remembered kissing her good night at the dorm door. Right then, he thought, he should've done something brave. He should've carried her up the stairs to her room and tied her to the bed and touched that left knee all night long. He should've risked it. Whenever he looked at the photographs, he thought of new things he should've done.

What they carried was partly a function of rank, partly of field specialty.

As a first lieutenant and platoon leader, Jimmy Cross carried a compass, maps, code books, binoculars, and a .45-caliber pistol that weighed 2.9 pounds fully loaded. He carried a strobe light and the responsibility for the lives of his men.

As an RTO, Mitchell Sanders carried the PRC-25 radio, a killer, 26 pounds with its battery.

As a medic, Rat Kiley carried a canvas satchel filled with morphine and plasma and malaria tablets and surgical tape and comic books and all the things a medic must carry, including M&M's for especially bad wounds, for a total weight of nearly 20 pounds.

As a big man, therefore a machine gunner, Henry Dobbins carried the M-60, which weighed 23 pounds unloaded, but which was almost always loaded. In addition, Dobbins carried between 10 and 15 pounds of ammunition draped in belts across his chest and shoulders.

As PFCs or Spec 4s, most of them were common grunts and carried the standard M-16 gas-operated assault rifle. The weapon weighed 7.5 pounds unloaded, 8.2 pounds with its full 20-round magazine. Depending on numerous factors, such as topography and psychology, the riflemen carried anywhere from 12 to 20 magazines, usually in cloth bandoliers, adding on another 8.4 pounds at minimum, 14 pounds at maximum. When it was available, they also carried M-16 maintenance gear—rods and steel brushes and swabs and tubes of LSA oil—all of which weighed about a pound. Among the grunts, some carried the M-79 grenade launcher, 5.9 pounds unloaded, a reasonably light weapon except for the ammunition, which was heavy. A single round weighed 10 ounces. The typical load was 25 rounds. But Ted Lavender, who was scared, carried 34 rounds when he was shot and killed outside Than Khe, and he went down under an exceptional burden, more than 20 pounds of ammunition, plus the flak jacket and helmet and rations and water and toilet paper and tranquilizers and all the rest, plus the unweighed fear. He was dead weight. There was no twitching or flopping. Kiowa, who saw it happen, said it was like watching a rock fall, or a big sandbag or something—just boom, then down—not like the movies where the dead guy rolls around and does fancy spins and goes ass over teakettle—not like that, Kiowa said, the poor bastard just flat-fuck fell. Boom. Down. Nothing else. It was a bright morning in mid-April. Lieutenant Cross felt the pain. He blamed himself. They stripped off Lavender's canteens and ammo, all the heavy things, and Rat Kiley said the obvious, the guy's dead, and Mitchell Sanders used his radio to report one U.S. KIA and to request a chopper. Then they wrapped Lavender in his poncho. They carried him out to a dry paddy, established security, and sat smoking the dead man's dope until the chopper came. Lieutenant Cross kept to himself. He pictured Martha's smooth young face, thinking he loved her more than anything, more than his men, and now Ted Lavender was dead because he loved her so much and could not stop thinking about her. When the dustoff arrived, they carried Lavender aboard. Afterward they burned Than Khe. They marched until dusk, then dug their holes, and that night Kiowa kept explaining how you had to be there, how fast it was, how the poor guy just dropped like so much concrete. Boom-down, he said. Like cement.

In addition to the three standard weapons—the M-60, M-16, and M-79—they carried whatever presented itself, or whatever seemed appropriate as a means of killing or staying alive. They carried catch-as-catch-can. At various times, in various situations, they carried M-14s and CAR-15s and Swedish Ks and grease guns and captured AK-47s and Chi-Coms and RPGs and Simonov carbines and black market Uzis and .38-caliber Smith & Wesson handguns and 66 mm LAWs and shotguns and silencers and blackjacks and bayonets and C-4 plastic explosives. Lee Strunk carried a slingshot; a weapon of last resort, he called it. Mitchell Sanders carried brass knuckles. Kiowa carried his grandfather's feathered hatchet. Every third or fourth man carried a Claymore antipersonnel mine—3.5 pounds with its firing device. They all carried fragmentation grenades—14 ounces each. They all carried at least one M-18 colored smoke grenade—24 ounces. Some carried CS or tear gas grenades. Some carried white phosphorus grenades. They carried all they could bear, and then some, including a silent awe for the terrible power of the things they carried.

In the first week of April, before Lavender died, Lieutenant Jimmy Cross received a good-luck charm from Martha. It was a simple pebble, an ounce at most. Smooth to the touch, it was a milky white color with flecks of orange and violet, oval-shaped, like a miniature egg. In the accompanying letter, Martha wrote that she had found the pebble on the Jersey shoreline, precisely where the land touched water at high tide, where things came together but also separated. It was this separate-but-together quality, she wrote, that had inspired her to pick up the pebble and to carry it in her breast pocket for several days, where it seemed weightless, and then to send it through the mail, by air, as a token of her truest feelings for him. Lieutenant Cross found this romantic. But he wondered what her truest feelings were, exactly, and what she meant by separate-but-together. He wondered how the tides and waves had come into play on that afternoon along the Jersey shoreline when Martha saw the pebble and bent down to rescue it from geology. He imagined bare feet. Martha was a poet, with the poet's sensibilities, and her feet would be brown and bare, the toenails unpainted, the eyes chilly and somber like the ocean in March, and though it was painful, he wondered who had been with her that afternoon. He imagined a pair of shadows moving along the strip of sand where things came together but also separated. It was phantom jealousy, he knew, but he couldn't help himself. He loved her so much. On the march, through the hot days of early April, he carried the pebble in his mouth, turning it with his tongue, tasting sea salt and moisture. His mind wandered. He had difficulty keeping his attention on the war. On occasion he would yell at his men to spread out the column, to keep their eyes open, but then he would slip away into daydreams, just pretending, walking barefoot along the Jersey shore, with Martha, carrying nothing. He would feel himself rising. Sun and waves and gentle winds, all love and lightness.

What they carried varied by mission.

When a mission took them to the mountains, they carried mosquito netting, machetes, canvas tarps, and extra bug juice.

If a mission seemed especially hazardous, or if it involved a place they knew to be bad, they carried everything they could. In certain heavily mined AOs, where the land was dense with Toe Poppers and Bouncing Betties, they took turns humping a 28-pound mine detector. With its headphones and big sensing plate, the equipment was a stress on the lower back and shoulders, awkward to handle, often useless because of the shrapnel in the earth, but they carried it anyway, partly for safety, partly for the illusion of safety.

On ambush, or other night missions, they carried peculiar little odds and ends. Kiowa always took along his New Testament and a pair of moccasins for silence. Dave Jensen carried night-sight vitamins high in carotene. Lee Strunk carried his slingshot; ammo, he claimed, would never be a problem. Rat Kiley carried brandy and M&M's candy. Until he was shot, Ted Lavender carried the starlight scope, which weighed 6.3 pounds with its aluminum carrying case. Henry Dobbins carried his girlfriend's pantyhose wrapped around his neck as a comforter. They all carried ghosts. When dark came, they would move out single file across the meadows and paddies to their ambush coordinates, where they would quietly set up the Claymores and lie down and spend the night waiting.

Other missions were more complicated and required special equipment. In mid-April, it was their mission to search out and destroy the elaborate tunnel complexes in the Than Khe area south of Chu Lai. To blow the tunnels, they carried one-pound blocks of pentrite high explosives, four blocks to a man, 68 pounds in all. They carried wiring, detonators, and battery-powered clackers. Dave Jensen carried earplugs. Most often, before blowing the tunnels, they were ordered by higher command to search them, which was considered bad news, but by and large they just shrugged and carried out orders. Because he was a big man, Henry Dobbins was excused from tunnel duty. The others would draw numbers. Before Lavender died there were 17 men in the platoon, and whoever drew the number 17 would strip off his gear and crawl in headfirst with a flashlight and Lieutenant Cross's .45-caliber pistol. The rest of them would fan out as security. They would sit down or kneel, not facing the hole, listening to the ground beneath them, imagining cobwebs and ghosts, whatever was down there—the tunnel walls squeezing in—how the flashlight seemed impossibly heavy in the hand and how it was tunnel vision in the very strictest sense, compression in all ways, even time, and how you had to wiggle in—ass and elbows—a swallowed-up feeling—and how you found yourself worrying about odd things: Will your flashlight go dead? Do rats carry rabies? If you screamed, how far would the sound carry? Would your buddies hear it? Would they have the courage to drag you out? In some respects, though not many, the waiting was worse than the tunnel itself. Imagination was a killer.

On April 16, when Lee Strunk drew the number 17, he laughed and muttered something and went down quickly. The morning was hot and very still. Not good, Kiowa said. He looked at the tunnel opening, then out across a dry paddy toward the village of Than Khe. Nothing moved. No clouds or birds or people. As they waited, the men smoked and drank Kool-Aid, not talking much, feeling sympathy for Lee Strunk but also feeling the luck of the draw. You win some, you lose some, said Mitchell Sanders, and sometimes you settle for a rain check. It was a tired line and no one laughed.

Henry Dobbins ate a tropical chocolate bar. Ted Lavender popped a tranquilizer and went off to pee.

After five minutes, Lieutenant Jimmy Cross moved to the tunnel, leaned down, and examined the darkness. Trouble, he thought—a cave-in maybe. And then suddenly, without willing it, he was thinking about Martha. The stresses and fractures, the quick collapse, the two of them buried alive under all that weight. Dense, crushing love. Kneeling, watching the hole, he tried to concentrate on Lee Strunk and the war, all the dangers, but his love was too much for him, he felt paralyzed, he wanted to sleep inside her lungs and breathe her blood and be smothered. He wanted her to be a virgin and not a virgin, all at once. He wanted to know her. Intimate secrets: Why poetry? Why so sad? Why that grayness in her eyes? Why so alone? Not lonely, just alone—riding her bike across campus or sitting off by herself in the cafeteria—even dancing, she danced alone—and it was the aloneness that filled him with love. He remembered telling her that one evening. How she nodded and looked away. And how, later, when he kissed her, she received the kiss without returning it, her eyes wide open, not afraid, not a virgin's eyes, just flat and uninvolved.

Lieutenant Cross gazed at the tunnel. But he was not there. He was buried with Martha under the white sand at the Jersey shore. They were pressed together, and the pebble in his mouth was her tongue. He was smiling. Vaguely, he was aware of how quiet the day was, the sullen paddies, yet he could not bring himself to worry about matters of security. He was beyond that. He was just a kid at war, in love. He was twenty-four years old. He couldn't help it.

A few moments later Lee Strunk crawled out of the tunnel. He came up grinning, filthy but alive. Lieutenant Cross nodded and closed his eyes while the others clapped Strunk on the back and made jokes about rising from the dead.

Worms, Rat Kiley said. Right out of the grave. Fuckin' zombie.

The men laughed. They all felt great relief.

Spook city, said Mitchell Sanders.

Lee Strunk made a funny ghost sound, a kind of moaning, yet very happy, and right then, when Strunk made that high happy moaning sound, when he went *Ahhooooo,* right then Ted Lavender was shot in the head on his way back from peeing. He lay with his mouth open. The teeth were broken. There was a swollen black bruise under his left eye. The cheekbone was gone. Oh shit, Rat Kiley said, the guy's dead. The guy's dead, he kept saying, which seemed profound—the guy's dead. I mean really.

ried Black Flag insecticide. Dave Jensen carried empty sandbags that could be filled at night for added protection. Lee Strunk carried tanning lotion. Some things they carried in common. Taking turns, they carried the big PRC-77 scrambler radio, which weighed 30 pounds with its battery. They shared the weight of memory. They took up what others could no longer bear. Often, they carried each other, the wounded or weak. They carried infections. They carried chess sets, basketballs, Vietnamese-English dictionaries, insignia of rank, Bronze Stars and Purple Hearts, plastic cards imprinted with the Code of Conduct. They carried diseases, among them malaria and dysentery. They carried lice and ringworm and leeches and paddy algae and various rots and molds. They carried the land itself—Vietnam, the place, the soil—a powdery orange-red dust that covered their boots and fatigues and faces. They carried the sky. The whole atmosphere, they carried it, the humidity, the monsoons, the stink of fungus and decay, all of it, they carried gravity. They moved like mules. By daylight they took sniper fire, at night they were mortared, but it was not battle, it was just the endless march, village to village, without purpose, nothing won or lost. They marched for the sake of the march. They plodded along slowly, dumbly, leaning forward against the heat, unthinking, all blood and bone, simple grunts, soldiering with their legs, toiling up the hills and down into the paddies and across the rivers and up again and down, just humping, one step and then the next and then another, but no volition, no will, because it was automatic, it was anatomy, and the war was entirely a matter of posture and carriage, the hump was everything, a kind of inertia, a kind of emptiness, a dullness of desire and intellect and conscience and hope and human sensibility. Their principles were in their feet. Their calculations were biological. They had no sense of strategy or mission. They searched the villages without knowing what to look for, not caring, kicking over jars of rice, frisking children and old men, blowing tunnels, sometimes setting fires and sometimes not, then forming up and moving on to the next village, then other villages, where it would always be the same. They carried their own lives. The pressures were enormous. In the heat of early afternoon, they would remove their helmets and flak jackets, walking bare, which was dangerous but which helped ease the strain. They would often discard things along the route of march. Purely for comfort, they would throw away rations, blow their Claymores and grenades, no matter, because by nightfall the resupply choppers would arrive with more of the same, then a day or two later still more, fresh watermelons and crates of ammunition and sunglasses and woolen sweaters—the resources were stunning—sparklers for the Fourth of July, colored eggs for Easter—it was the great American war chest—the fruits of science, the smokestacks, the canneries, the arsenals at Hartford, the Minnesota forests, the machine shops, the vast fields of corn and wheat—they carried like freight trains; they carried it on their backs and shoulders—and for all the ambiguities of Vietnam, all the mysteries and unknowns, there was at least the single abiding certainty that they would never be at a loss for things to carry.

After the chopper took Lavender away, Lieutenant Jimmy Cross led his men into the village of Than Khe. They burned everything. They shot chickens and dogs, they trashed the village well, they called in artillery and watched the wreckage, then they marched for several hours through the hot afternoon, and then at dusk, while Kiowa explained how Lavender died, Lieutenant Cross found himself trembling.

He tried not to cry. With his entrenching tool, which weighed five pounds, he began digging a hole in the earth.

He felt shame. He hated himself. He had loved Martha more than his men, and as a consequence Lavender was now dead, and this was something he would have to carry like a stone in his stomach for the rest of the war.

All he could do was dig. He used his entrenching tool like an ax, slashing, feeling both love and hate, and then later, when it was full dark, he sat at the bottom of his foxhole and wept. It went on for a long while. In part, he was grieving for Ted Lavender, but mostly it was for Martha, and for himself, because she belonged to another world, which was not quite real, and because she was a junior at Mount Sebastian College in New Jersey, a poet and a virgin and uninvolved, and because he realized she did not love him and never would.

Like cement, Kiowa whispered in the dark. I swear to God—boom, down. Not a word.

I've heard this, said Norman Bowker.

A pisser, you know? Still zipping himself up. Zapped while zipping.

All right, fine. That's enough.

Yeah, but you had to see it, the guy just—

I *heard*, man. Cement. So why not shut the fuck *up*?

Kiowa shook his head sadly and glanced over at the hole where Lieutenant Jimmy Cross sat watching the night. The air was thick and wet. A warm dense fog had settled over the paddies and there was the stillness that precedes rain.

After a time Kiowa sighed.

One thing for sure, he said. The lieutenant's in some deep hurt. I mean that crying jag—the way he was carrying on—it wasn't fake or anything, it was real heavy-duty hurt. The man cares.

Sure, Norman Bowker said.

Say what you want, the man does care.

We all got problems.

Not Lavender.

No, I guess not, Bowker said. Do me a favor, though.

Shut up?

That's a smart Indian. Shut up.

Shrugging, Kiowa pulled off his boots. He wanted to say more, just to lighten up his sleep, but instead he opened his New Testament and arranged it beneath his head as a pillow. The fog made things seem hollow and unattached. He tried not to think about Ted Lavender, but then he was thinking how fast it was, no drama, down and dead, and how it was hard to feel anything except surprise. It seemed unchristian. He wished he could find some great sadness, or even anger, but the emotion wasn't there and he couldn't make it happen. Mostly he felt pleased to be alive. He liked the smell of the New Testament under his cheek, the leather and ink and paper and glue, whatever the chemicals were. He liked hearing the sounds of night. Even his fatigue, it felt fine, the stiff muscles and the prickly awareness of his own body, a floating feeling. He enjoyed not being dead. Lying there, Kiowa admired Lieutenant Jimmy Cross's capacity for grief. He wanted to share the man's pain, he wanted to care as Jimmy Cross cared. And yet when he closed his eyes, all he could think was Boom-down, and all he could feel was the pleasure of having his boots off and the fog curling in around him and the damp soil and the Bible smells and the plush comfort of night.

After a moment Norman Bowker sat up in the dark.

What the hell, he said. You want to talk, *talk*. Tell it to me.

Forget it.

No, man, go on. One thing I hate, it's a silent Indian.

For the most part they carried themselves with poise, a kind of dignity. Now and then, however, there were times of panic, when they squealed or wanted to squeal but couldn't, when they twitched and made moaning sounds and covered their heads and said Dear Jesus and flopped around on the earth and fired their weapons blindly and cringed and sobbed and begged for the noise to stop and went wild and made stupid promises to themselves and to God and to their mothers and fathers, hoping not to die. In different ways, it happened to all of them. Afterward, when the firing ended, they would blink and peek up. They would touch their bodies, feeling shame, then quickly hiding it. They would force themselves to stand. As if in slow motion, frame by frame, the world would take on the old logic—absolute silence, then the wind, then sunlight, then voices. It was the burden of being alive. Awkwardly, the men would reassemble themselves, first in private, then in groups, becoming soldiers again. They would repair the leaks in their eyes. They would check for casualties, call in dust-offs, light cigarettes, try to smile, clear their throats and spit and begin cleaning their weapons. After a time someone would shake his head and say, No lie, I almost shit my pants, and someone else would laugh, which meant it was bad, yes, but the guy had obviously not shit his pants, it wasn't that bad, and in any case nobody would ever do such a thing and then go ahead and talk about it. They would squint into the dense, oppressive sunlight. For a few moments, perhaps, they would fall silent, lighting a joint and tracking its passage from man to man, inhaling, holding in the humiliation. Scary stuff, one of them might say. But then someone else would grin or flick his eyebrows and say, Roger-dodger, almost cut me a new asshole, *almost*.

There were numerous such poses. Some carried themselves with a sort of wistful resignation, others with pride or stiff soldierly discipline or good humor or macho zeal. They were afraid of dying but they were even more afraid to show it.

They found jokes to tell.

They used a hard vocabulary to contain the terrible softness. *Greased* they'd say. *Offed, lit up, zapped while zipping.* It wasn't cruelty, just stage presence. They were actors. When someone died, it wasn't quite dying, because in a curious way it seemed scripted, and because they had their lines mostly memorized, irony mixed with tragedy, and because they called it by other names, as if to encyst and destroy the reality of death itself. They kicked corpses. They cut off thumbs. They talked grunt lingo. They told stories about Ted Lavender's supply of tranquilizers, how the poor guy didn't feel a thing, how incredibly tranquil he was.

There's a moral here, said Mitchell Sanders.

They were waiting for Lavender's chopper, smoking the dead man's dope.

The moral's pretty obvious, Sanders said, and winked. Stay away from drugs. No joke, they'll ruin your day every time.

Cute, said Henry Dobbins.

Mind blower, get it? Talk about wiggy. Nothing left, just blood and brains.

They made themselves laugh.

There it is, they'd say. Over and over—there it is, my friend, there it is—as if the repetition itself were an act of poise, a balance between crazy and almost crazy, knowing without going, there it is, which meant be cool, let it ride, because Oh yeah, man, you can't change what can't be changed, there it is, there it absolutely and positively and fucking well *is*.

They were tough.

They carried all the emotional baggage of men who might die. Grief, terror, love, longing—these were intangibles, but the intangibles had their own mass and specific gravity, they had tangible weight. They carried shameful memories. They carried the common secret of cowardice barely restrained, the instinct to run or freeze or hide, and in many respects this was the heaviest burden of all, for it could never be put down, it required perfect balance and perfect posture. They carried their reputations. They carried the soldier's greatest fear, which was the fear of blushing. Men killed, and died, because they were embarrassed not to. It was what had brought them to the war in the first place, nothing positive, no dreams of glory or honor, just to avoid the blush of dishonor. They died so as not to die of embarrassment. They crawled into tunnels and walked point and advanced under fire. Each morning, despite the unknowns, they made their legs move. They endured. They kept humping. They did not submit to the obvious alternative, which was simply to close the eyes and fall. So easy, really. Go limp and tumble to the ground and let the muscles unwind and not speak and not budge until your buddies picked you up and lifted you into the chopper that would roar and dip its nose and carry you off to the world. A mere matter of falling, yet no one ever fell. It was not courage, exactly; the object was not valor. Rather, they were too frightened to be cowards.

By and large they carried these things inside, maintaining the masks of composure. They sneered at sick call. They spoke bitterly about guys who had found release by shooting off their own toes or fingers. Pussies, they'd say. Candy-asses. It was fierce, mocking talk, with only a trace of envy or awe, but even so the image played itself out behind their eyes.

They imagined the muzzle against flesh. So easy: squeeze the trigger and blow away a toe. They imagined it. They imagined the quick, sweet pain, then the evacuation to Japan, then a hospital with warm beds and cute geisha nurses.

And they dreamed of freedom birds.

At night, on guard, staring into the dark, they were carried away by jumbo jets. They felt the rush of takeoff. *Gone!* they yelled. And then velocity—wings and engines—a smiling stewardess—but it was more than a plane, it was a real bird, a big sleek silver bird with feathers and talons and high screeching. They were flying. The weights fell off; there was nothing to bear. They laughed and held on tight, feeling the cold slap of wind and altitude, soaring, thinking *It's over, I'm gone!*—they were naked, they were light and free—it was all lightness, bright and fast and buoyant, light as light, a helium buzz in the brain, a giddy bubbling in the lungs as they were taken up over the clouds and the war, beyond duty, beyond gravity and mortification and global entanglements—*Sin loi!* they yelled. *I'm sorry, motherfuckers, but I'm out of it, I'm goofed, I'm on a space cruise, I'm gone!*—and it was a restful, unencumbered sensation, just riding the light waves, sailing that big silver freedom bird over the mountains and oceans, over America, over the farms and great sleeping cities and cemeteries and highways and the golden arches of McDonald's, it was flight, a kind of fleeing, a kind of falling, falling higher and higher, spinning off the edge of the earth and beyond the sun and through the vast, silent vacuum where there were no burdens and where everything weighed exactly nothing—*Gone!* they screamed. *I'm sorry but I'm gone!*—and so at night, not quite dreaming, they gave themselves over to lightness, they were carried, they were purely borne.

On the morning after Ted Lavender died, First Lieutenant Jimmy Cross crouched at the bottom of his foxhole and burned Martha's letters. Then he burned the two photographs. There was a steady rain falling, which made it difficult, but he used heat tabs and Sterno to build a small fire, screening it with his body, holding the photographs over the tight blue flame with the tips of his fingers.

He realized it was only a gesture. Stupid, he thought. Sentimental, too, but mostly just stupid.

Lavender was dead. You couldn't burn the blame.

Besides, the letters were in his head. And even now, without photographs, Lieutenant Cross could see Martha playing volleyball in her white gym shorts and yellow T-shirt. He could see her moving in the rain.

When the fire died out, Lieutenant Cross pulled his poncho over his shoulders and ate breakfast from a can.

There was no great mystery, he decided.

In those burned letters Martha had never mentioned the war, except to say, Jimmy, take care of yourself. She wasn't involved. She signed the letters Love, but it wasn't love, and all the fine lines and technicalities did not matter. Virginity was no longer an issue. He hated her. Yes, he did. He hated her. Love, too, but it was a hard, hating kind of love.

The morning came up wet and blurry. Everything seemed part of everything else, the fog and Martha and the deepening rain.

He was a soldier, after all.

Half smiling, Lieutenant Jimmy Cross took out his maps. He shook his head hard, as if to clear it, then bent forward and began planning the day's march. In ten minutes, or maybe twenty, he would rouse the men and they would pack up and head west, where the maps showed the country to be green and inviting. They would do what they had always done. The rain might add some weight, but otherwise it would be one more day layered upon all the other days.

He was realistic about it. There was that new hardness in his stomach. He loved her but he hated her.

No more fantasies, he told himself.

Henceforth, when he thought about Martha, it would be only to think that she belonged elsewhere. He would shut down the daydreams. This was not Mount Sebastian, it was another world, where there were no pretty poems or midterm exams, a place where men died because of carelessness and gross stupidity. Kiowa was right. Boom-down, and you were dead, never partly dead.

Briefly, in the rain, Lieutenant Cross saw Martha's gray eyes gazing back at him.

He understood.

It was very sad, he thought. The things men carried inside. The things men did or felt they had to do.

He almost nodded at her, but didn't.

Instead he went back to his maps. He was now determined to perform his duties firmly and without negligence. It wouldn't help Lavender, he knew that, but from this point on he would comport himself as an officer. He would dispose of his good-luck pebble. Swallow it, maybe, or use Lee Strunk's slingshot, or just drop it along the trail. On the march he would impose strict field discipline. He would be careful to send out flank security, to prevent straggling or bunching up, to keep his troops moving at the proper pace and at the proper interval. He would insist on clean weapons. He would confiscate the remainder of Lavender's dope. Later in the day, perhaps, he would call the men together and speak to them plainly. He would accept the blame for what had happened to Ted Lavender. He would be a man about it. He would look them in the eyes, keeping his chin level, and he would issue the new SOPs in a calm, impersonal tone of voice, a lieutenant's voice, leaving no room for argument or discussion. Commencing immediately, he'd tell them, they would no longer abandon equipment along the route of march. They would police up their acts. They would get their shit together, and keep it together, and maintain it neatly and in good working order.

He would not tolerate laxity. He would show strength, distancing himself.

Among the men there would be grumbling, of course, and maybe worse, because their days would seem longer and their loads heavier, but Lieutenant Jimmy Cross reminded himself that his obligation was not to be loved but to lead. He would dispense with love; it was not now a factor. And if anyone quarreled or complained, he would simply tighten his lips and arrange his shoulders in the correct command posture. He might give a curt little nod. Or he might not. He might just shrug and say, Carry on, then they would saddle up and form into a column and move out toward the villages west of Than Khe.

BOBBIE ANN MASON
(1940–   )

Born and raised in western Kentucky, Bobbie Ann Mason has cultivated a distinctive art out of the materials of her region of America. Her forms are the short story and the short novel, in traditional structures, though often presented in a present-tense voice; her subjects are generally the clash of sub-cultures in a rapidly homogenizing late twentieth-century world. Typically, the clash is between men and women; or parents and children; in "Big Bertha Stories," included here, it is between a disturbed Vietnam War veteran and his family.

Bobbie Ann Mason was educated at the University of Kentucky, the State University of New York at Binghamton, and the University of Connecticut, and currently lives in western Kentucky. Her first book is Nabokov's Garden: A Guide to Ada *(1974). Though she is the author of two short novels,* In Country *(1985), which was made into a motion picture, and* Spence + Lila *(1988), she is best known for her short story collections* Shiloh *(1982) and* Love Life *(1989). The idiomatic yet poetic naturalism of Bobbie Ann Mason's prose voice is an art, unlike Nabokov's, so quietly forged as to seem at times artless; but it is precisely rendered, moving in subterranean ways to the final luminous detail, the powerful revelation of synecdoche.*

Big Bertha Stories

Donald is home again, laughing and singing. He comes home from Central City, Kentucky, near the strip mines, only when he feels like it, like an absentee landlord checking on his property. He is always in such a good humor when he returns that Jeannette forgives him. She cooks for him—ugly, pasty things she gets with food stamps. Sometimes he brings steaks and ice cream, occasionally money. Rodney, their child, hides in the closet when he arrives, and Donald goes around the house talking loudly about the little boy named Rodney who used to live there—the one who fell into a septic tank, or the one stolen by Gypsies. The stories change. Rodney usually stays in the closet until he has to pee, and then he hugs his father's knees, forgiving him, just as Jeannette does. The way Donald saunters through the door, swinging a six-pack of beer, with a big grin on his face, takes her breath away. He leans against the door facing, looking sexy in his baseball cap and his shaggy red beard and his sunglasses. He wears sunglasses to be like the Blues Brothers, but he in no way resembles either of the Blues Brothers. I should have my head examined, Jeannette thinks.

The last time Donald was home, they went to the shopping center to buy Rodney some shoes advertised on sale. They stayed at the shopping center half the afternoon, just looking around. Donald and Rodney played video games. Jeannette felt they were a normal family. Then, in the parking lot, they stopped to watch a man on a platform demonstrating snakes. Children were petting a 12-foot python coiled around the man's shoulders. Jeannette felt faint.

"Snakes won't hurt you unless you hurt them," said Donald as Rodney stroked the snake.

"It feels like chocolate," he said.

The snake man took a tarantula from a plastic box and held it lovingly in his palm. He said, "If you drop a tarantula, it will shatter like a Christmas ornament."

"I hate this," said Jeannette.

"Let's get out of here," said Donald.

Jeannette felt her family disintegrating like a spider shattering as Donald hurried them away from the shopping center. Rodney squalled and Donald dragged him along. Jeannette wanted to stop for ice cream. She wanted them all to sit quietly together in a booth, but Donald rushed them to the car, and he drove them home in silence, his face growing grim.

"Did you have bad dreams about the snakes?" Jeannette asked Rodney the next morning at breakfast. They were eating pancakes made with generic pancake mix. Rodney slapped his fork in the pond of syrup on his pancakes. "The black racer is the farmer's friend," he said soberly, repeating a fact learned from the snake man.

"Big Bertha kept black racers," said Donald. "She trained them for the 500." Donald doesn't tell Rodney ordinary children's stories. He tells him a series of strange stories he makes up about Big Bertha. Big Bertha is what he calls the huge strip-mining machine in Muhlenberg County, but he has Rodney believing that Big Bertha is a female version of Paul Bunyan.

"Snakes don't run in the 500," said Rodney.

"This wasn't the Indy 500, or the Daytona 500, none of your well-known 500s," said Donald. "This was the Possum Trot 500, and it was a long time ago. Big Bertha started the original 500, with snakes. Black racers and blue racers mainly. Also some red-and-white striped racers, but those are rare."

"We always ran for the hoe if we saw a black racer," Jeannette said, remembering her childhood in the country.

In a way, Donald's absences are a fine arrangement, even considerate. He is sparing them his darkest moods, when he can't cope with his memories of Vietnam. Vietnam had never seemed such a meaningful fact until a couple of years ago, when he grew depressed and moody, and then he started going away to Central City. He frightened Jeannette, and she always said the wrong thing in her efforts to soothe him. If the welfare people find out he is spending occasional weekends at home, and even bringing some money, they will cut off her assistance. She applied for welfare because she can't depend on him to send money, but she knows he blames her for losing faith in him. He isn't really working regularly at the strip mines. He is mostly just hanging around there, watching the land being scraped away, trees coming down, bushes flung in the air. Sometimes he operates a steam shovel, and when he comes home his clothes are filled with the clay and it is caked on his shoes. The clay is the color of butterscotch pudding.

At first, he tried to explain to Jeannette. He said, "If we could have had tanks over there as big as Big Bertha, we wouldn't have lost the war. Strip mining is just like what we were doing over there. We were stripping off the top. The topsoil is like the culture and the people, the best part of the land and the country. America was just stripping off the top, the best. We ruined it. Here, at least the coal companies have to plant vetch and loblolly pines and all kinds of trees and bushes. If we'd done that in Vietnam, maybe we'd have left that country in better shape."

"Wasn't Vietnam a long time ago?" Jeannette asked.

She didn't want to hear about Vietnam. She thought it was unhealthy to dwell on it so much. He should live in the present. Her mother is afraid Donald will do something violent, because she once read in the newspaper that a veteran in Louisville held his little girl hostage in their apartment until he had a shootout with the police and was killed. But Jeannette can't imagine Donald doing anything so extreme. When she first met him, several years ago, at her parents' pit-barbecue luncheonette, where she was working then, he had a good job at a lumberyard and he dressed nicely. He took her out to eat at a fancy restaurant. They got plastered and ended up in a motel in Tupelo, Mississippi, on Elvis Presley Boulevard. Back then, he talked nostalgically about his year in Vietnam, about how beautiful it was, how different the people were. He could never seem to explain what he meant. "They're just different," he said.

They went riding around in a yellow 1957 Chevy convertible. He drives too fast now, but he didn't then, maybe because he was so protective of the car. It was a classic. He sold it three years ago and made a good profit. About the time he sold the Chevy, his moods began changing, his even-tempered nature shifting, like driving on a smooth interstate and then switching to a secondary road. He had headaches and bad dreams. But his nightmares seemed trivial. He dreamed of riding a train through the Rocky Mountains, of hijacking a plane to Cuba, of stringing up barbed wire around the house. He dreamed he lost a doll. He got drunk and rammed the car, the Chevy's successor, into a Civil War statue in front of the courthouse. When he got depressed over the meaninglessness of his job, Jeannette felt guilty about spending money on something nice for the house, and she tried to make him feel his job had meaning by reminding him that, after all, they had a child to think of. "I don't like his name," Donald said once. "What a stupid name. Rodney. I never did like it."

Rodney has dreams about Big Bertha, echoes of his father's nightmare, like TV cartoon versions of Donald's memories of the war. But Rodney loves the stories, even though they are confusing, with lots of loose ends. The latest in the Big Bertha series is "Big Bertha and the Neutron Bomb." Last week it was "Big Bertha and the MX Missile." In the new story, Big Bertha takes a trip to California to go surfing with Big Mo, her male counterpart. On the beach, corn dogs and snow cones are free and the surfboards turn into dolphins. Everyone is having fun until the neutron bomb comes. Rodney loves the part where everyone keels over dead. Donald acts it out, collapsing on the rug. All the dolphins and the surfers keel over, everyone except Big Bertha. Big Bertha is so big she is immune to the neutron bomb.

"Those stories aren't true," Jeannette tells Rodney.

Rodney staggers and falls down on the rug, his arms and legs akimbo. He gets the giggles and can't stop. When his spasms finally subside, he says, "I told Scottie Bidwell about Big Bertha and he didn't believe me."

Donald picks Rodney up under the armpits and sets him upright. "You tell Scottie Bidwell if he saw Big Bertha he would pee in his pants on the spot, he would be so impressed."

"Are you scared of Big Bertha?"

"No, I'm not. Big Bertha is just like a wonderful woman, a big fat woman who can sing the blues. Have you ever heard Big Mama Thornton?"

"No."

"Well, Big Bertha's like her, only she's the size of a tall building. She's slow as a turtle and when she crosses the road, they have to reroute traffic. She's big enough to straddle a four-lane highway. She's so tall she can see all the way to Tennessee, and when she belches, there's a tornado. She's really something. She can even fly."

"She's too big to fly," Rodney says doubtfully. He makes a face like a wadded-up washrag and Donald wrestles him to the floor again.

Donald has been drinking all evening, but he isn't drunk. The ice cubes melt and he pours the drink out and refills it. He keeps on talking. Jeannette cannot remember him talking so much about the war. He is telling her about an ammunitions dump. Jeannette had the vague idea that an ammo dump is a mound of shotgun shells, heaps of cartridge casings and bomb shells, or whatever is left over, a vast waste pile from the war, but Donald says that is wrong. He has spent an hour describing it in detail, so that she will understand.

He refills the glass with ice, some 7-Up, and a shot of Jim Beam. He slams doors and drawers, looking for a compass. Jeannette can't keep track of the conversation. It doesn't matter that her hair is uncombed and her lipstick eaten away. He isn't seeing her.

"I want to draw the compound for you," he says, sitting down at the table with a sheet of Rodney's tablet paper.

Donald draws the map in red-and-blue ballpoint, with asterisks and technical labels that mean nothing to her. He draws some circles with the compass and measures some angles. He makes a red dot on an oblique line, a path that leads to the ammo dump.

"That's where I was. Right there," he says. "There was a water buffalo that tripped a land mine and its horn just flew off and stuck in the wall of the barracks like a machete thrown backhanded." He puts a dot where the land mine was, and he doodles awhile with the red ballpoint pen, scribbling something on the edge of the map that looks like feathers. "The dump was here and I was there and over there was where we piled the sandbags. And here were the tanks." He draws tanks, a row of squares with handles—guns sticking out.

"Why are you going to so much trouble to tell me about a buffalo horn that got stuck in a wall?" she wants to know.

But Donald just looks at her as though she has asked something obvious.

"Maybe I *could* understand if you'd let me," she says cautiously.

"You could never understand." He draws another tank.

In bed, it is the same as it has been since he started going away to Central City—the way he claims his side of the bed, turning away from her. Tonight, she reaches for him and he lets her be close to him. She cries for a while and he lies there, waiting for her to finish, as though she were merely putting on make-up.

"Do you want me to tell you a Big Bertha story?" he asks playfully.

"You act like you're in love with Big Bertha."

He laughs, breathing on her. But he won't come closer.

"You don't care what I look like anymore," she says. "What am I supposed to think?"

"There's nobody else. There's not anybody but you."

Loving a giant machine is incomprehensible to Jeannette. There must be another woman, someone that large in his mind. Jeannette has seen the strip-mining machine. The top of the crane is visible beyond a rise along the Western Kentucky Parkway. The strip mining is kept just out of sight of travelers because it would give them a poor image of Kentucky.

For three weeks, Jeannette has been seeing a psychologist at the free mental health clinic. He's a small man from out of state. His name is Dr. Robinson, but she calls him The Rapist, because the word *therapist* can be divided into two words, *the rapist*. He doesn't think her joke is clever, and he acts as though he has heard it a thousand times before. He has a habit of saying, "Go with that feeling," the same way Bob Newhart did on his old TV show. It's probably the first lesson in the textbook, Jeannette thinks.

She told him about Donald's last days on his job at the lumberyard—how he let the stack of lumber fall deliberately and didn't know why, and about how he went away soon after that, and how the Big Bertha stories started. Dr. Robinson seems to be waiting for her to make something out of it all, but it's maddening that he won't tell her what to do. After three visits, Jeannette has grown angry with him, and now she's holding back things. She won't tell him whether Donald slept with her or not when he came home last. Let him guess, she thinks.

"Talk about yourself," he says.

"What about me?"

"You speak so vaguely about Donald that I get the feeling that you see him as somebody larger than life. I can't quite picture him. That makes me wonder what that says about you." He touches the end of his tie to his nose and sniffs it.

When Jeannette suggests that she bring Donald in, the therapist looks bored and says nothing.

"He had another nightmare when he was home last," Jeannette says. "He dreamed he was crawling through tall grass and people were after him."

"How do *you* feel about that?" The Rapist asks eagerly.

"I didn't have the nightmare," she says coldly. "Donald did. I came to you to get advice about Donald, and you're acting like I'm the one who's crazy. I'm not crazy. But I'm lonely."

Jeannette's mother, behind the counter of the luncheonette, looks lovingly at Rodney pushing buttons on the jukebox in the corner.

"It's a shame about that youngun," she says tearfully. "That boy needs a daddy."

"What are you trying to tell me? That I should file for divorce and get Rodney a new daddy?"

Her mother looks hurt. "No, honey," she says. "You need to get Donald to seek the Lord. And you need to pray more. You haven't been going to church lately."

"Have some barbecue," Jeannette's father booms, as he comes in from the back kitchen. "And I want you to take a pound home with you. You've got a growing boy to feed."

"I want to take Rodney to church," Mama says. "I want to show him off, and it might do some good."

"People will think he's an orphan," Dad says.

"I don't care," Mama says. "I just love him to pieces and I want to take him to church. Do you care if I take him to church, Jeannette?"

"No. I don't care if you take him to church." She takes the pound of barbecue from her father. Grease splotches the brown wrapping paper. Dad has given them so much barbecue that Rodney is burned out on it and won't eat it anymore.

Jeannette wonders if she would file for divorce if she could get a job. It is a thought—for the child's sake, she thinks. But there aren't many jobs around. With the cost of a babysitter, it doesn't pay her to work. When Donald first went away, her mother kept Rodney and she had a good job, waitressing at a steak house, but the steak house burned down one night—a grease fire in the kitchen. After that, she couldn't find a steady job, and she was reluctant to ask her mother to keep Rodney again because of her bad hip. At the steak house, men gave her tips and left their telephone numbers on the bill when they paid. They tucked dollar bills and notes in the pockets of her apron. One note said, "I want to hold your muffins." They were real-estate developers and businessmen on important missions for the Tennessee Valley Authority. They were boisterous and they drank too much. They said they'd take her for a cruise on the Delta Queen, but she didn't believe them. She knew how expensive that was. They talked about their speedboats and invited her for rides on Lake Barkley, or for spins in their private planes. They always used the word *spin*. The idea made her dizzy. Once, Jeannette let an electronics salesman take her for a ride in his Cadillac, and they breezed down The Trace, the wilderness road that winds down the Land Between the Lakes. His car had automatic windows and a stereo system and lighted computer-screen numbers on the dash that told him how many miles to the gallon he was getting and other statistics. He said the numbers distracted him and he had almost had several wrecks. At the restaurant, he had been flamboyant, admired by his companions. Alone with Jeannette in the Cadillac, on The Trace, he was shy and awkward, and really not very interesting. The most interesting thing about him, Jeannette thought, was all the lighted numbers on his dashboard. The Cadillac had everything but video games. But she'd rather be riding around with Donald, no matter where they ended up.

While the social worker is there, filling out her report, Jeannette listens for Donald's car. When the social worker drove up, the flutter and wheeze of her car sounded like Donald's old Chevy, and for a moment Jeannette's mind elapsed back in time. Now she listens, hoping he won't drive up. The social worker is younger than Jeannette and has been to college. Her name is Miss Bailey, and she's excessively cheerful, as though in her line of work she has seen hardships that make Jeannette's troubles seem like a trip to Hawaii.

"Is your little boy still having those bad dreams?" Miss Bailey asks, looking up from her clipboard.

Jeannette nods and looks at Rodney, who has his finger in his mouth and won't speak.

"Has the cat got your tongue?" Miss Bailey asks.

"Show her your pictures, Rodney." Jeannette explains, "He won't talk about the dreams, but he draws pictures of them."

Rodney brings his tablet of pictures and flips through them silently. Miss Bailey says, "Hmm." They are stark line drawings, remarkably steady lines for his age. "What is this one?" she asks. "Let me guess. Two scoops of ice cream?"

The picture is two huge circles, filling the page, with three tiny stick people in the corner.

"These are Big Bertha's titties," says Rodney.

Miss Bailey chuckles and winks at Jeannette. "What do you like to read, hon?" she asks Rodney.

"Nothing."

"He can read," says Jeannette. "He's smart."

"Do you like to read?" Miss Bailey asks Jeannette. She glances at the pile of paperbacks on the coffee table. She is probably going to ask where Jeannette got the money for them.

"I don't read," says Jeannette."If I read, I just go crazy."

When she told The Rapist she couldn't concentrate on anything serious, he said she read romance novels in order to escape from reality. "Reality, hell!" she had said."Reality's my whole problem."

"It's too bad Rodney's not here," Donald is saying. Rodney is in the closet again. "Santa Claus has to take back all these toys. Rodney would love this bicycle! And this Pac-Man game. Santa has to take back so many things he'll have to have a pickup truck!"

"You didn't bring him anything. You never bring him anything," says Jeannette.

He has brought doughnuts and dirty laundry. The clothes he is wearing are caked with clay. His beard is lighter from working out in the sun, and he looks his usual joyful self, the way he always is before his moods take over, like migraine headaches, which some people describe as storms.

Donald coaxes Rodney out of the closet with the doughnuts.

"Were you a good boy this week?"

"I don't know."

"I hear you went to the shopping center and showed out." It is not true that Rodney made a big scene. Jeannette has already explained that Rodney was upset because she wouldn't buy him an Atari. But she didn't blame him for crying. She was tired of being unable to buy him anything.

Rodney eats two doughnuts and Donald tells him a long, confusing story about Big Bertha and a rock-and-roll band. Rodney interrupts him with dozens of questions. In the story, the rock-and-roll band gives a concert in a place that turns out to be a toxic-waste dump and the contamination is spread all over the country. Big Bertha's solution to this problem is not at all clear. Jeannette stays in the kitchen, trying to think of something original to do with instant potatoes and leftover barbecue.

"We can't go on like this," she says that evening in bed. "We're just hurting each other. Something has to change."

He grins like a kid. "Coming home from Muhlenberg County is like R and R—rest and recreation. I explain that in case you think

R and R means rock-and-roll. Or maybe rumps and rears. Or rust and rot." He laughs and draws a circle in the air with his cigarette.

"I'm not that dumb."

"When I leave, I go back to the mines." He sighs, as though the mines were some eternal burden.

Her mind skips ahead to the future: Donald locked away somewhere, coloring in a coloring book and making clay pots, her and Rodney in some other town, with another man—someone dull and not at all sexy. Summoning up her courage, she says, "I haven't been through what you've been through and maybe I don't have a right to say this, but sometimes I think you act superior because you went to Vietnam, like nobody can ever know what you know. Well, maybe not. But you've still got your legs, even if you don't know what to do with what's between them anymore." Bursting into tears of apology, she can't help adding,"You can't go on telling Rodney those awful stories. He has nightmares when you're gone."

Donald rises from bed and grabs Rodney's picture from the dresser, holding it as he might have held a hand grenade. "Kids betray you," he says, turning the picture in his hand.

"If you cared about him, you'd stay here." As he sets the picture down, she asks, "What can I do? How can I understand what's going on in your mind? Why do you go there? Strip mining's bad for the ecology and you don't have any business strip mining."

"My job is serious, Jeannette. I run that steam shovel and put the topsoil back on. I'm reclaiming the land." He keeps talking, in a gentler voice, about strip mining, the same old things she has heard before, comparing Big Bertha to a supertank. If only they had had Big Bertha in Vietnam. He says, "When they strip off the top, I keep looking for those tunnels where the Viet Cong hid. They had so many tunnels it was unbelievable. Imagine Mammoth Cave going all the way across Kentucky."

"Mammoth Cave's one of the natural wonders of the world," says Jeannette brightly. She is saying the wrong thing again.

At the kitchen table at 2 a.m., he's telling about C-5A's. A C-5A is so big it can carry troops and tanks and helicopters, but it's not big enough to hold Big Bertha. Nothing could hold Big Bertha. He rambles on, and when Jeannette shows him Rodney's drawing of the circles, Donald smiles. Dreamily, he begins talking about women's breasts and thighs—the large, round thighs and big round breasts of American women, contrasted with the frail, delicate beauty of the Orientals. It is like comparing oven broilers and banties, he says. Jeannette relaxes. A confession about another lover from long ago is not so hard to take. He seems stuck on the breasts and thighs of American women—insisting that she understand how small and delicate the Orientals are, but then he abruptly returns to tanks and helicopters.

"A Bell Huey Cobra—my God, what a beautiful machine. So efficient!" Donald takes the food processor blade from the drawer where Jeannette keeps it. He says, "A rotor blade from a chopper could just slice anything to bits."

"Don't do that," Jeannette says.

He is trying to spin the blade on the counter, like a top. "Here's what would happen when a chopper blade hits a power line—not many of those over there!—or a tree. Not many trees, either, come to think of it, after all the Agent Orange." He drops the blade and it glances off the open drawer and falls to the floor, spiking the vinyl.

At first, Jeannette thinks the screams are hers, but they are his. She watches him cry. She has never seen anyone cry so hard, like an intense summer thundershower. All she knows to do is shove Kleenex at him. Finally, he is able to say, "You thought I was going to hurt you. That's why I'm crying."

"Go ahead and cry," Jeannette says, holding him close.

"Don't go away."

"I'm right here. I'm not going anywhere."

In the night, she still listens, knowing his monologue is being burned like a tattoo into her brain. She will never forget it. His voice grows soft and he plays with a ballpoint pen, jabbing holes in a paper towel. Bullet holes, she thinks. His beard is like a bird's nest, woven with dark corn silks.

"This is just a story," he says. "Don't mean nothing. Just relax." She is sitting on the hard edge of the kitchen chair, her toes cold on the floor, waiting. His tears have dried up and left a slight catch in his voice.

"We were in a big camp near a village. It was pretty routine and kind of soft there for a while. Now and then we'd go into Da Nang and whoop it up. We had been in the jungle for several months, so the two months at this village was a sort of rest—an R and R almost. Don't shiver. This is just a little story. Don't mean nothing! This is nothing, compared to what I could tell you. Just listen. We lost our fear. At night there would be some incoming and we'd see these tracers in the sky, like shooting stars up close, but it was all pretty minor and we didn't take it seriously, after what we'd been through. In the village I knew this Vietnamese family—a woman and her two daughters. They sold Cokes and beer to GIs. The oldest daughter was named Phan. She could speak a little English. She was really smart. I used to go see them in their hooch in the afternoons—in the siesta time of day. It was so hot there. Phan was beautiful, like the country. The village was ratty, but the country was pretty. And she was beautiful, just like she had grown up out of the jungle, like one of those flowers that bloomed high up in the trees and freaked us out sometimes, thinking it was a sniper. She was so gentle, with these eyes shaped like peach pits, and she was no bigger than a child of maybe 13 or 14. I felt funny about her size at first, but later it didn't matter. It was just some wonderful feature about her, like a woman's hair, or her breasts."

He stops and listens, the way they used to listen for crying sounds when Rodney was a baby. He says, "She'd take those big banana leaves and fan me while I lay there in the heat."

"I didn't know they had bananas over there."

"There's a lot you don't know! Listen! Phan was 23, and her brothers were off fighting. I never even asked which side they were fighting on." He laughs. "She got a kick out of the word *fan*. I told her that *fan* was the same word as her name. She thought I meant her name was banana. In Vietnamese the same word can have a dozen different meanings, depending on your tone of voice. I bet you didn't know that, did you?"

"No. What happened to her?"

"I don't know."

"Is that the end of the story?"

"I don't know." Donald pauses, then goes on talking about the village, the girl, the banana leaves, talking in a monotone that is making Jeannette's flesh crawl. He could be the news radio from the next room.

"You must have really liked that place. Do you wish you could go back there to find out what happened to her?"

"It's not there anymore," he says. "It blew up."

Donald abruptly goes to the bathroom. She hears the water running, the pipes in the basement shaking.

"It was so pretty," he says when he returns. He rubs his elbow absentmindedly. "That jungle was the most beautiful place in the world. You'd have thought you were in paradise. But we blew it sky-high."

In her arms, he is shaking, like the pipes in the basement, which are still vibrating. Then the pipes let go, after a long shudder, but he continues to tremble.

They are driving to the Veterans Hospital. It was Donald's idea. She didn't have to persuade him. When she made up the bed that morning—with a finality that shocked her, as though she knew they wouldn't be in it again together—he told her it would be like R and R. Rest was what he needed. Neither of them had slept at all during the night. Jeannette felt she had to stay awake, to listen for more.

"Talk about strip mining," she says now. "That's what they'll do to your head. They'll dig out all those ugly memories, I hope. We don't need them around here." She pats his knee.

It is a cloudless day, not the setting for this sober journey. She drives and Donald goes along obediently, with the resignation of an old man being taken to a rest home. They are driving through southern Illinois, known as Little Egypt, for some obscure reason Jeannette has never understood. Donald still talks, but very quietly, without urgency. When he points out the scenery, Jeannette thinks of the early days of their marriage, when they would take a drive like this and laugh hysterically. Now Jeannette points out funny things they see. The Little Egypt Hot Dog World, Pharaoh Cleaners, Pyramid Body Shop. She is scarcely aware that she is driving, and when she sees a sign, Little Egypt Starlite Club, she is confused for a moment, wondering where she has been transported.

As they part, he asks, "What will you tell Rodney if I don't come back? What if they keep me here indefinitely?"

"You're coming back. I'm telling him you're coming back soon."

"Tell him I went off with Big Bertha. Tell him she's taking me on a sea cruise, to the South Seas."

"No. You can tell him that yourself."

He starts singing a jumpy tune, "Won't you let me take you on a sea cruise?" He grins at her and pokes her in the ribs.

"You're coming back," she says.

Donald writes from the VA Hospital, saying that he is making progress. They are running tests, and he meets in a therapy group in which all the veterans trade memories. Jeannette is no longer on welfare because she now has a job waitressing at Fred's Family Restaurant. She waits on families, waits for Donald to come home so they can come here and eat together like a family. The fathers look at her with downcast eyes, and the children throw food. While Donald is gone, she rearranges the furniture. She reads some books from the library. She does a lot of thinking. It occurs to her that even though she loved him, she has thought of Donald primarily as a husband, a provider, someone whose name she shared, the father of her child, someone like the fathers who come to the Wednesday night all-you-can-eat fish fry. She hasn't thought of him as himself. She wasn't brought up that way, to examine someone's soul. When it comes to something deep inside, nobody will take it out and examine it, the way they will look at clothing in a store for flaws in the manufacturing. She tries to explain all this to The Rapist, and he says she's looking better, got sparkle in her eyes. "Big deal," says Jeannette. "Is that all you can say?"

She takes Rodney to the shopping center, their favorite thing to do together, even though Rodney always begs to buy something. They go to Penney's perfume counter. There, she usually hits a sample bottle of cologne—Chantilly or Charlie or something strong. Today she hits two or three and comes out of Penney's smelling like a flower garden.

"You stink!" Rodney cries, wrinkling his nose like a rabbit.

"Big Bertha smells like this, only a thousand times worse, she's so big," says Jeannette impulsively. "Didn't Daddy tell you that?"

"Daddy's a messenger from the devil."

This is an idea he must have gotten from church. Her parents have been taking him every Sunday. When Jeannette tries to reassure him about his father, Rodney is skeptical. "He gets that funny look on his face like he can see through me," the child says.

"Something's missing," Jeannette says, with a rush of optimism, a feeling of recognition. "Something happened to him once and took out the part that shows how much he cares about us."

"The way we had the cat fixed?"

"I guess. Something like that." The appropriateness of his remark stuns her, as though, in a way, her child has understood Donald all along. Rodney's pictures have been more peaceful lately, pictures of skinny trees and airplanes flying low. This morning he drew pictures of tall grass, with creatures hiding in it. The grass is tilted at an angle, as though a light breeze is blowing through it.

With her paycheck, Jeannette buys Rodney a present, a miniature trampoline they had seen advertised on television. It is called Mr. Bouncer. Rodney is thrilled about the trampoline, and he jumps on it until his face is red. Jeannette discovers that she enjoys it, too. She puts it out on the grass, and they take turns jumping. She has an image of herself on the trampoline, her sailor collar flapping at the moment when Donald returns and sees her flying. One day a neighbor driving by slows down and calls out to Jeannette as she is bouncing on the trampoline, "You'll tear your insides loose!" Jeannette starts thinking about that, and the idea is so horrifying she stops jumping so much. That night, she has a nightmare about the trampoline. In her dream, she is jumping on soft moss, and then it turns into a springy pile of dead bodies.

JOHN EDGAR WIDEMAN
(1941–)

Though concerned as a writer with such issues as racial history and memory, and the paradoxes involved in being a black citizen in America, John Edgar Wideman is a highly experimental stylist, as the poetic prose work "Fever," included here, brilliantly demonstrates. Wideman's preoccupation with language as a living essence, and not as mere abstraction, relates him to such radically disparate precursors as Herman Melville, William Faulkner, and Jean Toomer; the material of his art is generally naturalistic, but his treatment is generally inventive. Wideman's is an art for both the eye and the ear: the musical cadences of his prose carry much of its meaning.

Born in Washington, D.C., Wideman grew up in Pittsburgh, graduated from the University of Pennsylvania, and studied at New College, Oxford, as a Rhodes scholar. He has been a celebrated basketball player as well as a celebrated writer, and has taught at a number of universities, including, at the present time, the University of Massachusetts. Perhaps best known for his fiction set in Homewood (the African-American section of Pittsburgh), Wideman is the author of the story collections Damballah *(1981) and* Fever *(1989), and the novels* A Glance Away *(1967),* Hurry Home *(1970),* The Lynchers *(1973),* Hiding Place *(1981),* Sent For You Yesterday *(1983),* Reuben *(1987), and* Philadelphia Fire *(1990). His memoir* Brothers and Keepers *(1984) is a nonfiction meditation, a double portrait, of the author and his younger brother, at that time serving a life sentence for murder.*

Fever

To Matthew Carey, Esq., who fled Philadelphia in its hour of need and upon his return published a libelous account of the behavior of black nurses and undertakers, thereby injuring all people of my race and especially those without whose unselfish, courageous labours the city could not have survived the late calamity.

Consider Philadelphia from its centrical situation, the extent of its commerce, the number of its artificers, manufacturers and other circumstances, to be to the United States what the heart is to the human body in circulating the blood.

Robert Morris, 1777

He stood staring through a tall window at the last days of November. The trees were barren women starved for love and they'd stripped off all their clothes, but nobody cared. And not one of them gave a fuck about him, sifting among them, weightless and naked, knowing just as well as they did, no hands would come to touch them, warm them, pick leaves off the frozen ground and stick them back in place. Before he'd gone to bed a flutter of insects had stirred in the dark outside his study. Motion worrying the corner of his eye till he turned and focused where light pooled on the deck, a cone in which he could trap slants of snow so they materialized into wet, gray feathers that blotted against the glass, the planks of the deck. If he stood seven hours, dark would come again. At some point his reflection would hang in the glass, a ship from the other side of the world, docked in the ether. Days were shorter now. A whole one spent wondering what goes wrong would fly away, fly in the blink of an eye.

Perhaps, *perhaps it may be acceptable to the reader to know how we found the sick affected by the sickness; our opportunities of hearing and seeing them have been very great. They were taken with a chill, a headache, a sick stomach, with pains in their limbs and back, this was the way the sickness in general began, but all were not affected alike, some appeared but slightly affected with some of these symptoms, what confirmed us in the opinion of a person being smitten was the colour of their eyes.*

Victims in this low-lying city perished every year, and some years were worse than others, but the worst by far was the long hot dry summer of '93, when the dead and dying wrested control of the city from the living. Most who were able, fled. The rich to their rural retreats, others to relatives and friends in the countryside or neighboring towns. Some simply left, with no fixed destination, the prospect of privation or starvation on the road preferable to cowering in their homes awaiting the fever's fatal scratching at their door. Busy streets deserted, commerce halted, members of families shunning one another, the sick abandoned to suffer and die alone. Fear ruled. From August when the first cases of fever appeared below Water Street, to November when merciful frosts ended the infestation, the city slowly deteriorated, as if it, too, could suffer the terrible progress of the disease: fever, enfeeblement, violent vomiting and diarrhea, helplessness, delirium, settled dejection when patients *concluded they must go (so the phrase for dying was), and therefore in a kind of fixed determined state of mind went off.*

In some it raged more furiously than in others—some have languished for seven and ten days, and appeared to get better the day, or some hours before they died, while others were cut off in one, two, or three days, but their complaints were similar. Some lost their reason and raged with all the fury madness could produce, and died in strong convulsions. Others retained their reason to the last, and seemed rather to fall asleep than die.

Yellow fever: an acute infectious disease of subtropical and tropical New World areas, caused by a filterable virus transmitted by a mosquito of the genus *Aëdes* and characterized by jaundice and dark colored vomit resulting from hemorrhages. Also called *yellow jack.*

Dengue: an infectious, virulent tropical and subtropical disease transmitted by mosquitoes and characterized by fever, rash, and severe pains in the joints. Also called *breakbone fever, dandy.* [Spanish, of African origin, akin to Swahili *kindinga.*]

Curled in the black hold of the ship he wonders why his life on solid green earth had to end, why the gods had chosen this new habitation for him, floating, chained to other captives, no air, no light, the wooden walls shuddering, battered, as if some madman is determined to destroy even this last pitiful refuge where he skids in foul puddles of waste, bumping other bodies, skinning himself on splintery beams and planks, always moving, shaken and spilled like palm nuts in the diviner's fist, and Esu casts his fate, constant motion, tethered to an iron ring.

In the darkness he can't see her, barely feels her light touch on his fevered skin. Sweat thick as oil but she doesn't mind, straddles him, settles down to do her work. She enters him and draws his blood up into her belly. When she's full, she pauses, dreamy, heavy. He could kill her then; she wouldn't care. But he doesn't. Listens to the whine of her wings lifting till the whimper is lost in the roar and crash of waves, creaking wood, prisoners groaning. If she returns tomorrow and carries away another drop of him, and the next day and the next, a drop each day, enough days, he'll be gone. Shrink to nothing, slip out of this iron noose and disappear.

Aëdes aegypti: a mosquito of the family *Culicidae,* genus *Aëdes,* in which the female is distinguished by a long proboscis for sucking blood. This winged insect is a vector (an organism that carries pathogens from one host to another) of yellow fever and dengue. [New Latin *Aëdes,* from Greek *aedes,* unpleasant: *a-*, not + *edos,* pleasant . . .]

All things arrive in the waters and waters carry all things away. So there is no beginning or end, only the waters' flow, ebb, flood, trickle, tides emptying and returning, salt seas and rivers and rain and mist and blood, the sun drowning in an ocean of night, wet sheen of dawn washing darkness from our eyes. This city is held in the water's palm. A captive as surely as I am captive. Long fingers of river, Schuylkill, Delaware, the rest of the hand invisible; underground streams and channels feed the soggy flesh of marsh, clay pit, sink, gutter, stagnant pool. What's not seen is heard in the suck of footsteps through spring mud of unpaved streets. Noxious vapors that sting your eyes, cause you to gag, spit, and wince are evidence of a presence, the dead hand cupping this city, the poisons that circulate through it, the sweat on its rotting flesh.

No one has asked my opinion. No one will. Yet I have seen this fever before, and though I can prescribe no cure, I could tell stories of other visitations, how it came and stayed and left us, the progress of disaster, its several stages, its horrors and mitigations. My words would not save one life, but those mortally affrighted by the fever, by the prospect of universal doom, might find solace in knowing there are limits to the power of this scourge that has befallen us, that some, yea, most will survive, that this condition is temporary, a season, that the fever must disappear with the first deep frosts and its disappearance is as certain as the fact it will come again.

They say the rat's-nest ships from Santo Domingo brought the fever. Frenchmen and their black slaves fleeing black insurrection. Those who've seen Barbados's distemper say our fever is its twin born in the tropical climate of the hellish Indies. I know better. I hear the drum, the forest's heartbeat, pulse of the sea that chains the moon's wandering, the spirit's journey. Its throb is source and promise of all things being connected, a mirror storing everything, forgetting nothing. To explain the fever we need no boatloads of refugees, ragged and wracked with killing fevers, bringing death to our shores. We have bred the affliction within our breasts. Each solitary heart contains all the world's tribes, and its precarious dance echoes the drum's thunder. We are our ancestors and our children, neighbors and strangers to ourselves. Fever descends when the waters that connect us are clogged with filth. When our seas are garbage. The waters cannot come and go when we are shut off one from the other, each in his frock coat, wig, bonnet, apron, shop, shoes, skin, behind locks, doors, sealed faces, our blood grows thick and sluggish. Our bodies void infected fluids. Then we are dry and cracked as a desert country, vital parts wither, all dust and dry bones inside. Fever is a drought consuming us from within. Discolored skin caves in upon itself, we burn, expire.

I regret there is so little comfort in this explanation. It takes into account neither climatists nor contagionists, flies in the face of logic and reason, the good doctors of the College of Physicians who would bleed us, purge us, quarantine, plunge us in icy baths, starve us, feed us elixirs of bark and wine, sprinkle us with gunpowder, drown us in vinegar according to the dictates of their various healing sciences. Who, then, is this foolish, old man who receives his wisdom from pagan drums in pagan forests? Are these the delusions of one whose brain the fever has already begun to gnaw? Not quite. True, I have survived other visitations of the fever, but while it prowls this city, I'm in jeopardy again as you are, because I claim no immunity, no magic. The messenger who bears the news of my death will reach me precisely at the stroke determined when it was determined I should tumble from the void and taste air the first time. Nothing is an accident. Fever grows in the secret places of our hearts, planted there when one of us decided to sell one of us to another. The drum must pound ten thousand thousand years to drive that evil away.

Fires burn on street corners. Gunshots explode inside wooden houses. Behind him a carter's breath expelled in low, labored pants warns him to edge closer to housefronts forming one wall of a dark, narrow, twisting lane. Thick wheels furrow the unpaved street. In the fire glow the cart stirs a shimmer of dust, faint as a halo, a breath smear on a mirror. Had the man locked in the traces of the cart cursed him or was it just a wheeze of exertion, a complaint addressed to the unforgiving weight of his burden? Creaking wheels, groaning wood, plodding footsteps, the cough of dust, bulky silhouette blackened as it lurches into brightness at the block's end. All gone in a moment. Sounds, motion, sight extinguished. What remained, as if trapped by a lid clamped over the lane, was the stench of dead bodies. A stench cutting through the ubiquitous pall of vinegar and gunpowder. Two, three, four corpses being hauled to Potter's Field, trailed by the unmistakable wake of decaying flesh. He'd heard they raced their carts to the burial ground. Two or three entering Potter's Field from different directions would acknowledge one another with challenges, raised fists, gather their strength for a last dash to the open trenches where they tip their cargoes. Their brethren would wager, cheer, toast the victor with tots of rum. He could hear the rumble of coffins crashing into a common grave, see the comical chariots bouncing, the men's legs pumping, faces contorted by fires that blazed all night at the burial ground. Shouting and curses would hang in the torpid night air, one more nightmare troubling the city's sleep.

He knew this warren of streets as well as anyone. Night or day he could negotiate the twists and turnings, avoid cul-de-sacs, find the river even if his vision was obscured in tunnellike alleys. He anticipated when to duck a jutting signpost, knew how to find doorways where he was welcome, wooden steps down to a cobbled terrace overlooking the water where his shod foot must never trespass. Once beyond the grand houses lining one end of Water Street, in this quarter of hovels, beneath these wooden sheds leaning shoulder to shoulder were cellars and caves dug into the earth, poorer men's dwellings under these houses of the poor, an invisible region where his people burrow, pull earth like blanket and quilt 'round themselves to shut out cold and dampness, sleeping multitudes to a room, stacked and crosshatched and spoon fashion, themselves the only fuel, heat of one body passed to others and passed back from all to one. Can he blame the lucky ones who are strong enough to pull the death carts, who celebrate and leap and roar all night around the bonfires? Why should they return here? Where living and dead, sick and well must lie face to face, shivering or sweltering on the same dank floor.

Below Water Street the alleys proliferate. Named and nameless. He knows where he's going but fever has transformed even the familiar. He'd been waiting in Dr. Rush's entrance hall. An English mirror, oval framed in scalloped brass, drew him. He watched himself glide closer, a shadow, a blur, then the shape of his face materialized from silken depths. A mask he did not recognize. He took the thing he saw and murmured to it. Had he once been in control? Could he tame it again? Like a garden ruined overnight, pillaged, overgrown, trampled by marauding beasts. He stares at the chaos until he can recall familiar contours of earth, seasons of planting, harvesting, green shoots, nodding blossoms, scraping, digging, watering. Once upon a time he'd cultivated this thing, this plot of flesh and blood and bone, but what had it become? Who owned it now? He'd stepped away. His eyes constructed another face and set it there, between him and the wizened old man in the glass. He'd aged twenty years in a glance and the fever possessed the same power to alter suddenly what it touched. This city had grown ancient and fallen into ruin in two months since early August, when the first cases of fever appeared. Something in the bricks, mortar, beams, and stones had gone soft, had lost its permanence. When he entered sickrooms, walls fluttered, floors buckled. He could feel roofs pressing down. Putrid heat expanding. In the bodies of victims. In rooms, buildings, streets, neighborhoods. Membranes that preserved the integrity of substances and shapes, kept each in its proper place, were worn thin. He could poke his finger through yellowed skin. A stone wall. The eggshell of his skull. What should be separated was running together. Threatened to burst. Nothing contained the way it was supposed to be. No clear lines of demarcation. A mongrel city. Traffic where there shouldn't be traffic. An awful void opening around him, preparing itself to hold explosions of bile, vomit, gushing bowels, ooze, sludge, seepage.

Earlier in the summer, on a July afternoon, he'd tried to escape the heat by walking along the Delaware. The water was unnaturally calm, isolated into stagnant pools by outcroppings of wharf and jetty. A shelf of rotting matter paralleled the river edge. As if someone had attempted to sweep what was unclean and dead from the water. Bones, skin, entrails, torn carcasses, unrecognizable tatters and remnants broomed into a neat ridge. No sigh of the breeze he'd sought, yet fumes from the rim of garbage battered him in nauseating waves, a palpable medium intimate as wind. Beyond the tidal line of refuge, a pale margin lapped clean by receding waters. Then the iron river itself, flat, dark, speckled by sores of foam that puckered and swirled, worrying the stillness with a life of their own.

Spilled. Spoiled. Those words repeated themselves endlessly as he made his rounds. Dr. Rush had written out his portion, his day's share from the list of dead and dying. He'd purged, bled, comforted and buried victims of the fever. In and out of homes that had become tombs, prisons, charnel houses. Dazed children wandering the streets, searching for their parents. How can he explain to a girl, barely more than an infant, that the father and mother she sobs for are gone from this earth? Departed. Expired. They are resting, child. Asleep forever. In a far, far better place, my sweet, dear, suffering one. In God's bosom. Wrapped in His incorruptible arms. A dead mother with a dead baby at her breast. Piteous cries of the helpless offering all they own for a drink of water. How does he console the delirious boy who pummels him, fastens himself on his leg because he's put the boy's mother in a box and now must nail shut the lid?

Though light-headed from exhaustion, he's determined to spend a few hours here, among his own people. But were these lost ones really his people? The doors of his church were open to them, yet these were the ones who stayed away, wasting their lives in vicious pastimes of the idle, the unsaved, the ignorant. His benighted brethren who'd struggled to reach this city of refuge and then, once inside the gates, had fallen, prisoners again, trapped by chains of dissolute living as they'd formerly been snared in the bonds of slavery. He'd come here and preached to them. Thieves, beggars, loose women, debtors, fugitives, drunkards, gamblers, the weak, crippled, and outcast with nowhere else to go. They spurned his church so he'd brought church to them, preaching in gin mills, whoring dens, on street corners. He'd been jeered and hooted, spat upon, clods of unnameable filth had spattered his coat. But a love for them, as deep and unfathomable as his sorrow, his pity, brought him back again and again, exhorting them, setting the gospel before them so they might partake of its bounty, the infinite goodness, blessed sustenance therein. Jesus had toiled among the wretched, the outcast, that flotsam and jetsam deposited like a ledge of filth on the banks of the city. He understood what had brought the dark faces of his brethren north, to the Quaker promise of this town, this cradle and capital of a New World, knew the misery they were fleeing, the bright star in the Gourd's handle that guided them, the joy leaping in their hearts when at last, at last the opportunity to be viewed as men instead of things was theirs. He'd dreamed such dreams himself, oh, yes, and prayed that the light of hope would never be extinguished. He'd been praying for deliverance, for peace and understanding when God had granted him a vision, hordes of sable bondsmen throwing off their chains, marching, singing, a path opening in the sea, the sea shaking its shaggy shoulders, resplendent with light and power. A radiance sparkling in this walkway through the water, pearls, diamonds, spears of light. This was the glistening way home. Waters parting, glory blinking and winking. Too intense to stare at, a promise shimmering, a rainbow arching over the end of the path. A hand tapped him. He'd waited for it to blend into the vision, for its meaning to shine forth in the language neither word nor thought, God was speaking in His visitation. Tapping became a grip. Someone was shoving him. He was being pushed off his knees, hauled to his feet. Someone was snatching him from the honeyed dream of salvation. When his eyes popped open he knew the name of each church elder manhandling him. Pale faces above a wall of black cloth belonged to his fellow communicants. He knew without looking the names of the men whose hands touched him gently, steering, coaxing, and those whose hands dug into his flesh, the impatient, imperious, rough hands that shunned any contact with him except as overseer or master.

Allen, Allen. Do you hear me? You and your people must not kneel at the front of the gallery. On your feet. Come. Come. Now. On your feet.

Behind the last row of pews. There ye may fall down on your knees and give praise.

And so we built our African house of worship. But its walls could not imprison the Lord's word. Go forth. Go forth. And he did so. To this sinful quarter. Tunnels, cellars, and caves. Where no sunlight penetrates. Where wind off the river cuts like a knife. Chill of icy spray channeled here from the ocean's wintry depths. Where each summer the brackish sea that is mouth and maw and bowel deposits its waste in puddles stinking to high heaven.

Water Street becomes what it's named, rises round his ankles, soaks his boots, threatens to drag him down. Patrolling these murky depths he's predator, scavenger, the prey of some dagger-toothed creature whose shadow closes over him like a net.

When the first settlers arrived here they'd scratched caves into the soft earth of the riverbank. Like ants. Rats. Gradually they'd pushed inland, laying out a geometrical grid of streets, perpendicular, true angled and straight edged, the mirror of their rectitude. Black Quaker coats and dour visages were remembrances of mud, darkness, the place of their lying in, cocooned like worms, propagating dreams of a holy city. The latest comers must always start here, on this dotted line, in this riot of alleys, lanes, tunnels. Wave after wave of immigrants unloaded here, winnowed here, dying in these shanties, grieving in strange languages. But white faces move on, bury their dead, bear their children, negotiate the invisible reef between this broken place and the foursquare town. Learn enough of their new tongue to say to the blacks they've left behind, *thou shalt not pass.*

I watched him bring the scalding liquid to his lips and thought to myself that's where his color comes from. The black brew he drinks every morning. Coloring him, changing him. A hue I had not considered until that instant as other than absence, something nonwhite and therefore its opposite, what light would be if extinguished, sky or sea drained of the color blue when the sun disappears, the blackness of cinders. As he sips, steam rises. I peer into the cup that's become mine, at the moon in its center, waxing, waning. A light burning in another part of the room caught there, as my face would be if I leaned over the cup's hot mouth. But I have no wish to see my face. His is what I study as I stare into my cup and see not absence, but the presence of wood darkly stained, wet plowed earth, a boulder rising from a lake, blackly glistening as it sheds crowns and beards and necklaces of water. His color neither neglect nor abstention, nor mystery, but a swelling tide in his skin of this bitter morning beverage it is my habit to imbibe.

We were losing, clearly losing the fight. One day in mid-September fifty-seven were buried before noon.

He'd begun with no preamble. Our conversation taken up again directly as if the months since our last meeting were no more than a cobweb his first words lightly brush away. I say conversation but a better word would be soliloquy because I was only a listener, a witness learning his story, a story buried so deeply he couldn't recall it, but dreamed pieces, a conversation with himself, a reverie with the power to sink us both into its unreality. So his first words did not begin the story where I remembered him ending it in our last session, but picked up midstream the ceaseless play of voices only he heard, always, summoning him, possessing him, enabling him to speak, to be.

Despair was in my heart. The fiction of our immunity had been exposed for the vicious lie it was, a not so subtle device for wresting us from our homes, our loved ones, the afflicted among us, and sending us to aid strangers. First they blamed us, called the sickness Barbados fever, a contagion from those blood-soaked islands, brought to these shores by refugees from the fighting in Santo Domingo. We were not welcome anywhere. A dark skin was seen not only as a badge of shame for its wearer. Now we were evil incarnate, the mask of long agony and violent death. Black servants were discharged. The draymen, carters, barbers, caterers, oyster sellers, street vendors could find no custom. It mattered not that some of us were born here and spoke no language but the English language, second-, even third-generation African Americans who knew no other country, who laughed at the antics of newly landed immigrants, Dutchmen, Welshmen, Scots, Irish, Frenchmen who had turned our marketplaces into Babel, stomping along in their clodhopper shoes, strange costumes, haughty airs, Lowlander gibberish that sounded like men coughing or dogs barking. My fellow countrymen searching everywhere but in their own hearts, the foulness upon which this city is erected, to lay blame on others for the killing fever, pointed their fingers at foreigners and called it Palatine fever, a pestilence imported from those low countries in Europe where, I have been told, war for control of the sea-lanes, the human cargoes transported thereupon, has raged for a hundred years.

But I am losing the thread, the ironical knot I wished to untangle for you. How the knife was plunged in our hearts, then cruelly twisted. We were proclaimed carriers of the fever and treated as pariahs, but when it became expedient to command our services to nurse the sick and bury the dead, the previous allegations were no longer mentioned. Urged on by desperate counselors, the mayor granted us a blessed immunity. We were ordered to save the city.

I swear to you, and the bills of mortality, published by the otherwise unreliable Mr. Carey, support my contention, that the fever dealt with us severely. Among the city's poor and destitute the fever's ravages were most deadly and we are always the poorest of the poor. If an ordinance forbidding ringing of bells to mourn the dead had not been passed, that awful tolling would have marked our days, the watches of the night in our African-American community, as it did in those environs of the city we were forbidden to inhabit. Every morning before I commenced my labors for the sick and dying, I would hear moaning, screams of pain, fearful cries and supplications, a chorus of lamentations scarring daybreak, my people awakening to a nightmare that was devouring their will to live.

The small strength I was able to muster each morning was sorely tried the moment my eyes and ears opened upon the sufferings of my people, the reality that gave the lie to the fiction of our immunity. When my duties among the whites were concluded, how many nights did I return and struggle till dawn with victims here, my friends, parishioners, wandering sons of Africa whose faces I could not look upon without seeing my own. I was commandeered to rise and go forth to the general task of saving the city, forced to leave this neighborhood where my skills were sorely needed. I nursed those who hated me, deserted the ones I loved, who loved me.

I recite the story many, many times to myself, let many voices speak to me till one begins to sound like the sea or rain or my feet those mornings shuffling through thick dust.

We arrived at Bush Hill early. To spare ourselves a long trek in the oppressive heat of day. Yellow haze hung over the city. Plumes of smoke from blazes in Potter's Field, from fires on street corners curled above the rooftops, lending the dismal aspect of a town sacked and burned. I've listened to the Santo Domingans tell of the burning of Cap François. How the capital city was engulfed by fires set in cane fields by the rebelling slaves. Horizon in flames all night as they huddled offshore in ships, terrified, wondering where next they'd go, if any port would permit them to land, empty-handed slaves, masters whose only wealth now was naked black bodies locked in the hold, wide-eyed witnesses of an empire's downfall, chanting, moaning, uncertain as the sea rocked them, whether or not anything on earth could survive the fearful conflagration consuming the great city of Cap François.

Dawn breaking on a smoldering landscape, writhing columns of smoke, a general cloud of haze the color of a fever victim's eyes. I turn and stare at it a moment, then fall in again with my brother's footsteps trudging through untended fields girding Bush Hill.

From a prisoner-of-war ship in New York harbor where the British had interned him he'd seen that city shed its graveclothes of fog. Morning after morning it would paint itself damp and gray, a flat sketch on the canvas of sky, a tentative, shivering screen of housefronts, sheds, sprawling warehouses floating above the river. Then shadows and hollows darkened. A jumble of masts, spars, sails began to sway, little boats plied lanes between ships, tiny figures inched along wharves and docks, doors opened, windows slid up or down, lending an illusion of depth and animation to the portrait. This city infinitely beyond his reach, this charade other men staged to mock him, to mark the distance he could not travel, the shore he'd never reach, the city, so to speak, came to life and with its birth each morning dropped the palpable weight of his despair. His loneliness and exile. Moored in pewter water, on an island that never stopped moving but never arrived anywhere. The city a mirage of light and air, chimera of paint, brush, and paper, mattered naught except that it was denied him. It shimmered. Tolled. Unsettled the watery place where he was sentenced to dwell. Conveyed to him each morning the same doleful tidings: *The dead are legion, the living a froth on dark, layered depths. But you are neither, and less than both.* Each night he dreamed it burning, razed the city till nothing remained but a dry, black crust, crackling, crunching under his boots as he strides, king of the nothing he surveys.

We passed holes dug into the earth where the sick are interred. Some died in these shallow pits, awash in their own vomited and voided filth, before a bed in the hospital could be made ready for them. Others believed they were being buried alive, and unable to crawl out, howled till reason or strength deserted them. A few, past caring, slept soundly in these ditches, resisted the attendants sent to rouse them and transport them inside, once they realized they were being resurrected to do battle again with the fever. I'd watched the red-bearded French doctor from Santo Domingo with his charts and assistants inspecting this zone, his *salle d'attente* he called it, greeting and reassuring new arrivals, interrogating them, nodding and bowing, hurrying from pit to pit, peering down at his invisible patients like a gardener tending seeds.

An introduction to the grave, a way into the hospital that prefigured the way most would leave it. That's what this bizarre rite of admission had seemed at first. But through this and other peculiar stratagems, Deveze, with his French practice, had transformed Bush Hill from lazarium to a clinic where victims of the fever, if not too weak upon arrival, stood a chance of surviving.

The cartman employed by Bush Hill had suddenly fallen sick. Faithful Wilcox had never missed a day, ferrying back and forth from town to hospital, hospital to Potter's Field. Bush Hill had its own cemetery now. Daily rations of dead could be disposed of less conspicuously in a plot on the grounds of the estate, screened from the horror-struck eyes of the city. No one had trusted the hospital. Tales of bloody chaos reigning there had filtered back to the city. Citizens believed it was a place where the doomed were stored until they died. Fever victims would have to be dragged from their beds into Bush Hill's cart. They'd struggle and scream, pitch themselves from the rolling cart, beg for help when the cart passed a rare pedestrian daring or foolish enough to be abroad in the deadly streets.

I wondered for the thousandth time why some were stricken, some not. Dr. Rush and this Deveze dipped their hands into the entrails of corpses, stirred the black, corrupted blood, breathed infected vapors exhaled from mortified remains. I'd observed both men steeped in noxious fluids expelled by their patients, yet neither had fallen prey to the fever. Stolid, dim Wilcox maintained daily concourse with the sick and buried the dead for two months before he was infected. They say a woman, undiscovered until boiling stench drove her neighbors into the street crying for aid, was the cause of Wilcox's downfall. A large woman, bloated into an even more cumbersome package by gases and liquids seething inside her body, had slipped from his grasp as he and another had hoisted her up into the cart. Catching against a rail, her body had slammed down and burst, spraying Wilcox like a fountain. Wilcox did not pride himself on being the tidiest of men, nor did his job demand one who was overfastidious, but the reeking stench from that accident was too much even for him and he departed in a huff to change his polluted garments. He never returned. So there I was at Bush Hill, where Rush had assigned me with my brother, to bury the flow of dead that did not ebb just because the Charon who was their familiar could no longer attend them.

The doctors believe they can find the secret of the fever in the victims' dead bodies. They cut, saw, extract, weigh, measure. The dead are carved into smaller and smaller bits and the butchered parts studied but they do not speak. What I know of the fever I've learned from the words of those I've treated, from stories of the living that are ignored by the good doctors. When lancet and fleam bleed the victims, they offer up stories like prayers.

It was a jaunty day. We served our white guests and after they'd eaten, they served us at the long, linen-draped tables. A sumptuous feast in the oak grove prepared by many and willing hands. All the world's eyes seemed to be watching us. The city's leading men, black and white, were in attendance to celebrate laying the cornerstone of St. Thomas Episcopal African Church. In spite of the heat and clouds of mettlesome insects, spirits were high. A gathering of whites and blacks in good Christian fellowship to commemorate the fruit of shared labor. Perhaps a new day was dawning. The picnic occurred in July. In less than a month the fever burst upon us.

When you open the dead, black or white, you find: the dura matter covering the brain is white and fibrous in appearance. The leptomeninges covering the brain are clear and without opacifications. The brain weighs 1450 grams and is formed symmetrically. Cut sections of the cerebral hemispheres reveal normal-appearing gray matter throughout. The white matter of the corpus callosum is intact and bears no lesions. The basal ganglia are in their normal locations and grossly appear to be without lesions. The ventricles are symmetrical and filled with crystal-clear cerebrospinal fluid.

The cerebellum is formed symmetrically. The nuclei of the cerebellum are unremarkable. Multiple sections through the pons, medulla oblongata and upper brain stem reveal normal gross anatomy. The cranial nerves are in their normal locations and unremarkable.

The muscles of the neck are in their normal locations. The cartilages of the larynx and the hyoid bone are intact. The thyroid and parathyroid glands are normal on their external surface. The mucosa of the larynx is shiny, smooth, and without lesions. The vocal cords are unremarkable. A small amount of bloody material is present in the upper trachea.

The heart weighs 380 grams. The epicardial surface is smooth, glistening, and without lesions. The myocardium of the left ventricle and septum are of a uniform meaty-red, firm appearance. The endocardial surfaces are smooth, glistening, and without lesions. The auricular appendages are free from thrombi. The valve leaflets are thin and delicate, and show no evidence of vegetation.

The right lung weighs 400 grams. The left lung 510 grams. The pleural surfaces of the lungs are smooth and glistening.

The esophageal mucosa is glistening, white, and folded. The stomach contains a large amount of black, noxious bile. A veriform appendix is present. The ascending, transverse, and descending colon reveal hemorrhaging, striations, disturbance of normal mu-

patriarch, son, son's wife, and three children, either dead or in the last frightful stages of the disease. Upon the advice of one of Dr. Rush's most outspoken critics, they had refused mercury purges and bleeding until now, when it was too late for any earthly remedy to preserve them. In the rich furnishings of this opulent mansion, attended by one remaining servant whom fear had not driven away, three generations had withered simultaneously, this proud family's link to past and future cut off absolutely, the great circle broken. In the first bedroom we'd entered we'd found William Spurgeon, merchant, son, and father, present manager of the family fortune, so weak he could not speak, except with pained blinks of his terrible golden eyes. Did he welcome us? Was he apologizing to good Dr. Rush for doubting his cure? Did he fear the dark faces of my brother and myself? Quick, too quickly, he was gone. Answering no questions. Revealing nothing of his state of mind. A savaged face frozen above the blanket. Ancient beyond years. Jaundiced eyes not fooled by our busy ministrations, but staring through us, fixed on the eternal stillness soon to come. And I believe I learned in that yellow cast of his eyes, the exact hue of the sky, if sky it should be called, hanging over the next world where we abide.

Allen, Allen. He lasted only moments and then I wrapped him in a sheet from the chest at the foot of his canopied bed. We lifted him into a humbler litter, crudely nailed together, the lumber still green. Allen, look. Stench from the coffin cut through the oppressive odors permeating this doomed household. See. Like an infant the master of the house had soiled his swaddling clothes. Seepage formed a dark river and dripped between roughly jointed boards. We found his wife where she'd fallen, naked, yellow above the waist, black below. As always the smell presaged what we'd discover behind a closed door. This woman had possessed closets of finery, slaves who dressed, fed, bathed, and painted her, and yet here she lay, no one to cover her modesty, to lift her from the floor. Dr. Rush guessed from the discoloration she'd been dead two days, a guess confirmed by the loyal black maid, sick herself, who'd elected to stay when all others had deserted her masters. The demands of the living too much for her. She'd simply shut the door on her dead mistress. No breath, no heartbeat, sir. I could not rouse her, sir. I intended to return, sir, but I was too weak to move her, too exhausted by my labors, sir. Tears rolled down her creased black face and I wondered in my heart how this abused and despised old creature in her filthy apron and turban, this frail, worn woman, had survived the general calamity while the strong and pampered toppled 'round her.

I wanted to demand of her why she did not fly out the door now, finally freed of her burden, her lifelong enslavement to the whims of white people. Yet I asked her nothing. Considered instead myself, a man who'd worked years to purchase his wife's freedom, then his own, a so-called freeman, and here I was following in the train of Rush and his assistants, a functionary, a lackey, insulted daily by those I risked my life to heal.

Why did I not fly? Why was I not dancing in the streets, celebrating God's judgment on this wicked city? Fever made me freer than I'd ever been. Municipal government had collapsed. Anarchy ruled. As long as fever did not strike me I could come and go anywhere I pleased. Fortunes could be amassed in the streets. I could sell myself to the highest bidder, as nurse or undertaker, as surgeon trained by the famous Dr. Rush to apply his lifesaving cure. Anyone who would enter houses where fever was abroad could demand outrageous sums for negligible services. To be spared the fever was a chance for anyone, black or white, to be a king.

So why do you follow him like a loyal puppy, you confounded black fool? He wagged his finger. *You.* . . . His finger a gaunt, swollen-jointed, cracked-bone, chewed thing. Like the nose on his face. The nose I'd thought looked more like finger than nose. *Fool. Fool.* Finger wagging, then the cackle. The barnyard braying. Berserk chickens cackling in his skinny, goiter-knobbed throat. You are a fool, you black son of Ham. You slack-witted, Nubian ape. You progeny of Peeping Toms and orangutans. Who forces you to accompany that madman Rush on his murderous tours? He kills a hundred for every one he helps with his lamebrain, nonsensical, unnatural, Sangrado cures. Why do you tuck your monkey tail between your legs and skip after that butcher? Are you his shadow, a mindless, spineless black puddle of slime with no will of its own?

You are a good man, Allen. You worry about the souls of your people in this soulless wilderness. You love your family and your God. You are a beacon and steadfast. Your fatal flaw is narrowness of vision. You cannot see beyond these shores. The river, that stinking gutter into which the city shovels its shit and extracts its drinking water, that long-suffering string of spittle winds to an ocean. A hundred miles downstream the foamy mouth of the land sucks on the Atlantic's teat, trade winds saunter and a whole wide world awaits the voyager. I know, Allen. I've been everywhere. Buying and selling everywhere.

If you would dare be Moses to your people and lead them out of this land, you'd find fair fields for your talent. Not lapdogging or doggy-trotting behind or fetch doggy or lie doggy or doggy open your legs or doggy stay still while I beat you. Follow the wound that is a river back to the sea. Be gone, be gone. While there's still time. If there is time, *mon frère*. If the pestilence has not settled in you already, breathed from my foul guts into yours, even as we speak.

Here's a master for you. A real master, Allen. The fever that's supping on my innards. I am more slave than you've ever been. I do its bidding absolutely. Cough up my lungs. Shit hunks of my bowel. When I die, they say my skin will turn as black as yours, Allen.

Return to your family. Do not leave them again. Whatever the Rushes promise, whatever they threaten.

Once, ten thousand years ago, I had a wife and children. I was like you, Allen, proud, innocent, forward looking, well-spoken, well-mannered, a beacon and steadfast. I began to believe the whispered promise that I could have more. More of what, I didn't ask. Didn't know, but I took my eyes off what I loved in order to obtain this more. Left my wife and children and when I returned they were gone. Forever lost to me. The details are not significant. Suffice to say the circumstances of my leaving were much like yours. Very much like yours, Allen. And I lost everything. Became a wanderer among men. Bad news people see coming from miles away. A pariah. A joke. I'm not black like you, Allen. But I will be soon. Sooner than you'll be white. And if you're ever white, you'll be as dead as I'll be when I'm black.

Why do you desert your loved ones? What impels you to do what you find so painful, so unjust? Are you not a man? And free?

Her sleepy eyes, your lips on her warm cheek, each time may be the last meeting on this earth. The circumstances are similar, my brother. My shadow. My dirty face.

The dead are legion, the living a froth on dark, layered depths.

Master Abraham. There's a gentleman to see you, sir. The golden-haired lad bound to me for seven years was carted across the seas, like you, Allen, in the bowels of a leaky tub. A son to replace my son his fathers had clubbed to death when they razed the ghetto of Antwerp. But I could not tame the inveterate hate, his aversion and contempt for me. From my aerie, at my desk secluded among barrels, bolts, crates, and trunks of the shop's attic, I watched him steal, drink, fornicate. I overheard him denounce me to a delegate sent 'round to collect a tithe during the emergency. 'Tis well known in the old country that Jews bring the fever. Palatine fever that slays whole cities. They carry it under dirty fingernails, in the wimples of lizardy private parts. Pass it on with the evil eye. That's why we hound them from our towns, exterminate them. Beware of Master Abraham's glare. And the black-coated vulture listened intently. I could see him toting up the account in his small brain. Kill the Jew. Gain a shop and sturdy prentice, too. But I survived till fever laid me low and the cart brought me here to Bush Hill. For years he robbed and betrayed me and all my revenge was to treat him better. Allow him to pilfer, lie, embezzle. Let him grow fat and careless as I knew he would. With a father's boundless kindness I destroyed him. The last sorry laugh coming when I learned he died in agony, fever shriven, following by a day his Water Street French whore my indulgence allowed him to keep.

In Amsterdam I sold diamonds, Allen. In Barcelona they plucked hairs from my beard to fashion charms that brought ill fortune to their enemies. There were nights in dungeons when the mantle of my suffering was all I possessed to wrap 'round me and keep off mortal cold. I cursed God for choosing me, choosing my people to cuckold and slaughter. Have you heard of the Lamed-Vov, the Thirty-six Just Men set apart to suffer the reality humankind cannot bear? Saviors. But not Gods like your Christ. Not magicians, not sorcerers with bags of tricks, Allen. No divine immunities. Flesh and blood saviors. Men like we are, Allen. If man you are beneath your sable hide. Men who cough and scratch their sores and bleed and stink. Whose teeth rot. Whose wives and children are torn from them. Who wander the earth unable to die, but men always, men till God plucks them up and returns them to His side where they must thaw ten centuries to melt the crust of earthly grief and misery they've taken upon themselves. Ice men. Snowmen. I thought for many years I might be one of them. In my vanity. My self-pity. My foolishness. But no. One lifetime of sorrow's enough for me. I'm just another customer. One more in the crowd lined up at his stall to purchase his wares.

You do know, don't you, Allen, that God is a bookseller? He publishes one book—the text of suffering—over and over again. He disguises it between new boards, in different shapes and sizes, prints on varying papers, in many fonts, adds prefaces and postscripts to deceive the buyer, but it's always the same book.

You say you do not return to your family because you don't want to infect them. Perhaps your fear is well-founded. But perhaps it also masks a greater fear. Can you imagine yourself, Allen, as other than you are? A free man with no charlatan Rush to blame. The weight of your life in your hands.

You've told me tales of citizens paralyzed by fear, of slaves on shipboard who turn to stone in their chains, their eyes boiled in the sun. Is it not possible that you suffer the converse of this immobility? You, sir, unable to stop an endless round of duty and obligation. Turning pages as if the next one or the next will let you finish the story and return to your life.

Your life, man. Tell me what sacred destiny, what nigger errand keeps you standing here at my filthy pallet? Fly, fly, fly away home. Your house is on fire, your children burning.

I have lived to see the slaves free. My people frolic in the streets. Black and white. The ones who believe they are either or both or neither. I am too old for dancing. Too old for foolishness. But this full moon makes me wish for two good legs. For three. Straddled a broomstick when I was a boy. Giddy-up, Giddy-up. Galloping m'lord, m'lady, around the yard I should be sweeping. Dust in my wake. Chickens squawking. My eyes everywhere at once so I would not be caught out by mistress or master in the sin of idleness. Of dreaming. Of following a child's inclination. My broom steed snatched away. Become a rod across my back. Ever cautious. Dreaming with one eye open. The eye I am now, old and gimpy limbed, watching while my people celebrate the rumor of Old Pharaoh's capitulation.

I've shed this city like a skin, wiggling out of it ten score and more years, by miles and els, fretting, twisting. Many days I did not know whether I'd wrenched freer or crawled deeper into the sinuous pit. Somewhere a child stood, someplace green, keeping track, waiting for me. Hoping I'd meet him again, hoping my struggle was not in vain. I search that child's face for clues to my blurred features. Flesh drifted and banked, eroded by wind and water, the landscape of this city fitting me like a skin. Pray for me, child. For my unborn parents I carry in this orphan's potbelly. For this ancient face that slips like water through my fingers.

Night now. Bitter cold night. Fires in the hearths of lucky ones. Many of us still abide in dark cellars, caves dug into the earth below poor men's houses. For we are poorer still, burrow there, pull earth like blanket and quilt 'round us to shut out cold, sleep multitudes to a room, stacked and crosshatched and spoon fashion, ourselves the fuel, heat of one body passed to others and passed back from all to one. No wonder then the celebration does not end as a blazing chill sweeps off the Delaware. Those who leap and roar 'round the bonfires are better off where they are. They have no place else to go.

Given the derivation of the words, you could call the deadly, winged visitors an *unpleasantness from Egypt.*

Putrid stink rattles in his nostrils. He must stoop to enter the cellar. No answer as he shouts his name, his mission of mercy. Earthen floor, ceiling and walls buttressed by occasional beams, slabs of wood. Faint bobbing glow from his lantern. He sees himself looming and shivering on the walls, a shadowy presence with more substance than he feels he possesses at this late hour. After a long day of visits, this hovel his last stop before returning to his brother's house for a few hours of rest. He has learned that exhaustion is a swamp he can wade through and on the far side another region where a thin trembling version of himself toils while he observes, bemused, slipping in and out of sleep, amazed at the likeness, the skill with which that other mounts and sustains him. Mimicry. Puppetry. Whatever controls this other, he allows the impostor to continue, depends upon it to work when he no longer can. After days in the city proper with Rush, he returns to these twisting streets beside the river that are infected veins and arteries he must bleed.

At the rear of the cave, so deep in shadow he stumbles against it before he sees it, is a mound of rags. When he leans over it, speaking down into the darkness, he knows instantly this is the source of the terrible smell, that something once alive is rotting under the rags. He thinks of autumn leaves blown into mountainous, crisp heaps, the north wind cleansing itself and the city of summer. He thinks of anything, any image that will rescue him momentarily from the nauseating stench, postpone what he must do next. He screams no, no to himself as he blinks away his wife's face,. the face of his daughter. His neighbors had promised to check on them, he hears news almost daily. There is no rhyme or reason in whom the fever takes, whom it spares, but he's in the city every day, exposed to its victims, breathing fetid air, touching corrupted flesh. Surely if someone in his family must die, it will be him. His clothes are drenched in vinegar, he sniffs the nostrum of gunpowder, bark, and asafetida in a bag pinned to his coat. He's prepared to purge and bleed himself, he's also ready and quite willing to forgo these precautions and cures if he thought surrendering his life might save theirs. He thinks and unthinks a picture of her hair, soft against his cheek, the wet warmth of his daughter's backside in the crook of his arm as he carries her to her mother's side where she'll be changed and fed. No. Like a choking mist, the smell of decaying flesh stifles him, forces him to turn away, once, twice, before he watches himself bend down into the brunt of it and uncover the sleepers.

Two Santo Domingan refugees, slave or free, no one knew for sure, inhabited this cellar. They had moved in less than a week before, the mother huge with child, man and woman both wracked by fever. No one knows how long the couple's been unattended. There was shame in the eyes and voices of the few from whom he'd gleaned bits and pieces of the Santo Domingans' history. Since no one really knew them and few nearby spoke their language, no one was willing to risk, et cetera. Except for screams one night, no one had seen or heard signs of life. If he'd been told nothing about them, his nose would have led him here.

He winces when he sees the dead man and woman, husband and wife, not entwined as in some ballad of love eternal, but turned back to back, distance between them, as if the horror were too visible, too great to bear, doubled in the other's eyes. What had they seen before they flung away from each other? If he could, he would rearrange them, spare the undertakers this vision.

Rat feet and rat squeak in the shadows. He'd stomped his feet, shooed them before he entered, hollered as he threw back the covers, but already they were accustomed to his presence, back at work. They'd bite indiscriminately, dead flesh, his flesh. He curses and flails his staff against the rags, strikes the earthen floor to keep the scavengers at bay. Those sounds are what precipitate the high-pitched cries that first frighten him, then shame him, then propel him to a tall packing crate turned on its end, atop which another crate is balanced. Inside the second wicker container, which had imported some item from some distant place into this land, twin brown babies hoot and wail.

We are passing over the Dismal Swamp. On the right is the Appalachian range, some of the oldest mountains on earth. Once there were steep ridges and valleys all through here but erosion off the mountains created landfill several miles deep in places. This accounts for the rich loamy soil of the region. Over the centuries several southern states were formed from this gradual erosion. The cash crops of cotton and tobacco so vital to southern prosperity were ideally suited to the fertile soil.

Yeah, I nurse these old funky motherfuckers, all right. White people, specially old white people, lemme tell you, boy, them peckerwoods stink. Stone dead fishy wet stink. Talking all the time 'bout niggers got BO. Well, white folks got the stink and gone, man. Don't be putting my hands on them, neither. Never. Uh-uh. If I touch them, be wit gloves. They some nasty people, boy. And they don't be paying me enough to take no chances wit my health. Matter of fact they ain't paying me enough to really be expecting me to work. Yeah. Starvation wages. So I ain't hardly touching them. Or doing much else either. Got to smoke a cigarette to get close to some of them. Piss and shit theyselves like babies. They don't need much taking care anyway. Most of them three-quarters dead already. Ones that ain't is crazy. Nobody don't want them 'round, that's why they here. Talking to theyselves. Acting like they speaking to a roomful of people and not one soul in the ward paying attention. There's one old black dude, must be a hundred, he be muttering away to hisself nonstop everyday. Pitiful, man. Hope I don't never get that old. Shoot me, bro, if I start to getting old and fucked up in body and mind like them. Don't want no fools like me hanging over me when I can't do nothing no more for my ownself. Shit. They ain't paying me nothing so that's what I do. Nothing. Least I don't punch 'em or tease 'em or steal they shit like some the staff. And I don't pretend I'm God like these so-called professionals and doctors flittin' 'round here drawing down that long bread. Naw. I just mind my own business, do my time. Cop a little TV, sneak me a joint when nobody's around. It ain't all that bad, really. Long as I ain't got no ol' lady and crumb crushers. Don't know how the married cats make it on the little bit of chump change they pay us. But me, I'm free. It ain't that bad, really.

By the time his brother brought him the news of their deaths . . .

Almost an afterthought. The worst, he believed, had been overcome. Only a handful of deaths the last weeks of November. The city was recovering. Commerce thriving. Philadelphia must be revictualed, refueled, rebuilt, reconnected to the countryside, to markets foreign and domestic, to products, pleasures, and appetites denied during the quarantine months of the fever. A new century would soon be dawning. We must forget the horrors. The mayor proclaims a new day. Says let's put the past behind us. Of the eleven who died in the fire he said extreme measures were necessary as we cleansed ourselves of disruptive influences. The cost could have been much greater, he said I regret the loss of life, especially the half dozen kids, but I commend all city officials, all volunteers who helped return the city to the arc of glory that is its proper destiny.

When they cut him open, the one who decided to stay, to be a beacon and steadfast, they will find: liver (1720 grams), spleen (150 grams), right kidney (190 grams), left kidney (180 grams), brain (1450 grams), heart (380 grams), and right next to his heart, the miniature hand of a child, frozen in a grasping gesture, fingers like hard tongues of flame, still reaching for the marvel of the beating heart, fascinated still, though the heart is cold, beats not, the hand as curious about this infinite stillness as it was about thump and heat and quickness.

BHARATI MUKHERJEE
(1940–)

Born in Calcutta, India, to a prominent family, Bharati Mukherjee received a bachelor's degree from the University of Calcutta and two master's degrees (in literature and ancient Indian culture) from the University of Baroda. She left India in 1961 to earn a Ph.D. at the Writers' Workshop at the University of Iowa. Married in 1966 to the Canadian writer Clark Blaise, Bharati Mukherjee lived in Montreal and taught at McGill University until 1979, at which time, according to her account, the rise of racial intolerance in Canada made living in that country increasingly difficult, and she, Clark Blaise, and their two sons moved to Saratoga Springs, New York, where she taught at Skidmore College. Since that time Bharati Mukherjee has taught at Columbia University, City University, and Queens College, and is currently a professor at Berkeley.

Bharati Mukherjee, who has described herself as imaginatively stimulated by the "exuberance of immigration," became an American citizen in 1988. The work for which she is best known draws upon the experience of immigration in America, not only her own but that of others, of diverse ethnic backgrounds. This alone would make her something of a special case as a writer; the extraordinary range of her authorial "voices" distinguishes her further. Her celebrated collection of stories, The Middleman *(1988), is inhabited by naturalized American citizens and refugees from Iraq, Afghanistan, Uganda, and Latin America, as well as India.*

Bharati Mukherjee is the author of an earlier short story collection, Darkness *(1985). Her novels are* The Tiger's Daughter *(1972),* Wife *(1975), and* Jasmine *(1989); her nonfiction books, co-authored with Clark Blaise, are* Days and Nights in Calcutta *(1977) and* The Sorrow and the Terror *(1987).*

The Management of Grief

A woman I don't know is boiling tea the Indian way in my kitchen. There are a lot of women I don't know in my kitchen, whispering and moving tactfully. They open doors, rummage through the pantry, and try not to ask me where things are kept. They remind me of when my sons were small, on Mother's Day or when Vikram and I were tired, and they would make big, sloppy omelets. I would lie in bed pretending I didn't hear them.

Dr. Sharma, the treasurer of the Indo-Canada Society, pulls me into the hallway. He wants to know if I am worried about money. His wife, who has just come up from the basement with a tray of empty cups and glasses, scolds him. "Don't bother Mrs. Bhave with mundane details." She looks so monstrously pregnant her baby must be days overdue. I tell her she shouldn't be carrying heavy things. "Shaila," she says, smiling, "this is the fifth." Then she grabs a teenager by his shirttails. He slips his Walkman off his head. He has to be one of her four children; they have the same domed and dented foreheads. "What's the official word now?" she demands. The boy slips the headphones back on. "They're acting evasive, Ma. They're saying it could be an accident or a terrorist bomb."

All morning, the boys have been muttering, Sikh bomb, Sikh bomb. The men, not using the word, bow their heads in agreement. Mrs. Sharma touches her forehead at such a word. At least they've stopped talking about space debris and Russian lasers.

Two radios are going in the dining room. They are tuned to different stations. Someone must have brought the radios down from my boys' bedrooms. I haven't gone into their rooms since Kusum came running across the front lawn in her bathrobe. She looked so funny, I was laughing when I opened the door.

The big TV in the den is being whizzed through American networks and cable channels.

"Damn!" some man swears bitterly. "How can these preachers carry on like nothing's happened?" I want to tell him we're not that important. You look at the audience, and at the preacher in his blue robe with his beautiful white hair, the potted palm trees under a blue sky, and you know they care about nothing.

The phone rings and rings. Dr. Sharma's taken charge. "We're with her," he keeps saying. "Yes, yes, the doctor has given calming pills. Yes, yes, pills are having necessary effect." I wonder if pills alone explain this calm. Not peace, just a deadening quiet. I was always controlled, but never repressed. Sound can reach me, but my body is tensed, ready to scream. I hear their voices all around me. I hear my boys and Vikram cry, "Mommy, Shaila!" and their screams insulate me, like headphones.

The woman boiling water tells her story again and again. "I got the news first. My cousin called from Halifax before six A.M., can you imagine? He'd gotten up for prayers and his son was studying for medical exams and heard on a rock channel that something had happened to a plane. They said first it had disappeared from the radar, like a giant eraser just reached out. His father called me, so I said to him, what do you mean, 'something bad'? You mean a hijacking? And he said, *Behn*, there is no confirmation of anything yet, but check with your neighbors because a lot of them must be on that plane. So I called poor Kusum straight-away. I knew Kusum's husband and daughter were booked to go yesterday."

Kusum lives across the street from me. She and Satish had moved in less than a month ago. They said they needed a bigger place. All these people, the Sharmas and friends from the Indo-Canada Society, had been there for the housewarming. Satish and Kusum made tandoori on their big gas grill and even the white neighbors piled their plates high with that luridly red, charred, juicy chicken. Their younger daughter had danced, and even our boys had broken away from the Stanley Cup telecast to put in a reluctant appearance. Everyone took pictures for their albums and for the community newspapers—another of our families had made it big in Toronto—and now I wonder how many of those happy faces are gone. "Why does God give us so much if all along He intends to take it away?" Kusum asks me.

I nod. We sit on carpeted stairs, holding hands like children. "I never once told him that I loved him," I say. I was too much the well-brought-up woman. I was so well brought up I never felt comfortable calling my husband by his first name.

"It's all right," Kusum says. "He knew. My husband knew. They felt it. Modern young girls have to say it because what they feel is fake."

Kusum's daughter Pam runs in with an overnight case. Pam's in her McDonald's uniform. "Mummy! You have to get dressed!" Panic makes her cranky. "A reporter's on his way here."

"Why?"

"You want to talk to him in your bathrobe?" She starts to brush her mother's long hair. She's the daughter who's always in trouble. She dates Canadian boys and hangs out in the mall, shopping for tight sweaters. The younger one, the goody-goody one according to Pam, the one with a voice so sweet that when she sang *bhajans* for Ethiopian relief even a frugal man like my husband wrote out a hundred-dollar check, *she* was on that plane. *She* was going to spend July and August with grandparents because Pam wouldn't go. Pam said she'd rather waitress at McDonald's. "If it's a choice between Bombay and Wonderland, I'm picking Wonderland," she'd said.

"Leave me alone," Kusum yells. "You know what I want to do? If I didn't have to look after you now, I'd hang myself."

Pam's young face goes blotchy with pain. "Thanks," she says, "don't let me stop you."

"Hush," pregnant Mrs. Sharma scolds Pam. "Leave your mother alone. Mr. Sharma will tackle the reporters and fill out the forms. He'll say what has to be said."

Pam stands her ground. "You think I don't know what Mummy's thinking? *Why her?* That's what. That's sick! Mummy wishes my little sister were alive and I were dead."

Kusum's hand in mine is trembly hot. We continue to sit on the stairs.

She calls before she arrives, wondering if there's anything I need. Her name is Judith Templeton and she's an appointee of the provincial government. "Multiculturalism?" I ask, and she says "partially," but that her mandate is bigger. "I've been told you knew many of the people on the flight," she says. "Perhaps if you'd agree to help us reach the others. . . ?"

She gives me time at least to put on tea water and pick up the mess in the front room. I have a few *samosas* from Kusum's house-warming that I could fry up, but then I think, why prolong this visit?

Judith Templeton is much younger than she sounded. She wears a blue suit with a white blouse and a polka-dot tie. Her blond hair is cut short, her only jewelry is pearl-drop earrings. Her briefcase is new and expensive looking, a gleaming cordovan leather. She sits with it across her lap. When she looks out the front windows onto the street, her contact lenses seem to float in front of her light blue eyes.

"What sort of help do you want from me?" I ask. She has refused the tea, out of politeness, but I insist, along with some slightly stale biscuits.

"I have no experience," she admits. "That is, I have an M.S.W. and I've worked in liaison with accident victims, but I mean I have no experience with a tragedy of this scale—"

"Who could?" I ask.

"—and with the complications of culture, language, and customs. Someone mentioned that Mrs. Bhave is a pillar—because you've taken it more calmly."

At this, perhaps, I frown, for she reaches forward, almost to take my hand. "I hope you understand my meaning, Mrs. Bhave. There are hundreds of people in Metro directly affected, like you, and some of them speak no English. There are some widows who've never handled money or gone on a bus, and there are old parents who still haven't eaten or gone outside their bedrooms. Some houses and apartments have been looted. Some wives are still hysterical. Some husbands are in shock and profound depression. We want to help, but our hands are tied in so many ways. We have to distribute money to some people, and there are legal documents—these things can be done. We have interpreters, but we don't always have the human touch, or maybe the right human touch. We don't want to make mistakes, Mrs. Bhave, and that's why we'd like to ask you to help us."

"More mistakes, you mean," I say.

"Police matters are not in my hands," she answers.

"Nothing I can do will make any difference," I say. "We must all grieve in our own way."

"But you are coping very well. All the people said, Mrs. Bhave is the strongest person of all. Perhaps if the others could see you, talk with you, it would help them."

"By the standards of the people you call hysterical, I am behaving very oddly and very badly, Miss Templeton." I want to say to her, *I wish I could scream, starve, walk into Lake Ontario, jump from a bridge.* "They would not see me as a model. I do not see myself as a model."

I am a freak. No one who has ever known me would think of me reacting this way. This terrible calm will not go away.

She asks me if she may call again, after I get back from a long trip that we all must make. "Of course," I say. "Feel free to call, anytime."

Four days later, I find Kusum squatting on a rock overlooking a bay in Ireland. It isn't a big rock, but it juts sharply out over water. This is as close as we'll ever get to them. June breezes balloon out her sari and unpin her knee-length hair. She has the bewildered look of a sea creature whom the tides have stranded.

It's been one hundred hours since Kusum came stumbling and screaming across my lawn. Waiting around the hospital, we've heard many stories. The police, the diplomats, they tell us things thinking that we're strong, that knowledge is helpful to the grieving, and maybe it is. Some, I know, prefer ignorance, or their own versions. The plane broke into two, they say. Unconsciousness was instantaneous. No one suffered. My boys must have just finished their breakfasts. They loved eating on planes, they loved the smallness of plates, knives, and forks. Last year they saved the airline salt and pepper shakers. Half an hour more and they would have made it to Heathrow.

Kusum says that we can't escape our fate. She says that all those people—our husbands, my boys, her girl with the nightingale voice, all those Hindus, Christians, Sikhs, Muslims, Parsis, and atheists on that plane—were fated to die together off this beautiful bay. She learned this from a swami in Toronto.

I have my Valium.

Six of us "relatives"—two widows and four widowers—chose to spend the day today by the waters instead of sitting in a hospital room and scanning photographs of the dead. That's what they call us now: relatives. I've looked through twenty-seven photos in two days. They're very kind to us, the Irish are very understanding. Sometimes understanding means freeing a tourist bus for this trip to the bay, so we can pretend to spy our loved ones through the glassiness of waves or in sun-speckled cloud shapes.

I could die here, too, and be content.

"What is that, out there?" She's standing and flapping her hands, and for a moment I see a head shape bobbing in the waves. She's standing in the water, I on the boulder. The tide is low, and a round, black, head-sized rock has just risen from the waves. She returns, her sari end dripping and ruined, and her face is a twisted remnant of hope, the way mine was a hundred hours ago, still laughing but inwardly knowing that nothing but the ultimate tragedy could bring two women together at six o'clock on a Sunday morning. I watch her face sag into blankness.

"That water felt warm, Shaila," she says at length.

"You can't," I say. "We have to wait for our turn to come."

I haven't eaten in four days, haven't brushed my teeth.

"I know," she says. "I tell myself I have no right to grieve. They are in a better place than we are. My swami says depression is a sign of our selfishness."

Maybe I'm selfish. Selfishly I break away from Kusum and run, sandals slapping against stones, to the water's edge. What if my boys aren't lying pinned under the debris? What if they aren't stuck a mile below that innocent blue chop? What if, given the strong currents . . .

Now I've ruined my sari, one of my best. Kusum has joined me, knee deep in water that feels to me like a swimming pool. I could settle in the water, and my husband would take my hand and the boys would slap water in my face just to see me scream.

"Do you remember what good swimmers my boys were, Kusum?"

"I saw the medals," she says.

One of the widowers, Dr. Ranganathan from Montreal, walks out to us, carrying his shoes in one hand. He's an electrical engineer. Someone at the hotel mentioned his work is famous around the world, something about the place where physics and electricity come together. He has lost a huge family, something indescribable. "With some good luck," Dr. Ranganathan suggests to me, "a good swimmer could make it safely to some island. It is quite possible that there may be many, many microscopic islets scattered around."

"You're not just saying that?" I tell Dr. Ranganathan about Vinod, my elder son. Last year he took diving as well.

"It's a parent's duty to hope," he says. "It is foolish to rule out possibilities that have not been tested. I myself have not surrendered hope."

Kusum is sobbing once again. "Dear lady," he says, laying his free hand on her arm, and she calms down.

"Vinod is how old?" he asks me. He's very careful, as we all are. *Is*, not was.

"Fourteen. Yesterday he was fourteen. His father and uncle were going to take him down to the Taj and give him a big birthday party. I couldn't go with them because I couldn't get two weeks off from my stupid job in June." I process bills for a travel agent. June is a big travel month.

Dr. Ranganathan whips the pockets of his suit jacket inside out. Squashed roses, in darkening shades of pink, float on the water. He tore the roses off creepers in somebody's garden. He didn't ask anyone if he could pluck the roses, but now there's been an article about it in the local papers. When you see an Indian person, it says, please give them flowers.

"A strong youth of fourteen," he says, "can very likely pull to safety a younger one."

My sons, though four years apart, were very close. Vinod wouldn't let Mithun drown. *Electrical engineering*, I think, foolishly perhaps: this man knows important secrets of the universe, things closed to me. Relief spins me lightheaded. No wonder my boys' photographs haven't turned up in the gallery of photos of the recovered dead. "Such pretty roses," I say.

"My wife loved pink roses. Every Friday I had to bring a bunch home. I used to say, Why? After twenty-odd years of marriage you're still needing proof positive of my love?" He has identified his wife and three of his children. Then others from Montreal, the lucky ones, intact families with no survivors. He chuckles as he wades back to shore. Then he swings around to ask me a question. "Mrs. Bhave, you are wanting to throw in some roses for your loved ones? I have two big ones left."

But I have other things to float: Vinod's pocket calculator; a half-painted model B-52 for my Mithun. They'd want them on their island. And for my husband? For him I let fall into the calm, glassy waters a poem I wrote in the hospital yesterday. Finally he'll know my feelings for him.

"Don't tumble, the rocks are slippery," Dr. Ranganathan cautions. He holds out a hand for me to grab.

Then it's time to get back on the bus, time to rush back to our waiting posts on hospital benches.

Kusum is one of the lucky ones. The lucky ones flew here, identified in multiplicate their loved ones, then will fly to India with the bodies for proper ceremonies. Satish is one of the few males who surfaced. The photos of faces we saw on the walls in an office at Heathrow and here in the hospital are mostly of women. Women have more body fat, a nun said to me matter-of-factly. They float better.

Today I was stopped by a young sailor on the street. He had loaded bodies, he'd gone into the water when—he checks my face for signs of strength—when the sharks were first spotted. I don't blush, and he breaks down. "It's all right," I say. "Thank you." I heard about the sharks from Dr. Ranganathan. In his orderly mind, science brings understanding, it holds no terror. It is the shark's duty. For every deer there is a hunter, for every fish a fisherman.

The Irish are not shy; they rush to me and give me hugs and some are crying. I cannot imagine reactions like that on the streets of Toronto. Just strangers, and I am touched. Some carry flowers with them and give them to any Indian they see.

After lunch, a policeman I have gotten to know quite well catches hold of me. He says he thinks he has a match for Vinod. I explain what a good swimmer Vinod is.

"You want me with you when you look at photos?" Dr. Ranganathan walks ahead of me into the picture gallery. In these matters, he is a scientist, and I am grateful. It is a new perspective. "They have performed miracles," he says. "We are indebted to them."

The first day or two the policemen showed us relatives only one picture at a time; now they're in a hurry, they're eager to lay out the possibles, and even the probables.

The face on the photo is of a boy much like Vinod; the same intelligent eyes, the same thick brows dipping into a V. But this boy's features, even his cheeks, are puffier, wider, mushier.

"No." My gaze is pulled by other pictures. There are five other boys who look like Vinod.

The nun assigned to console me rubs the first picture with a fingertip. "When they've been in the water for a while, love, they look a little heavier." The bones under the skin are broken, they said on the first day—try to adjust your memories. It's important.

"It's not him. I'm his mother. I'd know."

"I know this one!" Dr. Ranganathan cries out, and suddenly, from the back of the gallery. "And this one!" I think he senses that I don't want to find my boys. "They are the Kutty brothers. They were also from Montreal." I don't mean to be crying. On the contrary, I am ecstatic. My suitcase in the hotel is packed heavy with dry clothes for my boys.

The policeman starts to cry. "I am so sorry. I am so sorry, ma'am. I really thought we had a match."

With the nun ahead of us and the policeman behind, we, the unlucky ones without our children's bodies, file out of the makeshift gallery.

From Ireland most of us go on to India. Kusum and I take the same direct flight to Bombay, so I can help her clear customs quickly. But we have to argue with a man in uniform. He has large boils on his face. The boils swell and glow with sweat as we argue with him. He wants Kusum to wait in line and he refuses to take authority because his boss is on a tea break. But Kusum won't let her coffins out of sight, and I shan't desert her though I know that my parents, elderly and diabetic, must be waiting in a stuffy car in a scorching lot.

"You bastard!" I scream at the man with the popping boils. Other passengers press closer. "You think we're smuggling contraband in those coffins!"

Once upon a time we were well-brought-up women; we were dutiful wives who kept our heads veiled, our voices shy and sweet.

In India, I become, once again, an only child of rich, ailing parents. Old friends of the family come to pay their respects. Some are Sikh, and inwardly, involuntarily, I cringe. My parents are progressive people; they do not blame communities for a few individuals.

In Canada it is a different story now.

"Stay longer," my mother pleads. "Canada is a cold place. Why would you want to be by yourself?" I stay.

Three months pass. Then another.

"Vikram wouldn't have wanted you to give up things!" they protest. They call my husband by the name he was born with. In Toronto he'd changed to Vik so the men he worked with at his office would find his name as easy as Rod or Chris. "You know, the dead aren't cut off from us!"

My grandmother, the spoiled daughter of a rich zamindar, shaved her head with rusty razor blades when she was widowed at sixteen. My grandfather died of childhood diabetes when he was nineteen, and she saw herself as the harbinger of bad luck. My mother grew up without parents, raised indifferently by an uncle, while her true mother slept in a hut behind the main estate house and took her food with the servants. She grew up a rationalist. My parents abhor mindless mortification.

The zamindar's daughter kept stubborn faith in Vedic rituals; my parents rebelled. I am trapped between two modes of knowledge. At thirty-six, I am too old to start over and too young to give up. Like my husband's spirit, I flutter between worlds.

Courting aphasia, we travel. We travel with our phalanx of servants and poor relatives. To hill stations and to beach resorts. We play contract bridge in dusty gymkhana clubs. We ride stubby ponies up crumbly mountain trails. At tea dances, we let ourselves be twirled twice round the ballroom. We hit the holy spots we hadn't made time for before. In Varanasi, Kalighat, Rishikesh, Hardwar, astrologers and palmists seek me out and for a fee offer me cosmic consolations.

Already the widowers among us are being shown new bride candidates. They cannot resist the call of custom, the authority of their parents and older brothers. They must marry; it is the duty of a man to look after a wife. The new wives will be young widows with children, destitute but of good family. They will make loving wives, but the men will shun them. I've had calls from the men over crackling Indian telephone lines. "Save me," they say, these substantial, educated, successful men of forty. "My parents are arranging a marriage for me." In a month they will have buried one family and returned to Canada with a new bride and partial family.

I am comparatively lucky. No one here thinks of arranging a husband for an unlucky widow.

Then, on the third day of the sixth month into this odyssey, in an abandoned temple in a tiny Himalayan village, as I make my offering of flowers and sweetmeats to the god of a tribe of animists, my husband descends to me. He is squatting next to a scrawny sadhu in moth-eaten robes. Vikram wears the vanilla suit he wore the last time I hugged him. The sadhu tosses petals on a butter-fed flame, reciting Sanskrit mantras, and sweeps his face of flies. My husband takes my hands in his.

You're beautiful, he starts. Then, *What are you doing here?*

Shall I stay? I ask. He only smiles, but already the image is fading. *You must finish alone what we started together.* No seaweed wreathes his mouth. He speaks too fast, just as he used to when we were an envied family in our pink split-level. He is gone.

In the windowless altar room, smoky with joss sticks and clarified butter lamps, a sweaty hand gropes for my blouse. I do not shriek. The sadhu arranges his robe. The lamps hiss and sputter out.

When we come out of the temple, my mother says, "Did you feel something weird in there?"

My mother has no patience with ghosts, prophetic dreams, holy men, and cults.

"No," I lie. "Nothing."

But she knows that she's lost me. She knows that in days I shall be leaving.

Kusum's put up her house for sale. She wants to live in an ashram in Hardwar. Moving to Hardwar was her swami's idea. Her swami runs two ashrams, the one in Hardwar and another here in Toronto.

"Don't run away," I tell her.

"I'm not running away," she says. "I'm pursuing inner peace. You think you or that Ranganathan fellow are better off?"

Pam's left for California. She wants to do some modeling, she says. She says when she comes into her share of the insurance money she'll open a yoga-cum-aerobics studio in Hollywood. She sends me postcards so naughty I daren't leave them on the coffee table. Her mother has withdrawn from her and the world.

The rest of us don't lose touch, that's the point. Talk is all we have, says Dr. Ranganathan, who has also resisted his relatives and returned to Montreal and to his job, alone. He says, Whom better to talk with than other relatives? We've been melted down and recast as a new tribe.

He calls me twice a week from Montreal. Every Wednesday night and every Saturday afternoon. He is changing jobs, going to Ottawa. But Ottawa is over a hundred miles away, and he is forced to drive two hundred and twenty miles a day from his home in Montreal. He can't bring himself to sell his house. The house is a temple, he says; the king-sized bed in the master bedroom is a shrine. He sleeps on a folding cot. A devotee.

There are still some hysterical relatives. Judith Templeton's list of those needing help and those who've "accepted" is in nearly perfect balance. Acceptance means you speak of your family in the past tense and you make active plans for moving ahead with your life. There are courses at Seneca and Ryerson we could be taking. Her gleaming leather briefcase is full of college catalogues and lists of cultural societies that need our help. She has done impressive work, I tell her.

"In the textbooks on grief management," she replies—I am her confidante, I realize, one of the few whose grief has not sprung bizarre obsessions—"there are stages to pass through: rejection, depression, acceptance, reconstruction." She has compiled a chart and finds that six months after the tragedy, none of us still rejects reality, but only a handful are reconstructing. "Depressed acceptance" is the plateau we've reached. Remarriage is a major step in reconstruction (though she's a little surprised, even shocked, over *how* quickly some of the men have taken on new families). Selling one's house and changing jobs and cities is healthy.

How to tell Judith Templeton that my family surrounds me, and that like creatures in epics, they've changed shapes? She sees me as calm and accepting but worries that I have no job, no career. My closest friends are worse off than I. I cannot tell her my days, even my nights, are thrilling.

She asks me to help with families she can't reach at all. An elderly couple in Agincourt whose sons were killed just weeks after they had brought their parents over from a village in Punjab. From their names, I know they are Sikh. Judith Templeton and a translator have visited them twice with offers of money for airfare to Ireland, with bank forms, power-of-attorney forms, but they have refused to sign, or to leave their tiny apartment. Their sons' money is frozen in the bank. Their sons' investment apartments have been trashed by tenants, the furnishings sold off. The parents fear that anything they sign or any money they receive will end the company's or the country's obligations to them. They fear they are selling their sons for two airline tickets to a place they've never seen.

The high-rise apartment is a tower of Indians and West Indians, with a sprinkling of Orientals. The nearest bus-stop kiosk is lined with women in saris. Boys practice cricket in the parking lot. Inside the building, even I wince a bit from the ferocity of onion fumes, the distinctive and immediate Indianness of frying ghee, but Judith Templeton maintains a steady flow of information. These poor old people are in imminent danger of losing their place and all their services.

I say to her, "They are Sikh. They will not open up to a Hindu woman." And what I want to add is, as much as I try not to, I stiffen now at the sight of beards and turbans. I remember a time when we all trusted each other in this new country, it was only the new country we worried about.

The two rooms are dark and stuffy. The lights are off, and an oil lamp sputters on the coffee table. The bent old lady has let us in, and her husband is wrapping a white turban over his oiled, hip-length hair. She immediately goes to the kitchen, and I hear the most familiar sound of an Indian home, tap water hitting and filling a teapot.

They have not paid their utility bills, out of fear and inability to write a check. The telephone is gone, electricity and gas and water are soon to follow. They have told Judith their sons will provide. They are good boys, and they have always earned and looked after their parents.

We converse a bit in Hindi. They do not ask about the crash and I wonder if I should bring it up. If they think I am here merely as a translator, then they may feel insulted. There are thousands of Punjabi speakers, Sikhs, in Toronto to do a better job. And so I say to the old lady, "I too have lost my sons, and my husband, in the crash."

Her eyes immediately fill with tears. The man mutters a few words which sound like a blessing. "God provides and God takes away," he says.

I want to say, But only men destroy and give back nothing. "My boys and my husband are not coming back," I say. "We have to understand that."

Now the old woman responds. "But who is to say? Man alone does not decide these things." To this her husband adds his agreement.

Judith asks about the bank papers, the release forms. With a stroke of the pen, they will have a provincial trustee to pay their bills, invest their money, send them a monthly pension.

"Do you know this woman?" I ask them.

The man raises his hand from the table, turns it over, and seems to regard each finger separately before he answers. "This young lady is always coming here, we make tea for her, and she leaves papers for us to sign." His eyes scan a pile of papers in the corner of the room. "Soon we will be out of tea, then will she go away?"

The old lady adds, "I have asked my neighbors and no one else gets *angrezi* visitors. What have we done?"

"It's her job," I try to explain. "The government is worried. Soon you will have no place to stay, no lights, no gas, no water."

"Government will get its money. Tell her not to worry, we are honorable people."

I try to explain the government wishes to give money, not take. He raises his hand. "Let them take," he says. "We are accustomed to that. That is no problem."

"We are strong people," says the wife. "Tell her that."

"Who needs all this machinery?" demands the husband. "It is unhealthy, the bright lights, the cold air on a hot day, the cold food, the four gas rings. God will provide, not government."

"When our boys return," the mother says.

Her husband sucks his teeth. "Enough talk," he says.

Judith breaks in. "Have you convinced them?" The snaps on her cordovan briefcase go off like firecrackers in that quiet apartment. She lays the sheaf of legal papers on the coffee table. "If they can't write their names, an X will do—I've told them that."

Now the old lady has shuffled to the kitchen and soon emerges with a pot of tea and two cups. "I think my bladder will go first on a job like this," Judith says to me, smiling. "If only there was some way of reaching them. Please thank her for the tea. Tell her she's very kind."

I nod in Judith's direction and tell them in Hindi, "She thanks you for the tea. She thinks you are being very hospitable but she doesn't have the slightest idea what it means."

I want to say, Humor her. I want to say, My boys and my husband are with me too, more than ever. I look in the old man's eyes and I can read his stubborn, peasant's message: *I have protected this woman as best I can. She is the only person I have left. Give to me or take from me what you will, but I will not sign for it. I will not pretend that I accept.*

In the car, Judith says, "You see what I'm up against? I'm sure they're lovely people, but their stubbornness and ignorance are driving me crazy. They think signing a paper is signing their sons' death warrants, don't they?"

I am looking out the window. I want to say, *In our culture, it is a parent's duty to hope.*

"Now Shaila, this next woman is a real mess. She cries day and night, and she refuses all medical help. We may have to—"

"Let me out at the subway," I say.

"I beg your pardon?" I can feel those blue eyes staring at me.

It would not be like her to disobey. She merely disapproves, and slows at a corner to let me out. Her voice is plaintive. "Is there anything I said? Anything I did?"

I could answer her suddenly in a dozen ways, but I choose not to. "Shaila? Let's talk about it," I hear, then slam the door.

A wife and mother begins her new life in a new country, and that life is cut short. Yet her husband tells her: Complete what we have started. We, who stayed out of politics and came half way around the world to avoid religious and political feuding, have been the first in the New World to die from it. I no longer know what we started, nor how to complete it. I write letters to the editors of local papers and to members of Parliament. Now at least they admit it was a bomb. One MP answers back, with sympathy, but with a challenge. You want to make a difference? Work on a campaign. Work on mine. Politicize the Indian voter.

My husband's old lawyer helps me set up a trust. Vikram was a saver and a careful investor. He had saved the boys' boarding school and college fees. I sell the pink house at four times what we paid for it and take a small apartment downtown. I am looking for a charity to support.

We are deep in the Toronto winter, gray skies, icy pavements. I stay indoors, watching television. I have tried to assess my situation, how best to live my life, to complete what we began so many years ago. Kusum has written me from Hardwar that her life is now serene. She has seen Satish and has heard her daughter sing again. Kusum was on a pilgrimage, passing through a village, when she heard a young girl's voice, singing one of her daughter's favorite *bhajans.* She followed the music through the squalor of a Himalayan village, to a hut where a young girl, an exact replica of her daughter, was fanning coals under the kitchen fire. When she appeared, the girl cried out, "Ma!" and ran away. What did I think of that?

I think I can only envy her.

Pam didn't make it to California, but writes me from Vancouver. She works in a department store, giving makeup hints to Indian and Oriental girls. Dr. Ranganathan has given up his commute, given up his house and job, and accepted an academic position in Texas, where no one knows his story and he has vowed not to tell it. He calls me now once a week.

I wait, I listen and I pray, but Vikram has not returned to me. The voices and the shapes and the nights filled with visions ended abruptly several weeks ago.

I take it as a sign.

One rare, beautiful, sunny day last week, returning from a small errand on Yonge Street, I was walking through the park from the subway to my apartment. I live equidistant from the Ontario Houses of Parliament and the University of Toronto. The day was not cold, but something in the bare trees caught my attention. I looked up from the gravel, into the branches and the clear blue sky beyond. I thought I heard the rustling of larger forms, and I waited a moment for voices. Nothing.

"What?" I asked.

Then as I stood in the path looking north to Queen's Park and west to the university, I heard the voices of my family one last time. *Your time has come,* they said. *Go, be brave.*

I do not know where this voyage I have begun will end. I do not know which direction I will take. I dropped the package on a park bench and started walking.

AMY TAN

(1952–   )

Born in Oakland, California, two and a half years after her parents emigrated to the United States from Beijing, Amy Tan has become the most popularly acclaimed of Chinese-American writers of the present time. Her father was an electrical engineer who was also trained as a Baptist minister, and the family moved so often, when Tan was growing up, that she speaks of herself as a "local girl" from Fresno, Hayward, Santa Rosa, Palo Alto, Sunnyvale, Santa Clara, and San Jose, as well as Oakland. She and her husband now live in San Francisco.

Amy Tan attended numerous public schools in America, but completed her high school education in Montreux, Switzerland. Back in the United States, she worked for seven years to put herself through college; married young (at eighteen); and earned a master's degree in English from the University of California at Berkeley. Before beginning the sequence of interrelated stories that would constitute The Joy Luck Club, *Tan worked as a consultant to programs for disabled children, sat on numerous boards of directorships that required "minority" representation, and did freelance technical writing.*

Tan is the author of two best-selling and critically acclaimed novels: The Joy Luck Club *(1989), from which "Two Kinds" is taken; and* The Kitchen God's Wife *(1991). Her subject is the experience of growing up in America, from the perspective of the daughter of Chinese immigrants; her specific focus is often a complex emotional relationship between a Chinese-born mother with a strong personality and her American-born daughter.*

Two Kinds

My mother believed you could be anything you wanted to be in America. You could open a restaurant. You could work for the government and get good retirement. You could buy a house with almost no money down. You could become rich. You could become instantly famous.

"Of course you can be prodigy, too," my mother told me when I was nine. "You can be best anything. What does Auntie Lindo know? Her daughter, she is only best tricky."

America was where all my mother's hopes lay. She had come here in 1949 after losing everything in China: her mother and father, her family home, her first husband, and two daughters, twin baby girls. But she never looked back with regret. There were so many ways for things to get better.

We didn't immediately pick the right kind of prodigy. At first my mother thought I could be a Chinese Shirley Temple. We'd watch Shirley's old movies on TV as though they were training films. My mother would poke my arm and say, "*Ni kan*"—You watch. And I would see Shirley tapping her feet, or singing a sailor song, or pursing her lips into a very round O while saying, "Oh my goodness."

"*Ni kan,*" said my mother as Shirley's eyes flooded with tears. "You already know how. Don't need talent for crying!"

Soon after my mother got this idea about Shirley Temple, she took me to a beauty training school in the Mission district and put me in the hands of a student who could barely hold the scissors without shaking. Instead of getting big fat curls, I emerged with an uneven mass of crinkly black fuzz. My mother dragged me off to the bathroom and tried to wet down my hair.

"You look like Negro Chinese," she lamented, as if I had done this on purpose.

The instructor of the beauty training school had to lop off these soggy clumps to make my hair even again. "Peter Pan is very popular these days," the instructor assured my mother. I now had hair the length of a boy's, with straight-across bangs that hung at a slant two inches above my eyebrows. I liked the haircut and it made me actually look forward to my future fame.

In fact, in the beginning, I was just as excited as my mother, maybe even more so. I pictured this prodigy part of me as many different images, trying each one on for size. I was a dainty ballerina girl standing by the curtains, waiting to hear the right music that would send me floating on my tiptoes. I was like the Christ child lifted out of the straw manger, crying with holy indignity. I was Cinderella stepping from her pumpkin carriage with sparkly cartoon music filling the air.

In all of my imaginings, I was filled with a sense that I would soon become *perfect.* My mother and father would adore me. I would be beyond reproach. I would never feel the need to sulk for anything.

But sometimes the prodigy in me became impatient. "If you don't hurry up and get me out of here, I'm disappearing for good," it warned. "And then you'll always be nothing."

Every night after dinner, my mother and I would sit at the Formica kitchen table. She would present new tests, taking her examples from stories of amazing children she had read in *Ripley's Believe It or Not,* or *Good Housekeeping, Reader's Digest,* and a dozen other magazines she kept in a pile in our bathroom. My mother got these magazines from people whose houses she cleaned. And since she cleaned many houses each week, we had a great assortment. She would look through them all, searching for stories about remarkable children.

The first night she brought out a story about a three-year-old boy who knew the capitals of all the states and even most of the European countries. A teacher was quoted as saying the little boy could also pronounce the names of the foreign cities correctly.

"What's the capital of Finland?" my mother asked me, looking at the magazine story.

All I knew was the capital of California, because Sacramento was the name of the street we lived on in Chinatown. "Nairobi!" I guessed, saying the most foreign word I could think of. She checked to see if that was possibly one way to pronounce "Helsinki" before showing me the answer.

The tests got harder—multiplying numbers in my head, finding the queen of hearts in a deck of cards, trying to stand on my head without using my hands, predicting the daily temperatures in Los Angeles, New York, and London.

One night I had to look at a page from the Bible for three minutes and then report everything I could remember. "Now Jehoshaphat had riches and honor in abundance and . . . that's all I remember, Ma," I said.

And after seeing my mother's disappointed face once again, something inside of me began to die. I hated the tests, the raised hopes and failed expectations. Before going to bed that night, I looked in the mirror above the bathroom sink and when I saw only my face staring back—and that it would always be this ordinary face—I began to cry. Such a sad, ugly girl! I made high-pitched noises like a crazed animal, trying to scratch out the face in the mirror.

And then I saw what seemed to be the prodigy side of me—because I had never seen that face before. I looked at my reflection, blinking so I could see more clearly. The girl staring back at me was angry, powerful. This girl and I were the same. I had new thoughts, willful thoughts, or rather thoughts filled with lots of won'ts. I won't let her change me, I promised myself. I won't be what I'm not.

So now on nights when my mother presented her tests, I performed listlessly, my head propped on one arm. I pretended to be bored. And I was. I got so bored I started counting the bellows of the foghorns out on the bay while my mother drilled me in other areas. The sound was comforting and reminded me of the cow jumping over the moon. And the next day, I played a game with myself, seeing if my mother would give up on me before eight bellows. After a while I usually counted only one, maybe two bellows at most. At last she was beginning to give up hope.

Two or three months had gone by without any mention of my being a prodigy again. And then one day my mother was watching *The Ed Sullivan Show* on TV. The TV was old and the sound kept shorting out. Every time my mother got halfway up from the sofa to adjust the set, the sound would go back on and Ed would be talking. As soon as she sat down, Ed would go silent again. She got up, the TV broke into loud piano music. She sat down. Silence. Up and down, back and forth, quiet and loud. It was like a stiff embraceless dance between her and the TV set. Finally she stood by the set with her hand on the sound dial.

She seemed entranced by the music, a little frenzied piano piece with this mesmerizing quality, sort of quick passages and then teasing lilting ones before it returned to the quick playful parts.

"*Ni kan,*" my mother said, calling me over with hurried hand gestures. "Look here."

I could see why my mother was fascinated by the music. It was being pounded out by a little Chinese girl, about nine years old, with a Peter Pan haircut. The girl had the sauciness of a Shirley Temple. She was proudly modest like a proper Chinese child. And she also did this fancy sweep of a curtsy, so that the fluffy skirt of her white dress cascaded slowly to the floor like the petals of a large carnation.

In spite of these warning signs, I wasn't worried. Our family had no piano and we couldn't afford to buy one, let alone reams of sheet music and piano lessons. So I could be generous in my comments when my mother bad-mouthed the little girl on TV.

"Play note right, but doesn't sound good! No singing sound," complained my mother.

"What are you picking on her for?" I said carelessly. "She's pretty good. Maybe she's not the best, but she's trying hard." I knew almost immediately I would be sorry I said that.

"Just like you," she said. "Not the best. Because you not trying." She gave a little huff as she let go of the sound dial and sat down on the sofa.

The little Chinese girl sat down also to play an encore of "Anitra's Dance" by Grieg. I remember the song, because later on I had to learn how to play it.

Three days after watching *The Ed Sullivan Show,* my mother told me what my schedule would be for piano lessons and piano practice. She had talked to Mr. Chong, who lived on the first floor of our apartment building. Mr. Chong was a retired piano teacher and my mother had traded housecleaning services for weekly lessons and a piano for me to practice on every day, two hours a day, from four until six.

When my mother told me this, I felt as though I had been sent to hell. I whined and then kicked my foot a little when I couldn't stand it anymore.

"Why don't you like me the way I am? I'm *not* a genius! I can't play the piano. And even if I could, I wouldn't go on TV if you paid me a million dollars!" I cried.

My mother slapped me. "Who ask you be genius?" she shouted. "Only ask you be your best. For you sake. You think I want you be genius? Hnnh! What for! Who ask you!"

"So ungrateful," I heard her mutter in Chinese. "If she had as much talent as she has temper, she would be famous now."

Mr. Chong, whom I secretly nicknamed Old Chong, was very strange, always tapping his fingers to the silent music of an invisible orchestra. He looked ancient in my eyes. He had lost most of the hair on top of his head and he wore thick glasses and had eyes that always looked tired and sleepy. But he must have been younger than I thought, since he lived with his mother and was not yet married.

I met Old Lady Chong once and that was enough. She had this peculiar smell like a baby that had done something in its pants. And her fingers felt like a dead person's, like an old peach I once found in the back of the refrigerator; the skin just slid off the meat when I picked it up.

I soon found out why Old Chong had retired from teaching piano. He was deaf. "Like Beethoven!" he shouted to me. "We're both listening only in our head!" And he would start to conduct his frantic silent sonatas.

Our lessons went like this. He would open the book and point to different things, explaining their purpose: "Key! Treble! Bass! No sharps or flats! So this is C major! Listen now and play after me!"

And then he would play the C scale a few times, a simple chord, and then, as if inspired by an old, unreachable itch, he gradually added more notes and running trills and a pounding bass until the music was really something quite grand.

I would play after him, the simple scale, the simple chord, and then I just played some nonsense that sounded like a cat running up and down on top of garbage cans. Old Chong smiled and applauded and then said, "Very good! But now you must learn to keep time!"

So that's how I discovered that Old Chong's eyes were too slow to keep up with the wrong notes I was playing. He went through the motions in half-time. To help me keep rhythm, he stood behind me, pushing down on my right shoulder for every beat. He balanced pennies on top of my wrists so I would keep them still as I slowly played scales and arpeggios. He had me curve my hand around an apple and keep that shape when playing chords. He marched stiffly to show me how to make each finger dance up and down, staccato like an obedient little soldier.

He taught me all these things, and that was how I also learned I could be lazy and get away with mistakes, lots of mistakes. If I hit the wrong notes because I hadn't practiced enough, I never corrected myself. I just kept playing in rhythm. And Old Chong kept conducting his own private reverie.

So maybe I never really gave myself a fair chance. I did pick up the basics pretty quickly, and I might have become a good pianist at that young age. But I was so determined not to try, not to be anybody different that I learned to play only the most ear-splitting preludes, the most discordant hymns.

Over the next year, I practiced like this, dutifully in my own way. And then one day I heard my mother and her friend Lindo Jong both talking in a loud bragging tone of voice so others could hear. It was after church, and I was leaning against the brick wall wearing a dress with stiff white petticoats. Auntie Lindo's daughter, Waverly, who was about my age, was standing farther down the wall about five feet away. We had grown up together and shared all the closeness of two sisters squabbling over crayons and dolls. In other words, for the most part, we hated each other. I thought she was snotty. Waverly Jong had gained a certain amount of fame as "Chinatown's Littlest Chinese Chess Champion."

"She bring home too many trophy," lamented Auntie Lindo that Sunday. "All day she play chess. All day I have no time do nothing but dust off her winnings." She threw a scolding look at Waverly, who pretended not to see her.

"You lucky you don't have this problem," said Auntie Lindo with a sigh to my mother.

And my mother squared her shoulders and bragged: "Our problem worser than yours. If we ask Jing-mei wash dish, she hear nothing but music. It's like you can't stop this natural talent."

And right then, I was determined to put a stop to her foolish pride.

A few weeks later, Old Chong and my mother conspired to have me play in a talent show which would be held in the church hall. By then, my parents had saved up enough to buy me a secondhand piano, a black Wurlitzer spinet with a scarred bench. It was the showpiece of our living room.

For the talent show, I was to play a piece called "Pleading Child" from Schumann's *Scenes from Childhood.* It was a simple, moody piece that sounded more difficult than it was. I was supposed to memorize the whole thing, playing the repeat parts twice to make the piece sound longer. But I dawdled over it, playing a few bars and then cheating, looking up to see what notes followed. I never really listened to what I was playing. I daydreamed about being somewhere else, about being someone else.

The part I liked to practice best was the fancy curtsy: right foot out, touch the rose on the carpet with a pointed foot, sweep to the side, left leg bends, look up and smile.

My parents invited all the couples from the Joy Luck Club to witness my debut. Auntie Lindo and Uncle Tin were there. Waverly and her two older brothers had also come. The first two rows were filled with children both younger and older than I was. The littlest ones got to go first. They recited simple nursery rhymes, squawked out tunes on miniature violins, twirled Hula Hoops, pranced in pink ballet tutus, and when they bowed or curtsied, the audience would sigh in unison, "Awww," and then clap enthusiastically.

When my turn came, I was very confident. I remember my childish excitement. It was as if I knew, without a doubt, that the prodigy side of me really did exist. I had no fear whatsoever, no nervousness. I remember thinking to myself, This is it! This is it! I looked out over the audience, at my mother's blank face, my father's yawn, Auntie Lindo's stiff-lipped smile, Waverly's sulky expression. I had on a white dress layered with sheets of lace, and a pink bow in my Peter Pan haircut. As I sat down I envisioned people jumping to their feet and Ed Sullivan rushing up to introduce me to everyone on TV.

And I started to play. It was so beautiful. I was so caught up in how lovely I looked that at first I didn't worry how I would sound. So it was a surprise to me when I hit the first wrong note and I realized something didn't sound quite right. And then I hit another and another followed that. A chill started at the top of my head and began to trickle down. Yet I couldn't stop playing, as though my hands were bewitched. I kept thinking my fingers would adjust themselves back, like a train switching to the right track. I played this strange jumble through two repeats, the sour notes staying with me all the way to the end.

When I stood up, I discovered my legs were shaking. Maybe I had just been nervous and the audience, like Old Chong, had seen me go through the right motions and had not heard anything wrong at all. I swept my right foot out, went down on my knee, looked up and smiled. The room was quiet, except for Old Chong, who was beaming and shouting, "Bravo! Bravo! Well done!" But then I saw my mother's face, her stricken face. The audience clapped weakly, and as I walked back to my chair, with my whole face quivering as I tried not to cry, I heard a little boy whisper loudly to his mother, "That was awful," and the mother whispered back, "Well, she certainly tried."

And now I realized how many people were in the audience, the whole world it seemed. I was aware of eyes burning into my back. I felt the shame of my mother and father as they sat stiffly throughout the rest of the show.

We could have escaped during intermission. Pride and some strange sense of honor must have anchored my parents to their chairs. And so we watched it all: the eighteen-year-old boy with a fake mustache who did a magic show and juggled flaming hoops while riding a unicycle. The breasted girl with white makeup who sang from *Madama Butterfly* and got honorable mention. And the eleven-year-old boy who won first prize playing a tricky violin song that sounded like a busy bee.

After the show, the Hsus, the Jongs, and the St. Clairs from the Joy Luck Club came up to my mother and father.

"Lots of talented kids," Auntie Lindo said vaguely, smiling broadly.

"That was somethin' else," said my father, and I wondered if he was referring to me in a humorous way, or whether he even remembered what I had done.

Waverly looked at me and shrugged her shoulders. "You aren't a genius like me," she said matter-of-factly. And if I hadn't felt so bad, I would have pulled her braids and punched her stomach.

But my mother's expression was what devastated me: a quiet, blank look that said she had lost everything. I felt the same way, and it seemed as if everybody were now coming up, like gawkers at the scene of an accident, to see what parts were actually missing. When we got on the bus to go home, my father was humming the busy-bee tune and my mother was silent. I kept thinking she wanted to wait until we got home before shouting at me. But when my father unlocked the door to our apartment, my mother walked in and then went to the back, into the bedroom. No accusations. No blame. And in a way, I felt disappointed. I had been waiting for her to start shouting, so I could shout back and cry and blame her for all my misery.

I assumed my talent-show fiasco meant I never had to play the piano again. But two days later, after school, my mother came out of the kitchen and saw me watching TV.

"Four clock," she reminded me as if it were any other day. I was stunned, as though she were asking me to go through the talent-show torture again. I wedged myself more tightly in front of the TV.

"Turn off TV," she called from the kitchen five minutes later.

I didn't budge. And then I decided. I didn't have to do what my mother said anymore. I wasn't her slave. This wasn't China. I had listened to her before and look what happened. She was the stupid one.

She came out from the kitchen and stood in the arched entryway of the living room. "Four clock," she said once again, louder.

"I'm not going to play anymore," I said nonchalantly. "Why should I? I'm not a genius."

She walked over and stood in front of the TV. I saw her chest was heaving up and down in an angry way.

"No!" I said, and I now felt stronger, as if my true self had finally emerged. So this was what had been inside me all along.

"No! I won't!" I screamed.

She yanked me by the arm, pulled me off the floor, snapped off the TV. She was frighteningly strong, half pulling, half carrying me toward the piano as I kicked the throw rugs under my feet. She lifted me up and onto the hard bench. I was sobbing by now, looking at her bitterly. Her chest was heaving even more and her mouth was open, smiling crazily as if she were pleased I was crying.

"You want me to be someone that I'm not!" I sobbed. "I'll never be the kind of daughter you want me to be!"

"Only two kinds of daughters," she shouted in Chinese. "Those who are obedient and those who follow their own mind! Only one kind of daughter can live in this house. Obedient daughter!"

"Then I wish I wasn't your daughter. I wish you weren't my mother," I shouted. As I said these things I got scared. It felt like worms and toads and slimy things crawling out of my chest, but it also felt good, as if this awful side of me had surfaced, at last.

"Too late change this," said my mother shrilly.

And I could sense her anger rising to its breaking point. I wanted to see it spill over. And that's when I remembered the babies she had lost in China, the ones we never talked about. "Then I wish I'd never been born!" I shouted. "I wish I were dead! Like them."

It was as if I had said the magic words. Alakazam!—and her face went blank, her mouth closed, her arms went slack, and she backed out of the room, stunned, as if she were blowing away like a small brown leaf, thin, brittle, lifeless.

It was not the only disappointment my mother felt in me. In the years that followed, I failed her so many times, each time asserting my own will, my right to fall short of expectations. I didn't get straight As. I didn't become class president. I didn't get into Stanford. I dropped out of college.

For unlike my mother, I did not believe I could be anything I wanted to be. I could only be me.

And for all those years, we never talked about the disaster at the recital or my terrible accusations afterward at the piano bench. All that remained unchecked, like a betrayal that was now unspeakable. So I never found a way to ask her why she had hoped for something so large that failure was inevitable.

And even worse, I never asked her what frightened me the most: Why had she given up hope?

For after our struggle at the piano, she never mentioned my playing again. The lessons stopped. The lid to the piano was closed, shutting out the dust, my misery, and her dreams.

So she surprised me. A few years ago, she offered to give me the piano, for my thirtieth birthday. I had not played in all those years. I saw the offer as a sign of forgiveness, a tremendous burden removed.

"Are you sure?" I asked shyly. "I mean, won't you and Dad miss it?"

"No, this your piano," she said firmly. "Always your piano. You only one can play."

"Well, I probably can't play anymore," I said. "It's been years."

"You pick up fast," said my mother, as if she knew this was certain. "You have natural talent. You could been genius if you want to."

"No I couldn't."

"You just not trying," said my mother. And she was neither angry nor sad. She said it as if to announce a fact that could never be disproved. "Take it," she said.

But I didn't at first. It was enough that she had offered it to me. And after that, every time I saw it in my parents' living room, standing in front of the bay windows, it made me feel proud, as if it were a shiny trophy I had won back.

Last week I sent a tuner over to my parents' apartment and had the piano reconditioned, for purely sentimental reasons. My mother had died a few months before and I had been getting things in order for my father, a little bit at a time. I put the jewelry in special silk pouches. The sweaters she had knitted in yellow, pink, bright orange—all the colors I hated—I put those in moth-proof boxes. I found some old Chinese silk dresses, the kind with little slits up the sides. I rubbed the old silk against my skin, then wrapped them in tissue and decided to take them home with me.

After I had the piano tuned, I opened the lid and touched the keys. It sounded even richer than I remembered. Really, it was a very good piano. Inside the bench were the same exercise notes with handwritten scales, the same secondhand music books with their covers held together with yellow tape.

I opened up the Schumann book to the dark little piece I had played at the recital. It was on the left-hand side of the page, "Pleading Child." It looked more difficult than I remembered. I played a few bars, surprised at how easily the notes came back to me.

And for the first time, or so it seemed, I noticed the piece on the right-hand side. It was called "Perfectly Contented." I tried to play this one as well. It had a lighter melody but the same flowing rhythm and turned out to be quite easy. "Pleading Child" was shorter but slower; "Perfectly Contented" was longer, but faster. And after I played them both a few times, I realized they were two halves of the same song.

LOUISE ERDRICH
(1954–   )

Louise Erdrich was born in Minnesota, of German-American and Native American parents. She grew up in North Dakota, the mythopoetic setting for much of her work; received her bachelor's degree from Dartmouth; and returned to teach in the Poetry in the Schools program in North Dakota. She then studied in the writing program at Johns Hopkins University. Married to the writer Michael Dorris, who is also of Native American descent, Louise Erdrich has lived in New Hampshire where she and her husband (with whom she frequently collaborates) have been associated with Dartmouth.

Like a number of other writers in this volume, Louise Erdrich is a stylist whose language, while certainly prose, possesses the bold metaphors and musical cadences of poetry. "Fleur," included here, is a magical tale overlaid with a vision of history that is unsentimental and unsparing; it begins the author's account of the legendary Fleur Pillager, a figure of power and destructiveness, who is a presence, as an ancestor, in other, linked work by the author. Fleur and other members of two families of the Turtle Mountain Chippewas are the protagonists of a projected tetralogy set between 1912–84, consisting so far of Love Medicine *(1984);* The Beet Queen *(1986); and* Tracks *(1988), in which "Fleur" appears. The version of "Fleur" presented here appeared originally in* Esquire, *in 1986.*

Louise Erdrich is a magical realist ideally gifted to mediate between the Native American world and the Caucasian world. Her use of meticulously linked stories that form novels, and individual novels that, in sequence, provide an ongoing history of a time and a place, has proven a brilliant writerly strategy.

Fleur

The first time she drowned in the cold and glassy waters of Lake Turcot, Fleur Pillager was only a girl. Two men saw the boat tip, saw her struggle in the waves. They rowed over to the place she went down, and jumped in. When they dragged her over the gunwales, she was cold to the touch and stiff, so they slapped her face, shook her by the heels, worked her arms back and forth, and pounded her back until she coughed up lake water. She shivered all over like a dog, then took a breath. But it wasn't long afterward that those two men disappeared. The first wandered off, and the other, Jean Hat, got himself run over by a cart.

It went to show, my grandma said. It figured to her, all right. By saving Fleur Pillager, those two men had lost themselves.

The next time she fell in the lake, Fleur Pillager was twenty years old and no one touched her. She washed onshore, her skin a dull dead gray, but when George Many Women bent to look closer, he saw her chest move. Then her eyes spun open, sharp black riprock, and she looked at him. "You'll take my place," she hissed. Everybody scattered and left her there, so no one knows how she dragged herself home. Soon after that we noticed Many Women changed, grew afraid, wouldn't leave his house, and would not be forced to go near water. For his caution, he lived until the day that his sons brought him a new tin bathtub. Then the first time he used the tub he slipped, got knocked out, and breathed water while his wife stood in the other room frying breakfast.

Men stayed clear of Fleur Pillager after the second drowning. Even though she was good-looking, nobody dared to court her because it was clear that Misshepeshu, the waterman, the monster, wanted her for himself. He's a devil, that one, love-hungry with desire and maddened for the touch of young girls, the strong and daring especially, the ones like Fleur.

Our mothers warn us that we'll think he's handsome, for he appears with green eyes, copper skin, a mouth tender as a child's. But if you fall into his arms, he sprouts horns, fangs, claws, fins. His feet are joined as one and his skin, brass scales, rings to the touch. You're fascinated, cannot move. He casts a shell necklace at your feet, weeps gleaming chips that harden into mica on your breasts. He holds you under. Then he takes the body of a lion or a fat brown worm. He's made of gold. He's made of beach moss. He's a thing of dry foam, a thing of death by drowning, the death a Chippewa cannot survive.

Unless you are Fleur Pillager. We all knew she couldn't swim. After the first time, we thought she'd never go back to Lake Turcot. We thought she'd keep to herself, live quiet, stop killing men off by drowning in the lake. After the first time, we thought she'd keep the good ways. But then, after the second drowning, we knew that we were dealing with something much more serious. She was haywire, out of control. She messed with evil, laughed at the old women's advice, and dressed like a man. She got herself into some half-forgotten medicine, studied ways we shouldn't talk about. Some say she kept the finger of a child in her pocket and a powder of unborn rabbits in a leather thong around her neck. She laid the heart of an owl on her tongue so she could see at night, and went out, hunting, not even in her own body. We know for sure because the next morning, in the snow or dust, we followed the tracks of her bare feet and saw where they changed, where the claws sprang out, the pad broadened and pressed into the dirt. By night we heard her chuffing cough, the bear cough. By day her silence and the wide grin she threw to bring down our guard made us frightened. Some thought that Fleur Pillager should be driven off the reservation, but not a single person who spoke like this had the nerve. And finally, when people were just about to get together and throw her out, she left on her own and didn't come back all summer. That's what this story is about.

During that summer, when she lived a few miles south in Argus, things happened. She almost destroyed that town.

When she got down to Argus in the year of 1920, it was just a small grid of six streets on either side of the railroad depot. There were two elevators, one central, the other a few miles west. Two stores competed for the trade of the three hundred citizens, and three churches quarreled with one another for their souls. There was a frame building for Lutherans, a heavy brick one for Episcopalians, and a long narrow shingled Catholic church. This last had a tall slender steeple, twice as high as any building or tree.

No doubt, across the low, flat wheat, watching from the road as she came near Argus on foot, Fleur saw that steeple rise, a shadow thin as a needle. Maybe in that raw space it drew her the way a lone tree draws lightning. Maybe, in the end, the Catholics are to blame. For if she hadn't seen that sign of pride, that slim prayer, that marker, maybe she would have kept walking.

But Fleur Pillager turned, and the first place she went once she came into town was to the back door of the priest's residence attached to the landmark church. She didn't go there for a handout, although she got that, but to ask for work. She got that too, or the town got her. It's hard to tell which came out worse, her or the men or the town, although the upshot of it all was that Fleur lived.

The four men who worked at the butcher's had carved up about a thousand carcasses between them, maybe half of that steers and the other half pigs, sheep, and game animals like deer, elk, and bear. That's not even mentioning the chickens, which were beyond counting. Pete Kozka owned the place, and employed Lily Veddar, Tor Grunewald, and my stepfather, Dutch James, who had brought my mother down from the reservation the year before she disappointed him by dying. Dutch took me out of school to take her place. I kept house half the time and worked the other in the butcher shop, sweeping floors, putting sawdust down, running a hambone across the street to a customer's bean pot or a package of sausage to the corner. I was a good one to have around because until they needed me, I was invisible. I blended into the stained brown walls, a skinny, big-nosed girl with staring eyes. Because I could fade into a corner or squeeze beneath a shelf, I knew everything, what the men said when no one was around, and what they did to Fleur.

Kozka's Meats served farmers for a fifty-mile area, both to slaughter, for it had a stock pen and chute, and to cure the meat by smoking it or spicing it in sausage. The storage locker was a marvel, made of many thicknesses of brick, earth insulation, and Minnesota timber, lined inside with sawdust and vast blocks of ice cut from Lake Turcot, hauled down from home each winter by horse and sledge.

A ramshackle board building, part slaughterhouse, part store, was fixed to the low, thick square of the lockers. That's where Fleur worked. Kozka hired her for her strength. She could lift a haunch or carry a pole of sausages without stumbling, and she soon learned cutting from Pete's wife, a string-thin blonde who chain-smoked and handled the razor-sharp knives with nerveless precision, slicing close to her stained fingers. Fleur and Fritzie Kozka worked afternoons, wrapping their cuts in paper, and Fleur hauled the packages to the lockers. The meat was left outside the heavy oak doors that were only opened at 5:00 each afternoon, before the men ate supper.

Sometimes Dutch, Tor, and Lily ate at the lockers, and when they did I stayed too, cleaned floors, restoked the fires in the front smokehouses, while the men sat around the squat cast-iron stove spearing slats of herring onto hardtack bread. They played long games of poker or cribbage on a board made from the planed end of a salt crate. They talked and I listened, although there wasn't much to hear since almost nothing ever happened in Argus. Tor was married, Dutch had lost my mother, and Lily read circulars. They mainly discussed about the auctions to come, equipment, or women.

Every so often, Pete Kozka came out front to make a whist, leaving Fritzie to smoke cigarettes and fry raised doughnuts in the back room. He sat and played a few rounds but kept his thoughts to himself. Fritzie did not tolerate him talking behind her back, and the one book he read was the New Testament. If he said something, it concerned weather or a surplus of sheep stomachs, a ham that smoked green or the markets for corn and wheat. He had a good-luck talisman, the opal-white lens of a cow's eye. Playing cards, he rubbed it between his fingers. That soft sound and the slap of cards was about the only conversation.

Fleur finally gave them a subject.

Her cheeks were wide and flat, her hands large, chapped, muscular. Fleur's shoulders were broad as beams, her hips fishlike, slippery, narrow. An old green dress clung to her waist, worn thin where she sat. Her braids were thick like the tails of animals, and swung against her when she moved, deliberately, slowly in her work, held in and half-tamed, but only half. I could tell, but the others never saw. They never looked into her sly brown eyes or noticed her teeth, strong and curved and very white. Her legs were bare, and since she padded around in beadwork moccasins they never saw that her fifth toes were missing. They never knew she'd drowned. They were blinded, they were stupid, they only saw her in the flesh.

And yet it wasn't just that she was a Chippewa, or even that she was a woman, it wasn't that she was good-looking or even that she was alone that made their brains hum. It was how she played cards.

Women didn't usually play with men, so the evening that Fleur drew a chair up to the men's table without being so much as asked, there was a shock of surprise.

"What's this," said Lily. He was fat, with a snake's cold pale eyes and precious skin, smooth and lily-white, which is how he got his name. Lily had a dog, a stumpy mean little bull of a thing with a belly drum-tight from eating pork rinds. The dog liked to play cards just like Lily, and straddled his barrel thighs through games of stud, rum poker, vingt-un. The dog snapped at Fleur's arm that first night, but cringed back, its snarl frozen, when she took her place.

"I thought," she said, her voice soft and stroking, "you might deal me in."

There was a space between the heavy bin of spiced flour and the wall where I just fit. I hunkered down there, kept my eyes open, saw her black hair swing over the chair, her feet solid on the wood floor. I couldn't see up on the table where the cards slapped down, so after they were deep in their game I raised myself up in the shadows, and crouched on a sill of wood.

I watched Fleur's hands stack and ruffle, divide the cards, spill them to each player in a blur, rake them up and shuffle again. Tor, short and scrappy, shut one eye and squinted the other at Fleur. Dutch screwed his lips around a wet cigar.

"Gotta see a man," he mumbled, getting up to go out back to the privy. The others broke, put their cards down, and Fleur sat alone in the lamplight that glowed in a sheen across the push of her breasts. I watched her closely, then she paid me a beam of notice for the first time. She turned, looked straight at me, and grinned the white wolf grin a Pillager turns on its victims, except that she wasn't after me.

"Pauline there," she said, "how much money you got?"

We'd all been paid for the week that day. Eight cents was in my pocket.

"Stake me," she said, holding out her long fingers. I put the coins in her palm and then I melted back to nothing, part of the walls and tables. It was a long time before I understood that the men would not have seen me no matter what I did, how I moved. I wasn't anything like Fleur. My dress hung loose and my back was already curved, an old woman's. Work had roughened me, reading made my eyes sore, caring for my mother before she died had hardened my face. I was not much to look at, so they never saw me.

When the men came back and sat around the table, they had drawn together. They shot each other small glances, stuck their tongues in their cheeks, burst out laughing at odd moments, to rattle Fleur. But she never minded. They played their vingt-un, staying even as Fleur slowly gained. Those pennies I had given her drew nickels and attracted dimes until there was a small pile in front of her.

Then she hooked them with five-card draw, nothing wild. She dealt, discarded, drew, and then she sighed and her cards gave a little shiver. Tor's eye gleamed, and Dutch straightened in his seat.

"I'll pay to see that hand," said Lily Veddar.

Fleur showed, and she had nothing there, nothing at all.

Tor's thin smile cracked open, and he threw his hand in too.

"Well, we know one thing," he said, leaning back in his chair, "the squaw can't bluff."

With that I lowered myself into a mound of swept sawdust and slept. I woke up during the night, but none of them had moved yet, so I couldn't either. Still later, the men must have gone out again, or Fritzie come out to break the game, because I was lifted, soothed, cradled in a woman's arms and rocked so quiet that I kept my eyes shut while Fleur rolled me into a closet of grimy ledgers, oiled paper, balls of string, and thick files that fit beneath me like a mattress.

The game went on after work the next evening. I got my eight cents back five times over, and Fleur kept the rest of the dollar she'd won for a stake. This time they didn't play so late, but they played regular, and then kept going at it night after night. They played poker now, or variations, for one week straight, and each time Fleur won exactly one dollar, no more and no less, too consistent for luck.

By this time, Lily and the other men were so lit with suspense that they got Pete to join the game with them. They concentrated, the fat dog sitting tense in Lily Veddar's lap, Tor suspicious, Dutch stroking his huge square brow, Pete steady. It wasn't that Fleur won that hooked them in so, because she lost hands too. It was rather that she never had a freak hand or even anything above a straight. She only took on her low cards, which didn't sit right. By chance, Fleur should have gotten a full or flush by now. The irritating thing was she beat with pairs and never bluffed, because she couldn't, and still she ended up each night with exactly one dollar. Lily couldn't believe, first of all, that a woman could be smart enough to play cards, but even if she was, that she would then be stupid enough to cheat for a dollar a night. By day I watched him turn the problem over, his hard white face dull, small fingers probing at his knuckles, until he finally thought he had Fleur figured out as a bit-time player, caution her game. Raising the stakes would throw her.

More than anything now, he wanted Fleur to come away with something but a dollar. Two bits less or ten more, the sum didn't matter, just so he broke her streak.

Night after night she played, won her dollar, and left to stay in a place that just Fritzie and I knew about. Fleur bathed in the slaughtering tub, then slept in the unused brick smokehouse behind the lockers, a windowless place tarred on the inside with scorched fats. When I brushed against her skin I noticed that she smelled of the walls, rich and woody, slightly burnt. Since that night she put me in the closet I was no longer afraid of her, but followed her close, stayed with her, became her moving shadow that the men never noticed, the shadow that could have saved her.

August, the month that bears fruit, closed around the shop, and Pete and Fritzie left for Minnesota to escape the heat. Night by night, running, Fleur had won thirty dollars, but only Pete's presence had kept Lily at bay. But Pete was gone now, and one payday, with the heat so bad no one could move but Fleur, the men sat and played and waited while she finished work. The cards sweat, limp in their fingers, the table was slick with grease, and even the walls were warm to the touch. The air was motionless. Fleur was in the next room boiling heads.

Her green dress, drenched, wrapped her like a transparent sheet. A skin of lakeweed. Black snarls of veining clung to her arms. Her braids were loose, half-unraveled, tied behind her neck in a thick loop. She stood in steam, turning skulls through a vat with a wooden paddle. When scraps boiled to the surface, she bent with a round tin sieve and scooped them out. She'd filled two dishpans.

"Ain't that enough now?" called Lily. "We're waiting." The stump of a dog trembled in his lap, alive with rage. It never smelled me or noticed me above Fleur's smoky skin. The air was heavy in my corner, and pressed me down. Fleur sat with them.

"Now what do you say?" Lily asked the dog. It barked. That was the signal for the real game to start.

"Let's up the ante," said Lily, who had been stalking this night all month. He had a roll of money in his pocket. Fleur had five bills in her dress. The men had each saved their full pay.

"Ante a dollar then," said Fleur, and pitched hers in. She lost, but they let her scrape along, cent by cent. And then she won some. She played unevenly, as if chance was all she had. She reeled them in. The game went on. The dog was stiff now, poised on Lily's knees, a ball of vicious muscle with its yellow eyes slit in concentration. It gave advice, seemed to sniff the lay of Fleur's cards, twitched and nudged. Fleur was up, then down, saved by a scratch. Tor dealt seven cards, three down. The pot grew, round by round, until it held all the money. Nobody folded. Then it all rode on one last card and they went silent. Fleur picked hers up and blew a long breath. The heat lowered like a bell. Her card shook, but she stayed in.

Lily smiled and took the dog's head tenderly between his palms.

"Say, Fatso," he said, crooning the words, "you reckon that girl's bluffing?"

The dog whined and Lily laughed. "Me too," he said, "let's show." He swept his bills and coins into the pot and then they turned their cards over.

Lily looked once, looked again, then he squeezed the dog up like a fist of dough and slammed it on the table.

Fleur threw her arms out and drew the money over, grinning that same wolf grin that she'd used on me, the grin that had them. She jammed the bills in her dress, scooped the coins up in waxed white paper that she tied with string.

"Let's go another round," said Lily, his voice choked with burrs. But Fleur opened her mouth and yawned, then walked out back to gather slops for the one big hog that was waiting in the stock pen to be killed.

The men sat still as rocks, their hands spread on the oiled wood table. Dutch had chewed his cigar to damp shreds, Tor's eye was dull. Lily's gaze was the only one to follow Fleur. I didn't move. I felt them gathering, saw my stepfather's veins, the ones in his forehead that stood out in anger. The dog had rolled off the table and curled in a knot below the counter, where none of the men could touch it.

Lily rose and stepped out back to the closet of ledgers where Pete kept his private stock. He brought back a bottle, uncorked and tipped it between his fingers. The lump in his throat moved, then he passed it on. They drank, quickly felt the whiskey's fire, and planned with their eyes things they couldn't say out loud.

When they left, I followed. I hid out back in the clutter of broken boards and chicken crates beside the stock pen, where they waited. Fleur could not be seen at first, and then the moon broke and showed her, slipping cautiously along the rough board chute with a bucket in her hand. Her hair fell, wild and coarse, to her waist, and her dress was a floating patch in the dark. She made a pig-calling sound, rang the tin pail lightly against the wood, froze suspiciously. But too late. In the sound of the ring Lily moved, fat and nimble, stepped right behind Fleur and put out his creamy hands. At his first touch, she whirled and doused him with the bucket of sour slops. He pushed her against the big fence and the package of coins split, went clinking and jumping, winked against the wood. Fleur rolled over once and vanished in the yard.

The moon fell behind a curtain of ragged clouds, and Lily followed into the dark muck. But he tripped, pitched over the huge flank of the pig, who lay mired to the snout, heavily snoring. I sprang out of the weeds and climbed the side of the pen, stuck like glue. I saw the sow rise to her neat, knobby knees, gain her balance, and sway, curious, as Lily stumbled forward. Fleur had backed into the angle of rough wood just beyond, and when Lily tried to jostle past, the sow tipped up on her hind legs and struck, quick and hard as a snake. She plunged her head into Lily's thick side and snatched a mouthful of his shirt. She lunged again, caught him lower, so that he grunted in pained surprise. He seemed to ponder, breathing deep. Then he launched his huge body in a swimmer's dive.

The sow screamed as his body smacked over hers. She rolled, striking out with her knife-sharp hooves, and Lily gathered himself upon her, took her foot-long face by the ears and scraped her snout and cheeks against the trestles of the pen. He hurled the sow's tight skull against an iron post, but instead of knocking her dead, he merely woke her from her dream.

She reared, shrieked, drew him with her so that they posed standing upright. They bowed jerkily to each other, as if to begin. Then his arms swung and flailed. She sank her black fangs into his shoulder, clasping him, dancing him forward and backward through the pen. Their steps picked up pace, went wild. The two dipped as one, box-stepped, tripped each other. She ran her split foot through his hair. He grabbed her kinked tail. They went down and came up, the same shape and then the same color, until the men couldn't tell one from the other in that light and Fleur was able to launch herself over the gates, swing down, hit gravel.

The men saw, yelled, and chased her at a dead run to the smokehouse. And Lily too, once the sow gave up in disgust and freed him. That is where I should have gone to Fleur, saved her, thrown myself on Dutch. But I went stiff with fear and couldn't unlatch myself from the trestles or move at all. I closed my eyes and put my head in my arms, tried to hide, so there is nothing to describe but what I couldn't block out. Fleur's hoarse breath, so loud it filled me, her cry in the old language, and my name repeated over and over among the words.

The heat was still dense the next morning when I came back to work. Fleur was gone but the men were there, slack-faced, hung over. Lily was paler and softer than ever, as if his flesh had steamed on his bones. They smoked, took pulls off a bottle. It wasn't noon yet. I worked awhile, waiting shop and sharpening steel. But I was sick, I was smothered, I was sweating so hard that my hands slipped on the knives, and I wiped my fingers clean of the greasy touch of the customers' coins. Lily opened his mouth and roared once, not in anger. There was no meaning to the sound. His boxer dog, sprawled limp beside his foot, never lifted its head. Nor did the other men.

They didn't notice when I stepped outside, hoping for a clear breath. And then I forgot them because I knew that we were all balanced, ready to tip, to fly, to be crushed as soon as the weather broke. The sky was so low that I felt the weight of it like a yoke. Clouds hung down, witch teats, a tornado's green-brown cones, and as I watched one flicked out and became a delicate probing thumb. Even as I picked up my heels and ran back inside, the wind blew suddenly, cold, and then came rain.

Inside, the men had disappeared already and the whole place

was trembling as if a huge hand was pinched at the rafters, shaking it. I ran straight through, screaming for Dutch or for any of them, and then I stopped at the heavy doors of the lockers, where they had surely taken shelter. I stood there a moment. Everything went still. Then I heard a cry building in the wind, faint at first, a whistle and then a shrill scream that tore through the walls and gathered around me, spoke plain so I understood that I should move, put my arms out, and slam down the great iron bar that fit across the hasp and lock.

Outside, the wind was stronger, like a hand held against me. I struggled forward. The bushes tossed, the awnings flapped off storefronts, the rails of porches rattled. The odd cloud became a fat snout that nosed along the earth and sniffled, jabbed, picked at things, sucked them up, blew them apart, rooted around as if it was following a certain scent, then stopped behind me at the butcher shop and bored down like a drill.

I went flying, landed somewhere in a ball. When I opened my eyes and looked, stranger things were happening.

A herd of cattle flew through the air like giant birds, dropping dung, their mouths opened in stunned bellows. A candle, still lighted, blew past, and tables, napkins, garden tools, a whole school of drifting eyeglasses, jackets on hangers, hams, a checkerboard, a lampshade, and at last the sow from behind the lockers, on the run, her hooves a blur, set free, swooping, diving, screaming as everything in Argus fell apart and got turned upside down, smashed, and thoroughly wrecked.

Days passed before the town went looking for the men. They were bachelors, after all, except for Tor, whose wife had suffered a blow to the head that made her forgetful. Everyone was occupied with digging out, in high relief because even though the Catholic steeple had been torn off like a peaked cap and sent across five fields, those huddled in the cellar were unhurt. Walls had fallen, windows were demolished, but the stores were intact and so were the bankers and shop owners who had taken refuge in their safes or beneath their cash registers. It was a fair-minded disaster, no one could be said to have suffered much more than the next, at least not until Fritzie and Pete came home.

Of all the businesses in Argus, Kozka's Meats had suffered worst. The boards of the front building had been split to kindling, piled in a huge pyramid, and the shop equipment was blasted far and wide. Pete paced off the distance the iron bathtub had been flung—a hundred feet. The glass candy case went fifty, and landed without so much as a cracked pane. There were other surprises as well, for the back rooms where Fritzie and Pete lived were undisturbed. Fritzie said the dust still coated her china figures, and upon her kitchen table, in the ashtray, perched the last cigarette she'd put out in haste. She lit it up and finished it, looking through the window. From there, she could see that the old smokehouse Fleur had slept in was crushed to a reddish sand and the stockpens were completely torn apart, the rails stacked helter-skelter. Fritzie asked for Fleur. People shrugged. Then she asked about the others and, suddenly, the town understood that three men were missing.

There was a rally of help, a gathering of shovels and volunteers. We passed boards from hand to hand, stacked them, uncovered what lay beneath the pile of jagged splinters. The lockers, full of the meat that was Pete and Fritzie's investment, slowly came into sight, still intact. When enough room was made for a man to stand on the roof, there were calls, a general urge to hack through and see what lay below. But Fritzie shouted that she wouldn't allow it because the meat would spoil. And so the work continued, board by board, until at last the heavy oak doors of the freezer were revealed and people pressed to the entry. Everyone wanted to be the first, but since it was my stepfather lost, I was let go in when Pete and Fritzie wedged through into the sudden icy air.

Pete scraped a match on his boot, lit the lamp Fritzie held, and then the three of us stood still in its circle. Light glared off the skinned and hanging carcasses, the crates of wrapped sausages, the bright and cloudy blocks of lake ice, pure as winter. The cold bit into us, pleasant at first, then numbing. We must have stood there a couple of minutes before we saw the men, or more rightly, the humps of fur, the iced and shaggy hides they wore, the bearskins they had taken down and wrapped around themselves. We stepped closer and tilted the lantern beneath the flaps of fur into their faces. The dog was there, perched among them, heavy as a doorstop. The three had hunched around a barrel where the game was still laid out, and a dead lantern and an empty bottle, too. But they had thrown down their last hands and hunkered tight, clutching one another, knuckles raw from beating at the door they had also attacked with hooks. Frost stars gleamed off their eyelashes and the stubble of their beards. Their faces were set in concentration, mouths open as if to speak some careful thought, some agreement they'd come to in each other's arms.

Power travels in the bloodlines, handed out before birth. It comes down through the hands, which in the Pillagers were strong and knotted, big, spidery, and rough, with sensitive fingertips good at dealing cards. It comes through the eyes, too, belligerent, darkest brown, the eyes of those in the bear clan, impolite as they gaze directly at a person.

In my dreams, I look straight back at Fleur, at the men. I am no longer the watcher on the dark sill, the skinny girl.

The blood draws us back, as if it runs through a vein of earth. I've come home and, except for talking to my cousins, live a quiet life. Fleur lives quiet too, down on Lake Turcot with her boat. Some say she's married to the waterman, Misshepeshu, or that she's living in shame with white men or windigos, or that she's killed them all. I'm about the only one here who ever goes to visit her. Last winter, I went to help out in her cabin when she bore the child, whose green eyes and skin the color of an old penny made more talk, as no one could decide if the child was mixed blood or what, fathered in a smokehouse, or by a man with brass scales, or by the lake. The girl is bold, smiling in her sleep, as if she knows what people wonder, as if she hears the old men talk, turning the story over. It comes up different every time and has no ending, no beginning. They get the middle wrong too. They only know that they don't know anything.

DAVID LEAVITT

(1961–)

David Leavitt, born in Pittsburgh, Pennsylvania, was raised in Palo Alto, California, and graduated from Yale in 1983. One of the first of American gay writers to have found a sympathetic mainstream audience, he has divided his time in recent years between East Hampton, New York and Barcelona, Spain, where he is foreign writer-in-residence at the Institute of Catalan Letters. He has also taught at Princeton University.

David Leavitt's first collection of short fiction, Family Dancing *(1984), was published when the author was only twenty-three, and received a good deal of acclaim. A second collection,* A Place I've Never Been *(1990), from which the story included here has been taken, develops themes explored in the earlier work, presented in voices of admirable versatility and boldness. David Leavitt's novels are* The Lost Language of Cranes *(1986),* Equal Affections *(1989), and the forthcoming* While England Sleeps.

Among the many imaginative works—poetry, prose, plays, memoirs, polemics—written in an epoch of AIDS, when the very source of all creativity in certain quarters of our culture has been threatened, none is more powerfully succinct and more humanly moving than David Leavitt's "Gravity," in which the unspeakable is depicted in domestic and wholly convincing terms. The victory that constitutes the story's epiphany is a small one, but it is a victory.

Gravity

Theo had a choice between a drug that would save his sight and a drug that would keep him alive, so he chose not to go blind. He stopped the pills and started the injections—these required the implantation of an unpleasant and painful catheter just above his heart—and within a few days the clouds in his eyes started to clear up, he could see again. He remembered going into New York City to a show with his mother, when he was twelve and didn't want to admit he needed glasses. "Can you read that?" she'd shouted, pointing to a Broadway marquee, and when he'd squinted, making out only one or two letters, she'd taken off her own glasses—harlequins with tiny rhinestones in the corners—and shoved them onto his face. The world came into focus, and he gasped, astonished at the precision around the edges of things, the legibility, the hard, sharp, colorful landscape. Sylvia had to squint through *Fiddler on the Roof* that day, but for Theo, his face masked by his mother's huge glasses, everything was as bright and vivid as a comic book. Even though people stared at him, and muttered things, Sylvia didn't care, he could *see.*

Because he was dying again, Theo moved back to his mother's house in New Jersey. The DHPG injections she took in stride—she'd seen her own mother through *her* dying, after all. Four times a day, with the equanimity of a nurse, she cleaned out the plastic tube implanted in his chest, inserted a sterilized hypodermic and slowly dripped the bag of sight-giving liquid into his veins. They endured this procedure silently, Sylvia sitting on the side of the hospital bed she'd rented for the duration of Theo's stay—his life, he sometimes thought—watching reruns of *I Love Lucy* or the news, while he tried not to think about the hard piece of pipe stuck into him, even though it was a constant reminder of how wide and unswimmable the gulf was becoming between him and the ever-receding shoreline of the well. And Sylvia was intricately cheerful. Each day she urged him to go out with her somewhere—to the library, or the little museum with the dinosaur replicas he'd been fond of as a child—and when his thinness and the cane drew stares, she'd maneuver him around the people who were staring, determined to shield him from whatever they might say or do. It had been the same that afternoon so many years ago, when she'd pushed him through a lobbyful of curious and laughing faces, determined that nothing should interfere with the spectacle of his seeing. What a pair they must have made, a boy in ugly glasses and a mother daring the world to say a word about it!

This warm, breezy afternoon in May they were shopping for revenge. "Your cousin Howard's engagement party is next month," Sylvia explained in the car. "A very nice girl from Livingston. I met her a few weeks ago, and really, she's a superior person."

"I'm glad," Theo said. "Congratulate Howie for me."

"Do you think you'll be up to going to the party?"

"I'm not sure. Would it be okay for me just to give him a gift?"

"You already have. A lovely silver tray, if I say so myself. The thank-you note's in the living room."

"Mom," Theo said, "why do you always have to—"

Sylvia honked her horn at a truck making an illegal left turn. "Better they should get something than no present at all, is what I say," she said. "But now, the problem is, *I* have to give Howie something, to be from me, and it better be good. It better be very, very good."

"Why?"

"Don't you remember that cheap little nothing Bibi gave you for your graduation? It was disgusting."

"I can't remember what she gave me."

"Of course you can't. It was a tacky pen-and-pencil set. Not even a real leather box. So naturally, it stands to reason that I have to get something truly spectacular for Howard's engagement. Something that will make Bibi blanch. Anyway, I think I've found just the thing, but I need your advice."

"Advice? Well, when my old roommate Nick got married, I gave him a garlic press. It cost five dollars and reflected exactly how much I felt, at that moment, our friendship was worth."

Sylvia laughed. "Clever. But my idea is much more brilliant, because it makes it possible for me to get back at Bibi *and* give Howard the nice gift he and his girl deserve." She smiled, clearly pleased with herself. "Ah, you live and learn."

"You live," Theo said.

Sylvia blinked. "Well, look, here we are." She pulled the car into a handicapped-parking place on Morris Avenue and got out to help Theo, but he was already hoisting himself up out of his seat, using the door handle for leverage. "I can manage myself," he said with some irritation. Sylvia stepped back.

"Clearly one advantage to all this for you," Theo said, balancing on his cane, "is that it's suddenly so much easier to get a parking place."

"Oh Theo, please," Sylvia said. "Look, here's where we're going."

She leaned him into a gift shop filled with porcelain statuettes of Snow White and all seven of the dwarves, music boxes which, when you opened them, played "The Shadow of Your Smile," complicated-smelling potpourris in purple wallpapered boxes, and stuffed snakes you were supposed to push up against drafty windows and doors.

"Mrs. Greenman," said an expansive, gray-haired man in a cream-colored cardigan sweater. "Look who's here, Archie, it's Mrs. Greenman."

Another man, this one thinner and balding, but dressed in an identical cardigan, peered out from the back of the shop. "Hello there!" he said, smiling. He looked at Theo, and his expression changed.

"Mr. Sherman, Mr. Baker. This is my son, Theo."

"Hello," Mr. Sherman and Mr. Baker said. They didn't offer to shake hands.

"Are you here for that item we discussed last week?" Mr. Sherman asked.

"Yes," Sylvia said. "I want advice from my son here." She walked over to a large ridged crystal bowl, a very fifties sort of bowl, stalwart and square-jawed. "What do you think? Beautiful, isn't it?"

"Mom, to tell the truth, I think it's kind of ugly."

"Four hundred and twenty-five dollars," Sylvia said admiringly. "You have to feel it."

Then she picked up the big bowl and tossed it to Theo, like a football.

The gentlemen in the cardigan sweaters gasped and did not exhale. When Theo caught it, it sank his hands. His cane rattled as it hit the floor.

"That's heavy," Sylvia said, observing with satisfaction how the bowl had weighted Theo's arms down. "And where crystal is concerned, heavy is impressive."

She took the bowl back from him and carried it to the counter. Mr. Sherman was mopping his brow. Theo looked at the floor, still surprised not to see shards of glass around his feet.

Since no one else seemed to be volunteering, he bent over and picked up the cane.

"Four hundred and fifty-nine, with tax," Mr. Sherman said, his voice still a bit shaky, and a look of relish came over Sylvia's face as she pulled out her checkbook to pay. Behind the counter, Theo could see Mr. Baker put his hand on his forehead and cast his eyes to the ceiling.

It seemed Sylvia had been looking a long time for something

like this, something heavy enough to leave an impression, yet so fragile it could make you sorry.

They headed back out to the car.

"Where can we go now?" Sylvia asked, as she got in. "There must be someplace else to go."

"Home," Theo said. "It's almost time for my medicine."

"Really? Oh. All right." She pulled on her seat belt, inserted the car key in the ignition and sat there.

For just a moment, but perceptibly, her face broke. She squeezed her eyes shut so tight the blue shadow on the lids cracked.

Almost as quickly she was back to normal again, and they were driving. "It's getting hotter," Sylvia said. "Shall I put on the air?"

"Sure," Theo said. He was thinking about the bowl, or more specifically, about how surprising its weight had been, pulling his hands down. For a while now he'd been worried about his mother, worried about what damage his illness might secretly be doing to her that of course she would never admit. On the surface things seemed all right. She still broiled herself a skinned chicken breast for dinner every night, still swam a mile and a half a day, still kept used teabags wrapped in foil in the refrigerator. Yet she had also, at about three o'clock one morning, woken him up to tell him she was going to the twenty-four-hour supermarket, and was there anything he wanted. Then there was the gift shop: She had literally pitched that bowl toward him, pitched it like a ball, and as that great gleam of flight and potential regret came sailing his direction, it had occurred to him that she was trusting his two feeble hands, out of the whole world, to keep it from shattering. What was she trying to test? Was it his newly regained vision? Was it the assurance that he was there, alive, that he hadn't yet slipped past all her caring, a little lost boy in rhinestone-studded glasses? There are certain things you've already done before you even think how to do them—a child pulled from in front of a car, for instance, or the bowl, which Theo was holding before he could even begin to calculate its brief trajectory. It had pulled his arms down, and from that apish posture he'd looked at his mother, who smiled broadly, as if, in the war between heaviness and shattering, he'd just helped her win some small but sustaining victory.

SANDRA CISNEROS

(1954–   )

One of the most poetic and dramatic of emerging Latina writers, Sandra Cisneros was born in Chicago to a Mexican father and a Chicana mother, the only daughter in a family with six sons. Her family moved frequently, back and forth from Chicago to Mexico City, living always in urban neighborhoods; Cisneros attended a number of schools as she was growing up. She received her B.A. in English from Loyola University of Chicago in 1976, and her MFA in Creative Writing at the Iowa Writers' Workshop in 1978.

Cisneros is both a poet and a short story writer. Her books of poetry are Bad Boys *(1980) and* My Wicked, Wicked Ways *(1987); her short story collections are* The House on Mango Street *(1984), from which the selections included here have been taken, and* Woman Hollering Creek *(1991). By way of her forceful writing and her outspoken views, Sandra Cisneros has emerged as a spokeswoman for Latina writers, and has involved herself in numerous educational projects, including teaching in the Latino Youth Alternative High School in Chicago. More recently, she has taught creative writing at the University of California at Berkeley, the University of California at Irvine, and the University of Michigan in Ann Arbor. She lives in San Antonio.*

Cisneros' gift is for the luminous image, the revelatory phrase. Her emotionally rich subject is the Latino community, specifically the experience of growing up female in a male-dominated society; her work, as these selections suggest, might be as readily classified as prose poetry as prose fiction.

The House on Mango Street

We didn't always live on Mango Street. Before that we lived on Loomis on the third floor, and before that we lived on Keeler. Before Keeler it was Paulina, and before that I can't remember.

But what I remember most is moving a lot. Each time it seemed there'd be one more of us. By the time we got to Mango Street we were six—Mama, Papa, Carlos, Kiki, my sister Nenny and me.

The house on Mango Street is ours, and we don't have to pay rent to anybody, or share the yard with the people downstairs, or be careful not to make too much noise, and there isn't a landlord banging on the ceiling with a broom. But even so, it's not the house we'd thought we'd get.

We had to leave the flat on Loomis quick. The water pipes broke and the landlord wouldn't fix them because the house was too old. We had to leave fast. We were using the washroom next door and carrying water over in empty milk gallons. That's why Mama and Papa looked for a house, and that's why we moved into the house on Mango Street, far away, on the other side of town.

They always told us that one day we would move into a house, a real house that would be ours for always so we wouldn't have to move each year. And our house would have running water and pipes that worked. And inside it would have real stairs, not hallway stairs, but stairs inside like the houses on T.V. And we'd have a basement and at least three washrooms so when we took a bath we wouldn't have to tell everybody. Our house would be white with trees around it, a great big yard and grass growing without a fence. This was the house Papa talked about when he held a lottery ticket and this was the house Mama dreamed up in the stories she told us before we went to bed.

But the house on Mango Street is not the way they told it at all. It's small and red with tight steps in front and windows so small you'd think they were holding their breath. Bricks are crumbling in places, and the front door is so swollen you have to push hard to get in. There is no front yard, only four little elms the city planted by the curb. Out back is a small garage for the car we don't own yet and a small yard that looks smaller between the two buildings on either side. There are stairs in our house, but they're ordinary hallway stairs, and the house has only one washroom. Everybody has to share a bedroom—Mama and Papa, Carlos and Kiki, me and Nenny.

Once when we were living on Loomis, a nun from my school passed by and saw me playing out front. The laundromat downstairs had been boarded up because it had been robbed two days before and the owner had painted on the wood YES WE'RE OPEN so as not to lose business.

Where do you live? she asked.

There, I said pointing up to the third floor.

You live *there?*

There. I had to look to where she pointed—the third floor, the paint peeling, wooden bars Papa had nailed on the windows so we wouldn't fall out. You live *there?* The way she said it made me feel like nothing. *There.* I lived *there.* I nodded.

I knew then I had to have a house. A real house. One I could point to. But this isn't it. The house on Mango Street isn't it. For the time being, Mama says. Temporary, says Papa. But I know how those things go.

What Sally Said

He never hits me hard. She said her mama rubs lard on all the places where it hurts. Then at school she'd say she fell. That's where all the blue places come from. That's why her skin is always scarred.

But who believes her. A girl that big, a girl who comes in with her pretty face all beaten and black can't be falling off the stairs. He never hits me hard.

But Sally doesn't tell about that time he hit her with his hands just like a dog, she said, like if I was an animal. He thinks I'm going to run away like his sisters who made the family ashamed. Just because I'm a daughter, and then she doesn't say.

Sally was going to get permission to stay with us a little and one Thursday she came finally with a sack full of clothes and a paper bag of sweetbread her mama sent. And would've stayed too except when the dark came her father, whose eyes were little from crying, knocked on the door and said please come back, this is the last time. And she said Daddy and went home.

Then we didn't need to worry. Until one day Sally's father catches her talking to a boy and the next day she doesn't come to school. And the next. Until the way Sally tells it, he just went crazy, he just forgot he was her father between the buckle and the belt.

You're not my daughter, you're not my daughter. And then he broke into his hands.

Linoleum Roses

Sally got married like we knew she would, young and not ready but married just the same. She met a marshmallow salesman at a school bazaar, and she married him in another state where it's legal to get married before eighth grade. She has her husband and her house now, her pillowcases and her plates. She says she is in love, but I think she did it to escape.

Sally says she likes being married because now she gets to buy her own things when her husband gives her money. She is happy, except sometimes her husband gets angry and once he broke the door where his foot went through, though most days he is okay. Except he won't let her talk on the telephone. And he doesn't let her look out the window. And he doesn't like her friends, so nobody gets to visit her unless he is working.

She sits at home because she is afraid to go outside without his permission. She looks at all the things they own: the towels and the toaster, the alarm clock and the drapes. She likes looking at the walls, at how neatly their corners meet, the linoleum roses on the floor, the ceiling smooth as wedding cake.

A House of My Own

Not a flat. Not an apartment in back. Not a man's house. Not a daddy's. A house all my own. With my porch and my pillow, my pretty purple petunias. My books and my stories. My two shoes waiting beside the bed. Nobody to shake a stick at. Nobody's garbage to pick up after.

Only a house quiet as snow, a space for myself to go, clean as paper before the poem.

PINCKNEY BENEDICT

(1964–)

Born in Ronceverte, West Virginia, Pinckney Benedict grew up and continues to live on his family's dairy farm north of Lewisburg, West Virginia. He graduated from Princeton University magna cum laude *in 1986 with a B.A. in English, and received his MFA in 1987 from The Writers' Workshop of the University of Iowa. After an appointment to the Hill School, a prep school in Pottstown, Pennsylvania, Benedict spent two years on the Creative Writing Faculty of Oberlin College.*

One of the most gifted of contemporary American writers of his generation, Pinckney Benedict writes almost exclusively of his West Virginia background. His carefully crafted stories have the air of being tales in the process of their very telling; *in Benedict's most characteristic work, as in "Town Smokes," included here, protagonist and landscape are deeply bonded. Like a number of other writers in this volume, including Eudora Welty, Bobbie Ann Mason, Leslie Silko, and Louise Erdrich, Benedict raises "regional" writing to a transcendental level.*

Pinckney Benedict's first short story collection, Town Smokes, *was published in 1987; his second,* The Wrecking Yard, *in 1992.*

Town Smokes

My daddy been in the ground a couple hours when it starts to rain. Hunter's up on the porch, strippen away at a chunk of soft pine wood with his Kaybar knife, and I'm setten out in the yard to get away from the sound, chip chip chip like some damn squirrel. Hunter moves in his seat as he whittles, can' sit still.

It's big drops that are comen down, and starten real quick, like you wouldn' of expected it at all. I look up when it comes on to rain, and what I see of sky's just as blue and clear. Happen like that up here sometimes, my daddy's told me, that you get your hard rain and your blue sky, and both together like that. First time I seen it though, that I recall.

You gonna drown out there Hunter says to me, and I can just hardly hear him over the rain pounden into the dirt of the yard and spangen off the tin roof.

What's that I say. He's not more'n ten yard from me but there's rain like a sheet between us, getten in my eyes and my ears and down my collar. I like the way the cool rain feels as it soaks my shirt. I catch a couple drops in my mouth, and they got no taste to them at all. The rain washes the sweat and the dirt off me.

Drown like a turkey in the rain Hunter says. Out there and mouth open. He gets up to go inside, drops the wood and the knife down into the chair. The heavy knife sticks in the seat, blade down. Hunter moves like an old man, older than my daddy, fat and tired. He ran the sweat like a hog when we was diggen before, because the dirt was hard and packed where we put the grave, out behind the house. I thought his heart might vapor-lock on him there for a while, all red and breathen through the mouth as he was.

Hunter slips the straps of his overalls as he goes inside and I know he will spend the rest of the day in his underwear sluggen bourbon and listenen to the radio.

Get in out the rain he says to me back over his shoulder. I stay out in the yard until the door swings shut behind him. The ground is getten soft under my sneakers but I know that is just the top dirt. It hasn' rained for a good long while and the clay dirt has got dry. The rain comes down too fast and hard to soak in. I know it will not get down deep at all.

I go to the door and I can smell the piece of wood Hunter's been cutten on, the sharp pine sap. It's a tooth he's carven out, like a big boar's tusk, all smooth and curved comen out of the rough wood. He carves a lot of things like that.

He's my daddy's brother that lives with us at the camp up on Tree Mountain. He's a big man, has this small head that sits on his body like a busted chimney on a house. He don' talk much. Old Hunter'll surprise you, how good he is with whittlen. He's sold some things in town.

Water rollen off the roof runs deep around the edges of the porch. Out of the rain, my wet clothes are heavy on me. Against my leg, cold in my pocket, I feel the arrowhead I found in my daddy's grave. Flint hunten point with the edges still sharp. It wasn' very far down, only mebbe five inches. I didn' know this's a good place to find arrowheads. I'll dig again later in other spots to look for some more. I lick my lips, want a smoke, a Camel mebbe.

You got a cigarette I say, goen into the house.

Get your fucken shoes off, bringen wet in the house Hunter says. He's standen in the front room in his shorts, and his hair stands up like he's been runnen his hands through it. The radio he keeps back in his room is on to a news station. What's a fourteen-year-old boy want with a cigarette anyway he says.

Fifteen I say. My shoes come off my feet with a wet noise. I got no socks on, and the wood floor is rough. I know to be careful in bare feet or get a sliver.

I ain' got a cigarette he says.

You got a pinch then I say. I know he's got no snuff but I ask anyway.

Hunter sits down. He's got the bottle in his hand. Christ Jesus he says. You visit whores too?

These are things a man does I say. I guess I just feel like a smoke.

I laugh but Hunter don' join in. He looks at me. When I keep my eyes on him he looks away, out the window. The hard rain throws up a spray of mist and you can' see for more than a couple yards. The roof of the camp is fairly new and tight and it don' leak at all. Hunter and my daddy put it on just the last summer before this one and they did a good job. I carried tacks and tin sheets for them, always scared of slippen and fallen off the roof.

Real gulley-washer Hunter says. They got to watch for them flash floods down to the valley. Farms goen to lose a lot of dirt to the river, this don' let up.

He keeps on looken out the window and all the time the rain is getten harder. It's finally dark out there, clouds coveren the sun. We are high up and it is strange to see it dark in the middle of day. Generally we get hard bright mountain light that makes you squint to look at it.

Your daddy used to make his own smokes Hunter says.

I say I know.

Mebbe you look through his traps, you find you the fixens he says.

That's a thought I say. I don' make any move to the room my

daddy and I share, did share. I stand and drip on the floor and listen to the rain. Hunter looks at me like watchen a snake or mebbe a dog that you ain' sure of. The rain outside the windows makes it look like it ain' any place in the world but the camp and us in it. We're alone here. I think mebbe the rain won' let up for a while yet.

Hunter says You do what you want. Always done it that way anyhow didn' you.

He stands, works his shoulders back and forth. He is sore from the diggen and would like his muscles rubbed I know. Rain throbs him some these days.

I'm gonna listen to the radio for a time he says.

I make a bet with myself he will be asleep before long.

The door to Hunter's room don' shut just right, so when he closes it I can still get the sound from the radio in his room. It is a station from in the valley. The announcer says to watch for flash floods in the narrow, high-banked creeks comen down off the mountain. He says it like it is the mountain's fault.

The tower of the radio is on top of a ridge not far from the camp. The place where they put it is a couple hunnerd feet higher than where we are and you can see it from the porch of the camp on a good day. They took out a whole big stand of blue spruce to get it in.

From where we are, the clearen looks smooth and clean and well took care of, like a yard, but I have been up there a couple time—it ain' such a hard climb as it looks, just a couple hours scramble—and it is a mess around the base of that tower. Vines and creepers around the base and grass to your knees. The blue spruce are comen back too and they are fast-growen trees.

Hunter snaps off the radio and I hear him stretch out on to his bed. He keeps moven around like he will never get to sleep.

My daddy's things is all over the room in no particular order. It is like he is still there, in all them traps, though I know that he is cold and dead and under the earth not a dozen yards away.

These things are mine now I say but it is not like they belong to me at all. Some of them should go to Hunter. I ain' sure that I want that Hunter should have them, though I would be hard put to say why not.

I move the rifle that is layen on my daddy's bed, the heavy

lever-action Marlin, and the cartridge belt that is layen there too. My fingers touch the cool blued metal of the barrel and I know I will have to clean the metal where I touched it, rub it down with a patch of oiled cloth. There is nothen that is worse for any good piece of metal than the touch of a man's hand my daddy would always be sayen.

It is two guns that are in my family, both my daddy's, his old Marlin and the single-action Colt .38 that his grandaddy used sometime way back in the Philippine Insurrection. I put the Colt down on the bed next the rifle, fish out a box of rounds for it as well. From the feel, there ain' too many cartridges left to the box, which is tore up and very old. Beside the guns and his clothes, there is not much else of his in the room.

In the top of the old chifferobe I find his little sack for tobacco. There is not much that is left in the sack, and I can bet that it is pretty old and dry. He was not much for a smoker and a sack of tobacco had a long life around him. There is a paper book of matches next the tobacco with all but two of the matches gone. It is from the Pioneer, which is a bar I have seen down to the valley. There is also a couple bills, a five and a one. I pocket the money.

I scratch through the rest of his stuff in the drawer—a dog whistle and a couple loose .410 rounds for a gun that we ain' even got; needles and thread in a sewen kit; some Vietnamese money that he used to keep around for a laugh—and come up with his old Barlow clasp knife and his Gideon's. The clasp knife I toss down with the rest of the pieces that I figure I might take with me. It clicks off the barrel of the Colt and leaves a mark on the metal. That is one mark that I won' get a hiden for.

The Gideon's is old and slippery in my hand and missen many pages. My daddy has used it for a lot of years. The paper is thin and fine for rollen your own; if you are good you can get two smokes to the page. As I say, he was not a heavy smoker and he is not even gotten up to the New Testament yet, just somewhere in Jeremiah.

I pull out the next page and crease it with my middle finger, tap tobacco onto the paper. The tobacco is crumbly with age and breaks into small pieces; it is very dark brown and cheap-looken. Some of it sticks to my skin. I lay down on the bed and put the home-rolled cigarette in my mouth. Pieces of tobacco stick to my tongue. I spit out, light the smoke.

Christ I say. The cigarette don' taste good at all, like the tobacco has rotted. I flick it out onto the floor and sparks fly off from the lit end. They stick to the wood floor and smolder there, and one by one the sparks burn themselves out.

I figure I will go into town for a time I say to Hunter's back.

He is face down on the narrow cot in his room and I figure him for asleep. The bottle is by the bed and it is several fingers down from where it was earlier. Hunter's back is pale and wide, and there is a mole I never took notice of before in the deep track that his backbone makes.

He says Goen where? and rolls over so sudden it startles me. His face is wet with tears and it surprises me that this old man has been cryen. For a minute I can' remember why. The bed sags under him.

Down the mountain I say. Get me some smokes mebbe.

He is wipen at his face with his arm, drunk and embarrassed that I seen him cry. You can cry for your brother I want to say.

You ain' comen back are you Hunter says.

He puts a foot on the floor and the bottle goes over. I pick it up for him, set it back where it was. It is all but empty with haven been dumped out. The floor is damp and the room smells of bourbon. I look out the little window in Hunter's bedroom and the rain has slacked off some. That is a help.

The rifle's in on the bed I say. He would of wanted for you to have it.

I walk out into the front room and Hunter comes after me, walken in his underwear and bare feet. I got the .38 and the clasp knife and all in my kit with me, ready to go.

Why is it that you're goen now Hunter says. With the rain and all. It's a bad day to be goen down to the valley.

I think about that. It is not somethen I have thought about much before this. I look at him.

Because I am tired I say. Tired of the mountain and smoken shitty tobacco. Mebbe I just want to smoke a real cigarette for a change.

Want you some town smokes I guess Hunter says.

I say I guess.

Mebbe want to kiss all them pretty girls down to the valley too Hunter says. I don' say anythen.

Yeah he says. Bring me back a bottle when you come.

I'll do that I say. You bet.

I go outside and the air is cool for a day in the middle of summer. The rain has turned the dust to mud, and water runs in streams in the yard, has bit into the dirt. A hard rain for just a couple hours I know can raise the creeks and cut right through the banks and dirt levees down below. I wonder what they are doen with all the water down in the town. The air feels damp but the rain is mostly stopped.

Hunter has followed me out into the yard and his feet are all over mud. How you goen down? he says.

Railroad right of way I say. It's the quickest way.

Hunter follows me the next couple of steps and I cut from the yard into the underbrush so he will stop followen. The leaves on the bushes are wet and soak my shirt, my kit. I know the damp will be hard on the gun.

Ought not to of happened to your daddy that way Hunter says. He is looken in the bushes like he can' see where I am at, but he wants me to hear him.

When the tree falls I say best the man that cut it should be out the way.

That is hard Hunter says to the bushes. That a boy should say that about his daddy that brought him up and fed him.

I know that Hunter will see me if I keep on talken. I don' want that he should see me. I turn and go, headen toward the right of way down the mountain.

We should of had someone to say the words Hunter calls after me. It ain' right that there wasn' nobody to say the words for him.

I keep goen through the brush. I guess I would of said the words if I knew them. I ain' got the least idee what words he would of wanted though.

The last time I seen my daddy he tells me a story. He has the old two-stroke loggen saw over his shoulder and is headed out to where he known there's some trees that has come down, or are ready to come down anyhow. You want some help daddy I ask and he says no.

Then he looks over at where Hunter is sitten on the porch and this time Hunter is carven a great horned owl out of a big piece of oak that would have gone well in the fire in the winter.

Hunter wasn' always so fat and lazy he says loud enough that he knows Hunter can hear him. Hunter don' stir from his carven, usen a chisel instead of the Kaybar knife. That's how he works on the ones he figures to sell.

Nawsir my daddy says, was a time when he and I used to run and raise some hell in these parts. When we was about your age. I 'member one time down to Seldomridge's place, little shorthorn farm next the river. You recall that Hunter?

Hunter keeps quiet, just gouges a long chunk of wood out the owl's back. It kind of ruins how the owl looks I think.

The river was froze over, couple three feet thick out near the banks my daddy says. Ice got all thin and black out toward the middle though where the water's deep and fast.

He shifts the chain saw from one shoulder to the other and I see where a little gas mixed with oil has leaked onto his shirt. He don' seem to mind.

So Hunter here riles up Seldomridge's cattle and about a dozen shorthorns go plowen out onto the ice my daddy says.

My daddy's starten to laugh and there are these tears formen in the corners of his eyes. I can hardly stand to look at him because he thinks the story is so funny and I don' get it at all yet.

And they're shiveren out there my daddy keeps on. Can hardly stand, all spraddle-legged and tryen to stay up on the ice, blowen and snorten, scared and full of snot and droolen, them whiteface. Hunter's yellen and holleren at them from the bank, just to keep them on the move, keep them up and off from the shore. Hunter's voice sounds loud out there with everthen else so quiet and covered in snow.

Then the first one goes through my daddy says and he can hardly keep the saw on his shoulders for laughen.

It sounds like a pistol shot when the ice gives and the steer disappears down and it's just black black water shooten up through the hole in the ice like a geyser. That sets them off, stompen and bellowen and the next goes through the ice, skitteren and scrabblen, and the next after that one. Prob'ly half a dozen, one after the other, they get out on the thin ice in the middle and don' have time to look surprised 'fore they go down.

And you was laughen Hunter says from behind his carven.

You damn right I was too my daddy says. I was laughen like a son of a bitch he says and he wheels and heads off into the woods after the tree that fell on him. As he goes, me and Hunter can hear him in the woods there, laughen and laughen about the whiteface that went through the ice in the middle of the river.

Them cattle showed up as far down the river as Teaberry Hunter says after my daddy is gone.

Drownded I ask.

Dead as hammers he says. You bet.

About halfway down the mountain a pig runs across the right of way just a couple feet in front of me. Scares the bejesus out of me, cutten out of the brush on one side and nearly steps on me goen past. It gets stuck for a second goen across the rails and I see that it is young, just a little spotted sucklen and haven a hard time of it. It is whinen a little as it gets over the belly-high steel rails, tail twitchen like a dog's. When it gets over the far rail it turns toward me a second and its eyes are rolled way back in its head. Then it gets into the brush on the other side of the right of way and it's gone.

Two boys come out of the brush after it and they are right on top of me too. Christ one of them says and shoves at me. He is not very big and I knock him down with my kit. The other is big and red-haired and carryen a rifle. He rushes across the right of way and stares into the brush. Goddam it to hell he says.

He raises the rifle, pointen into the brush after the sucklen, and I think for a minute that he is goen to let go. Then I realize the pig must be in under cover now and he'd be a fool to shoot. Still his finger curves on the trigger a second, tugs and almost fires.

It is a short-barrelled Winchester carbine that he is carryen with a shrouded front sight for brush-beaten. The stock is wrapped around with black electric tape and there is rust all on the receiver. They are rough-looken boys. The big one is about my age and the little one some younger I figure.

The big red-headed one turns around to me and his eyes are cold. I figure he is mad because they lost the pig that they had been tracken. He drops the hammer back into half-cock, holds the rifle easy in the crook of his arm. His clothes are dirty and too small on his big frame.

Le's get a move on Okie the little one says. His teeth are gone rotten on him and make him talk odd, real soft like his mouth pains him. He says mebbe we can still get us that 'ere pig.

You hush Darius the big one says and he is still looken at me. It makes me nervous and I turn to head on down the cinder roadbed. The cinders are soft with the rain. They stick to the bottoms of my shoes, make my feet feel heavy. It is hard to walk on the railroad ties though, because they are too close together to make for an easy stride.

When I look back the big one, Okie, is still staren at me from under the long red hair. He licks his lips.

Hold up there a minute he says.

The little one trots after me a couple steps and I see there is somethen wrong with his legs, how they are too short for the rest of his body is what makes him so small. He is mebbe not so young as I first thought, mebbe older than me or Okie too. The ties are just right for him and he moves from one to the next without any trouble at all. Okie stays where he is.

We lost that 'ere shoat Darius says and he sounds like on the edge of cryen about it. You seen it he says.

Darius is right up on me now where I can smell him and I stop.

You boys want to let me alone I say. I ain' botheren you none.

Who says you was Okie calls out.

He's got the rifle pointen up at the gray sky now, held in both hands. He spits on the cinders, got a pinch of snuff in the right side of his mouth. He comes down the track a way, smilen, and I see his teeth are gone bad on him too. The snuff'll do that to you in time.

What you got Darius is sayen and I catch him looken at my kit. He's got his hands out like a kid asken for a candy. I drop the bag, push it back behind me. Darius is hoppen back and forth from one railroad tie to the other. He's got mud to the knee on his old corduroy pants, but it seems like he don' want to touch foot down on the roadbed.

He don' want you messen with his stuff Okie says to Darius. It is like a man talken to a kid.

He looks at me. You headen down into town he says. You live up on the mountain? He points back up the way I came with the carbine.

Yeah I say.

He looks at Darius and snorts, spits again. Goddam ridge runner he says. Come down from up on top and don' know nothen. Darius laughs.

What you want to go into town for, ridge runner? Okie says. He pokes the rifle barrel into my chest real sudden. It clunks against my ribs and hurts like a son of a bitch. I can hear Darius goen in my kit but I don' look.

Ain' nothen for you in town, boy Okie says. Best you go on back up the mountain and stay with the rest of the runners.

Just take the whole fucken thing Darius he says, ain' no use to go rooten through there. It don' stop Darius. Okie turns back to me.

You turn out your pockets he says and he taps me with the rifle again. We could do you he says. Kill you just as easy as killen that shoat and nobody to know any differ'nt about it. Who'd care what happens to a ridge runner like you anyhow.

I know I say. We're about fifteen hunnerd feet above the valley and I figure he is right.

You turn out your pockets and keep your mouth shut and you be all right Okie says. Darius is goen through my stuff still and I can hear the Colt clink against somethen. I hate to think of these two with it but there is nothen to do about it. I wish I had left the thing with Hunter.

My daddy's dead I say. I don' know why I say it.

Looky here Darius says and holds up the Barlow knife. He has got it open and the blade looks shiny even under the cloudy sky. He tests it against his hairy forearm. Sharp he says. Okie holds the rifle on me but he is looken off somewheres else, after where the pig went. I dig in after the money I got in my pockets.

Tree fell on him I say. When he was cutten it down.

Okie takes the six dollars from me, shoves it in his pants. I think about what a 30-30 could do to you this close up. I seen one take the whole hind end off a groundhog one time at about two hunnerd yards, just tore it off and threw the 'hog about ten feet. I hold out the arrowhead to him, turn out my pockets so's he can see they ain' nothen in them. He takes he arrowhead, holds it out from him with his left hand, squinten. He knows I ain' goen to give him any trouble.

Leave me some to get a pack of smokes down to the valley I say. And a bottle for my uncle.

Shoot Okie says. He tosses the arrowhead back over his shoulder. It hits the smooth steel rail and gives out a pretty sound, like a note on my daddy's old jew harp. The flint busts into about twenty pieces.

That was a pretty old arrowhead I say. I don' know how old it was but I want to say somethen.

Gimme his shoes Darius says.

He's standen and looken at my feet. His shoes look like bags tied with string or somethen. Mine ain' much but they are better than that, an old pair of sneakers that was my daddy's.

His shoes ain' about to fit you, clubfoot Okie says. Darius is bouncen up and down, still standen on a railroad tie. He's got my kit in his hand. He just looks at Okie and sticks his lip out. He is retarded some I see.

Get out your shoes Okie says. He seems like he is tired of the whole thing now. Just go on and get on out of them he says. He ain' even holden the rifle on me now.

I take my shoes off and hand them to Darius. He don' even try to put them on. He just stuffs them in the kit and laughs, sound like a dog barken. The roadbed is cold with the rain and the cinders stick to the soles of my feet, stain them black.

Darius goes to the edge of the right of way, looks off into the brush. Le's see can we get that pig now Okie he says. He goes off into the brush carryen my kit with him. After a minute I can' see him anymore, just hear him crashen around in there.

Okie looks me up and down and his eyes are still hard. The smell of him that close up is greasy, like somethen fat cooked on an open fire.

You go back on up he says. That's best for ridge runners, the top of the mountain.

I'm headed into town I say.

He looks mad at me and I think for a minute he may shoot me, but he don' even bring the gun around to bear. He looks at me some more, then heads on into the brush after Darius.

I wait a minute to see if they're comen back but they're both gone. No use tryen to follow them into the brush with no shoes. I start down the right of way again, on into the valley. The walken is easier without my kit. The rain has started up again, lighter this time. It don' feel like the kind of a rain that goes on for too long.

The cinders make my feet sore and black. I walk that way for a while, then change to walken on the ties. It is strange the small steps you have to take, but easier than stretchen to skip a tie every time. I get used to it.

When we find my daddy he's been dead for quite a while. The tree just caught him across the chest with one thick branch. He must of been on his way to dodge the fall when it caught him. His face looks surprised; his body don' look like anythen I ever seen before, all a different shape from what it was, crushed ribs and tore cloth, somethen terrible to look at. Hunter covers him with a good thick tarpaulin right after we jack the tree up off of him and I don' have a chance to look at him after that. We bury the tarpaulin along with him.

The loggen saw's down on the ground next to him. It didn' get caught by the tree at all, looks just like it had when he walked out with it. All the gas in it ain' gone so it must of stalled after he got hit. Hunter and me talk about it but can never figure what it was about that old oak that made it fall the wrong way or why my daddy didn' figure how it was goen to come down. He must of made the cut wrong somehow and just not seen his mistake until it was too late.

Lot of folks lost everthen says the man who owns the drugstore. He is a heavy man wearen a white apron tied behind his back. Houses, stock, barns, the whole kitten caboodle down the river and on into Monroe County. He is talken to a skinny man in overalls who nods.

You betcha the drugstore man says. We awful lucky to be this high up. He is sweepen at a puddle of water near the door of his store, pushen the water out into the street. He wears glasses and the glass flashes as he moves his head in time with the broom. The bristles of the broom have soaked up a lot of the dirty water and he works like they are heavy.

The town is quiet, like it's a Sunday, and the streets are wet from the rain. When I walk in the store the men look at me. They see I got no shoes on.

Sucked the pilens right out from under the bridge the drugstore man says. Craziest thing you ever saw. Help you he says to me. I got no money so I don' say anythen back.

The Dodge dealership down to the river the skinny man says. You know, Sims'. Say the cars was floaten up near around the ceilen. Water came in so fast nobody had time to move nothen. Earth dam couple miles up let go and that was all she wrote.

Don' I know the drugstore man says. He sweeps some water past my feet, looks at me again. You need somethen he says.

I was looken for some smokes I say. Cigarettes.

We got them the drugstore man says. All kinds. What was you looken for?

Camels I say.

It's a bunch of miles down the mountain and I feel tired, sick. I want to sit down and have a smoke. I wish I had some money. My feet hurt.

Yo Carl the drugstore man says. You want to go in there back of the counter and get a pack of Camels for me.

Sure the skinny man says. He gets the cigarettes and tosses them to me. I catch them against my chest and the pack crushes a little.

I got no money I say.

The drugstore man stops sweepen a minute. Some of the water he just got out the door trickles back in. It's dirty river water, brown on the white floor.

Day like today I guess that's all right he says. He grins at me and I know how dirty I am. I know how I look. He figures I got wiped out by the flood.

My daddy's dead I say.

The drugstore owner shakes his head.

What a day Carl says behind the counter. He shakes his head too, snags himself a pack of smokes. What a day. I don' tell them that my daddy was dead before the rain even started.

That's hard son the drugstore man says. Awful goddam hard.

You got to wonder what the Lord is up to the skinny man says. Leave a boy 'thout a father.

I figure that is the nicest thing I ever heard. All I want to do right then is sit down and cry. I tear the wrap off the pack of cigarettes and the drugstore man hands me his lighter, a plastic Cricket. Coleman's Since 1942 it says on the side, the name of his drugstore. I turn the striken wheel with my thumb and the lighter catches, sends up a good strong flame the very first time.

I suck in the smoke and the third cigarette tastes just as good as the first. There is nothen like a butt that somebody else has rolled in a machine for you and that don' leave pieces of tobacco on your tongue.

I sit out near the end of the bridge that must of used to connected the two parts of the town across the river. It was an old steel bridge that sat up on stone pilens, and the drugstore man was right: the supports are clean gone and the span is down by the middle in the dark rushen river. Right near where I sit there's a sign that says Weight Limit 2 Tons.

I pull on the cigarette until it burns down near my fingers. I seen men that smoked so much they built up yellow callus on their thumb and pointer finger, could burn a smoke all the way down if they wanted to and never feel it at all. I can' do that and besides I got a whole pack yet to go. No use to be hard on myself. I flick the butt into the river and it is gone in the fast water almost even before I see it hit.

I have heard that in floods you will sometimes see animals and trees that got caught in the water goen downstream. I have not seen any by this time and figure they must all of been pushed down the river right at first when the water was highest. There probably won' be any again until the next time the river rises.

It is starten the hard rain again, not just the soft drizzle now, and I have to shield the fourth cigarette against the water to get it to light. The lighter catches the first try. I figure the cigarette will burn pretty well in the rain once I manage to start it goen. I am wet again but this time it is not so pleasant as it was this mornen. This time it is just cold and nasty. I ain' sure what I will do. It is sure as hell I won' go back up the mountain.

After a while I may go up the river and look for the earth dam that let go and did all the damage. It must look pretty awful, busted open in the middle and oozen the river water over the lip of the hole, brown and thick with bottom mud. Not like the creeks up on the mountain but a real river and comen through just the way it wants with nothen to hold it back. Yessir, that would sure be somethen to see.

AUTHOR INDEX